BOOK 1:
ASCEND ONLINE

LUKE
CHMILENKO

Editor: Robert Ciechanowski and Vera Chmilenko
Proofer: Evan Mears
Cover Illustration: Yongjae Choi
Cover Design and Interior Layout: STK·Kreations

Hardcover ISBN: 978-1-7752413-6-2
Trade paperback ISBN: 978-1-7752413-7-9
Ebook ISBN: 978-0-9953378-0-0
Worldwide Rights.

2nd Edition, April 2020

Published by Aetherworld Productions Inc.
www.lukechmilenko.com

ASCEND
ONLINE

ACKNOWLEDGEMENTS

Few novels are created in a vacuum and this one is no exception. I would like to extend my most heartfelt gratitude to those who have helped shape this novel into what it is today.

To my wife Christina, for encouraging and supporting my desire to write this story. Without you, this story would have never even started.

To Robert Ciechanowski and Vera Chmilenko for your endless patience in reviewing, editing and providing feedback. Your hard work and diligence has helped find countless errors and continuity mistakes that I've managed to hide in this novel.

To 'The Gang', you are all awesome.

To my parents, for encouraging a lifelong obsession with reading and for indulging me every time I packed five books to tie me over a two-day vacation.

To all my readers on Royal Road Legends, your support and feedback over the last five months has been nothing short of amazing, it's because of all of you that this story has finally made it out of my head and into the world.

ONE

Sunday, February 3rd, 2047 - 6:43 am
24-Hour Fitness - Augmented Reality Exercise Simulator
(ARES)

"**R**AH!" I LET OUT A loud grunt as I swung my fist through the air, feeling the telltale buzz of my haptic glove shoot up my arm as my fist passed through the jaw of the shimmering opponent in front of me. A heartbeat later the simulation reeled backwards as I quickly followed up with a combination of punches, breaking through my virtual opponent's defense.

I ducked under a wild punch, feeling a slight buzz in my headgear, telling me the attack had barely grazed the side of my head. My leg shot forward, landing a vicious strike against the simulated boxer's side, sending him crashing into the ground. I raised my fist to strike down at my fallen opponent when the program paused itself, a sudden buzzing sound filling my ears as a message scrolled across the augmented reality goggles I wore.

INCOMING CALL: PETER

ACCEPT? / REJECT?

"Ugh, Peter has to be the only person who still uses a phone to call people." With a small grunt of annoyance, I sucked in a deep breath, feeling sweat run down my back as I forced myself upright. I cleared my throat before answering the call. "Accept."

"Peter?" I said after my earpiece beeped, indicating the line was connected.

"Yo, Marc." The voice behind the phone sounded rushed, excited. "Where are you?"

"Eh? I'm exercising in the ARES at my gym. What's up? You're up pretty early for you, is everything okay?" I asked, concerned. Peter was one of my best friends, but he was a night owl. Having him awake this early in the morning was unusual.

"The ARES?" Peter sounded confused for a moment. "Oh right, that augmented reality training thing!"

"Yeah, and I was winning too." I breathed, letting some of the annoyance creep into my voice. "What's up? You okay?"

"Yeah, man, I'm fucking great! I'm calling because I've got news! Huge news!" He paused for a moment to take a breath. "Creative Tech just announced a new title. This time, it's a VRMMORPG!"

"Sweet shit, Peter! Did you just call me for that?!" I said, rolling my eyes as I looked at the frozen simulation in front of me. "Announcing means they're still years away from a product, and VR is a flop. VisionQuest tried it, failed miserably, and that was in development for fifteen years! Hell, the best they could do with their tech was to repurpose it for these ARES rooms, anyway."

"Why all the hype now?" I asked, while internally thinking *Why are you calling me about this?*

"Because they are releasing tomorrow." I could hear the smugness in Peter's voice.

"*What?! How?*"

"I know, right?" Peter spoke quickly, excitement evident in his voice. "The only bit of information we have is that there's a stream scheduled for noon today, and that more information will be available afterwards. A ton of hype has started building on the net about it already, and the news has only been out less than an hour."

I looked at the frozen simulation before me, remembering the slight delay that all ARES had. I sighed and began stripping my haptic gloves off. "All right, man. Color me interested. I've been looking for a new fix anyway. What's the game called?"

"Ascend Online."

FIVE HOURS LATER, MY CONDO was the site of an impromptu gathering. After taking a quick nap, Peter brought over our entire gaming group: Deckard, Misha, Heron, and Zach to watch the upcoming stream together.

The six of us had been friends all our lives, having met in early grade school and consistently staying in touch as the years went by. During our university years, when we all scattered to different cities to pursue our studies, games kept us together. Between late night marathons to *traditional* MMORPG launch day rush-to-the-level-cap sprints, the long distances between us were bridged. There was rarely a day we didn't speak to one another in some way, shape, or form.

"You didn't know anything about this Marcus?" Deckard asked me as I sat down on the couch with a cup of coffee.

"Nah...nothing. No reviews requests or leaks...not even a peep." I shook my head as I took a sip of my drink and looked for a place to set my mug down. I made my living as an independent game designer and freelancer and had just finished a major project. Unfortunately, that meant that there were half-finished doodles of artwork, maps, and notes scattered around the room that I had yet to clean up and organize. Apparently, I was still one of the few people left that thought better on paper before moving to a digital tablet.

"Hold this." I gave Deckard my mug as I quickly stacked a pile of papers on top of one another and found a spot to put my cup down.

"How could they have made a game in a vacuum without anyone getting wind of it?" Zach asked while pulling a gaming forum up on his phone.

"Well…like my right hand on a Sunday night—" Heron began before a flying tissue box hit him on the side of the head.

"No," Misha said.

"Quiet! It's starting!" Almost as soon as Peter arrived, he had commandeered the monitor I had mounted on the wall and brought up a timer leading to the stream.

00:00:04

00:00:03

00:00:02

00:00:01

00:00:00

We all watched as a black screen replaced the countdown; it gradually faded into a first-person perspective of someone traveling through a forest accompanied by a wistful and soothing music score. The detail in the scene was breathtaking, indistinguishable from real life. The stream followed our mystery protagonist as it showcased the scenery of the surrounding forest.

"Is this…a live action trailer?" Deckard asked before we all shushed him down.

The musical score suddenly changed as a growl broke the serenity of the scene, and the perspective spun quickly to see a massive gray wolf leap upon the protagonist, knocking them to the ground. We saw arms attempting to hold the wolf at bay as the vicious wolf snarled and snapped at our—the protagonist's—face. The massive maw of the wolf was all we could see.

I heard someone whisper, "Oh, shit."

The music took on a more desperate tone. The arms were appearing to get weaker as the fight went on, and the wolf inched closer to the screen. We could see the saliva covering the wolf's teeth as it moved in for the kill.

Two arrows suddenly burst into the wolf's head with a spray of blood, and the protagonist shoves the dead wolf off. A leather-gloved hand then enters the scene and moves to help the protagonist up.

"It's not safe out here. You should be more careful," a smooth voice admonishes, before the perspective shifts to reveal a leather-clad man carrying a large bow. "Come with me."

The scene and musical score changes to a montage of travel, showing the protagonist stumbling after the man. In a moment the forest is gone, showing a rolling grassland with something massive in the distance. The view pans around generously, showing merchants carrying goods on a cart, another showing a distant farmhouse with people working in the field.

"We're here." The man's smooth voice causes the protagonist to look forward once more, revealing a massive medieval city that stretched wide enough to take up the entire screen. There were suddenly hundreds of people milling about as the view went on to pan around in a circle. Huge muscle-bound orcs inspected weapons while haggling with a smith; a human woman held bread in both hands while shouting to passersby, all while a trio of elves walked by, girded in gleaming armor.

The view stopped on the man we had been following, and he

greeted us with a smile. "Welcome home, adventurer."

The screen focused on the man for a heartbeat before it cut to black and displayed:

ASCEND ONLINE
02/04/47 – 8:00 AM
19:54:59

"Hoooly shit!" Heron exclaimed just as the second countdown began. "That was incredible!"

"Nothing like VisionQuest!" Peter said with a grin. "Though it didn't tell us that much."

"That was a disaster," Misha replied, then indicated the screen. "But that…fuck! That was…awesome!"

"It looked so real." Zach shook his head. "I hope it wasn't fake. Are we sure it wasn't live action?"

"Shit, it was glorious!" Deckard grunted. "Bring up their website. How do we get in on this?"

"Sure." I nodded as I enabled the sync feature on my tablet, automatically casting everything on my phone to the monitor. A quick search brought up Ascend Online's website. It was bare at best. It featured a repeat of the stream we just watched, with the countdown taking over the majority of the page. There were only two small paragraphs of information on the page.

Ascend Online is a fantasy-based, full immersion VRMMORPG. To find out how to join us for our upcoming worldwide release, please click here!

To curb meta-gaming, the Ascend Online development staff has decided against providing an excessive amount of information at the start of the game. We have prepared a basic primer on the world information to better coordinate the initial game start with friends and guild members. Please click here for more details!

Additional content and information will be added to this page as the game progresses. We hope to see you in game soon!

"Full immersion?" I asked aloud.

"Who cares? Get the primer!" Misha yelled at me, her expression already wild.

"Listen to the woman, Marc! Heron already has it up on his phone!" Deckard joined in.

"I'm doing it, I'm doing it!" I impatiently grunted as I brought up the primer on the big screen. "Hold onto your socks."

Everyone ended up staying at my condo that night.

TWO

I WAS GRINNING IN MAD ANTICIPATION as the six of us walked through the main doors of CTI. Everything was a blur since I'd loaded the primer last night. Six hundred pages long, it detailed an incredible wealth of lore and background to the game world—without revealing a single scrap of information when it came to mechanics, gameplay, or even what to expect from the game itself. We spent the better part of the day--and night—reading and debating the little information that we could parse from it.

"Calling group three-eighty-four. Calling group three-eighty-four. Please proceed to Processing," a crisp voice called over the lobby speakers. Already a massive crowd had formed within the building's lobby as groups of prospective players all milled about until their group number was called.

Geez! There has to be close to two thousand people here! I looked around the lobby, seeing Peter waving us onwards.

"That's us!" Peter called as he pointed towards a sign hanging on the other side of the room. "Over there! That sign says Processing! We'll need to push our way through!"

The first thing that the primer explained to us was that Ascend Online didn't use the traditional virtual reality (VR) as we understood it. We wouldn't be expected to throw on a VR headset, place a few sensors on us, and play. That was what VisionQuest tried to do about ten years ago—the development cost and the odd disconnect between body and game never attracted a large enough player base to keep it afloat, and it flopped. Hard.

Ascend Online was pioneering Full Immersion Virtual Reality (FIVR) technology, which, thanks to the recent advances in nanotechnology, we would be able to experience a video game directly—without having to rely on a screen, headset or computer. All the information would be fed directly into our brain through the use of nanobots or nanites while our physical bodies were placed into a sort of artificial hibernation. From our perspective, our new reality would be one of the game world.

The one downside to this level of immersion was the overhead required. Because we needed constant monitoring during our unconscious state, we needed to play the game from within a capsule or pod, housed at a CTI Player Housing Facility. The pod would regularly inject our comatose bodies with the required nanites to maintain our connection with the Ascend Online universe, as well as provide the needed nutrients to keep our physical bodies alive. It wouldn't do to let players die while they were playing your game, right?

"Ow!" I yelped as an elbow accidently jabbed itself into my ribs as we pushed through the dense crowd.

I can't believe just how many people are here! I was a little taken aback at how popular Ascend Online was shaping up to be, becoming a little concerned about the potential economic and social impact of the game. As I pushed through the crowd I noticed that nearly everyone was around my age or younger, only spotting a handful of prospects appearing to be in their fifties or older.

Figures that there are mostly younger people here. It's not like they have anything better to do, I thought to myself bitterly as I received a second elbow to the ribs. Society as a whole was in the middle of a massive overpopulation crisis, with close to ten billion souls now clinging to life here on Mother Terra, which only exacerbated an already rampant unemployment problem as very few of the 'Millennial' generation were choosing to retire.

I really couldn't blame people my parents' age for wanting and needing to continue working. In the last ten years since nanotechnology became commercially available, modern science had been working overtime to catch up on the last six decades of promises. Things like cancer, heart disease, and even obesity were starting to be ailments of the past. Some early studies were even predicting that we might be able to get a few extra decades of life with the right mix of nanites in our blood—if you could afford to pay for them of course.

What's an extra five or ten years of working compared against living another eighty in near perfect health? I thought to myself and I shoved through the last bit of the crowd. *It just means the rest of us younger people will need to wait even longer to get into the job market.*

"Group 384?" a woman queried as we approached, bringing me back into the moment. "Six of you in total? I will need to see your IDs, of course."

"Yep, six of us are all here," I said as I presented my ID.

"Perfect! My name is Carol, and on behalf of CTI, I am excited to get you all oriented and into the game world." Carol quickly scanned our IDs and made a note on her tablet. "I see you have all signed and submitted your Terms of Use forms and everything else seems to be in order. Please follow me, we will need to register you with security and then we'll get you settled in your section."

The woman led us past a set of doors and through a security station, where we were prompted to present our IDs once more as we enrolled in the building's security system. At the end of it all, we were given a plain metal bracelet to wear on our wrist.

"Can't be too careful," Carol told us as we patiently waited for everyone to finish. "We take security seriously since the majority of our residents will be unconscious in their section."

"Makes sense." Zach nodded. "And makes me feel better, knowing I'll be safe."

After passing through security, Carol led us into an elevator which quickly whisked us away to the ninth floor. Carol led us out of the elevator and into an adjoining room. "This will be your section for the duration of your stay with us. Again, as a confirmation—all of you have indicated that you are onboard for long-term play on a monthly subscription, correct? I also understand you've all designated a third party as your stream producer?"

"Yep!" I replied as everyone echoed in chorus behind me.

Despite Ascend's requirement of needing to be physically in a pod to play the game, CTI did attempt to cater to a wide range of playstyles and priced their rentals accordingly. Subscriptions were classified into daily, weekly, and monthly durations with both short-term and long-term play options. Short-term play was geared more towards the casual market—play for a few hours a week with frequent logins and logouts.

Long-term play, however, was dedicated to the hardcore market who would stay logged in for multiple days at a time. The only stipulation with long term play was one twenty-four-hour cycle of "reality" out of every ten days of play. The reason for this "rest period" was to ensure that the brain maintained an appropriate baseline and to allow for proper non-stimulated rest.

The ten-day rotation also fed into another interesting feature—everything within Ascend Online was recorded and made available to the player. The recording not only caught the first person's perspective of the player but also of the surrounding area, allowing for multiple perspectives of anything a player experienced.

The recordings could even be posted publicly; the only stipulation being a ten-day delay between when the video was recorded and released. So, for anything we did today once we got in game, we would be able to show it publicly ten days from now. The idea for the delay was to contain the spread of meta-gaming and to give players time to play out any events or quests without any real-world interference.

For us, however, we were looking at these recordings as a potential money source. We were hoping that by playing together, and by being reasonably entertaining, we would be able to attract a high enough viewership to help fund our time playing. To help with that, we hired an eager management service ready to capitalize on this new content stream, to receive, edit, manage, and post our player streams on our behalf.

"Great!" Carol said as she then quickly gave us a tour of the room. "Your pods are here," she said indicating a wall covered with panels and displays. The pods were organized three across and two high, the better to conserve space. "They each slide out of the wall independently, and the upper level does have a ladder to climb down.

"The rest of your section is fairly self-explanatory. Think of it as a shared apartment. You have four monitors that you can sync to your private devices while you are out of your pod, as well as a pair of dedicated desktop machines. There are enough beds for all of you, plus a couple of full bathrooms just in case you all decide to have your downtime at the same time."

We all looked through our new home if somewhat half-heartedly whispering between ourselves before Carol laughed. "Don't worry! I won't keep you all from the game any longer. Stow any things you have and we can get you all in the pods."

Ten minutes and a change of clothes later, we were all lying down flat in our pods as they quietly whirred to life. "Hello? Can you hear me?" I heard Carol's voice come through the speakers in the pod. "Raise your hand if you can hear me."

I lifted my hand.

"Good! Everyone's system seems to be working. You should all be able to talk amongst yourselves now, too." I shuffled myself inside the pod to get more comfortable. "Basic diagnostics are starting now, just relax."

"Hello?" I spoke into the air. "Anyone there?"

Everyone quickly replied, and I could feel their excitement building. "All right, so that everyone knows. Where are we starting again?"

"Eberia!" Misha's voice came over the speakers the fastest.

"Hopefully it's a decent place. The primer didn't give all that much information..." Deckard spoke softly.

"It'll be okay. If not, we can just make our way to another city," Peter's voice replied confidently.

"Yeah. I'm not worr-OW!" I gasped as I felt something pinch me in the neck and, from the sounds of it, so did everyone else.

"Sorry for not warning you all!" Carol's voice sounded completely unapologetic. "I find it's best not to warn when the nanites are being injected. Don't worry, the IV and any additional wires will be applied once you are in hibernation."

"Before we can complete the log in process, CTI's legal team requires me to remind you that by signing the Terms of Agreement papers you have fully agreed to all aspects of CTI's Terms of Use Policy which outlines your rights and responsibilities as players. Furthermore, you have agreed not to seek legal action against CTI or its holdings due to in-game experiences that are of a non-technical nature. This includes but is not limited to, pain, torture, dismemberment, burning, drowning, and repeated simulated death. Also any emotional and/or psychological harm incurred by playing Ascend Online is taken at the player's risk. In the event of a mental break or descent into sociopathy, CTI is happy to provide PTSD, grief counseling, personality editing and limited memory wipes, at a nominal fee."

"Wait!" I heard Heron's voice squeak over the comm system. "Sociopathy?"

"I told you to read the papers before you signed them!" I yelled at Heron. "I did!"

"Ugh, you're the only one who must have ever bothered to read those things!"

"Thank you for choosing CTI and for subscribing to Ascend Online." Carol's voice continued undeterred from Heron's angst.

"Corporeal detachment in 3...2...1..."

THREE

Corporeal detachment – Complete
Integrating into Creativity – Complete
Running Pod Diagnostic – Complete
Creating Randomly Generated Feature – Complete
Loading Purgatory – Character Creation – Complete

"*W*ELCOME, MARCUS.*" A FEMALE VOICE greeted me as I shook off the transition between reality and virtual reality. I found "myself" floating in an endless starry night completely alone.

"Hel…hello?"

"*Do not be afraid,*" The voice spoke soothingly. "*I am Creativity, the Goddess of Creation. The disorientation will fade momentarily. Please tell me when you are ready to proceed.*"

"Oh…" I floated a moment while I digested the news. *Goddess? I must be in the game already!* "I'm ready."

"*Excellent! Let's begin!*"

The starry night swirled away as I felt my incorporeal body starting to move. Across my vision a menu appeared:

Choose a Race and Gender.

All right, here we go! I thought as I shook my head and started to page through the list of offered races. Practically every single race ever seen in a fantasy world was available here: catfolk, dwarves, elves, gnomes, gnolls, halflings, humans, orcs, goblins, saurians, ogres, even ratfolk.

Even though I typically didn't like playing the bestial races, as they tended to start with harder reputation penalties to enter major cities or far off in the wild, I decided to take a closer look at their racial information and see what was available. Waving a mental hand to select one of the options, I began paging through the races to look at their racial bonuses.

ORC:

Race Ability: Passive - Relentless – Stunning and movement slowing durations are reduced by 20+(lvl*0.35)%.
Passive – Night Vision – Grants ability to see in daylight conditions up to 100 feet in total darkness.
Racial Modifiers: - +5 Strength, +5 Constitution. Gain an additional +2 Strength, +2 Constitution per level.

More information kept scrolling, but I paged to the next race without reading. I wasn't interested in playing an orc. Not for this game at least.

ELF:

Race Ability: Passive – Magical Resistance – Any hostile arcane damage is reduced by 5+(lvl*0.1)%

Passive – Low Light Vision – Grants ability to see in daylight conditions up to 100 feet in reduced lighting.
Racial Modifiers: +5 Agility, +5 Intelligence. Gain an additional +2 Agility, +2 Intelligence per level.

I mentally frowned. The orc's racial was powerful, especially from a PvP perspective! But then on the flip side, reduced magical damage taken for an elf player could be the difference between surviving a magic attack or not.

I was still unsatisfied; I paged through a few more races trying to find out more about the new world I was about to become a part of. Usually by the time a game was released I was already armed with build suggestions, critiques, and in some cases, boss strategies. I quickly found it to be a sobering experience for me, barely knowing anything about the game.

"Do you have any recommendation on choosing race, Creativity?" I asked the goddess halfheartedly, not expecting a reply.

"It is not my place to advise. This choice must be yours and yours alone."

"Are you sure? I won't tell anyone!"

"Unfortunately, I am forbidden to interfere. Perhaps I may advise you to continue looking through the options before you?"

"Hm." I mentally nodded at Creativity's advice, continuing to scan through a few dozen more races available to me before giving into inevitability and bringing up Human as my starting race.

HUMAN:

Race Ability: Passive - Diplomatic Reputation – All positive reputation gains are increased by 10%. All negative reputation gains are decreased by 10%.
Passive – Ambitious – Receive a 5% experience bonus when gaining experience.
Racial Modifiers: +5 to two stats of player's choice, +2 to

previously chosen stats per level.

"Flexibility is essential," I said to myself when I saw the ability to customize my stats. Other races seemed to have a more "favored" path due to their locked in stats. But as a human I could build exactly what I wanted. I hovered my imaginary hand over the "next" button as I read over everything again.

> *Do you wish to select a Sub-Race or Regional specialization of your race?*
> *Warning: May restrict your starting location.*
> *Yes / No*

Intrigued, I selected "Yes," and a massive menu unfolded before my eyes, listing dozens of sub-races. Half-elf, half-orc, half-dwarf, half-troll—the variations were endless. I scrolled further down the menu only to start finding regional differences. My brain started to drool as I paged through all the variations. Half-breed races had a mix of both human and their other half racial abilities, but it was a regional specialization that I was looking for specifically.

HUMAN – EBERIAN

Coming from the fledgling kingdom of Eberia, Eberians are recent immigrants from the Ascendant Empire to the continent. After several decades of war, Eberia has just recently ended a bitter war with the orc tribes, resulting in a massive age of expansion. A very militant society, Eberians typically follow either Arcane or Martial roles, as they are blessed with both a brilliant intellect and a healthy constitution. Compulsory physical training and military service from a young age has resulted in a hardy and tough citizenry.

Racial Ability: Military Conditioning (Passive) – All defenses are increased by 5% and total hit points are increased by 10%

Racial Modifiers: Constitution: +5, Intelligence: +5 to base attributes. Constitution: +2 and Intelligence: +2 per level. The player may choose one Trait.

"Yes! It's here!" A regional specialization right in the city I wanted to start in! "Awesome!"

I was more than happy to exchange the reputation bonus in favor of the extra defense, and no sane player would ever pass up bonus hit points. *Military Conditioning* wasn't a scaling bonus like the other classes had, though I would argue that the orc's "Relentless" racial trait was probably just as powerful. What was a "trait," though? Would I be able to choose it myself?

Eager to find out, I selected "Male" as my gender and hit the "next" button, which had been glowing softly in the corner of my vision all this time.

I was prompted with:

Do you wish to use your stored appearance?

A mirror gradually appeared in front of me as I sped through space which displayed a figure based loosely off of my features, wearing a simple pair of underwear. Short blonde hair, light beard, tall, and in reasonably good shape. I wouldn't call myself a particularly vain person, but the first and only thing I did, was add more muscle than a realistic person could ever hope to have.

"If only losing fifteen pounds, then gaining twenty in muscle was that easy," I muttered wistfully as I accepted my character's appearance, eager to see what traits I could choose.

The mirror quickly faded away and my vision was replaced with another menu:

Select (1) Character Trait:

Followed by hundreds of entries. My mind reeled at it all as I tried to absorb what a trait was…it seemed like an innate buff to your character. They all ranged in power and usefulness from entries such as:

Augmented Vision – Magical enhancements to the Player's eyes now allow to see Daylight quality up to a distance of 100 feet, regardless of the surrounding ambiance.

Or:

Were-blood – Lycanthrope blood courses through the Player's body, granting +5% regeneration of total hit points every 30 seconds. Damage by Silver Weapons halts this regeneration until the player is fully healed through natural or magical means.

Could I get all of these in-game? I quickly lost track of time as I paged through the trait list. At first I tried to commit everything I could to memory but found it to be a losing battle. There were simply too many traits to choose from! How could I know what was useful?

I looked at the in-game clock and cursed. I'd been on the character creation screen for three hours already? Where was I?

Open Minded – Accepting of racial differences and radical ideas, you have learned to accept wisdom and the opportunity to learn no matter what form it takes, allowing you to make intuitive insights where others would give up in frustration. Grants a substantial increase in learning new skills, and the ability to learn all race locked traits, skills, crafting recipes, and abilities that are not otherwise restricted.

Oh, wow! My virtual mouth hung open; this was an amazing trait! The potential to learn race-locked traits and skills, on top of racial crafting? The faster skill gain was just a bonus at this point! In the past I'd always been huge on crafting; it was how I made my in-game money and kept me wearing the best gear I could craft.

Making my choice, I continued to the next section of character development, not believing that I'd already spent three hours making my character! I suddenly couldn't help but feel behind compared to all the other players who may have been faster in making their characters. I eagerly advanced to the next stage of character creation.

Character progression:
Level 1: Novice (Tutorial levels 1 – 4)
Level 10: Basic Class
Level 30: Advanced Class
Level 70: Prestige Class
Choose a Premade Starting Package (Optional):
Warrior – *Strength: +5, Constitution: +5.*
Equipment: Worn Chain Shirt, Rusty Sword.
Ability: Power Attack I
Mage – *Intelligence: +5, Agility: +5.*
Equipment: Moth-Eaten Robe, Cracked Wand, Spellbook
Spell: Arcane Missile I
Rogue – *Agility: +5, Intelligence: +5.*
Equipment: Patched Leather Tunic, Rusty Dagger.
Ability: Feint Attack I
Priest – *Willpower: +5, Strength: +5.*
Equipment: Moth Eaten Robe, Rusty Mace, Prayer Book
Spell: Holy Smite I
Create Custom Starting Package

I mentally nodded, ten novice levels and I could then choose my basic class. That should be enough to figure out whatever play style I wanted, looking at the options before me, I decided to take the custom path and design my character *exactly* how I wanted it to be.

Create Custom Starting Package:

You have 10 attribute points unspent.

Choose a starting weapon and/or armor.

Choose a starting skill.

Enter your Character Name.

Current Attributes:

Strength: 10

Agility: 10

Constitution: 17

Intelligence: 17

Willpower: 10

Looking good so far! My character had a good start in the surviv-ability aspect of the game. I looked for some more information on what the stats did before I made my final choices.

Strength *– Increases melee damage, chance to block or parry an attack, carrying capacity and skill gain of offensive melee abilities.*

Agility *– Increases ranged damage, evasion, accuracy, chance to score a critical hit, movement speed, and skill gain of offensive ranged abilities.*

Constitution *– Increases hit points (1 Point grants 10 hit points), hit point regeneration, physical resistances, lung capacity and stamina.*

Intelligence *– Increases the potency of Arcane Spells, mana pool, and skill gain of all non-combat abilities.*

Willpower *– Increases the potency of Faith Spells, mana pool, mana regeneration and mental resistances.*

All right, simple enough. But what direction do I want to go in? The game was hinting at a huge amount of flexibility for those who were willing to look for it. I paused to think for a moment, I wanted to use magic, but not be limited to *only* using magic. I especially enjoyed being able to hit things with a sword and being in the thick of the action. I assigned +5 to both Strength and Intelligence.

Next, I chose a rusty sword as my primary weapon, Power Attack I as my ability, and a spellbook to round things out. I had to make a choice between a spellbook and armor; I was sure I could scrounge up some basic armor when I got into the game. I was more than eager to start *playing* by now. I finished and double checked my selections. Ah, I forgot the character name! I didn't hesitate; I used the same name for all the games I played. *Lyrian Rastler*. After checking to see if the name was available, I was presented with my full character sheet.

LYRIAN RASTLER – LEVEL 1 NOVICE

Human Male (Eberian)

Statistics

HP: 209

Stamina: 170

Mana: 240

Attributes:

Strength: 15

Agility: 10

Constitution: 17

Intelligence: 22

Willpower: 10

Racial Ability:

Military Conditioning (Passive) – All defenses are increased by 5%. Total hit points are increased by 10%.

Abilities:

Power Attack I (Active: 50 Stamina) - You slash viciously at the target, putting extra strength behind the blow. Deal weapon damage +7.

Skills:

(None)

Traits:

*Open Minded: Accepting of racial differences and radical ideas,
the player accepts wisdom and the opportunity to learn no matter
what form it takes, allowing him to make intuitive insights where
others would give up in frustration. Grants a modest increase
in skill gain and the ability to learn all race-locked traits, skills,
crafting recipes, and abilities that are not restricted otherwise.*

Starting Equipment:

Rusty Sword

Spellbook

"Are you sure you wish to proceed without armor?" Creativity's voice
broke my reverie. *"Review your choices closely; you will not be able to make
any further changes."*

"I don't need anything to wear right now. I want that spellbook!"
I replied to the goddess. "But…can you tell me if I missed anything
important?"

"As I said before, I am forbidden from interfering," the voice replied
regretfully.

"I know," I said slowly after looking over my sheet carefully. "I'm
happy with my choices."

As I accepted the system's warning, my character sheet vanished,
and it was replaced by a huge map that took up my entire vision.

*"Due to your choices, you are required to start your journey in the King-
dom of Eberia,"* Creativity's voice spoke aloud once again. *"Do you accept
this choice?"*

"Yep!" I stated confidently, itching to get started.

"Very well, Lyrian. If you will close your eyes for just a moment," Creativity said to me as I began to move. *"The next time you open them, you
shall be at your destination."*

I felt myself beginning to pick up speed as I flew through the cosmos, the stars blurring past me faster and faster. Closing my eyes before I started to feel sick, I heard Creativity's voice whisper into my ear.

"Good luck, adventurer."

Loading, please wait…

FOUR

Loading, please wait…
Loading, please wait…
Warning: The Capital City - Eberia has been locked for an Event!
Transferring Player Spawn to closest open settlement.
Tutorial levels are engaged. You will not be able to message other players
until the tutorial is completed.
The tutorial will end at Level 4.
Welcome to Ascend Online!

THE FIRST FEW SECONDS AFTER I materialized into existence were disorienting. I don't honestly know what I was expecting with FIVR, and for a moment I thought that I'd been logged out. Everything felt *real!* The wooden floor under my feet, a gentle breeze on my chest, even my heart beating in my chest. *Wait, I'm holding a sword!*

I paused to take an experimental swing with the rusty blade. "Neat! This is so real!"

I looked around and saw that I was in a room of some sort. A castle room maybe? The detail was even better than the trailer! Was this what Ascend Online promised? I just couldn't beli—

"DIIIIIIIE!!!!!!"

A wicked, high-pitched screeching broke my thoughts, and I spun to the noise. A dirty, vile-looking creature was running straight at me!

"Oh, shit!" I shouted in surprise, swinging my sword out of reflex at the charging creature only to drop it straight on the ground as the creature evaded my swing and stabbed me in the arm with a crude-looking shiv.

"Aaaaaah! What the fuck?" I screamed as pain coursed through my arm, just as if I had been stabbed with a real knife! "Fucking shit! That hurts!"

The pain brought me to my senses and I barely managed to dodge the creature's second attack. It barely came up to my waist in height, but so far it was doing a great job of kicking my ass! As I focused on it, a small prompt in my vision identified it as a *[Young Goblin Raider] – Level 1.*

Anger quickly replaced the pain as I lashed out with my fists, ignoring the fallen sword. My fist connected hard with the goblin's face, sending it staggering backwards as teeth flew from its mouth. I watched as the blow took a third of the goblin's health away. Not giving the goblin a chance to recover, I followed up with two quick jabs and a fierce kick that sent the goblin sprawling to the ground, dead. System messages appeared in the corner of my vision.

A [Young Goblin Raider] Stabs you for 12 damage!
You punch a [Young Goblin Raider] for 9 points of damage!
You punch a [Young Goblin Raider] for 5 points of damage!
You punch a [Young Goblin Raider] for 7 points of damage!
You critically kick a [Young Goblin Raider] for 14 points of damage!
You killed a [Young Goblin Raider]!
*You have learned a new skill - **Unarmed Combat!***
You have gained 10 experience! 10/300

Looking at the dead goblin, my mind quickly flashed back to

my morning in the ARES yesterday. *This is a million times better than having to wear all that stupid haptic body gear! But holy hell does it hurt to get stabbed!*

Beating a goblin to death with my bare hands wasn't the way I had expected to start the game, but I wasn't one to argue with results. When the goblin stabbed me, I noticed that a small health bar had appeared in the corner of my vision; a quick check now showed that I had recovered already from the wound.

"Okay, while it hurts to get stabbed, it seems like I heal quickly enough," I muttered to myself, rubbing a bloody patch on my arm. Oddly enough, the pain was already a distant memory. Was the game helping me forget the pain? "And my brain has no hang-ups against murdering goblins in self-defense."

Picking up the sword I had artlessly dropped, I looked around to find out exactly where I was. This place didn't seem like Eberia; the system messages told me I spawned somewhere else. *Did everyone go through this, or just me?*

The room I arrived in looked like an office of some sort: a desk with papers strewn about and quills for writing, a few chairs. Nothing out of the ordinary, except, you know, the goblin. *Wait! What's happening?*

The corpse of the goblin turned a pale green and slowly dissolved into pixels. In its place remained a plain sack.

It dropped loot! My eyes widened in surprise as I quickly darted forward to find out what the goblin had dropped.

Crude Goblin Shiv
  Slot: Main Hand or Off-Hand
  Item Class: Common
  Item Quality: Poor
  Damage 3-8 (Piercing)
  Durability 20/20
  Weight: 0.4 kg

Favored Class: Novice
Level 1

Nothing particularly exciting, I thought to myself as I added the shiv to my inventory, after comparing the dagger's stats with my rusty sword.

Rusty Sword
  Slot: Main Hand or Off-Hand
  Item Class: Common
  Item Quality: Poor
  Damage 6-12 (Slashing)
  Durability 60/60
  Weight: 1 kg
  Favored Class: Novice
  Level 1

The sword certainly wasn't Excalibur, but it was good enough for the time being, allowing for a much better reach than the shiv. Taking a firm grip of the sword, I walked carefully out of the room trying to keep low to the ground. As I made my way down the hallway I began to hear people yelling, followed by the sounds of battle.

Where the hell did I spawn?! I thought as I hurried my way down the hall trying to keep as quiet as possible. With all the noise, I didn't have to try very hard.

*You have learned a new skill – **Stealth**.*

Happy that I was doing something right, I slowed my pace as I came to a stairway. The sounds of battle were louder down here. Hefting my sword, I crept quietly down the stairs. I entered into a hall filled with chaos; a dozen goblins were trying to batter down a makeshift barricade comprised mostly of piled tables and chairs, manned by a quickly dwindling number of defenders. An alert popped up in my vision:

▷**NEW QUEST! THE GOBLIN RAID!**

Goblin Raiders have assaulted the village. Save the villagers and drive away the goblins!

Warning! This quest will fail if all the villagers die!

12/12 Villagers alive.

30/30 Goblins in the village.

Difficulty: Average

Reward: Experience and ???

My first quest! I looked over the details with excitement as my heart started to pound in my chest. *Geez, there are thirty goblins in the village? Did I just spawn in the middle of a warzone?*

Maybe if I catch them in small groups or individually, I'll be able to take them. Right now the bulk of the goblins seemed to be concentrated at the head of the barricade by the hall doors. Closer to me, however, were three goblins that I would have to take care of before I could move any further.

A scream from a villager brought me back to the moment as a spear-wielding goblin found a hole in the barricade. Focusing on not being seen, I cautiously crept as close as I dared behind a *[Young Goblin Raider]* before I lunged forward and swung my sword with all my strength.

You Sneak Attack a [Young Goblin Raider] for 24 points of damage!

You have learned the Stealth Skill - Sneak Attack I!

Sneak Attack I - Passive:

Attacks made before the target is aware of you automatically deal weapon damage + 13.

You slash a [Young Goblin Raider] for 8 points of damage!

You kick a [Young Goblin Raider] for 10 points of damage!

You killed a [Young Goblin Raider]!

My vicious dispatch of the goblin caught the attention of two of its friends. They both charged me, screaming goblin obscenities as I set myself to receive their charge.

This is going to hurt, I thought to myself, wishing I had taken armor instead of a spellbook. *Shit! I forgot to check my spellbook!*

My temporary lapse cost me a spear thrust to the ribs, taking a solid ten percent of my hit points away. Grabbing the spear, I pulled the attacking goblin off balance as I slashed back at the second goblin, keeping it at bay.

I kicked the feet out from under the overbalanced goblin, sending it crashing to the ground, quickly followed by a sword thrust to the neck to ensure it stayed down for good. Surprised by my brutal assault, the second goblin shrunk away from me, turning to flee towards its other comrades. Taking quick aim with the spear I'd torn from the other goblin's grasp, I threw it, watching it bury itself into the fleeing goblin's back and slowing it down enough for me to catch up and run it through with my sword.

"You! Help us!" a red-haired woman shouted at me from behind the barricade of tables. "They're about to break through!"

"Because all I'm doing is standing here right?" I snapped back at the woman, as I watched the little bit of missing health regenerate itself and the pain fade away. *I only took a single scratch, and it hurts like hell! The pain settings here are far too realistic! Shit!*

Right now it seemed my health took care of itself reasonably quickly. The later levels I was sure I'd need bandages or healing of some sort. My health quickly hit a hundred percent, and I continued my efforts to clear the goblins out of the hall. I moved away from the makeshift barricade of piled furniture, towards the wall as I tried to flank the horde of goblins. Thankfully, the goblins were far too focused on a trio of spearmen holding the barricade from being breached to see me as I crept along.

"Give it all you got, men! Help is on the way!" I heard a voice shout from behind the barricade. "Stand fast!"

Taking the shout as a cue, I sprang forward, hitting the rear ranks of the assembled goblins. My newly learned Sneak Attack ability gave me the edge to kill two of the goblins quickly before the horde turned my way.

"Here's our chance boys! Chaaarge!" the voice shouted out again, followed by a guttural war cry as the spearmen leaped over the table they were using as a shield.

The spearmen's charge distracted the goblins long enough for me to slide my sword through a third goblin. The sounds of our battle brought more goblins from the other side of the barricade, the fight quickly descending into chaos. I fought wildly, swinging my sword with more strength than skill; at one point I even used a goblin as an impromptu shield as I slowly choked it to death with one hand. The battle took its toll, with two of the spearmen having fallen back from a dozen weeping wounds. I found myself fighting back to back with the last spearman and an older, dark-haired villager wielding an ax.

With the last fleeting bits of my stamina, I swung my sword in a two-handed chop and connected with a goblin's head, killing it in a spray of blood. Exhausted, I looked around the room seeing nothing but goblin corpses littering the ground.

> ▷QUEST UPDATE! THE GOBLIN RAID!
> *Goblin Raiders have assaulted the village. Save the villagers and drive away the goblins!*
> *Warning! This quest will fail if all the villagers die!*
> *12/12 Villagers alive.*
> *17/30 Goblins in the village.*

The quest update flashed again in my vision. Almost half of the goblins were dead, and the villagers were still safe.

Everything hurts. I fought to catch my breath while looking at my health bar, seeing it flash at forty-seven percent. With combat over, it gradually began to climb as my body healed itself.

"Ahem. Adventurer?" I heard a voice call me back to my new reality.

"Yes?" I turned to see an older, dark-haired, bearded man looking at me, along with some other villagers, mouths slightly agape. A pair of women were blushing heavily.

"Thank you for your help…but. Erm," the older man said, looking slightly above my head. "Are you aware you are naked?"

My mouth opened as I looked down. *Yep. I'm naked.*

I just killed a baker's dozen worth of goblins with my cock hanging out. I shut my mouth with a snap, looking the old man in the eye. *I swear I had underwear at the character creation screen! Hang on, didn't I say to Creativity that I didn't need anything to wear?*

"It seems I've misplaced my clothes. You know, the goblins…" I trailed off.

"Of course." The older man nodded. "The goblins."

Achievement Unlocked – Nudist
 For you, clothes are "optional".

As I mentally waved away the intrusive system alert, I swear I heard a distant feminine laugh. *Creativity has quite the sense of humor for a goddess.*

"I don't suppose I could ask for a set of armor?" I asked, trying to return to the business at hand. "There are still more goblins around. I can't fight them as effectively if I'm…hanging in the wind."

He looked blankly at me for a moment until he broke out in a short laugh at the absurdity of it all. "Ha! Indeed!"

He looked back towards the villagers and over at the two spearmen who had made it back to their feet. "We should be safe for the moment. The barracks are part of the town hall, just this way. We should have some spare clothes there."

He led me out of the town hall and into an adjoining room as if having a naked, blood-covered, adventurer nearby was a regular occurrence. "Your arrival is fortuitous, adventurer. We would not have held out much longer. I would have preferred to welcome the first adventurer to Aldford another way."

"I am the first?" I said in surprise. "My name is Lyrian, by the way. Lyrian Rastler."

"Bann Aldwin." Bann was a noble title of sorts, often for those formally recognized as a mayor of a village or township. More often than not they owed direct allegiance to the nobility that sponsored them.

We quickly made it to the barracks without any goblins impeding our progress. The bann pointed to a chain mail shirt hanging from a rack. "This was Steven's. I was told he was one of the first to fall when the raiders broke gates. It does us no good hanging here. Help us drive away the goblins, and it's yours for good."

I took a closer look at the armor while the bann provided me with a set of trousers and boots.

Militia Chain Shirt
  Item Class: Common
  Item Quality: Normal
  Slot: Chest
  Armor: 10
  Armor Type: Light
  Durability: 60/60
  Weight: 5 kg

A few moments later, my shame was hidden. The bann had given me a pair of plain black trousers, dark leather boots, and a linen shirt which covered me up for the time being, even if they didn't give any stats. Remembering my train of thought from earlier, I took a moment to pull out my spellbook—essentially what I had traded my starting armor in for. I glanced at the first page. *Empty.* Frowning, I paged through the whole thing. I didn't even get a spell to start with? A frustrated growl escaped my mouth.

"Problem?" Aldwin queried me.

"No. Just my stupidity," I replied, remembering the character sheet details now. I assumed I'd start with a spell in my spellbook. Shoving the book back into the pack with a sigh, I promised myself I would deal with it later. "How did the goblins assault the town?"

"I don't rightfully know," the bann admitted as we started walking back to the town hall. "I was speaking with one of our foremen about our construction plans, then I heard a loud explosion. Next thing I knew, we were under attack."

"Have you had many problems with goblins before?"

"We didn't even know there were goblins here! We just settled here a month ago. I bought the land rights from the Surveyors Guild for a small fortune. They promised that there was nothing here of any concern for new settlers." Aldwin looked at me. "We are bordered by river on three sides, with a double wide slate bridge we brought with us connecting to the southeast. We were in the process of finishing a stone gateway at the bridge's mouth to control access. Had we known danger was lurking by, I'd have started on a palisade instead!"

"They used magic to bring down the gate and charged across the bridge," interjected the red-haired woman I had seen earlier as we reached the town hall again. "A caster of some sort. I saw it happen."

"Lyrian, this is Shelia. She is a Sister of the Dawnfather. Without her, we would have lost many more villagers," Aldwin said, introducing us. "You saw them bring down the gate?"

"It didn't just bring down the gate. It blew the entire gate to pieces!" Shelia said, shaking her head. "I was watching the sunrise from the side of the river when I saw a single figure approach the gates. Truthfully, I thought it was just a villager returning from gathering some herbs or hunting and paid it no mind. My mind was preparing for the morning's prayers. The next thing I saw was a ball of fire streak from the corner of my eye, and the gate was gone."

"Was it a goblin that cast the spell?" I asked curiously.

"I couldn't tell. Does it matter?"

"It might later," I said with a shrug. "We need to drive the remaining goblins out of the village."

"We don't have much help to spare," Aldwin began. "I can't leave these villagers alone."

"No, I don't need your help," I said, hoping it was true. "I will do my best to drive the goblins out on my own. What I need you to do is to barricade yourselves in again. If I don't need to worry about trying to protect any villagers, I can focus on killing the goblins."

"We can't expect you to risk your life by yourself. Let me come wi—" Shelia began.

"Yes, you can take that chance. I'm an adventurer. I'm expendable by nature. If I find any other villagers, I will be sending them back here for you to tend to," I said as I interrupted the cleric. "Though if you could heal my current wounds…"

Shelia's eyes rose, then she nodded. "Oh! Of course!"

Shelia gripped a sunburst symbol that hung from her necklace while holding her hand out at me. "By the grace of the Dawnfather, *heal!*"

I felt a rush of energy swell into me, as a faint orange glow covered my body. I saw a system alert appear as the pain faded away.

Shelia cast [Heal I] on you! You have been healed for 54 points of damage!

"Thanks! That feels much better." The added bit of healing plus what I had regenerated so far was enough to take me back to full health.

"We still have a dozen villagers unaccounted for," the bann said to me as he nodded in thanks to Shelia. "Jenkins, our smith, and Ritt, a merchant, were out by the workshop—just to the east of the hall. It's the only other building in the village without a straw roof. They may have had a chance to barricade themselves inside. There were other guards at the gate, but if they didn't make it here…"

▷QUEST UPDATE! THE GOBLIN RAID!
New Objective! (Optional)
Rescue Jenkins and Ritt
Reward: Bonus Experience and ???

I looked at the villagers before me and nodded. "Don't worry. If they're alive, I'll find them and bring them back."

AFTER I LEFT THE VILLAGERS barricaded inside the town hall, I quickly found the workshop, a dull, mostly stone structure with a large chimney and clay roof. The primary point of interest, however, was the four goblins looking to break the door down. The door looked worse for wear as the goblins' weapons took small pieces off of it with every blow.

I quickly scanned the group of goblins, seeing that all of them were lowly level one *[Young Goblin Raiders]. Hopefully, this will hurt less now that I have armor!*

I made stealth a priority as I carefully crept towards the workshop. Thankfully, the goblins weren't trying to stay quiet, so their noise covered any missteps that I may have made on the way.

I stealthily closed the distance until I was only a few feet away, then quickly exploded into action. Leaping forward, I led with a heavy boot to the back of a goblin's head, sending it sprawling into one of its companions with a crash. Using my forward momentum, I chopped my sword viciously into the shoulder of another goblin, nearly splitting it in two as the blade sliced its way through the goblin's body.

I wretched my sword out of the dying goblin in a spray of blood, quickly cleaving an arm off the nearby goblin beside it. The armor the bann had given me easily caught a feeble spear thrust as I backhanded the offending goblin to the ground and stabbed it until it stopped moving. I whirled on the now one-armed goblin that had pressed itself against the door in fear and quickly put it out of its misery with a stroke.

"Starting to get the hang of this," I muttered to myself as I finished off the dazed goblin I had kicked at the beginning of the fight. Looking around, I paused to witness the results of my brutality, and to ensure none of the goblins remained alive. A moment later, the goblin bodies all dissolved in a spray of green pixels.

"Is someone out there?" a voice called from the inside.

"Yes! Ritt? Jenkins?" I called back. "The bann sent me to rescue you and get you to the town hall!"

"You don't sound like a goblin. Hold a moment…" I heard a bar being moved from behind the door, and it was pulled open slowly. A young, pale-skinned man holding a spear peered back out at me and, after a moment, waved me in quickly. "Come inside, quick!"

I stepped inside the workshop, cautiously looking around as the door closed behind me and the bar was set back in place. A second dark-skinned man standing behind the now closed door looked at me wearily. "Who are you? Why are you wearing militia armor?"

"I'm an adventurer. I saw the goblin attack and came to help," I said, somewhat twisting the truth as I looked at the dark-skinned man. I noticed that he was dressed in similar style armor as me but carried a nicer looking sword with a matching shield. "As for the armor, I had none of my own, so the bann gave it to me for helping drive out the goblins in the Town Hall. He said it belonged to Steven."

"Shit, Steven didn't make it? I'm Ritt, by the way," the pale-skinned man said. "He's Jenkins."

"I only know what the bann told me," I quickly replied with a sorrowful expression on my face. "We can't stay here, though. The bann sent me to see if I could find you two and take you back up to the town hall. We've cleared out the goblins attacking the hall, and they have a pretty solid defense set up in there."

"There's no time for a defense," Jenkins said hotly while peering out of a finger-sized hole in the door, courtesy of the goblins remodeling efforts. "The goblins are up to something. We saw them dragging villagers out of their homes."

"I'll take care of that," I stated confidently. "I fought my way here, after all."

"Bullshit! I don't know you. Why would you care about these villagers, anyway?" Jenkins spat while tightening the fastenings on his shield as he spoke. "I'm going out there to rescue as many as I can."

"Slow down, Jenkins! You can't go alone! If you die, I'll never hear the end of it." Ritt waved the big man to a stop as he quickly set his spear against the wall, picking up a bow and quiver. Ritt looked at me, motioning me to follow. "Come on, he's not going to take no for an answer!"

"Um." The pair quickly threw the bar off the door a second time and darted outside, leaving me in the workshop by myself. *Shit! These NPCs sure are more independent than I'm used to!*

Snapping back to the present, I checked my journal as I moved to follow the pair; there were thirteen more goblins left in town. Easy enough to do now that I had help. *Hopefully they won't run too far off without me.*

Chasing after the smith and merchant, I caught up with the pair as we approached the broken gate, hearing desperate shouts for help echoing through the air, intermixed with merciless goblin laughter.

"There are villagers still alive!" Ritt exclaimed as we saw several goblins herding captive villagers into a barred wagon. Four large horses stood ready to pull the wagon away at a moment's notice. "They're kidnapping them!"

"Is that uncommon?" I asked.

"Sure as shit, it's uncommon!" Jenkins was already on the move towards the group. "Let's go!"

"Hold up! We need a plan!" I said as I ran to catch up with Jenkins, pulling him aside. "We can't just run into there, they'll eat us alive!"

"Those are *my friends* in that wagon!" Jenkins hissed, shrugging my hand off. "The plan is to kill them! Hard and fast! I thought you had *stones*, adventurer!"

"Hard and fast is exactly what your ass is going to get if you wander right into that mess!" I retorted, not backing down from the angry smith. "Listen, we need to do this smart. We can save the villagers *and* live through this. Trust me."

Jenkins made an annoyed sound but nodded.

You have learned a new skill – Wordplay

Wordplay: Increases chance to persuade Non-Player Characters, resolve differences, and/or get information.

▷**QUEST UPDATE! THE GOBLIN RAID!**

New Objective! (Optional)

Rescue the Captured Villagers!

Reward: Bonus Experience and ???

"Good! First, you and Ritt can back up a few steps so they can't clearly see you. In the meantime, I'm going to go hide behind those crates." I pointed to a stack of crates with building material strewn around it about thirty feet away. "Once I'm in place, Ritt will fire off a few arrows to get their attention. At that point, Jenkins, you get to put on a show. Make them want you enough to come chasing over this way. With any luck, they'll take the bait and string themselves out as they run. Once they're past my hiding spot, I'll pop out and start killing them from behind. From there, we'll just chop our way through them until we meet in the middle."

Looking at Ritt, Jenkins nodded, a smile forming on his face. "Sounds like a plan, adventurer."

"Call me Lyrian," I said with a smile, then motioned them away as I crept my way towards my hiding spot.

Sword in hand I quickly stalked over to the hiding spot I had picked out for myself: a stack of two crates roughly shoulder level high. Ten seconds later, I heard Ritt's bow twang.

A loud cry told me that it had landed in the midst of the goblins and caused some pain. I crouched further behind the crates as I heard Jenkins start yelling while banging his sword and shield together. "Over here, you filthy beasts! Come and get me!"

Predictably, the goblins took the bait and charged towards Ritt and Jenkins without any regard to subterfuge or tactics, screeching the entire way. Crouching behind the boxes, I saw a few arrows hit the leading goblins, causing them to stumble as they ran. As soon as I counted the last goblin passing by my hiding spot, I moved. I quickly caught up to the rear of the goblins and began slashing out at the goblins wounded by Ritt's arrows, my passive sneak attack ability giving me an edge as I cut my way through the unaware goblins.

Four straggling goblins later, I caught up to the horde as they swarmed Jenkins. He maintained a desperate defense, swinging his sword in wide arcs, doing his best to keep the goblin horde from flanking him. Meanwhile, I saw Ritt playing for distance as he shot down a goblin that threatened to flank Jenkins.

Running in a full sprint, I crashed into the goblins, using my size to bully two of them to the ground. I sank my sword deep into the side of a third, giving Jenkins a chance to behead it as it recoiled in pain. Combat blurred as we hacked and stabbed the goblins to pieces. The fight only lasted seconds, but by the end of it both Jenkins and I were covered in blood. I was nursing a particularly nasty bite when I heard three separate *dings* as the system prompt exploded across my vision:

> *You have gained Experience!*
> **Congratulations! You have reached Level 2!**

> ▷**QUEST COMPLETE! THE GOBLIN RAIDERS!**
> *Optional Complete! Rescue Ritt and Jenkins!*
> *Optional Complete! Rescue the captured villagers!*
> *You have gained Experience!*
> *You have gained Experience!*
> *You have gained Experience!*
> **Congratulations! You have reached Level 3!**
> **Congratulations! You have reached Level 4!**
> *You have 15 Attribute Points Unspent!*
> *You have completed the Tutorial levels!*
> *Your resurrection point has been set to Aldford.*
> *Player Messaging has been unlocked.*
> *You have friend requests pending.*

That's more like it! I thought to myself as I scanned through all the messages.

"That's the last of the goblins," I said, smiling. The levels I gained had restored my health instantly. Jenkins looked quite worse for wear, however. "Let's go get the rest of the villagers out of the wagon and get you healed."

"Phew! I may have been wrong about you, adventurer...Lyrian," Jenkins said in between hurried breaths. "You adventurer types don't care about us common folk."

"Well, I'm not that kind of adventurer," I said flatly as I turned to make my way to the captive villagers.

"We will see."

FIVE

THE AFTERMATH OF THE GOBLIN raid resolved itself reasonably quickly. Jenkins, Ritt, and I released the captive villagers from the wagon and informed the bann of the all clear. The villagers weren't shy about heaping praise and thanks for helping kill the goblins, but I could still see the fear in their eyes. Their home had been invaded, and five of their own were dead. With how small this village was and how closely everyone knew one another, the mood was understandably depressed.

"Your timely assistance is much appreciated Lyrian." Things had finally calmed down enough for the bann and me to talk, ironically enough, in the very office I had first spawned in. "There was talk about sending out a call for all able-bodied adventurers to help tame these frontiers, but we had left Eberia before a decision was made. We are in your debt for helping us, though I am about to ask for even more of your assistance."

"What sort of help do you need?" I asked, torn between curiosity and hesitation.

At least Eberia is nearby. I still have no idea why I was spawned here, I thought as I listened to the bann speak.

I was hoping to have some time to catch my breath and sort out my character. Right now I was a somewhat inept rogue/warrior hybrid with high intellect for my level. I needed time to train, read my character sheet, and find a spell or two. Not to mention getting in touch with the group.

"Supplies. More specifically, any and all help you can offer in helping us get back on our feet again. The horses we captured from the goblins will go a long way to helping move goods and plow the fields, but we still need everything from meat to pelts to help replenishing the stores the goblins spoiled." The bann sighed and looked at me with concern in his eyes. "It is imperative that we get this village in shape before the next round of settlers arrive at the end of the month."

"The end of the month?" I exclaimed with surprise. "That isn't a lot of time! What happens if it isn't?"

"Then I stand a very good chance at being removed as bann," Aldwin replied softly. "And thrown into a debtor's prison or worse."

"What?" I nearly shouted. "Why?"

The bann looked at me for a moment, as if mulling something over in his mind. "In order to fund this village, I was forced to take out a loan from a noble house. House Denarius, in fact. As part of the agreement, they allow me considerable freedom to run the village as I see fit. However, the agreement also stipulates that I must have a prosperous village to show for their investment within a month's time as they are putting a considerable amount of effort into recruiting settlers and obtaining supplies on my behalf."

"That's reasonable, I suppose," I said to Aldwin, understanding his predicament.

"It would have been, if not for the goblin attack," the bann agreed with a sigh. "Which is why I'm turning to you for help. Any aid you could offer us would be greatly appreciated."

"I'll see what I can do," I replied earnestly, seeing a new quest appear in my vision.

> ▷NEW QUEST! REBUILDING ALDFORD (EVOLVING-QUEST)
>
> *The village of Aldford needs your help in getting more supplies*
> *and rebuilding after the goblin raid! They are in dire need of*
> *Food, Crafting Materials and Defenses!*
> *Warning! This quest is timed! 30 Days Remaining!*
> *Objective: Find Food and Supplies for Aldford.*
> *Difficulty: Hard*
> *Reward: Experience and Reputation with Aldford.*

"I haven't forgotten what you've done for us during the attack, however," Bann Aldwin continued as I accepted his quest with a nod. "We collected everything we found on the goblins. Hopefully, you can make use of them. If not, I'm sure Ritt and Jenkins will scavenge or burn them later. The villagers aren't keen on seeing or using anything they saw in the goblins' hands."

> *You have received a [Sturdy Backpack - 30 slots] from Bann*
> *Aldwin.*
> *Warning! [Sturdy Backpack] is currently full!*

Oh, geez! I completely forgot about the loot during all the fighting! I peered inside the bag and saw that it was filled with random items from the goblins. A few spears, a fair number of shivs, similar to the one I found before, and some scrap leather armor pieces. The biggest prize however, was the bag itself! Thirty slots tripled my carrying capacity! "Oh, wow! Thank you! I'll see what I can do to put this to use in helping out Aldford."

"No, thank *you*, adventurer. You helped us out of a bind with the goblin raid. We were caught unprepared, and that was my fault. I'll not let it happen again. I've spoken with Jenkins and Ritt. I've asked that they help you out should you need any spare tools or instructions to get you started."

I nodded at the bann as I stood to leave, sensing the implied dismissal. "I'll go see them right away and see what I can do to help Aldford."

WALKING DOWNSTAIRS, I FOUND A spot in the town hall to take a break. The barricade had been disassembled, with the tables and benches now organized into rows. Taking a seat at a table, I pulled up my character sheet and began mentally reviewing the battle against the goblins.

I need to be faster and stronger. I had some success in using my size against the goblins, but I was fairly confident it wasn't going to last. Right now my innate bonuses to Constitution and Intelligence kept my health and mana pool growing, not that I had anything to use my mana with yet. With fifteen attribute points to use, I carefully looked over my sheet before assigning ten points to Agility and the other five points to Strength. Accepting my changes, I took a moment to look at my updated sheet.

LYRIAN RASTLER – LEVEL 4 NOVICE

Human Male (Eberian)
Statistics
HP: 341

Stamina: 310

Mana: 360

Armor: 10

Attributes:

Strength: 20

Agility: 20

Constitution: 23

Intelligence: 28

Willpower: 10

Abilities:

Stealth – Sneak Attack I *(Passive) – Attacks made before the target is aware of you automatically deal weapon damage +13.*

Power Attack I *(Active: 50 Stamina) - You slash viciously at the target putting extra strength behind the blow. Deal weapon damage +7.*

Skills:

Unarmed Combat – Level 1 – 1% *(Increases knowledge of hand-to-hand fighting and improves related Abilities.)*

Stealth – Level 1 – 66% *(Decreases chance of being detected while attempting to stay hidden. Improves related Abilities.)*

Swords – Level 1 – 90% *(Increases knowledge of sword fighting and improves related Abilities.)*

Wordplay – Level 1 – 15% *(Increases chance to persuade others, resolve differences and/or get information.)*

The moment I assigned my stats, I felt…different. My arms instantly felt a little thicker, and my body just a bit more energetic, like I suddenly had an extra spring in my step, and everything was just a little bit easier. Would my body change as I gained levels and assigned my stat points? What about my mind, if I added more to my intellect? I shook my head; this was too much to think about right now.

Looking at my character sheet, I noted that my stats were relatively balanced for the moment, but I had to pick a path soon. Sneak attack was reliable as ever, though it was unlikely I'd be able to get the opening blow consistently, and unless I focused in stealth, the damage bonus would likely remain small.

Scrolling down my sheet, I saw the little progression I had made in my skills, noting that the more I used a skill, the better it got. Seeing how I was at level four already, and all of my skills a measly level one, I considered myself seriously behind.

A message appeared in the corner of my vision:

Constantine: Yo. It's Peter! Are you finally out of the tutorial?

During our night of reading and debating the information that was given in the primer, we'd all made sure to trade a list of character names that we'd try to take when we made it in game. Peter chose Constantine, Deckard chose Drace, Zach chose Caius, Heron chose Halcyon, and Misha chose Sierra.

Lyrian: Yeah. Shit. Character creation overwhelmed me a bit. I ended up with tunnel vision and just kept reading through the character menus. Odd thing though, I got blocked from starting in Eberia. What about you guys?

Constantine: Eh? No, we all loaded in here fine. Wait, how are you level four already if you've practically just started? Where are you?

Lyrian: I got bumped to a different village. When I finished making my character, the system tried to load me into Eberia, but all I got was a message the area was "locked due to an event". So I was dropped into the middle of a village called Aldford under attack from a horde of goblins. I just finished clearing them out of here.

Constantine: You've already been in combat? All they've had us do are fetch type quests and then we had to sit through this stupid "Call to Arms" ceremony the king put on; that's probably what blocked you. He's a massive twat by the way, but it got us three silver and a starter's kit. Any idea where Aldford is?

Lyrian: No idea. I don't have a map. It's near Eberia, though. One of the locals just mentioned it.

Constantine: Let me check with the Surveyors Guild here. They have a free map everyone can use.

Lyrian: Sure.

I idly waited for a few minutes, reading over my character sheet until Constantine replied.

Constantine: Okay. From the looks of it, Aldford is about seven days travel on foot, but I just heard another group talking about a shortcut that we'll check out. With any luck, we can cut it to two days if it pans out and if we walk late into the night. Eberia is crowded as fuck right now anyway, probably close to ten thousand people here if not more. Fewer players will be out your way.

Lyrian: Works for me. Be careful in combat, though. It really hurts if you get hit.

Constantine: Really? Shit. We saw a guy take a dive off a balcony because he was too lazy to go down the stairs. Broke both his legs and was screaming the whole time until he was healed. I thought he was just playing it up.

Lyrian: The pain is very real at the moment, but the memory of it
fades fast.

We chatted for a few more minutes before they set off, during which we both found out that player messaging was only enabled when both players were in a safe zone. If a player was out adventuring in the wild, the messages would be held in limbo until they returned.

Makes sense to limit communication, I thought to myself. *It forces people to cooperate closely and gives them another incentive to return to a city.*

I stood up with a stretch; it was time to see Ritt and Jenkins about the bann's promise for assistance. *Maybe they'll be able to teach me a trade skill or two.*

A FEW MINUTES LATER, I found Ritt outside the workshop. "Hey, Lyrian, I was about to look for you. The bann have a chance to talk to you yet?"

"Yeah, he mentioned that you had tools for me?" I asked hopefully.

"I have a few tools and a handful of tradeskill primers here too," Ritt replied handing me a stack of books.

"Primers?" I asked taking the books.

"The trade guilds decided it was easier and cheaper to write out the instructions for the more common trades and basic recipes and sell the primer books than it was to have their workers training each and every adventurer that threw coin at them. Once the scribe's guild caught wind of the idea..." Ritt rubbed his fingers together in the universal "money" motion. "Sure helps us out here in the middle of nowhere, though, or if you can't easily find someone that'll teach you."

"Definitely! Thanks, Ritt," I said as I looked closer at the books.

Tradeskill Primer – **Blacksmithing**
Tradeskill Primer – **Leatherworking**

Tradeskill Primer – Cooking

Tradeskill Primer – Mining

Do you wish to learn these Tradeskills?

This will consume the Tradeskill Primers

Yes / No

Blacksmithing - *A Crafting skill used to work metal.*

Leatherworking - *A Crafting skill used to work leather.*

Cooking - *A Crafting skill used to cook meats and plants into tasty meals.*

Mining – *A Gathering skill used to spot and identify raw stone and ore in the world. Minable nodes will be highlighted with a green outline.*

Yes! Now we're getting somewhere! The books crumbled into dust, and I saw messages fly by as the novice level blacksmithing, leatherworking, and cooking recipes were added to my recipe book.

"Here's a pickaxe you can use as well," Ritt continued, completely ignoring the dissolving books.

"I appreciate the help getting started," I said as I accepted the tool, then pointed towards the workshop. "I was thinking to take a few minutes to look over the things the goblins had on them. Maybe I can learn something useful from them."

"Sure, be my guest and use the forge. Jenkins said you could have free reign. He's…busy at the moment." Ritt smirked, eyebrows raised, silently begging me to follow up with more questions.

"Thanks, Ritt," I replied, pushing past the young merchant. I wasn't in any mood to pry right now; I had better things to do.

I FIGURED THINGS OUT QUICKLY once I sat myself down in the workshop. I didn't have the material I needed to craft just yet, but after unlocking the different tradeskills, I found out I was also able to deconstruct items and gain resources and experience from them.

Wasting no time, I quickly deconstructed the bag of goblin loot. As a whole I was somewhat disappointed with the result: half a level in both blacksmithing and leatherworking, a few leather scraps from the armor, some low-quality copper metal, and a number of miscellaneous items like bone, plant fibers, and wood.

> **You have learned the Goblin Skill - Improvisation.**
> *You are the first player to learn this skill! Congratulations!*
> *Improvisation - Goblins are often scavengers, making do with*
> *whatever they can find. Your study of goblin craftsmanship has*
> *given you the insight to make adjustments to standard and*
> *learned recipes by replacing required materials with something else.*
> *E.g., Replacing metal with wood in an armor recipe will create*
> *a set of wooden armor instead of metal. The higher your level*
> *in Improvisation, the more changes can be made and the fewer*
> *materials they will require.*

My jaw dropped. That was an incredible skill! *The Open-Minded trait was paying dividends already*! I felt my palms start to sweat as my mind raced at the thought of crafting unique items. First things first, though, I needed to get crafting materials. Unfortunately, a quick look over the basic recipes I'd managed to unlock after learning my tradeskills showed me that I didn't have enough materials to make anything at all.

Time to go hunting, then. I started to throw the mess of deconstructed items into my backpack as I stood up and left the workshop.

Outside, I ran into Ritt again. Apparently, he had nothing better to do for the moment but sit on a crate outside the workshop. "Hey, Ritt. I don't suppose you have any spells for sale?"

"Spells?" Ritt frowned. "I didn't take you for a caster while you were laying about with that sword. I have a single scroll actually, but won't do you any good without a spellbook, though."

"I have a spellbook," I said, pulling the book out of my pack excitedly. I was finally going to rectify my haste in character creation. "What spell is it?"

"Flare." Ritt stood and pulled a scroll out of the crate he was just sitting on. He waved it in the air, baiting me with it. "I'm going to need something in exchange for it. Five silver."

"Seriously? I'm going to be going out there into the wild trying to get supplies for this village, and you're hocking me five silver pieces for a spell no one in this town has a spellbook to even learn?"

"Demand has suddenly skyrocketed." Ritt grinned greedily. "You know…market forces are hard to predict now that adventurers are about. Might go up even further. Besides, with the primers and tools I've given you, I'm already out double that."

As greedy as the NPC was being, he had a point. "How about this. Give me the spell now; it'll help me out while I'm out there in the wild, and I'll pay you seven silver pieces worth of pelts and ore."

I could see the wheels turning inside Ritt's head. "Fine. That works too."

He handed over the scroll.

Arcane Spell – Flare (Evocation)
Favored Class: Novice
Mana: 30
Range: 50 feet
The player conjures a ball of fire in their hand and throws it at the target, dealing 13 damage.
Do you wish to scribe this spell? Yes / No

Once again I was rewarded with the scroll crumbling away into dust, and I saw the magical script slowly appear on the first page of my spellbook. Mentally selecting the spell, I activated it, conjuring a small ball of fire in my left hand with a bright orange glow.

"Oh, shit!" Ritt yelped, hopping off his crate. "You learned it already? Don't do that in the village! Put it out!"

"Right! Sorry." I flinched, waving my hand to cancel the spell. It looked like I could conjure this spell on the fly, something I appreciated. Standing still was a sure way to get yourself into trouble. I would have to practice more with it once I left the village. "Thanks, Ritt. I'll be sure to put this to good use!"

I waved goodbye to Ritt. It was time to go hunting before I got roped into the rebuilding efforts at the gate.

SIX

THE LANDS SURROUNDING ALDFORD WERE lush and fertile. I figured it was only a matter of time before the coming wave of players cleared the land and settled it for farming. It had the perfect mix of trees, greenery, and scattered ponds without being too hilly. You could drop a seed on the ground here, and it would happily grow in no time. I had even found a few veins of copper ore while I was exploring the area. Truthfully, the only downside of the area was that it was absolutely crawling with animals and other creatures.

"Rah!" I threw my newly learned spell in the [Fire Beetle]'s face and quickly followed up with a stab to finish the creature off. I'd been exploring the area for roughly two hours, tracing a small circle around Aldford. I found it difficult to move further than twenty feet without tripping over a snake, fox, or beetle, but it let me train the skills I was already behind in, due to my earlier level gain.

I had another odd moment when my "Swords" skill rose to level two. I immediately felt like I knew *more* about the art of swordplay; it was hard to explain. In an instant, I knew I was gripping the hilt wrong, and I could now envision different attacks or parries. The same happened when my skill reached level three. *If FIVR can replace everything we see and feel with this virtual reality, can it not implant skills and knowledge in our head?*

My consistent use of Flare had unlocked the *Evocation* skill as well, which provided a similar influx of knowledge. I could concentrate just a *little* better, and I felt like I was scratching at the *rules* of magic within the game. Even the blinding pain I had originally felt when I was first stabbed by the goblins was somehow easier to bear. All this was a strange and addicting feeling.

You have run out of food and drink!
You are Hungry and Thirsty!
Regeneration of Health and Mana has stopped.
Regeneration of Stamina reduced by 50%.

Oh, shit! I cursed mentally, snapping out of my daydream as my stomach rumbled. I had forgotten about food! Here I sat at fifty percent health, in an area where creatures were ready to take a bite out of me, and my health had stopped regenerating!

Wait, I learned cooking, didn't I?

I opened my recipe book; only a single recipe was listed:

Charred meat - Food - Meal
  Benefit: Satiate Hunger for 2 hours.
  Requirements: Meat (any), Fire.

It was a basic meal, but I had plenty of snake meat on me, or heaven forbid, beetle meat. I just needed fire. I frowned, wishing I had thought to buy a tinderbox from Ritt before I left town, then it hit me. *I'm a magical lighter.*

I quickly gathered some deadfall from a nearby tree—thankfully without attracting the attention of a nearby creature—and threw it into a pile. I tossed my tiny orange fireball into the pile of sticks and was rewarded with a small glowing fire.

"Ha! There we go!" I started skewering bits of snake and beetle meat onto a stick and held it over my makeshift campfire. I was sure I would remember this day with fond nostalgia a year from now, hopefully, while chewing on a finely cooked dragon meat steak. My first day in Ascend, cooking snake and beetle meat in front of a fire.

I carefully watched the meat as I cooked it, trying not to cook the meat any longer than necessary. After a few minutes of cooking, the juicy aroma of the meat made its way to my nose, and I began salivating. It didn't taste half bad, to be honest,.bBth the meats tasted oddly close to chicken.

"RAWR!" Something heavy slammed into me from behind, knocking me forward and my shoulder exploded in pain as I took a vicious bite to the shoulder.

I saw my health bar take a dive as I reacted out of instinct, grabbing the biting creature and rolling my body forward as I threw it over my now bloody shoulder onto the makeshift fire I'd started.

"Shit!" I cursed while I scrambled to get my footing, drawing my sword as I watched the *[Young Puma] – Level Five*, whirl from my throw and snarl in rage. *This is just like the trailer, except with a big fucking cat and ME!*

Reacting desperately, I slammed my fist into the puma's nose, stunning it for a moment. I had enough time to scorch it once with a hasty flare before it was on me again. I could barely keep ahead of the puma as it mauled my thigh with a swipe of its paw which knocked me onto my knees. I threw another flare at the creature as it coiled to spring, scorching a patch of fur.

Undeterred, the animal leaped at me, sending us both to the ground in a heap, my sword falling from my grasp as I fell. I pummeled the angry cat with my fists, managing to knock a single tooth out of its maw.

Enraged, a paw slapped down on my chest, and claws dug through my armor as the puma struggled for leverage to put an end to me. The first person view of the feral cat definitely trumped the mangy wolf in the trailer! I tried reaching behind me to find my sword lying on the ground. *So close!* I could just feel the edge of the hilt.

Gritting my teeth at the pain in my chest I pushed against the cat, moving me enough to reach my sword while its claws tore at my flesh. Grabbing my blade I stabbed out and into the creature's ribs, landing three solid thrusts before the fourth found something important, and the puma collapsed on me, all fight going out of it in an instant.

"Phew. That was close." The battle had taken a great deal out of me; my health flashed red at a measly six percent, and I could hear my heart thundering in my ears. A stiff breeze could do me in at this point, and while I had managed to make food for myself, I was still thirsty, which meant I wasn't about to regenerate anytime soon.

Pushing the puma's corpse off of me, I stood up, and out of habit, grabbed the loot on the creature as it faded away, finding a *[Normal Quality Puma Pelt]* and a *[Chunk of Meat]* on the creature.

With a sigh I began looking around for the food I had dropped in the scuffle. I was still a little hungry, and my health wasn't about to regenerate itself.

Did the five-second rule apply in virtual reality? I laughed mentally at the thought as I traced around the area.

"Ah! There!" I saw the stick lying half under a bush.

Bending down, I grabbed the stick to pick it up, only to have a paw reach out from the bush and slap it back to the ground with a growl. Blinking, I saw an even larger puma's face poke itself from out of the bush; in its mouth, it held a piece of meat I had previously skewered on the stick.

"Nice...kitty." The puma scowled around the chunk of meat in its mouth and growled even louder as it began shoving itself through the bush.

My meager health bar had yet to recover beyond six percent; there was no way I would stand up to a second fight so soon. Swallowing any shame I had, I spun on my heels and sprinted off into the woods, raw digital adrenaline fueling my flight. The sound of claws and growling as the puma extracted itself from the bush and gave chase only sped me along.

Shit! Shit! Shit! Shit! Where am I going?

I dodged branches and ankle-sized pitfalls as I sprinted out of the plains and into a small forest. In a straight sprint the puma would catch me quickly. I had to keep it twisting and turning to have a chance. The puma already found one free meal today; I wasn't ready to give it a second! The small forest was starting to clear as I made it towards the other side. *Just a little further to go!*

You have run out of Stamina.

On second thought, it looked like I was going to end up as a meal after all! My pace dropped drastically as my stamina hit zero. I could barely move faster than walking speed as my lungs began to wheeze. I could hear the sounds of the cat closing in on me.

"Welp. I guess that's that," I wheezed to myself as I continued pushing through the woods, trying to stay ahead of the puma.

I pushed my way through the last few branches and bushes that were blocking my way out of the forest, and my heart fell. Ten paces away the land simply ended. I was overlooking the edge of a cliff; I had nowhere to go other than back into the forest, or down.

"Well, shit." I peered over the edge. *Was that water?*

It looked like something had taken a massive bite out of the land here ages ago, forming a crater lake with a forest surrounding it. It was at least a hundred feet straight down to the water.

"RAWR!" The puma finally caught up to me. I turned to see it rush out of the forest, claws helping it skid to a stop as its yellow eyes fixated on me. Going back into the woods wasn't an option anymore. That only left one way.

I looked behind me, over the edge of the cliff and came to a decision.

"Not today, you little fucker," I said as I flipped the puma off with both hands.

Satisfied with my act of petty defiance, I fell backward off the cliff.

SEVEN

I HAD A LITTLE OVER TWO seconds to watch the cliff blur away from me as I fell before I hit the water with a thunderous splash. Thankfully falling into the water had led to no falling damage. Had I fallen on land, I would have splattered everywhere, making my reckless escape of the puma pointless.

Nemesis Added
Your actions have marked a [Young Puma] – level 6, as a personal enemy!
Your Nemesis will continue to gain strength and hunt you until it is defeated! Beware!

"Nemesis?" I gasped, still trying to catch my breath. "Well...I guess that's a problem for the future."

There is so much we don't know about this game. I hope it doesn't come back to bite me later. Literally!

Either way, I was happy to still be alive as I tread water. The cliff I had jumped off of was to my right, large and imposing. There wasn't really anywhere to scramble ashore there. Looking forward, I could see a distant shore. It would be a long swim, but I would be able to make it eventually. To my left, I saw an island of some sort, not that far away.

With nothing of interest behind me but another distant shoreline. I swam my way towards the island; I wanted to have a chance to sit and recover before more trouble found me. Seeing that I was likely the first person to ever swim in this lake, I drank as I swam. It finally got rid of the annoying thirst notification in the corner of my vision and boosted my regeneration to a measly two percent every few seconds.

As I made my way closer to the island, I could see that it was small, barely more than thirty feet across, covered solely in grass. I kept a sharp eye out for danger the closer I swam to the island, the nemesis warning already making me a little paranoid.

After watching the island for a few minutes, I didn't see any creatures and deemed that it looked safe enough to swim closer. Interestingly, the island didn't have a shore and didn't get any shallower as I approached, forcing me to drag my wet self onto the island. Happy to have a few minutes to finally catch my breath, I lay on my back while I watched my health and stamina recover.

Isolated away from the mainland, the island felt serene, peaceful even. All I could hear was the gentle sound of the lapping water around me. Yawning, I felt the mental stress of my fight fade away. How long had it been already since I started playing Ascend Online? Six or seven hours? Time flew by fast.

I allowed myself a few minutes of rest before I started to move again. Back to full health and feeling re-energized for the swim back to shore, my biggest challenge now would be finding a way back to higher ground. From what I could see in the distance I would either need to scale the cliff or find a dogleg path once I got over there.

"Might as well get moving," I grunted to myself as I slipped back into the water and began the swim to shore.

"OH WOW!" I GAPED AS I saw the pale green outline of what had to be a fifteen-foot-long vein of copper ore running along the cliff. I'd been swimming steadily towards the shore for about fifteen minutes before the vein highlights appeared in my vision. "Hm…"

I might be able to get all of it, if I can balance myself between those two rocks…

An hour, two skill ups in mining, three slips back into the water, and a lot of cursing later, my pack was literally overflowing with raw copper ore and a fair amount of tin ore. I was ecstatic and a bit confused as to why the two metals were found in such close proximity to one another.

Splashing back into the water, I couldn't wait to get back to Aldford and sit in front of the forge. With how tattered my *[Militia Shirt]* was getting, it was past time that I found myself a better set of gear!

I continued my swim back to the shore until finally stumbling my way onto land. As my feet touched solid ground beneath me, the hunger notification appeared again, much to my annoyance.

Figures. I hadn't had a chance to finish my whole meal before the first puma attacked me. After taking a moment to gather some dry wood, I repeated my earlier trick with the fire, this time cooking the chunk of meat I took from the puma.

While I was eating I looked through the system menus that were available to me. I saw the familiar options such as journal, character sheet, and map. When I attempted to open my map, I was given an error message:

> *You must have a map equipped in order to use this menu. In order to create a map, you must learn the **Cartography** skill.*

I shrugged. I could try my hand at making a map if I got some parchment, though that didn't help my being any less lost right now. *Another problem for the future,* I thought wistfully.

Thankfully, I was able to finish my meal and drink my fill from the lake without anything getting the jump on me. After taking some time to mentally retrace my earlier exploring, I figured Aldford was somewhere to the northeast, if at a much higher elevation.

With a sigh, I pushed myself up off the ground and started following the nearby ridge. I had no idea how long it would take me to get back to the village, and I wasn't eager to be stuck in the wild for the night. I paused for a moment to glance at the sun; it was already making its way to the west, and the best I could tell was that it was sometime between early and mid-afternoon. That meant I had anywhere between three to five hours of daylight left.

With a spring in my step, I set off north, deeper into the forest adjoining the ridge, looking for a way out of the crater-lake I had fallen into.

OVER THE NEXT FEW HOURS, I quickly found that the forest was packed with just as many animals and creatures as before. I ran into countless snakes, foxes, beetles, and even a few lone wolves as I made my way through the forest trying to find higher ground.

Thankfully none proved to be as difficult as the puma I'd fought earlier, and my skills quickly improved. I managed to collect quite a few animal pelts, enough that I was sure to fulfill my debt with Ritt, along with enough experience to hit level five. With barely a glance,

I dumped my five attribute points into strength, bringing it up to a mighty twenty-five, and the now-familiar feeling of thickening muscles followed.

As I stumbled up the gentle incline of the forest, I was starting to get a little concerned at the state of my gear. My pants were ragged, boots waterlogged, and my militia shirt? Well, it looked like it had lost a fight with a puma. Even my rusty sword felt off as I swung it.

As the sun waned, it gradually became harder and harder to see in the forest, and I grumbled at not choosing a race that could see in the dark, such as an elf or a dwarf. I was starting to have problems seeing anything further than ten feet in front of me.

"Some adventurer I am," I muttered to myself as I stumbled over an exposed tree root. "Wandering through the forest using my sword like a blind man's cane, hoping nothing decides to eat me for a snack. Ugh. Why didn't I bring a torch?"

The idiocy of my statement hit me about twenty strides and an unexpected fall later. With my eyes looking up high, trying to make the best of my better peripheral night vision, my foot stepped into nothing, causing me to pitch forward as I fell into a hidden fissure in the rocks. My face hit something hard, followed by my knees as I tumbled blindly, landing on my shoulder with a crash against hard stone.

"Fuck! Ow!" I cursed as debris continued to fall from above, along with my sword, which thankfully fell hilt first nearby. "Ugh, I'm an idiot! This is the tinderbox all over again! I'm a magical torch!"

I continued to swear as my battered brain finally caught up to the situation. Raising a hand high, I conjured and held my flare spell in my hand. The orange glow of the tiny fireball gradually illuminated the area I had just fallen into as I moved my hand around. Both the walls and floor were made of hewn stone, rough and unfinished.

"A passageway or maybe a tunnel?" I whispered to myself as I stood up slowly, checking my health. This time, the fall had taken a solid thirty-five percent off my health! I shook my head as I held my hand up high, trying to make the best use of my meager light to get my bearings. "I'd be the one to fall into a hole that you couldn't climb out of."

The little bit of directional sense I had left after my fall made me think that the passage behind me led south, back towards the lake. I lifted my flare and took a few tenuous steps down the southern path; it only led a short distance before it was filled in with dirt and rubble.

"Was this here before the crater formed?" I asked aloud. There was no way out this way.

I turned back to the area where I had fallen in and glanced upward at the ceiling. Climbing out didn't seem like an option either; as rough as the stone walls were, they proved to have few handholds to climb out. Not to mention I would have to make the climb in the dark as there was just no way I could hold the flare and climb at the same time.

"Onwards the inept adventurer goes!" I muttered to myself, choosing the northern path. At least I was able to see where I was going now.

With my flare in one hand and my sword in the other, I walked down the tunnel in hopes of finding another way out. I took it as a good sign that the further I walked the more I noticed a slight incline to the tunnel. I figured if I got close enough to the surface, I could always take my pickaxe out and dig myself through a little bit of rubble or backtrack and try digging myself out at the other blockage.

As I walked down the tunnel, I started to notice large gashes and burns that adorned the walls. To my untrained eye it looked like a running battle was fought here once, a long time ago. With still only one way to go, I followed the signs of battle until I came to a doorway. A heavy iron door that once used to bar the passage lay twisted against the ground. From the amount of corrosion on it, I had to guess that this door had been lying here for ages.

I quietly stepped over the door and entered into what appeared to be an ancient storeroom or staging area. Everywhere I looked I could see burn marks and shattered pieces of weapons and armor. Whatever this place used to be, its inhabitants certainly didn't go down without a fight. I bent down to take a closer look at a scrap of metal on the floor, but unfortunately for me, it didn't even register as an item.

Skreet, skreet

What was that sound? I lifted my meager torch higher into the air as I turned to where I heard the noise coming from.

Skreeeet, skreeet

Out of the dark, a shambling skeleton appeared, slowly shuffling towards me. It was covered in tattered, decaying armor with a long broken sword in hand. Standing from my crouched position, I brought my torch higher and readied my sword. With the added light, I noticed that the skeleton was missing its right arm and foot, forcing it to walk oddly slumped due to the missing bones. In fact, it looked as if the entire right side of the skeleton was covered in burns. Warily, I focused on the creature to gauge its strength.

[Decaying Commander – Rare – Level 5]

A rare creature! I thought to myself excitedly as I gripped my sword tight, watching it shamble into range. *I wonder what loot it'll have!*

Leaping forward, I smashed my sword into the skeleton's side while trying to send it stumbling with my boot.

You slash a [Decaying Commander] for 10 points of damage!
You kick a [Decaying Commander] for 4 points of damage!
A [Decaying Commander] hits you with [Heavy Slash] for 173 points of damage!

The blow from the skeleton sent me flying across the room before I crashed into a wall.

Aaaah! What the hell was that ability? It took off nearly half of my health in one hit! I wheezed as I gasped for breath; the blow had knocked the air out of me. Wincing in pain, I groped around in the darkness as I forced myself to stand up blindly. I had lost control of my Flare spell when I was hit.

Skreeeet, skreeet

It was on the move again! I hastily conjured my flare again, bathing the area in a dim orange light.

How was I going to kill this thing? The skeleton lumbered towards me slowly on its unsteady limb. *It's not that fast. Plus it's missing an arm—maybe I can get around it!*

I stood ready as the decaying commander closed the gap between us, I waited until it wound up for an attack and rolled hard to its right. The skeleton's broken sword sailed over my head, leaving a brand-new scar on the wall as it lumbered to turn after me slowly. *Shit, it's strong! But slow too.*

Taking advantage of the slow turning rate of the creature, I shoved the skeleton, sending it stumbling off balance. I slashed out, landing four solid hits before I backed away from the creature.

I can fight this! I smiled to myself for a moment before I saw that the hits I had landed so far only accounted for three percent of the skeleton's health! *Tough bugger! But then again, using a sword to cut a skeleton apart probably isn't the smartest idea!*

I drew the skeleton away from the wall and into the slightly more open area in the middle of the room. I glanced around the chamber to see if there was anything I could use to better fight the skeleton.

Nothing! All I could find in the room was rubble and shards of broken metal. I ducked under another powerful blow as the skeleton closed the gap and landed a few more hits on the monster. This time I darted in close to the skeleton as it attempted to turn on its broken leg and threw my shoulder into it, trying to knock it to the ground.

When I made contact, I found the skeleton to be much lighter than I expected and ended up tackling it straight to the ground. I lost my flare as I landed atop the skeleton, plunging the room back into darkness. I flailed with a fist and was rewarded with the sound of snapping bones.

Conjuring a flare once more, I barely managed to duck a swing of the skeleton's blade. Reaching out instinctively I grabbed the skeleton's remaining arm to hold the sword at bay, dropping my flare yet again. Despite its lack of actual mass, a wicked strength surged from the skeletal arm. It was all I could do to hold it at bay.

A [Decaying Commander] bites you for 34 points of damage!

"Aaaah!" I felt teeth crunch into my shoulder and tear through my armor. I fumbled in the dark for my blade, but my hand only came down on loose rubble.

A [Decaying Commander] bites you for 36 points of damage!

Blinded by pain at the second bite, I grabbed a chunk of rubble and swung it in an arc, hearing a satisfying *crunch*. I swung again, and again and again. I kept swinging until I saw a burst of messages appear on my screen.

You have slain a [Decaying Commander]!
You are the first person to kill the rare creature - [Decaying Commander]!
You have gained Experience!
You have gained Bonus Experience for defeating a Rare Creature for the first time!
You have gained 50 Renown for defeating a Rare Creature for the first time!
Congratulations! You have reached Level 6!
You have 5 Attribute Points Unspent!

"Ugh!" I gasped from the rush of killing the creature and the pain vanishing the moment I gained a level. "How...?"

I checked the combat logs.

You crush a [Decaying Commander] for 41 (+200%) points of damage!

You crush a [Decaying Commander] for 49 (+200%) points of damage!

A damage bonus? I slowly lifted myself off the commander's remains and conjured a flare. My half-dozen blind attacks had ended up crushing the skeleton's head nearly to dust. *Aren't skeletons typically weak to blunt damage? I thought I was done for!*

Brushing myself off, I assigned my newly gained attribute points into strength again.

Being the first to kill a Rare creature certainly pays off in experience! I thought to myself as I bent down to pick up the loot from the skeleton.

Commander's Broken Sword
Slot: Main Hand or Off Hand
Item Class: Relic
Item Quality: Normal
Damage 1-1 (Slashing)
Strength: +2 Agility: +2
Durability 0/0
Weight: 1 kg
Note: A skilled smith might be able to re-forge this item.

"Oh! Bonus stats!" I admired the looted sword. It was certainly worse for wear. I idly wondered if Jenkins would be able to help repair the sword for me.

Deciding to keep moving, I explored my surroundings a little further. Before whatever battle forced this place to be abandoned, this room used to be a combined sleeping area and storage room. I could see the remnants of a few bed frames along with a number of long since rotted crates. The signs of the battle disappeared as I walked further into the room, keeping a sharp eye for anything else that could be lingering in here.

At the far end of the chamber, I found a second hallway with yet another mangled door on the ground. The hall appeared to split in two different directions. To my right there was a rubble filled passage that seemed to lead deeper down, followed by another that led to a series of gentle switchbacks that led upwards.

Might be worth coming back down here one day and dig further down, but I really want to get back to the village, I mused to myself. Choosing the upward route, I continued up the switchbacks until I eventually felt a cool breeze.

There's a way out somewhere here! I started to walk a little faster until the tunnel I was following evened out.

"Ah, shit." I cursed as more and more rubble began to fill the tunnel until it was impossible to go any further. The breeze I felt was the strongest here as it floated in from along the ceiling "Well, it looks like I'll have to dig after all."

Holding the flare in one hand and using the pickaxe proved to be a difficult, slow, and annoying task. Eventually, after an hour's work, I was able to one-handedly dig my way through all the loose dirt and rubble that had accumulated over the tunnel's entrance, pushing all the excess further down the switchbacks. The moment I saw my mining skill hit level four though, I didn't mind digging my way clear. Whatever structure the tunnel led into was long gone, but with only bits of rubble and dirt remaining, I pushed my way through the gap I had dug, and out into the fresh evening air.

"What a day!" I gasped, as I paused to catch my breath and brushed myself off. The switchbacks led me back up to the plains and out of the crater. I took a few steps away from the hill I had dug myself out of and looked to the sky. The last lights of the sun poked over the western horizon, along with small wisps of white smoke rising into the air.

"That must be Aldford," I said to myself, happy to have a direction to walk in. "Time to get back and get some sleep."

And so ended my first day in Ascend Online.

EIGHT

Good morning, players!

Due to numerous complaints of Ascend Online's pain settings, we have implemented Patch 1.01 - All maximum pain thresholds have been reduced by 58%.

Thank you, and enjoy your time in Ascend Online!

-CTI Development Team

THE NEXT DAY I WOKE feeling refreshed and excited. By the time I'd made it back to Aldford, night had fallen, and if it weren't for the gate's rebuilding efforts and the extra lighting Jenkins's needed, I'd have probably ended up getting lost once more. I was especially thankful that I was left alone by the roaming creatures during my trek back too. My guess was nothing in the immediate Aldford area was willing to tangle with a level six player.

I sat up in the cot the villagers had given me in the corner of the town hall, then stood with a stretch. I heard noise coming from elsewhere in the hall along with the smell of food—*tasty, delicious smelling food!*

With a rumble from my stomach, I followed my nose and made my way to the kitchen.

As I turned the corner, I heard a snarl. "Hey! What you doing here?" A large, elderly half-orc woman holding a spoon stared at me. "Yous not supposed to be here!"

"Um…I smelled the food." The kitchen looked like a bomb had gone off inside it; a number of pots had been trashed and were piled into a corner. Bits of food were swept into another pile. I was surprised anything was capable of being cooked here. "I was hoping for a bite…"

"Oh no! I don't be having enough to be feeding the villagers, let alone lay-about adventurers!" The woman began to advance on me with the spoon. "Your lot are as bad as the goblins that trashed mine kitchen! No. Nope. Out! Out! OUT!"

"Wait! Wait! I have food, lots of food!" I shouted as I opened my inventory with a gesture, taking out the beetle and snake meat I had from hunting yesterday. They appeared as simple slabs of white meat. A counter in the corner of each indicated how much I had.

Chunk of Beetle Meat x 37
Chunk of Snake Meat x 19

The woman stopped her advance when she saw what I was holding. "Meat!" There was a tinge of respect in her voice. "Okay, maybe yous isn't useless. Give."

"Sure. Do you need help?" I handed over the meat to the half-orc cook. "I can cook, a little. My name is Lyrian, by the way."

"I's Ragna," the woman grunted as she snatched the beetle meat from my hands. "Yes, need help! Last assistant eaten by goblins, hope not happen to you. You useful so far. Take pan, fry snake meat with oil. Watch."

Ragna grabbed a single chunk of snake meat from my hands and threw it into a pan on the stove, along with some oil. A moment later she pulled the meat out of the pan with a fork and ate it whole. "Tasty. Now you, fry all. Break pan, I break you. Last pan."

Following Ragna's instructions, I repeated her actions and fried the snake meat in the pan. A few seconds later a system alert popped up.

> **You have learned the recipe: Fried Snake**
> *Fried Snake - Food - Snack*
> *Benefit: Satiate Hunger for 45 minutes.*
> *Regenerate 3 health every 5 seconds for 45 minutes when not in combat.*
> *Requirements: Chunk of Snake Meat, Cooking Oil, Pan.*
> *Level 1*

It certainly was an improvement over the charred meat I made yesterday! The extra bonus to regeneration would be a great help during solo adventuring. Currently, I regenerated about eight hit points every five seconds. I quickly continued frying the remainder of the snake meat that I had.

> *Your Cooking skill has increased to level 2!*
> *Your Cooking skill has increased to level 3!*

"Good. Much still learn. But not burning meat." Ragna looked over the pile of snake meat I had fried. "Beetle stew next. Mix with herbs. Already cut, watch."

The half-orc chef pointed at a large pot that I had barely noticed. It was filled with water, beetle meat and a green herb.

"Cut meat into bits, add water and hollyleaf. Simple, but taste well, helps with sickness and health." She handed me a spoon and pointed to another bowl with all the ingredients already prepared. "Add slowly, cook until almost boiling."

Setting myself to the task at hand, I added the meat and herbs to the stew, stirring it carefully. At first, it didn't look all that appetizing, but as the minty hollyleaf smell took over, my mouth started to water.

"Pay attention!" Ragna shouted at me and swatted me hard enough with a spoon to inflict a single point of damage. "Boiling!"

"Errr...right! Sorry." I quickly took the pot off the stove to cool.

> *You have learned the recipe: Beetle Stew*
> *Beetle Stew - Food - Meal*
> *Benefit: Satiate Hunger for 3 Hours.*
> *Regenerate 10 health every 5 seconds for 3 Hours when not in combat.*
> *Remove one Poison or Disease debuff when used.*
> *+10% Resistance to Poison and disease damage.*
> *Requirements: Chunk of Beetle Meat, Water, Hollyleaf, Pot.*
> *Level 3*
> *Your Cooking skill has increased to level 4!*
> *Your Cooking skill has increased to level 5!*

My eyes shot up. Now this was a meal! It would certainly make adventuring easier, though I had no idea where I could get hollyleaf. I said as much to Ragna.

"Hollyleaf? It grows everyplace, like weed. You not spot?" She frowned at me as she began to ladle the stew into wooden bowls.

"No, I haven't learned how to spot or harvest herbs." I watched as Ragna ladled the soup into smaller bowls.

"Heh. Was right! Layabout adventurer!" Ragna grunted and gave me a horrifying fang-filled smile. "Still, yous helpful. Ragna make you more helpful."

Wiping her hands on a cloth Ragna pushed away some of the clutter—broken pots and dirty food left over from the goblin attack—and reached up onto a shelf, grabbing a book.

"Here, Herbing Primer. Ragna has no time to show you properly. Bring more meat, herbs. Ragna show you how to make cook."

Surprised at having been given a reward without a matching quest, I activated the book in my hand without a further thought.

> **Tradeskill Primer - Herbalism**
> *Do you wish to learn this Tradeskill?*
> *This will consume the Tradeskill Primer.*
> *Yes / No*

The book crumbled to dust again as soon as I confirmed my selection. So far I hadn't found any indication that there would be a limit to the amount of tradeskills I could learn; likely the only limit would be the actual cost of materials.

I was painfully aware that at this moment I didn't even have a coin to my name, but from looking at the empty values in my wallet, I could see that the currency scale went from Copper to Silver to Gold and finally to Platinum. However, what the exchange rates between them all was still a mystery to me.

"Good. You learn fast." Ragna interrupted my train of thought. "You not needed anymore. Here extra foods you cook."

> *You have received Fried Snake x 10*
> *You have received Beetle Stew x 10*

"Thank you, Ragna," I replied graciously. "I'll be sure to bring back some more meat for you!"

As I left the kitchen, I checked out the new skill I had just learned.

> **Herbalism** - *Allows for the identification and harvesting of plants found in the wild. Harvestable plants will be highlighted*

with a green outline. Plants can be eaten for minor benefits.

I made a mental note to myself to start paying attention for herbs the next time I went out of the village. I was always on the lookout for things I could use for crafting or sell to other players.

My hunger getting the better of me, I quickly ate three fried snake snacks as I walked towards the forge. It was still early, barely past 6 a.m. by my best guess, and the village was still asleep. I could see faint rays on the horizon; the sun would be rising soon. I let myself into the workshop and started to sort out my haul from yesterday. After a quick look through my pack I had:

[Copper Ore] x 147
[Tin Ore] x 45
[Puma Pelt] x 1
[Fox Pelt] x 22
[Snake Skin] x 20

I brought up my crafting menus and began to sort through everything to see what I was capable of making. First I would have to reduce the pelts and skin into *[Raw Leather]*, from there I could use it directly in crafting either a set of leather armor or refine it further into *[Leather Straps]*, which I could see was needed for crafting a few of my Blacksmith recipes. I had enough to smelt forty-five *[Bronze Ingots]*, at a rate of two *[Copper Ore]* and one *[Tin Ore]*, which would then leave me enough to smelt twenty-eight *[Copper Ingots]*, at a rate of two *[Copper Ore]*, with a single piece of ore left over.

Taking a moment to sort out my workspace, I dug right into my work. The learning process was difficult at first, and the first few pelts and ingots I made were misshapen and uneven, but as my leatherworking and blacksmithing skills increased, new knowledge slowly trickled into my head, and I quickly got the hang of refining the materials.

*Your skill in **Leatherworking** has increased to Level 2!*

*Your skill in **Blacksmithing** has increased to Level 2!*
*Your skill in **Blacksmithing** has increased to level 3!*

Within an hour I finished refining all of my gathered material and was ready to get started making *actual* armor and weapons for myself. With a gesture, I opened up my character sheet to see what I could equip.

*Main Hand - **Rusty Sword***
Off Hand - (Empty)
Arm - (Empty)
Back - (Empty)
*Chest - **Militia Chain Shirt***
Ear - (Empty)
Face - (Empty)
Feet - (Empty)
Hands - (Empty)
Head - (Empty)
Legs - (Empty)
Neck - (Empty)
Ring 1 - (Empty)
Ring 2 - (Empty)
Ring 3 - (Empty)
Ring 4 - (Empty)
Ring 5 - (Empty)
Ring 6 - (Empty)
Ring 7 - (Empty)
Ring 8 - (Empty)
Shoulders - (Empty)
Waist - (Empty)
Wrist 1 - (Empty)
Wrist 2 - (Empty)

It was a whole lot of empty at the moment, but I was hoping I would be able to fill out the majority of the body slots by the time I finished this crafting session. Right now, however, I was still a Novice, which meant I could choose between Cloth and Light armor. It was my guess that proficiency in heavier armor types would open up depending on your basic class and advanced classes in the future. Since I wasn't able to do anything about it at the moment, I opened up my recipe book and took a look at what I was able to craft right now.

Bronze Studded Leather Tunic

Slot: Chest

Item Class: Common

Item Quality: Normal

Armor: 30

Armor Type: Light

Durability: 90/90

Weight: 3 kg

Favored Class: Novice

Level: 5

Ingredients Required: 2 Bronze Ingots, 4 Raw Leather

Bronze Studded Bracers

Slot: Arms

Item Class: Common

Item Quality: Normal

Armor: 5

Armor Type: Light

Durability: 60/60

Weight: 1 kg

Favored Class: Novice

Level: 5

Ingredients Required: 1 Bronze Ingots, 2 Raw Leather

Bronze Studded Cap

Slot: Head

Item Class: Common

Item Quality: Normal

Armor: 10

Armor Type: Light

Durability: 60/60

Weight: 1 kg

Favored Class: Novice

Level: 5

Ingredients Required: 1 Bronze Ingots, 1 Raw Leather

Hardened Leather Boots

Slot: Boots

Item Class: Common

Item Quality: Normal

Armor: 7

Armor Type: Light

Durability: 60/60

Weight: 1 kg

Favored Class: Novice

Level: 5

Ingredients Required: 2 Raw Leather

Hardened Leather Gloves

Slot: Hands

Item Class: Common

Item Quality: Normal

Armor: 5

Armor Type: Light

Durability: 60/60

Weight: 0.5 kg

Favored Class: Novice

Level: 5

Ingredients Required: 2 Raw Leather

Bronze Studded Leather Pants

Slot: Legs

Item Class: Common

Item Quality: Normal

Armor: 20

Armor Type: Light

Durability: 80/80

Weight: 2 kg

Favored Class: Novice

Level: 5

Ingredients Required: 2 Bronze Ingots, 4 Raw Leather

Bronze Studded Leather Shoulder Guards

Slot: Shoulders

Item Class: Common

Item Quality: Normal

Armor: 10

Armor Type: Light

Durability: 60/60

Weight: 1 kg

Favored Class: Novice

Level: 5

Ingredients Required: 2 Bronze Ingots, 2 Raw Leather

It took me another hour to finish crafting all the armor and shape it into something useful to wear. I carefully worked each piece of leather as the crafting system slowly walked me through the steps of stitching and assembling each piece. With every armor piece I crafted, I gained experience, and with every level I gained, I felt more knowledge seep into my head. I was starting to get used to the eerie feeling of remembering something I had never learned before. With a mental rush as I finished my last armor piece and reached level four in my leatherworking, I smiled. *I'll always remember this first armor set!*

Taking a quick inventory of my crafting so far, I used six out of my forty-five bronze ingots and seventeen pieces of leather. *I'll need a lot more leather if I'm going to make a set of armor for everyone else.*

I sighed and then put the remainder of the bronze ingots and my newly crafted armor into my inventory for the time being. I was about to do the same with my copper ingots before an idea took hold of me. *I wonder…*

Grabbing the forge hammer, I began to hammer away at my idea. I worked without following any specific recipe, attempting to envision the end result and hoping for the best with the knowledge that the game had given me. I discarded several poor prototypes, smelting them back down to ingots and hammering them back into the shape I desired until I was finally happy with the end result.

You have successfully created a new recipe!
You have created a [Copper Frying Pan]!
You gain Bonus Blacksmithing Experience for creating a unique recipe!

"Ragna is going to love this," I whispered to myself as I created a pot to match the pan, along with a number of knives. Realizing how useful a pan could be while traveling, I made a second one for myself, now that I had the recipe firmly fixed in my mind.

I quickly found that all my experimenting paid off experience-wise; for each and every broken prototype I created, I gained twice the amount of experience I gained when I followed the earlier armor recipes, bringing my blacksmithing level up to level six. Following a set recipe only got you so far. I idly wondered how far my imagination could take me.

It was then that Jenkins walked through the door.

"Ho, and I thought I was an early riser," he greeted me, seemingly in a much better mood than yesterday though I could still see signs of exhaustion in his eyes.

"Ah. Good morning, Jenkins," I replied, slightly startled when he walked in. "Sorry about hopping on the forge without asking…"

"Don't worry about it." Jenkins waved a hand dismissively as he stifled a yawn. He looked at me with a grin on his face.

"I heard the story yesterday, you slaying goblins without a stitch of clothes on you. I'd be a fool not to let you make some armor to help cover yourself up! Besides, it looks like you had a tumble with a bear." He indicated my tattered-looking armor and clothes.

"Erm." I shook my head at the memory. "Guess that will take a while to live down. As for the armor, it was a puma, not a bear."

"Ha! Wait, you're not lying?" Jenkin barked an even louder laugh. "We don't have that much entertainment here. Well, at least before the goblins came."

"They won't be bothering anyone else anymore now," I offered before changing the subject. "Say, while I have you here, I was actually hoping for your help in something."

"Oh?" Jenkins's eyebrows went up.

"I was hunting yesterday, and I found this." I gave Jenkins the general outline of my day yesterday and took out the broken sword I had found. "Any idea how I can fix this?"

"Ruins by the lake, goblins at our door…" Jenkins shook his head, but I could see his excitement when he looked at the broken blade in my hand. "That used to be a fair blade in its time. Thankfully, the core is still strong, and you should be able to Re-Forge it easily enough. Won't be as strong as it used to be, though. It's far too damaged," Jenkins told me as he joined me at the forge. "First clean and prepare the item. The cleaner you can make it, the better. Grab that whetstone—once you're done with that, you'll need to choose a metal to fill the chips…"

Jenkins spoke softly and guided me through the process. It was a long process and expensive process, one that cost me ten bronze ingots and three pieces of leather to re-forge the sword. But when I was finished, the system alert prompted me with a series of messages.

You have gained the Crafting Trait: **Re-Forge**

Re-Forge – *You have learned the basics of how to recreate a broken relic and are able to bring back some of its former glory. This skill will function across any and all Tradeskills you acquire. Beware! Some Relics are better lost to time!*

You have successfully Re-Forged the Commander's Broken Blade into:

Razor

Slot: Main Hand or Off Hand

Item Class: Relic

Item Quality: Fine (+10%)

Damage 15-25 (Slashing)

Durability 120/120

Weight: 1 kg

Favored Class: Novice

Base Metal: Bronze

Minor Enchantment: +2 Strength, +2 Agility

Level 5

I gaped at the long black and bronze blade I had just forged for myself. "Wow."

"Wow indeed." Jenkins nodded.

"Thank you!" My luck had certainly paid off! The sword was a fair bit better than what I would normally be able to craft, and it even gave minor boosts to my stats.

"No problem! You did all the work anyway. Are you finished here?" Jenkins asked as he sat down at the forge and began sorting a few tools after I had moved them, a subtle hint to make myself scarce. "I ought to get to work on materials for the gate."

"Yep, I'm done! I won't keep you longer." I collected the remainder of my things and placed them into my pack. "Going back out hunting, I promised Ragna that I would bring back more meat for her tonight!"

"Ah! You're the one that I have to thank for the beetle stew then!" Jenkins smiled. "We were worried that we wouldn't have enough for everyone, but everyone managed to get fed without a problem! You have my thanks!"

"Happy to help!" I said as a waved goodbye to Jenkins. "I'll be back!"

I walked out of the building and off to the side as I organized my newly crafted gear. With a grunt, I pulled off my tattered [*Militia Chain Shirt*] and clothes before putting on the armor that I had crafted. Two minutes later I felt like a half-decent adventurer properly clothed in armor. I eagerly brought up my character sheet to look over my new level and stats.

LYRIAN RASTLER – LEVEL 6 NOVICE

Human Male (Eberian)
Statistics:
 HP: 429
 Stamina: 390
 Mana: 484
 Armor: 87 (91)
 Critical Hit Chance: 11.5%
Attributes:
 Strength: 30 (32)
 Agility: 20 (22)
 Constitution: 27
 Intelligence: 32
 Willpower: 10

Abilities:

Stealth – Sneak Attack I (Passive) – Attacks made before the target is aware of you automatically deals weapon damage +13.

Swords - Power Attack I (Active: 50 Stamina) - You slash viciously at the target putting extra strength behind the blow. Deals weapon damage +7.

Skills:

Evocation – Level 4 – 8% (Increases knowledge of Evocation Magic and improves related Abilities.)

Unarmed Combat – Level 3 – 14% (Increases knowledge of hand-to-hand fighting and improves related Abilities.)

Stealth – Level 2 – 14% (Decreases chance of being detected while attempting to stay hidden. Improves related Abilities.)

Swords – Level 5 – 43% (Increases knowledge of sword fighting and improves related Abilities.)

Wordplay – Level 1 – 15% (Increases chance to persuade others, resolve differences and/or get information.)

Tradeskills:

Blacksmithing – Level 7 – 1%

Herbalism – Level 1 – 0%

Leatherworking – Level 4 – 8%

Mining – Level 4 – 11%

Cooking – Level 5 – 4%

Traits:

Open Minded

Re-Forge

Improvision

Equipped Items:

*Main Hand - **Razor***

Off Hand - (Empty)

*Arm - **Bronze Studded Bracers***

Back - (Empty)

*Chest - **Bronze Studded Leather Tunic***

Ear - (Empty)

Face - (Empty)

*Feet - **Hardened Leather Boots***

*Hands - **Hardened Leather Gloves***

*Head - **Bronze Studded Cap***

*Legs - **Bronze Studded Leather Pants***

Neck - (Empty)

Ring 1 - (Empty)

Ring 2 - (Empty)

Ring 3 - (Empty)

Ring 4 - (Empty)

Ring 5 - (Empty)

Ring 6 - (Empty)

Ring 7 - (Empty)

Ring 8 - (Empty)

*Shoulders - **Bronze Studded Leather Shoulder Guards***

Waist - (Empty)

Wrist 1 - (Empty)

Wrist 2 - (Empty)

Armored up and a new weapon in hand, I took a moment to admire my accomplishments since being dropped completely naked in the middle of a goblin infested Aldford. With a quick smile to myself, I set off towards the gate. "Back out into the wild we go."

NINE

UNFORTUNATELY, BEFORE I COULD MAKE my way out of the village, Ritt crossed my path. "Ho, Lyrian! Nice armor! Where'd you manage to find that?"

"Hey, Ritt. Didn't find it anywhere! Made it myself!" I was more than happy to boast at my accomplishments right now.

"You found that much ore out there in one day?" Ritt stopped and asked me intently. "Where did you find it? Do you still have more ore left?"

"Hm?" I was confused at what the big deal was. "Yeah, I dug it up yesterday, I lucked out on a large vein. There is plenty of ore around in the hills here if you can survive the creatures."

"Can you find more?" Ritt asked looking over my armor, envy

clear in his appraisal. "The village needs it badly. I've heard more than a few villagers talking about getting weapons and armor of their own. The militia armor we came here with was barely better than cloth against the goblins. Plus, we need more for repairs. Are you taking commissions?"

"Commissions? For armor?" I asked eyebrows raised.

"Yeah. Armor, weapons, ore, everything." Ritt nodded. "The bann has opened the village coffers to me. Whatever you can find or make, the village will buy it. If not, I might personally."

"Why me and not Jenkins? Isn't he the smith?" I asked, hoping I hadn't just shot myself in the foot.

"He is. But he's also our carpenter, leatherworker, and now militia captain, now that Steven is…well, he has plenty enough to do already. Plus we can't be risking him to go out and prospecting for metals either," Ritt explained.

"Ah…well, that makes sense then," I replied to him with a nod. "If you're buying now, I was actually hoping to repay that debt for the spell yesterday," I said, changing the subject. "I have ten copper ingots, which should be enough to settle our debt. I also want some parchment and ink to start making a map of the area."

"Eh, normally ten wouldn't be enough, but we need the metal badly enough." Ritt hedged as he looked over the ingots that I had handed to him. "All right, this is pretty good quality metal. Consider our debt even. I have a few sheaves of parchment stored in a crate."

"Thanks, Ritt." I put the parchment into my pack; I'd take some time to draw out the area later on and design a better map of the area. Maybe once the players started to flood the area, I would be able to trade or sell copies of my map. Not to mention be able to find my way around much easier.

"How much are you offering for a full set of armor?" I asked Ritt.

Ritt rubbed his face while inspecting my armor. "I can go just shy of a gold piece, nine silver for a set. eleven silver if you include a bronze weapon."

"Hm. What's the gold to silver exchange rate?"

"Right now, I can exchange at twelve silvers to one gold, since we're far from the capital and gold pieces are pretty rare. If you're at the capital, though, it's almost always fixed at ten to one," Ritt answered with a shrug. "Unless there's a vampire or werewolf outbreak. Then you'll be hard pressed to find silver anywhere."

"I'll keep that in mind, Ritt. Thanks." With our transaction done, I waved Ritt goodbye and set back off into the wild, idly wondering how often vampire or werewolf outbreaks occurred if Ritt felt it was worth mentioning.

MY SECOND ADVENTURE OUTSIDE THE village had me feeling much more confident than my first. With the added levels under my belt and my new sword, I was easily burning through the low-level creatures surrounding the village, and thanks to my new armor, any damage they did to me was negligible if they even landed a hit at all.

Hoping to find a challenge, I directed my hunting back towards the area I'd mentally named Crater Lake. With how overpopulated the area was with creatures, I netted myself forty-three *[Fox Pelts]*, sixteen *[Snake Skin]*, and four *[Puma Pelts]*.

Unfortunately, though, none of the puma pelts belonged to my nemesis; I idly wondered what had happened to the puma I'd escaped from yesterday and if I would see it again today. I'd be ready to give it a better fight this time!

Ragna wasn't kidding about hollyleaf, I thought to myself as I bent down yet again to tear the herb out of the ground. I'd made good use of the herbalism skill so far and managed to collect fifty pieces of *[Hollyleaf]*, along with bringing my herbalism skill to level three. As much as it slowed me down, the properties of the leaf had me stopping every chance I got.

Hollyleaf - Herb - Level 1
Use: Cure one lesser poison effect.
Tastes extremely minty.

An hour later I arrived at Crater Lake, having found a roundabout way to descend to the lower elevation. Sitting on a rock on the shore of the lake, I took a moment to eat a bowl of *[Beetle Soup]* as I began to sketch out the outlines of my new map. I had some experience drawing maps from a few design projects in the past, so the process went reasonably quickly and before long, I had a basic map to help me keep track of the way I came. I drew out the route I had taken, detailing the ridge wall and an outline of the lake. I made a mental note to return to the outcropping I'd leaped from to get a bird's eye view of the surrounding area.

I made personal notes of the areas where I'd found the large vein of copper and tin. It might be worth taking a closer look at the area one day. Happy with my budding map, I added a pair of markers to the map indicating "Aldford - Village" and another at my current position, "Crater Lake (Levels 1-5)."

Achievement Unlocked – Explorer I
You are the first person to explore and name a location!
Movement Speed: +1%
Renown: 5
Next rank: Discover and Name 5 Locations.
You have learned a new skill – Cartography
Your skill in Cartography has increased to Level 2!

I grinned at the system message and the flood of knowledge a new skill level always brought.

Excited, I decided to flesh out my budding map, and I started on a small circuit of the area, pausing every so often to draw additional detail on the map. While following a small vein of metal that netted me ten [Tin Ore], I lucked out and even found the hole I fell into the previous night. With half a thought I named it "Underground Ruins?" with the note (Digging Required). It might be another thing worth exploring one day—or selling the location to another adventurer.

I was happy to have something to focus on other than just sense-lessly killing creatures as they crossed my path. As it was, they hardly gave me any experience now thanks to diminishing returns. The creatures in this area ranged from level one to three with the rare level four or five. Keeping Aldford's food issues in mind, I made a point to kill a decent quantity of creatures, managing to collect about forty slabs of beetle and snake meat, along with a more few generic [Chunks of Meat] from the foxes and pumas I'd killed earlier.

Having exhausted the hunting on the Aldford side of the lake as I started to call it in my head and wanting a break from detailing my map, I decided to follow the lake's shoreline and see if I could find a more challenging spot to hunt. I spent the next half hour walking around the lake, ignoring the weak, low level creatures in my path.

The further I walked around the lake, the more I noticed a dif-ferent tone to the forest. The trees became grayer and grayer, and I couldn't remember the last time I saw a creature cut across my path. I stopped to take a closer look at one of the gray trees, and as I got closer, I noticed that countless webs were strewn about between the branches of the tree. I wasn't any sort of expert, but it was obvious even to my untrained eye that it was choking the growth of the tree.

"If this area doesn't scream spiders, I don't know what does," I muttered to myself as I looked around the area. Truthfully, I was glad. It was starting to get a little boring killing low-level creatures so easily. I was ready to see what I could do to a more powerful creature.

I looked at the forest line carefully, channeling all my years of gaming experience, attempting to spot anything moving. In my experiences, spiders were ambush predators by nature, and I wasn't about to go wandering blindly into its web. I stared intently at a nearby tree until I finally spotted a dark brown smudge…nestled inside a tree. I readied a tiny ball of fire in my hand and threw it at my target.

The tiny flare easily burnt through the fine webs hanging from the tree and splashed against the spider I'd spotted. Almost immediately the forest quickly burst into painful chitters and screeching as a pair of dog-sized spiders leaped from the tree and charged towards me.

"Here we go!" I grinned, summoning another ball of fire. I focused on the spiders: *[Small Spiderling] - level seven*. I tossed a flare at the second spider, causing it to halt, hissing in pain as it momentarily burned. I charged to meet the other spider, my new sword Razor in hand. I quickly found out that the spiderlings were much faster and more nimble opponents compared to the creatures I'd fought before, easily dodging my opening swings with Razor and moving far too fast for me to land a solid kick on.

I channeled another flare in my palm and tossed it at the spider I had burnt earlier. The flare splashed across it, causing it to squeal in pain once more. A follow-up Power Attack quickly finished it off. The second spider that I had ignored made its presence known as it bit into my forearm. I felt a burning sensation run down my arm.

A [Small Spiderling] bites you for 4 damage!
You have been poisoned!
You take 4 damage from a [Small Spiderling]'s Venom!
You take 3 damage from a [Small Spiderling]'s Venom!

I saw the messages appear quickly across my combat log as the venom began to rapidly drain my health. With a flick of my arm, I managed to dislodge the spider, and a vicious kick gave me some space to breathe.

"Shit!" I cursed as the side effect of the venom started to make my vision blurry. I conjured another flare and tossed it at the spider, missing horribly.

The spider, sensing my weakness, leaped at me and managed to land another venom-filled bite as it bit into my leg. This time, instead of kicking it away, I had enough presence of mind to stomp on it instead, pinning it to the ground long enough for my blade to find it and kill it.

"Ugh." Fighting these spiders was going to be a tedious task. It didn't appear that they had a large amount of health, but their speed and venomous attack more than made up for it! The two venomous bites the spiderlings managed to land on me brought my health down twelve percent after they ran their course.

Had I been less lucky and suffered a few more bites, I would have been in trouble. The only factor that had me excited was that killing the two spiders brought me seven percent closer to my next level.

That much experience per kill is worth a little bit of pain and suffering, I told myself.

> **You have learned a new skill – Perception.**
> **Perception** – *You are skilled in spotting hidden creatures and places. Depending on your skill level, hidden creatures, and places will be highlighted in red.*

"That'll help in spotting damn things before they sneak up on me. This would really be a good place to grind if it weren't for the venom," I thought aloud before I remembered the beneficial effects of the hollyleaf I'd been gathering a few hours earlier. *I'm going to hate the taste of mint pretty quickly.*

Two glowing bags reminded me that I had yet to check the loot from the spiderlings that I had just killed.

[Spider Silk Webbing] x2

[Meaty Spider Legs] x 4
[Venom Pouch] x2

Stowing the loot in my pouch, I decided to take a closer look at the tree I had seen the spiders on, hoping that I hadn't set it on fire. Thankfully, there were only a handful of scorch marks on the branches, the fire not having fully caught to set the rest of the tree aflame. Deciding not to waste any more time, I set off in search of more spiders nestled in the trees above.

Two hours, and seventy some-odd spiders later, I blew past level seven and hit level eight. For both levels, I chose to invest my attribute points into Agility in an attempt to boost my speed and accuracy against the spiderlings. I barely noticed now the speed advantage the spiderlings had on me earlier, finding it much easier to predict and follow their movements.

Unfortunately, levels weren't the only thing I managed to get in the forest. It was all I could do not to throw up after chewing down a hollyleaf sprig, a few dozen close calls with a swarm of spiders having given me a new dislike for the taste of mint.

With a scowl on my face, I forced down the last bit of hollyleaf down, happy to see the venom debuff fade away as it was neutralized. I opened my inventory to take a closer look at what I had looted during my grind session against the Webwood spiders, having named the area "The Webwood" on my map as I waited for my health to regenerate between fights.

[Spider Silk Webbing] x44
[Meaty Spider Legs] x 488
[Venom Pouch] x48
[Spider Carapace] x 65
[Spider Fang] x31
[Chewed Leather Boot] - Quest Item

Wait, a Quest item? Where did I get that boot from? I paused to take a closer look at it and, my quest log quickly filled my vision.

> *Chewed Leather Boot – Quest Item*
> *This single boot carries a single bite mark from a spider and is covered in what appears to be blood. Whoever lost this boot didn't do it on purpose.*
> ▷**NEW QUEST! A MISSING BOOT.**
> *You've found a half-chewed boot in the forest, and you definitely know that spiders don't wear boots. Find the missing owner of the leather boot before it's too late!*
> *Difficulty: Average*
> *Reward: ???*

"A quest?" I shook my head at the mental picture of a spider wearing boots. Quests in Ascend Online had far less hand holding than games I played in the past. Earlier MMORPGs would even have golden trails and an autorun feature to lead me from goal to goal.

"Hrm. Let's think a moment. The boot has a hole in it, bloody too. Probably caught in one of the spider's webs, I imagine. Spiders wrap their prey in webs…before they eat them."

I had looked around the area while hunting spiders and had largely ignored the cocoon-like sacs that hung from the odd tree. It made sense to me now that the spiders likely wrapped their prey until they were hungry enough to eat. I would have to cut open a few of sacs, but hopefully, I would find the owner of the boot.

Armed with a more concrete goal aside from the systematic genocide of the forest's spider population, I continued further into the Webwood, stopping to cut down every cocoon I came across. Inside, I found the remains of the forest creatures I had hunted near Crater Lake—foxes, beetles, and even a puma. The deeper I went, the more and more forbidding the forest became.

Thick webs hung high in the sickly, light-starved trees, and the forest itself was filled with an eerie silence. As good a home as it was for the spiders, they were slowly choking and killing the forest. The absence of any real predator caused their spawn rate to jump out of control. Before long, they would likely start harassing the villagers of Aldford.

In truth, however, I thought it was a perfect set up. A massive overpopulation of monsters was an adventure magnet; the local NPCs would generate quests as needed, and poof! adventurers get experience, monsters are defeated, and the region becomes safer. It was a happy circle, unless you happened to be a monster, of course.

Speaking of monsters.

"Where is everything?" I whispered to myself, keeping a sharp eye on the surrounding trees. The Perception skill had given me a great edge in spotting hiding spiders, but right now, I didn't see a thing. My wandering through the Webwood had led me to a small clearing, complete with a copse of trees in the center of it covered so thickly in webs that I could barely make out their outline.

A spot between my shoulders began to itch.

▷QUEST UPDATE! A MISSING BOOT
Objective: Survive

I flinched at the system message. *Shit! I must have stumbled onto an event!*

I held my sword and flare up high, waiting to see what would come my way. A burst of movement from the copse caught my eye, and dozens upon dozens of tiny palm-sized spiders exploded forth and swarmed towards me! I played for distance as I conjured flare after flare, tossing it into the seemingly endless swarm. That swarm would devour me in no time if they got too close!

Where my flare spell would be enough to slightly scorch a single normal-sized monster, here it burned the tiny spiders by the handful, three in one blast, a lucky five in another. It was all I could do to stay out of range of the spiders, quickly running around the clearing as I threw flare after flare into the swarm until I suddenly realized I'd spent nearly half of my stamina and mana pool, barely making a dent in the swarm.

"Shit! What am I supposed to do?" I cursed as I looked around the place. Webs had sprung up, almost by magic, blocking any exit out of the clearing. If I ever left this place, it would be as a victor, or feet first into a grave. "Time to try something different..."

Fighting the swarming spiders didn't seem to be working for me; I could still see more pouring out of the web covered copse of trees.

"Damn!" I cursed. "Flare, don't let me down now!"

Paying heed to the swarm, I stopped any attempt at conserving my mana and started tossing every flare I could muster at the webs surrounding the copse of trees. The first few spells I threw splashed against the webs, smoldering without truly catching fire, then on my seventh flare, it was as if an invisible hand poured gasoline on the trees causing it to explode in flames.

The effect was immediate on the swarm chasing me. It ground to a halt and began to scatter. I paused for a moment to catch my breath and regain some of the stamina I had lost while running. "Is that it?" I looked around, still seeing the web barriers blocking my exit from the clearing.

"SKREEEEEEEEEEEEEEEEE!"

I flinched as the sound assaulted my ears.

From the burning webs of the copse, a massive spider barreled out while shrieking. Burning webs had fallen all over it, sending it into a frenzy. I barely saw the name of the creature before it was on top of me.

[Giant Webwood Spider – Quest – Level 8]

I dodged frantically, trying to get away from the massive spider. It was easily over six feet long! Hell, it was bigger than my *car*!

I'm in the right place! This is a quest monster! I slashed at the spider landing two wild hits before I was forced to back off.

You slash a [Giant Webwood Spider] for 31 points of damage!
You slash a [Giant Webwood Spider] for 37 points of damage!

The spider recoiled from my attack, giving me the chance to see that the spider's health had dropped five percent.

"I can do this!" I whispered to myself as I conjured a flare in my palm, waiting for the spider to make its next move.

Realizing I had some teeth to me, the spider took a moment to size me up before it quickly turned and shot a string of web at me. The move caught me by surprise, and the web hit me right in the chest. Before I knew what was happening I was sailing through the air right at the spider!

A [Giant Webwood Spider] hit you with [Web Grab]! You are immobilized!
A [Giant Webwood Spider] has pulled you close!

"Aaaaaah!" A distinctly unmasculine scream escaped me as I was yanked off my feet, sending me flying through the air.

I landed painfully on my stomach in front of the spider as it spun to pounce on me. I rolled over quickly, to see a pair of fangs descending at my head. Flinching and twisting wildly, I brought up my hand holding my flare and threw it at the spider's face just as the fangs grazed my head and shoulder!

A [Giant Webwood Spider] bites you for 42 points of damage!
Your [Flare] spell burns a [Giant Webwood Spider] for 15 damage!

Blinded momentarily by my spell, I had enough time to roll to my feet before the spider attacked again. This time, it struck out with its two front-most legs, which I painfully learned had sharp claws at the end of them. The first claw was poorly aimed and missed me entirely. The second, however, found a spot in my side and stuck there.

A [Giant Webwood Spider] critically stabs you for 61 points of damage!

Wincing at the massive blow, I instinctively slashed out with Razor at the leg embedded in my side. Guided by my desperation, the blade sliced clean through the spider leg, spraying dark spider ichor all over me as the spider pulled a severed stump of a leg back screeching wildly!

You slash a [Giant Webwood Spider] in a vulnerable location for 76 points of damage!

"Shit!" I cursed as I pulled the clawed end of the spider leg out of my side out of reflex. Thankfully, they had lowered the pain threshold this morning. Even then, the pain was distracting.

So far the spider was winning the bout. I was down about twenty-five percent of my health while the spider was only down eleven percent. The only advantage I could see was that the partial loss of a leg had decreased the reach of the spider. Seizing the initiative, I charged the spider, leading with a flare to obscure my attack. It was impossible to miss the spider with the spell this close, and the tiny fireball singed the creature as I closed in.

I leaped over a meaty leg that attempted to skewer me with its sharp claw and landed a vicious kick in what I thought to be the spider's face, stunning it momentarily. I slashed out with weight behind my attack, severing the outstretched leg that had just missed me.

Howling with pain, the spider then swatted me away with a vicious swing of a leg, sending me sprawling to the ground once again a short distance away from the spider. I sprung up to my feet once again, barely dodging another attempt at a *[Web Grab]*. Needing a moment for my stamina to recover after all my sprinting, I conjured flares and peppered the giant spider from afar.

Not willing to have me scorch it from afar and unable to pull me close, the spider growled and then leaped at me. Its six remaining legs were more than enough to launch itself into the air as it pounced at me, knocking me off my feet and sending my health below the fifty percent mark.

In a panic, I rolled under the creature's body, slashing somewhat ineffectively with my sword. The spider *skittered* angrily as I evaded its probing legs and cut deeper into its body, drawing forth a foul-smelling black ichor.

Unable to fish me out with its claws, the spider attempted to crush me with its bulk. Fortunately enough for me, I anticipated the move and managed to roll myself clear from under the arachnid and get my feet under me. When the spider crashed to the ground, I leaped—directly onto its back. Truthfully, it wasn't graceful enough to be called a leap, more like an extremely awkward lunge.

Thankfully, I had enough presence of mind to lead with my sword as I leaped. Razor sunk deeply into the spider, and I used it mercilessly, pulling myself up onto the creature as its shrieks reached new levels of volume.

Tearing my sword out in another spray of gore, I stabbed and sliced everything that I could reach atop the giant spider as it tried to buck me off. Holding onto the spider as tightly as I could with my legs, I shifted forward until I was just behind the creature's eyes. The two stumps I had severed earlier flailed wildly in an attempt to dislodge me, but no longer had the reach.

"I've had enough of your shit!" I grabbed Razor with both my hands and stabbed down with the last reserve of stamina I had.

You critically [Power Attack] a [Giant Webwood Spider] in a

vulnerable location for 224 points of damage!
You have slain a [Giant Webwood Spider]!
You gain Experience!

My vicious swing with Razor bit deep into the spider's carapace, opening a massive wound that immediately gushed with ichor. I felt the spider go completely slack under me as it collapsed to the ground in a heap. A few heartbeats later the corpse turned faintly green, and I was sitting on the ground with yet another loot sack waiting for my perusal.

"Phew! What a fight!" I gasped to myself looking at my status bar.

LYRIAN RASTLER – LEVEL 8 NOVICE

Human Male (Eberian)
Statistics:
HP: 160/517
Stamina: 22/470
Mana: 166/572
Experience to next level: 3132/5400

I was sure happy that that this particular spider didn't have a poisoned attack, or else the fight would have quickly gone the other way. I shrugged and grabbed the loot sack "To the victor…the spoils!"

[Meaty Giant Spider Legs] x6
[Wicked Spider Claw] x6
[Giant Spider Carapace] x1
[Black Spider Ichor Vial] x1
[Spider Silk Webbing] x 10
[Giant Spider Fang] x2

Not seeing anything that required my immediate attention, I pocketed the loot and took a moment to eat a piece of food to help my regeneration. The webs that had locked me into the clearing now hung tattered and loose. The copse of trees smoldered slightly, the web having burned clearly away, but leaving the trees reasonably intact.

A few minutes later, with my health recovered enough to feel confident to continue exploring, I made my way to the copse of trees. Inside I could see the havoc that the fire had wreaked. Dozens of egg sacs were burnt and ruptured. There certainly weren't going to be any spiders hatching from here anymore. Looking past the charred mess, I spotted a burrow large enough to hold the massive spider I had just slain.

I moved closer and peered into the burrow; I could still see something covered in webs inside.

"A cocoon?" I slowly slid feet first into the burrow.

"Probably another half-eaten puma..." I muttered to myself as I gently sliced the cocoon open with the tip of Razor. "Oh!"

This time, it wasn't a puma.

TEN

I PEELED BACK THE WEB COCOON to reveal an ashen face of a young woman; a tag appeared in bright letters across my vision:

[Unconscious Huntress – Level 7]

At the same time my quest log decided to update:

▸**QUEST UPDATE! THE QUEST A MISSING BOOT IS NOW UNIQUE!**
Objective: Rescue the Unconscious Huntress.
Reward: Experience

I shook my head to clear the overload of information. *Apparently seeing her is enough to trigger the quest! What is this about a unique quest?*

I guess someone can't rescue her if I'm already rescuing her...

I tore at the web cocoon covering her until I had managed to get the majority of it removed from her body, revealing hunting leathers—and of course, a missing boot. I attempted to shake her gently. "Hey...wake up! Are you okay?"

Unfortunately for me, however, whatever was afflicting her kept her firmly unconscious. I sighed. I didn't have any healing or first aid abilities, and I doubted that force feeding the huntress hollyleaf would cure her of whatever was keeping her unconscious. That left only one option: get her back to Aldford.

Getting myself and the huntress out of the burrow wasn't an easy or graceful process, but thanks to the mighty thirty-two strength I had, I managed to get the both of us out of the hole. With a moment to catch my breath, I picked the huntress up in a fireman carry position and set off towards Aldford with Razor in my other hand.

While what I would like to say happened is that I carried her back to Aldford in a full sprint the entire way without any issues, the actual reality of the trek back was comprised of several stops for me to slowly regenerate my stamina and fend off a few opportunistic creatures. Maybe in a few levels I wouldn't have such issues carrying a heavier load, but for the time being, it was slow going.

The rough map I had made of the area helped me keep on track towards Aldford, and by early afternoon I made it back to the village.

"Lyrian! What happened?" Shelia was the first to greet me, her white and red robes billowing as she ran towards me, followed closely by a few villagers who had heard the commotion.

"I found her in the far forest on the other side of the lake; there are giant spiders infesting the forest. She's been bitten and won't wake up." I explained how I had found her half-eaten boot in the forest, and the giant spider I had killed.

"*Giant spiders?*" A villager shrilled. "Aren't goblins enough?"

"This place isn't safe!" another villager shouted. "We should never have settled here!"

"I'm leaving in the morning!"

"Don't do that! You'll get eaten by the spiders or enslaved by the goblins!"

"Enough!" Shelia shouted to the growing crowd. "We won't get eaten or enslaved! The Dawnfather sent Lyrian here in our darkest hour to protect us from the goblins. Have patience and faith!"

Shelia looked at me with a sharp glance. "There's no time for this. We need to get her to a bed."

Pushing through the growing crowd, Shelia led me to the town hall in the center of the village.

"Put her there." She pointed to a spare cot in the corner of the room while ordering another female villager to set up blinds for some privacy.

I set the huntress gently on the bed to hear a familiar *ding* and a number of notices appear in the system prompt.

> ⊳A MISSING BOOT (UNIQUE)
> QUEST COMPLETED!
> *Objective: Rescue the Unconscious Huntress.*
> *Reward: Experience*
> *You have gained experience!*
> **Congratulations! You have reached Level 9!**
> *You have 5 Attribute Points Unspent!*
> *You will not be able to advance to level 10 without receiving*
> *training for a Base Class.*

"I need some privacy to tend to her and to clean the rest of the webs off her." Shelia began stripping pieces of gear off the huntress and shouted an order for some hot water. "You should tell the bann about the spiders."

"Right. If you need me, I'll be around here somewhere." I nodded as I turned and walked around the blinds that had been set up beside the cot.

I paused long enough to assign my newly gained attribute points to Strength before I continued walking towards the kitchen. The bann could wait for a few minutes.

"Ragna?" I called out. "Are you here?"

"Ho. Where else I be?" I heard a snort from the kitchen as I rounded the corner. "Is useful assistant back with more meats, or does Ragna need to beat with spoon?"

I glanced about the kitchen; Ragna had done an admirable job cleaning and re-arranging the kitchen from the disaster it was in the morning, and she was busy with her back turned towards me, mixing something.

"No need for a spoon Ragna! I brought more meat!" I smiled and pulled out an item I made earlier in the day. "I brought gifts too!"

"Silly adventurer…why you waste time bringing Ragna gif—" Ragna stopped when she saw what I was holding in my hand. "Copper pan!"

"Not just a pan!" I told Ragna as I pulled out two pots of varying sizes and the copper knives, setting them on the table.

Ragna looked at me for a moment before wiping an invisible tear away and moving to embrace me.

"Maybe not so layabout after all," she said, holding the copper pan and testing its weight. "You too nice to Ragna…"

"But wait! There's more!" I was in such a hurry to show Ragna the meat I had collected while hunting; I pulled out a *[Meaty Giant Spider Leg]*. "Oh. Whoops! I also found spider legs. Maybe not best for cooking. I have more me—"

"Oh! Spider legses?" Ragna *squealed* in delight. "They make very tasty treats! This leg so big! You have spider venoms? Yes?"

Taken aback at the loud noises coming from the matronly half-orc, it was all I could do to nod.

"Ye-yeah, I have some venom, a lot of it actually!" I handed over my stash of meat, spider legs, and venom to Ragna.

"Ragna make foods! Aldford not be hungry for long while!"

"I am happy to hear that, Ragna!" My face betrayed concern as I saw her begin slicing the chitin off the giant spider leg I had given her. I decided it was time to beat a hasty exit. "I need to go see the bann; I will see you later, Ragna."

"Bye-bye, assistant. You come back and help Ragna cook when yous have time! Ragna will set foods asides for yous."

▷QUEST UPDATE! REBUILDING ALDFORD

Thanks to your efforts, Aldford will no longer go hungry for the time being!

Having escaped being press-ganged by Ragna, I waved down a villager in the town hall to see where the bann was.

"Sir, last I saw of him was them gathering the militia and getting set for some drilling in the far yard."

I thanked the villager and left in search of the bann. I didn't need to go far before I heard shouting and concerned voices. Unfortunately, word of my arrival and rescue of an unknown huntress had traveled fast, and a number of villagers had gone to the bann in search of answers.

"Who else is out there?"

"We were supposed to have the only settlement rights in the area!"

"What are you going to do about the spiders?"

I saw the bann and Jenkins standing behind a number of the guardsmen, trying to address the crowd without success.

"Lyrian! Lyrian!" The bann saw my approach and waved at me. "Let him through!"

The crowd parted around me as I made my way to the bann, and they began to fall quiet. Whispers of my earlier arrival with the un-known huntress filled the air as I approached the bann and Jenkins.

"Lyrian! What is going on?" the bann whispered fiercely to me. "The wood is infested with giant spiders? You found someone too?"

"Not all the wood…" I paused to give the bann an outline of my adventures in the Webwood, finishing with the discovery of the huntress.

"They are still far enough away then." The bann sighed, more to himself than me. "I had no idea there was anyone else nearby. Hope-fully this huntress will wake and tell us exactly what she was doing in the area."

"We'll have to deal with the spiders eventually." Jenkins broke into the conversation. "Between me and the militia, we barely have enough people to form a watch to cover the entire day and night. Let alone go hunting for marauding spiders."

"What can we do, Jenkins?" The bann held his hands up and shrugged. "If we leave the village uncovered to search for spiders, then we leave it wide open for the goblins to swoop in behind us!"

"I have friends, other adventurers like myself who should arrive here tomorrow, and countless more behind them as well," I offered quickly before Jenkins could reply. "Once they arrive, we can work on thinning the spiders and beating them back."

The bann's eyebrows shot up at the mention of more adventurers arriving, but I could see that he was nervous about that fact as well. Adventurers always brought their own sort of trouble with them. "Very well. I'll leave the spiders in your hands for the moment."

"May I have your attention please?" Moving to address the crowd, Bann Aldwin spoke in a loud and clear voice. "The rumors that you have all heard are indeed true! There are giant spiders living in the forest, to the west of Crater Lake in an area now known as the Webwood! However, have no fear! Our goblin-slaying hero Lyrian has already called on other adventurers for aid and is expecting them to arrive soon, to help thin the ranks of the arachnid menace! Please go on about your regular business, everything here is well in hand."

The crowd listened to the bann's short speech, placated by the promise of the coming adventurers. I overheard some further nervous remarks about the spider infested forest, but the crowd began to disperse quickly. At that moment, my quest log chimed with a new quest alert:

> ▷**NEW QUEST! CLEANSING THE WEBWOOD.** *(Open) (Group)*
> *The village of Aldford is threatened by the encroaching spiders of the Webwood. Slay as many spiders as possible to relieve the threat against the village.*
> *Spiders Slain: 0/1000.*
> *Difficulty: Hard*
> *Reward: Experience, Reputation, 100 gold pieces. (Reward proportional to percentage contributed)*

I read over the quest log and gaped. *What had I just gotten myself into?*

ELEVEN

AFTER THE VILLAGERS HAD FULLY dispersed, the bann thought it was best to return to the town hall for a bit of rest and to be on hand if the huntress awoke, the three of us retreating to the bann's study on the upper floor of the hall.

"Lyrian, I've noticed that your skill has been steadily increasing since you've arrived, and your time as a novice is nearly over. I was wondering if you had given any thought to choosing a class?"

"I had thought of it, but I didn't quite know what was available to me just yet." I paused for a moment, looking at both the bann and Jenkins. It was slightly surreal to have NPCs talking to me this way, but at the same time, with Ascend Online being a closed system, what other way could the player get that sort of information? "Is it rude to ask what classes you've chosen?"

"Not at all!" Jenkins exclaimed shaking his head. "I'm a warrior."

"The same as me," Bann Aldwin echoed Jenkins.

"What other base classes are there?"

"Well…" The bann started to speak, just as an information box appeared across my vision.

> *Tutorial – Choosing a Base Class*
>
> *Congratulations on nearly completing your novice class! The Ascend development team hopes that you have managed to experience a wide variety of play styles in order to make an informed choice about your Base Class. Once a Base Class is chosen, you will not be able to change your class in the future. Proceed carefully!*
>
> *Note: In order to prevent excessive meta-gaming, specific class abilities are not shown in this Tutorial.*
>
> *Based on the detected playstyle your recommended Base Classes are:*
>
> *Mage*
> *Monk*
> *Rogue*
> *Scout*
> *Spellsword*
> *Warrior*

I looked over the list of base classes the system had recommended for me.

Ascend has a branching class system, I reminded myself, remembering the level progression that appeared when I was creating my character. At level ten I would choose my base class, and again at level thirty, I would have a chance to branch into an advanced class, and eventually at level seventy into a prestige class.

In my previous games, I had traditionally gravitated towards either a rogue or warrior role. However, this time, was the first time I had the option to play a hybrid melee/arcane caster. Intrigued to see what waited for me down each road, I brought up the class formation for the rogue, spellsword, and warrior.

BASE CLASS: ROGUE

A cunning and deadly adventurer relying on surprise and crippling blows to take down their enemies. Masters of stealth, they can often enter and exit a battlefield without ever being seen.

Role: Damage, Recon.

HP Progression: Moderate

Armor: Light

Weapon Skills: Sword, Dagger, Unarmed, Crossbow, Short Bow, Throwing.

Class Difficulty: High

Requirements:

Any Above Weapon Skill Level 9

Learned Two Martial Weapon Skills (Complete!)

Stealth Level 9

Learned Two Stealth Skills

BASE CLASS: SPELLSWORD

A mobile, melee-oriented warrior that blends magic and martial prowess into a unique fighting style. Can learn a mix of Martial Skills and Arcane Spells, resulting in a deadly storm of steel and magic.

Role: Damage, Recon, Support.

HP Progression: Moderate

Armor: Light

Weapon Skills: Sword, Dagger, Axe, Mace, Unarmed, Polearm.

Arcane Trees: Evocation, Abjuration, Alteration, Conjuration.

Class Difficulty: High

Requirements:

Any Above Weapon Skill Level 9

Learned Two Martial Weapon Skills (Complete!)

Any Above Arcane Tree Level 9

Scribed Two Arcane Spells

BASE CLASS: WARRIOR

Masters of combat that take on the deadliest foes head-to-head without any hesitation. They are able to shrug off blows that would leave others crippled—or dead.

Role: Damage, Tank.

HP Progression: High

Armor: Light, Medium, Heavy, Shields.

Weapon Skills: Sword, Dagger, Axe, Mace, Polearm, Unarmed, Crossbow, Short Bow, Longbow, Throwing.

Class Difficulty: Average

Requirements:

Three Above Weapon Skills Level 7

Learned Five Martial Weapon Skills

I read through the class information, noting the requirements to unlock the class. While I did like the rogue, the spellsword spoke loudest to me. Bringing both support and damage would make me reasonably high in demand when it came to grouping with others, and it fit my character's stat growth perfectly. I selected *Spellsword* as my base class choice.

Are you sure you wish to become a Spellsword? This choice is irreversible! Yes/No

Pausing for only a heartbeat, I selected *yes*.

‣**NEW QUEST! BECOMING A SPELLSWORD.**

*Welcome to the path of the Spellsword! In order to unlock the
Spellsword class you must complete the following:
Any Spellsword Weapon Skill Level 9
Any Spellsword Arcane Tree Level 9
Scribed Two Arcane Spells.*

"I've chosen to become a spellsword." I finally said aloud to the
bann and Jenkins.

"A spellsword?" The bann looked at me thoughtfully, as if he was
going to say something. "Are you close to meeting your requirements?"

"I still need to work on both my sword work and arcane skills."
I shook my head slightly. "I need one more additional spell as well."

"That doesn't sound too bad," Jenkins spoke up. "Though I'm not
sure where you will find any spells around here. I heard you bought
the one Ritt had."

"I might be able to help with one," the bann chimed in, standing
to pull a sheet of parchment from a bookshelf. He placed it on the
desk in front of me. "I had a few of these scribed before we left. I'm
sure it'll help you out."

"Really? It can't be easy getting any spells out here..." I started to
say as I mentally brought the information up for the parchment the
bann had set in front of me.

Arcane Spell – Light (Evocation)
Favored Class: Novice (1)
Mana: 10
*The player temporarily creates light centered on themselves,
illuminating up to 30 feet away for 1 hour.*
Do you wish to scribe this spell? Yes / No

"Oh." I had thought back to the last day of me walking around the
forest, Flare in hand, with its meager illumination. "That'll certainly
help!" I wouldn't be limited to hunting during the day anymore!

"It's nothing. I have more." Bann Aldwin waved me off. "Also, when you have time, come spar with me. I may be an old warrior, but I can certainly help you out with your blade work and help you meet your class requirements."

I nodded at the bann. "That would be great!"

"It's the least I can do to help after all you've done."

"Speaking of help, I had a good hunt." I pulled a few leathers and ore out of my pack to demonstrate to the bann and Jenkins. "I also temporarily solved our food problems for the time being as well."

"Oh?" Both Jenkins and the bann looked quite interested in that bit of information.

"Ragna apparently has quite a few recipes for spider meat. In fact, she was ready to prepare the meat I brought her as a delicacy." I watched the two carefully to see what their reaction would be after I dropped that bit of news.

"Hm. Well…Ragna has made us do on much less." The bann didn't seem overly excited about my news but was willing to take it in stride.

Jenkins, on the other hand, was bursting at the seams. "I've heard of a few spider meat recipes during my travels! When properly prepared, I've heard that it can give you an extra spring in your step."

"Are you sure that extra spring wasn't to get away from the meal itself?" The bann grunted, then sighed. "I'm sorry, Lyrian, I'm sure it'll be more than adequate. I've never considered spiders as a food source before."

You should have played some of the games I've played, I thought to myself before replying. "I have some other ideas as well about the militia's armo—"

A knock sounded at the door, interrupting my train of thought. "Bann Aldwin? The huntress has awoken."

WITH NO TIME TO WASTE, we left the study, proceeding to make our way downstairs. The voice belonged to one of the villagers Shelia had conscripted to help her treat the huntress. "Shelia says she's well enough to answer questions."

"I still wonder why she was out here in the first place," Jenkins grumbled. "Maybe she's a member of the Surveyors Guild?"

As we made our way downstairs, we were thankful to find that the town hall was empty of any curious villagers; it would hopefully let us keep any new information from panicking anyone else today.

"She was poisoned pretty seriously, but I've managed to get the toxins out of her," Shelia informed us. "She is fairly weak but should be back on her feet in a day or two. Keep the questioning short. I'd like her to get some rest tonight. She needs it."

Coming around the blinds, I saw that Shelia's healing efforts greatly improved the huntress's complexion. Her gray face had regained a more natural-looking olive complexion, and I could tell her hair was a dark raven color now that the webs had been removed from it.

I looked back at Jenkins and Bann Aldwin. Both hung back half a step, with the bann indicating to me to take the lead.

"Hi there. My name is Lyrian. I found you in the forest. You're safe in the village of Aldford now." I tried to sound warm and soothing as I introduced myself. "What's your name?"

"Hello, Lyrian." The huntress said weakly as I knelt down beside her cot. Despite her being awake, I could see that her eyes were glassy and exhausted. Being trapped in the spider's cocoon had certainly taken its toll on the young woman. "My…name is…Natasha. Thank you for…finding me."

"What were you doing in the forest, Natasha? Did you come from another settlement?"

"I…I…was running…from…goblins! Oh!" Natasha started to become more animated as she spoke. "You…have to get ready! Goblins are coming! They may have followed me!"

I exchanged sharp looks between Bann Aldwin and Jenkins before looking back at Natasha. "I'm sorry, you're too late. Goblins have already tried to raid the village, but we killed them all."

"Too...late?" Natasha looked confused. "I..."

"Tell me more of why you were running. Where did you come from?"

"I don't know...where I am..." Natasha paused to think about it, her exhaustion clearly weighing on her. "We had a camp, twenty of us."

"What were you doing out here?" The bann finally decided to enter the conversation. "Were you looking for Aldford?"

"N-no." Natasha shook her head. "We were searching for a ruin. The Mages Guild sponsored us as a research expedition."

"What happened, Natasha? Did the goblins attack you?" I asked, trying to get back on track.

"Yes. We were camped at night. They attacked. They cast a spell that caused our campfire to explode, quickly followed by our tents." Natasha closed her eyes as she started to fade. "I couldn't do anything. I just...ran. I'm still a novice. This was my first time away from Eberia. I grabbed what I could and ran. The goblins always sounded like they were close behind. I remember something biting my foot...and falling..."

Natasha sleepily rubbed her face as she tried to recall the details of the last few days. "I remember waking up. I couldn't move much, or see anything. If I moved too much, something...bit me."

"You ran into the Webwood, an area infested with giant spiders," I explained to Natasha, "I found you tucked away into a cocoon."

"Spiders? Oh...then I would have been—" Natasha's eyes shot open. "Eaten."

"I think that might be enough for now!" Shelia broke in as Natasha started to get visibly upset. "Natasha needs to rest. She'll be better to answer more questions later."

The three of us gave Shelia some space as she went to console Natasha and took a seat at one of the tables at the far side of the hall. "Any idea what she could have meant by expedition?" I asked.

"Not really," Jenkins started. "Despite how close we are to Eberia, this area hasn't been explored all that much. It was only recently that the Surveyors Guild declared this land free of serious threats and opened land for settlement and further exploration."

"The Mages Guild might have had a lead in particular for something in the area." The bann shrugged. "They are well within their rights to do so."

"I did find a small underground ruin by Crater Lake," I offered, remembering the previous day's adventure. "It was mostly destroyed."

"Hm..." Bann Aldwin sat quietly with his hands clasped together.

"The goblins concern me. They attacked that expedition before raiding us," Jenkins pointed out, bringing us back on track. "Why are the goblins raiding the area? Did they try to take prisoners there too?"

"It might not have been the same group of goblins," I offered, "How would they have crossed the Webwood?"

"Well..."

We dissected the results of the questioning for a short while, but it became apparent to me that nothing would actually be solved here. Threads like these were designed to get adventurers like me intrigued and out looking for quests. Hell, with everything going on here, I was willing to bet Razor that an event was brewing.

That could wait for later. Right now, I wanted to get ready for my gang's arrival tomorrow. It'd finally be the end of solo play, and we'd finally be able to get some real work done. For what I had planned, though, it wouldn't do to have them wandering around undergeared. I bid farewell to the bann and Jenkins and made my way to the workshop.

It was time to start crafting again.

TWELVE

Good morning, players!

Great and unique secrets await the players who carefully pay attention to their surroundings! Leave no stone unturned!

Thank you, and enjoy your time in Ascend Online!

–CTI Development Team

I AWOKE GROGGILY THE NEXT DAY on the floor of the workshop. *Shit. Must have fallen asleep,* I thought to myself as I picked myself up off the floor. I had spent the rest of the afternoon and evening refining the materials I'd collected, then worked late into the night assembling a few sets of armor and weapons. Stifling a yawn, I quickly glanced over the fruits of my labor over the last night.

[Bronze Studded Leather Tunic] x5

[Bronze Studded Leather Pants] x5

[Hardened Leather Boots] x5

[Hardened Leather Gloves] x5

[Bronze Studded Cap] x5

[Bronze Longsword] x2

[Bronze Short Sword] x2

[Bronze Mace] x1

With the refining and crafting, my leatherworking skill doubled to reach level eight, along with slight progress in my blacksmithing skill also reaching level eight. The biggest experience gain in crafting seemed to come from making items I hadn't made before, or successfully creating a new prototype design. Something I made sure to keep in mind for the future.

Out of idle curiosity, I brought up the stats for the weapons I had crafted:

Bronze Longsword

Slot: Main Hand or Off-Hand

Item Class: Common

Item Quality: Normal

Damage 10-20 (Slashing)

Durability 120/120

Weight: 1 kg

Favored Class: Novice

Base Metal: Bronze

Level 5

Bronze Shortsword

Slot: Main Hand or Off-Hand

Item Class: Common

Item Quality: Normal

Damage 8-15 (Slashing)

Durability 90/90

Weight: 0.5 kg

Favored Class: Novice

Base Metal: Bronze

Level 5

Bronze Mace

Slot: Main Hand or Off-Hand

Item Class: Common

Item Quality: Normal

Damage 14-22 (Crushing)

Durability 120/120

Weight: 1.5 kg

Favored Class: Novice

Base Metal: Bronze

Level 5

I mentally nodded at the expected differences in weapon types, something that I knew was important after the fight with the skeleton. It would pay to have a few decent weapons on hand that could bypass damage reduction.

I needed more materials to do that, though, at least I had enough to give everyone a basic set of armor and a weapon to start. Plus this was still the novice levels, no use in burning through all my materials just yet.

With a huge yawn, I shrugged to myself. *Might as well get moving…*

I picked myself up off the ground, stashing my crafted goods and then grabbing some *[Fried Snake]* from my inventory, tossing it in my mouth. It wasn't really food, here in the digital world, but it made me feel better and more alert. I pushed the workshop door open as I wandered outside into the gray morning. *I wonder if coffee exists in Ascend Online. If I could corner the market in this world…*

"Hold! Identify yourselves!" A distant voice called out, causing me to start.

I looked around and saw a bit of commotion stirring towards the gate as a pair of guards were motioning at something on the other side of the river bordering the village; I was too far away to hear what was happening at the other end of the conversation.

Moving quickly, I jogged through the village towards the noise as other villagers nervously peeked their heads out of their homes, many were still understandably on edge. A third guard heard my rapid approach and beckoned me with a look of relief on his face.

"Lyrian! There are people here asking for you by name." The guard eyed me cautiously. "They look a bit worse for wear. I think they may be bandits!"

I frowned a moment, before laughing. "*Bandits?* Well, let me have a look at them."

As I peered through the gate, a ragged group of adventurers came into view. With each of them covered in dirt, mud, and wearing burnt clothes, I could definitely understand the guard's caution.

On the other hand, I could have a bit of fun...

"Well, aren't you the filthiest group of casuals I've seen this week!" I smiled at my friends. "'Bout time you all made it! Did that shortcut have you all swimming through dirt to get here?"

"Is that you, Lyrian?" I heard Misha's—Sierra's—voice reply. "Please tell me it's you, so I can fire an arrow right into your face and not feel bad about it."

"Sierra, no." Zach's—Caius's—voice replied. "Let me strangle him a bit first."

"Ugh. Fine."

Aren't friends great?

The guard beside me looked at me in bewilderment. "Sir...?"

"They're expected, and despite their looks, not bandits," I whispered to the guards.

I laughed and waved at the group. "Fine. I guess I'll let you all in. Try not to dirty up the place, though."

A moment later, the guards had the semi-repaired gate open, and we were all patting one another on the back while trying to catch up since we'd logged in.

"You guys look like you had a rough trip." I eyed them carefully and saw that their gear looked fairly damaged. I waved them to follow me as we made our way into the village and towards the town hall. I quickly took a moment to get my bearings and a closer look at their character choices.

Peter, now known as Constantine, looked to be a pale-skinned half-elf with long dark hair. Armed with a single shortsword and a backpack, he walked confidently without a single care in the world as his eyes took in the village.

Misha, having chosen the name Sierra, caused my heart to skip a beat. Flame-red hair flared behind her as she moved with unearthly grace—there was no doubt in my mind she was a full-blooded elf. In her hands, she held a bow, making her earlier threat much more believable to me.

Zach chose the name Caius and was also a half-elf, though in contrast to Constantine he was dark-skinned and almost unhealthily thin. I idly wondered how he would have followed through with his desire to strangle me; he barely looked strong enough to stand up under the weight of his clothes! The only item of note I saw on him, was a plain wooden club.

Heron, taking the name Halcyon, was human through and through, tall, dark haired with a full beard. I was confident that he took the same regional specialization as I did. He didn't seem to have any weapons on him, just a single backpack slung over his shoulders.

Deckard, now known as Drace, was an absolute mountain of a man, standing taller than everyone else in the party, including me. He looked to be human, but I was fairly sure he had chosen some sort of sub-race due to his size. He had a backpack strapped to his shoulders as well, in addition to a plain wooden shield and shortsword.

"Yeah, I'm not interested in making that trek again." Constantine looked around the village as we walked. "Eberia is placed in a weird spot geographically, despite not being too far distance-wise."

"What do you mean?" I hadn't thought about it until now, but a two-day journey from a capital city wasn't really that far to travel or for the area not to be already settled.

"The city is built on the coast," Halcyon explained. "But it's also in a bit of a cul-de-sac due to a cliff range that blocks it off to the north and northwest with the ocean being directly towards the west and south."

"The only natural way to higher elevation is to detour three or four days east, and then to make it here you'd have to cut back northwest and backtrack for another three or four days."

"That still isn't that far, though," I mused. "Shouldn't this place be already settled then?"

"You're forgetting about *the war*," Sierra said.

"Oh, right! What was that all about?" I asked, the primer only having mentioned that Eberia had just ended a war with a nearby orc tribe.

"Oh, boy…where to start? They gave us a pretty big history lesson during the '*Call to Arms*' event back in Eberia." Sierra shook her head as she started to explain. "Let's take a step back first. Eberia, the nation, was founded by a group of refugees from the Ascendant Empire roughly forty years ago. Led by a handful of major noble houses after the empire began to fall apart."

"What happened to the empire?" There had been no mention at all about the Ascendant Empire in the primer.

"Well, the Ascendant Emperor was apparently obsessed with the idea of achieving godhood, and the entire empire was built around the near fanatical belief that the emperor was a god." Sierra continued to fill me in as we took seats at a table in the town hall. "As the legend goes—and I'm paraphrasing here—on the day that the emperor was destined to Ascend, something *otherworldly* took offense at the idea of a mortal ascending to godhood, and within the span of a few weeks, the entire empire was razed to the ground."

"Shit."

"I know, right?" Sierra took a breath before continuing. "So during the fall, it was pretty much a mad scramble to get off of the old continent, people dying left and right. Cities vanishing overnight. That's where our noble houses come in. They put aside their differences and evacuated an entire city, loading it up into barges, ships and boats, setting off into the blue."

"Eventually, they landed on this continent, and as luck would have it, found a completely abandoned ruin of a city: Eberia. Complete with a massive wall blocking access from the sea straight to the mountains, all protecting fertile farmland within."

"Well, that's convenient."

"I'm sure the developers thought it'd make for a great story," Sierra said, shrugging the coincidence away. "Anyway, they set up shop in the city, declared a noble king, and began to rebuild the city. The problem was, the orc tribes got wind of the settlement, and as it turns out, the ruins were kind of a holy city to them. A memory of their past masters, the Nafarr."

"So they went to war."

Sierra bobbed her head in acknowledgment. "They did. The orc tribes are largely scattered throughout the southeast, which put them in a prime location to block access to the greater continent. They bottled up the Eberians and tried to dig them out. From all accounts, it was a brutal war," Sierra explained. "But with the war on Eberia's doorstep and their supply lines protected by massive fortifications, it ended up as a massive stalemate for decades."

"So what changed all of that? The orcs came to their senses and decided to leave?"

"The dark elves did, if indirectly," Sierra answered. "Over the decades the orc tribes were at war with Eberia, the dark elf empire continued to expand westward. They simply ran over whatever few minor tribes remained behind, putting them to the sword and burning their villages.

"Eventually that news made it back to the major orc tribes, and they were forced to abandon their campaign here to save what they could of their home. Not all the tribes agreed to that, and a great deal of infighting broke out during the withdrawal."

"Don't forget about the Eberian prince going off and killing himself," Constantine added helpfully.

"Oh, I'm getting to that!" Sierra hissed, raining down half a dozen blows on Constantine. "Don't ruin my story!" She cleared her throat. "*Right*. So Prince Rainier, Heir to the Throne. Decides that on seeing the orc tribes withdrawing that it would be a great idea to sally forth with the entire Eberian Army and crush them individually. It turns out it was a flawless idea." Sierra made a chopping motion with her hand. "The army absolutely devastated the divided orc forces, and Rainier was rumored to have personally killed half a dozen orc chieftains during the battle. In a single battle, he completely cut the head off of the orc leadership.

"Problem was that a lifetime of war breeds a lot of hate, and he didn't want to allow a single orc to escape and lost sight of the battle. He pulled ahead of the army and just like that." Sierra snapped her fingers "He was surprised by an ambush, filled full of arrows and left for dead."

"Just like that?" I was surprised at the anti-climactic ending.

"That's war," Sierra said bluntly. "It doesn't care who you are."

"With the prince dead, Rainier's son, Swain became heir. Just in time too, because age finally caught up with King Cyril, leaving the very young twenty-year-old king."

"Twenty? Can he even be left alone unsupervised?" I started to get a better idea of the political landscape of Eberia. "How can they expect him to run a kingdom?"

"Poorly, most likely, since he comes off as a colossal dick," Constantine grunted. "Kept going on and on about himself during the event, and how we should be so thankful for his leadership and all the money the crown spent on training the adventurers. I give him less than a year before he's killed by a player."

"You think so?" I asked as the group nodded their assent empathetically. "So quickly?"

"You didn't see Eberia, so you didn't see the other players," Constantine explained "We saw a blacksmith get robbed by mob—simply because his gear was on display and easy to take. Another vendor was stabbed to death in the street because someone liked the hat they were wearing."

"Sure, the guards came in, broke some heads, and threw the offenders in jail. Apparently killing an NPC unprovoked will get you thirty days of online jail time. If you log out, the timer stops."

"That's harsh, but a good idea I think." I nodded. "NPCs won't re-spawn like we do."

"Yeah. Players are slowly getting the message, but by majority people are acting like this is just any other MMORPG and that NPCs are made to be walked over. It'll take time for the consequences to sink in. Right now, the only rule players are playing by is the rule *might makes right*."

I sighed and nodded. "Then we need to make sure we're the strongest players around until they do."

THIRTEEN

"SO WITH THE WAR, IT makes more sense why this place hasn't been settled until recently. But how did you guys get here so soon?" I asked, hoping to get answers to their threadbare appearances.

"Well, while we were messaging a few days ago, I overheard a few members of the Surveyors Guild talking about a network of ropes that they had set up to help scale the cliff without having to trek around the ridge," Constantine explained. "Long story short, we had a few issues, but we made it up without too many problems."

"I almost died!" Caius exclaimed.

"Bah, you're fine." Constantine waved a hand dismissively. "Besides, you'll probably die a ton of times in this game.

"That's not the point! You could have waited before setting fire to the ropes!" Caius continued, now glaring at Drace.

"That wasn't my fault!" Drace grunted. "I just did what I was told!"

"Wait, what happened?" I gaped at my friends.

"Oh, he's just annoyed because we lost some gear." Constantine shrugged. "Nothing too serious."

"And that we may technically be kill on sight for the Surveyors Guild now," Sierra deadpanned. "Or face jail time if we're ever caught by them."

"*Wait, WHAT?*" I shouted.

"Okay, so maybe they were going to use those ropes to create a lift." Constantine continued to wave his hands around dismissively. "And maybe it wasn't so much as just setting the ropes on fire, but the entire supporting structure."

"And other players," Halcyon chimed in.

"Why...would you just decide to burn it?" I shook my head at the story unfolding before me.

"Because they wouldn't listen, even after I threw one of them off," Constantine explained as if it made perfect sense.

"Okay." I rapped my knuckles on the table, getting everyone's attention. "I'm going to need the full story here, because what we've got so far...just isn't adding up."

"Ugh." Constantine rolled his eyes. "So we weren't the only ones that found out about the rope system, and there was another group of people that were making the climb with us. Follow?"

"So far so good," I said giving Constantine a thumbs-up.

"Right, so during the climb we were mixed in with the other group of players climbing with us. The thing is, once we got to the top. They decided they didn't want to play nice anymore and killed the two guards stationed there. Then they told me to strip and drop all my gear onto the ground."

"So naturally you told them to suck a bucket of dicks," I said, still following the story.

"So naturally I told them to suck a bucket of dicks." Constantine nodded. "They didn't take my advice and tried to get handsy. So I decided to throw one of them off the platform."

"Seems appropriate," I replied in full agreement.

"Well, they decided that they didn't like that either and by that point, two more had finished their climb." Constantine mimed fighting with his sword. "I kept them at bay long enough for Drace to finish his climb."

"Not with a sword," Drace cut in. "But by smashing a lantern against the side of one of their heads in a wooden structure."

"Okay, so maybe that wasn't the best idea at the time. But I barely knew what end of a sword to hold back then." Constantine shrugged. "I'm better at it now."

"Right." I rubbed my face. "So you're fighting for your life and now the place is catching fire."

"So then I yelled at Drace to grab something that's burning and to set the ropes on fire."

"So I did." Drace nodded. "And set the rope the other members of their party were climbing on fire."

"I was climbing it too!" Caius yelled.

"Bro, calm down. Sierra caught you. You're fine." Constantine waved at Caius's complaint dismissively. "You worry too much."

"Right, so after that the gloves came off," Constantine continued to explain. "Drace and I managed to keep them from killing either of us until Halcyon made it up the other rope, and once he did, they didn't have a chance."

Constantine ran a hand through his hair. "But by that point..." He made a whooshing sound. "The place was completely aflame. Caius lost his pack when he fell, and Sierra had to cut hers loose when she caught him."

"Then it all burnt down," I finished.

"Pretty much." Constantine nodded. "After that, we had to split supplies on our way up here. With the five of us, roaming creatures weren't much of a problem…"

"Until we ran out of food and water," Halcyon added. "Did you know that you stop regenerating health if you haven't eaten?"

I nodded. "Yeah, found out the hard way too."

"Thankfully Sierra managed to find us some wild potatoes." Caius acknowledged with a nod in her direction. "Kept us going until today."

"Well, we have plenty of food here you all can have." I smiled at the group while I collected my thoughts. "So—are you sure you're kill on sight with the Surveyors Guild? Or you think you might be?"

"We…might be?" Sierra said. "I didn't get a message, and my character sheet still lists me as neutral. But it wasn't a real secret that we were making the climb."

"It's not like there was a sign-in sheet either!" Constantine exclaimed, before a thoughtful expression came over his face. "They might be able to piece it together. Technically the other group killed the guards, then we killed them."

I sighed, while rubbing my forehead. "Yet another problem for the future, then." I leaned back in my seat as I looked over the group. "Okay. First things first. Let's grab you all a bite of food."

I pulled out a *[Beetle Soup]* out of my inventory for everyone and was met with cheers.

"Ah!" Drace exclaimed at the sight of food.

"Oh, we needed that." Constantine sighed with relief as he inhaled the soup.

"Did you cook this?" Sierra asked between sips. "It's good!"

"Yeah. I learned the recipe from one of the cooks here," I explained. "Managed to get a few other tradeskills too."

"Hah!" Constantine laughed. "Spawned days away from the starting area, and here we thought you'd be behind. What level are you?"

"Uh. I just hit level nine yesterday, and now I need to train my skills before I qualify for the spellsword class requirements." I motioned to my hand, summoning a Flare momentarily before canceling the spell.

The group looked at me blankly for a moment.

"You're…level nine. Of course you are." Sierra barked a short laugh. "We just hit level seven."

"How the hell have you hit level nine already?" Caius hissed. "We've been killing monsters the whole way here and haven't seen anything higher than level five!"

"Well—" I started.

"Yeah, what gives Lyr?" Constantine broke in. "You somehow spawned here and now, you're level nine? I see you have some fancy new armor you're wearing, and I noticed how those guards deferred to you at the gate. You start a cult?"

"Ha. It's been a busy few days…" I gave the group a rundown of everything since I spawned in the middle of the goblin attack, not leaving anything out. By the end of my story, the group was shaking their heads.

"Well, you certainly don't waste time." Halcyon was the first to speak after I finished my story; the rest of the group was silently admiring Razor, which I had brought out to show off.

"Don't worry, I thought of you guys too." I stood up and started pulling the items I had crafted earlier from my pack, handing out the set of bronze studded leather armor and weapons I'd crafted earlier to the party. "I ran out of materials for bracers and shoulder pads. I figured you'd all appreciate some weapons instead."

There was another round of excitement as everyone discarded some remnants of their old gear or simply slipped the new gear atop the clothes they already wore. Drace and Sierra grabbed the two longswords, and Constantine and Caius split the pair of shortswords, which left Halcyon holding the mace.

"Unfortunately, I can't make bows, Sierra," I said while handing the weapons out. "I haven't learned that tradeskill."

"No worries, I actually can." Sierra smiled back at me while fastening her new sword onto her belt. "We were all given a choice of two tradeskills in Eberia. I chose carpentry and mining."

"Great! What did everyone else get?" I couldn't help but already start planning a trade empire if I could get everyone else on board with crafting.

Having finished putting on his new equipment the quickest, Halcyon filled me in on the group's choices. "I picked up tailoring and herbalism. Caius chose alchemy and herbalism, and Drace and Constantine both took mining and logging."

"There are a few other advanced tradeskills we didn't qualify for just yet but might be interesting," Caius added. "Runecrafting, enchanting, gemcutting, and spellcraft. Though I don't know what the requirements are to learn them."

"Hm. We'll have to keep an eye out." I nodded at Caius. "We'll need to have all the core trades covered."

"You said you ran out of materials for the armor? What do you need to make more?" Drace asked me while pulling his new chest piece on.

"Metals, mostly. I have a fair bit of leather, but I'll need more of that as well if I start mass producing stuff," I replied taking a quick look through my inventory. "A lot more."

"We have a decent amount of leather. Not that much ore, though." Reaching into his pack, Drace pulled out a few items and set them on the table. "Is this any help?"

[Copper Ore] x 14
[Tin Ore] x 4

[Puma Pelt] x 17
[Fox Pelt] x 67
[Snake Skin] x 76

"Perfect!" I exclaimed, looking over the materials. "We'll need to find more metal, but I'll be able to find a use for all of this!"

Grabbing the items, I put them in my backpack. I'd find some time to sort through all of it later.

"So," Constantine began once everyone had finished putting on their new gear. "What's our plan now?"

I thought for a moment before answering, an idea forming in my head.

"Have any of you tried to learn how to cook?" I asked while motioning for us to move towards a communal fire pit just outside the town hall.

"I burned water once." Halcyon shrugged. "I stick to pre-packs now."

"Ugh." I shook my head as I grabbed a few pieces of wood from a stack and tossed them into the pit. I carefully lit it with a Flare and kindled a small fire. "I meant in-game."

"Sorry, Lyr, haven't had the chance." I was met with shrugs and negative head shakes from the others.

"Well, that's going to end now. Like you all know, you can start a fire easily enough." I brought out the *[Copper Frying Pan]* I'd crafted the other day and handed it to Constantine. "Not having food means not regenerating."

"And not regenerating can mean death," Sierra finished with a nod looking at the rest of the men. "We've been down that road."

Over the next half hour, I showed everyone the basics of cooking, or at least Ascend Online's version of it. It only took a few minutes of frying meat for Constantine to learn the basics of the craft, and when he did, a wonderful message appeared in my vision.

You have successfully taught Constantine the basics of Cooking!
You have gained Tradeskill Experience!

"Ah!" I exclaimed at the same time Constantine did. "I just got experience for teaching you how to cook!"

"Neat! I didn't know you could do that!"

"Neither did I! I was hoping it would work, though!" I took a moment to think about the skills I had acquired so far. "There's so little we know about this game, hell. You could probably make a living just being a teacher in this game!"

"It makes sense," Sierra said, taking the frying pan from Constantine. "This world is huge. How often would you run across an NPC with the skills you wanted? Let alone one willing to teach you."

"Good point," I said thinking about the implications, especially with my Open Minded trait. Would I be able to teach others the same skills I learned?

Just as I finished teaching Drace the basics of cooking, Shelia came walking by, still dressed in her formal robes from her morning prayers. "Good morning, Lyrian! I just heard about your friends arriving. Ah! Are you putting them to work already?"

"Ha! Just introducing them to the realities of frontier life!" I laughed as I introduced everyone to the priestess.

"No doubt! Aldford welcomes you all!" Shelia smiled at the group. "I understand you have all come from the city? Do you wish to have your souls bound to this village?"

I cocked my head at the odd question. "Bound?"

"Oh, yes." Shelia nodded. "We know you adventurers are gifted with the ability to return from death, to wherever your soul is anchored. I sense yours is bound here Lyrian, but your allies, they are bound far to the southwest. It could be problematic to return to life so many days of travel away."

We all exchanged confused glances before Caius shrugged and

stepped forward. "I don't want to make the trek here again! Please, bind my soul."

"Of course!" Shelia clasped a small sunburst symbol and murmured a prayer causing a cool blue aura to briefly envelop Caius before fading away. "It is done."

With Caius leading the way, the rest of the party quickly jumped at the chance to ensure their respawn at Aldford.

"We are all happy to have a trustworthy group of adventurers watching our village," Shelia spoke as she bound the party to Aldford. "Not all adventurers are so kind. Some think their ability to return from death makes them better than those who cannot."

"We've seen a few like that." Constantine nodded. "Though they quickly learned the consequences, if they weren't lucky enough to be cut down where they stood."

"Perhaps they will learn," Shelia mused, then shuddered. "At times I wonder if returning from death is truly a gift. Adventurers don't tend to die peaceful deaths."

The conversation stalled a moment as Shelia's words echoed in our minds. Thankfully, the arrival of Jenkins broke us from our mental spiral.

"Morning, Shelia, Lyrian." Jenkins looked exhausted as he half-heartedly waved to the group. "These must be the other adventurers I heard about."

Jenkin's distrust of adventurers could barely be felt through the sheer exhaustion his body projected. His head merely nodded at the party as introductions were made.

"You look exhausted, dear!" Shelia fussed over Jenkins. "You're going to work yourself into the ground!"

"No way about it." Jenkins sighed. "Not enough bodies to cover the night watches or help with the work around the village."

"How much sleep did you get tonight?" On seeing Jenkins, Shelia had fallen into healer mode as she peered into his eyes.

"I finished my watch at third bell. I think maybe three hours? Can't sleep anymore, though, need to make some bows for the guard." Rubbing his face, Jenkins muttered, "All we have to throw at an enemy outside the village is harsh language."

"I think not!" Shelia grabbed Jenkins by the arm. "If you pick up a tool in this state, I'll be sewing your fingers back on by the end of the day. You're going to get something to eat and get some more sleep."

"Shelia," Jenkins began. "I have so much to do…"

"I've heard enough!" Shelia started to pull the overworked man into the town hall. "One more word and I'll hex you to sleep!"

"Nice meeting you all, and I hope to see you around!" Shelia waved back at us dragging a semi-compliant Jenkins. "I need to make sure this dolt takes care of himself before he hurts something!"

"That man looked dead on his feet," Drace mused as he ate a freshly cooked piece of meat.

"He's the only crafter the village has." I shrugged, turning back to the group. "Also probably their second-best fighter too."

"Shit, really?"

I nodded at Drace as I put the copper pan back into my pack and motioned everyone to get moving. "All right, you guys up for heading back out in the wild? I want to get you all introduced to the area and see if we can get you caught up to me today."

FOURTEEN

I NOTICED AN EXTRA SPRING OF confidence from my friends as we walked out of Aldford and back into the wild. A half hour of relaxation, some new gear, along with a decent meal went a long way to cure the beaten down and tired-looking adventurers that arrived earlier.

"Yo, party up." Constantine's voice broke my thoughts as a notice appeared in my vision.

Constantine has invited you to the group.

"Sure." I mentally accepted the invite with a nod. A moment later, I felt a new awareness emerge from the back of my mind. I could vaguely tell what direction everyone was from me, along with a general understanding of their health.

Gone are the days of seeing everyone's health bars, I guess, I thought to myself as a pair of alerts appeared in my vision.

You are now the Party Leader.
You now have access to the Leadership menu.

"Passed you party Lead," Constantine said at the same time as the new notices appeared. "So, where are we off to? You must have found a good spot to hit level nine so fast!"

"Ye—ah!" I stumbled on a rock as I instinctively opened the leadership menu mid conversation, only to have my vision taken over by a wall of text.

Congratulations on forming your first Adventuring Party! You have taken the first step in developing your Leadership skills! Leadership skills are Passive Skills that will benefit all members of the party. In order for Leadership abilities to take effect and to earn Leadership experience, you must be in a party of 6 or more players. All effects immediately end if the Leader is knocked unconscious, killed, or moves out of range of the party.
In order to develop Leadership skills, you must devote a portion of Adventuring experience earned to unlock a Leadership Skill Point. You cannot have more Leadership Skill Points than 5 times your level.
  The current rate is set to: 10%
  Next Leadership Skill Point: 0/1000 XP
  Current Leadership Skills Available:
  Increased Health Regeneration – Increase amount of Health Regenerated by 1.   0/10
  Increased Mana Regeneration – Increase amount of Mana Regenerated by 1.   0/10
  Increased Stamina Regeneration – Increase amount of Stamina

Regenerated by 1. 0/10

Increased Movement – Increase mounted and unmounted speed by 1%. 0/10

Additional Leadership Skills may become available when certain Adventure Levels and/or Skills are met.

"Sorry." I blinked furiously as I mentally moved the wall of text into a corner of my vision. "When you made me Party Leader, it unlocked the Leadership Menu for me."

"Hm?" Caius asked as everyone stopped to look back at me. "What's that?"

I quickly explained to the party what the menu outlined and the options we had, getting more excited as I read. "This is pretty awesome!"

"No kidding!" Halcyon grinned. "Movement speed should be our first priority!"

"Definitely!" Drace agreed. "We're going to be constantly on the move, especially with overland travel."

"The extra regeneration will help with downtime eventually too," Caius chimed in. "But yeah, with how far we had to travel to get here, anything that has us moving faster is a plus."

I nodded as I adjusted the leadership experience rate to one hundred percent. I wasn't gaining any experience right now—due to being locked at level nine until I finished my base class requirements, I might as well put it towards something useful.

"So," Constantine asked again once we resumed walking. "Where are we off to?"

"There's a lake not far from here that I'll show you all." I motioned in the direction we were walking while explaining how I first found the lake, as well as briefly describing the underground ruins that I'd fallen into. "I think there must have been something where the lake is now, at least something that would explain why the ruins existed."

"Sounds like it may have been a supply tunnel to get in or out of whatever used to be there," Constantine suggested.

"Good explanation as any." I shrugged. "It's definitely been ages since whatever it was happened."

"Is there anything worth exploring there?" Sierra asked.

"Not sure to be honest." I explained the general layout of the ruin and the fight with the skeleton guardian. "There was a blocked off section, but we'd need to dig through it all or get a team of NPCs to excavate it."

Sensing that no one was eager to spend the day digging, I continued on with my original plan. "I was actually going to take you to the Webwood. We should be able to get all of you up to level nine quickly, so we can figure out our base classes."

A thought struck me as I walked. I didn't really know what everyone was attempting to build class-wise. "Hey, what races did you all choose, and how are you building your characters? Have you found out what base classes are available yet?"

"Yeah." Constantine was the first to answer. "During our tutorial in Eberia, they had us jumping through a few hoops, which gave us a few recommended classes based on our playstyle."

"I'm half-Eberian and half-high elf, and I'm planning on taking the rogue class since I have fairly good growth in Agility and Intelligence," Constantine continued. "Plus, I'm all about the sneaky, stabby, thief-in-the-night thing. I also have an elf racial ability that gives low-light vision. I didn't expect how much we'd need it in this game."

"I hear you there," I told Constantine, just as Sierra spoke up.

"Since I'm enjoying archery more than I thought I would, I'm planning on taking the scout class," Sierra said excitedly. "I chose pure high-elf for my race, which gives me a strong Agility and Intelligence as well along with low-light vision too."

"Warrior all the way for me!" Drace exclaimed. "I'm half-human and half-giant with a huge boost to Strength and Constitution, and

I get special bonuses on certain martial abilities due to my size. No special see-in-the-dark vision for me, though."

"It was an easy choice for me! I'm half-Eberian and half-dark elf, which gives me complete night-vision, along with a high Intelligence and Willpower progression." Caius grinned as he waved his fingers in the air. "I'm going right into dark magic and aiming to become a warlock."

"Well, I've always been a spellcaster, and don't see a reason to change now!" Halcyon spoke as he conjured a blue missile in his hand. "Choosing mage on my end, and I am a pure Eberian human like you, Lyrian."

"Ah! What trait did you pick?" I asked Halcyon excitedly.

"*Magical Aptitude*. All of my magic skills level faster in general and are considered a level higher when it comes to determining their effect!"

"Awesome!" I was interested to see how that would scale towards the later levels.

We gradually made our way towards Crater Lake, killing a few dozen creatures unfortunate enough to cross our path. I took pains to show Sierra, Drace, and Constantine the basics of herbalism, and after a few failed attempts each, they managed to figure out the basics and successfully unlocked the gathering skill.

"Anything we need to know about this 'Webwood' you're taking us to?" Sierra asked as she pulled a sprig of hollyleaf from the ground. "It sounds…spidery."

"It's a good spot." I started to explain as the lake came into view. "It's an area of forest not too far from here that's slowly being choked to death by an overpopulation of spiders. The worse thing about this place is the poison the spiderlings have. If you're not quick, they'll wear you down fast. That plant—" I motioned to the hollyleaf everyone had been collecting, "—will help you recover from mistakes. Make sure to keep some on hand and call out if you start to run low. If for whatever reason you bite the dust, well, we'll meet you back in Aldford at the end of the day."

"We're also here for another reason." I opened my journal menu and shared the quest the bann gave me yesterday.

> *You have shared the quest:* **CLEANSING THE WEBWOOD.**
> *(Open) (Group) with the party.*
>
> *The village of Aldford is threatened by the encroaching spiders of the Webwood. Slay as many spiders as possible to relieve the threat against the village.*
>
> *Spiders Slain: 0/1000.*
>
> *Difficulty: Hard*
>
> *Reward: Experience, Reputation, 100 gold pieces. (Reward proportional to percentage contributed)*

There was a pause as everyone digested the quest's information.

"You don't do things by half measures, do you, Lyrian?" Halcyon gasped with exasperation. "A thousand spiders!"

"That's a silver a spider!" Constantine exclaimed excitedly. "Hey, if we killed more, do you think we'd get more money? Maybe we could just set the forest on fire?"

"What is with you and fire?" Caius yelled back. "And what on Earth makes you think that's a good idea?"

"Just thinking out loud. Besides, are we even on Earth anymore?"

"I can't believe I need to say this." I sighed, rubbing my face. "No setting forest fires."

"But..." Constantine started. "We could—"

"No. Setting. Forest. Fires," I repeated myself slowly.

"Okay! Okay!" Constantine threw his hands up in defeat. "I'm just trying to save time, that's all."

"*Riiiight.*" Sierra rolled her eyes, voice full of sarcasm.

"We're going to be here for a while. How hard are these spiders to kill?" Halcyon asked a slight tinge of nervousness to his voice.

"Eh, they should be easy enough to take out. We can probably pull them by the dozen easily, the trick is...finding them." I paused as a red highlight appeared in my vision. "Ah! Perfect! Time to learn another useful skill."

FIFTEEN

"AAAAAAAAAH! GET IT OFF! GET it off!" Halcyon's voice shrilled as he wildly bucked about, trying to dismount the [Webwood Spiderling] that had pounced on him from above. We'd spent the last two hours crawling through the Webwood as I taught everyone the Perception skill.

Constantine, Drace, and Caius managed to pick up the skill fairly quickly, but for whatever reason, both Halcyon and Sierra were having a rather difficult time in learning the skill, so I sent the others to bring back a few critters to kill while I spent some more time training the pair.

To be fair, I was having quite a bit of fun at their expense.

"Damn it, Lyrian! Why?" Sierra joined in shouting as she swung her sword, splitting another spiderling in two. "You said these spiders were nothing to worry about! I'm never going to sleep again!"

I laughed as I tore the creature off of Halcyon's back, crushing it under my boot. "These things? Pah! They're barely worth our time. I'm hoping Constantine will find the bigger ones while we're out here!"

"*Bigger ones?*" Halcyon sounded on the verge of becoming unhinged as he attempted to dislodge himself from a web he'd gotten draped across his face. "*I hate spiders!*"

"Hey, are you okay? I thought you were okay with these sorts of things? Didn't you have a pet snake?"

"Sneks—" Halcyon coughed as he pulled a web out of his mouth. "Snakes are not spiders! First of all, they are cute. They just want boops on the snoo—"

"INCOMING!" Constantine's voice shattered the relative silence of the forest, followed by the sound of running feet. I quickly felt the other half of the party sprinting towards us.

"Oh, fuck!" I heard Sierra gasp. "Did they just pull the entire fucking forest?"

I cocked my head towards the noise. "Sure sounds like it."

"Lyr, you're being an ass!"

"Well, I have to get you scrubs to my level quickly." I couldn't help but smirk at their distress. "This seemed like the best and fastest way."

Caius, Constantine, and Drace finally broke into view, sprinting wildly towards us with a veritable horde of spiderlings in tow.

"Oh, fuck you, Lyrian!" Sierra had drawn her bow and started firing arrows into the horde. "If we live through this, I am going to kill you!"

Winded, the other half of the party arrived ahead of the swarm. "I think we overdid it!" Caius gasped as he spun to face the swarm.

"No shit!" Halcyon hissed as he started to conjure and throw glowing missiles into the swarm.

"Aren't you going to draw your sword?" Sierra shouted at me.

"Nah. I've been meaning to work on my hand to hand." I shrugged the question away as I cracked my knuckles. "Seems like the best time for it."

"REALLY?"

The spiderling swarm slammed into Drace, sending him back half a step before a vicious cleave cleared the ground in front of him. Stepping up beside him, Caius streamed a steady cone of fire as he set fire to anything crossing his gaze. I heard Constantine swear, but before I could turn to see what was happening, the swarm was on me.

I dodged and weaved around the spiderlings that attacked me, having already had plenty of experience fighting the creatures. My fists shattered the carapace of a spiderling that was unlucky enough to come within range, quickly followed by a vicious kick that stomped the creature into the ground. A quick Flare singed a spider attempting to flank Constantine, while another was enough to kill a mortally wounded one threatening Caius.

"Heads up!" Constantine shouted. "We've got big ones coming!"

I barely had enough time to register Constantine's warning before a *[Giant Webwood Spider]* trampled Drace, knocking him to the ground. A second giant spider came charging behind the first, straight at Constantine and Halcyon. Sierra quickly launched two arrows that sunk deep into the creature before a thick strand of web hit her shoulder.

"Sierra!" My hand shot out reflexively, grabbing the sticky web. My eyes, quickly following the strand, revealed a third giant spider attacking from behind, having used the chaos of battle to flank us and catch us unaware.

With a twist of its body, the spider yanked the web, yanking both Sierra and me off our feet as it struggled to pull us closer. Hand stuck to the sticky strand, I fumbled to draw Razor as we were dragged across the ground but couldn't reach the blade at my hip.

"Aaah! What's happening?" Sierra thrashed, trying to dislodge herself from the web.

"Hold on!" I shouted as I conjured a Flare in my trapped hand, the tiny fireball immediately beginning to burn through the web. A strong yank from the spider caused the strand to snap, leaving Sierra and me in a pile on the forest floor. I barely had a moment to collect myself before I heard the spider growl in frustration.

Oh, shit! I cursed to myself. This situation was rapidly getting out of hand!

"Get up!" I shouted at the stunned form of Sierra. I knew what that growl meant. "Move! It's going to jump!"

"What?" Sierra shouted, her head staring at the giant arachnid.

I barely had enough time to shove Sierra off me before the giant spider leaped onto me, pinning me to the ground. A fang pierced my shoulder as it landed, with a trio of claws, fortunately, being stopped by my armor as it attempted to disembowel me. I viciously kicked up at the spider, landing a pair of punishing blows on its thorax while my hand grabbed and crushed a claw-tipped pedipalp in a spray of gore.

Howling, the spider bore down onto the one fang still stuck deep in my shoulder, causing me to scream in pain as my health bar shrank quickly. A sword flashed inches away from my face, slicing through the fang pinning me and a nearby leg. Sierra, wielding the longsword in both hands, swept the blade in an arc, gashing the creature along its maw and obliterating a set of eyes in its passage.

I hammered the stunned beast with another kick and managed to get my legs between myself and the spider, heaving with all my might as I attempted to force the creature off me.

"Sierra! Kill it!" I bellowed as I struggled to keep it at bay. "I can't hold this!"

Screaming wordlessly, Sierra lunged forward with her blade, stabbing deep into the spider's head. The sword pierced through the carapace as Sierra forced it right up to the hilt, ichor streaming freely from around the blade.

With a gurgling whimper, the giant spider went limp on top of me and began to twitch wildly, forcing me to clumsily kick the dying carcass off to one side. Grabbing the blade and wrenching it free, I held the blade out to Sierra, who was staring at the now still giant spider in shock.

"Thanks." I handed her the sword while wincing at the giant fang still embedded in my shoulder. "Let's get back into the fray."

Sierra looked at me blankly for a moment before the words reached her. "Lyrian—"

Without warning, a blue, football-sized missile struck Sierra in the back, sending her sprawling to the ground. Flinching, I barely dodged a second, smaller missile as I scrambled to find the source of the attack.

A third missile flew from a nearby bush, and immediately my Perception skill kicked in, highlighting a hiding creature. The missile grazed my already wounded shoulder, sending a searing pain through it.

A [Webwood Aberration]'s Arcane Missile grazes you for 26 damage!

Gritting my teeth through the pain, I broke into a sprint towards the creature, finally drawing Razor as I ran. I tore through the bush, sweeping Razor in a wide arc to catch the hiding beast. I felt the tip of the blade catch on something, followed by a hissing scream. Shoving myself through the bush, I gasped as I finally saw the aberration.

It looked like a grotesquely mutated spiderling, hairless and covered in eerie glowing boils. No leg was the same size or length, and it was covered in far too many eyes, at least a dozen more than even a spider should have; it was almost as if this creature was mutated due to radiation exposure.

Continuing to hiss at me, the boils on the creature flared a bright blue as its pedipalps traced a pattern in the air. A heartbeat later, another blue missile hit me directly in the chest.

"Aaah!" I screamed as the missile tore through my armor as if it wasn't even there, sending my health to dangerous levels. It was all I could do to stand on my feet as I fought through the pain.

My heartbeat hammering in my ears, I desperately swept Razor at the aberration's oversized legs, severing a pair of them. With a wail of pain, the creature bounded away from me, its unusual shape and size making it difficult to land a follow-up blow.

Oozing a pale blue stream from the wound, the aberration's boils dimmed slightly as I chased it, not letting up. The boils flared once more as the creature turned to fight. Eager to end the fight, I closed in on the creature, feinting with Razor then suddenly lunging, stomping on a misshapen leg to keep it from escaping.

The aberration flared even brighter as it struggled to tear its leg free and began to emit a keening cry. I slashed down into the creature, coating Razor in bright blue ichor as I carved the misshapen beast to pieces. With a final thrust, deep into a glowing boil, I put the creature out of its misery.

Only to have the spider erupt in a spray of glowing gore.

Without warning, I was thrown to the ground with a wet burst of glowing ichor covering me. My skin burned unbelievably wherever it touched. I felt what little health I had remaining slowly ebb away.

"Fuck…I need help," I muttered to myself, wincing through the pain. I could barely see a sliver of health in the corner of my display. *What sort of spider casts spells?*

I let out a gasp as I attempted to sit up, my head starting to spin.

I tried to wipe as much of the glowing ichor off me as I could with my good arm, the other still having a wicked fang embedded deep inside. A rustling noise nearby caught my attention causing me to turn my head. "Sierra?"

A pair of green cat eyes regarded me with curiosity, sniffing the air. Recognition dawned in the creature's eyes.

"Oh, shit." My hand groped the ground for Razor, but I was too slow. The puma leaped at me with a growl, teeth gleaming, claws outstretched.

Then I died.

Loading, Please Wait…

INTERLUDE

Purgatory

CREATIVITY WATCHED THE GRAND TAPESTRY silently, her senses fully outstretched. Billions of threads slowly wove themselves into place, guided by countless golden threads, her agents or, as the mortals called them, gods.

A gray, decaying, thread caught her eye.

Poor thing missed again…

With a gesture she pulled the thread from the tapestry, pruning the now defunct story arc. Cradling the thread like a tender child in need of soothing, she gently caressed it while cooing softly. The thread quivered under its mother's touch, and slowly, color returned to it until it shone a bright and vibrant violet.

Satisfied, Creativity turned to regard her grand work, reading each individual strand with infinite care.

Perhaps this will be a better place for you this time.

She wove the now-brilliant thread high into the tapestry, where it would have the greatest chance to touch an active thread. Creativity paused as she considered the potential of the reborn thread; she was reluctant to meddle and get lost in the minutia of her design, but what mother did not wish the best for her children?

With a gentle tug, she pulled free a single translucent hair from her head and attached it to the base of the violet thread. She then drew the hair around a number of copper-colored threads, before finally anchoring it to a silver one. It still wasn't certain that the thread would be touched, yet now its potential was greater than ever before.

Creativity lovingly ran her finger down the silver strand, the color representing adventurers with the greatest potential to affect the world. Her fingers touched an unexpected knot.

Oh, no! She gasped in surprise as she turned her full attention towards the unexpected presence.

A black thread had intercrossed with the silver one, and now began to weave itself tightly around it. No other threads would be able to attach for as long as the pair were intertwined.

"Do you like my work, sister?" Discordance rang through Creativity's mind as an intruder slithered into her domain.

"Destruction!" Creativity snapped as she turned her attention from the tapestry. "What have you done?"

"Right to business already?" Destruction spoke with a laugh akin to the sound of shattering glass. "Aren't you happy to see me, sister?"

"You are not allowed to touch the tapestry! You meddle outside your purview!"

"I think not, sister. Death and Destruction are entirely within my rights. Be it by hand, or by weave." Destruction laughed as she motioned to the black thread. "Perhaps you are angry my pawn bested one of yours?"

"You have loosed a nemesis! It is far too early in the weave for that!" Creativity hissed as she moved to block Destruction from seeing the tapestry. "You could tear everything apart!"

"Ah, but that is exactly what I want to do." Destruction fixed her predatory gaze on Creativity. "I find your orderly vision sickening. You stifle all that you touch, forcing it to follow your rules. With my touch, I merely set them free to be as they truly are."

"Your actions skew the Balance!" Creativity shouted. "You have gone too far!"

"And if I have?" Destruction waved a hand dismissively. "You cannot stop me from carrying out my duties, Creativity. You need me for your existence to have meaning. I am the Death to your Life, Chaos to your Order. Without me, you are nothing. But on the other hand," Destruction's voice grew darker, "without you, I am everything."

"I tire of this, Destruction! I must undo your poison before it spreads!" Creativity advanced towards Destruction, anger burning in her eyes. "Leave!"

"Of course, sister. All you had to do was ask." Destruction's gaze went to the tapestry. "It seems to me that you are about to become quite busy."

"What?" Creativity whirled as she looked back at her work in terror. "What have you done?"

Black threads now sprouted in the thousands, weaving like poisonous vines through the Grand Tapestry, strangling all that they touched. Countless dozens of copper threads, mere adventurers of little note, now shone blood red as they embarked on a path of Discord, leaving hundreds of threads pale as they fought and killed with little reason.

As Creativity watched the tapestry reshape itself, a massive black thread arose from the mass, snaking itself around a golden thread. The golden thread trembled for a split instant, before succumbing and beginning to fade.

"No!" Creativity's eyes flowed with tears as she rushed to salvage what she could.

Destruction laughed. "Goodbye for now, sister."

SIXTEEN

Somewhere

I FOUND MYSELF SOARING OVER A vast field of broken bones stretching as far as the eye could see. Infinite shades of grey coated the land, leaving it devoid of a single sign of life. A seeping, pervasive, cold crept over me as a massive black sun rose in the distance.

...*dead?* I struggled to form even the simplest thought as the corrupted star tore the light of life from me.

I lost track of time as I flew over the horizon, drawn towards something in the endless field of bones. In the distance, I began to see something...*massive*. As the distance diminished, I slowly began to realize that it was moving, that it was *alive*.

Colossal beyond scale, I witnessed a massive, eight-armed creature claw the ground as it picked up bones by the hundreds, heaping them into a pile.

...building, something? I struggled to form the thought in my death-addled mind, as I noticed a growing square being cleared of bones.

As if hearing my thoughts, the colossus halted in its work and turned its body to the sky. An impossibly pale eye fixed on me.

"**BEGONE.**"

The mental voice shattered what little control I had over myself, rending my shade to pieces.

My mind spiraled into darkness.

Aldford

I AWOKE IN A FIT of terror, my mind trying to make sense of what I'd just experienced, only to find myself standing just outside the town hall in Aldford with the sun beating down on me. I'd been dead for less than a minute.

"Ugh." My heart hammered in my chest as I rubbed my eyes, trying to come to terms with my death and the disjointed vision I'd just experienced.

What the hell was that? Where was that? A few deep breaths helped settle me down, and within a minute the experience was beginning to fade into a distant memory. I tried to focus on the rest of the party, but all I could sense was their general direction, towards where I knew Crater Lake to be. If they died, they'd show up here with me. When I finally opened my eyes, several alerts hung in my vision.

> **You have died at the hands of your Nemesis!**
> *As a badge of your failure, you will bear the scars of your death wound!*
> *As a result of your death, your Nemesis grows in skill and power, beware!*

Your Spirit feels weakened after your death!
Due to being under level 10, you do not experience any additional
death penalty.

I pulled a glove off and touched my face, recalling my last moments of life before the puma pounced onto me. My fingers found a thick line of scar tissue crossing the left side of my mouth, followed by another line on the right side of my forehead.

"Ho, Lyrian." The bann's voice interrupted my thoughts. "You're back already? Where are your companions?"

"They're still out there." I turned to face the bann as I spoke. "I… died, unfortunately."

The bann's eyebrows shot up as he glanced over my new scars. "Ah, unfortunate indeed. The *adventurer's curse*, as I call it, though I am more than happy to have you still among the living."

"Right now, I'm not sure if I feel the same way…"

"Are you going to head back out again?" Aldwin asked, indicating in the direction of the gate with a nod.

I mulled over the bann's question, trying to evaluate how it was I felt. Compared to my last moments, I felt hale and full of energy. A quick glance showed me I still had my equipment as well. I just felt *off*. As if my very spirit had stretched thin. "No. I think I'll be staying in for the rest of the day and wait for my friends to return."

The bann nodded, though after seeing my downcast expression, he frowned. "There is no sense in brooding. Come, we will spar then."

"I'm not sure if I'm up for that," I hedged, not feeling particularly enthusiastic about the idea. All I wanted to do at the moment was sit and collect myself.

"Nonsense!" The bann waved my complaints away. "The best way to get over death sickness is to either get under someone or to get your blood up and shake off the cobwebs. I'm sure you've noticed the village is a bit sparse, regardless of preference for the former."

"What—" I coughed at the bann's lewd suggestion, quickly realizing he was doing his best to get me out of my funk. "I-I suppose a little bit of sparring would help me get my mind off dying."

"Good! The last thing the villagers need to see is you moping around like you just found a bag of drowned kittens." Aldwin laughed as he led me towards the yard set aside for militia practice. "They'd probably take to the hills, to be honest. Your presence is more soothing to them than you may realize."

"Is it?" I paused, thinking over the last few days. Had I not spawned here during the goblin attack, a good portion of the villagers would have surely been kidnapped. Not to mention providing food for everyone after the attack.

"Enough wool-gathering," the bann said as we arrived at the bare patch of dirt that was the drill yard. "Let's see what you've learned out there."

The bann stalked across the field, pulling his hand ax free from his belt loop. "We will fight until one submits. Don't hold your blows, either; we'll call Shelia over to heal us between bouts."

Fixing me with an eager smile, Aldwin spread his arms out wide. "Come at me, adventurer."

Bann Adwin has challenged you to a duel!

"Are you sure?" I hedged, still feeling the lethargy of death hanging over me. "I don't—"

"Lyrian! On this field, I am *Sir* Fredric Aldwin, Knight of Eberia!" The bann's calm and friendly persona had vanished as if a switch was flicked. "When I give an order on this field, I expect it to be obeyed! If you don't attack me this instant, I am going to cut your arm off and use it to beat you back to death!"

A knight?

"Lyrian!"

Not waiting for the bann to follow through on his threat, I instantly broke into a charge, drawing Razor in stride. I slashed out upwards, looking to split *Sir Fredric* from hip to shoulder. But before I could even get Razor fully drawn, he darted forward, shoulder first, using his body to block my draw. His body check completely negated my charge, sending me sprawling to the ground.

"Come on, Lyrian!" he yelled at me as he slashed downward with his ax. "My senile mother would have seen that coming! It's no wonder to me why you died!"

Instinct had me urgently rolling to the side as I slammed into the ground, saving me from the ax that would have ended up in my chest. The swing had enough strength behind it to bury itself into the dirt right up to shaft. *Shit! He isn't fooling around! That could have killed me!*

I kicked out at the back of the bann's knee and was rewarded with a meaty thump as he lost his balance, going down to one knee. I rolled to my feet, barely missing a slash as he tore the ax from the ground in a spray of dirt. As I leaped away to build space between us, I felt the specter of death hanging over me, sapping my strength and slowing my movements. Nothing was as easy or fast as it should have been.

"That's more like it!" Aldwin roared as he launched himself at me.

Fighting through the lethargy, I quickly drew Razor, parrying a handful of probing attacks as the bann closed in, sweeping his hand ax in short, and controlled arcs as he attempted to close the gap between us. He wielded the hand ax like a smith wielding a hammer. Short but punishing swings forced me to constantly backpedal as he attempted to overpower my defenses with brute force.

He's even stronger than he looks! I winced as fervent parries sent jarring quakes of pain up my arm. We were evenly matched with speed, but with the bann's greater strength and the skill he wielded his ax with, he was a world beyond me. *Time to do something reckless!*

I stopped backpedaling under the bann's furious assault and retaliated with a flurry of blows as I closed the gap. Aldwin easily knocked my attacks aside but was surprised as I stepped forward with a vicious elbow across the jaw. The effort cost me a wicked chop across the knee, even as Razor nicked the inside of the bann's arm.

Before I could even begin to celebrate landing a blow, I found myself sliding across the ground, propelled by a wicked kick that caught me in the chest. For the second time in the fight, I gasped for air as I got my feet under me and forced myself to stand, only to wince in pain as the wound on my knee made it impossible.

"Do you...shubmit?" the bann slurred through a cracked lip as he cradled his right arm against his chest to stem the flow of blood.

"I..." I winced again as I tried to stand up, my knee was in definite trouble. "I submit."

Bann Aldwin was victorious in your Duel!
Your skill in Swords has increased to Level 6!

"Good fight," Aldwin grunted as he knelt down beside me. "You have the speed and strength to compete. However, your blade skill is sorely lacking. You wield your sword like a club."

I nodded as I absorbed a new inflow of knowledge the new skill level brought. He was right; I might be level nine, but my weapon skills had been left far behind. Ever since I'd found Razor, I'd had to worry less about my actual skill in combat, and focused more on just swinging the sharp end of the blade around.

Despite the death sickness and trouncing at the bann's hand, I was thrilled that skills could improve through dueling! It sure beat having to run out into the wild and senselessly murder creatures until I reached a certain skill level.

Summoning my character sheet with a mental command, I double checked how my skills were progressing. "I have quite a bit to learn."

Skills:

Evocation – Level 5 – 34% (Increases knowledge of Evocation Magic and improves related Abilities.)

Unarmed Combat – Level 4 – 11% (Increases knowledge of hand-to-hand fighting and improves related Abilities.)

Stealth – Level 2 – 14% (Decreases chance of being detected while attempting to stay hidden. Improves related Abilities.)

Swords – Level 6 – 2% (Increases knowledge of sword fighting and improves related Abilities.)

Wordplay – Level 1 – 15% (Increases chance to persuade others, resolve differences and/or get information.)

Perception - Level 3 - 35% (You are skilled in spotting hidden creatures and places. Depending on your skill level, hidden creatures, and places will be highlighted in red.)

I noticed I made small improvements in both Evocation and Unarmed Combat, likely during the fight with the spiders before I had died. I also remembered that in order to qualify for my spellsword class I had to reach level nine in both Swords and Evocation.

"Indeed." Aldwin waved at a figure in the distance. "Here comes Shelia now."

"Ready for another?"

A WOODEN SHAFT SLAMMED INTO the side of my face, filling my mouth with blood as I desperately brought up my wooden sword to block the blows following behind it. I knocked two shafts out of the way while sidestepping a third.

"Hit!" the bann shouted. "We start again at four minutes!"

I let out a roar of frustration as I parried the endless avalanche of attacks directed at me. The bann was an evil man! Born from the blackest pits of Hell! Spawned from the union of pain and despair! I swore if he and the devil crossed paths, the devil would give him the right of way!

"Focus, Lyrian!" Aldwin called from the side of the field as he ran a whetstone along Razor's edge, having traded it for a weighted training blade. "Unless you'd rather take another turn with me!"

Gone was the witty, quiet leader who offered to take my mind off of death sickness with friendly sparring. In his place stood a knight, intent on honing my broken, sweat covered body with the calm patience of a blacksmith sharpening a rusty knife.

The only solace I took at this moment, was that I wasn't the only target of his wrath, if only indirectly.

Four of Aldford's guards—two-thirds of the village militia—had been summoned from their duty to aid me in training. At the moment, Loren, Ioun, Caleb, and Wallace were armed with blunted spears, doing their best to hit me as hard and often as they could. I didn't even have the luxury of my armor to fall back on, the knight having insisted that I fight bare-chested.

If only I hadn't opened my fat mouth! I berated myself as I blocked a swing from Wallace and stepped past him, using his body to block the others from having a clear view of me.

An eternity ago, after a pair of lost duels at the bann's hand, I had foolishly asked: "Couldn't you have killed all the goblins yourself during the attack?"

Without missing a beat, the bann fully agreed that he probably could have, he then asked Shelia to call over the day shift's militia members. "Killing the goblins wasn't my concern; protecting every villager near me was."

Knight Aldwin looked at me carefully. "What is more important to you, Lyrian? Is it killing your enemies? Or is it protecting those dearest to you? Take it from an old man who wishes he'd learned that lesson earlier in life. If you try to do both, you *will* fail."

It may have been my imagination at the time, but I swore I saw a ghost cross Aldwin's face as he spoke.

He then ordered the militia to attack me, with the stipulation that I wasn't allowed to attack back until I had survived four consecutive minutes without them landing a hit on me.

So far, even after the death sickness faded away, I had failed a total of twenty-six times.

THWACK!

Twenty-seven times.

Argh! I sucked in a deep lungful of air as I shook the stinging pain out of my arm. *Damn it!*

I leaped away as the bann restarted the count once again, backing to the very edge of the practice field. Instinctively, the two younger militia members, Loren and Ioun, followed. They had been among the villagers surprised by the goblins during the raid and nearly kidnapped to parts unknown. They burned for a chance to prove their worth and redeem themselves, if only in their own eyes.

They rushed in, attacking without any coordination. First in line, Loren stabbed out with his spear, looking to catch me high in the chest. Anticipating the attack, I shifted to the side, letting the thrust pass harmlessly beside me and feinted forward. Ioun, a step behind, twirled his spear and swung it horizontally like a staff as he attempted to keep me from escaping the corner.

I may not be able to hit them. I planted my foot and leaped backward.

THWACK!

"Aaah! I'm sorry!"

...but they can hit each other! Ioun's wild blow caught Loren full in the side, bending the man double from the unexpected blow.

"Fair play!" Aldwin shouted, a faint frown showing on his face. "Always control your weapon!"

Seizing the distraction, I dashed past the two militiamen, slapping the spear from Ioun's hand as I passed, kicking it behind me.

Wiser than the younger pair, Wallace and Caleb had taken the time to form up together, shoulder to shoulder, and attacked with coordinated thrusts, one high, the other low. I was forced to give ground under their relentless advance, unable to parry both spears simultaneously.

As my feet found the edge of the practice field once again, I conjured a Flare in my hand, whipping it at the ground in front of the more experienced militiamen. The Flare burst with an unexpected snap, causing both of them to flinch. My sword swept out at Caleb's outstretched spear, smashing into it with all the fury I could muster, causing it to fly from his hands and off the field.

"You are disarmed!" The bann's shout halted Caleb's instinctive reaction to chase his weapon. "Fight!"

At that moment, Ioun chose to rejoin the bout.

He charged in from my flank, leading with a powerful thrust that was sure to pierce straight through me, blunt edge or not. At the same time, Wallace lunged, sending a weak thrust towards my ribs. Desperately I reached out, grabbing Wallace's spear and tugging it, pulling it in line with Ioun's charge. With my sword I chopped down at Ioun's thrust, redirecting it downwards, causing it to bury itself into the ground so that it trapped Wallace's spear.

Before either man could react, I stomped on the two intercrossed spears, jamming my boot in place and preventing either Ioun or Wallace from pulling free their weapon. A quick glance showed Loren crouched in pain, clutching at the ribs on his side with Shelia already kneeling beside him. I hefted my blade, ready to threaten any advance by Caleb.

"Hold!" Aldwin shouted, disgust evident in his voice. "That's enough! It seems my militia is more dangerous to one another, rather than to the enemy! Take a break! You lot need it!"

I heaved as I stepped off the spears and fell to the ground, gasping for air. *It's finally over. I think I'm going to die again. Here I thought I exercised hard in real life...*

"Lyrian! What the hell are you doing?" Sir Fredric Aldwin's voice rang out. "The rest break is for them! Not you! Get up!"

I liked him better before I knew he was a knight.

SEVENTEEN

The Webwood
Nemesis

THE TRANSITION FROM SENTIENCE TO sapience was one filled with fear and confusion.

Bloody paws tracked through the Dark Forest, eyes and ears ever alert for threats. The Many-Legged-Ones ruled the Dark Forest. It was an interloper here and knew danger could come from any direction. If not from the Many-Legged, then from the Two-Legged. It knew there was a chance the other Two-Legs could come searching soon, so it hurried deeper into the woods in search of safety.

It had been compelled to find a specific Two-Leg, somehow knowing the Two-Leg would be in the Dark Forest. It was easy prey to stalk, stampeding through the Dark Forest with other Two-Legs, no regard for stealth. It waited patiently, watching as the Two-Legs hunted the

Many-Legs, biding its time until it could strike without fear.

Now the Two-Leg's blood covered its maw, and the mysterious compulsion was sated, it was eager to leave the Dark Forest and return to the ridge.

Why?

The alien thought caused it to freeze mid-stride, ears straining to hear where it came from. Had the Two-Legs followed it?

What?

It quickly dropped to all fours, heart racing as it pressed itself down into the ground. It didn't hear anything, but it could *hear* something.

How?

Instinct warred with the birth of new thoughts that it had no reference for, sending it into a panic. With a yowl of fear, it took off, sprinting wildly through the woods as it tried to outrun its own mind.

Where am I?

Aldford

THE EVENING FOUND ME SLUMPED over a table inside the town hall, holding my head, with my face hovering inches away from a steaming [Webwood Casserole] Ragna had prepared for me. I breathed deeply, taking in the ever-so-slight minty aroma, mixed with a hint of venom-infused spider meat that had my mouth watering. For the last minute, I'd been carefully working up the focus to pick up my fork to begin the meal.

My head felt like it was ready to *explode.*

I sighed as I finally summoned enough energy to lean back in my bench and grab my utensil. I scooped a portion of the dish and took a bite. Instantly, the venom set fire to my mouth as I methodically chewed the meal.

It was the best meal I had ever tasted.

I looked down at the meal in surprise, forgetting the pain in my head, for a moment wondering how I even managed to arrive at the hall. The bann had been relentless in his sparring, only pausing long enough between duels for Shelia to cast a healing spell on the two of us. I scooped another bite into my mouth, savoring the flavor. Between his ax and the militiamen's spears, I had been pummeled for nearly nine hours straight.

If I hadn't frozen after that skill increase, I'd probably still be out there. I closed my eyes as my head still struggled to make sense of all the information that had been loaded into it today. Under the bann's punishing tutelage, I had reached level ten in Swords, level seven in Unarmed Combat, and level seven in Evocation, once he allowed no-holds-barred dueling.

When I hit my last skill up in Swords at level ten, it was as if an ice pick stabbed itself through my forehead, instantly forming a massive migraine as my brain attempted to assimilate the newest level of skill. It caused me to freeze mid-duel with Aldwin, who thankfully managed to pull a vicious blow directed at my head in time.

Otherwise, I'd likely be sitting at this table with another round of death sickness *and* an even worse migraine.

"Looks like you've surpassed your limit for the day," was all the knight said, looking at me with approval. "Go get some rest."

Truthfully, I wasn't sure if the migraine was because I learned too many skills in a day, or because I had leveled a combat skill's level past my class level.

Possibly a combination of both? The bann had essentially power-leveled my skills through non-stop training over the course of a day. *Maybe there's a limit for taught skills?*

It would easily trivialize the game if higher level players could infinitely teach lower level players. At some point, after all, you just had to go into the wild and get first-hand experience.

My fork scraped the bottom of the plate at the same moment the party walked in.

"Lyrian!" Caius was the first to call out as the group rushed over. "Ah! What happened?"

"What did you do to your face?!" Halcyon gasped as he saw my new scars.

"It's been a long day," I began as the others quickly grabbed seats at the table.

"Lyrian…" Sierra's eyes were fixated on my scars. "I'm sorry, I froze. I—"

I shook my head waving her off. "It's okay, Sierra. I threw you all into the fire today to see how you'd handle it. If anything, I should be the one apologizing!"

"But your face…"

"Besides, dying isn't so bad." I shrugged, deciding to keep the odd vision to myself for now. "You just feel like crap for an hour, then it sort of…fades away."

"I'm glad you're okay. I didn't know what to expect after we found you."

I smiled at Sierra and to the rest of the group. "So what happened after I died? The fight go well? Did you see any more of those Webwood aberrations?"

The party shook their heads as they looked at Drace to speak. "It was touch and go with the horde Constantine pulled. The larger spiders were a pain to deal with, and they nearly killed us. But we managed to pull through without seeing any more aberrations."

Conversation paused as everyone relived their piece of the fight.

"After the fight, we noticed you weren't with us, and when we realized we couldn't sense you nearby, we looked around and found your body, covered in strange glowing…goop." Drace motioned to

Sierra, who pulled something from her inventory.

"This was all I found in a loot sack near your body." She handed me a blue glowing vial in her hand, eyes going to my scars once more. "What happened to you? It looked like something had...mauled you."

"Yeah." I nodded as I began to explain my side of events, describing my brief fight with the aberration and its spellcasting abilities, finishing off with the nemesis's attack. Despite it attacking Sierra, no one had seen the creature or came across another one during the day's hunt.

As I spoke, I looked down at the vial in my hand, a tag in my vision identifying it as *[Strange Glowing Ichor] x5*. I pocketed it for later investigation.

"Your body just...*dissolved* a moment after we found it." Sierra shrugged as she made an exploding motion with her hands. "A moment after that, we sensed you again in the direction of Aldford."

"After that, it took us a bit of time to rest up. Then we decided to continue hunting like we agreed earlier. Much more carefully, though." Drace glanced over at Constantine, as he continued to outline their day. "Long story short, we're all level nine now!"

"That's great!" I beamed at everyone, ecstatic that they were able to progress without me.

"Lyr." Drace looked at me intently. "Do you think that this... nemesis...of yours will be a problem?"

"I'm not sure." I frowned as I considered the warrior's question. "It caught me inches away from dying today, so I have no idea how strong it really was, and my death supposedly made it even stronger. Maybe?"

"Hm." Drace exhaled as he collected his thoughts. "I think we should focus on getting our base classes as soon as possible then."

"Yeah, definitely." Halcyon agreed.

"I think it's a good idea too, but we also have another thing to consider." I spoke quietly as I rubbed my temples, trying to banish the still present migraine. "Aldford itself."

"What about Aldford?" Sierra asked, but she frowned as she saw me rubbing my head. "Wait, are you okay?"

"Ugh, sort of." I winced as the pain in my head flared. "I had a bit of a development with the bann today..."

I gave everyone the highlights of my day after resurrecting in Aldford, everything from the moment that the bann revealed himself as a knight of Eberia to the brutal training that he put the militia and myself through.

"...and now it feels like the morning after an entire bottle of vodka," I finished with a sigh, after explaining my theory on training limits.

"Huh. A knight," Constantine mused. "Makes sense, I suppose. They wouldn't hand out land to just commoners."

"Not poor commoners at any rate," Caius added. "Good to know about training limits, though."

"I wonder why he doesn't have more retainers, though," Halcyon commented. "Don't knights usually have big familial houses that support them?"

"Maybe he earned his title during the war?" Sierra replied. "Have to start from somewhere."

"Could be..."

"I can't imagine how hard it'll be to hit the limit as time goes on," Drace said, moving away from the topic of the bann's knighthood. "Skills are easy enough to level right now. It's bound to slow down the higher they get."

"That's true." I nodded in agreement.

"So what did you mean about Aldford?" Sierra asked.

"We need to decide if we're going to put roots down here in Aldford or find somewhere else to go," I began, taking a deep breath. "And if we do stay, it'll mean work."

"You want to leave?" The table groaned as Drace leaned to rest his massive bulk on it. "There isn't anywhere else to go, short of going back to Eberia, or an aimless trek through the wild. What's on your mind?"

"The coming adventurers," I said with a sigh. "I hadn't really given it much thought until today. Well, just now, actually, after training with the militia."

"You're afraid they're going to try and take the village when they get here." Following my train of thought, Constantine had reached the same conclusion.

"This village is somewhat defensible, thanks to the river surrounding it," I continued with a nod at him. "But we have what? A total of twenty NPCs, with maybe nine capable of combat? That'd be a tempting target for any group. Not to mention that the stone gate is a wreck, allowing anyone to just wander over that tiny bridge, and the northern part of the village is completely open."

"So what do you want to do?" Sierra asked while everyone else looked at me.

"I was actually going to ask you all the same thing." I made eye contact with everyone, one at a time. "If we stay, I have a plan of what I'd like to do, but we're going to have to work hard to start building up the village defenses and prepare for when other adventurers start coming. Not to mention we still have raiding goblins in the area, a missing expedition to find, unknown ruins, and a forest full of spiders to deal with.

"I know we all jumped at the chance to play together, but I'm not going to pull you all down a road that you all don't want to get into."

Everyone looked at me incredulously for a moment before they burst out laughing.

"Lyrian! We scaled half of a mountain and clawed our way through the wild to get here!" Drace scolded me. "If we didn't want to get involved in any of that, we'd have told you before we left Eberia!"

"Yeah, shit! Do you even hear what you're saying?" Constantine added. "Here we have the chance to get in on the development of the only settlement in the area, plus you seem to have a lock on *four* different story arcs! Like hell, we'd give that up just because it's going to be *hard*!"

"I think you have our answer, Lyr," Sierra said, followed by nods from Halcyon and Caius. "We're with you in whatever you have planned."

"I'm happy to hear that!" I couldn't help but smile at their words and the trust they put in me. "There's a hell of a lot I want to do too, and I'm going to be leaning on you all pretty hard."

Despite the promise of hard work, everyone looked visibly excited.

Sierra spoke eagerly. "So what's the plan?"

EIGHTEEN

Good morning, adventurers!

Due to numerous complaints, we would like to remind all players that Ascend Online is designed to be a social and dynamic experience! If you find yourself on a difficult story arc and can't accomplish it by yourself, try partnering up or forming a group!

Happy Hunting!

-CTI Development Team

THE NEXT MORNING, WE WOKE up with the speed of a lightning bolt, barely able to contain our excitement for the day to come. By the time the sun began to peak over the distant horizon, we had eaten and were standing on the practice field with weapons in hand.

The first step of my plan was to admit to the party that I was wrong with my approach yesterday. As soon as they arrived, I had fallen back into the traditional MMORPG approach: *go forth and kill.* While a reasonably effective tactic in itself, there was a massive difference between sitting at a keyboard and playing a game as opposed to actually *living a game.*

Just as there was a difference between fighting together and fighting *together.*

It had taken a lot of thought and a full night's sleep for the revelation to properly crystallize, but when I awoke in the morning, I understood the subtle message the bann was trying to tell me when he pitted me against the militia yesterday.

This is not a world where you can stand alone.

I thought back to our battle in the Webwood. Sure, we fought competently, but we fought also independently, concerned only for our tiny sliver of the overall battle.

Today, I wanted to start working on how to fight as a team. I knew it wasn't going to be something that happened overnight, no matter how hard we trained. It would be a slow and subtle process, one reenforced with constant training every single day.

However, with the way our first training session was going so far, all I hoped for at the moment was that the six us of would reach a point where we weren't an active danger to one another.

"Ah, mah nose!" I winced, completely bent over as I reflexively clenched my shattered septum, eyes watering. "Nat door falt Draae!"

Being the three frontline melee fighters, Drace, Constantine, and I had been working together on how to form an efficient battle line, one that wouldn't interfere with any of our individual styles but also allow us to support and protect one another.

Drace's massive size and reach, however, made it difficult to judge where my support should start or end, resulting in an inadvertent elbow to my face on his backswing. As I spat a mouthful of blood out, I silently envied Constantine's choice to be on Drace's shield side.

Funny how they never show the heroes in stories getting coldcocked by a training accident.

"Shit, Lyr! I didn't realize you were so close!" Drace apologized profusely.

I shook my head as I exhaled through my mouth, already feeling the cartilage re-arranging itself as I healed the damage. "Joor—you're not supposed to. I'm still getting used to your swing with a mace."

Adding onto the difficulty of judging Drace's reach were the subtle and not-so-subtle differences between attacking with a sword, mace, or spear. I wanted us to be ready to switch weapons at a moment's notice if we fought a creature resistant to a type of damage. Not to mention that Drace's base class requirements to become a warrior required that he at least have three weapon skills at level seven.

After an hour of practice, slip ups, and a handful of minor injuries, I added Sierra, Halcyon, and Caius into the equation. They had spent the morning carefully watching our quirks, stances, and positioning as we drilled together. Now their job, as ranged combatants, was to find holes to shoot through.

"One, two, three, step, and fire!" Sierra called out the cadence as we ran through a drill at quarter of combat speed.

Constantine, Drace, and I slowly attacked our imaginary enemies, and on Sierra's cue took a single step away from Drace. An arrow whizzed by the spot I just vacated, followed by two magical bolts in Constantine's. The second the ranged attacks passed by Drace, he sent his weapon in a wicked cleave, clearing the ground in front of him, followed by Constantine and I quickly collapsing back into line with him.

Ideally, if we could successfully execute similar drills in combat, we could quickly devastate a line of enemies while keeping one another safe from counter attacks.

"Good!" I called. "Again!"

As before, there were mistakes and slip ups as we trained, but before long, we were able to run through the drill at nearly full speed, reasonably confident that we wouldn't accidentally stab, scorch, or shoot one another.

As an added bonus, everyone reported multiple skill increases to boot.

"Lyrian! I see you have taken a liking to my practice field," the bann's voice called out at the end of a drill. "Perhaps my lessons yesterday weren't wasted on you after all!"

"Good morning, sir!" I greeted the knight as we broke formation, all happy for a bit of a break. "We still need quite a bit of practice, but we're getting there!"

The bann had brought a small entourage with him to the practice field this morning: the same group of militiamen from yesterday, as well as a much healthier-looking Natasha.

A slight wince passed across Aldwin's face as he heard my greetings. "Please, just Aldwin or even Fredric, if you prefer. This is a frontier village, after all! We have far too much work to do than worry about silly honorifics all day!"

I sensed there was a *great* deal more behind those words than the bann was letting on, but I nodded in agreement. There would be another time to find out more about Aldwin's history. At the moment, though, he was absolutely right. There was a ton of work to do.

"We didn't have a chance to meet everyone yesterday, but these are my friends." I quickly introduced everyone as they stepped forward to shake hands. After our sparring wound down yesterday, the bann had retreated to his study, even having his meal sent up to him. Though seeing Natasha here, it now occurred to me that he may have been keeping her company.

"It's good to see you on your feet, Natasha! Are you feeling better today?" I noticed that the dark-haired novice seemed a little cautious at meeting everyone all at once and stepped to the side as everyone continued with their greetings.

"Good morning, Lyrian!" She smiled at me with a nod, looking more comfortable talking to someone she knew. "Ah! Yes, I feel like my old self again. Shelia has been taking great care of me."

"I'm happy to hear that!" I said honestly as I looked back at the party. It seemed Drace had quickly hit it off with the bann and mili-tiamen, having formed their own semi-circle as they spoke. Caught between two groups, Sierra and Halcyon gradually began to edge their way towards us as they debated which conversation to join. "So what are your plans now? Are you going to set off looking for your comrades?"

"Well, I want to, but Aldwin doesn't seem to think I should." Natasha's demeanor became visibly frustrated as she spoke. "And truthfully, I don't even know where to begin looking."

"What do you mean?" Sierra asked, having turned her full atten-tion to our conversation.

"I don't remember where our camp was," Natasha admitted with a frustrated sigh. "We spent days trekking through the forest, and when the goblins attacked in the middle of the night, I couldn't even tell you what *direction* I ran in, thanks to the trees. I just grabbed the first backpack I saw and ran into the night once I saw they were tak-ing prisoners. I didn't even get a chance to open the pack before I got caught by those spiders!" Natasha said as she gestured to me. "If it wasn't for Lyrian, I'd have ended up as spider food."

"We? You were with others?" Halcyon joined in on the conversa-tion, having shifted over from the other conversation. "Err, sorry for interrupting."

"Oh, no worry! I was part of an Eberian Mages Guild expedition exploring the area," Natasha explained to Halcyon, shrugging off his interruption. "I don't really know too much about it. The expedition leader, Adept Donovan Kaine, kept referring to a 'ruptured ley line', and was trying to find a ruin that the Surveyors Guild casually noted a few months back in a report."

"A ley line?" Sierra repeated. "I don't do magic, what's that?"

"I'm not sure. Something, magical? Can't be any good if it's ruptured, though." Natasha shrugged.

"It's like a magical pathway," I said. "Probably not a good thing if it's ruptured."

"Definitely not a good thing if it's ruptured!" Halcyon exclaimed. "It's more like a magical river, or a highway!"

"So what will happen if it stays ruptured?" Sierra asked, looking at Halcyon with a bit of alarm.

"Do I look like a wizard?" Halcyon grunted in exasperation. "How am I supposed to know?"

"Uh, Halcyon." I cocked an eyebrow at the mage. "You kinda-sorta *are* a wizard."

"Shit!" Halcyon cursed under his breath. "I kinda-sorta *am* a wizard now. Uh, well. I would consider a ruptured ley line as being a bad thing."

"What kind of advice is that?!" I hissed at Halcyon's unhelpful information as I swatted him in the arm. "Anything *ruptured* is a bad thing!"

"It's wizardly advice," Halcyon hedged as he reached out and tugged on Caius's arm. "My wizardly advice is also telling me that this would be a perfect time to leave!"

I slapped the fleeing mage on the shoulder again as he made his escape with Caius. "Go train your shit! Smartass…"

For Halcyon and Caius's base classes, mage and warlock respectively, they had a similar wide range of requirements as Drace did for his warrior class. In their case, they had to reach at least level seven in three of the five arcane trees – Abjuration, Alteration, Conjuration, Divination, or Evocation. Since I had other plans for my day, I told them to focus on leveling their skills together for the time being.

"What?" Natasha shook her head in confusion as Caius and Halcyon made their escape. "What just happened?"

"Just Halcyon being…himself," Sierra said to Natasha with a shrug. "You'll get used to him."

"Yeah, I keep telling myself that too…" I muttered under my breath as the bann's circle shifted to fill the gaps left by the two mages.

"Everything all right, Lyrian?" Aldwin asked, nodding his head in the direction of the departing spellcasters.

"Yeah, there's no problem…" I paused for a moment. "Well, not a problem we can do much about right now."

"Oh?" The bann looked at me cautiously, and understandably so. I was starting to develop a reputation for bringing him problems.

"Has Natasha told you what their expedition was looking for here?"

"Yes, something about a ruptured ley line and a ruin." Aldwin fell silent for a moment. "Though I confess, I really don't have any idea what that means."

"Neither do we." Sierra sighed. "Probably not good, though."

"Hm…." Aldwin looked to the sky for a moment, likely praying to, or berating, his deity of choice. "I see."

"We'll look into it *eventually*—it'll just have to be another problem for the future for the moment." I echoed Sierra's sigh, starting to realize just how *many* problems my future was filled with. "We have more immediate things we want to sort out."

Aldwin smiled as he motioned to Drace, clearly happy to be on more familiar ground. "Ah yes! Drace here was telling me about your plan to take my militia out into the wild?"

"Yeah." I nodded, looking at the group of semi-eager militiamen. "Training will only get them so far, and now is a good time for more practical experience. I was hoping you would be willing to assign them to Drace for the day." I motioned to the half-giant. "He would take them on a circuit around Aldford, clearing out creatures and prospecting for metals. With any luck, they'll come back having been bloodied, and we'll have some more material to go around for Aldford."

"If it helps, Sierra and I will also be on hand nearby." Constantine finally spoke, having been content to listen up until now. "The both of us need to practice our stealth skills and can shadow them from afar."

"Oh! Can I come?" Natasha's request caught everyone off guard. "I've been cooped up too long, and I could use the practice."

"Sure!" Sierra nodded excitedly. "We'll need to find you a weapon, though."

"Jenkins made a few bows yesterday evening," Aldwin said, nodding at Natasha. "They should be stored in the workshop. Just help yourself to one."

"Ah! Thank you, Aldwin!" Natasha replied graciously.

"So what do you think?" I prompted the bann. "Can we borrow the militia?"

"Hm…" the bann mused as he turned over the idea in his head, clearly pleased. "I like it."

He looked to Drace and nodded. "Bring them back in one piece, but don't coddle them either."

"Will do!" Drace said with a grin as he beckoned the militiamen to follow him.

"So where does that leave us today, Lyrian?" Aldwin looked over at me. "Seems to me we're the only ones without a task."

"Well now, Aldwin, funny you should ask." I grinned at the knight. "How many shovels do we have?"

NINETEEN

"HAD I KNOWN I'D BE spending my morning digging a shit pit, I'd have slept another hour or three!" the bann grumbled as he shoveled a mound of dirt out of the ditch.

With the second step of my plan complete, the party now focused on training the last few skills needed to unlock their base classes. I was in the process of beginning step three, building the defenses of Aldford.

Right now that had me, the bann, and practically every other villager in Aldford, save Ragna and Shelia, digging a ditch around the perimeter of the village.

"Ha! And miss out on some *honest* work? What sort of country knight are you? I thought this is why you settled out here in the frontier?" I laughed as I paused my own shoveling to wipe the sweat off my brow and look back at the work we'd completed so far. A few hours of work had given us nearly a hundred feet long and four and a half feet deep ditch, though we still had about twice that much to go lengthwise, just for the northern side of the village alone.

That we even made that much progress was because Ascend Online *thankfully* struck a balance between realism and practicality, as well as accounting for superhuman strength when it came to digging. "Besides, a common shit pit or a *latrine*, for those with gentle ears, wouldn't be nearly as helpful as this ditch will be."

"There is that," Aldwin admitted grudgingly as he continued to shovel. "Though, it's been forty-five years since even the *idea* of a real country knight existed, let alone one with practical experience."

"There are no country knights in Eberia?"

"No. Not really, at any rate." The bann shook his head. "Anyone with the skill or standing to be considered a knight was needed on the wall—the Bulwark—that protected us from the orcs. If they weren't there, they were busy training the next generation. Or dead," he added grimly. "Between the fall of the empire and the war, we've lost a great deal since we had to abandon Assara, the old continent."

"You lived on the old continent?" I was *extremely* curious to hear more about this world's history and hadn't considered that Aldwin had likely been born before the Ascendant Empire's fall. "How old were you when the empire fell?"

"Me? Hm..." He stopped shoveling as he thought. "I must have been seven...or eight years old. It was a long, long time ago."

"What happened?" I asked. "During the fall?"

"I don't really know." Aldwin sighed as his eyes took a faraway look. "I was too young to truly understand what was happening at the time. I remember that we first lost contact with the capital, and then shortly after, entire *cities* started disappearing.

"I was told some vanished like they were never there, cities hundreds of years old, suddenly replaced with wheat fields or fully-grown forests. While others were torn and shattered beyond recognition. The most terrifying thing I remember, though, was hearing about the cities where the *people* simply vanished without even a sign of where they went."

"I remember my parents grabbing me one day, and before I knew what was happening, we were on a ship." The bann spoke softly as he resumed shoveling. "It took us eighty-four days to make landfall here… things became so desperate aboard the ships that had it been another few days, we might have not made it at all. As it was, we barely had a chance to catch our breath before the orcs found us."

We dug for a few minutes silently as the knight wrestled with his memories. "As the war escalated, and more bodies were needed to hold the orcs at bay, we started to make compromises in teaching and training. If it wasn't related to actively fighting the war, then it wasn't taught."

"By the time we realized our mistake, all the experts were dead, and their knowledge gone with them." Aldwin paused in his shoveling to gesture at me. "That's why we all tolerate and encourage you, adventurers. Whatever spark it is that allows your kind to transcend death also gives you a unique font of knowledge to draw from. One that we pray will be used to help us recover what was lost and not held over our heads."

Now it was my turn to dig silently as I contemplated the bann's words. "I appreciate your trust," I said finally, starting to understand *how* and *where* adventurers fit in this world.

"I think you've more than earned it by now."

"Yo, Lyrian," Jenkins called from nearby. "Spare a minute to look over the plan?"

"Yeah, hold on." I waved goodbye to Aldwin as he resumed digging through the soft dirt as I heaved myself out of the ditch. Jenkins and

Ritt had set up a table nearby where they had sketched out a rough outline of the village, along with the proposed plan that I'd set up.

"All right." Ritt greeted me with a simple nod as he indicated the paper. "So with my rough pacing, we're looking at about three hundred feet across the north part of the village, three hundred and forty-five feet to the southwest, and three hundred and fifty-five feet to the southeast. The river takes a bit of a jink along the way that we'll have to avoid."

"Looks good to me." I nodded at the young merchant. "It'll give us plenty of room inside the village to expand."

"Judging on how fast we're going today, that'll take us roughly three to four days to dig...if we do nothing but dig," Jenkins calculated. "When are you expecting other adventurers to start arriving?"

"No earlier than three days from now," I replied. Based on what the others told me about the lay of the land it'd take roughly a week to dogleg around from Eberia, up the ridge and over here. If a group was dedicated enough, they could be here as early as Sunday afternoon or evening. "Likely four to five."

"All right, that gives us time then." Jenkins scribbled Ritt's numbers on the paper, with question marks beside them. "Show me that design you were talking about?"

"Sure, let's head over to the workshop," I said, waving him to follow me as I led the way.

When I had first conscripted the bann this morning, my plan had been to start building a palisade around the village. But when I presented the plan to Jenkins, he...*kindly*...pointed out the error in my thinking when we asked him how feasible the idea was.

"Lyrian, are you off your *fucking* gourd? Do you have any idea how many trees and work that's going to take?"

It turns out I didn't.

Jenkins explained to me that even if we took trees a foot in diameter, it would take *at least* a thousand trees to build a proper wall around the village. They'd have to be reasonably tall trees, too, which would make hauling them back to Aldford a colossal pain. Not to mention we'd have to ensure that any of the work parties going out to cut the wood, stayed safe from all the roaming creatures. Even if we somehow surpassed those obstacles, it would take an incredible amount of time to cut, strip, and stake the sheer quantity of trees we needed to circle the village. Time we didn't have.

In short, building a palisade just wasn't anywhere close to feasible with the manpower and time we had available to us. We would have to find another way to build up Aldford's defenses against the initial rush of adventurers and hope we found enough trustworthy souls to help with further developing the village at a later date.

What we *could* do right now, though, was start to lay the groundwork for the future palisade, and thanks to an idea of mine, still have a defensible perimeter around the village.

"Okay," I started once we were in the workshop and indicated a pile of wood. "It's called a tribuli, but I guess you could also call it a giant caltrop. If we wanted to make a quick and dirty version, we can lash three sharpened stakes together and set it up," I continued talking as I used a few lengths of scrap wood to show Jenkins the general design of what I pictured in my mind. "What do you think?"

"Hm…yeah. I think this can work!" On seeing my idea, Jenkins started to nod. "I get it now, you're hoping to put them in and around the ditches. That way if anyone tries to jump the ditch, they get an ass full of wood. Or if they try to creep through, they're going to make enough noise to alert someone."

"That's the plan!"

"It's still going to take a hell of a lot of these to fill the perimeter," Jenkins mused as he started clearing a workspace.

"Less than a thousand trees worth?" I asked with a grin. "It's not like we have enough metal lying around either."

"Good point," Jenkins grunted as he pointed to a nearby tool. "Grab that drawing knife over there. You're going to be helping me with these."

Your skill in Carpentry has increased to level 4!

"PHEW." I FINISHED ANOTHER TRIBULI and carefully set it down to the side. It was slow going at first, as Jenkins had to take the time to show me the basics of the carpentry, but once I'd managed to learn the skill, progress picked up. "Another one done!"

"And many more still to go…" Jenkins sighed as he worked on his own tribuli at another nearby bench.

"I have to ask, Lyrian. What exactly are you expecting from these coming adventurers, a siege?" Jenkins asked. "You seem intent on making sure that Aldford is defended, hell, even *fortified* before their arrival."

"Honestly?" I shrugged, grabbing another length of wood to start shaping. "I expect the best and the worst people that have to offer."

"I'm not sure what to make of that."

"Think of it from an adventurer's perspective." I turned to look at him. "You just spent seven days traveling here from Eberia, through all the wild has to offer. Likely also *unprepared* for what the wild has to offer. You're tired, hungry, maybe you have no idea where you even are. Then you find Aldford, a safe haven, the first sign of civilization you've seen in a week. Some adventurers, most adventurers even, will respect the difficulty, the simple *challenge* of setting up and simply surviving long enough to build a community here and integrate neatly. Those I'm not overly concerned about.

"It's the few who will do anything to achieve power who I worry about." I waved my hand to indicate the village around us. "Anyone with an ounce of cunning would know that Aldford is in a prime location for travel and trade. They'll look to be here the quickest and take it over. They won't care if they have to kill people or even burn half the village to the ground, so long as they have control."

"Isn't that what you've done already, though? Taken control of Aldford?" Jenkins whispered as he shook his head. "Isn't all this work, just to protect what you have?"

"What?" A dark expression crossed my face and my jaw dropped as I realized what Jenkins was implying. I couldn't help but get angry.

Where the hell is this coming from? I'm just trying to help Aldford survive the coming wave of adventurers, and he thinks I'm taking over? "I've just done my bes—"

"Whoa! Don't get me wrong!" Jenkins hastily interrupted as he saw my expression. "I definitely appreciate everything you've done for us! The whole town appreciates it!" He met my eyes, surprised at the emotion he saw there. "Gods, Lyrian. You didn't even realize it! I am so sorry for thin—"

"Realize what?" I barked angrily. "Think what? That I'm not any different than any other adventurer? I thought you buried this shit after the goblin attack!"

"I did, but—"

"But what, Jenkins?" I was off my bench and looming over the dark-skinned man. "What?"

"I want to propose to Shelia!"

"What? What the fuck does that even have to do with me?" I shouted, taken aback, my anger quickly turning to confusion. "Or this?"

"I want her to be safe! I want to build a *life* here with her!" Jenkins yelled back at me. "Everything that we're doing here will make Aldford safer, sure! But only for as long as you and your friends are here! I need to know that you aren't going to cut out on us, on the village," Jenkins continued softly. "You just don't get it. You barely spoke for ten minutes today outlining your plan for Aldford. Then everyone *went with it*."

Jenkins pointed outside in the direction where everyone was still digging.

"There are over a dozen people out there, including a *knight of Eberia* who happens to be the *legal* leader of this settlement, digging a three-hundred-foot ditch because you told them it'd be a good idea. Lyrian, in every way that matters, this village is as good as yours already." Jenkins looked up at me. "I need to *know* that you're going to be the same adventurer you were the very first day you got here. That you're actually going to *care* about us, regular people. Even when the other adventurers start coming. *Especially* when the other adventurers start coming."

Shit, he's right. The anger vanished quickly and was replaced with a crushing sense of responsibility. All I had tried to do up to this point was keep everyone in Aldford safe and make a few suggestions along the way. But over the last few days, I'd grown to actually *care* about the people here and didn't want to see them come to harm. *I keep forgetting that I can't think of these people as simple NPCs.*

"I can't promise that my friends and I will stay in Aldford forever, Jenkins," I answered sincerely. "But if and when that day comes when we decide to leave, it will be because *Aldford* no longer needs *us*, not the other way around. But if anyone, *ever*, raises a hand against the village of Aldford in anger, I promise you—it will be the last thing they do."

Jenkins nodded, relief showing on his face as he heard my answer. "Thank you, Lyrian."

"Don't mention it."

"So." I sat down on my bench and broke into a smile. "You and Shelia, eh?"

TWENTY

CONSTANTINE AND SIERRA WERE THE first of the party members to unlock their base classes. They both strode into Aldford with joy on their faces with an exhausted, but happy-looking Natasha not far behind. Having entered the village from the north, they walked right into the middle of our excavation project as we began to wind down for the day. They found us as we were about to finish emplacing the last of the tribuli we'd managed to make so far.

"We did it, Lyr!" Constantine was grinning wildly as he spoke. "We're finally level ten!"

"Congrats!" I beamed at the pair, taking in their dirty and disheveled appearances. *What the hell happened to them?* "How did your day work out?" I asked hesitantly.

"We kept up a good tempo." I couldn't recall a time when I saw Sierra as happy as she was right now, speaking excitedly with a huge smile on her face. "We played a few wargames with Drace and his militia group for most of the morning and afternoon. I'd say they're *sharp* now and finally not green enough to be considered a tree!"

"They downplay how relentless they were to those boys!" Natasha exclaimed shaking her head at Sierra's version of the day. "We'd spend fifteen, twenty, or even forty minutes creeping in on the militiamen, just to goose them with arrows!"

"Those poor boys are going to be seeing hidden dangers in their sleep!"

"That was kind of the point," Constantine freely admitted to Natasha. "They *need* to see dangers both for their own good and for Aldford's good too. I'd rather have an overly paranoid guardsman that needs to be reined in than one who needs to be kicked in the ass."

"I suppose…" Natasha agreed hesitantly, seeing the wisdom in that approach.

"We understand your training methods a bit better now, Lyr." Sierra looked at me intently as she nodded at Constantine's statement. "Yesterday…we needed a harsh perspective on what it takes to survive and what the cost is if we were to *fail*. We'll always come back to life, others won't be so lucky."

"Well, I'm happy you feel better about that. Though I didn't die on purpose yesterday just to teach you all that." A part of me felt happier knowing that they understood *why* I did things the way I did, even if they didn't turn out the way I intended. "So what can you tell me about being level ten? Is it everything we were hoping for?"

Constantine and Sierra shared a look before Constantine answered. "Actually, Lyrian, we want to keep quiet about that…"

"What? *Why?*"

"Because…" Sierra started as she tried to find words to explain.

"We don't want to ruin the experience."

"It's worth it." Constantine nodded. "Trust me."

"Ugh. You two are such teases." I shook my head at the pair with frustration before fixing them with an evil eye. "Fine! Keep your secrets! I have enough on my plate as it is!"

"No shit! We saw your work today," Constantine said as he waved at the ditch. "I thought we were aiming for a wooden wall, though?"

"That...didn't really pan out," I said as I began to explain what actually building a palisade entailed. "We're going to keep it a bit simpler right now, and this does the trick."

"This reminds me of something I saw from a documentary on the Roman Empire once," Sierra said as she examined a tribuli, turning it over in her hands as she admired the craftsmanship. "Shit, Lyrian, this has your name carved on it here! When the hell did you have time to learn carpentry today?"

"Ha! Yeah, it's Roman in inspiration!" I finished tying the straps to the tribuli I was assembling and set it aside. "As for the carpentry part, Jenkins taught me. The rest I kind of picked up on my own."

"Are you some sort of skill learning prodigy?" Constantine shook his head as he nudged an oversized caltrop. "Seems every time I turn around you've learned something new!"

"Actually, now that you mention it," I started to say before I grinned and changed my mind. "On second thought, I don't really want to *ruin the experience* for you two."

"You walked into that one." Sierra laughed as she shook her head at Constantine.

"Ugh," Constantine grunted. "I did."

"*Anyway...*" I said with a sigh as I changed topics. "Did you three manage to get any metals or herbs while you were out for the day? Or just add to the militiamen's nightmares?"

"Herbs mostly." Natasha was unexpectedly the first to reply. "We found a great deal of hollyleaf since it's native to the area. But we also found a good amount of yellowthorn as well!"

"Yeah, Lyr!" Constantine exclaimed excitedly. "Natasha is a bloodhound when it comes to finding herbs! I have no idea how she does it, but we managed to get nearly three hundred sprigs of hollyleaf throughout the day, and about ninety sprigs of a new herb called yellowthorn. We didn't find all that much metal, though, only about fifty pieces of copper ore throughout the entire day."

"Awesome!" The more hollyleaf we had, the less worried I became about the spiders in the Webwood. It canceled out poison during combat and was a central cooking ingredient for spider meat. The discovery of yellowthorn and a handful of metal ore was just an added bonus as far as I was concerned. "Any idea on what yellowthorn can be used for?"

"Nah." Constantine shrugged. "Doesn't have any consumable benefits like hollyleaf does."

"It requires distilling," Natasha said, obviously happy to contribute. "It's primarily used by alchemists, though I'm not quite sure what for."

"Hrm. I guess we'll have to pass it onto Caius," Sierra said. "He's the alchemist of the group."

"Till Lyrian learns it," Constantine added teasingly.

"Feh! Like I have time to learn everything under the sun!" I replied with a bit of exasperation.

"Maybe, maybe not." Constantine shrugged as he motioned to the town hall. "Do you want all the stuff we've collected for the day? We're going to find a bite to eat and sit down."

I shook my head. "Nah, I don't have room for all that. Jenkins cleaned out a crate in the workshop for us to use, just drop all of it in there and I'll sort it out."

"All righty, can do!"

"While you're there, hang up your armor on a rack or something."

I'd been subtly inspecting their armor since they arrived back to town, and it was *quite* worse for wear. "Did you guys purposefully decide to crawl through every single thorn bush and sharp rock you found out there today?"

Constantine, Sierra, and Natasha all looked down at their armor. "You think this is bad? Wait until you see Drace and his militiamen tonight! They had a *much* more exciting day than we did!"

"WHAT THE EVER-LIVING FUCK happened to you all?" I gaped at Drace and the militiamen as they stumbled their way into the town hall, having just finished dropping off a package of hollyleaf and meat for Ragna when I ran into the group.

I couldn't believe what I saw when I looked at the group. Their armor hung in tatters, chainmail links broken every which way. Drace was even missing an entire sleeve of armor that was supposed to cover his right arm. "Hold on, what's going on with your spear, Ioun?"

"Sir! It's technically a stick now!" Ioun replied with extreme formality as if I were some sort of military officer. "It was broken during combat with a wolverine, sir! I, unfortunately, left my spear buried six inches in its hindquarters before it snapped!"

A wolverine? I stared at the group at a loss for words. "Uh...well done?"

"Thank you, sir!"

"Drace." I looked at the half-giant warrior. "What the hell?"

"Hey, Lyr!" Drace gave me a mock salute. "How's your day working out? Saw the work outside, seems like you guys have been pretty busy!"

"Quit stalling! What the hell is this about a *wolverine*? I thought you spent the day wargaming with Sierra and Constantine?"

"Yeah...we started off the day like that." Drace broke into a smirk as he started to describe his day. "But after a while, these guys needed something a bit more interesting. So we went wandering."

"Right. And a tiny little…*wolverine* did all this to your armor? What did you do? Call its mother names?"

"Lyr, wolverines are eight-foot-tall, level ten murder machines in this game," Drace said firmly. "There's nothing little about them."

"Why the hell did you decide to fuck with one, then?" I was shocked that they had managed to find a level ten creature wandering anywhere close to the town, let alone engaged one. "Where the hell did you even find it?"

"Well, you *did* tell us to go looking for metals," Drace began. "So we decided to poke our heads into whatever caves we came across. Third one we looked into, was the beast, all cozied up and taking a nap."

"Do wolverines even live in caves?" I couldn't believe how literal everyone had been taking my suggestions lately.

"Like fuck I even know," Drace replied dryly. "I didn't bother to ask it about living arrangements, seeing how badly it was trying to redecorate using my intestines."

"I'll say it again. Why did you even decide to fuck with it in the first place?"

"Because of what was behind it!" A wicked grin broke over Drace's face. "We found the motherlode, Lyr! Four hundred pieces of copper ore! Nearly half that in tin! Just from that shallow cave alone!"

"Holy shit!" That sort of haul would solve a great deal of problems for us in the short term. If nothing else, I'd have enough to repair our armor and make a few sets for the militia. "*That's awesome!*"

"I figured it was worth the risk!" Drace said happily after hearing my excitement. "That's not all, though! I hit level ten too!"

"Ah! Congrats! Sierra and Constantine did too!"

"Yeah! We ran into them outside." Drace smiled as he spoke. "They told me to keep the details of level ten a secret, so you're out of luck to get anything from me!"

"Damn it!" I cursed. Everyone *knew* that my curiosity would always get the better of me. "You're all conspiring against me!"

"Just a little," Drace said. "But you'll understand why."

"Yeah, one day, maybe. Seems like I have an endless list of shit to do before I get something as *mundane* as my base class." I shook my head with a huff. "There's a crate in the workshop you can drop your stuff into, leave your armor on a rack while you're there. I'll see if there is any way I can fix some of it up."

"After that…" I eyed the group of militiamen, who had all been standing stoically while Drace and I chatted. *Hang on.* "Wait. Loren, are you okay? Your jaw looks a bit…off. Gods, is it dislocated?"

"Gah," was all that Loren managed to say. "Gnat go gad."

"Shit, Drace!" I looked at the rest of the men and noticed one cradling his shoulder, and another leaning on his spear like a crutch. "Your men are all broken and you have them standing here like it's nothing!"

"They haven't complained." Drace looked at the men proudly.

"I don't care! Go get Shelia!"

"SO YOU HAVE TO GO out into the wild and make some sort of fautian snack?" Constantine asked.

"Ugh, no," Caius said with a touch of exasperation. "I need to go out into the wild and make a *Faustian Pact* after I find and sacrifice a creature."

"Then you'll gain your dark powers?" Drace cut in.

"That or be damned for all eternity if I get it wrong."

"Wait, what?" I just clued into the conversation happening around me. I finally managed to get enough work done for the day that I didn't feel bad calling it quits and was in the middle of enjoying a Webwood casserole with everyone, save Halcyon, who had already gone to bed, when the topic of Caius's base class came up.

I *still* had more than enough work on my plate, from repairing everyone's armor to getting more crafting done and somehow finding the time to level my Evocation skill to finally unlock my base class. But at the moment, I was doing the best to enjoy my evening without feeling bad about it.

"Damned for all eternity? Do you want us standing by just in case?"

"Huh?" It took a moment for Caius to realize I was talking to him. "Nah, I'll be fine. It's all the typical arcane mumbo jumbo stuff. *Be afraid of demons…they'll fuck your shit up…*Blah, snore. I'm honestly not worried."

"If you're sure…" I wasn't completely convinced of Caius's bravado, but there were some things that could only be faced by oneself.

"Yeah, don't worry about it," Caius said without a concern. "You really worry about us too much, Lyrian. You should worry about hitting level ten yourself. You've been working yourself to the bone trying to take care of the village. Don't forget about yourself, eh?"

"Heh, I'll take that under consideration."

"If you're anything like Halcyon, you have enough to look forward to," Caius spoke softly. "He's feeling a bit…overwhelmed right now."

"Yeah." I nodded with a bit of sympathy. Halcyon was the fourth of our group to reach level ten today, but for whatever reason when he hit level ten, he was immediately overwhelmed with an influx of arcane knowledge and afflicted with a similar type of migraine to the one I had yesterday. "Hopefully we'll be fortunate enough to avoid that."

"Yeah, shit," Caius agreed, tapping his head. "I have my immortal soul to worry about here. I don't need a headache clogging up the works when I'm negotiating with a demon."

"Don't you mean digital soul?" Sierra quipped with a raised eyebrow.

"S'long as it gets me level ten," Caius said excitedly. "You can call it whatever kind of soul you want."

"I hear you there!" Constantine laughed.

"So what's the plan for tomorrow?" Drace cut in. "More drilling?"

"Yeah." I nodded. "We need to get used to working together. Then after that, we'll keep working on Aldford's defenses."

"Sounds good to me." Drace nodded. "We should be able to burn through the next ditch tomorrow if we're all on it."

"Hopefully…" I added softly. "Gods know I have enough shit to do."

The rest of the evening broke down into simple chatter and catching up about our day. There was an energy about the village that I hadn't felt before. Hope, excitement, *joy* even. Sometimes an honest day's work was all it took to raise people's spirits, and today was one of them.

It was the first day I went to bed thinking that everything would work out perfectly, that I could handle all the work that I'd piled onto myself.

At least until the screaming started and threw all my plans out the window.

TWENTY-ONE

Friday, February 8th, 2047 - 1:58 am
Aldford

I T STARTED WITH A SINGLE shriek of surprise echoing over the sleeping village, leaving its inhabitants struggling to discern if they *dreamed* the noise or had actually *heard* the noise.

The second shriek banished all doubt from the sleeping villagers. *Aldford was under attack.*

"Lyrian! Wake up!" Sierra's voice had me leaping off my cot, still half tangled in my blanket.

"What the fuck is happening?" I shouted as I reflexively conjured Light on myself. In the dim lighting, I saw the rest of the party scrambling out of their cots as another scream pierced the night. "Shit!"

I tore the blanket off myself, my hand shooting to where I had left Razor. I grabbed the cool hilt of the blade as I pulled it free of its sheath. *Shit! Everyone's armor is still in the workshop waiting for repairs!* "We're under attack, somewhere outside! Let's get moving!"

Weapons already in hand, we rushed towards the town hall door. Drace slammed through the large door with his shoulder and charged through.

"Spiders!" Caius shouted as his night vision was the first to pierce the darkness. "Holy shit! A ton of spiders!"

"Fuck!" I heard Halcyon swear as he conjured Light on himself as well. "What are we going to do?"

"Start killing them!" Sierra shouted as she began to fire arrows into the horde. "Lyrian, we need to start finding the villagers!"

"Yeah!" Adrenaline was coursing through my body as my sleeping mind went into overdrive. "Drace! Constantine! Let's go! House to house!"

"Right!" Drace shouted as he broke into a run.

We barely made it twenty feet before we found a trio of villagers being swarmed by over a dozen spiders as they pressed themselves into a doorway in an attempt to hide from the creatures. Two wielded simple short knives as they tried to keep the creatures at bay, while the third shakily held a lantern, casting a dim orange glow over the spiders. Seeing our approach, they quickly called out. "Hey! Help!"

"There! Go! Go! Go!" I ordered Drace as the three of us dashed to the rescue.

We closed the gap between us and the spiders in a heartbeat and trampled over the swarm, desperation fueling our assault. Razor slashed through a quartet of legs as I forced myself through the swarm, trying to place myself between the villagers and horde.

A thunderclap of magefire flared for the briefest moment as Halcyon joined the fight, his spell incinerating three spiderlings instantly in a burst of fire.

Shit! I need to learn that one! Halcyon's attack blew a hole in the spiderling swarm, which Drace quickly filled as he swung his blade in a mighty cleave.

An arrow and bolt of magic crashed into a spiderling beside me, killing it instantly before it was able to bite me. With the path mostly cleared before me, and I was able to reach the huddling villagers. A pair of spiders appeared but were swiftly slashed down by two quick strokes from my sword.

"Go! Retreat back to the town hall! Wake the bann if he isn't already! He'll know what to do!" The irony of my words struck me hard. *Of course, he'll know what to do! This is the second attack Aldford has suffered!*

As the villagers broke off to run to the town hall, I took a moment to look at the few spiderlings still alive and saw that they were all *[Webwood Spiderlings]*, level seven.

"These are all Webwood creatures!" I called out to the party as Constantine and Drace butchered the remaining spiderlings nearby.

"What are they doing all the way out here?" Halcyon shouted as he sent another magical blast towards a group of spiders.

"They're expanding," Sierra guessed as she fired another arrow into the darkness. "Doesn't matter right now! We have incoming! "

"So quickly?" I couldn't believe that the spiders could expand through the forest so fast. *Did they follow us somehow?*

I quickly snapped back into the present as I heard Drace yell and point at something *glowing* in the distance. "What the hell is that?"

WOOD SPLINTERED INTO A THOUSAND pieces as I flew through the side of the building, coming to a rest in front of two *very* terrified looking villagers. "Get...to the town hall!" I wheezed as I checked my health and struggled to get my feet under me.

Down 27% health with just a graze!

It had taken just a handful of minutes for everything to go to hell. Seconds after saving our first trio of villagers, we were overrun by a massive horde of spiderlings. Lacking armor and being generally unprepared for a late-night invasion, the battle was desperate until Ritt, Jenkins, and Shelia, along with all six members of the militia charged into battle to relieve us.

With the bulk of the spider horde destroyed, we had a few precious minutes to comb through the village in search of any trapped villagers as the ominous blue glow marched closer to Aldford. Thankfully, after being victim to one invasion, the villagers had a first-hand understanding of the benefits to have a sharpened weapon at hand, or in most cases a sharpened pitchfork or spade.

The militia helped us direct and even carry the rest of the villagers we found to the town hall. There we quickly found the bann organizing a defense. Happy to have defenders in place to ensure the villagers wouldn't be overrun, we turned our attention to the strange glow that had steadily been advancing on Aldford.

"Fuck!" Sierra hissed as she could finally make out details through the bright blue glow. "Is that a giant glowing spider?"

"It's fucking nightmare fuel, is what it is!" Halcyon's voice trembled as his fear of spiders reached new heights.

[Webwood Horror – Rare – Level 10]

Glowing like a blazing furnace, the many-legged horror was like no other we had seen before. It towered above the rest of its kin, easily twice the size of the larger spiders but with even more legs. It put the Webwood aberration that I had fought yesterday to shame. With no regard for the freshly dug ditch below it, the vile creature crossed the threshold of our defences the same way we effortlessly crossed street curbs in the real world. I cursed as I saw a day's worth of work go completely to waste.

To be fair, I didn't build it with the intention of defending against something like this!

Stumbling through the wreckage that was once a wall, I moved to rejoin the fight. The creature shone like a miniature blue star, forcing my eyes to squint as I took in its massive, twelve-legged form. Judging by the damage I had taken, its spellcasting ability was more potent than an aberration's. The monstrosity had none of the strange deformities the other creatures had. I swore that the behemoth of a spider had to be at least ten feet tall!

On top of it all, it's a fucking rare creature! Which means it's going to be a ridiculous pain in the ass to kill!

I grimaced as a wave of Caius's magic splashed harmlessly in front of the creature, caught by some sort of unseen barrier. To make matters even worse, the creature seemed to possess some sort of *shield* when it came to ranged and magical attacks.

"Lyr! You okay?" Caius panted as he wove another spell together to throw at the horror.

"Yeah, that didn't quite work out." A moment ago, I had tried to close with the creature and get into melee range but had misjudged my timing and gotten myself thoroughly clobbered. Judging from the lack of anyone else being close by, none of the other melee fighters managed either.

"Shit!" Caius cursed as another one of his spells splashed harmlessly off the creature's shield. "I'm fucking useless here. What can I fucking do to help?" He turned to eye me for a moment, taking in my injuries and slapped a hand to my shoulder. "Oh, fuck. This is going to suck…"

"Caius, what are you—oh!" I flinched as my wounds instantly faded. "What the hell did you do?"

"Ugh." Caius was gasping as he clutched his side. "I took them away…d-don't worry, though."

Caius saw one of the numerous spiderlings still roaming the village and quickly slammed his hand onto the creature's rough chitin.

A heartbeat later, a red pulse of energy enveloped, the spider and it quickly dried to a husk. "Ahh…much better!"

"Caius, what the fuck? I thought you were a warlock?!" I couldn't quite believe what I'd just seen, momentarily forgetting about the Webwood horror.

"I am." Caius's voice sounded *different* than it usually was, but I couldn't place how. "I made a pact with blood demon, and it allows me to heal, in a way. But that's a story for later."

A flash of blue energy drew my attention away from Caius. I turned in time to see the Webwood horror cast a massive blue missile at the town hall, only to be intercepted by Halcyon, as he caught the missile on some sort of ward and directed it straight into the ground.

The resulting blast threw dirt everywhere and sent the mage flying backwards into the hall. "Damn it!"

We need to do something! Or we're going to lose the fucking village!

Leaving Caius behind, I charged at the horror again, leading the way with my measly Flare spell. *Fuck! Everyone else is throwing level ten magic around, and all I can do is throw around a tiny little fireball.* I saw my Flare splash against the creature's shield and cursed at its ineffectiveness.

My charge quickly had me re-entering melee range with the creature, breaking into a full out sprint as I closed with the creature. I somersaulted over a sweeping leg, rolling across the ground, forcing my momentum back into a run through sheer athleticism and determination.

Barely ten feet away from the massive creature, I was close enough to be attacked, yet far enough to still be ineffective against the creature. Not willing to give up on at least doing *something*, I continued to throw Flares at the creature.

[You scorch a Webwood Horror for 19 points of damage!]

What? I actually managed to land an attack on the creature? I rolled to the side as I slashed out at an attacking limb and threw another Flare to confirm my result.

[You Power Attack I a Webwood Horror for 48 points of damage!]
[You scorch a Webwood Horror for 20 points of damage!]

The shield only extends as far as its reach!

"THE SHIELD ENDS AT MELEE RANGE!" I screamed at the top of my lungs, praying to all the gods I knew that my friends would understand what I meant. For the moment, I was more concerned with staying alive, while in the belly of the beast, so to speak.

The next thirty seconds of my life were probably the most intense and stressful that I had experienced to date. I went into a full defensive panic, trying to stay alive as I desperately evaded a maelstrom of legs and *two-foot long* claws directed at ending my life. With me crouched in so close to the creature, my only saving grace was that it was unable to physically *see* where I was as I danced my way towards its flank.

Drace was the first to come to my rescue, taking full advantage of the fact that the spider's attention was focused on me. Charging straight into melee range unmolested, he unleashed a mighty two-handed swing, brutally chopping through a leg the spider had braced its weight on.

With a gush of blue-glowing ichor, Drace cut the horror's leg in two, the spider's balance momentarily faltering as it shifted its weight to its other legs, long enough to allow a close following Constantine a chance to charge down its gullet. At the last moment, I saw him jump, higher than I thought was possible, landing on the spider's face and continue running up the creature's thorax.

Far too caught up in observing Drace and Constantine, I was too late to dodge a leg as it slapped me to the ground. Fortunately I was far enough away for the attached claw to barely miss disemboweling my unarmored form.

Drace, on the other hand, wasn't so lucky.

The claw punctured him through the lower torso just as he finished cleaving through the horror's claw-tipped pedipalp. His face was a mix of pain and utter shock, but to his credit he managed to retaliate by slashing down on the leg piercing through his body. The spider's leg was cut cleanly in half, blue ichor seeping out of its stump as it let out an eerie screech. Freed from the creature's embrace, Drace tried to get away, but the colossal spider pierced him from behind with yet another leg.

The Webwood horror's body pulsed with a blue light as it turned its head to its captured prey and released a projectile stream of blue goo onto Drace's captive form.

For a brief instant, I saw Drace's figure silhouetted in the spray before his form completely evaporated from sight.

"Drace!" I couldn't help but shout as I witnessed my friend's demise, feeling him vanish from our party sense. "Damn it!" The words were barely audible from my mouth.

My gut twisted as I tried to comprehend Drace's death. *There's nothing you can do right now but try to make sure he has a place to respawn!* I mentally reassured myself, knowing I had already gone through a similar experience.

A roar from the creature promptly brought me back to the present as Constantine found something sensitive to stab, causing it to thrash in pain as one of its legs suddenly fell limp. I quickly added to the creature's worries by cutting open another chunk of chitin, letting fresh blue ichor gush from the wound. Hoping it would make a difference, I conjured with my other hand and hurled Flare after Flare at the beast.

A thunderclap of magefire heralded Halcyon's arrival as the explosion blew a chunk of flesh off another one of the creature's legs, rendering it functionally useless. The destructive magic was quickly followed by two wickedly precise arrows, slamming directly into the creature's face as both Sierra and Natasha braved melee range of the creature and shot it point-blank.

Howling with pain, the creature thrashed as it found its primary defenses negated. It feverishly stumbled backwards in an attempt to create space away from us. Conjuring rapidly, it fired blue missiles into the ground, spraying dirt everywhere as it retreated, forcing Halcyon and the others to scramble for cover.

Barely able to dodge the creature's attacks and still manage to keep up, I stabbed my sword deep into a nearby leg, using it as an anchor as I wrapped myself around the limb. I felt the hard hairs of the spider's leg pierce through the simple shirt I was wearing and dig deep enough into my flesh to cause my health to plummet to fifty percent, but I didn't dare let go as it dragged me along.

Splashes of light played across the creature's shield once more as it moved out of range of Sierra and the others, forcing them to chase the creature as it retreated.

The creature flinched and roared once again as Constantine did something to break its concentration and stride. Eager to dislodge myself before I bled to death, I heaved on the hilt of Razor, causing it to slice and tear through half the leg's chitin. With a quick glance as I landed on my feet, I figured any pressure on the creature's leg would cause the hairy limb to quite literally, break in half.

Heaving to catch up, Caius ran through the horror's shield and quickly let loose with twin streams of fire from his hands. The flames bathed the horror's body, charring the chitin until it blackened and cracked under the heat of the conjured fire.

Taking a moment to check my surroundings, I saw the running forms of Halcyon, Sierra, and Natasha as they attempted to close with the creature once again. *Need to slow this fucker down!*

With a deep breath, I sprinted under the creature as I ran towards its head, in hopes of getting it to focus solely on me. I held Razor high as I ran, carving a shallow furrow along the creature's chitin covered belly.

A pedipalp stabbed out at me as I entered the spider's line of sight, forcing me to pirouette to the side as I instinctively chopped it in two. As the limb fell away streaming glowing ichor, the beast screeched in pain and began to *pulse* with a blue glow.

Having bought myself some space, I tossed yet another handful of fire at the Webwood horror's face as I charged directly towards its maw. Surprised by my near suicidal charge and without any intact pedipalp to attack me with, I was able to leap up high and chop Razor down in a devastating two-handed slash.

My blow split the creature's mouth vertically, the same instant it spat another torrent of ooze. Blue glowing goo sprayed wildly from the ruined maw of the beast, searing my flesh as a few droplets sprayed the sky.

[A Webwood Horror's Arcane Venom sears you for 16 points of damage!]
[A Webwood Horror's Arcane Venom sears you for 23 points of damage!]
[A Webwood Horror's Arcane Venom sears you for 15 points of damage!]

Shit! That burns! I swore as I reflexively tried to brush the burning venom off my skin without prevail. Out of the corner of my eye, I saw the rest of the venom splash harmlessly on the ground with a substantial glob bouncing off a hastily cast ward that Halcyon managed to conjure in time.

It was at that moment Caius changed the course of the fight. Not being content to simply barbecue the horror, he had carefully crept forward while its attention had been focused on me and touched one of the creature's legs. The leg rapidly began to wither into a desiccated husk as Caius stole the life energy from it. Unable to support the weight of its hulking form, the leg buckled and caused the horror to flail to one side.

In an attempt to save its balance, the horror instinctively planted the leg I had damaged earlier in the fight, forcing it to snap entirely and sending the beast crashing down to the ground. Still having *far* too many legs available to it, the beast scrambled to stand up once more.

Having smashed to the ground right before me, I was in a perfect spot to see Constantine *riding* the horror's back, his arms working like pistons as he continuously drove his blades into the same spot in the creature's spine. Even from here I could see the glowing ichor covering his hands as it slowly seared his flesh.

Another thunderclap of magefire exploded as Halcyon came into range once again. This time, the blast was directed at the creature's maw and blew a massive chunk of chitin and flesh off the creature, exposing tender innards.

I forced myself forward as two more arrows flew past me to bury themselves deep in the gap Halcyon had made. Screaming, I lunged with Razor, thrusting the blade deep into the open wound. Viciously, I twisted my sword in hope of inflicting even more damage.

The horror suddenly flared an even brighter blue as it began to keen. *Shit! I know what that means!*

"GET AWAY FROM IT! IT'S GOING TO EXPLODE!" I screamed at the top of my lungs as I tore Razor free and began to run. "CONSTANTINE! RUN!"

Propelled by experience, I sprinted past Sierra, Halcyon, and Natasha with Caius close in tow. I don't know if Constantine didn't hear me or had disregarded my shout, but by the time I realized he wasn't moving it was already too late.

The Webwood horror exploded with a muffled *splort* as its shields managed to stay intact long enough to keep the worst of the blast contained. It didn't do anything to save Constantine, though, and I felt him vanish from our party sense.

> *Your skill in Evocation has increased to Level 9!*
> *Your Spellsword Class Requirements have been met!*
> *You are the first group to slay the rare creature - [Webwood Horror]!*
> *You have gained Leadership Experience!*
> *You have gained Bonus Leadership Experience for defeating a Rare Creature for the first time!*
> *You have gained a Leadership Skill Point!*
> *You have 4 Leadership Skill Points Unspent!*
> *You have gained 50 Renown for defeating a Rare Creature for the first time!*
> *Congratulations! You have reached Level 10!*
> *You have learned a new skill – Abjuration!*
> *You have learned a new skill – Alteration!*
> *You have learned a new skill – Conjuration!*
> *You have learned a new skill – Divination!*
> *Please see the class tab for more information about unlocking your Base Class!*
> *You have 5 Attribute Points Unspent!*
> *You have 3 Class Skill Points Unspent!*

The sudden cascade of information stunned me as I tried to process everything that had just happened, along with Constantine's death. I felt my injuries vanish as I hit level ten, along with the familiar feeling of various attribute increases that I couldn't quite discern. Before I could even begin to read all the information being thrown at me, I felt Constantine's and Drace's presence return near the town hall.

I looked at the glowing puddle of ooze where the Webwood

horror had died.

I don't know what Constantine and Sierra had in mind when they decided to keep quiet about level ten, but I definitely don't think this is what they had in mind!

TWENTY-TWO

I T TOOK TIME FOR THE chaos of the spider invasion to sort itself out after we killed the Webwood horror. Apparently during our battle with the creature, the spiderlings made a concerted and desperate attempt to swarm the town hall to get to the villagers. The swarm of vile creatures was met by the militiamen, who with the help of Drace's extra training were more than up to the task of defending the hall with the support of the bann, Jenkins, Shelia, and Ritt.

Expecting to hear of multiple casualties, I was happy to hear that Drace and Constantine were our only fatalities, temporary as they were. Injuries, on the other hand, were plentiful, especially among the villagers. There were dozens of spider inflicted bites throughout the citizenry, which resulted in more than a few serious cases of poisoning.

It was absolutely dumb luck that I had brought a bundle of hollyleaf for Ragna earlier in the night and was the deciding factor in helping Shelia save a number of villagers' lives.

So far I hadn't had a chance to review all the alerts crying for my attention since I hit level ten. From the moment that Drace and Constantine resurrected and said the words aloud, I'd been distracted by a terrifying, blood curdling, and anger inducing pair of words to all adventurers everywhere.

Death Penalty.

The pair had resurrected with the same morose depression I experienced myself. However, they were both cursed with something they called *torn soul*. A tiny fragment of their soul had been left behind at the scene of their death, waiting and hoping for its eventual recovery. They both said they had lost a full twenty percent progress in five of their best skills, along with a twenty percent experience debt for the current level.

"There's a timer," Drace spoke softly as we walked through the village towards the *still* glowing patch of soil where the Webwood horror had been slain. "We have seven days to recover our soul fragment before it dissipates, and the longer we take to recover it, the greater the permanent penalty to our skills."

When we arrived at the glowing mess, Drace and Constantine simply raised their hands as they grabbed something invisible to the rest of us. Within a heartbeat, they breathed a deep sigh of relief.

"Phew, hardly any loss at all," Constantine breathed.

"Maybe a percent or two across each skill." Drace nodded. "Not that bad, experience debt is gone too."

We all stood there quietly looking at the glowing mess.

"Well," Drace said, still sounding depressed. "I'm going to go back to bed. Sleep this death sickness off."

"Yeah…" Constantine echoed. "Me too."

With only the four of us standing near the eerie blue glow, Halcyon broke the silence. "So...what did it drop?"

"Huh?" Sierra asked, completely caught off-guard. "What drop?"

"The creature. It's a rare, right? Did it drop any loot?" Halcyon motioned towards the goo without looking directly at it. "I wonder if that stuff will despawn, or will we have a glowing nightlight out here now? It...really hurts to look at, magically speaking."

"I don't know," Sierra said, her eyes a bit glazed over. "I'm too tired to think straight right now."

"Yeah, me too," Halcyon mumbled in agreement.

"I'll look," I volunteered after I realized Caius wasn't going to contribute to the conversation. I turned towards the blue glow, spotting a loot sack within easy reach.

[Massive Glowing Spider Legs] x10
[Wicked Glowing Spider Claw] x11
[Massive Glowing Spider Carapace] x1
[Strange Glowing Ichor] x100
[Glowing Spider Silk Webbing] x 30
[Massive Glowing Spider Fang] x2

"Glowing?" I said aloud as I looked over the items and finding that they all had non-standard names. "I wonder what that means?"

"Seeing that the spider is *glowi*—" Halcyon started to mutter sarcastically. "Oh, I'm too tired for this, even for me. I'm going back to bed. Heads up, Lyr. Aldwin's coming."

"No shi—" I bit off my reply as I also saw the bann approach. "Right."

"I'm out too, Lyr." Sierra sighed in exhaustion as she moved to follow Halcyon. "I can barely stand."

"Night, Lyrian," Caius said quietly as he followed the group. Between tonight's events and the ritual he had to undergo for his base class, he likely had next to no sleep at all.

"Yeah, no worries." I waved everyone to bed as the bann approached.

"Lyrian." He sighed as he looked at my departing friends. "Thankfully, with you and your friends' help, we have no casualties."

The bann looked as exhausted as I felt and was still covered in black ichor from defending the town hall. "Two major attacks a handful of days apart. The defenses we'd spent the day building, ignored."

I shook my head, even though I *knew* how Aldwin felt. "We didn't build defenses in mind to repel spiders—*magical spiders*—but we still survived."

"True…"

We silently watched the glowing mass of ooze that the horror had left behind before Aldwin spoke again. "I'm going to have to ask you and your friends to return to the Webwood and thin out the spiders' numbers."

"Do you really think that'll make a difference? What about the work for the village defenses?"

"We'll manage. I daresay everyone will be a bit more motivated to ensure we have *something* to defend us." Aldwin sighed as he chewed a corner of his beard.

"There's that, though I'm concerned about the appearance of the Webwood horror. And the aberration I found yesterday," I said as I considered the two creatures I had fought. "Instinct has me thinking their appearance may be related to Natasha's expedition."

"Eh? That ruptured ley line business, you mean?" The bann frowned as he considered my train of thought.

The longer I thought about it, the more pieces began to fall into place. The aberration I found in the forest yesterday displayed a similar spellcasting ability as the horror, if to a lesser extent, but at its core it was still a Webwood spiderling.

The Webwood horror, on the other hand, reminded me of a giant Webwood spider, or possibly another type of creature we hadn't yet come across. Magic had clearly warped the beast, turning it into a truly overwhelming monster.

Had the beast stayed in the forest, the terrain would have made it nearly impossible to get close and get past its shield.

"I need you to get to the bottom of this, Lyrian," the bann whispered. "I know you're concerned what the other adventurers may do once they get here." Aldwin paused, mulling over his next words before speaking again. "But if we don't do *something* about the Webwood, there won't be a village left to defend!"

▷QUEST UPDATED! THIS QUEST IS NOW UNIQUE!
CLEANSING THE WEBWOOD. *(Unique) (Group)*
  Bann Aldwin wants you to return to the Webwood to cleanse
  the forest of spiders and find the source of whatever is granting
  spiders magical powers—then destroy it.
  Spiders Slain: 321/1000
  Source found: 0/1
  Difficulty: Very Hard
  Reward: Experience, Reputation, 100 gold pieces. (Reward
  proportional to percentage contributed)
  Bonus: ???

I looked over the updated quest quickly before dismissing it from my vision. At this point, I felt too invested in Aldford to let it be destroyed, be it by spiders or adventurers, and I didn't really need a quest as motivation. Though it did tell me just how *seriously* the bann wanted it done, especially since the system updated the quest to be unique and was no longer available to any other groups!

"We'll figure it out," I told the bann, trying to sound as confident as I could. "What are you going to do about this?" I indicated the glowing ichor still on the ground. "It doesn't seem to be disappearing."

"I'll get a few villagers to help me throw some dirt on it." Aldwin shrugged as if it were a trivial matter. "I doubt anyone will want to build a house on that plot now. Maybe I'll throw down a few acorns, and something good will come of it. Blue glowing acorns," he chuckled half-heartedly.

"Hopefully." I nodded as I tried to stifle a yawn.

"You should go back to bed, Lyrian. You certainly deserve it."

"I wish I could." I shook my head, knowing that despite being tired, there was no way my mind would let me sleep. "I'm going to go to the workshop. I need to work on a few repairs before we're set to go back into the Webwood."

"I understand." Aldwin nodded, still fixated on the glowing goop. "Good night, Lyrian."

CONJURING LIGHT ON MYSELF, I sat down in the workshop, happy to have a moment to catch my breath. With a sigh, I saw everyone's armor hanging from several different racks. *It's going to take a while to fix this all—wait! I hit level ten!*

A burst of energy cleared my sleep-addled mind as I excitedly brought up my newly available class menu.

> ***Congratulations on unlocking the Spellsword Base Class!***
> *You have successfully completed the first step in honing your magical ability and martial prowess!*
> *You have gained a permanent increase to the following attributes:*
> *Strength: +5*
> *Agility: +5*
> *Intelligence: +5*
> *Willpower: +5*
> *For every level you gain after level 10, you will gain an additional*

+1 in each of the above attributes, this increase is in addition to any racial increases that you already may have.

I paused for a moment as I digested the information I'd read so far. If I understood it correctly, when I leveled I would be getting: +1 Strength, +1 Agility, +2 Constitution, +3 Intelligence, and +1 Willpower. All in addition to the free five attribute points I could at assign each level. *Awesome!*

At first glance, I felt the bonus attributes for achieving your base class and the added boost to attribute gain would create a massive statistical imbalance between the novice levels and the base class levels, at least when it came to player versus player conflict. But I quickly understood *that was the point.*

Reaching and unlocking your base class was supposed to be an important achievement and had to be rewarded accordingly. The way I saw it, the presence of such an imbalance was to motivate lower level players to work harder, or if that wasn't possible, group up together.

Eager to see what else was waiting for me, I continued reading.

As a new Spellsword, you have been granted 3 Class Skill Points to help define your playstyle! These skill points can be used to learn Traits, Martial Arts, or Spells. All skills are divided into three different categories, General, Class, and Racial.

General Skills can be learned or taught to any class as long as the required skill level has been reached.

Class Skills can only be learned or taught to a valid class, as long as the required skill level has been reached.

Racial Skills can only be learned or taught by members of an applicable race, which can include General or Class Skills, as long as the required skill level has been reached.

Please note that there are exceptions to these rules that can be obtained via quest rewards, traits, and other special events.

Please choose three of the following options:

Traits:

Arcane Sight

Type: Trait, Class Skill

Duration: Permanent

Skill Requirement: Any Arcane Tree Skill Level 9 or Higher.

Description: Endless practice and exposure to magic has given you the ability to physically see Arcane Energy.

Effect: Any Arcane based energy or magic within 60 feet of you is automatically highlighted by a pale blue aura. This ability can be suppressed at will.

Iron Mind

Type: Trait, General Skill

Duration: Permanent

Skill Requirement: Any Weapon Skill Level 9 or Higher.

Description: Practitioners of this style of fighting strive to eliminate every single unnecessary movement, both in and outside of combat. This mastery allows them to strike with sudden ferocity while dodging blows with inches to spare.

Effect: While in this Stance and not immobilized, you gain a passive 5% boost to dodge and attack speed. This ability can be suppressed at will.

Spells:

Jump

Type: Spell, General Skill

Duration: 30 Seconds

Arcane Tree: Abjuration

Spell Mastery: Abjuration - Level 9

Mana Cost: 80

Description: You temporarily reduce gravity's hold on you, giving you increased buoyancy.

Effect: For the duration of the spell, you are able to jump up to four times your normal maximum.

Flame Dagger:

Type: Spell, Class Skill

Duration: Instant

Arcane Tree: Conjuration

Spell Mastery: Conjuration - Level 9

Mana Cost: 100

Description: You instantly conjure a foot-long dagger made of fire centered on your fist. After you attack, it vanishes in a puff of smoke.

Effect: You instantly conjure a dagger made of fire. This can be used for one attack dealing 100-150 Fire and Piercing Damage.

Minor Shielding

Type: Spell, General Skill

Duration: 1 Hour

Arcane Tree: Abjuration

Spell Mastery: Abjuration - Level 9

Mana Cost: 110

Description: You create a shield of force around your body that deters both physical and magical attacks.

Effect: You create a temporary, invisible shield around you that grants you +30 to armor and +5% Spell Resistance.

Shocking Touch

Type: Spell, Class Skill

Duration: Instant

Arcane Tree: Evocation

Spell Mastery: Evocation - Level 9

Mana Cost: 70

Description: You charge your hand with electricity, discharging it through the first thing you touch.

Effect: Your shock the next thing you touch for 30-55 points of Electricity Damage. This attack can be conducted through metallic weapons, items, and water.

Blink Step

Type: Spell, Class Skill

Duration: Instant

Arcane Tree: Alteration

Spell Mastery: Alteration - Level 9

Mana Cost: 110

Description: You vanish from one place and immediately reappear nearby.

Effect: You can instantly travel up to 30 feet to any direction in your line of sight. Minor Intervening obstacles such as people, creatures, or light foliage will not impede the spell. Other obstacles will cause the spell to fail.

Martial Arts:

Power Attack II

Type: Martial Art, General Skill

Upgrade to: Power Attack I

Skill Requirement: Any Weapon Skill Level 9

Stamina Cost: 75

Description: You attack viciously with your weapon, putting more power behind it at the expense of accuracy and energy.

Effect: You slash viciously at the target putting extra strength behind the blow. Deal weapon damage +25.

Shoulder Tackle

Type: Martial Art, General Skill

Skill Requirement: Unarmed Combat Skill Level 7

Stamina Cost: 40

Description: Seeing an opportunity, you charge forth and slam your shoulder into your enemy, breaking their stride.

Effect: When successfully used, Stun enemy for 1-2 seconds with chance to knock enemy down based on Strength and/or Agility attribute.

Cleave

Type: Martial Art, General Skill

Skill Requirement: Any Weapon Skill Level 5

Stamina Cost: 75

Description: With a mighty swing, you swipe your weapon in a wide arc in front of you, carving through your enemies.

Effect: Attack all enemies in front of you, dealing Weapon Damage +11.

Kick

Type: Martial Art, General Skill

Skill Requirement: Unarmed Combat Skill Level 5

Stamina Cost: 50

Description: You send your enemy reeling back with a powerful kick.

Effect: You kick your enemy for 10-20 points of damage and knock them back 1-2 yards. Depending on your Strength/Agility score, you may also knock down the target.

My mouth fell open at the *sheer variety* of options available to me. *I want them all! How can I just choose three of them?*

I grumbled as I started to think through my options. *Okay! Think of what you need to learn now and what you can bug someone else to teach you later.*

I eliminated the Martial Arts portion of what was available to me. As useful as those abilities were, I knew that both Drace and Aldwin already had similar, if not the same abilities already. I wasn't about to waste my precious class skill points just to learn what they could teach me later.

That had me focusing on spells, which the longer I thought about it the more I realized that there was no wrong option.

Blink Step and Jump would give me absolutely insane mobility but would practically force me to take an offensive ability to compensate. Shocking Touch is great to use with a weapon, but Flame Dagger does more damage.

I compared Arcane Sight and Iron Mind next, trying to determine which better fit my playstyle and personal goals. *The Stance would be great to have, but I generally don't want to be in the position where things can hit me anyway, and if I am, what would a measly five percent difference do? Seeing magic on the other hand—that's just useful no matter what and has great use outside of combat!*

Hold on though, what's Spell Mastery? Shit! I completely forgot about the other arcane trees! I took a deep breath as I brought up an explanation.

> **Spell Mastery** – *This field represents the overall complexity of a spell, as well as the tree of magic that the spell belongs too.*
> *A caster who attempts to cast a spell for which they have not yet attained Mastery carries a 10% chance of outright failing to cast the spell for every skill level that they are below the Mastery level. Furthermore, there is an additional 10% chance, plus 1% for every skill level below the Mastery level, that when failing a spell that the caster will lose control of the spell and take damage equal to half the amount of mana the spell cost.*
> *For Example: A caster attempting to cast a spell with a Spell Mastery of Abjuration Level 9, while their own Abjuration skill is Level 4, will have a 50% chance to fail every time they cast the spell and a 14% chance that on a failure, they will take half the spell's mana cost in damage.*
> *A caster cannot cast a spell that has a Mastery Level 10 or more skill levels above their own.*

I struggled to wrap my head around the idea of Spell Mastery and found it to be a reasonably fair process and thought it added a level of realism to the casting process. It gave casters a *reason* to focus on training their skills, much like the other classes had to train their weapon skills, both so as not to be a danger to themselves and others around them.

Armed with that knowledge, I looked over my choices once more and finally came to a decision. I would take Arcane Sight, Shocking Touch, and Blink Step. It was a balanced approach, giving me the ability to get into and out of a fight quickly, cause a few problems while I was there, then hopefully survive long enough for my friends to save me. It also meant I had to start training in an entirely new school of magic, to have a hope in not hurting myself. *Thankfully leveling at least taught me all the arcane trees!*

With that in mind, I wasn't looking forward to a ninety percent failure rate in learning how to cast Blink Step and how painful that process was likely going to be.

With my choices selected, I looked to see if there was anything else left to do because I'd figured out where to assign my remaining attribute points.

You will gain an additional Class Skill Point once every 5 levels. Class Skill Points can also be obtained via quest rewards and special events.

Additional options to further specialize your class and play style can be achieved through Class Challenges, which are available at Levels 19 and 29. Rumors have also been heard of hidden Class Challenges available at any level! Be on the lookout!

Further information about Advanced Classes will be made available once reaching Level 29.

"Phew." I rubbed my eyes as I digested the rest of the information available. "Now, what to do about those attribute points…"

Attributes:
 Strength: 40 (42)
 Agility: 35 (37)
 Constitution: 29
 Intelligence: 39

Willpower: 15

Hm. I don't particularly need much Willpower, at least right now. I think it'd be a better decision to add it into Constitution. I assigned the points without a second thought and instantly felt my health improve ever so slightly. *It will definitely help when I'm blowing myself apart with spell failures!*

"Next…leadership points," I said aloud as I dismissed my character sheet and opened the Leadership menu, assigning all four points into *Improved Movement.*

I must have gained all these points during the fight with the horror, I thought, remembering that I had set my leadership experience ratio to one hundred percent.

Resetting the leadership experience rate to zero percent for the time being, I decided to check just how much experience I needed to reach level eleven for curiosity's sake.

Current Experience 0/21,300

"Gah! Twenty-one thousand!" I gasped when I saw the massive number. "Wasn't level eight around fifty-four hundred?"

I guess things are about to slow down now that we're in the meat of the game and through the novice levels!

Truthfully though, I was happy to have a gradual leveling process. Practically every single game I had ever played was an all-out sprint to maximum level; to just be scratching level ten after a few days of nonstop play was a refreshing change of pace.

Not to mention that levels actually seem to matter in this game too!

Extremely happy to know Ascend Online was shaping up to be a long-term home, rather than a few weeks of hardcore play, I dismissed all the alerts and menus I still had open in my vision.

Where did Jenkins put that crate? Let's see if I can make anything useful for level tens…

TWENTY-THREE

AFTER FINDING THE CRATE, I took a few minutes to come up with a crafting plan. Thanks to everyone's efforts in hunting, harvesting, and mining, we had a fairly decent amount of raw metals and materials to work with.

So what am I doing first? I thought to myself as I mentally started calculating what I needed. First, the militia needed proper armor and spears. Then I needed to repair the group's armor and see if I could upgrade any of it. *Probably better to start with the militia armor and see if I can hit level ten in blacksmith and leatherworking. The party is also missing out on bracers and shoulder guards...*

Doing a bit of mental math to figure out how much material I needed, I came to the total of 128 pieces of leather, along with ninety-three bronze bars, just for the militia's armor alone. I'd likely need a bit more once repairs were factored in.

All right, you're wasting time. Let's get started!

Diving right into the process of refining the materials, I found it much easier than I remembered. In fact, with both leatherworking and blacksmithing at level eight, I found the process of refining the leather and metal downright trivial and didn't gain a single shred of experience during the entire process.

What used to take me three swipes with a knife to clean a hide properly now only took me one, leaving the hide clean and the cut straight. Similar being the case with pouring the bronze ingots into their molds, I no longer had to visually check to see how full it was. I simply just *knew* how much to pour before moving onto the next one. It saved me much more time than I was expecting.

Little over an hour and a half later I was slurping a bowl of beetle stew as I waited for the last batch of bronze ingots as they cooled.

"Well, that both did and didn't take long, considering how much I did…" I muttered to myself as I wiped my face with a sleeve.

Makes sense that crafting would speed up a bit as my skill increases, not to mention I feel pretty confident in plain refining, having done it over a hundred times now! I doubt that'll stay the same if I get my hands on more difficult materials.

Now with a veritable mountain of leather and bronze, I started on crafting the militia's gear. Starting with the items I had to make the most of—bracers and shoulder guards—I grabbed a tool and began working away at the material. Unlike the refining process, however, I was happy to see my tradeskill experience slowly improving for every item I crafted.

The eleven pairs of bracers took me an hour to finish, propelling my leatherworking skill just twenty-five percent shy of level nine. Stashing them off to the side, I then moved onto crafting the shoulder guards. Since I was only making a single item, rather than a pair, the process flew by *much* faster. By the time I finished my fourth shoulder guard, the familiar and now addictive inflow of knowledge told me I'd hit level nine.

As expected, the new knowledge made the crafting easier, smoother, and most importantly, *faster*. I finished crafting the shoulder guards in no time. The crafting process wasn't quite yet *trivial*, as the refining one was, but I felt on the verge of the items being beneath my skill.

These are still novice recipes, though, I thought to myself as I shifted a tunic I was working on. *How will level ten recipes change? Maybe we'll need to find iron, or a new material? Will I learn a whole new batch of recipes with new materials I'll need to look for, or maybe the recipes will stay the same and I'll just be able to substitute other materials?*

I gradually worked my way through the rest of the armor as I created and discarded theories in my head, crafting tunics, helmets, and pants. Roughly forty-five minutes later, with me eying my experience bar the entire way, I was rewarded with another skill up in leatherworking, followed by a wall of information.

> ***Your skill in Leatherworking has increased to Level 10!***
> *Congratulations! You have completed the Novice crafting levels and have begun the journey to master your craft!*
> *You have earned the right to call yourself an: Apprentice Leatherworker!*

"Ah!" I broke into a smile as I quickly read the information appearing in my vision, quickly focusing on the next paragraph.

> *Crafting progression is broken up into seven separate tiers, which reflect the amount of skill you possess in a given Tradeskill.*
> *The tier and skill progression is as follows:*
> *Novice – Skill Levels: 1 to 9*
> *Apprentice – Skill Levels: 10 to 29*

Journeyman – Skill Levels: 30 to 49

Expert – Skill Levels: 50 to 69

Master – Skill Levels: 70 to 89

Grandmaster – Skill Levels: 90 to 99

Legendary Grandmaster – Skill Level: 100+

As an Apprentice, a new crafting attribute is now available on all crafted items – Item Quality.

Item Quality represents the craftsmanship that has gone into the item as well as the potency of materials used to construct it. This attribute can positively or negatively affect the end item's statistics, attributes, and durability. In order to ensure the highest item quality, it is advisable to craft items well within your skill range and to use the highest quality materials available.

Item Quality and the impact that they can have on an item ranges from:

Poor (-10%)

Average (+0%)

Fine (+10%)

Good (+15%)

Mastercraft (+20%)

Mythical (+30%)

In order to progress from one tier to the next (E.g. Apprentice to Journeyman) on the final skill level of a tier (Skill Levels: 29, 49, 69, 89, and 99). The crafter must create at least one 'Mastercraft' quality item as proof of their growing skill. This Mastercrafted item must be any finished product appropriate for the Tradeskill. (E.g., a piece of armor, jewelry, weapon, etc.)

"Item quality?" My eyes jumped as I read over the information. *Ah! That's awesome! It means crafters won't just be repetitively grinding out ten thousand iron daggers or something equally useless just to raise their skill! We'll have something useful to work towards every time we pick up a tool!*

I had my fair share of games that had made crafting simple beyond measure, or so needlessly complex and interdependent you had to level practically every single tradeskill in parallel, which left you feeling overwhelmed and frustrated as you constantly had to switch between tradeskills just to create a simple pair of boots.

As an Apprentice Leatherworker, you are now able to create new items via Modular Recipes. This allows you to take an existing recipe that you have learned and modify the recipe to use different materials of the same type or to add additional properties to other items already created.

For Example:

The Novice recipe - [Bronze Studded Cap]

1 x [Raw Leather]

1 x [Bronze Ingot]

Has now been replaced as:

[Studded Cap]

1 x [Leather]

1 x [Metal]

This process allows a crafter to experiment with different materials as they explore and hone their craft. Different combinations of materials will produce drastically different results!

"Ah! That makes sense!" I said to myself as I pieced together *what* exactly a modular recipe was. "If I already know how to make a helmet out of scrap leather and bronze, it's not going to be a completely revolutionary change to make a similar helmet out of a different type of leather, or another metal like iron. The difficulty will be in working the material itself, since iron I imagine is *very* different to work with than bronze." I paused to think about it for a moment. "Though I'm sure if I wanted to make a full plate helmet or something similar, that would be its own recipe."

Armed with a better understanding of modular recipes I continued to read the final bit of information that was still hovering in my vision.

Keep in mind, a true crafter is not limited by the recipes that they have learned, but by the limits of their very imagination! Recipes are intended to be simple guidelines to follow; those who experiment beyond the simple assembly of recipes have the potential to create truly wondrous and unique works never seen before!

That's how I made the pots and pans! I thought to myself as I finished reading. *I had a picture in my head of what I wanted to achieve, and eventually with a few prototypes, work, and clarity of what I wanted as an end result, I created my own item!*

I was excited to see how far I would be able to push the limits of crafting and what sort of items my Improvisation skill would allow me to craft. Where other people would be limited to following the modular recipes with leather and metal, I could replace those base materials with bone and wood if I wanted to! Imagination would truly be my only limit when it came to crafting!

And I have a pretty wild imagination! I smiled as ideas started to pop into my head.

Before I could start experimenting, though, I had to finish the rest of the militia's armor. My most recent skill up made the task of crafting the armor trivial. Quickly and smoothly, I used my knife to cut out the needed patterns without a single wasted motion, allowing me to quickly finish the remainder of the boots and gloves in just under forty minutes.

With the armor finished, I moved on to the spears, slowly drawing them out of solid bronze. They would be heavier than the wooden ones used by the militia, but much more durable as well. Not to mention being all around more lethal. By the time I finished making the spears, the sun's rays were starting to poke up over the horizon, leaving me blearily surprised at the amount of time that had passed.

"Shit. The sun's almost up," I said with a bit of surprise as I put the final spear down. "Gah, I haven't even started on repairs…or upgrades!"

I quickly inhaled two fried snake snacks to curb my growing hunger as I smelted five more bronze ingots, then carved out a few pieces of leather before getting to work on quickly repairing everyone's armor.

The repair process was fairly straightforward and quick as I sewed tears in the leather together and added patches to cover the stitching. In Drace's case, it was easier for me to completely replace the missing sleeve his tunic had lost than try to recover the few remaining shreds of leather that remained.

Once the armor was repaired, I hung each of them on the armor racks, trying to discern a method of upgrading them somehow. *I could possibly add in a few sheets of leather around the knees to give it better padding…and maybe make a shin guard out of bronze.*

Turning away from the armor, I walked over to the crate of supplies and began to rustle through for inspiration. Nothing catching my eye, I opened my pack and began to transfer materials I'd been carrying into the crate. *Hell of a lot of spider shit still in my pack.*

I sighed as I began to transfer [Spider Fangs], [Spider Carapaces], and other various spider parts into the crate, until I pulled out the stack of [Strange Glowing Ichor] I had looted from the Webwood horror.

As soon as I pulled it out of my bag, it was immediately engulfed in a pale blue aura, which only served to intensify the pale blue it already shone.

You have identified a [Strange Glowing Ichor] as [Mana-Infused Ichor]!

Wait…what?

I looked at the item with surprise as it blazed with arcane energy. "Holy shit."

I quickly put the ichor down as I reached into my pack to pull out the other items I'd looted from the horror. One by one, each and every single piece shone with a brilliant blue aura, and before long, I had everything set in front of me, barely believing the sight.

100 x [Mana-Infused Ichor]
10 x [Massive Mana-Infused Spider Legs]
11 x [Wicked Mana-Infused Spider Claw]
1 x [Massive Mana-Infused Spider Carapace]
30 x [Mana-Infused Spider Silk Webbing]
2 x [Massive Mana-Infused Spider Fang]

"I was right!" I hissed to myself. *These spiders have to somehow been getting in contact with the ruptured ley line! What else could be filling them full with mana?* I looked at the pile of glowing spider parts. *Maybe I can test this somehow?*

With a shrug, I grabbed a smelting pan and put a *[Spider Carapace]* in it, then poured a vial of *[Mana-Infused Ichor]* on it. The carapace hissed as it quickly absorbed the ichor, gaining a very slight aura to it, seemingly on the verge of fading away. Curious, I poured a second vial onto the carapace and saw the aura brighten then begin to dim once more. I quickly poured a third vial onto the carapace.

You have created a [Mana-Infused Spider Carapace]!

"Yes!" I exclaimed as the carapace now shone with energy. "It worked!"

Taking it out of the pan, I carefully inspected the carapace with my Arcane Sight to see if the energy would begin to fade, but after a few minutes, I didn't see any dimming of the aura.

I think I've stumbled onto something here!

"Now, what can I do with this I wonder…?" I held the chitin in my hand as I squeezed and bent it, finding it tough, yet much more flexible than it was previously. "Hm, this is pretty light, too."

I looked at the party's armor pieces that were hanging on nearby racks. Walking closer to the rack where my armor hung from, an idea started to take shape in my head. Placing the carapace on a piece of the armor, I broke into a smile.

"This could work…"

"LYRIAN? *LYRIAN!*" SIERRA AND CONSTANTINE burst into the workshop in a rush. "There you are! You have to come se—"

They both stopped in their tracks as they saw what I was working on. "Lyrian, what…*is that?*"

"Oh, hey!" I turned to wave at the pair, then looked back to the last bit of stitching I was working on. "Is it time for everyone to be up already?"

"*Time to be up?*" Constantine echoed as he walked towards an armor rack, having completely forgot what he came in here for. "Lyrian, did you even go to bed?"

"Bed? Nah." I shrugged as I finished my last stitch and took a step back to admire my work. "No time for that, not today at least." I turned around to regard my friends and gestured towards the armor. "So what do you guys think?"

I waited patiently as Sierra and Constantine wordlessly inspected the armor. "Lyr…"

"I know, I know. Armor just isn't enough," I said with a sigh as I waved at another workbench. "That's why I also made these."

I waved my hand to indicate what looked like a pile of spider parts, but on closer inspection were…

"Weapons," Sierra whispered with a little awe and disbelief. "You made weapons and armor from spider…parts?"

"Yeah, it seemed like a good idea at the time." I shrugged as I indicated the item Constantine was now holding. "Careful, that's sharp! I sliced through a corner of the bench...uh...*accidentally*...while making it."

Constantine made a coughing sound as he put it down. "I don't ev—"

"Hey, did you find him?" A rustle of feet followed by Drace's voice interrupted whatever Constantine was about to say as he walked into the workshop. "What's going—" Drace's mouth fell open when he saw the armor. "—on. Oh!"

"Hey, Drace." I waved at the speechless warrior as I cocked my head in the direction of the door. "Something going on?"

"Yeah, uh. Wow." Drace crossed the workshop, instinctively going towards his set of armor. I could barely make sense of what he was saying. "Oh...Aldwin, Town Hall."

"Hm?" I shook my head confused. "He wants to see me?"

"Sure, that'd be great." Constantine had just indicated the pile of weapons to Drace, and he was *visibly* drooling over them.

"Wait, what?"

"Hey! Why is everyone just disappearing into here?" Halcyon's voice called from the outside.

"It's like the start to a bad joke," I heard Caius begin. "Three adventurers walk into a building..."

"Ugh." I heard Halcyon grunt just before he poked his head into the workshop. "What are yo—oh!"

I'd given up trying to get a response from Drace as he inspected his armor and looked at the two new arrivals. "Oh good! You're all here now!"

"Lyr..." Caius and Halcyon both gasped as they found everyone fixated on their individual sets of armor, also forgetting whatever purpose drove them here in the first place. Their gaze eventually landed on me.

"*What did you do?*" Halcyon whispered in awe. "I can *see* the magic in it, but I don't understand *how* you could have—"

"I upgraded our armor!" I smiled while puffing my chest out with pride. "I think you'll all appreciate what I've managed to come up with!"

"This is still our armor?" Sierra said with some disbelief as she inspected a glove. "But…"

"…why?" Caius finished. "I thought we were digging today?"

I shook my head. "No. Aldwin wants us to head back into the forest and try to find out what caused the horror to attack."

"Oh," Caius said as he nodded. "Probably a good idea, now that I think about it. We can't afford another attack."

"How'd you do it, Lyrian?" Constantine asked, cutting into the conversation. "This looks like…spider chitin."

"That's because it is!" I started to explain excitedly. "Earlier this morning, after I finished repairing our armor, I tried to come up with a way of enhancing it."

"Uh…*curious*. How many other things did you try before you thought that adding the flesh of our enemy onto the armor would be considered enhancing it?" Halcyon asked a bit squeamishly. "I don't think the spiders are smart enough to respond to this level of intimidation, but if they are, I don't want to give them ideas."

"Oh, relax scaredy-pants," I chided Halcyon as I went on to explain my discovery of the mana-infused ichor, and how I could combine it with various other spider parts. "Then with my Improvisation skill, I was able to essentially re-enforce the existing armor using non-standard crafting materials."

"All right," Constantine said nodding slowly, "But it looks like there are three different designs here? How did that work out?"

"Well, when I was working on the armor, I had a slightly different vision in mind depending who it would be for." I pointed to three sets of armor that all shared a similar design. "I call this one, the Webwood Striker Armor Set, intended for you, Sierra, and myself. For this armor set, as you can see, I added several carapace segments across the armor for some extra protection, plus a pair of bronze shin guards to keep the lower legs protected without losing any mobility. I think you'll also be happy once you see the set bonus for the armor." I finished with a smile as I called up the armor's stats to look over myself.

Webwood Striker Armor Set
Slots: Arm, Chest, Feet, Hands, Legs, Head, Shoulders
Item Class: Magical
Item Quality: Good (+15%)
Armor: 175
Set Bonus (7/7):
Strength: +5
Agility: +5
Armor Type: Light
Weight: 7 kg
Favored Class: Any Martial
Mana-Infused: +15% Resistance against Arcane spells and abilities.
Level: 10

"Holy shit, Lyr!" Sierra gasped as she called up the armor's information. "Stat boosts and resistances?"

"Yeah! Only thing is, you need to have the entire set on for it to get the bonuses," I said with a shrug. "If nothing else, the extra armor is a huge bonus."

"No kidding!"

I motioned to Halcyon and Caius while indicating another armor design. "This armor set is for you two. I call this one the Webwood Adept Armor Set. Similar sort of idea as the other set when it came to adding in some extra protection, but instead of loading you guys up so you couldn't move, I used mana-infused spider silk in your stitching, which should help you focus and channel mana a bit better."

Webwood Adept Armor Set
Slots: Arm, Chest, Feet, Hands, Legs, Head, Shoulders
Item Class: Magical
Item Quality: Good (+15%)
Armor: 125
Set Bonus (7/7):
+5 Intelligence
+5 Willpower
Armor Type: Light
Weight: 5 kg
Favored Class: Any Arcane or Divine
Mana-Infused: +15% Resistance against Arcane spells and abilities.
Level: 10

"Oh, man. Awesome!" Halcyon exclaimed with Caius adding, "This is great, Lyr!"

Lastly, turning to Drace. "And this last one here is for you, man. The Webwood Defender Armor Set. I went a bit crazy on this one, extra carapace all over, bronze Shin guards, bronze arm guards, gorget as well as a—"

"A shield!" Drace cut me off as he hefted a massive piece of spider carapace, covered in thorny spikes. "Oh, man! Thanks so much, Lyr! This is great!"

"No worries at all, man!" I beamed at the large warrior's happiness, calling up his armor set information for one last look.

Webwood Defender Armor Set
Slots: Arm, Chest, Feet, Hands, Legs, Head, Shoulders, Shield
Item Class: Magical
Item Quality: Good (+15%)
Armor: 300
Set Bonus (8/8):

+5 Strength

+5 Constitution

Armor Type: Medium

Weight: 12 kg

Class: Any Martial

Mana-Infused: +15% Resistance against Arcane spells and abilities.

Level: 10

"What are the other things over here, Lyrian?" Constantine asked, having gone as far to dress himself in the new armor already.

When did he even take his pants off? I wondered before snapping back into the moment.

"Oh! Right!" I quickly walked over to Constantine while motioning Sierra and Drace over to the bench. "Hey, there's more for you two over here!"

"What?" Sierra asked a bit numbly. "*More?*"

"I didn't stop at just armor!" I said with a smile, grabbing a massive pair of spider fangs off the bench and handing them to Constantine. I then picked up a massive spider claw from the bench and *very* gently handed it to Drace. Last, but not least, I then picked up a smoothly finished bow, strung with a faintly glowing string, giving it to Sierra.

In addition to being able to use the spider carapace as armor reinforcement, my Improvisation skill also allowed me to make slight modifications *directly* to some of the spider parts I'd found on the Webwood horror. All it took was scratching away some unneeded chitin on an already sharp claw or fang and then sinking a makeshift hilt deep into it to give a good place to grip.

"So..." I prompted everyone as I double checked the item stats I had just handed out. "Happy?"

Webwood Daggerfang

Slot: Main Hand or Off Hand

Item Class: Magical

Item Quality: Good (+15%)

Damage 13-20 (Piercing)

Agility: +3

Durability 120/120

Base Material: [Massive Mana-Infused Spider Fang]

Weight: 0.3 kg

Favored Class: Any Martial

Level: 10

Webwood Bladeclaw

Slot: Main Hand or Off Hand

Item Class: Magical

Item Quality: Good (+15%)

Damage 15-25 (Slashing)

Strength: +2 Agility: +2

Durability 120/120

Base Material: [Massive Mana-Infused Spider Claw]

Weight: 0.5 kg

Class: Any Martial

Level: 10

Spruce Silkstring Bow

Slot: Main Hand and Offhand

Item Class: Magical

Item Quality: Good (+15%)

Damage 20-35 (Piercing)

Agility: +6

Durability 120/120

Base Material: [Spruce Stave]

Weight: 1 kg

Class: Any Martial

Level: 10

"If I didn't know better," Constantine said as he made a show of checking the time, "I'd say it was Christmas!"

"It's awesome, Lyrian!" Drace exclaimed as he tested his grip on the bladeclaw. "Just plain awesome!"

"I love it," Sierra exclaimed as she ran her hand along the bow, then hugged it close to her chest. "It's perfect!"

"Great!" I clapped my hands together, before calling over to Halcyon and Caius. "Unfortunately, I don't have any new weapons for you two unless you want a new melee weapon at some point?"

"Nah, I'm okay." Halcyon shook his head. "Rather not be any closer to critters than I absolutely need to be."

"Yeah, I'm cool too." Caius shrugged. "Any idea if you can make magic staves?"

"Maybe," I said after thinking about it for a moment. "I'd need to have magic-infused wood of some sort most likely. Plus some time to work on my carpentry. I outright stole the wood for Sierra's bow from Jenkins's pile."

The moment I said the word "magic wood," it was as if I shocked everyone in the room.

"Shit!" Constantine cursed as they all remembered what had them looking for me in the first place.

"Lyrian, we have something to show you," Halcyon began.

"HUH," I GRUNTED AS I arrived to at the town hall, looking upwards in awe. "Neat."

"*Neat?*" I heard Halcyon say, everyone else electing to stay behind and get dressed in their new gear. "That's all you have to say?"

I turned to frown at the mage with an eyebrow raised. "Uh, neato?"

"I was expecting something with a bit more *gravity*," Halcyon said with a sigh as he shook his head in annoyance. "Let it be known:

the first word said by Lyrian when witnessing a true wonder of magic was 'Neat.'"

"Oh." I turned to look back at the oak tree that had erupted from the same patch of ground that the horror had died on and assumed a mocking pose. *"Astounding!"* I smirked back at Halcyon. "How's that for gravity?"

"If it weren't for the armor you made me today, I'd be telling you to go fuck yourself right now." Halcyon flipped me off as he turned on his heel and strode back towards the workshop. "I'm off to get dressed, be back in a bit."

"Ha!" I barked a laugh before I turned my gaze back to the tree, happy to have a chance to annoy the mage.

True to his word, Aldwin had buried the glowing ichor while planting an acorn atop it, and over the course of the night, the seed had taken root. Now, next to the very heart of Aldford, stood an eight-foot-tall oak sapling.

This in itself would not be a very troubling or even unexpected development, given that I now knew of the magical properties of the Webwood horror's ichor. But the fact that the tree happened to be faintly glowing *blue*, as well as radiating magic in my Arcane Sight— that made it an *interesting* development and another link to the ruptured ley line.

"Ho, Lyrian." Aldwin strode over, seeing me circling the tree. He indicated the tree with a nod, seeming slightly at a loss for words. "So, this is…?"

"Quite," I agreed, still watching the magical aura shine across my vision. "Though I suppose you did get your wish for a tree. People should quickly forget about the horror now."

"Perhaps…though I hadn't expected that it would grow so quickly." The bann's eyebrows rose as I strode forward to place my hand on the tree. "Sdomething wrong?"

"No." The tree was slightly warmer under my palm than I expected, but as far as I could tell, it was just a simple tree.

It also just happened to be a glowing tree.

"A bit warmer than I expected, but I think it may also still be growing?" I said with a shrug as I took a step away from the tree.

"It is," Aldwin confirmed with a slight sigh. "About a hand span over the last hour."

"I'm curious to see how large it will get."

"Oh?" The bann looked at me hesitantly. "You don't want to cut it down right away?"

"No! Why should we?" I shook my head quickly, then realized that I hadn't told Aldwin about discovering the mana-infused ichor earlier in the morning. "I don't think the tree is a danger to the village." I quickly explained what I'd discovered about the glowing ichor that the spider had left behind when it died. "I think that whatever mana there was left in the ichor fueled the growth of the tree the same way it fueled the growth of the spider...and why it turned out *blue*."

My explanation ended with a deep sigh coming from the country knight.

"Life was so much simpler when I was still in Eberia. Magic was left to the mages and the fighting to the knights," Aldwin spoke softly while staring blankly at the tree. "Very well, Lyrian. We'll leave the tree be, then. At least until it appears dangerous. Thankfully, it's rather pleasing to look at in the meantime. Is there anything else I should tell any villagers that ask about the tree?"

"I don't think they have anything to fear," I said as I shook my head, then I broke into a slight smile. "Though it may be a good idea to start making shades for windows to keep the glow out."

"Ha!" Aldwin let out a snort. "That may not be a bad idea, actually."

We watched the tree silently for a moment before I spoke. "Are you sure that you'll all be okay for the day today?"

"We'll manage," Aldwin said confidently. "Thanks to Drace, I've never seen the militia in better form. We'll keep the village safe and keep working on the digging."

"The militia!" I exclaimed as I knocked on my head with a fist, remembering the armor and weapons I'd spent a good part of the night crafting. "I have a new set of armor and spears waiting for them in the workshop."

"Ah!" the bann exclaimed. "Thank you, Lyrian! They'll be even more effective with better equipment! They aren't on duty just ye—" Aldwin's voice fell flat as he saw Drace, Constantine and Halcyon approaching all decked out in their new Webwood armor. "Good gods, Lyrian! What is that?"

"Ah! A new type of armor I made!" I replied excitedly, still happy to boast about my accomplishments.

"Good morning, sir," Drace greeted as he entered conversation range. "Great armor, Lyr. Barely feels like I'm wearing anything!"

"Is that…spider chitin?" The bann's closely inspected the armor. "What—"

"It's an excellent fit, sir! And the protection is unmatched!" Drace continued to sing my praises as he slowly turned to show the bann the full view of his armor.

"Never would I have even *tried* to use chitin as armor…" The bann shook his head in awe.

"We're just about ready to go, Lyr," Constantine told me while Drace and the bann continued to talk between themselves.

"Sierra and Caius went to grab some hollyleaf and food from Ragna, just to make sure we're properly stocked up before we go stick our dicks into a spider den," Halcyon explained a little sourly.

"Uh, thanks for that mental picture," I said as I tried to shake it out of my head. "I could have gone several lifetimes without imagining that."

"Yeah…well. It's pretty obvious that I fucking hate spiders. So I'm going to do my best to make all of you as uncomfortable as possible today."

"Oh, good. It's going to be that kind of day today."

"You should go change, Lyr," Constantine cut in with a sigh. "He's just going to keep going."

"Doesn't he always?" I waved a quick goodbye as I jogged over to the workshop to change into my armor.

A FEW MINUTES LATER I was on my way back to the tree and saw that Sierra and Caius had returned from their errand. With them, however, was Jenkins, Shelia, and Natasha as word of our impending departure had spread.

"Hey, Lyrian," Jenkins greeted me as I got close. "We're just here to see you off. Ritt would say bye too, but he doesn't usually wake before ten."

"Of course." I laughed.

"You guys be careful today," Natasha started. "I really wish I were coming with you all."

"You're more needed here, Natasha," Sierra said, shaking her head. "If something were to happen, you're the best scout the village has."

"Yeah." Natasha still didn't seem overly happy, but clearly understood what her role was. "Come back as soon as you can!"

"Definitely!" Sierra agreed as she gave the younger woman a quick hug. "Don't sweat it!"

"We are more than able to manage for a day!" Shelia said with a smile. "So don't go worrying about us. There's plenty enough work to go around without adding extra onto your plates! Just…be safe!"

"Do your best to sort *whatever* may be happening out there, Lyrian." Aldwin spoke to me softly as he offered a hand in farewell. "We won't be as lucky a second time."

I nodded to the bann as I clasped his arm and shook firmly. "We'll get to the bottom of it."

The rest of the party quickly bid farewell, and within a few minutes we were past the ditch we'd dug yesterday and out into the wild.

Despite having only five hours of sleep this last night, I was excited as we set off towards Crater Lake, feeling ready for anything the day threw at us.

"So, I've been thinking," Halcyon started. "Since we all match in this armor, shouldn't we have some sort of cheesy team name?"

"Like what?" I heard Caius reply hesitantly.

"I don't know. *Spider Dungeon Force* or something."

"That doesn't even make sense!" Constantine said.

"Your face doesn't make sense!" Halcyon retorted.

"Oh my god, are you twelve?" Sierra exclaimed. "Who even says that anymore?"

I sighed to myself. *This was going to be a long day.*

TWENTY-FOUR

"**D**AMN IT!" I SWORE IN pain as mana coursed through me, filling me with the feeling of being burnt, frozen and electrocuted all at once. Yet another attempt to raise my Alteration skill spectacularly failing. "Fuck, that hurts!"

Ever since we left Aldford, I'd been steadily practicing my new Blink Step spell whenever my mana allowed.

Unfortunately, the process was proving to be just as painful and frustrating as I anticipated, and I hadn't even managed to successfully cast the spell *once*. The frequent failures had me trailing behind the party a few dozen steps as we made our way steadily downhill towards Crater Lake, with only Halcyon hanging back with me.

"You're still doing it wrong," Halcyon said with a bit of frustration.

"You're not properly accounting for the trans-positional variables."

"What...the hell does that even *mean*?" I barked a bit testily. For whatever reason, after a few failures, Halcyon had taken it upon himself to tutor me in magic.

"It means exactly what I said!" Halcyon retorted, struggling to find words to explain. "When you hit level ten, didn't you get a huge injection of magical knowledge?"

"Like the bit about Spell Mastery?"

"No, not just that. I mean...literal *knowledge* about magic." Halcyon waved his hands around as he tried to find a way to explain. "When I hit level ten, it felt like something stuck a fire hose into my brain and then turned it on. That's why I crashed to bed so early the other night. Now when I cast a spell, I need to and I'm able to account for every single piece of what the spell is going to do as I cast it." He continued to explain. "That includes where the spell is taking effect, how far is it going, along with how fast it is moving. I think with enough practice, I might be able to start doing little things like changing the colors of certain spells. Hell, give me enough time, and I can maybe even change the element of the spell!"

"No, I didn't get anything like that at all." I shook my head slowly, a little overwhelmed at Halcyon's excitement. "I just think of the spell, then it happens. Like this." I raised my hand as I conjured a Flare. "I think of the Flare in my hand and poof."

"Okay, and when you think of the Blink Step spell, do you still think of your hand?"

I glanced at Halcyon as we walked, frowning. "Well, yeah. That's how I always cast magic. I figured I'd cast the spell, then choose where to go."

"Well, that's your fucking problem right there!" Halcyon exclaimed with a laugh. "No wonder it's not working. You're trying to Blink Step right into your palm! You're basically trying to dismember yourself with the spell!"

"Are you fucking kidding me?" I growled as I triggered the spell, this time focusing on something in the distance. "It can't be that easy!"

Instantly everything blurred as I teleported myself to the spot I had focused on, then I immediately felt myself falling forward until I landed on my chest and skidded to a stop.

Wheezing to get the air back into my lungs, I felt a footstep on my back.

"Oh!" Sierra said with a bit of surprise. "Hi Lyrian, taking a dirt nap? Or did you get your spell to work?"

"Can't it be both?" Caius laughed as Drace helped me up. "I take you didn't mean to land on your face?"

"I don't even..." I spat while shaking my head. "Mleh, dirt." As I rubbed the dirt off my tongue, I caught an alert in my vision. "At least I'm making progress. Alteration level three!"

"Nice!"

"Hey! You did it, Lyr!" Halcyon exclaimed happily as he caught up to us. "Well, aside from appearing a foot off the ground. I think you forgot about the downhill slope here. Can you see what I mean now about the variables in the spell?"

"No." I wheezed as I took a deep breath to help regain my wind. "No, nothing like that, unfortunately. I...just picked a spot and thought *very hard* that I wanted to go there."

"Oh." He sounded a bit disappointed.

"I only have one arcane tree at level nine so far, Halcyon," I said, trying to soothe him. "You have what, three all over level seven?"

"True." He sighed with a shrug. "Probably once you get a few more trees leveled up it'll kick in."

"Here's to hoping."

After taking a moment to brush myself off from my impromptu face plant, we set off walking again, ignoring the few creatures that crossed our path, but still taking the time to grab any hollyleaf we came across.

"Never hurts to have extra" was my motto, which probably also explained why I normally beat video games while having an inventory full of unused potions.

"So," I began. "Everyone care to explain what sort of new skills they got at level ten now? Or are we still keeping secrets?"

"Heh." Drace laughed before he started to explain his class choices. "I think we can spill the beans now. I chose warrior, obviously, as my base class and grabbed a racial *and* class trait called Roots of the Mountain, which gives me decent bonuses against being knocked down or bull rushed out of the way. Plus a small bonus against physical stunning attacks.

"After that, I grabbed Shield Slam skill, which judging from the spikes on this shield is going to *hurt* anything it hits and possibly knock it down. Then I also grabbed the second rank of Power Attack."

Constantine began next. "As for me, I picked up a passive trait called Acrobatics, which gives me a crazy amount of flexibility and natural agility, along with a pretty decent boost to my jump height."

"After that, I grabbed the second rank of Sneak Attack, along with the second rank of Power Attack. I'm ready to go full stabby-stabby on whatever decides to get in my way."

"Oh?" I rose an eyebrow in slight surprise at Constantine's choices. "No lockpicking or trapfinding abilities that rogues usually get?"

"Lockpicking was an option." Constantine nodded as he began to explain. "But with us being all the way out in the wild, I figured it wasn't the best choice. I was thinking with how popular we are back in Aldford, we could probably just ask whomever to unlock whatever it is we need to get into. Oh, also, lockpicking was listed as a general skill, meaning anyone can learn lockpicking if they wanted to."

"Hm…good to know!" I filed that bit of information away for later.

"We should all definitely learn that when we get a chance."

As soon as I finished that statement, I was met with exaggerated groans and grumbling.

"Lyr! This is one of the reasons why we wanted to keep our skills a secret!" Sierra exclaimed mockingly "We know that as soon as you get wind of something useful that we can all learn, you give us a well-reasoned argument that somehow forces us to!"

"Yeah!" Caius laughed loudly. "You're going to turn us into some sort of Renaissance adventurers!"

"Well, if you rather let me keep all the loot from chests or doors I unlock," I said slyly. "I could agree to that."

"Fuck that!" they all said at once.

"Ha!"

"Fine. Add it to the list." Sierra sighed begrudgingly. "I assume you have a *list*, right?"

I laughed and evaded Sierra's question by nodding my head at Constantine. "So no traps?"

"Nothing available to me," Constantine said with a shrug. "I think it might be tied into Perception, to be honest, and possibly whatever voodoo sight you magic users have for magical traps…"

"It's *Arcane Sight*," Halcyon breathed with a bit of exasperation. "With how much variety this game has, I actually wouldn't be surprised if there was a Voodoo Sight of some sort."

"Take a bet?"

"Sucker's bet." Halcyon shook his head at the rogue. "No way."

"*Anyway*," I interrupted trying to get back on track. "How about your skills, Hal?"

"Well, as you know, Arcane Sight, for one," Halcyon said as he started to list his abilities. "Which gives me the ability to see magic as a pale blue aura around things. I also grabbed a defensive spell called Force Shield, which is a channeled spell that lets me deflect, push, or block anything directly in front of me, up to a point. It saved my ass this morning with the horror, that's for sure.

"My other offensive spell if you remember, is Pyroclap. It's an instant explosion of arcane energy that I can conjure at a specific location. Super useful and self-explanatory I think."

Seeing that Halcyon was finished, Sierra jumped in. "As for me, I also upgraded my Sneak Attack to the next rank and picked up a new ability called Rapid Shot, which lets me fire arrows faster at the expense of slightly reduced damage and accuracy. And I also chose a racial and class ability called Windrunner's Stride, which when activated lets me shoot arrows while running at no penalty, along with a pretty good speed boost too! And before you ask, no, there wasn't a tracking ability to take either. I'm of the same mind as Constantine that it's somehow rolled into the Perception skill."

"You know me too well, Sierra." I laughed. "That sounds great! You'll have a ton of mobility to get around and be wherever you need to be!"

"That's my plan! Staying still is always a good way to get killed."

"How about you, Caius?" I prompted the warlock. "I remember you did something...*odd* this morning and healed me."

"Yeah," he began. "A warlock is largely defined by what he chooses for a patron, and like I mentioned to you this morning, I formed a pact with a blood demon. What happened this morning wasn't quite *healing* you, but more of just...giving you *my* health," Caius said, slightly wincing at the memory. "It's from a new ability I have called Transference, which lets me transfer my life energy to anything that I'm touching."

"So you lose hit points when you use it?" I asked.

"Yeah, I can roughly choose how much, though." Caius nodded. "*But* for a short while, after I use it, I get an awesome buff called Lifevoid, which gives me a huge bonus to my next life draining spell depending on how much life I transferred. Which is why for my second spell, I picked Lifetap. Depending on the fight, I can nearly or sometimes completely heal myself with a single tap."

"That's so cool!" Sierra exclaimed, "Good thing this game isn't brutally heavy on needing healing, but I'm happy we have some heals available!"

"For sure," Caius said. "It'll take me a while to be more reliable with heals, though. I saw a few other curses that do damage over time *and* life-drain, but they didn't scale that well at this level, so I didn't get any of them just yet."

"Eh?" Drace asked. "What was your third skill then?"

"Bloodsense."

"Sounds...ominous?" Constantine said a bit hesitantly.

"It..." Caius paused as he tried to find the right words. "The best way I can describe it is as if I can *hear* the blood in living things close to me. I can hear all of your heartbeats since you're all so close to me." He paused, then waved to his right. "Over there, it's faint, but I hear a gentle sort of swishing. I think there's some sort of creature further away. It's hard to say."

"So if something were to sneak up on you, you'd pretty much just hear them coming?" I asked with a frown. "That sounds powerful!"

"Well...maybe." Caius shrugged. "It's like standing in the middle of a crowd. You *hear* everything, but everyone is saying the same thing, how can you figure out which is which? If I were somewhere where there usually isn't any life, then sure, I'd notice right away. Otherwise, it could just get lost in the noise of everything else around it."

"I still think that's pretty awesome!" I said, going through mental scenarios where such a skill would be useful.

"So what exactly is our plan right now, Lyr?" Sierra asked. "Anything more concrete than just going on a spider killing rampage?"

"Hey, sign me up for that!" Halcyon said excitedly. "Bad enough I'm *wearing* spider skin..."

"Not really to be honest." I shook my head as I tried to come up with a mental map of how much of the Webwood we'd explored. "I sort of remember the direction I hunted in a few days ago when I first found Natasha. I figured to head in that direction and go from there."

"Makes sense." Sierra nodded, then perked up as the trees started to clear. "Finally, we're out of the trees! Let's stop for a drink. I'm thirsty."

With a spring in our steps, we made our way out of the forest and to the shore of Crater Lake, when something caught my eye. "Hang on, are those webs?"

I squinted at the nearby trees, watching silky strands billow in the wind.

"Damn!"

"What's wrong, Lyr?" Drace asked, following my gaze.

"I think the Webwood is growing."

TWENTY-FIVE

Somewhere
Nemesis

I EXTENDED MY CLAWS AS I stretched, raking deep furrows into the ground while I shook myself awake. Out of habit, I began to groom myself, licking down stray fur and cleaning dirt off my body. It was only then that I realized something was different, and finally understood what I had experienced the day before.

I am! I exist! I can think! The revelation caused my fur to stand on end as a new emotion flooded me.

Ecstasy.

Eyes closed in bliss, my mind thought back to the Two-Leg I had killed, the one whose death had gifted me with this newfound awareness of self. I remembered the whispers starting in my mind moments after sinking my teeth into its head, the next thing I knew,

I was running across the woods as if chased by a stampede, everything afterward just a blur.

As the ecstasy of the kill began to fade, I opened my eyes, looking about the den that I found myself in. I was surrounded by dirt, with several thick tree roots growing from the earth above me. The entire burrow was riddled with claw marks, *my claw marks*, I realized as a brief memory of fear surfaced, one that led me to hide here.

Sniffing fresh air, I left the burrow and pushed myself out into the forest. It was different than I remembered, the trees now covered in silky strands.

The Many-Legs encroach. It is no longer safe here. I realized it would be time to leave this forest for another hunting ground soon.

My eyes played across the surrounding area as I carefully searched for threats. Finding nothing, I turned to stride back towards the Ridge, where I knew things would be safer.

A familiar *compulsion* suddenly struck me, freezing me in place as invisible strands coiled around my body. I felt the presence of the *Two-Leg* in the distance.

How? My mind reeled, I had tasted the creature's blood, felt it die beneath my claws! Why did it still live?

The compulsion fanned my instinct, to find the Two-Leg, to attack it once more, and ensure its proper demise, whatever the cost may be. My newfound reason, however, bade me to flee, far away from what I didn't understand and the strange Two-Leg that would not die.

The compulsion intensified, forcing itself deep into my mind. I felt a paw move, a halting step forward, as control was taken from me, quickly followed by another. I struggled to regain control, but there was nothing I could do.

I was trapped.

The Webwood

"SKREEEEEEEeeeeeeeeeeee!"

"Not bad!" Drace congratulated me as a splashing sound echoed from the distance. "My turn!"

SPLORT

"Oh dear…"

"Ugh. Oh, god… *WHY?*" Halcyon started to shout as Drace, Caius, and I started laughing.

In the day since we'd last hunted in the Webwood, it had drastically expanded. Fresh webbing covered trees all the way to the Aldford side of Crater Lake, and after taking a moment to reflect, it had been quite a while since I remembered seeing a snake, beetle, or fox cross our path.

After pausing for a drink at the lake, we followed the shoreline towards our old hunting grounds. It didn't take long before we started spotting spiderlings nestled high in the trees or inside bushes. Initially, our plan was to bypass all the spiders we could and make our way deeper into the woods, hoping that the level difference would keep the critters off of us.

Unfortunately, we ran into a problem.

The second we approached the tree line, a horde of spiderlings leaped from the trees to attack us, in numbers that were far too great for even a group of level tens to safely ignore.

The forest was quite literally *crawling with angry spiders*.

That horde quickly multiplied as we instinctively pulled back to the shoreline, catching the attention of dozens of other spiderlings perched on nearby neighboring trees. A somewhat hectic battle later had us reconsidering our approach as we recovered from the surprising aggressiveness the spiderlings had displayed.

"Let Constantine and I sneak around quietly through the forest," Sierra suggested. "I can't quite place it, but something feels *off* to me about the way the spiders are acting."

Happy to leave it in Sierra's hands, Drace, Halcyon, Caius, and I stayed behind near the shore while she and Constantine crept north into the Webwood expertly evading the spiderlings notice.

I should really work on my stealth skill, I thought wistfully to myself as I saw them disappear into the brush, the level difference finally working in our favor.

For a while, we stayed vigilant, prepared to rush forward in aid if a horde of spiderlings fell on them, but their practice and patience served them well, and we quickly felt them make their way deeper into the woods.

Whatever skill they had at evading notice, though, it didn't transfer to the rest of us. Even as we stood still near the shoreline, a handful of spiderlings would occasionally catch sight of us and spring from the forest in a suicidal attack.

After getting over the excitement of the first few spiderling assaults, the lack of challenge and experience caused boredom to quickly set in. So to help pass the time, until Sierra and Constantine returned we invented a new sport, Spider Punting, which unfortunately Halcyon had found himself on the worse end of.

"I...ugh." Halcyon was knee deep into the lake, feverishly trying to wash off the ichor covering his face and armor.

"Sorry, Hal." Drace shrugged in slight mock apology. "I didn't think the critter would...*explode* like that. I guess I must have kicked it too hard!"

"*You guess?*" Halcyon shrilled sarcastically. "By all the gods that exist in this game and in reality, I am going to put *so many* fucking snakes in your bed when I can find ones big enough."

"I think you got a solid twenty-five feet on that one, Lyr." Caius chuckled. "Though I think Drace may have beat you if his spider hadn't, uh...malfunctioned."

"Heh." I laughed. "I was going to go with *lost containment.*"

"I can hear you two!" Halcyon called as he began shuffling out of the water.

"Uh. I think they're on their way back now," Drace said, suddenly looking off into the woods.

"Yeah," I agreed, sensing Sierra and Constantine gradually approaching. "They're getting closer."

We watched the tree line, steadily feeling our two scouts make their way back to us. Before long, I spotted a glimpse of Sierra's red hair peeking from her helmet as she and Constantine stealthily crept from the forest edge and made their way over.

"Hey! We found—" Sierra started to report, greeting us with a wave, right before her eyes went to the water. "Hang on. Why are there so many spiders in the water?"

"Hm?" I looked behind me and shrugged. "Oh! We kept having stragglers attack us in singles or pairs, and we got bored of just killing them. So Drace and I just started punting them into the water to see who'd get one the furthest. They'll all de-spawn in a minute or two."

Sierra stared at me in slight disbelief, waiting for me to tell her I was kidding. "You—you're not joking?"

"Not at all. Anyway, what'd you find?"

"Um…well." I saw a slight smile cross her face as she shook her head and muttered "*Boys.* We didn't find what was causing it, but there's something in the forest that is forcing the spiders to push east en-masse, almost as if they were fleeing from something."

"Well, I guess that explains their aggression and why there are so many of them out this way." I paused to scratch under my helmet as I thought. "What do you recommend we do? If they're running away from something, then we should definitely look into it, else they'll push right into Aldford."

"Yeah, that was my thought too." Sierra nodded and then turned to look at the forest, mentally retracing her steps. "We should keep going further west, then make our way back northeast once we can find a way into the forest without getting swarmed."

"Sounds like a plan to me," I said, waving everyone else over. "Let's get moving."

"Whoa, whoa, whoa, hold up there," Sierra said, holding a finger up as she spotted an approaching spiderling. "We can't leave yet."

"Hm? Why not?"

"Because I haven't punted a spider yet."

"GOT IT!" SIERRA EXCLAIMED IN triumph as her bow sang and a spiderling fell from the tree. "Move up! There's a small group ahead we'll need to take down too."

"Good shot," I said as I mentally triggered my Blink Step spell, successfully managing to blink forward five feet and reaching Alteration level six in the process. Following Sierra's and Constantine's lead, we circled Crater Lake and entered the forest from the west and had steadily been making our way back north towards the Webwood.

So far the spider density in this part of the woods was drastically lower than the roaming hordes we were constantly encountering earlier, re-enforcing Sierra's theory that the spiders were migrating east.

"Look." I pointed ahead as we hustled forward, indicating a tattered, web-covered tree ahead of us. "This tree is dying and looks like it has been choked by the webs for a while. We're almost into the heart of the Webwood."

"What are we going to do then?" Constantine asked. "Wander until we trip over the ley line?"

"That or whatever is driving the spiders crazy," I replied while watching Sierra nock an arrow and take aim. "Assuming they're not the same thing..."

"Incoming!" Sierra whispered urgently as she loosed an arrow, quickly followed by another one. The two arrows flew through the air before piercing two spiderlings hiding in the nearby tree, killing them instantly.

Four more spiderlings fell from the tree chittering angrily as they sprinted towards us. A pair of magical bolts flashed past me, sending one spider to the ground smoldering. Drace, Constantine and I quickly sprang forward and effortlessly dispatched the remaining three.

"These things are hardly even worth the effort," Constantine grumbled as he flicked his daggers clean. "Thirteen experience points... bah! It's going to take nearly, uh, sixteen-hundred more of these just to hit level eleven."

"The critter is only level seven," Drace said with a shrug. "Considering how easily we can squish one of them now, I'd say that's pretty generous."

"Yeah, I'm just putting everything into leadership experience for the time being." I spoke while checking our surroundings for telltale glows of red or blue, which would indicate either something of interest or something hostile. "Just a few dozen more spiders away from another leadership skill point!"

"Sweet," Constantine said with a smile as he grabbed the loot off the dead spiderlings. "I can definitely feel that speed buff already."

"Hey, Lyr. Check this out." Caius waved me over to the tree that the spiders had been hiding in, where Halcyon and Sierra were looking at something.

"Eh? What's up?" I asked as I approached the tree.

"We found...claw marks on the tree," Halcyon said pointing to deep gashes all along the tree base. "Judging by the ragged webbing here, I'd say it happened fairly recently too."

Following Halcyon's hand, I bent down to take a look at the gashes, finding dozens of them, ranging from a few inches to over two feet in length. "Looks pretty vicious, maybe from a wandering bear or another Wolverine like Drace found?"

"I…don't think so," Sierra said, shaking her head as she pointed to the claw marks. "These are barely shoulder high. If it were a bear or a giant wolverine, there'd be markings higher up the tree."

"Hm."

"That's not all, though." She traced the claw marks with a finger. "None of these are parallel to one another or grouped together."

"What does that mean exactly?" Drace asked while keeping an eye on the surrounding forest.

"My guess…that whatever did this only had one claw."

"A spider, then?" Constantine said aloud. "Plenty of them have just a single claw…per claw. Ugh, you know what I mean."

"I have no idea, but I think the spiderlings tried to get away from something, but whatever was chasing it couldn't follow them up the tree."

"Hrm." I scratched my head as I digested Sierra's assessment. "I guess we're going the right way."

"Shall we push forward then?" Sierra asked, quickly scanning the woods. "I don't see any spiderlings hiding nearby anymore. We should be able to move faster now."

"Yeah, let's see if we can find more marked up trees like this." I motioned for Sierra to take the lead. "Maybe we'll be able find whatever's doing this."

NO LONGER FORCED TO STOP every few paces to deal with a nest of spiders, we quickly flew through the oldest parts of the Webwood as we headed northeast. The sound of our crunching boots was all that filled the air, as the trees were far too encumbered with webs to even whisper in the wind.

It's like the entire forest has been suddenly abandoned, I thought to myself.

The eerie silence began to weigh on us as we moved through the woods, eventually spotting other trees with claw marks on them. At first, it was a single tree every few dozen meters, then a handful every ten meters, until at some point we passed an invisible wall, and it became impossible to find a tree that *wasn't* clawed in some way.

"Well, this is getting a bit creepy," Caius commented nervously as we approached an area free of trees, yet still covered by all the forest's canopy. "I can hear all of your heartbeats and *only* your heartbeats by the way, so I know I'm not the only one that thinks so."

"It's as if everything just…*left*," Constantine replied. "Did this start happening yesterday when the spiderlings invaded Aldford?"

"Who knows?" Sierra whispered, holding an arrow nocked to her bow as she looked around. "I'm just wondering: why didn't we see any spiderlings earlier in the day when we descended towards Crater Lake?"

"Maybe whatever was chasing them stopped here?" I suggested as we approached the clearing. Web-covered branches littered the ground here.

My eye spotted something jutting from a tangle of leaves and web. *Is that fabric?* I grabbed at the piece and gave it a sharp tug pulling free a large brown sheet free from the pile. "Hang on. Is this a tent?"

"Shit! This is a tent!" Broken support sticks tumbled out of the tent as I turned it over in my hands. "What is it doing here?"

"Well, I am totally *spooked* now," Halcyon muttered as he nervously conjured a ball of blue fire in his hand after he saw me pull up the tent. "And I'd really appreciate it if we dialed back the spookiness back down to manageable levels."

"Dude, you can't use that word unless there's a skeleton around," Constantine chided Halcyon nervously.

"This isn't the time to joke!" Halcyon snapped.

"Quiet!" I hissed as my eyes scanned the clearing. "Check the area out!"

Sierra and Drace quickly moved forward and began picking through the broken branches in the clearing. *Who tried to hide this and who did they hide it from?*

"Lyr," Sierra said as she dragged a torn pack from a pile of branches. "This was the expedition camp Natasha was a part of!"

She quickly made her way over to me and showed me an emblem on the bag. "This is the Eberian Mages Guild Insignia! It's stitched right onto the bag! We saw this on flying banners when we were in Eberia!"

"Shit! This camp was attacked by goblins!" I exclaimed remembering Natasha's recollection of the attack. I quickly looked around at what I now knew to be a campsite, trying to envision the attack. "Why did they try to hide the campsite? There's no one here for miles... especially if they were set to attack Aldford."

"Maybe they didn't," Drace mused as he cleared away some debris. "Check out these branches. They're all broken. Hell, some of them even look mangled like they were crushed by something." He paused to look up into the forest canopy. "Look up there. There are a ton of branches that are all broken too."

Curious, I walked over to Drace's vantage point and followed his gaze. "Huh, you're right. I wonder how that happened."

We stood silently for a moment as we tried to puzzle the sequence of events out.

"A spider stampede?" Sierra suggested after a moment. "We know something was chasing them, the spiders probably tried to escape by running tree to tree, but when they got to this clearing, they had no other branches in reach."

"And with enough spiders on a branch..." Drace trailed off.

The longer I stay in this world, the harder it becomes to remember it's just a game. I thought to myself as I shook my head with a sigh, trying to banish the terrifying vision of a spider stampede. *Events just happen, with or without us.*

"Uh, guys? I hate to interrupt," Caius called out urgently, "but we aren't alone anymore…"

TWENTY·SIX

SNAPPING BACK TO THE PRESENT, I whirled on Caius's words as I drew Razor. "Where?"

Caius shook his head as he struggled to make out what his Bloodsense ability was telling him. "Everywhere."

We quickly formed up back-to-back in the center of the clearing as we nervously stared out into the forest.

"It's getting closer," Caius whispered as he readied a glowing blue missile in his hand.

My eyes scanned the forest around us, looking for whatever it was that Caius could hear. A faint aura of blue caught my eye, outlining a strange crawling shape in the distance, followed by another, and another.

Shit! We're surrounded! I turned around, scanning the entirety of the forest around us, seeing pale blue auras all around us.

"*Halcyon...*" I started to say.

"Yeah, I see it too, Lyr," he said nervously.

"See what?" Sierra hissed as she drew her bow, ready to fire.

"Magic auras," I explained. "Spider-sized, I think. All around us."

"Oh, fuck!"

The auras started to increase in brightness as the circle around us tightened, giving better clarity to the shape beneath the aura.

"Guys, these don't look like they're *spiderling* sized," Halcyon said nervously as he took half a step backwards into our circle.

He's right. My head spun as I looked all around us, the auras coalescing into a dozen, three-foot-tall, multi-limbed creatures. I conjured a flare in my hand as I mentally prepared myself for combat.

No sense in waiting for them to jump us.

"Sierra, shoot where you see my Flare go!" I started barking out orders as I readied to toss my tiny fireball. "Halcyon, paint your target! Caius follow his lead! Be careful, they may explode if they die!"

I threw my flare at the brightest target I could see, the tiny missile blazing through twenty feet of air unerringly before splashing against the creature. A pair of expertly shot arrows quickly thudded deep into the creature as Sierra found her mark.

There was a single heartbeat of silence before the entire forest *screamed* in pain.

Blue light flared as a horde of creatures illuminated themselves and immediately shot forward from the nearby brush with an unexpected burst of speed, covering the intervening distance in less time than it took to blink.

In the split instant as a pair of creatures launched themselves at me, I *saw* what they were.

It was a spider unlike I had ever seen before, completely night black and sleeker than anything its size had a right to be. Blue veins traced over the spider's carapace, pulsing with a malevolent energy that both the aberration and horror had lacked. Oversized and barbed pedipalps framed an equally massive pair of fangs.

Then there were the claws.

They were massive, almost beyond comprehension for a creature of the spider's size. Two wicked scythe-like claws comprised the entirety of the spider's front-most legs, which were gleaming with the same pale blue malevolence that the body shared.

Everything about the spider screamed *danger*, instinct shouting at me to flee.

As a pair of these creatures sailed through the air towards me, I had enough time to read a single tag that appeared in my vision.

[Webwood Predator – Level 10]

I caught a pair of the glowing claws with Razor as the two predators leaped on me, trying to bear me down to the ground. The second pair of claws bit through my armor and sliced into my upraised forearm, drawing blood and making me hiss in pain. It was all I could do not to flinch away, from the pain and bring the spiders crashing down directly on me. Weathering the impact, I felt my feet slide across the ground until I felt my shoulders bump Halcyon in the back.

A [Webwood Predator] slices you for 21 points of damage!
A [Webwood Predator] slices you for 24 points of damage!

Gritting my teeth I shoved back at the spiders with a yell, as I struggled to cancel their momentum, feeling yet another hot wave of pain as the claws sawed deep into my arm. Barely dodging a flailing pedipalp, I felt it scrape across my helmet ineffectively, inches away from blinding me, as I threw the two predators off me.

"Aaaah!" I heard Constantine scream in pain behind me as the predators crashed to the ground before me. Not willing to chance a glance behind me, I quickly uttered the trigger word for Shocking Touch, filling the hand that held Razor full of electricity.

I felt the charge course through my arm as I slashed down with my sword, putting extra power behind the blow.

You [Power Attack 1] a [Webwood Predator] for 41 points of damage!
Your [Shocking Touch] discharges into a [Webwood Predator] for 39 points of damage!

I felt Razor cut easily through the spider as the spell discharged itself through the metal blade. The creature froze momentarily as the electricity shot through it.

"I'm going to need help here!" I heard Halcyon shout. "I can't hold this shield much longer!"

"Constantine needs healing!" Caius yelled directly after Halcyon. "And I need a victim to drain! They are too fast for me to catch!"

My response was taken from me as my two enemies had recovered *blindingly* fast and slashed out at me furiously. *Gods! It's like fighting a pair of angry blenders!* I feverously worked Razor through a set of dizzying parries as I tried to deflect their claws into one another's path. Even then they still scored half a dozen glancing blows.

If something doesn't change quickly, I'm going to die from a thousand paper cuts!

Little did I know that Sierra was about to answer my prayer.

"Caius!" Sierra shouted. "How long do you need to heal Constantine?"

"Uh, three seconds!" he replied, slightly unsure. "Maybe four!"

"I'm going to try and give you five!" Sierra yelled and suddenly sprinted out of the circle with an unearthly grace as she activated Windrunner's Stride, effortlessly dodging past a trio of predators in her way.

"Sierra, no!" Drace boomed as we saw her take off, catching the attention of nearly all of the nearby spiders.

Oh, shit, Sierra! I swore to myself as her flight triggered something in the Webwood predators as they turned to focus on a lone target, including the pair that had been threatening me.

"I NEED A MOB!" Caius's scream tore through our surprise.

"Raaaaaaah!" Fueled by rage, Drace *slammed* his shield into a wheeling predator, practically flattening it against the ground before it could run after Sierra. His wicked bladeclaw chopped into the creature, sending out a glowing spray of ichor as he dragged it backwards, tossing it behind him.

"Lyrian! Keep it down!" he bellowed right before he *roared* at another hesitating predator and launched into a brutal assault before it could chase after Sierra.

"*Fuck yeah!*" I screamed mindlessly as I stabbed Razor straight through the stunned predator, burying it a hand's length in the ground. As I slammed my armored knee into the creature's back, I finally chanced a glance over to Caius and Constantine.

Constantine was lying flat on the ground, twin holes *gushing* blood from his neck and side, his face pale and filled with pain. Caius was kneeling beside him with a hand on his chest.

"Caius, now!" I shouted as I twisted my blade to keep the creature from writhing out under me.

On my word, the wounds instantly vanished from Constantine as Caius activated Transference. I was close enough to hear him gasp in pain before his other hand slapped the smooth chitin of the predator and flared red.

Like a dying man finding an oasis, Caius drank in the predator's life energy as its struggles grew weaker under my blade. When Caius finally drew his hand away, the blue glow of the creature was gone, and the body crumbled under my weight.

"What the fuck?" I exclaimed as I practically fell *through* the creature.

"*Incoming!*" I heard Sierra scream over the screeching of the predators chasing her.

Standing up, I whirled on her voice and saw her sprinting towards us with the swarm of predators in tow. Blood flowed freely from a deep cut on the cheek, spraying in the air as she ran.

"Halcyon, Force Shield in front of Drace as soon as Sierra passes by!" I barked, seeing Drace brutally dismember a spider in front of him, the glow fading away from the creature, as it too crumbled to dust. *At least these aren't exploding!*

Seeing Constantine on his feet, I motioned for him to take Drace's shield side. "You okay, buddy?"

"Yeah, completely fucked up..." He shook his head. "I'm okay."

"Good, let's go!" Moving up to stand beside Drace, I saw Sierra's long strides quickly eating up the distance between us as the horde of predators nipped at her heels.

Halcyon is going to need to be fucking quick on this! I worried to myself, remembering Halcyon's fear of spiders as he planted himself in front of Drace to receive the spiders' charge. *Hopefully he doesn't choke.*

Eyes wild, Sierra charged towards us as the predators tore the ground up behind her, wicked claws gleaming eerily in the forest gloom. At the last moment before running headlong into Halcyon, she dropped into a slide, skidding just past his legs.

The moment Sierra was safe, Halcyon's shield slammed into place, a slight distortion marking the arc of the shield.

Caught running full stride, the chasing predators had no chance or warning to slow down. They violently collided into Halcyon's shield with a vicious *crunch* as the momentum sent them all piling into one another. The impact sent Halcyon sliding backwards into Drace as the warrior's massive form helped keep the mage steady.

"Shields down, Halcyon! Attack while they're stunned!" I shouted as I moved forward trusting Halcyon to bring the shield down in time.

I saw the mage sidestep Drace, ducking under the warrior's outstretched shield arm as he wound up for a sweeping cleave.

A thunderclap of magefire announced the departure of Halcyon's Force Shield, washing over nearly the entire pile of spiders. Drace's wicked bladeclaw quickly swept through the tangle of spiders, easily severing half a dozen limbs in a single pass.

Ducking under Drace's follow through, Razor crackled with electricity as I skewered a pair of predators, sinking my blade right to the hilt and wrenching it violently for maximum damage.

Out of the corner of my eye, I saw Constantine land two thunderous blows that punctured deep into a predator that already carried twin arrows lodged deep into its carapace. Even as the creature began to dissolve, he had already torn his daggerfangs free, seeking another target.

Moving with incredible speed, the horde of predators finally managed to untangle themselves from one another, each bearing at least a single wound or burn as they redoubled their attack.

All that and we just got two! I grimaced while doing a quick mental count of the spiders still standing. *Eight left! We can do this!*

"Push forward! Don't let them flank!" I shouted out as the predators began to spill over the sides of our formation. I kept Razor moving in a blur as I parried or deflected a seemingly endless avalanche of glowing claws. Finding an opportunity, I sliced through an offending leg, then quickly twisted my body to slap away yet another claw that would have completely pierced through Drace's side.

"STEP!" Sierra bellowed.

It took half a second for the training to kick in, promptly reminding me to take a step to the right.

Two arrows whistled past my vacated spot thudding into a surprised predator, quickly followed by another burst of magefire that sent it disintegrating.

Another one bites the dust. I grinned to myself as I glided back to my usual spot at Drace's right side, carving a wicked gash across a carapace.

"What the hell?" Halcyon shouted in surprise.

"Lyr, behind you!" Sierra screamed.

I spun wildly, ready to slash out at a flanking predator. I barely noticed that Sierra and Halcyon had broken formation, as my mouth fell open in shock.

"Oh, fuck!" I felt icy tendrils of terror shoot through my veins.

A massive puma soared through the air at me, claws outstretched, maw open.

As it slammed into me and knocked me off my feet, my mind snapped back to my death, filling me with dread.

I felt a single thought cross my mind.

Not again.

TWENTY-SEVEN

THE IMPACT KNOCKED THE WIND out of me, sending me sailing through the air and landing on top of a pair of predators. I felt chitin crunch under me as my nemesis slammed its weight down onto me, pinning me down.

Fuck! Did this thing get even bigger? The thought crossed my panicking mind as I reflexively punched the giant cat in the face. I grabbed the creature's throat as its head rocked back, trying to simultaneously strangle the beast single-handedly and keep it from adding another collection of scars to my face.

Massive claws dug into my chest, thankfully unable to pierce through the re-enforced carapaces that I had stitched onto my armor as it lunged forward to take a bite of me. My hand struggled to keep its grip on the creature's throat as powerful muscles drove the head towards me. Remembering my other hand still held Razor, I stabbed inwards, hoping to drive my blade deep into my nemesis's side.

The tip of the blade barely punched into the side of the puma, before it ground against the creature's ribcage. The beast roared in pain on top of me as it tried to shrug itself off my blade. Its hind claws dug deep into my legs as it raked deep furrows in my flesh.

Why is this thing so dead set on killing me? My mind reeled in pain as I tried to suck in a breath of air. I felt the two predators writhing under me as they struggled to escape. A flash of blue caught my eye as I saw a predator's gleaming scythe-claw break free from under me and begin to flail wildly.

Damn it! I can't catch a break! I gasped as the puma's claws finally managed to pierce through my chest armor. I had to make a move *fast* if I was going to survive this. *Alteration, please don't let me down!*

Chancing a quick glance to my right, I fixated on a distant patch of brush, free from anything nearby. Taking a quick breath and sending a quick prayer to all the gods I knew, I let go of the puma's throat and triggered Blink Step.

The world blurred as I teleported out from under the puma and the wild scythe-claw, appearing in the air a short distance away. I landed onto the ground with a sigh of relief.

That was too close! I gasped a desperate breath as I rolled to my feet, looking back at the pile of creatures. My nemesis looked confused as it found itself biting down into a predator instead of my throat. Committed, it shook its head viciously as it thrashed the creature around on the ground, sending another spider crumbling to dust.

"Lyr! Are you okay?!" I heard Caius shout from nearby.

The party had momentarily scattered when the puma attacked from behind and knocked me out of our line. Despite falling on two of them, the rest of the predators had taken advantage of the distraction and redoubled their attack. I saw that Sierra had dropped her bow in favor of her sword to keep the creatures from flanking Halcyon and Caius.

"Y-y-yeah!" I lied, trying to hide how much the memory of my death had unsettled me. I quickly started to move back towards the group. "Fucking cat! This is going to end here!"

On hearing my voice, the puma's head instantly fixated on me and bared its teeth in a roar. Slapping away the second predator with a paw, it sprang forward towards me, ready for blood. But before it could cover more than a single stride, a pair of spiders peeled away from the party blocking the puma's path.

Skidding to a halt, the big cat hissed with fury as it swiped a claw at a spider that *dared* to cross its path, rending five jagged lines into the creature's carapace that began to spew glowing ichor.

Welcoming the distraction, I sprinted back towards the relative safety of the party, still wheezing for air as my lungs struggled to settle themselves. Seeing Sierra under assault by a pair of predators, I angled my charge to sneak attack the pair from behind, electricity crackling through Razor as I cast Shocking Touch yet again. My blade brutally pierced through an unsuspecting predator's abdomen, splitting the creature open as my momentum drove the blade forward.

"Get your bow!" I shouted at Sierra as I took her place in the line, now on Constantine's left side as the predator I had just trampled evaporated into dust.

"Thanks, Lyr!" Sierra gasped as she backpedaled, quickly sheathing her sword, then stooping to pick up her bow.

Faced with only a single predator this time and a wounded one to boot, I unleashed a furious combination of blows designed to bully the creature into the ground, smashing it with relentless overhand attacks. The predator desperately attempted to block and deflect my attacks with its massive claws, but with it fighting alone and no longer having the benefit of surprise, it began to flag under my assault.

With a snap, I shattered a claw into pieces and chopped Razor deep into the predator's thorax, sending yet another spurt of glowing ichor in the air. At that moment, Constantine's daggerfang seized an opening, burying itself deep between the spider's cluster of eyes. I kicked out at the creature, sending it sliding off Constantine's daggerfang and quickly disintegrating as it collapsed to the ground.

"I need help here!" I heard Drace shout out behind me. "Cat is coming to dance!"

"Go, Lyr!" Constantine shouted as he caught a claw on his daggerfang. "I got this!"

"Right!" I stepped backwards as I turned, moving to Drace's right side.

On my way through the defensive pocket we'd formed, Caius clapped me on the shoulder, and I felt my wounds vanish.

"Ah!" He winced as he removed his hand and moved to fill the spot I had just left. "Go get it, Lyr!"

"Constantine!" I heard him grunt. "Line the critter up for me!"

As I stepped up towards Drace, I saw the puma sinking its teeth into another Webwood predator and violently whipping the spider around. In the brief instant, I had lost sight of the creature it had acquired a pair of long gashes along its body, with one of Sierra's arrows firmly entrenched in its hindquarters.

Doing a quick count, I saw only three more predators remaining. One by Constantine, one by Drace, and another in the pum—*Shit, scratch that! It's already dead!*—the angry cat having just killed its spider.

"Bring it, kitty!" I taunted the puma as a blue missile flew past by me and splashed across the creature's shoulder.

Hissing in pain, the puma glared at me and then roared in anger and frustration. For the briefest of moments, I made eye contact with the beast and saw a glint of intelligence behind the bright amber eyes.

Then it was gone.

As quickly as the puma had tried to ambush me, it turned to flee, running off deep into the forest.

"No!" I screamed as hot rage welled up inside me. I sprang forward as the creature fled. "Get back here, you fucking cat!"

"Lyr!" Drace yelled as I took off to chase the wounded creature. "Wait for us!"

Breaking into a full sprint, I left the clearing and the party behind. I pumped my legs furiously as I began to gradually close the gap with the fleeing puma, Sierra's arrow greatly slowing down its maximum speed.

"Hey!" I shouted at the creature, trying to get its attention, anger completely overriding the wisdom of taunting such a massive cat. "You fucking want me? Here I am! I'm not going to be afraid of you!"

"Let's see how you fucking like it when something fucking tackles you out of nowhere!" I lunged forward as I triggered Blink Step once more. *Oh, please don't let me face plant!*

The world blurred as I instantly teleported thirty feet forward, directly on top of the fleeing puma. *Fucking right!* My mind roared with glee.

I slammed into the beast with the best flying tackle I could muster, completely breaking its stride and sending the both of us skidding to the ground.

"How the fuck do you like that?!" I roared in triumph as I rode the creature to a stop. My fist crackled with electricity as I viciously punched the creature in the back of the head, completely forgetting I still held Razor in my other hand. "A Thunder Punch right upside the head might teach you to *leave me the fuck alone!*"

It was at this point that I realized that I was straddling a *very* angry, seven-hundred-plus-pound mountain lion.

Completely by myself.

"Oh, fuck!" The creature twisted under me as it planted its feet on the ground, coiling its muscles in preparation to leap.

The puma launched itself a solid eight feet into the air, even as it dragged my not inconsiderable *two-hundredish-pound* body into the sky. Twisting wildly in a way only a cat can, it slipped out from under me and we both crashed to the ground in a heap.

I instantly sprang to my feet, just in time to dodge a swiping claw as the puma regained its balance. We both took half a step backwards as we collected ourselves and began to test one another's defenses.

My eyes drank in every detail of the creature as I looked for weaknesses. I saw a number of weeping wounds running along the creature's body, marring the golden fur with blood. A slight lean to one side told me it was favoring its rear left leg. A probing tongue flicked over a broken fang.

There! I saw my opening and charged forward, at the same instant the creature coiled to attack.

With a thunderous crash, we slammed together in a tangle of blood, teeth, and metal, neither of us holding an ounce of energy in reserve as we each did our absolute best to kill one another.

I fought purely on instinct, my body reacting faster than my mind could process.

A slight shift of my leg let a swiping claw sail harmlessly by, followed by quick step forward to slice a thin line across it as it passed. An open palm, slapping away the creature's maw, turned a potentially crippling bite to the arm into a minor graze as the teeth missed their mark.

Minutes felt like lifetimes as neither of us dared to slow our tempo, lest the other seize a decisive advantage. We fought past endurance, past reason.

Reality snapped back into focus as I found myself driving Razor deep into the puma's side, the same instant I felt teeth close down on my leg. Pain exploded through my body as teeth tore through flesh and muscle, leaving me screaming louder than I ever thought I could. Like a puppet with its strings cut, I fell to the ground in a heap.

With a twist, the puma pulled itself off of my sword, whimpering as it let go of my leg. Blood leaked freely from the wound as it backed away from me. I looked at the creature, expecting to see anger and hatred flicker in its amber eyes right before it killed me a second time.

For a fleeting instant, as we locked eyes, I saw a profound *sadness* cross the puma's eyes before the emotion vanished, leaving the creature's gaze blank for the briefest of moments. Then the anger arrived.

As I struggled to comprehend what I had just seen, the puma let out a long hiss and began to move forward.

Grasping Razor tightly, I prepared myself for one last attack. I didn't care if I survived anymore. Death was a small price to pay to make sure that I took the creature with me. Only then would I truly be *safe* again.

Only one chance at this, I told myself as the creature crept closer. *Wait until it's committed, then kill it, before it kills me.*

I exhaled a ragged breath as I waited for the puma to make its move, watching it intently.

Closer... Closer... Closer...

"Lyrian!" A voice shouted out behind me. I heard a dull *twang* echo a heartbeat after.

The puma flinched as a black arrow whizzed past it, barely missing its head. It snarled as it looked past me and then quickly abandoned its approach. Whirling out of my reach, it turned and limped off into the forest at a slow trot.

"Noooo!" I shouted, voice suddenly hoarse as I tried to force my tattered leg to stand, but promptly fell to the ground.

No! No! No! It's going to escape! My expression was wild with pain as I dragged myself forward after the creature. *I have to get it! I won't be safe until its dead!*

Fixing my eye on the departing creature, I triggered Blink Step. *I have to kill it!*

The spell instantly came apart as I cast it, the mana bleeding into the air around me. *No! Not like this!*

I desperately tried to trigger the spell again, gripping Razor so tight that my hand began to cramp. I felt the world begin to blur, then pain blossomed through my body as the spell came apart, the mana rebounding into my body.

My vision blurred as I lost consciousness, leaving me with a single fleeting thought.

Damn...

"LYRIAN! LYRIAN!" MY RETURN FROM darkness was slow and disorienting. I felt something slapping at my face, aggravating the wounds across my head. "Shit! He's bleeding out! Caius, see what you can do!"

"Oh man, this isn't good!"

"Mrahh...staahp." I struggled to ward off whatever was hitting me in the face. I felt a flash of pain as something touched my chest, then the pain instantly vanished.

"Lyrian, what the fuck?" I heard Drace's voice carve through the darkness, and I opened my eyes, quickly followed by Sierra's voice asking, "What were you thinking?"

My sight slowly began to clear and after a moment I saw Caius and Sierra kneeling close by with Drace looming over me. I pegged the other blurry shapes nearby that I couldn't quite make out just yet as being Halcyon and Constantine.

"I had it," I croaked as I tried to sit up. "Fuck. We need to find it."

"Damn it, Lyrian! Why didn't you wait for us?" Sierra practically shouted at me.

It took a moment for the words to penetrate my head as my brain struggled to fully reboot. I stared at her blankly for a moment before I finally caught on. "It's going to keep hunting me. I had to stop it."

"And didn't you think that by running away from us you did exactly what it wanted?" Sierra asked hotly.

"I didn't think…"

"Fucking right, you didn't think!" Sierra yelled as she closed the verbal trap. "Goddamn it, Lyrian. We spent all that time practicing to work as a team because *you* said it was a good idea! Then you run off solo and nearly get yourself killed!"

"It *killed me*, Sierra," I mumbled as I rubbed my eyes to help clear them. "It killed me and got stronger. What if it jumps me halfway through a battle again? When I'm even more wounded?"

"Then you need to trust us to be there to help you," Sierra said. "Just like you'd be there for us if one of us were in your shoes."

"Don't try to do everything all the time, Lyr," Drace added softly. "Let us help out where we can too. We have your back."

I thought about bringing up Sierra's earlier suicidal charge, but with a sigh I thought better of it, knowing in my heart that they were both right. "Thank you…and I'm sorry. I'm not used to being *hunted*. I reacted badly."

Sierra looked at me in the eye for a moment before nodding. "It's okay."

"Spiders taken care of?" I asked as I mentally checked my health in the corner of my vision.

HP: 234/594

Well, I guess that explains why I still feel like shit.

"Yeah. We killed them," Drace replied. "Truthfully, your nemesis helped us out. I don't know how or why, but quite a few of the creatures peeled off to attack it. We'd have been in trouble otherwise."

"Isn't that…odd?" I asked, trying to recall pieces of the fight. "Monsters don't usually do that."

"I don't—" Caius said with a wince, not yet having recovered from healing me, "—think that I'm going to complain about that. We lived; spiders died. Works for me."

"No loot on the spiders, though," Constantine said with a grumble, finally coming into focus for me. "They just…poofed into dust."

"Shit experience too." I heard Halcyon's voice add glumly. "Not even a hundred points each. I think the leveling speed is going to slow way the hell down if all level ten creatures are like this."

"That doesn't matter right now," Sierra said shaking her head, at the pair then looked back to me. "You okay to move?"

"I…don't know," I said as I tried moving the leg that the puma had mangled. I quickly found out that it hurt, but no longer was immobilized. I motioned for help to stand up, Sierra and Drace both grabbing an arm to pull me up. "Ugh. Yeah, I'll be okay. I can feel it starting to heal."

"Good!" Sierra broke into a smile. "Then we need to start moving. Fast."

"Huh?" I looked at her confused. "Why?"

"Because your puma friend happened to leave a nice blood trail going that way." Sierra's grin widened as she pointed north into the woods. "I figured you'd want to follow it before it gets too far away."

TWENTY-EIGHT

GIVEN THE NEED TO TRACK down my fleeing nemesis before it could fully heal, we all agreed to put off fully investigating the expedition site for the time being. Sierra was confident that she could find her way back to the camp once we caught up with the beast, or, gods forbid, lost the trail.

We had taken off on the puma's trail at a jog, keeping our pace steady as Caius and I recovered from our more serious wounds. Or, more aptly put, my *very serious wounds* which Caius had graciously taken a portion of. I had even gone as far as assigning the one leadership skill point that I had earned after the fight with the Webwood predators into the increased health regeneration option in hopes of making it back to full health as soon as possible.

The forest was quiet as we jogged northwards with Sierra in the lead, her eyes focused on the ground as her Perception skill helpfully outlined the puma's blood trail as it fled. The webs covering the trees gradually thinned as we ran, despite nearly all the trees still being covered with wicked gashes and scars.

We must be leaving the original part of the Webwood. I looked at the web covered canopy as I ran. *Doesn't seem like this part of the forest has been part of the Webwood for long.*

"So." Constantine puffed with relief as the ground began to level out slightly. "Think those predators drove the spiderlings out of the Webwood?"

"Does a bear shit in the woods?" Halcyon asked sarcastically. "Made *me* want to fucking run, and I only have a near-crippling fear of *regular* spiders. Let alone ones that have glowing greatswords for arms!"

"And yet you stood up and took a horde of charging spiders to the face, like a man!" Drace said proudly. "I'll make a proper tank out of you yet."

"Fuck, I don't get paid enough for this," Halcyon muttered.

"Wait, you get paid?" Caius grunted in mock outrage. "I'm the one bearing everyone's wounds, do I get thanks? *Noooo.* Everyone's all 'Touch me and make me feel better, Caius'."

"Are we still doing phrasing?" Sierra asked cautiously from the front of the group. "Because that didn't sound right."

"Uh, how does a bag of my good coffee sound?" I offered with a smirk. "For services rendered."

"Do you have *bad* coffee, if you need to say *good* coffee?" Caius asked hesitantly.

"Don't fuck around, Caius. Lyr knows his coffee," Drace warned, half serious. "Take the offer and run."

"Maybe I should keep running until I get a better offer."

"Hold up!" Sierra called us to stop, a worried expression on her face.

"Aw." Caius sighed as we came to a halt.

"Wait here." Sierra's held up her hand as she ran ahead of us and circled the area, her elven eyes easily piercing through the shadowy gloom of the Webwood. "We're just about at the edge of the forest. I can see a ridge wall ahead of us, though, running southwest to northeast."

"Did you lose the trail?" I asked hesitantly, hoping that chasing the puma hadn't been a colossal waste of our time.

"No, but...it's getting harder to follow," Sierra said while shaking her head. "That's not why I stopped, though."

"What's up?"

"Look at these trees." Sierra pointed at a nearby tree that had been clawed. "The majority of the claw marks are on the northeast facing side of the tree."

"And then take a look at the ground and dirt around us," Sierra continued to explain. "It's all chewed up."

"Well, the spiderlings and predators would have done that, right?" Drace asked as he glanced around at the nearby trees. "These scratches look the same as the ones we saw before, near the camp."

"Yes, but actually *look* at the dirt," Sierra said. "It took me a while to notice it while we ran. It's all marred in the exact same way."

"What does that mean, though?" Caius asked, shaking his head.

"It means we're about to stick our dicks into a spider den, as Halcyon would say," I replied with a sigh, looking at the torn-up dirt.

Thanks to Sierra's explanation, the pieces finally started to come together. The predators had spawned somewhere to the northeast and had spread out from there. When they began to invade the Webwood they would have come this way en-masse, churning and carving up everything in their path.

"We're getting close to the point where the predators *started* to chase the spiderlings. The trees are marred on one side because that's the side they came from."

"And the dirt tells us where they went," Sierra finished with a nod.

"Then that also means we're nearly on top of the ley line," Halcyon stated. "That's probably where the spiderlings...*mutated*...into whatever they are now."

We fell silent for a moment as we digested that bit of information.

"Okay." I exhaled, mentally coming to a decision. "Let's keep following the blood trail, but if we trip over the ley line first, we'll drop the chase and deal with my nemesis another day."

"You sure, Lyr?" Sierra asked.

"Yeah. If we don't do something about the spiders now, we may not get another chance before they hit Aldford again."

"All right." Sierra nodded and motioned us to follow as we broke into a run again, following the puma's blood trail northeast.

"What if your nemesis finds the ley line?" Constantine whispered to me as we ran.

"Shit, don't joke about that!" I gasped, not having considered the possibility.

"Why else would it be going this way?"

"Hopefully because it knows all the spiders are hiding out to the east." My imagination began to take off at the possibility of having to deal with a *mutated* puma as my nemesis.

"Hopefully..." Constantine replied optimistically.

I ran faster.

WE MOVED WITH A NEWFOUND sense of urgency as we jogged through the Webwood, keeping the ridge to our left. Scree and loose rubble slowly began to replace the dirt as the trees thinned, causing our boots to crunch with every stride. Looking up at the ridge I had to guess that there'd been a landslide or something similar recently, or at least *recent* on a geological timeframe, as the soil had yet to reclaim fallen rocks.

Unfortunately the scree and harder surface made tracking the puma more difficult, the blood trail had just about vanished and I had just about given up hope that we would be able to catch it. I was a handful of seconds away from calling a stop to our hunt when Sierra called out.

"There it is!" She broke into a sprint.

Following her line of sight, I spotted a prowling shadow in the distance that took off running at her shout.

"Yes!" My heart boomed in my chest as I drew Razor and charged forward, risking the extra burst of speed on the unstable ground.

You're not getting away this time!

I saw the puma come into focus as I gained speed. A number of the wounds had vanished from the creature, and it no longer freely bled. Based on it not leaving us in the dust, however, I could only assume Sierra's arrow was still slowing it down.

We crashed through the undergrowth of the forest, tearing through low-lying webs, foliage, and branches with ease. I saw Drace simply trample a sapling in his path, tearing it right from the ground as it struck his shoulder, rather than break his stride.

A loud feral yelp had my head snapping quickly forward as I saw an explosion of webs and foliage burst in the distance.

"Shit! I think it just ran into a spider!" I practically shouted at Caius who was struggling to keep pace with me.

"Uh…good! Yeah! We canna staph den!" Caius panted as he struggled to gasp for air.

The sounds of battle quickly greeted my ears as we approached where I had seen the puma vanish. Without pausing to break my stride, I leaped through a scrap of foliage blocking my path and promptly came crashing down on top of my nemesis.

"How do you like me now?" I yelled, masking my surprise as I turned my leap into an awkward tackle, nearly taking off my nose as

Razor whirled by my face. In the split second before I knocked the surprised puma off its feet, I quickly counted six equally surprised Webwood predators surrounding it.

Oh, fuck! I rode my nemesis down on top of a slow-moving predator, flattening the critter to the ground with a crunch. I found myself sitting right on top of the puma's stomach as its paws flailed wildly in the air. *I'm getting a strong déjà vu feeling right about now!*

"Not so much fun when I tackle you out of nowhere, is it?" I shouted at the beast as I slammed Razor's hilt into its face.

Ah! Shit! My leg is pinned! I realized as a sharp stab of pain shot through my knee when I tried to move.

At that moment, Drace entered the battle with a shout, still running at full speed he unleashed a thunderous kick right into a predator's side, sending it sailing high through the air.

"Aw yiss!" Drace exclaimed, taking half a second to admire the predator's flight, before chopping his bladeclaw into a startled predator. "It held up this time! I think I win for longest distance, Lyr!"

The puma went momentarily limp under me as it lay stunned by my blow, leaving me with a moment to admire Drace's epic spider punt. I even had enough time to mentally compose my reply to Drace, which was going to be along the lines of *Awesome kick, man! Care to help me out with this giant cat?*

But at that moment, the two other predators that had evaded getting crushed under the puma rejoined combat.

By leaping right at me.

So unfortunately, my reply to Drace ended up coming out as: "Aaaaaaaaaaaaaaaah!"

One predator landed right on top of my chest, gashing me in the face with its barbed pedipalp as it readied to sink its blade-arms into my back. The other predator, landing on top of the puma, sliced a wicked line across its chin and cheek as it spun to attack the fallen cat. I slammed a hand onto the smooth predator's chitin and shoved it away from me, feeling the predator's blade-arms scrape across my back as it fell away to the ground, but thankfully not piercing my armor.

Then the rest of the party arrived on the scene.

Two arrows slammed into the predator that Drace had already wounded, quickly followed by two blue missiles. Drace followed up with a pair of brutal blows that had the predator disintegrating to dust.

I felt the puma begin to stir under me as my stunning punch wore off, at the same instant the predator I had thrown off me recovered and redoubled its attack. With half my leg still pinned under my nemesis, I awkwardly twisted my body to catch a single gleaming blade on Razor before it could bury itself into my chest but couldn't reach the second one in time.

The predator's blade-arm pierced through my armor and dug deep into my shoulder. Immediately I felt my left arm fall limp as the blade sliced through something important. I screamed as the predator twisted the blade, nearly losing my grip on Razor as the pain shot through my body.

It was then that Constantine burst from the bush, having seen my awkward landing on top of my nemesis. It took half a heartbeat for him to assess the scene, then he quickly sprang into action. A daggerfang shot forth like a bolt of lightning, stabbing deep into the unprotected side of the predator that had stabbed me. Using the blade as leverage, he slid behind the creature and *pulled*, yanking the predator's blade-arm out of my shoulder.

Using the momentum of his maneuver, Constantine brutally shanked his second daggerfang into the creature's back, spraying glowing ichor across him as he repeatedly began stabbing his blade into the creature.

Breathing a sigh of relief as the blade-arm left my shoulder with a faint sucking sound, I barely had enough time for the pain to fade before I felt hot claws pierce through my armor and scrape along my buttocks and lower back. Arching forward away from the pain I saw that the puma had bitten into the predator standing on its chest with both front claws rending massive wounds across the creature's carapace.

Fuck! Time to get off this thing! I kicked off with my good leg, sending myself sprawling on the ground in a burst of pain as I landed on my wounded left shoulder. I felt my trapped leg straighten in relief as I fell, planting a solid kick in the puma's hindquarters as I yanked it free.

With my weight off of it, the puma brought its hind legs into play as it ravaged the predator that it had caught. It tossed the spider into the air like a deadly ball of yarn before catching the creature again in its claws and killing it in a spray of dust.

I quickly scrambled to my feet the same instant that Constantine finished off the predator that he had pulled off of me, taking a step back to fall in beside him I winced as pain flared from the new wounds on my back. While I moved, I heard an echoing thunderclap and the faintest glimpse of magefire as Halcyon's Pyroclap detonated on top of the pair of predators near Drace.

"Lyr!" Constantine shouted seeing the puma roll off of the predator that it had landed on when I tackled it. I saw its head whirl around as it quickly absorbed its surroundings then immediately fixated on Constantine and me, eyes going wide with surprise.

Its gaze darted to the predator that was still struggling to stand, wheels quickly turning in its head. The puma took a quick glance back at us, and swiped out with a paw, scooping the predator up *and batting it right at us.*

Too surprised to react, Constantine and I didn't have any time to avoid the predator before it crashed to the ground in front of us.

"Gah! What—?" My cry was cut off as the rightfully angry predator scrambled to its feet, whirling its massive blade-arms in a circle as it screeched in rage, forcing Constantine and I to take a step backwards.

"Did it just—*urk*—" Constantine's words were cut off as the puma slammed into Constantine's hip, sending him spinning into me and knocking the both of us off balance.

Not bothering to stop, the puma ran past us, fleeing the battle once more as it scrambled towards the ridge.

Damn it! Not again! The thought echoed through my mind as I turned to look where it was running to. *Where the hell is it going? There's nothing there but the Ridge.*

As I turned my head to follow the puma, the entire side of the ridge began to bloom with a dull blue aura. In the distance, about halfway up the incline a single point was noticeably brighter than the rest of the Ridge.

Directly where my nemesis was charging towards.

Oh, fuck! The ley line! My eyes filled with fear as Constantine's earlier words crossed my mind, which then quickly magnified as I realized that my nemesis could *see* magic. *How the hell did it learn that?*

"The ley line is in the Ridge!" I shouted. "The cat is after it!"

"Lyr, fuck! Pay attention!" Constantine barked as I heard a screeching sound, followed by a sharp burst of pain across my arm.

"Ah!" I had completely forgotten about the predator that my nemesis had dumped in our lap, its blade-arm slicing through a gap in my increasingly damaged armor.

Taking my eyes off the fleeing puma, I saw Constantine trap a blade-arm with both his daggerfangs and unleash a violent kick at the base of limb. A sickening crack greeted my ears as the limb fell uselessly to the ground, followed by a loud scream of pain. I took a step wide, moving to flank the predator as Constantine held its attention.

Before I could take a second step a hail of arrows and magic slammed into the creature from behind, the rest of the party having finished off the other Webwood predators.

"Lyrian! Constantine! Go!" Drace shouted as his bladeclaw rent a massive wound across the predator's carapace. "We're right behind you!"

"Okay!" I quickly spun on the ball of my foot and charged after the puma.

"Right behind you, Lyr!" Constantine shouted as he turned to follow me.

Glancing up at the glowing Ridge, I just hoped I wasn't too late.

TWENTY-NINE

I HAD BARELY GIVEN THE RIDGE a second thought while we were hunting for my nemesis, aside from accepting it as a direction the creature couldn't escape to. At first glance, it didn't look any different than the Ridge separating the higher elevation of Aldford, and the lower elevation of Crater Lake. But now, as I burst through the foliage and up the incline, praying that I wouldn't lose my footing on the loose scree, I started catching stray details my mind had missed.

The greatest of these details being that the Ridge near Aldford and Crater Lake had been sheer, almost smooth, in comparison. As if a laser from the sky had perfectly carved a slice through the rocks, leaving no loose rubble or jagged marking across the ridge. Here in the Webwood however, the ridge face looked like it had been beaten into submission by a drunk giant, leaving countless pockmarks and fractures across it, filling the ground with rubble.

There was definitely an avalanche at one point in time here.

"Lyr!" Constantine exclaimed with a gasp. "Are you seeing what I'm seeing?"

"Eh? Nothing but magic and rocks..." I started to say, suppressing Arcane Sight for a moment, the magic auras permeating the area vanishing from my vision. I looked to the spot where I remembered seeing the brightest glow, my eyes widening in surprise. "*Oh!*"

Carved into the side of the rock I saw what had to be at least a thirty-foot statue, rising up from the rubble that came up to its chest, whatever details that it once carried having been long lost to the ravages of time, leaving it smooth and featureless. To its left was an archway that rose just shy of the statue's chin, partially filled with rubble, tattered webs billowing in the air. Flanking the opposite side of the archway was a depression, where I assumed another statue once stood.

"It's like one of those Egyptian tombs or temples that were carved into the side of hills or mountains," I said with awe as my eyes drank in the sight. "Did you see where the puma went?"

"Yeah, it does, doesn't it?" Constantine breathed as we slowed down, before pointing at the web covered archway. "I saw it go inside."

"Shit." We quickly ran over to the mouth of the archway, finding even more webs now covering the rubble at our feet.

Whoever built this place, carved it right out of the rock, the ceiling inside here has to be at least twenty-five feet high!

Peering inside, I saw that the rubble led to a sharp decline that vanished into the darkness. I could make out ragged tears and marks in the webs covering the rubble from something heavy sliding down. "Ugh, that's a long way down. We're going to have to slide down on our asses."

"We should wait for the others," Constantine said, looking behind him and seeing the rest of the party quickly running towards us.

"Definitely, no telling what we'll find in there," I agreed, willing to give my nemesis a head start into the ruin rather than go charging in unprepared.

"Looks like a rockslide or something partially buried this place," Constantine said as he looked around. "If this ceiling wasn't so high, we'd have never known anything was buried under here."

"Yeah." I idly wondered *why* this place needed such a high ceiling as I looked into the gloom. "You know, this is the second ruin I've found in this area."

"Hm?" Constantine looked confused for a moment before he nodded emphatically. "Oh, right! You found that other one closer to Crater Lake. You think they're connected?"

"Don't know," I said with a shrug. "I think there used to be something where Crater Lake is now; the ruin I found had a ton of damage. Maybe whatever was once in the middle of Crater Lake exploded?"

"That would explain the avalanche along the ridge here," Constantine added with a nod. "Shockwaves would travel far."

"Hm, that's true too," I mused, making a mental note to take a second look at the other ruin I had found.

Maybe I'll have time to get to it in five or six days. I thought with a sigh, remembering just *how much* I still had on my to-do list. *Assuming that other adventurers don't fuck up my plans too drastically.*

"Oh, wow!" Drace exclaimed as he and the rest of the party came up to us.

"Shit, my eyes!" Halcyon muttered, clasping a hand over his face, overwhelmed by the magical aura permeating the area. "This place *bleeds* magic."

"Did the puma go inside, Lyr?" Sierra asked, immune to the surprise of the ruin.

"Yeah, Constantine saw it run in. Just wanted to wait for you guys before we rushed in." I quickly took the time to explain the magic aura that I had seen when looking in the area, pointing deeper into the ruins. "I think the ley line is somewhere in here, and judging from the webs, so are a ton of spiders."

"Perfect! We'll skin that cat, squash the critters and stick a Band-Aid on that ley line all in one swoop." Sierra said confidently before quickly looking everyone over. "With any luck, we'll be back in Aldford for a late dinner! Everyone good to move?"

"Ye-yep!" Caius exclaimed as he tried to still catch his breath.

"Ready!" Drace called, having already moved forward, preparing to slide down the rubble.

"Ugh," Halcyon grunted, grudgingly moving to follow Drace.

"Good to go!" I said after seeing Constantine give Sierra a thumbs-up.

"Okay! Get those asses in gear then!" Sierra laughed, seeing Drace slide away into the darkness. "*Literally.*"

ONE RATHER UNCOMFORTABLE SLIDE DOWN the rubble later, we were brushing ourselves off as our eyes slowly adjusted to the sourceless illumination Halcyon's and my Light spell produced.

"Bah! I have rubble everywhere..." Halcyon whispered to himself as he adjusted his pants, unaware his voice was echoing through the massive hall we found ourselves in. "Bad enough I can fucking *taste* the rocks we just slid down..."

"*Ahem.* Caius, can you *hear* anything with your Bloodsense?" I asked while clearing my throat to get everyone's attention.

"Uh...no, just you guys," Caius said, hesitantly at first, then with more confidence after he had a moment to think about it. "It's quiet right now."

"All right, you mind taking the lead for now?" I asked Caius, indicating the darkness ahead of us. "Between your Bloodsense and Night Vision, you're probably the best to catch any dangers before we trip over it."

"Yeah, no worries Lyr!" Caius said with a smile. "Happy to help."

With weapons in hand and Caius in the lead, we pushed further into the ruins. The hall was easily twenty feet wide, allowing us to walk without any concern of bumping into one another, each of us straining to catch a whisper of a spider's feet or the soft patter of the puma's paws. As we moved deeper into the ruin, the rubble and webs that covered the entrance gradually disappeared, leaving a smooth and even floor with matching chiseled walls.

"This place was well cared for at one point," I said, running my hand along the smooth wall. "Busy place too, look at the floor."

Having moved away from the rubble, I now saw that the smoothness of the floor went beyond simple chiseling. It was gradually worn and smoothed from the repeated passage of hundreds, maybe thousands of feet over a long period of time.

"Wonder what this place was," Sierra whispered, looking around in the gloom. "No carvings on the wall or anything like that, so probably not a temple or tomb."

We continued walking down the massive hall for another fifty feet or so until Caius held up a hand.

"More rubble ahead and…a pair of stairs?" he said, slightly confused as we cautiously approached. "Oh, darn! They're blocked."

Bisecting the hallway was a pair of stairs facing one another, which at one point in time must have led to an upper level in the ruin. Today, they both overflowed with rubble, spilling out into the hall.

There's no way anything could have gone up those stairs, I noted as we walked by, a part of me greatly relieved that nothing could be sneaking down the stairs behind us once we passed by.

Continuing onwards, we picked our way through the broken rocks, moving further down the hall. We had barely traveled ten feet past the stairs before Caius spoke again.

"Huh, the walls are gone," he whispered quietly. "A massive chamber is coming up ahead, I can't even see the far wall."

Without any noticeable warning, the hallway we had been walking in had widened into a monstrously huge chamber, the stone walls that had flanked us widening and vanishing into the darkness beyond the meager radius that my Light spell covered. The ground in front of us began to slope downwards, forming a small ramp that joined the chamber floor.

"Caius, what do you see?" I asked the warlock somewhat nervously. "More importantly, what do you *hear?*"

"Just you guys, nothing else," Caius replied, scanning the darkness carefully as he took few steps down the ramp. "But, I see...*statues?* Of spiders, I think. All in the center of the room, hell of a lot of them. Big ones too."

"Statues?" I frowned, confused. *Why would there be a room full of spider statues here?* "What do you mean?"

"I don't know, they haven't moved, and I can't hear them...so, statues." Caius had walked to the edge of my Light spell, holding a hand up for us to wait at the base of the ramp. "Oh! That's so weird..."

"A little bit more explanation would be great, Caius," I called out to him impatiently, deciding to reactivate Arcane Sight for a quick glimpse around the room.

"There's a statue of a man here, along with...a goblin?" Caius sounded confused as he vanished into the darkness. "Oh, shit! Is that a—"

Brilliant magical auras snapped into existence as my Arcane Sight overlaid itself on my vision, causing me to flinch for a split second as the rest of the party shouted out Caius's name and began to move forward to his rescue.

"Wait!" I shouted as the magical auras came into focus, the party halting in their tracks, just a few feet shy of a bright crescent of magic that was embedded into the floor, stretching across the entire room, or at least as far as my vision could see. "There's a magic circle right by your feet! Don't cross it!"

I quickly moved towards the foot thick, glowing aura on the ground, finding an intricate design carved onto the floor. "There's a design here!"

"I see it too," Halcyon said, having re-activated his Arcane Sight too. "What the hell happened to him? I can still feel him via party sense."

"I don't know." I looked towards Constantine and Sierra. "You guys have low light vision—can you see him at all?"

"Uh." Constantine came right up to the line, peering into the darkness. "Yeah, I see him just over there."

"He's frozen...mid-stride," Sierra spoke slowly, slightly confused at what she was seeing. "It's like he's paralyzed?"

"He should have fallen down then," Constantine said shaking his head. "One foot is halfway in the air as he's walking forward."

The magic aura in the floor began to fade.

"The magic is fading!" Halcyon exclaimed as he quickly scanned the area.

"Shit." All traces of magic had quickly faded, leaving the room pitch dark to my magical vision once more.

Why isn't this room bleeding magic?

"Caius still isn't moving," Sierra said with a bit of worry in her voice. "I think whatever sort of trap this is just reset itself."

"Well, fuck." I cursed, rubbing my face, thinking quickly. "Okay, Sierra, come with me. Let's take a circuit around this room. The rest of you hold up here. We'll use your light as a reference point for where we are."

"You heard him mention something about a man and goblin?" Drace spoke softly. "You think there'll be trouble?"

"I think we're not the only people to fall into this trap," I said with a sigh.

"Seems like it." Drace agreed. "Be careful. If there's trouble, we'll come running."

Keeping an eye on the carved design that ran along the floor, Sierra and I followed it as it curved south, keeping it on our right-hand side.

"The walls here are rougher," I said, seeing the jagged, coarse walls gleam in the meager illumination that my Light spell produced. "They didn't smooth out the walls in this chamber, this looks like it used to be a natural cave that was carved out."

"Maybe they didn't have time," Sierra answered with a shrug, squinting into the darkness ahead. "Hrm, more rubble ahead."

As we reached what I expected to be the southern-most portion of the magic circle, we found that a large portion of the southern wall and ceiling had collapsed, sending tons of debris and stone to the ground and burying the carvings that we had been following. Continuing on would mean climbing through the rubble and hoping that it didn't trigger the magical trap.

"Damn," Sierra cursed as the mess became clearer. "No idea where the circle is now, should we turn back?"

"Hm, do you see any of those statues Caius was talking about?"

"Hm?" Sierra squinted into the darkness again. "My eyes aren't as good as his, but no. I don't see anything at all."

"It should be safe enough to cross. We'll just have to be careful," I said, moving towards the rubble.

"What are you hoping to find Lyrian?" Sierra asked with a bit of exasperation creeping into her voice.

"Don't know." I shrugged as I stepped out onto a rock. "I'll know it when I see it."

"Of course, how silly of me."

We gingerly climbed and picked our way through the fallen debris, moving slowly to ensure that Sierra could keep up with my Light spell, which was centered on me. We had only climbed for a short distance when a wispy blue aura appeared near the ceiling, followed by another one in the distance, but at ground level.

"There's something magical up there." I pointed into the dark, forgetting for a moment that Sierra couldn't see magic the same as me, but then remembering she had better low light vision. "And another one further ahead."

"Hm, I see something faintly shiny? Glass, maybe, or crystal," Sierra replied looking towards the ceiling where I had pointed, moving her head side to side as she tried to catch a reflection in her eye. "Want me to try shooting it?"

"Let's take a look at that other magic source first, I don't know what shooting at it may do." I shook my head at Sierra's question.

"All righty."

We continued to climb along the rubble, trying to hug the collapsed wall as close as possible and eventually made our way through to the other side. Back on solid ground once more, I quickly found the intricate carvings of the magic circle and we resumed following it as it began to curve back towards north. Taking a glimpse backwards, I could see a faint glow from Halcyon's Light spell as the rest of the party waited for our return.

This room is pretty big, I thought as I walked towards the other magical aura that I had spotted. *I can't imagine what they could have used this room for...*

Almost at the exact opposite side of the room from where we had arrived, we found another ramp, this one leading downwards, even deeper into the ruins. Flanking the ramp on both sides was a carved stone railing, likely intended to prevent unwary individuals from simply walking off the edge and falling down the gentle slope.

My attention, however, was drawn to a small box carved out of the wall that held three fist-sized crystals cut into a diamond shape, suspended on their points, blazing with magic.

"This looks promising," Sierra commented. "Is this the magic aura you saw before?"

"Yeah." I nodded as I moved towards it, stepping over scattered chunks of stone. "All three of them are glowing, maybe they're switches of some kind?"

"Your guess is as good as mine. Give it a poke," Sierra suggested with a shrug, indicating my sword. "What's the worst that can happen? It's probably here for a reason."

Reaching out I gently tapped the crystals with Razor. They didn't budge in the slightest or react in any way that I could perceive.

"Maybe by hand?" I said, thinking out loud and reached out to touch one of the crystals. Placing a finger on it at first and then followed by my entire palm.

Even through my glove, the crystal felt warm to the touch. Carefully, I grasped the crystal and tried to pull it free of its place, to no avail.

"I have no idea what I'm even supposed to be doing," I told Sierra as I grabbed the next crystal in line, trying the same thing, with the same result.

Sighing, I touched the third crystal and instantly felt a shock of electricity shoot up my arm.

"Ow! Shit!" I cursed as my arm spasmed momentarily, letting go of the crystal.

The entire chamber suddenly lit up, completely bathed in a sourceless light.

"Hey! That worked!" Sierra exclaimed, giving me a playful punch in the shoulder. "Good job!"

Without warning, a thunderous cacophony of voices echoed

through the chamber.

TRANSLOCATION GRID INACTIVE
WARNING: ÆTHERWARPED LIFEFORMS PRESENT
DISENGAGING TEMPORTAL LOCK
EXECUTING PURGE PER STANDING ORDER #66

"I take that back!" Sierra looked at me, eyes wide open in shock. "What did you do?"

I didn't answer Sierra right away, my mouth working to find the words while I pointed towards the middle of the room. "Those weren't statues Caius saw, Sierra. Those were creatures frozen in time."

THERE WAS A SINGLE INSTANT of silence before all hell broke loose. To me, the instant stretched on endlessly, lasting years, decades, centuries even, as my brain moved with the glacial awareness of a brain that completely and irrevocably knew *that it had somehow just screwed up.*

Looking out into the massive chamber, I saw row after row of spiders snap back to life, continuing their stride as if nothing had happened. Some were just lowly spiderlings, others were the more formidable giant spiders.

Were it just those creatures alone, I wouldn't have worried as much.

But as pale blue auras from dozens of aberrations, predators, and even larger shapes started to appear, my stomach did a flip.

Oh…this is going to suck. I tapped Sierra on the arm as I started to sprint the way we'd come, not caring whether I crossed over the magic circle at this point. "Back to the party!"

The room exploded into shrieks of surprise, and dozens upon dozens of spiders found themselves surprised by countless others of their species. Recovering with blinding speed, I saw a quartet of predators launch themselves at a cluster of spiderlings easily five times their number, tearing through a dozen of them in the blink of an eye. A trio of giant spiders instinctively moved to aid the overrun spiderlings but were in turn assaulted by a small horde of aberrations.

As Sierra and I ran, I saw the scene magnify as normal spiders quickly ganged up on top of the mutated ones and the mutated spiders quickly returning the favor.

"They're fighting one another!" Sierra slowed not to outpace me. "We have a chance to get out! Let's find Caius and let them fight it out!"

"What about the man and goblin he saw?"

"Fuck it! Let them die!" Sierra sliced her hand through the air. "They probably started all this shit!"

"But—" My sentence was cut off as a burst of fire caught the corner of my eye, followed quickly by several flashes of light. Primal reflexes kicked in, turning my head towards the source of the disruption. Standing near the center of the room, I saw the man squaring off with the goblin.

In his hands he held whips of molten fire, slashing them furiously at the goblin, having them glance harmlessly off a translucent shield surrounding it. The goblin held one hand up high, while another was holding something I couldn't make out.

Did we just walk into a fucking mage duel on top of a spider war?

"Sierra! They—" I started to say.

"I see it, Lyr! What the fuck did we stumble into?" Sierra gasped as a bolt of lightning shot from the goblin's hand, forcing the human mage to roll out of the way.

ACTIVATING FIRE SWEEP CONTAINMENT

"What?" Sierra and I stared at one another in confusion as the voice thundered through the air once more. "Fire sweep?"

What kind of place is this?

A massive wall of fire erupted from the ground ahead of us, stretching from the center of the magic circle to the outer edge, trapping us on the inside of the magic circle. Flinching from the sudden burst of heat in front of us and to our right, we ground to a halt in surprise. Before we could acknowledge our way out being taken away from us, the wall of fire started to move.

Towards us!

"Oh, fuck!" I shouted with instant understanding. "Fire sweep!"

"Lyr! Backwards and towards the middle!" Sierra yelled, yanking my arm. "Move!"

Spinning on our heels, Sierra and I turned to sprint diagonally towards the middle as the massive wall of fire began to move. The wall had barely traveled six feet before I saw it claim a cluster of spiders, sending them bursting into flames as they flailed wildly before being consumed by the fire.

You've done this before, Lyr! I told myself as I ran. *It's just like the countless raids you've done before. Just stay out of the fire!*

Propelled by desperation and the sheer animal desire of *not wanting to be on fire,* Sierra and I tore through the pre-occupied breeds of spiders warring between one another, quickly finding ourselves at the heart of the chamber just past where the wall of fire ended.

Here I finally caught a proper glimpse of the mage and goblin as they continued to battle one another, oblivious to the chaos that raged around them.

I noted that the man was a human of an olive complexion, and reasonably young-looking too, perhaps only in his early to mid-thirties. His head was a mop of thick brown hair with a matching full beard. He appeared to have haphazardly dressed himself before somehow making his way to this chamber, wearing a thin, white undershirt with the sleeves cut off, loosely tucked into a pair of brown, travel-worn leather pants, which in turn were tucked into a similarly colored pair of leather boots.

First guess tells me that he didn't come here willingly. My eyebrows shot up in surprise as the man tossed a whip at the goblin, only to have it turn into a fiery snake the moment it left his hand.

The snake shattered the translucent shield that the goblin had conjured, forcing it to backpedal quickly. The goblin quickly traced a symbol in the air before touching its throat and exhaling directly at the snake. A magically aided burst of frost coated the flaming serpent, putting it out instantly. The goblin hissed as it made eye contact with Sierra and I, but quickly focused its attention back on the mage.

"Lyr, the goblin! It's blue!" Sierra noted with surprise.

Dressed in a patchwork array of furs and leather, I quickly noted that the goblin's coloration was indeed a pale sky color, a stark contrast from the grey-green skin the goblins invading Aldford had. Furthermore, despite the furs adding quite a bit of bulk to the goblin's stature, I had to guess it was easily twice the size of a normal goblin.

In its hands, the goblin wielded a length of bone, quickly twirling it in its hand as it conjured a trio of purple glowing balls. With a flourish of the wand, the glowing missiles shot forth, each of them divided between the mage, Sierra, and myself.

"Ah, shit! Aggro!" I leaned forward on the balls of my feet, starting to move towards the goblin, cursing that I had been caught standing still. I dared a glance at the mage, who in turn looked stunned to find other people nearby.

"Who the fuck are you people?" I heard him shout as the purple orb quickly closed towards me, suddenly splitting into three more orbs as they picked up speed, slamming into me before I had a chance to dodge.

A [Blue Goblin Shaman]'s Spirit Bolt strikes you for 26 points of damage!

A [Blue Goblin Shaman]'s Spirit Bolt strikes you for 29 points of damage!

A [Blue Goblin Shaman]'s Spirit Bolt strikes you for 32 points of damage!

"Aaaah!" I yelled in pain as the bolt of energy sliced through my armor, cooking my flesh. A similar scream behind me told me Sierra fared no better.

Ignoring the mage I charged the goblin shaman, now drawn into whatever conflict they had between one another. *At least the other mage didn't just outright shoot me! That earns him the benefit of the doubt for now!*

"TRAIN TO MIDDLE!" Drace's voice boomed over the chaos of battle. The words immediately sent my brain into red alert, adrenaline shooting through my body in response. Years of gaming instinct had my head snapping toward Drace's voice.

Somehow, the rest of the party had not only managed to also get trapped inside the magical circle but had also managed to somehow aggro the entirety of the spider horde in their immediate proximity as they attempted to escape from a similar moving wall of fire. To further add to my surprise, I saw my nemesis keeping pace directly beside Drace.

"CHOO-CHOO! THE PAIN TRAIN COMING THROUGH!" Drace continued to bellow as he sprinted past the outer edge of the Fire Wall. "NEXT STOP, ANYWHERE BUT HERE! OH GOD, SOMEONE SAVE ME!"

"Who the fuck are you people?" I heard the mage shout again in panic as he saw the party break through one of the several, clockwise rolling walls of fire, which now divided the outer edges of the magic circle into five different sections. "Where the *hell* did all these spiders come from? What the hell is happening?"

Ignoring the screaming mage, I fervently signaled Drace towards the goblin shaman while yelling, "Goblin is not on our team!"

"Right!" he yelled as he shifted his sprint to intercept the surprised shaman, who had literally seen him just burst from a wall of fire.

I then noticed the puma peeling away from Drace's side, as it cut through the middle of the room, running ahead of another wall of fire as it attempted to find safety away from the growing chaos the middle had to offer in another pocket of spiders.

"Incoming!" Constantine's voice shouted out, "From everywhere!"

Driven by wild instinct, the assembled hordes of spiders had all attempted to flee the spinning walls of fire by running towards the single spot where they saw safety, the middle. Some, already far too wounded to run fast enough to escape the wall's relentless passage, burnt to ashes as it passed over them. Others, too slow to start moving, found themselves trampled by their brethren, leaving them stunned or maimed allowing the burning wall to claim them as well.

Thankfully for us, that only left the quick and the lucky descending upon us, our lives becoming flashes of terror intermixed with copious amounts of blood and ichor.

My scope of the battle quickly shrank to the reach of my blade as I swung Razor in a desperate attempt to keep the horde of spiders at bay. At one point I felt Constantine fall in beside me, quickly followed by Sierra.

I caught a brief glimpse of Drace catching a bolt of lightning on his shield before punching the goblin shaman in the mouth with the hilt of his blade. A repeated thunderclap of magefire caught my attention as Halcyon and Caius shared a desperate defense with the unnamed mage, barely fifteen feet away from us.

I kicked out at a keening aberration, sending it sailing a short distance before it impacted another trio of aberrations and exploded with a vicious *splort*, quickly setting off a chain reaction as a pair of the aberrations erupted in sympathy, quickly followed by the third.

Chaos roamed everywhere I looked, seeing normal spiders wage a brutal war against the mutated kind. I had long since lost any semblance of *what* was happening in battle, just trying to focus on my tiny little pocket as we slowly edged our formation towards the trio of mages.

"Break forward!" I ordered, seeing a gap form in the chaos of creatures that would allow us to bring the mages within our defensive reach. Caius, seeing our advance, laid down a stream of fire from his hands to keep our path clear.

Constantine and I effortlessly cut through a cluster of singed Webwood spiderlings, the weakened creatures far too overwhelmed to stand up to us. We fell into a defensive circle around the mages, finally giving them a moment to catch their breaths from the constant flow of battle.

"Who the hell are you people?" The unknown mage repeated for a third time, breathing heavily just behind my ear.

"We're adventurers!" I shouted over the chaos, a marauding predator unwilling to give me a moment to turn my head and talk politely. "Pleased to meet you! Perhaps introductions can wait until this is all sorted out?"

"Yes! On second thought, I think that may be prudent!" the mage shouted back as I threw a ball of fire at a giant spider that lumbered close by.

ACTIVATING LIGHTNING NOVA

The ground under us suddenly pulsed blue, eliciting a cry of surprise from myself, Halcyon and the mage.

"You've got to be kidding me!" Halcyon voice shrilled over the sounds of combat. "We need to fucking move! Back out into the fire!"

"Drace! We need to get out of the middle!" I shouted at the warrior. "Finish it off and let's go! We need a trail!"

"No!" The unnamed mage shouted. "I need the creature alive! It attacked my camp!"

Wait, what? I cocked my head backwards to take a look at the mage for a split instant and then it clicked. *Shit! He must have been part of the expedition!*

"Drace!" I shouted, "Move!"

"Raaaah!" Drace roared as he kicked the goblin shaman to the ground, sending it skidding out of the circle. "Going to need some heals after this!"

Drace launched himself into a run as he thundered towards us. He didn't stop for anything in his path as the ground began to crackle with the smell of ozone, stomping a spiderling flat with a wet squishing sound. "Fall in!"

Continuing to gain speed, Drace charged through a wall of spiders with the relentless fury of a linebacker, crunching through anything and everything in his path. Fueled by necessity, he absorbed blows against his body, ignored wicked cuts that gouged his limbs, and forced himself to continue on as his blood began to boil from half a dozen venomous bites.

"Go! Go! Go!" I shouted the instant that Drace blazed a path.

"But—"The mage began, looking towards the goblin.

"Go, you idiot!" I shouted shoving the mage ahead of me. "Can't do shit if you're dead!"

There was barely fifteen feet left to go before I felt my hair rise up under my helmet, the charge building up in the air. An explosion of light flashed behind me.

Aw, shit, this is going to—

You have been hit by [Lightning Nova] for 294 points of damage!
You have been stunned!

I slammed into the ground face first, skidding to a halt just shy of Drace's feet.

"Shit, Lyr!" Sierra shouted, bending down to check on my trembling form. "Are you okay?"

"Fuck, man!" Constantine was right behind her. "How hard is it to stay out of AoE?"

"F-f-f-f-fuck y-y-y-ou, s-s-crub!" I stammered out as the aftershocks left my body twitching as nerves continued to misfire.

"See? He's doing great!" Constantine smiled as he stooped to help me up. "Bit salty, though."

ACTIVATING FIRE SWEEP PHASE TWO

"Oh, fuck! There's that voice again!" Halcyon shouted. "What the fuck caused it to go crazy?"

"Lyr touched a switch." Sierra helpfully supplied.

"Lyr, why?" Constantine asked.

"S-S-Seemed like a good idea to do at the time," I replied somewhat defensively. "Plus, Caius was trapped."

"You're the one responsible for this?" The mage asked with wide eyes. "Why did you touch things you didn't understand?"

"That sure doesn't sound like 'Thanks for getting me out of a Temporal Lock,'" I started to say hotly before Sierra cut us off.

"Measure your dicks later! We need to move! It spawned a second set of fire walls moving counterclockwise!"

"Back to the middle!" Drace yelled wearily as he pointed ahead. "Critters here are realizing they can't keep ahead of the wall anymore!"

Faced with two colliding walls of fire the remaining horde of spiders had turned to flee towards the center.

Right at us.

"Well, we know how this song and dance goes," I said, grabbing Razor off the ground as I checked my health, finding myself just below fifty percent. *Going to have to be more careful!*

"Shall we mosey back to the middle?"

"You people are *insane*." The mage looked at us incredulously. "You are far too cavalier with your lives!"

"Pff…" Caius waved a hand dismissively as we began to move. "This is just another Wednesday for us."

"Caius, it's Friday," Sierra deadpanned.

"Oh," Caius said with a bit of surprise. "That explains *everything* then doesn't it?"

"Wait!" the man hissed. "It's Friday today?"

"All day long." Caius nodded helpfully.

"But—" I didn't hear the rest of the chronologically challenged mage's reply as I ran ahead towards the center of the chamber again.

"Caius, fix Drace up when you have a chance! I'm going to need a spot of healing too!" I called out, seeing the goblin shaman charge into the relative safety of the middle, looking worse for wear.

With my puma half a step behind it.

"Oh, this is going to get dicey," I muttered, seeing the puma leap at the goblin shaman, quickly followed by hordes of spiders that had begun to flood into the relative safety of the middle, trying to get away from the colliding walls of fire.

"Stay close to the fire's edge and move with it!" Drace called out as the rest of the party moved. "If we need to dip out again, we won't be running far."

Following Drace's lead, we slowly walked ourselves along the edge of a rotating wall of fire, hoping that any fleeing creatures would give us a wide berth as they passed.

"How do we finish this?" Halcyon called out as he channeled his shield, protecting our flank.

"Wait it out?" Caius suggested as he reached out to slap a fleeing spiderling, reaving the life out of it as it passed.

"How about option number two?" Halcyon yelled, rocking back on his heels as spiders glanced off his barrier. "Anyone?"

"Lyr! What about the magic crystal you saw up here?" Sierra called out, pointing upwards. "Maybe we can start shooting at it now?"

"Uh." I stalled as I looked towards the ceiling, seeing it for the first time in the light.

The roof bulged ever so slightly inwards forming a dome, perfectly aligned with the center of the chamber. Set into the sides of the dome, I noticed four large depressions. Three were empty, glistening with what appeared to be shattered glass. In the fourth, however, was a large crystal, cut into a similar diamond shape as the others I had seen previously. It burned with a near white tint of blue, leaving afterimages in my eyes as I looked away.

"Crystal?" The nameless mage looked up to the ceiling, spotting the glowing shard. "Yes! That shard must be channeling magic for the circle!"

"Good enough for me!" Sierra shouted as she powerfully drew back her bow, aiming nearly straight up and firing an arrow. "Halcyon, Caius, and whatever your name is! Help me out with this!"

"Lyr! Swap out!" Halcyon called as he moved to follow Sierra's orders.

Wearily, I filled Halcyon's spot as our mages began to rain a flurry of magical energy upwards at the crystal anchoring the chamber's defense. Once more my world shrank into a mechanical array of parries, cuts, and scything limbs, losing the goblin shaman and puma in the chaos of battle. As the fight raged on, the horde began to dwindle, giving my beleaguered lungs a chance to suck in air and recover the precious stamina I hadn't realized I was missing.

I was about to shout out for an update when the broken cacophony of voices echoed out again, even more, distorted than before.

A-A-ACTIVATING L-LIGHT-LIGHTNING N-N-NOOOV-

"It's working!" Halcyon shouted, throwing another blue bolt up into the air.

"Move!" Constantine shouted as we timed our step out of the middle once again.

This time, there was no buildup of electricity as the circle flared with magical energy or the warning smell of ozone before the nova detonated itself. Without any sort of warning at all, a thunderous clap of magefire sprayed over the center of the chamber with so much force that it knocked all of us off our feet, sending us sprawling across the ground.

I saw brilliant shards of crystal rain down from the ceiling as a massive arc of blue lightning discharged itself along the walls and ground, gouging scars everywhere it touched. Then just as quickly as it had started, it was over, the walls of fire winking out, the room immediately beginning to dim.

Phew. My mind echoed with relief as I took a deep breath, rolling onto my back.

"Well…" Drace groaned as he sat up. "That was a ton of fun. Let's never do it again."

THIRTY

"WHERE IS IT?" THE MAGE was the first on his feet, with me not far behind. "The goblin! I need to catch it! If five days have truly passed…"

He scanned the rapidly dimming room urgently, trying to see where the goblin shaman had ended up after the blast. My eyes scanned the room eagerly as well, though in my case, trying to spot the puma before it could escape. I didn't know what had happened during the battle, but I was certain that the puma had taken a bite out of the goblin at one point.

A flash of violet light from across the chamber cast the room into a brief purple haze, silhouetting a pair of shadows across the far wall.

"There!" the mage and I both shouted, breaking into a run. "Let's go!"

We stared at each other in surprise for a moment, before the mage finally asked. "You! What is your name?"

"Lyrian, Lyrian Rastler!" I shouted back at the mage, already suspecting who he was. "Yours?"

"Donovan Kaine!"

"I think the puma is after the ley line!" I shouted back at him. "It's possessed by some sort of intelligence."

"Goblins attacked my camp while we searched for the ley line! I don't know what happened to them!" he shouted back.

By this point, the goblin and puma had noticed our reckless charge towards them. Sparing a quick glance at one another, forming a temporary truce, they turned about and ran deeper into the ruins.

"Damn it!" I cursed, seeing the pair fade away into the growing darkness as they descended down the ramp that Sierra and I had spotted what seemed like a lifetime ago. "Why. Does. Everything. Keep. Running?"

With Donovan and me leading the charge and the rest of the party not far behind, we charged across the chamber, my Light spell faithfully illuminating the way. We quickly began to descend down the ramp, moving deeper into the ruins. The moment that I stepped out of the massive chamber, the walls began to glow with a bright blue energy once more. Blinking my eyes quickly, I dismissed Arcane Sight before I tripped over something I couldn't clearly see.

As we ran down the ramp, we found that gentle plateaus had been cut in the decline, leveling out our descent every twenty feet or so, likely used to ensure that anyone losing their footing, wouldn't continue to gain speed as they tumbled their way down the passage.

Doorways and passages flanked the sides of each level we descended, expanding the ruin deeper into the ridge. At first, I noted that the passageways were blocked with rubble, having completely collapsed from the same event that affected the upper levels, but as we delved deeper, more of the passages gaped ominously unaffected by whatever caused the others to collapse.

"A light!" Donovan gasped, somewhat winded from the sprint.

Ahead, a brilliant blue light spilled from the final level of the ramp with scattered bits of rubble littering the floor. In addition to the rubble, I noted the tattered remains of webby cocoons and egg sacs scattered everywhere, even stuck to the walls.

The instant that Donovan and I stepped onto the final level of the ruin, into the blue light, a nauseous feeling struck my stomach, followed by the onset of a headache.

You have entered an area permeated with Æther!
You are affected by [Æther Sickness] for 1 point of damage.
You are affected by [Æther Sickness] for 1 point of damage.

"Ugh." I heard Donovan slow with a grunt as the symptoms hit him full force. "What...?"

Squinting ahead as my eyes adjusted to the brilliant glow, I saw the goblin shaman and puma just ahead, focused on something I couldn't make out. The passage had opened into yet another larger room, greatly dwarfing the massive chamber above.

"Come on, Donovan." I tugged on the flagging mage's arm. "We're almost there."

A massive roar echoed through the chamber, clenching my heart with such an existential dread I was certain that I had wet myself both in game and in reality. I even saw both goblin and puma fall to the ground in terror.

"What the hell was that?" Halcyon screamed as the party came charging down the ramp.

Stumbling forward I saw the goblin desperately begin to push itself backwards, struggling to both stand up and get away from the puma while something massive came at them. Reacting faster, the puma twisted, biting deep into the goblin's leg before it sprinted forwards, deeper into the room.

"Nooo!" Donovan screamed as a *massive* claw stabbed through the goblin, pinning it right to the floor, a second claw quickly skewering it from the other side. The mage ran forward into the room, intent on somehow rescuing the goblin.

"Donovan! Stop!" I chased the mage, having missed my chance to grab him.

I arrived into the room just in time to see a living nightmare pluck the struggling goblin off the ground, my mind at first refusing to accept what it was seeing. Whatever type of spider this once was before it had made its home here, in the bowels of this æther-filled room had long since changed. It was mutated grotesquely, almost beyond comprehension. No longer mobile, it was fused with the stone floor of the room, its flesh glowing with arcane energy as its corpulent form straddled a brilliant river of energy that had cut a chasm through the stone floor.

Gone were most of the creature's limbs, leaving only the two massive claws that held the helpless goblin impaled on them. Lifting the hapless creature to its tooth filled maw, dozens of flame red eyes regarded it for a heartbeat before it *crunched* on the goblin whole. Its deformed chest writhing as it swallowed the creature, the thick leathery skin barely able to keep itself from tearing apart.

Immediately the creature's name came up in my vision.

[Ætherwarped Webwood Queen – Boss – Level 11]

A boss creature! I gasped as I saw the tag appear. *That has to be the ley line under it, filled with…raw magic!*

"Damn it!" Donovan yelled with despair as the goblin disappeared into the queen's gullet. "Fuuuuck!"

"Quiet!" I hissed, grabbing the mage by the shoulder, while craning my head around, having lost sight of my nemesis in the split instant that it had taken me to chase after Donovan.

Looking around the room, I spotted nothing but countless more empty egg sacs everywhere I looked, not finding the puma anywhere in sight.

"This...is what we came for?" Drace gasped, terror intermixing with disbelief. "This...*queen?*"

"There isn't enough fire in the world to kill this," Halcyon whimpered, eyes wide, taking a step backwards. "Oh...nope, nope, nope."

"Hey! Where are you going?" Sierra shouted, giving Halcyon a slap. "Focus! You can do this!"

"Whatever I did in a previous life, I am *so sorry,*" Halcyon muttered while rubbing a red mark on his face. "Okay...let's do this. Then I can start therapy."

"We're running out of time!" Constantine hissed. "I feel like I'm ready to throw up everything I've ever eaten!"

"Okay!" Drace shouted, working up his own confidence before sprinting at the queen. "Let's do this!"

"All out!" I shouted, quickly moving to follow Drace. "Don't hold anything back! We need to kill the bug before the æther kills us!"

"Watch your spells!" Donovan suddenly shouted the instant that I had run past him, snapping out of his despair. "This place is full of raw äther! They will have unpredictable effects!"

Oh, shit! Like we need those sorts of complications!

"Oh, no!" I heard Halcyon yell as a strobing ball of multicolored light corkscrewed through the air towards the queen, slapping weakly across the creature's body, exploding like a fluffy snowball. "Shit!"

The spot then erupted with a fountain of glowing ichor.

"On second thought—oh, yeah!"

Wailing in pain, the queen's eyes fixated on us, as if noticing us for the first time, her massive scythe-claws slicing out toward Drace, Constantine and me as we charged towards her.

"She has a fixed reach!" I shouted as I leaped over one claw and rolled under the second. I heard a shout of pain as the massive claw struck Drace. "Get in close and she won't be able to attack us!"

As if hearing my words, six balls of blue energy coalesced in front of the queen's face, shooting out towards Drace, Constantine, and myself.

"Oh, maybe not!" I quickly cursed myself for jinxing the fight, paying the price as one of the orbs slammed into me.

A [Ætherwarped Webwood Queen] hits you with [Arcane Bolt] for 34 (40) points of damage!

Oh, thank you resistances for blunting that, even a little bit! I winced as the bolt sent me down to just over fifty percent of my total health, kicking myself for not having found a way to heal in between fights. *Deal with it best you can!*

A few strides more had me practically on top of the Webwood queen, leaving me staring upwards at the humungous bulk that stretched nearly twenty feet tall. *How the fuck do I even attack this thing?*

I saw a pair of arrows thud high into the creature's throat, Sierra able to easily pepper the creature from a distance. The beast cried in pain as it withdrew a massive claw, holding it in front of its face as a shield to Sierra's arrows. To Sierra's credit, she adjusted by lowering her aim to shoot into the creature's deformed abdomen, though for some reason the arrows didn't cause the beast as much pain.

"Lyr! Boost!" Constantine's voice snapped me back into the present, quickly turning to see Constantine running right at me.

"Right!" Following whatever Constantine had planned, I quickly fell to one knee, dropping Razor to the ground as I interlaced my fingers. "Ready!"

Constantine stomped into my hands at a full sprint, and at the same instant I heaved to throw him into the sky. Leaping through the air like a flying praying mantis, Constantine sailed under the defending claw and slammed into the bulk of the warped queen, burying his daggerfangs right up to the hilt in the creature's abdomen.

Digging his knees into the roiling skin, Constantine yanked downwards, rending a massive hole in the queen's gut as the skin tore with ease. Black bile began to pour from the glowing wound, covering the creature's front as Constantine pulled his daggerfangs free, landing on his feet.

I think he's onto something here!

Picking up my blade, I charged at the creature, burying it halfway into the lower half of the queen's abdomen and began to saw upwards, more bile gushing out at my feet. Out of habit, I cast Shocking Touch, only to have the spell fizzle as it came apart.

Stupid, æther distortion! I swore as a second cast simply caused my hand to flicker with a green light then vanish. *Fuck!*

"Move, Lyr!" Drace barked his voice barely masking pain. "Coming through!"

With barely a second thought, I tore Razor from the creature's belly, stepping to the side as Drace leaped at the queen with his bladeclaw held high over his head. My eye noted that Drace was missing the upper third of his shield, along with a fair chunk of his shoulder.

That didn't stop the half-giant warrior from quite literally splitting the queen in two. Drace's bladeclaw caught the lower lip of the tear that Constantine had started in the creature's abdomen and aided by his strength and weight, carved straight through the leathery skin to the weeping wound I had just torn Razor from.

The result had the queen's abdomen splitting open like a ripe fruit as it erupted with rotting viscera and bile. The torrent of black liquid washed over Drace and I, sweeping the both of us off our feet as the queen's bulging abdomen rapidly shrank, Constantine somehow being fortunate enough to get out of the way.

I splashed through the vile liquid, my stomach instantly clenching to vomit so hard I was concerned I would shatter my spine. I rolled over, trying to find some way I could wipe my face clean before I threw up a second time.

"Drace…" I called his name, loud enough to be heard over the wounded screams of the queen.

"Yeah, Lyr?" Drace gurgled, clearly affected the same way.

"Fuck you."

"Heh. Yeah." Drace spat to clear his mouth. "Fuck me…I saw that going differently in my head."

Pushing myself off the floor and onto my feet, I felt them skid on the loose spider entrails covering the ground, my gorge rising in response.

Just kill the queen, then you can throw up all you want and maybe burn this armor, I started to repeat to myself as I squished through the gore.

Looking back at the Webwood queen, she now looked like a deflated balloon, her chest split right open, exposing a huge empty cavity within the creature that glowed a bright blue.

The magic was rotting her from the inside out. My eye noticed something moving rhythmically inside the cavity. *Holy shit! Is that her heart?*

Engorged beyond belief, the massive heart pulsed urgently, sending glowing blue blood throughout the creature's body.

"By the Father…" I heard Donovan retch.

"Shoot the heart!" I shouted while pointing.

"Fucking, magic isn't doing—" Caius shouted right before a brilliant red line shot from his palm, scarring the wall behind the queen, then a portion of her head before winking out. "Shit! How do I do that again?!"

"Someone fucking help me!" Halcyon was stuck levitating a foot off the ground, seemingly completely unaffected by gravity and thrashing as he tried to find a way to move.

"Halcyon stop moving!" Sierra yelled as she bumped the flailing mage, sending him gliding through the air. "Oh, shit!"

"Sierra, shoot the heart!" I yelled, moving to intercept the floating mage. "I got him!"

The queen conjured another wave of glowing missiles through the air, this time targeting Sierra, Caius, and Donovan, forcing them all to scramble. It was then she spotted Halcyon floating helplessly in the air.

"Halcyon! Brace yourself!" I shouted, instantly wondering *how* he would do such a thing.

Scything out a massive claw, the queen aimed to slice the levitating mage completely in two. Leaping just before the claw hit the mage, I grabbed him and bore him straight to the ground, canceling out whatever magic perverted his original spell.

A roar of pain told me that one of Sierra's arrows had found the creature's heart, quickly followed by Halcyon thrusting his hands out in the air behind me, successfully conjuring his Force Shield.

The same instant the queen brought both of her claws down on us.

Halcyon grunted as he was pressed into the ground from the fury of the blows but managed to keep his shield intact.

"Shit! Thanks!" I gasped, knowing that the blade would have gone through me like butter.

"No worries," Halcyon gasped. "But, can you get off me, please? You're heavy."

"Right!" I rolled off the mage, catching a glimpse of Constantine leaping into the split open chest of the queen.

Instantly, the queen roared in pain as her massive claws retreated to guard her chest, a spray of multi-colored magic glancing off a claw.

"Got to go!" I called out to Halcyon as I rolled back onto my feet, running to get back into melee range. I quickly scanned the room, trying to spot Drace, but instead saw a tan-colored blur sprinting straight towards the queen's gaping chest cavity.

I had no idea what the puma was hoping to achieve by killing the queen, but at this point, I was happy that it had decided to finally reveal itself. My boots squelched with bile as I sprinted after the beast, trying my best not to lose my footing as I ran.

I can't let it kill the queen! No idea what that will do to it!

Barely ten steps behind the creature, I saw my nemesis tear past the queen's defensive claws before it could react, leaping inside the gaping chest cavity unmolested. As I desperately tried to catch up, a massive claw slammed down in front of me, blocking my path.

"Dammit!" I swore, grinding to a halt as the scythe-claw swung forward to sweep me away with the flat of the blade, only to be intercepted by a charging Drace, stopping it cold as he caught it on his shield.

"I got you, man," he croaked as he leaned into the creature's arm. "Go! Quick!"

"Thanks!" I called to Drace as I leaped over the spider queen's arm, finding myself right at the edge of the ley line.

What the? My eyes bulged in surprise as I saw the raging river of energy that was the ley line streaming straight through the queen's innards. *She...grew, right over it. Her heart is literally suspended over the ley line!*

Looking into the gaping wound, I saw the queen's heart hammering at a desperate rate, spurting æther infused blood wildly from a number of wounds. Clenching onto the heart with a daggerfang thrust deep into it, I saw Constantine holding on for dear life, hanging barely a foot over the ley line. All this while the puma tried to dislodge him from his precarious perch, its claws digging deep into the inner walls of the queen's chest as it bit furiously at Constantine's hands.

"Lyr!" he shouted once seeing me. "Help! I'm going to fall in!"

"On it, buddy! Just hold on!" I called back, my mind trying to come up with a plan.

The major problem wasn't just rescuing Constantine, but finding a way to do so without having him fall into the ley line or letting the puma kill the queen.

My brain froze. I had nothing.

"Lyrian!"

Oh, to hell with it. I leaped forward, arms outstretched as I slammed into my nemesis, quickly wrapping my arms and legs around its body.

"Kill the queen, Constantine!" I shouted, throwing my weight against the puma's grip, tearing it free of the wall.

Taking it with me as I fell into the ley line.

RAGING ENERGY COURSED THROUGH MY body as we sunk into the ley line, sending lightning bolts of pain through every single nerve my body had. I felt my nemesis thrash wildly in my grip as it struggled to find a way to escape. It burned to keep my eyes open, the vibrant blue energy of the river distorting everything I saw.

Oh! It burns! I felt the æther shoot through my mouth and lungs as my body took a deep breath out of shock, inhaling the bright liquid. The pain was unbearable, past anything I had ever experienced in the game before.

Why aren't I dying? The thought raged through me as I felt the puma escape my grip. *Please, just let me re-spawn! I can't take this!*

I felt the puma bite into my shoulder, sinking its teeth deep inside me, my collarbone snapping under the pressure. Its front paws wrapped around me, claws digging into my back as it latched onto me and began to shred my stomach with its hind claws.

Screaming and breathing in even more æther, I flailed uselessly at the beast. My one good arm trapped at my side. *Stop!*

Before I knew what I was doing, my head shot forward, fueled by a deep primal instinct I never knew I had.

I bit into the side of the puma's throat, using the only weapon I had left, my teeth. I felt the fur give way, biting harder until I felt hot blood spill into my mouth. I felt the creature buck under the unexpected assault and bit even deeper. Red blood billowed into the ley line all around us, before being whisked away by the current.

Now panicking, the puma kicked off me, pulling its teeth out of my ruined shoulder and slapping me in the face with a massive paw as it floated away.

My head snapped back as the claws tore through my face, my vision suddenly going dark.

Oh, fuck! He got my eyes! My heart flipped in terror, as my hand touched ruined bits of flesh and bone. *Why won't I die?*

The blinding pain of losing my sight quickly magnified to even greater heights. The æther began to seep into my open wounds. Writhing in pain, I paddled my working arm aimlessly as the ley line current slowly spun me, trying to find some reference to where I was.

Waving uselessly through the burning river, I was a hair's breadth away from giving up and forcefully logging myself out of the game when I felt a gentle caress across my face, right along my missing eyes. Startled, my hand waved in front of my face to ward away the unexpected touch but found nothing as it passed.

Gradually, the constant burning sensation of the coursing æther began to mute, and a pinprick of light appeared in my vision. I gasped with relief as my sight began to return, showing me a crystal-clear torrent of energy, the distortions that marred my vision before completely gone.

There! I saw the puma, paddling wildly, biting at something on its body. Wait... *what is that?*

Coiled all along the creature I now saw countless black strands, wrapped around its body, constricting every time a limb moved. Around its head I saw a mane of broken strands, billowing in the current around it. I could see the puma struggling to crane its neck to bite at the strands covering its paws, each bite tearing a handful off itself. The strands visibly tightened, causing the puma's expression to grimace in pain.

What am I seeing? I asked myself, waving my good arm to steady myself in the current as my legs touched something solid. *It's trying to free itself from the strands! But...what are they?*

For a dozen heartbeats, I watched the puma struggle to tear the ink black strands off of it. Slowly it began to tire, the strands then beginning to re-attach themselves around the beast. A look of defeat crossed the puma's eyes.

Oh, fuck me if I'm wrong about this!

I kicked off the ground as I swam along the current, flying towards my nemesis. Sensing my motion the beast looked at me, eyes echoing with the familiar sadness I had seen earlier in the day. This time, the eyes did not change to anger, watching me with the detached acceptance of something that had given up all hope.

The rest of the body, however, twisted in preparation for impact, black strands straining to move the creature's limbs. Just before I collided with the creature, its head shot out, biting into its own arm. I slammed into the puma's shoulder, weakly hooking my ravaged arm around it. The black strands *shivered* with what I could only describe as fury, my good hand reaching towards the mane of broken strands I had seen before.

My hand raked through the tattered strands, feeling a sticky, tar-like consistency as I tore them free from the puma's body. The creature's eyes widened in surprise, having expected to feel a killing blow. It bit deeper into its paw, struggling to keep it under control.

Hissing in pain as I felt the hind claws pierce into my legs, I continued to claw at the inky strands coating the puma's body, feeling them dissipate the moment I tore them free. For every handful I tore off the creature, the remaining strands constricted even tighter, forcing me to physically dig my nails into its flesh, sending clouds of blood billowing around us.

I lost track of how long I tore the corrupting strands off the creature, wrestling with limbs, not under its control. The more strands I removed, the less the creature fought me, even going as far to assist in tearing the threads off of it before they could regrow. My hand came down on a particularly thick nest of strands, my fingers sinking deeply into it as I struggled to tear it free.

I felt something inside the strands bite at my fingers, sending shooting pains up my arm. Gritting my teeth, I pulled, gradually ripping the mass free. Underneath, gleaming like a pearl, I spotted a single silver strand, pulsing with a weak light. Without hesitation, I grasped it, feeling it mold to my hand.

A prompt appeared in my vision, surprising me so much that I almost let go.

Yes! I screamed, feeling a searing warmth shoot up my arm. Instantly the remaining tar colored strands flared white, burning away from the creature in a flash of light. A second wave of energy shot through me, as a new awareness dawned upon me.

< *Thank you, Two Leg.* >

INTERLUDE

Purgatory

"**S**ISTER!" DESTRUCTION'S VOICE RAGED ACROSS the cosmos, a delightful treat to Creativity's ears. "*YOU HAVE CHEATED ME!*"

"Why hello, sister!" Creativity cheerfully beamed at Destruction's arrival. "What an unexpected delight! Shall I conjure some tea? You *must* tell me about your day!"

"You have broken the rules!" Destruction frothed as she approached Creativity, almost daring to strike her. "I *demand* recompense!"

"Broken a rule?" Creativity cocked her head in confusion, not the least bit intimidated. "Are you certain? It would be *quite* serious if I did, as I'm sure you know. *I cannot break the rules.*"

"So you admit it!" Destruction thrust a finger in Creativity's face.

"I admit nothing Sister, for I do not know what you're talking about."

"You have stolen a *nemesis* of mine, and...*given* it to your pawn!" Destruction continued to rage. "You have meddled beyond your scope!"

"Ah, is that what has your feathers in such a twist?" Creativity asked with a raised eyebrow, "I do not believe I have meddled at all, I merely presented opportunities. If I recall correctly, quite a number of them were in your...nemesis's favor."

"You lie!" Destruction spat. "I *rode* the creature the entire time! The creature was far too adept at resisting me for such a mindless beast, and your pawn should have never been able to do what it did to free it!"

"You *rode* the beast?" Creativity replied in mock surprise. "Have you considered that this is no one's fault but your own? Perhaps you are not as skilled as you believe yourself to be, even after *cheating* yourself and granting the beast magical sight."

"You try my patience, sister, and I tire of repeating myself! *I demand recompense for your meddling!*"

"You may demand all you wish, sister, but it will get you nothing." Creativity waved a hand dismissively. "I would offer you a chance to glimpse at the Weave to prove my innocence, but your last visit proved you cannot handle that sort of responsibility so, I have hidden it from you."

"You cannot do that!" Destruction screamed with fury. "Reveal it to me at once!"

"You seem to enjoy telling me what I can and cannot be doing." Creativity spoke slowly, as if to a child. "But in reality, I can do whatever it is I wish in order to preserve the balance."

"I—" Destruction began before Creativity cut her off with a gesture.

"The balance that your actions have skewed," Creativity continued to speak, now advancing on Destruction. "You taught me a valuable lesson after your last visit, sister. I will even admit you got the better of me.

"But I am not so naïve anymore, to think that we will be anything other than enemies." Creativity waved her hand in dismissal, her voice turning to ice. "Leave my domain, Destruction. You are no longer welcome here under any circumstances. If I see you here again, it will be as a broken corpse at my feet."

With fear in her eyes, Destruction turned and fled.

THIRTY-ONE

I GASPED WITH RELIEF AS MY hands came down on hard stone, heaving myself out of the raging energy of the ley line with a heroic surge of strength. I scrambled on my knees as my lungs and stomach began to rebel from the copious amounts of æther I had both inhaled and swallowed. I didn't even have a chance to scan the room before my body began retching violently, forcing itself to expel the glowing liquid.

Gods, that burns! My head spun as the æther began to sizzle on the stone floor. Gasping for air, my ears told me that the puma had also found its way out of the ley line, and based on the raspy growls I could hear, was also experiencing the same discomfort as it vomited out raw æther.

Where is everyone? I glanced around the room, not seeing any of the party members nearby. Even the massive form of the spider queen was gone, a fossilized skull now sitting in the place where her massive bulk once joined the floor.

With the æther leaving my system, my mind was slowly beginning to process the turn of events I had just experienced. Rubbing my mouth free of spittle, I began to take slow, deep breaths to calm myself as I quickly reviewed a list of alerts that were hovering in my vision. Starting with the one that had changed my relationship with the puma forever.

> *Congratulations on bonding an [Ætherwarped Puma – Level 10] as your familiar!*
>
> *Against all odds, you have freed the [Ætherwarped Puma] from the Nemesis Spirit possessing it! As such, you have gained the undying loyalty and gratitude of the rare creature. Bound together with both magic and blood, you and your familiar now share a unique and near unbreakable bond between one another. This bond allows you and your familiar to constantly understand where the other is, regardless of intervening distance, so long as you are both on the same plane of existence. As you both gain experience and strengthen the bond between the two of you, specialized abilities will become available.*
>
> *Beware! The [Ætherwarped Puma] you have bound as a familiar is an intelligent creature, subject to its own wants, needs, and desires. Should your personalities clash, or you perform actions outside the creature's moral code, it may choose to dissolve the familiar bond of its own accord.*
>
> *Current Familiar Abilities*
>
> *Mental Link – The magical bond linking you and your familiar has created an intimate mental link between the two of you, allowing each of you to communicate mentally between one*

another for a distance of up to one mile, regardless of intervening objects. Magical wards, however, will block this form of mental communication.

Soul Bound *– During the familiar bonding process, you have anchored the being's soul directly to your own. Should the familiar be slain in your service, you will immediately suffer a 10% penalty to all attributes and skills for the next 24 hours until the familiar is reborn. Should the familiar survive your death, it does not suffer any penalties, but will be compelled to travel to your place of rebirth as quickly as possible.*

Additional familiar abilities can be obtained through the use of Class Skill Points, Training, or Special Events.

Ætherwarped? My heart flipped in panic, seeing the leading prefix in the puma's name. My mind fearing that I had bound a creature as unstable as the spiders we'd spent our day fighting. I quickly turned to take a look.

My mouth fell open as I spotted the puma. It had indeed been warped by its swim in the æther.

The creature had grown, its size now rivaling one of a large tiger. It stood now at just under four feet high to the shoulder and nearly ten feet long from snout to tail. The once tan pelt that it wore now gleamed a vibrant azure, thick muscles visibly bulging from under the creature's fur. Massive claws protruded from dinner plate-sized paws, as the creature bared them out of reflex while it continued to cough.

Sensing my surprise through the link, a sapphire colored eye fixed on me in concern.

<Is something wrong, Two Leg?>

<Y-your fur is blue now!> I said haltingly, unused to the new form of mental conversation. *<And you're larger!>*

The puma paused its hacking cough and looked towards a massive paw. *<So it is.>*

<Are you okay with that?> I asked cautiously, trying to gauge the creature's state of mind. Nothing in my life had ever prepared me to speak with a…mutated wild cat, mind to mind.

<It is what it is,> the cat replied philosophically. *<I have undergone many changes over the last few nights. What are a few more?>*

The puma brought itself up into a regal pose as it sat on the ground, watching me carefully. I felt a wave of surprise and concern flow through our link. *<Two Leg…your eyes burn with the color of the sky!>*

What? I flinched at the urgency of the puma's mental voice, remembering its claws blinding me just a few moments earlier. *My eyes?*

I quickly rubbed my hand across my face, feeling nothing amiss, yet the panicked motion reminded me that there were two more alerts still waiting for my attention. Cautiously selecting one, I hoped for answers to whatever the puma saw in my eyes.

You have gained the Trait – Ætherwarped

Ætherwarped – Due to high exposure of Raw Æther, your body has undergone unpredictable changes! You have gained the following Sub-Trait and Abilities as part of your condition. Further exposure to Æther can result in further effects!

> *Mana Starved – Your body now has an innate hunger for Arcane Energy in order to fuel its normal bodily processes. For as long as you have mana, you do not require to eat or drink. However, if your mana reaches 0, your body will immediately begin to starve. All mana regeneration is permanently reduced by 50%.*
>
> *True Sight – Your eyes have been enhanced by exposure to Æther to the point where they are able to pierce through natural darkness and all facets of magic to see things as they truly are. This ability replaces Arcane Sight and can be suppressed at will. When this ability is active, the player's eyes will visibly glow a bright blue.*

"Fuck!" I cursed out loud as I read the first half of the alert. *Now I'm ætherwarped too, and I've completely gutted my mana regeneration! How the hell am I supposed to be an effective spellsword now?*

I felt some relief as I continued to the second half of the alert, realizing just how much my Arcane Sight had been augmented.

*Okay, maybe this isn't all bad. But I probably wouldn't have made this trade if I had an option...*I looked towards the giant cat regarding me with concern. *Okay, maybe I would have.*

<I'm fine.> I sent to the big cat, trying to find words that I thought it would understand. *<The enchantment allowing me to see magic has changed; my eyes now glow and allow me to see in the dark.>*

<Very useful.> The puma replied with an approving flick of an ear.

"Lyri—*holy shit!*" Constantine's voice shouted in surprise. "Run, Lyr! Why are you just sitting there?"

My head snapped up to see a shocked Constantine drawing his daggerfangs as he called for help from the ramp behind him. Beside me the puma leaped into action, putting itself between me and Constantine as it bared its fangs with a roar.

<Order your littermate to sheath his claws!> The puma's mental voice hissed through my mind. *<I am no longer a threat against them.>*

"Whoa! Whoa! Wait up!" I stumbled up onto my feet as the rest of the party charged down the ramp, weapons at the ready. "The cat isn't a threat! It's my familiar now!"

"Familiar?" Constantine exclaimed, relaxing ever so slightly. "That cat tried to kill me and it *did* kill you! Why the hell would it be your familiar now?"

"It was under *something's* control, and I freed it while we were in the ley line, then it was bound to me!" I started to explain. "I don't quite understand *how* I did it, but it happened!"

"How the hell did it turn *blue* and grow even larger then?"

"Because it's *ætherwarped*...the same as me now," I replied hesitantly.

Constantine stared at me in confusion. "Ætherwarped? Like the spiders?"

"Enough!" Sierra cut in while eying the puma carefully. "This isn't the best place to talk. *Æther* sickness is slowly poisoning us here. We're going to *carefully* move out of this room where it's safe." Sierra thrust a finger at me. "Then you have some explaining to do!"

WE HAD LEFT THE ROOM containing the ley line, moving up to the next highest plateau along the ramp to get away from the æther sickness. Still somewhat hesitant of the puma, the rest of the party stood across from me, while the big cat sat coolly by my side. Apart from both groups, Donovan watched all of us, carefully sitting with his back against the wall, his eyes glazed over and visibly exhausted.

"So that's all of it," I finished, having explained everything from the moment I'd dragged the puma into the ley line to the discovery of my new condition. "I don't know how effective I'm going to be with a completely shot mana regeneration going forward, though."

"I think you're too focused on the negatives, Lyr," Drace said shaking his head. "You have a...giant cat as a *friend*, don't need to eat or drink, and can see in the dark and through all illusions."

"I'd say you're pretty fucking lucky, Lyrian," Constantine grunted. "I bet if anyone else tried to do what you just did, they'd be eating a twenty percent penalty to skills and experience because their soul fragment is stuck at the bottom of the ley line with no way of recovering it."

"Believe me," I said softly, remembering the searing pain of the ley line. "While I was in there, death would have been a blessing. I have no idea why I didn't die."

"What happ—"

"What's his name?" Sierra interrupted suddenly, not having taken her eyes off the warped puma. "Does he have a name?"

"Uh. I'm not sure." Caught off guard by the sudden question, I turned to look at my familiar. *<Do you understand us when we speak out loud?>*

<I do.>

<Do you have a name that you wish us to call you?> I mentally asked the creature.

<What is this…name, you speak of?> The puma's tail swished, as it cocked its head towards me in confusion.

I frowned at the creature's confusion, and the surreality of explaining the concept of a name to a cat. *<A name is a word that identifies something or someone. When my friends arrived, they called out my name, Lyrian. It is something that belongs only to me, and no one else. Such as identifying a very specific Two Leg.>*

<I think I understand, Two Le—Lyrian,> my familiar replied cautiously as it adjusted to the concept. *< Then the fire-haired one who asked must be Sierra?>*

"Lyrian?" Sierra asked me impatiently, seeing me just staring at the cat. "Does it?"

"Sorry…" I shook my head. "I was just explaining *what* a name was to the cat."

"Oh."

<Yes! That's right!> I sent back enthusiastically. *<Do you have a name like that?>*

<No.> The cat sent back with a mental shrug. *<I have only recently become aware of myself. I have yet to discover my name.>*

<Your name isn't discovered.> Once more I struggled, trying to find a way to explain clearly to the creature. *<A name is either chosen by one's self or given by a parent or guardian during the creature's birth.>*

The puma regarded me with great interest as my words sunk in. *<Our bond brings us closer than a parent or guardian. I ask you to grant me a name.>*

<Uh...> Caught off guard for a moment, my mind quickly thought through dozens of names in my mind. *<Are you sure? A name is important.>*

<Indeed, I am.> The puma replied back somewhat impatiently.

< Then I name you Amaranth,> I sent back to the puma with confidence after thinking for a moment. *<It means "Immorta"' or "Unfading".>*

<A powerful name,> Amaranth replied graciously, as he started to purr. *< Thank you.>*

"His name is Amaranth," I finally told Sierra, the conversation having taken a handful of seconds.

"Amaranth..." Sierra said slowly, testing the name. She slowly took a step forward, holding her hand out for the cat to sniff. "My name is Sierra. It is...nice to meet you. I'm happy you're on our side now."

Amaranth regarded her coolly for a moment, before rubbing its face across her open hand, purring even louder.

Whatever spell held everyone in suspicion broke at that moment, each of the party members stepping forward to introduce themselves to my new familiar. Once more I shook my head at the surreal scene, but considering that I had just fought a massive spider queen in the bowels of an abandoned ruin, surreal was quickly becoming...rather ordinary.

I guess this is my life now.

While everyone was focused on Amaranth, I noticed Donovan still sitting with his back to the wall, completely unfocused on everything going on around him.

"Hey, Donovan, are you all right?" I called out as I approached the dazed mage, seeing that his shirt was soaked through with blood. Some time after I had jumped into the ley line, he must have taken a sizeable wound to the chest that had since healed.

"Huh? Oh. I'm okay...Lyrian, was it?" Donovan spoke softly, his mind clearly miles away. "It's just been a long night. Day. I don't even know *when* it is."

"It's...probably getting to be late afternoon, depending on how long I was in the ley line," I offered a bit more sympathy to the mage's temporal displacement now that we were out of combat. "On *Friday*, mind you."

"*Friday*." The mage sighed again. "Damn..."

"What happened, Donovan?" I prompted, wondering just how much to reveal. "How did you end up here in the middle of a temporal lock? In fact, what are you doing this far north at all?"

"That...is a long story." The mage sighed before looking up at me. "And much I am not at liberty to discuss."

"Tell me what you can, then," I told him with a shrug. "I have nowhere to be."

Taking a deep breath, Donovan steeled himself and nodded at me. "I am a member of the Eberian Mages Guild, and I was charged to lead an expedition north of Eberia to determine the location of a ley line that was believed to be in this area."

"How did you even know where to begin looking?"

"I can't say." Donovan shook his head. "That is a secret belonging to the guild."

"Okay, go on."

"We arrived in this area a few weeks ago, deigning to start our search much further to the north, then make our way southward. Our plan was to investigate a number of ruins that the Surveyors Guild had noted in the surrounding area. However, we did not anticipate that their maps were based on poor observations and a great deal of guesswork." The way that Donovan described the Surveyors Guild was one filled with scorn and derision. "Their maps proved to be near useless in the field, and we were forced to search the area ourselves."

"Why didn't you just go back and get better maps?" I asked.

"One does not return empty-handed to the house when it sponsors an expedition," Donovan said sternly. "It is bad. For your health."

"House? I thought the guild sponsored it?" I asked, my interest piqued.

"Huh? They did," Donovan replied, realizing that he had just misspoke.

"You just said a house sponsored it."

"Did I?" Donovan said slightly nervously. "I meant guild, my apologies. I am quite tired."

"I'm not sure I believe you," I responded flatly, meeting the mage's eyes and staring at him intently. "What house?"

Staring back at me, I could see a number of emotions play across Donovan's face before he sighed. "I guess it's no real harm to tell you this far from civilization. House Denarius sponsored the expedition through the Mages Guild."

*Your **Wordplay** skill has increased to Level 3!*

Huh, that's the same house that sponsored Aldwin's founding of Aldford.

"Interesting." I nodded at Donovan, sensing that the rest of the party had turned their attention to our conversation.

"Occasionally, when a noble house needs to have something taken care of or *acquired* that they cannot *officially* take notice of, or be associated with, it is usually handled through one of the Eberian guilds in exchange for a…monetary donation."

"They bribed you to do their dirty work." Drace entered the conversation bluntly. "No need to dress it up."

Donovan winced at Drace's brutal assessment but nodded. "Yes, at its heart that's what it is."

"Okay." I began, realizing that there was a huge can of worms surrounding this mess. "Leaving aside the fact that the guild *allowed* itself to be bribed, why does House Denarius want control over a ley line?"

"I'm afraid I don't know," Donovan replied, honestly this time.

"My directive was to find it and secure it. Then report back to the guild for their disposition."

Donovan took a deep breath before continuing to explain. "But… once we arrived to this area, I noticed that there was something wrong with the ley line, and seeing it here confirmed it for me."

"Noticed?" Halcyon spoke up for the first time. "How? You couldn't even find the place."

"True." Donovan nodded, "But we brought tools with us in hopes of being able to locate the ley line, finely tuned mana dowsing rods, ætherscopes, and so forth."

"And they were supposed to help you locate this place?"

"In normal circumstances, yes." Donovan spoke with calm patience now that he had started talking. "However, what we found was an extreme abundance of magic permeating the area for countless miles around us. It made our tools next to useless."

"Why?" Halcyon asked, genuinely interested in the theory of magic this world used.

"They were too sensitive for this type of work; no matter where we pointed them, all they would detect was magic. I hypothesized this was because æther was somehow leaking into the ground, outside of the regular channels a ley line should run. Seeing the ley line below has confirmed it."

"So the ley line is ruptured then," Halcyon stated.

"Yes!" Donovan nodded empathetically. "Very seriously so."

"As fascinating as this detour is…" I cut back into the conversation. "That doesn't tell us how you ended up trapped here…in your nightshirt, with an angry goblin after you."

Donovan's face fell as he looked to the ground. "Well."

<He smells of fear and guilt,> Amaranth interjected, sniffing the air in front of him.

Fixing my gaze on Donovan, I waited quietly, letting the silence weigh him into speaking.

"It was late," he began. "We found a clearing in the woods and set up camp, where it is in relation to here, I don't know."

But we do, I thought to myself.

"I was about to bunk down for the night after speaking to one of the scoutmasters when balls of fire struck from the woods." Donovan's eyes glazed over as he relived events that had just happened a few hours ago from his perspective. "They caught us completely unprepared, having evaded our night watch. Before I knew what was happening, dozens of goblins had broken into the camp. There was nothing I could do."

"I saw one of our scouts take off into the woods in an effort to escape, I and tried to follow..." the Eberian mage shook his head. "I barely made it a dozen steps into the woods before I was ambushed by a pair of goblin shamans.

"They chased me through the forest for what seemed like half the night." Donovan sounded tense as he continued his story. "Eventually, we ran into spiders. Large spiders. I had no idea any inhabited the forest this far south." Donovan let out a sigh. "We had dozens of spiders on our tail as we ran through the woods and I used the opportunity to land a paralytic curse on one of the shamans chasing me. His companion didn't even stop to help him..."

"Brutal," Caius whispered while glancing at a pale Halcyon.

"After that, the second shaman was too crafty. He maintained a shield for the rest of the chase, waiting for me to tire as we circled through the woods." Donovan shook his head as he indicated the ruin around us. "As if an answer to my prayers, I saw this mountain ridge bloom with magic—the irony that I would find the ruin I was looking for as I was sprinting wildly in the dark. Anyway, I had gained enough distance from the goblin to climb the scree and break the ward covering the entrance in hopes of hiding and ambush—"

"Hold on," I interrupted, a spark of anger kindling in my stomach.

"There was a ward on the entrance?"

"Yes, a primitive one, barely strong enough to protect a favorite privy stall, let alone anything valuable. Anything stronger and the shaman would have caught up with me."

"Would it have kept the spiders out?" I asked, trying to carefully hide the anger in my voice.

"Spiders? Oh, certainly! A good thing too, otherwise, they may have become..." Comprehension dawned on Donovan's face. "Oh, gods, what have I done?"

"You survived," Sierra soothed, shooting me a sharp look. "And as I understand, no *great* harm has been done."

"Only through dumb luck that the temporal lock caught most of—"

Sierra dug her elbow into my side. "No *great* harm done."

"Thank the gods!" Donovan sounded relieved. "Don't worry, I can ward this place once more and ensure that nothing else makes its way inside. At least until we can get members from the guild up here to properly assume control of this place and perhaps repair the ley line."

"Donovan," I grunted brusquely. "You seem to be mistaken. I'm not turning over this place to the guild."

"What?" Donovan shouted, anger crossing his face. "Why not? You don't have the skills to repair the ley line! What use would it be to you all?"

"Because I don't fucking trust you, your guild, or *House Denarius*," I told the mage bluntly. "And I'm not about to let Eberian politics dictate what I should be doing with a ruin that we fought, bled, and nearly died for."

"What right do you think you have to—" the mage started to shout before Sierra cut him off with a sharp slice of her arm.

"Shut up, and wait here," Sierra told Donovan. "I need to speak with Lyrian."

"Lyr, are you sure about this?" she asked me with concern, after taking a moment to lead me out of Donovan's hearing range.

"Do you remember what the magic voice said when I poked those crystals?" I asked countering Sierra's question with my own. "It said 'Translocation Grid Inactive.' *Translocation.* This place has to be a hub of some sort, a method of fast travel."

"I remember." Sierra nodded, a thoughtful look on her face "You think the House Denarius or the Mages Guild has a way of repairing this place? Fast travel sounds like a good thing."

"Maybe, but under the control of someone we don't know about?" I asked. "Someone who Donovan openly admitted takes and gives out bribes?"

"Shit. Good point," Sierra conceded. "Okay, what's your plan?"

"Stall. I need to talk to Aldwin about something."

"Oh?"

"He founded Aldford based on coin lent by House Denarius," I whispered.

"Are you fucking kidding me?" Sierra hissed.

"Not even a little bit."

"Okay," Sierra said after taking a deep breath. "I'll follow your lead."

Sierra and I rejoined the party, who had stayed behind to keep Donovan company. "We'll discuss more about what will and will not happen with this place later. As I'm sure you can understand, we're not about to give this place up without *considerable* recompense."

"That's very...*prudent* of you," Donovan said carefully, his anger fading slightly.

"In the meantime. Halcyon and I are going to watch you *carefully* ward this place to make sure nothing else can get in here."

"And then what?" Donovan asked.

"Then we're going to take you to your camp."

THIRTY-TWO

DESPITE THE FAILINGS DONOVAN HAD displayed so far, thankfully, a sense of responsibility for the members of his expedition was not among them. The exhausted mage nearly *cried* with joy after we told him that Natasha had survived the goblin attack and was safe in Aldford at the moment. Almost instantly, his demeanor changed to one of gratitude, despite the argument we just had and having been told we didn't trust him.

He isn't cut out for this, I realized while carefully watching Donovan ward the entrance of the ruin as the sun began to set along the Ridge.

I leaned heavily to one side as I paid attention to Donovan's warding, my foot resting on the rather large, fossilized skull of the spider queen that I had taken as a souvenir. I had no idea if it was because the spider queen was a boss creature that it had left something behind, or if it had something to do with being so drastically warped by magic. But I figured it would make an appropriate statement when we returned to Aldford. The only downside was that for whatever reason the skull didn't register as an item, so I wasn't able to magically stuff it into my inventory. I would have to lug it back by hand, one step at a time.

Donovan seems competent enough when it comes to magic, even battle, but as a leader or speaker, he is lost. He doesn't have the temperament or presence for it. He'd be better off to be given a technical task to do without interference.

I understood the majority of Donovan's work as he wove thick strands of magic across the ruin's entrance, building the ward that would keep any interlopers out. Unfortunately, though, complete understanding was beyond me. It was like being able to read a programming language and vaguely understand what it was trying to do, yet not understand it enough to be able to code something useful myself.

In the end, I was confident enough that if I had to break the ward I would be able to figure out a way to do so, although it'd likely be an exhausting and time-consuming process, akin to breaking down a cement wall with a sledgehammer.

Donovan was quiet as we walked through the abandoned forest towards the ruined camp, his eyes flitting to every scarred tree we passed. It was obvious that the destruction and silence weighed on him heavily.

"So Lyr, we finished that quest." Constantine slid beside me as we walked.

"Oh?" I exclaimed with a bit of confusion before I caught on. "The spider quest!"

I remembered that I still had one more alert pending that I had yet to read, I quickly brought up the quest update.

▷QUEST COMPLETE!

CLEANSING THE WEBWOOD. *(Unique) (Group)*

You have successfully thinned the spiders infesting the Webwood
and killed the [Ætherwarped Webwood Queen]! Return to Bann
Aldwin for a reward!
Spiders Slain: 1000/1000
Ætherwarped Webwood Queen Slain: 1/1
Difficulty: Very Hard
Reward: Experience, Reputation, 100 gold pieces. (Reward
proportional to percentage contributed)
Bonus: Unknown

I quickly scanned over the quest details, a smile breaking out on my face. *Finally! We'll have some gold to our name!*

"—don't know exactly what they are, but I'm sure they are used for crafting." Constantine had continued to speak while I was looking over the quest details. "Plus, we also found that bone wand that the shaman was using, which Halcyon claimed. He said that it had pretty decent stats on it."

"Here's all the loot," Constantine finished, handing me a bunch of goods. "There really wasn't much…"

[Colossal Mana-Infused Spider Claw] x2
[Massive Mana-Infused Spider Carapace] x4
[Mana-Infused Ichor] x200
[Vial of Raw Æther] x 50

"Uh…thanks," I replied, catching on, then juggling to add everything to my inventory while carrying the massive skull. "If nothing else I can use it for repairs and maybe something neat with the *æther.*"

"Hopefully," Constantine said. "We have a raging river of it after all."

"Yeah, I guess we do," I said thoughtfully.

As we walked towards the abandoned expedition camp, Caius and Constantine caught me up on the end of the spider queen fight.

"After you fell into the ley line with the puma, I was able to take care of the queen's heart without any problem," Constantine said.

"It went berserk with pain at that point, though," Caius added. "It really gored Donovan, and Drace took a few more hits too."

"Soon as the heart stopped beating, I lit out of the cavity." Constantine mimed a leaping motion with his hand. "A good thing too, since the entire thing just kinda caught fire."

"Well…caught magefire?" Caius tested the word. "It was blue fire, the same sort Halcyon conjures."

"Yeah, we didn't know what was happening, and with you gone, we grabbed Donovan and ran out of the room to heal." Constantine continued to explain. "A few more seconds and the æther sickness would have done Donovan and Drace in."

"After a while, the queen must have burnt herself out," Caius finished. "Because we got a thousand experience points for the fight! Plus a small bit for the hundreds of spiders caught in the trap! We're almost halfway to level eleven!"

"Sweet!" I exclaimed, happily summoning my experience bar. "Compared to what we've been getting before, that's amazing!"

Current Experience: 1303/21,300

Hang on, that's not right. I frowned, looking at my bar. *Oh, shit! I left leadership experience on!*

You have 8 Leadership Skill Points Unspent!

"Well, shit." I sighed with conflicting emotions. "I left leadership experience on, and now I have eight points."

"Ouch!" Constantine winced and then shrugged. "Levels can always come later, though. The leadership buffs are pretty powerful!"

"I suppose," I said as I opened the leadership menu and split my newly gained leadership points between increased health regeneration and increased mana regeneration. I quickly looked over the final point assignments before committing the changes, noting that all future increases to health regeneration would now require two leadership points per rank.

Increased Health Regeneration – Increase amount of Health Regenerated by 5. 5/10

Increased Mana Regeneration – Increase amount of Mana Regenerated by 4. 4/10

Increased Movement – Increase mounted and unmounted speed by 4%. 4/10

"Well, maybe that'll curb just a little bit of the loss in mana recovery," I grumbled to myself as I waved the menu out of my vision.

When we arrived back to the expedition camp, I was somewhat surprised to see that very little had changed since we rushed away in a hurry. I could see a number of disturbances in the fallen branches that vaguely lined up with what I remembered from the pitched battle against the predators earlier in the day today.

That battle feels like it was ages ago. The exhaustion of a long day suddenly hit me like a truck. *Was it this morning the Webwood horror invaded Aldford?*

I sighed as I set the queen's skull on the ground in front of me, then sat on its brow as a makeshift chair. Sierra and Drace were busy showing Donovan the remains of the camp, each poking through the fallen brush as they pulled free the remains of a scorched tent or a torn pack.

<The Dirty Ones preyed upon this camp,> Amaranth sent as he lay down beside me. *<Their scent is faint, yet still lingers.>*

<Dirty Ones?> I queried. *<Goblins?>*

<I know not. Goblins…the scent is similar to the Dirty One found in the magic cave we just departed.> Amaranth replied.

<Those are called goblins.> I explained to the cat. *<That is what their*

kind is named, just like my kind is referred to as umans.>

<Goblins…humans.> Once more my familiar tested the words. *<Names are indeed useful things.>* The puma sniffed the air in front of it. *<There are other scents here, cleaner, yet, not goblin.>*

<That must be the rest of the expedition!> I thought to Amaranth excitedly. *<Can you tell where they went? By their scent?>*

Without a word, the cat stood up and began to prowl around the camp, sniffing the air and pawing at the ground. Donovan looked at the familiar with a bit of nervousness, but Amaranth quickly circled the camp and left the clearing towards the east.

<The scent fades.> Amaranth sent with a notable tinge of disappointment as it trotted back towards the camp. *<It has been too long, and the Many-Legs' musk obscures the trail. I do not smell any blood or death, however.>*

<Damn, at least the expedition members might still be alive. Thanks for trying.>

<Worry not,> Amaranth replied. *<The scent is notable. I will recall it if it crosses my path again.>*

"Are we done here?" I called out tiredly to the group, though my attention was focused on Donovan. "We're burning light and still have a long way to go."

Donovan shook his head in despair. "There's nothing here for me…"

"Yeah, let's go home, Lyr," Sierra breathed, echoing my exhaustion. "I think I'm done with this day."

Home. Sierra's comment echoed through my mind as we set off to Aldford.

Yeah, this is home now.

WE RETURNED TO ALDFORD LIKE heroes. Tired, dirty, grumpy

heroes.

When we had left the village this morning, our armor was new, clean, with the pleasing scent of worked leather. Now it was tattered, covered in dirt, sweat, and bile. Each of us smelling like a charnel house.

Our journey back to Aldford was uneventful, if long. We took the dogleg path once again, traveling southward to the western side of Crater Lake and skirting the shoreline as we made our way back east. Burnt out from a day of nervous aggression, the majority of the spiderlings nesting along the forest line were content to leave us be as we passed, the few that didn't, we mechanically slew with barely a second thought.

As we climbed out of Crater Lake, we emerged into the final rays of the day as the sun began to set in the distant horizon. The sight of Aldford in the evening light warmed our hearts, giving us an extra spring in our step. Even from far away, we could still see villagers hard at work, intent on using every last second of light to finish digging the ditches around the village.

From what I could see at this distance, they had made great progress since we left. The first ditch was now filled with tribuli, a formidable obstacle that no invader would be able to cross without paying a steep price in blood. The second ditch was well on its way to being completed, with perhaps another fifty or sixty feet left to be dug out.

I let out a sigh of relief that I didn't realize I'd been holding. *The village is safe.*

"Halt! Identify yourselves!" An alert voice belonging to Ioun shouted from the distance.

"Ioun!" Drace shouted with a smile on his face. "It's us!"

"Sir, you're back!" Ioun's voice exclaimed happily, then shouted something towards the village.

Immediately, we saw all the villagers laboring in the distance perk up, then speed towards the northern side of Aldford to greet us. Before long the entire village had turned out, excitedly waiting for our arrival.

We were greeted with exuberant cheers as we crossed the fortified northern entrance and entered Aldford proper. The militia greeted us with a formal salute, standing at attention in their fine new armor. I saw the bann standing just off to the side, clapping along with the crowd, relief at our safe return evident on his face.

"The Webwood queen has been slain!" I shouted, tossing the massive skull to the ground in front of the roaring crowd with a thump, sending up a small spray of dust. "The spiders of the Webwood will no longer threaten Aldford!"

The villagers cheered even louder, the good news causing them to temporarily glaze over the fact that our group had grown by two members, one of them being a giant, azure-furred puma.

"Sir, your guests!" Loren exclaimed after allowing the crowd to cheer for a moment, clearly eying my familiar as he shouted above the noise of the crowd.

"Ah! You're right!" I knocked a knuckle to my forehead and indicated both Donovan and Amaranth to the crowd, enjoying the theater I was putting on. The cheers quickly faded as they spotted the wild cat, filling the air with a pregnant silence as some in the crowd took half a step back.

"Allow me to introduce a pair of new guests to the village!" I called out loudly to the village, making a point to speak clearly. "First we have Donovan Kaine, of the Eberian Mages Guild. He is of the same expedition as Natasha and was instrumental in the death of the Webwood queen."

I heard a few faint grumbles from the crowd with their attention still focused on Amaranth.

"Next, we have Amaranth." I indicated the puma, who flicked an ear at the crowd. "He is a creature of this land, and I have bonded him as my familiar. On my word, he will not harm anyone, save in self-defense."

More whispers emerged from the crowd as they watched the azure furred cat intently.

"Furthermore, an item I feel that is important to point out. Amaranth is an *intelligent* creature and can understand every word we say. I ask that you treat him as any other member of our group."

There was a pause of silence as the villagers absorbed that last bit of information.

"May I be the first to welcome you both to Alford!" Aldwin exclaimed as he stepped forward from the crowd before the silence could get awkward. I noticed a flare of recognition cross Donovan's face as he shook the bann's hand, but the bann didn't seem to notice or respond in any way I could see.

Well…I wonder what that's all about.

Aldwin then walked over to Amaranth, who had since sat down to regard the crowd around us. For a heartbeat, Aldwin seemed confused as to how to properly greet the cat but then held out a hand anyway.

To all of our amazement, Amaranth's ears flicked twice in amusement, then he lifted a massive paw that enveloped the bann's hand.

<*Strange,*> Amaranth sent. <*Why does he grasp a paw in greeting?*>

I could not help but smile slightly at my familiar's question. <*It is a sign of peace and trust. Also used to demonstrate that you are not carrying a weapon.*>

<*Have I broken trust then?*> Amaranth asked with concern. <*My claws are part of my paw!*>

<*I do not think you have anything to worry about,*> I soothed. <*So long as it was done in good faith.*>

Aldwin stepped back after shaking Amaranth's paw and addressed everyone. "I suppose we can all turn in for the night now that our faithful adventurers have returned! I'm sure they're more than looking forward to a hot meal, and rest for the night…"

The crowd let out another cheer, happy to be finished digging for the day.

"…along with a bath!" Aldwin coughed, close enough for me to hear. "Gods!"

AFTER A QUICK DIP IN the river at Aldwin's *polite* insistence, we soon found ourselves crammed into the bann's private study above the town hall to fill him in on our day. It had taken a bit of jostling to get the entire party, plus Donovan, Natasha, and Jenkins into the small room at first. Once we all sat down and stopped moving we each had enough space not to feel overly crowded.

I had explained our portion of the day first, giving the bann the major highlights of our adventure along with the events surrounding Amaranth and the spider queen, leaving out the business about House Denarius for the time being, in addition to my suspicions of the ruin being a translocation hub. Those matters I planned to bring up without Donovan being present.

"…then the next thing I knew, I was surrounded by spiders." Donovan shook his head tiredly as he explained his half of the story. "And lost five days in the blink of an eye. After that, well, all passed as Lyrian explained."

"Were there no other clues at the camp, telling us what happened to the rest of our people?" Natasha asked plaintively.

"Nothing we could find," I answered shaking my head, slowly stroking Amaranth's fur. "Amaranth could smell goblins in the area, but there was no trace that anyone was killed at the clearing."

"They may still be alive then," Natasha said softly as she shook her head "But why would the goblins take prisoners?"

"We don't know," Jenkins replied. "When they attacked here, they tried to do the same. They even had an enclosed wagon and horses to whisk everyone away."

"Hang on, goblins use horses?" Caius asked aloud with confusion. "Isn't that...*strange* in itself?"

"Not particularly," Aldwin explained with a shrug. "During the war, it wasn't uncommon to see a handful of goblin archers on horseback supporting the orcs. Truthfully speaking, we feared a dozen goblin skirmishers on horseback more than an equal number of orcs on foot."

"That is true." Jenkins nodded in agreement. "There were a handful of goblin tribes that realized horses had more practical uses aside from food and glue. Hell, even some orcs figured it out...when they could find horses large enough at least."

"Well...uh." Caius coughed at Jenkin's explanation. "I didn't think they were that smart."

"They may appear to be primitive, savage even," Aldwin spoke, his eyes recalling something from his past. "But they are far from stupid."

"I suppose," Caius conceded.

"Hang on a minute," Sierra began, seeing an opportunity to jump into the conversation. "If they brought a wagon, that means they had an overland route to get it here. A wagon wouldn't be convenient to pull over rocky or broken ground."

"Hm..." Jenkins grunted thoughtfully. "That's a good point. I hadn't thought of that."

"That would discount Crater Lake and the surrounding forest to the northwest in the lower elevation," I added, recalling the layout of the area. "Unless they cut a path through the forest we haven't managed to come across."

"Perhaps, but aside from the forest, the rest of the land is reasonably smooth, if not hilly, in all directions," Aldwin replied with a sigh. "The only real exception being *much* further to the west, where it eventually becomes a network of ridges and cliffs that make the land unpassable, at least by convenient means."

"What direction did the goblins attack from again?" I asked Jenkins and the bann. My mind was weary and it was difficult to recall the details of the last few days.

"They attacked through the gate with the bridge that leads over the river," Jenkins replied slowly. "That would be the southeast corner of the village."

"Then it would make the most sense that they came from somewhere from that direction," I reasoned. "If their plan was to abduct everyone, they would have come the most direct way."

"True," Aldwin agreed after a moment of thought. "I would have done the same against an unsuspecting enemy. Speed would be essential."

"Sure happened fucking fast," Jenkins muttered under his breath.

"With the adventurers a few days away and knowing nothing about the goblins..." Sierra spoke up, nodding her head towards Constantine and Natasha. "We should set up some roving patrols covering everything from the southeast to the northeast."

"That's a good idea," I said in full agreement. "Maybe we'll get lucky and trip over one of the two groups early."

"Great!" Sierra said happily. "The three of us will head out first thing in the morning."

<Explain the name 'adventurer' to me.> Amaranth asked me as Sierra spoke. *<These are...interlopers to our territory?>*

<Of a kind,> I replied, searching for the right words. *<Adventurers are those who seek fame, fortune, and power, often wandering far and wide to find it. Each is motivated by different desires; it is difficult to predict what they will want when they arrive. Some may seek to join our village peacefully. Others may decide to drive us from it, or even destroy it.>*

<So you seek to protect your den and littermates until their intentions are known?> Amaranth asked, a sense of understanding coming across the link we shared.

< We do, and we take steps to ensure we are not caught off guard by their arrival.>

< Wise,> The puma commented. *< I will assist in this. I am not one to lay about the den like a fat kitten on a teat.>*

"Amaranth has volunteered to help as well," I told the scouts. "You can arrange between one another how best to cover your ground tomorrow."

Sierra looked at Amaranth with surprise, then nodded. "We'll be happy to have him along!"

"How was the day here?" I turned to ask the knight. "I saw great progress on the defenses."

"Indeed." Aldwin nodded happily. "Everyone was *quite* motivated today and a bit more experienced at the task, so we made exceptional progress. That's even after Jenkins conscripted a pair of villagers to assist in his crafting of the tribuli and help repair the damage from the attack this morning."

"Wait, there was an attack?" Donovan asked with confusion.

"Yeah." Drace sighed, recalling this morning's events. "An æther-warped spider invaded the village this morning—"

"—and two of us died in order to keep it from destroying the village," Constantine finished tersely while looking at Donovan.

"Ah." I could tell that new bit of information added to the weight Donovan was carrying. "I see."

"You did what you had to, in the heat of the moment," I told the mage, realizing it was time to put this issue to rest, then looked around the room as I spoke. "We sit here now with the luxury of hindsight, and we can't truly say that we would have done it differently if we were in your shoes."

"What is important is that we survived."

"Indeed," the bann spoke with a nod.

"Thank you," Donovan breathed with a sigh of relief as he stood out of his chair. "I appreciate your...understanding in this."

Donovan swayed slightly on his feet as he turned to look back at the door.

"If I may beg permission to excuse myself for the night, I really must retire. I am no longer sure how long I've been awake, and I feel like I may collapse at any moment."

"Oh, certainly!" The bann rose with his arm outstretched indicating the door as he attempted to walk around his desk, to find that any path out of the room was blocked by at least three adventurers. "Erm."

"We could all probably use a bite to eat then some sleep," Halcyon said hopefully. "We can all shuffle out if there is nothing else?"

"Nothing that can't wait until morning!" Aldwin replied graciously. "After the day you've all had, I certainly won't begrudge you some rest!"

As everyone rose and began to extract themselves from the room, I quickly signaled the bann that I wished to speak with him privately.

"I'll be down in a bit," I told Constantine as he closed the door behind him, leaving only Aldwin, Amaranth, and myself in the room. With everyone having left the room, Amaranth had chosen to curl up near the center of the study, no longer pressed against me.

"Is everything all right, Lyrian?" Aldwin asked while smiling at Amaranth then myself. "I didn't expect for you to return with a...puma of all things! Nor the leader of the missing expedition!"

"It's been an interesting day," I replied with a sigh, looking at Amaranth settle into his new spot. "Do you know anything of Donovan? Have you met him before?"

"Him?" The bann shook his head. "Not at all. To be honest, he doesn't seem to be the type that should have been assigned to lead such an expedition."

"I agree." I rubbed my tired eyes as I recalled Donovan's expression when he first met Aldwin. "He seemed to have recognized you, however."

"Me?" Aldwin replied with some surprise. "It's been a while since I was in the capital, but I am one of the few knights of Eberia to actually *survive* the war. Perhaps he has a good memory for faces."

<He speaks in half-truths,> Amaranth commented from his spot on the floor, chin resting on his paws. *<I can hear his heart quiver from here.>*

"Perhaps," I offered, as my mind mulled over Amaranth's secret insight. "There is an issue I wanted to raise with you, however."

"Oh?"

"Donovan let slip that his expedition was funded by proxy through the Mages Guild by House Denarius. They were searching for the ley line and, indirectly, the ruin that we had found today. At first glance, it appears to be a translocation hub, something that I believe could be used to greatly speed travel across the continent, or between here and Eberia."

I didn't know what I expected Aldwin's reaction to be when I told him of the house's involvement, but him slamming both hands onto his desk and practically shouting, "What does that bitch have her hands in now?" wasn't high on my list.

Okay, it wasn't even on it at all.

"Uh…*what?*" I asked, shocked by the bann's sudden outburst.

"I am sorry, Lyrian." The knight's face was completely red with anger. "It appears that no matter how far we push the frontiers, Eberian politics are not far behind! Something I had thought I left for good."

"Why don't you tell me what's going on," I offered calmly. "Then I can be appropriately outraged on your behalf as well. First of all, who is 'that bitch'?"

"That *bitch* happens to be Matriarch Emilia Denarius of House Denarius, the dowager queen, or the Queen Mother of Eberia," Aldwin spoke evenly after taking a deep breath. "She is King Swain's mother and the late Prince Rainier's wife."

"Okay," I said slowly, nodding at Aldwin to continue.

"She and I have had a rather *tumultuous* history over the years." The bann seemed to be lost in thought as he spoke.

"You knew the queen?" I asked with a bit of surprise in my voice.

"Aye, you could say that!" Aldwin scowled as he spoke. "I was forced to see that foul harpy nearly every day of my life for nearly twenty years! If it weren't for the prince, I would have leaped off of *The Bulwark* and prayed for a yard of steel in my gut!"

"The prince?" I leaned forward in my chair, waving hands up in a calming motion. "Aldwin...*Fredrick*. Calm down, you're not making any sense!"

"I had hoped to find a fresh start here, as much as an old man like myself could find." The bann slumped back into his chair with a loud sigh, still clenching his fists. "But it seems like my past is determined to keep pace with me no matter where I go!"

"Aldwin, help me out here," I asked the knight. "Slow down, and start at the beginning."

"Are you sure? It is a long story," Aldwin warned. "And involves a great deal of politics..."

"I can't help if I don't know what's going on," I replied, leaning back into my chair.

"Okay." Aldwin inhaled a deep breath before continuing. "For the last...twenty-seven years, up until a year ago, I had the honor of being one of Prince Rainier's bodyguards before he died." Aldwin began to deflate as he spoke. "A royal knight charged with his safety."

"*A royal knight?*" I echoed in surprise. *I suspected there was more to Aldwin's past than he let on...but this?*

"I first met him when he turned thirteen." Aldwin nodded at me as he began to reminisce. "I was young, barely twenty-five, when they pulled me off the wall to assist in teaching the prince the ways of war. In many ways, he was both the brother and son I'd never had." The bann continued to dig through his memories. "We became close friends, at least as much as the heir of a kingdom could be to one of his subjects.

"Years flew by, the prince growing to become a fine young man and a fierce commander against the orc invaders. But as King Cyril's health declined, the nobility began to insist that the prince be wed and ensure that the dynasty be preserved. Lest some tragedy befall both king and prince and leave the kingdom in turmoil."

"Hm." I nodded to show the bann I was still following.

"After a great deal of politicking, Emilia was chosen as the best candidate, largely in part because the crown needed House Denarius's coffers and magical backing to counterbalance the growing political discord the other houses were displaying, in hopes of keeping the kingdom unified.

"Unfortunately that meant Emilia had to be pulled from her study of magic at the Mages Guild in order to fulfill her role as a scion of her house. Once Emilia found out, she was—*understandably*—enraged. Instead of doing her duty, however, let's just say I'm certain Thaddeus, Emilia's father, would have gladly bankrupted his house just to rid himself of that banshee at that point."

"So Emilia, I take, was difficult to get along with once she arrived at the palace?" I asked hesitantly.

"Gods! If she were just merely difficult to get along with, it would have been an incalculable improvement over her true disposition." Aldwin snorted with mock laughter. "She was a right terror to anyone who could not harness magic, believing them to be sub-sentient, little better than furniture. The idea that she would be *married* to a magi-cless, brute of a warrior was abhorrent to her. Within a month after the wedding, she had all but physically chased every courtier from the palace and alienated practically every other house."

"She didn't want to marry the prince just because he didn't have magic?" I said with a bit of surprise. I could understand outrage at being torn from a world you loved, and a political marriage was far from ideal, but eventually becoming queen had to count for *something*, especially to someone who grew up in a noble house and knew such things were possible.

But hating people just because they didn't have magic? That just sounds exhausting!

"She did not want to marry *at all!*" Aldwin exclaimed. "Rainier made it abundantly clear she was able to pursue other romantic interests should she have wished. But for all the interest she showed in men—*or women*—she might as well have had a fiery pit leading straight to Hell between her legs.

"I never knew the details, but I'm certain the better part of a brewery was needed to give Rainier the courage to bed her." The bann made a gesture with his hands implying the mechanics of the night. "Then, months later, barely an hour after Swain was born, the woman had the nerve to *test* the child for magical aptitude."

"When the test showed no spark of magic within the new ball of life she held in her hands, she gave it away to a retainer, barely even deigning to look at the baby and ordered them to leave."

"She did not!" I exclaimed, shaking my head at the picture the bann had painted. "What did she do with her time then? If she'd driven everyone away around her and didn't even take interest in her child…"

"She locked herself away in the royal apartments, studying whatever magic caught her fancy. Remember, Eberia itself is a ruin, from a civilization ages past. Even after all these years, hidden chambers and repositories are still being found somewhat regularly." Aldwin shook his head at the digression. "At first we kept Swain nearby, hoping that she would reconsider her attitude towards the child. But one day, a relic she was researching *activated*, nearly consuming the infant. When pressed for details her only comment was to apologize that she had *missed.*

"The boy was kept separate after that, and he never grew up right for it." Aldwin sighed. "Rainier was too caught up in the war and shouldering his father's duties to give the boy the proper attention he needed, and I'm saddened to say that young Swain took very much after his mother. He regards people as mere playthings and was far from ready to be king when Rainier died."

A silence fell upon the room as I slowly digested what Aldwin had just told me, the sudden revelation surprising me.

"I was with him that day, not so long ago," Aldwin said giving me a haunted look as tears gleamed in his eyes. "Our dreams were coming true all around us. For the first time in four decades, the orc tribes were in full retreat, the losses they had sustained large enough to keep them at bay for at least a generation, maybe two, until their numbers grew again. We would finally be able to see the lands the orcs hid from us beyond the Ridge, to have a chance to explore. It was not meant to be." A tear rolled down Aldwin's face as he rubbed his face. "Four hundred men and women rode with the prince's vanguard. Six of us returned to Eberia. Within a day of our return, three put themselves into a noose, another fell into the bottle, the last simply disappeared."

"And you made it here," I said, if only to myself.

"I did," Aldwin affirmed as he wiped his hands on a handkerchief. "After a while."

"So…" I ventured carefully. "How did the queen react?"

"She departed from the palace almost immediately after Rainier's death, returning back to the House Denarius estates," Aldwin replied, acknowledging my question. "I don't know if young Swain threw her out, or if she left of her own accord; I didn't care enough to find out, as King Cyril's heart finally broke when he heard of Rainier's death."

"Oh." I sat up in my chair, remembering Sierra's description of events a few days ago when they first arrived.

"We celebrated the bitter end of a four-decade-long war by burying father and son together, the first, and second of the royal line to lay within the Crypt of Kings." Aldwin's voice broke as he relived the events. "At the funeral, everywhere I looked, I saw eyes that resented my survival, wishing that I had traded places with the prince. Were it possible, I would have.

"Within a week of the funeral, Thaddeus Denarius also *conveniently* passed away, the other scions of the House abdicating in favor of Emilia Denarius who was installed as matriarch of the house at the ripe old age of thirty-nine. Her first action was to denounce the king, her very son, and distance herself from the throne."

Aldwin sat in silence for a moment as he lost himself in thought.

"For a time, it seemed like we were going to descend into civil war. None of the noble houses stood directly with the crown. Some were even pitted against one another as long buried feuds grew bloody. Without an external enemy to unify us, we quickly turned on one another." Aldwin then indicated himself. "Then the rumors began, centering on *me*."

"You?" I said with some surprise. "*Why?*"

"I don't truly know." Aldwin shrugged once again. "I had retired from active service, content to wallow in my own grief and misery by myself. The rumors began harmlessly, that I was secretly a bastard of this house or that house, laughable things really. Before long however, they turned darker, suggesting that I had been a paid assassin to infiltrate the royal guard, and to see the prince dead if the opportunity presented itself."

"That's insane!" I exclaimed with surprise. "You served your country to the best of your ability! How could they even think that?"

"I don't know, Lyrian, but there were far too many rumors to rebuke, and before long I wasn't even able to find a baker that would sell me a loaf of bread, no matter the coin I paid. Within a season, I found myself no longer welcome in Eberia." I could hear the pain and frustration in Aldwin's voice as he spoke. "Then one day, I received a letter, penned by Matriarch Denarius's hand. She...*berated me*, for becoming such a divisive figure in Eberia, for *allowing* the houses to use me as they pit themselves against one another in their feuds—"

"What world does this woman live in?" I interrupted the bann, my heart roiling at the woman's gall to accuse such a thing. "You were grieving! You didn't allow anything!"

"She was content to remain aloof while the other houses squabbled, but once the feuds began to affect her house..." Aldwin mimed a chopping motion. "She addressed the problem with a brutal finality. Terrifying the other houses into compliance."

"So how did that affect you, then?"

"In her letter, she determined that I was a painful reminder of days lost." It visibly pained Aldwin to say those words. "And that it would be better for everyone if I retired somewhere out of public sight to let the kingdom heal in peace. It was promised that she would put a swift end to the rumors that plagued my name, then offered me a loan to secure a distant plot of land, far away from Eberia, along with a handful of tenants, villagers."

"So...you left," I said stating the obvious.

"Oh, I took her offer, all right." The bann sounded angry at himself. "What choice did I have? I hadn't eaten in days by the time her letter arrived. I couldn't even leave my home without being beset by thugs. I was so angered by my kingdom's abandonment of me. I took the poisoned fruit she was offering and swallowed it whole!"

"What were her terms?"

"Surprisingly...fair. I was granted rights as the legal head of the settlement and the freedom to name it as I wished. I also secured the promise of additional settlers, with favorable dispositions to my leadership to come in about a month's time from now, if the village was progressing adequately." Aldwin recited softly. "Her requirements included a substantial return on her investment and the promise to never return to Eberia."

"So she exiled you, in all but name," I said.

"She did," Aldwin affirmed with a bitter laugh. "It is ironic, all my life I had wondered what was over the Ridge to the north of Eberia, and now that I'm here—" He indicated the walls around him and sighed, "—all I'm reminded about is Eberia."

We sat in companionable silence for a few minutes as Aldwin mulled through his memories, and I considered the day's events.

"What do you recommend we do about the ruin we found?" I asked Aldwin, after giving him a sympathetic nod. "Donovan wants to claim it for the Mages Guild, and House Denarius by extension. I am not so sure I wish to hand it over to them. If they discover a way to repair the translocation grid…"

"You are right not to trust them. Emilia plays by rules we lesser mortals can barely understand. She had a chance to rule Eberia and found it not worth her time. If she has turned her gaze here, it is most certainly for her *own* benefit, not the kingdom's." The bann explained with a wave of his hand. "Donovan isn't the one to negotiate with in this matter. He may be the titular head of this lost expedition, but I am all but certain House Denarius has included an agent of their own that holds the true power. Emilia wouldn't have sent such an expedition without including someone firmly in her camp."

"And with that mystery person potentially dead or captured by goblins?"

"Then do nothing, until approached by the house. Or…" Aldwin's face broke into a smile as an idea crossed his mind. "Claim it for yourself! Gods! That would piss her off to no end!"

"Claim it?" I frowned. "With just the seven of us to defend it?

To what end? Even if we could repair it, how long would it stay in our hands?"

Aldwin shook his head as if chiding a small child. "Lyrian...you think too small. I didn't mean for *you* to claim it."

"I meant for you to form a *guild* and claim it."

THIRTY-THREE

R HYTHMIC POUNDING WOKE ME UP from a night of strange and disjointed dreams. Despite my exhaustion, I had stayed up longer than I had hoped thinking about Aldwin's words. Creating and managing a guild was a difficult process on its own, but creating one and leaping headfirst into politics you didn't quite understand?

That was a recipe for trouble.

I rubbed my eyes while collecting my wits, a broken dream of me chasing a spiderling wearing a golden crown surfacing in my mind. I vaguely recalled that it had stolen something from me but couldn't quite remember what. As I tried to catch it, a strange goblin carrying a jar of blue honey laughed at me, slowly disappearing as I chased the spider.

"Ugh." Catching up on missed sleep always gave me weird dreams, today being no exception. Considering how long the day was yesterday, my brain definitely needed the rest. *What is that hammering noise? If we're going to stay in Aldford any length of time, we really need to build our own house.*

A quick look around told me that the rest of the party was already up and out of bed and that I was the last one to wake. Standing up off my cot with a stretch, I peered around the blinds set up around the cots, spotting the skull of the Webwood queen being held up high by three villagers on ladders as Jenkins fastened it to the wall.

"Morning," I greeted the villagers as I made my way across the town hall, quickly smoothing down stray hairs as I crossed the room. "Need any help?"

"Ho, Lyr." Jenkins greeted me with a slight echo, half of his upper body thrust into the skull's maw as he worked on something out of my sight. "There's a plaque down there on the table, pass it up in a moment."

"Plaque?" I asked, spotting a dark piece of wood on a nearby table. Curious, I picked it up and read the inscription.

The Ætherwarped Webwood Queen
Slain on Friday, February 8th, 2047
Amaranth, Caius Vail, Constantine Black, Donovan Kaine, Drace Kross, Halcyon Catos, Lyrian Rastler, Sierra Rain.

"Oh, wow." I turned the plaque over in my hand and ran my fingers over the inscription. "This is amazing!"

"Glad you like it, Lyr," Jenkins replied, then quickly addressed his helpers as he pulled himself out of the skull's mouth. "Looks good! Set it down slowly and see if it bears the weight."

Jenkins's assistants gradually let go of the skull, letting it settle onto the mounting. As Jenkins made a few adjustments, I took a step back to admire the trophy. With its massive size, it effortlessly dominated the room, looking down on everyone in the town hall. Placed in the center of the wall, it would forevermore hold the place of honor, being the first boss creature killed near Aldford.

I couldn't help but look forward to the day when the entire wall was filled with trophies and stories to go with them.

"Perfect! Thanks for the help, guys." Jenkins dismissed his helpers, grabbing the plaque from my outstretched hand.

With their part of the work done, the other villagers gave me a wave as they set off towards their other tasks, carrying their ladders with them.

"Just about finished here."

"Thanks for putting this up Jenkins," I said, watching him install the plaque where it could easily be read from the ground.

"Hey, no worries," he replied with a shrug. "You had to fucking *fight* the thing. I'd rather nail a hundred of these skulls to the wall than do that."

"Ha! Remind me to show you one of its claws!" I exclaimed with a laugh. "Large enough to make a greatsword out of it!"

"Gods." Jenkins shook his head. "I believe you, even without seeing it."

"There!" It didn't take long for Jenkins to fix the plaque firmly on the wall and hop down from his ladder.

"Any idea where everyone is this morning?" I asked Jenkins. "I slept in a bit longer than I was expecting."

"You needed it." Jenkins nodded at me understandingly. "Everyone's already moved on with the day. I saw Sierra, Natasha, and Constantine head out this morning, along with your cat, *err*, familiar. Amaranth."

"Oh," I said as I tried to send a thought over to Amaranth but found that he was out of range. I vaguely sensed that he was somewhere off to the east. "They must have gotten an early start."

"Early enough," Jenkins said with another shrug. "Drace and

Halcyon were getting set in helping with the digging, and Caius oddly enough asked to drill with the bann and the militia."

"Really?" I asked with some surprise. "I wonder why."

"Not sure." Jenkins motioned for me to follow him as he grabbed his tools and ladder. "Haven't seen that other mage you brought back today yet. Probably still sleeping."

"He's had a rough week," I offered.

"Around here, who hasn't?" Jenkins grunted with a fair bit of derision. "Anyway, what's your plan for the day? Your friends hung up all their armor in the workshop, which I can see needs a hell of a lot of mending. But I'm also going to need the space to keep crafting those tribuli."

"I can actually start on the repairs right now, then help out with the tribuli," I replied, happy to get that task out of the way first. "We can air the armor out afterward outside."

"Don't you want to grab a bite first?" Jenkins asked me with a raised eyebrow. "You just got up."

"Uh." I stalled, while I assessed how I felt. The regular feelings of hunger or thirst just, not being there. In fact, I couldn't remember the last time I had eaten something, yet I felt perfectly satiated. All thanks to my new Mana Starved trait. "I'm doing okay actually, plus I'd rather get started on work. I've already slept through half the morning!"

"Ha! All right, thanks." Jenkins barked a short laugh then nodded. "I need to go check that house that you partially demolished yesterday anyway, so I'll be out of your hair for a bit. I just need to grab a few tools from the shop."

"That wasn't entirely my fault!" I exclaimed fruitlessly. "The stupid thing clobbered me!"

"Uh-huh," Jenkins replied flatly. "You should have had the decency to miss the house and make less work for me then."

"*Right*. By the way, on an unrelated note, which one is your house again?" I made a mock motion of looking around. "Purely out of curiosity, of course…"

"Bah!" Jenkins exhaled sarcastically as he rolled his eyes. "Here, grab my tool box. I need to set this ladder down. I'll meet you inside."

Our short journey complete, I grabbed the box out of Jenkins's hand while he set the ladder against the side of the workshop and went inside. True to Jenkins's word, there were four sets of armor hung up on armor racks looking like they'd been, well, mauled by a horde of spiders and in my suit's case, a puma.

Guess it served its purpose. The thought crossed my mind as I inspected the battle damage to my suit of armor.

"Morning, Lyrian!" Ritt popped up from behind a crate, then began pushing it back into the corner.

"Oh!" I yelped, startled by the young merchant's appearance. "Ritt, what the fuck?"

"Sorry, Lyrian!" Ritt quickly exclaimed, giving me a wave. "Just organizing all the stuff around here a bit better. I sorted your stuff too in case you're looking for it."

Without even giving me a chance to reply, he started pointing out crates. "That one there is for ore, that one for smelted bars, herbs can sit in that one, spider…parts go into that one there."

"Thanks, Ritt," I said with a bit of surprise as I tried to quickly absorb the new layout. "Aren't you awake rather early for your schedule?"

"I dumped him out of bed," Jenkins said as he briskly walked in through the door, quickly grabbing a handful of tools.

"Jenkins dumped me out of bed," Ritt echoed, rolling his eyes. "The bastard."

"Because you had to have him organize the workshop?" I asked, slightly confused.

"No, because I need his *lazy ass* to pace off and string the final ditch measurements so we can get started on it today!" Jenkins pointed a hammer threateningly at Ritt. "You're standing still, did you find that string?"

"Y-yeah!" Ritt squeaked nervously, holding up a spool of twine.

"Did you give Lyrian his money?" Jenkins shook the hammer once more, as he turned to leave.

"N-Not yet!"

"I will be back here in an hour," Jenkins called over his shoulder as he left the workshop. "That ditch best be strung by the time I get back. Or else."

"Wait, money?" I asked Ritt. "Hold on, why is he—and what exactly did he threaten you with?"

Ritt sighed as he tossed the spool down onto the workbench with a thump. "He threatened to toss me into the water unless my work ethic improved."

"Eh, that's not so bad," I said with a shrug as I looked at the lazy merchant. "River's like what, six to nine feet deep here?"

"Not the river, Lyrian, *Crater Lake*, from the Ridge." Ritt shook his head. "I hate heights, and I can't swim."

"Oh, I see." I blinked in surprise. "I've done that trip, was a ton of fun. I plan to never do it again. So, what's this about money?"

"Ugh," Ritt grunted as he pulled out a bulging sack of coins and handed it over to me, it visibly paining him to let it go. "That Bann told me to give you this as your reward for taking care of the spider queen and the Webwood spiders."

Wordlessly, I opened the bag, revealing one hundred shiny gold coins gleaming back at me, the same instant a quest alert appeared across my vision.

▷**QUEST COMPLETE!**
Cleansing the Webwood
 You have claimed your reward!
 Reward: 10,000 Experience Points, 100 gold pieces.

Sweet! Halfway to level eleven with just a single quest! If the experience boost hadn't been enough, my head spun at the realization that I finally had money to my name! Without even trying, ideas began to filter their way into my head on how I could best put the money to use.

"He threw in something extra in there too," Ritt said, indicating the bottom of the bag.

"Hm." I shook the bag gently as I reached inside, my fingers finding something that was *definitely* not a coin. Grabbing onto it, I pulled out a finely cut ruby slightly bigger than my thumbnail. "Oh!"

"Don't lose it," Ritt cautioned. "Probably worth at least fifteen gold pieces, depending on demand, possibly more."

"Shit, really?" I looked at the tiny little gem in my hand.

"Yeah." Ritt nodded emphatically. "They hold value extremely well and as I'm sure you can tell are much lighter than gold coins."

I hefted the bag in my hand, still marveling at the pile of coins I'd acquired, finding them rather substantial in weight. "Yeah, I see what you mean."

"So any idea what you're going to use all that coin for?" Ritt asked optimistically as he began to pile sharpened stakes, markers, on top of one another.

"Uh, yeah," I replied without missing a beat, grabbing a sharp knife off the workbench and starting to slice through torn stitching in my armor. "Actually, since you're here, I might possibly need your help."

"Me?" Ritt exclaimed with surprise. "What for?"

"It might be premature to think about this, but I had a thought to use these coins to kick off Aldford's economy once the adventurers get here," I explained while pulling off a completely shredded piece of chitin from my armor.

"By doing what? Paying the adventurers to leave?" Ritt snorted, shaking his head. "Soon as they see that amount of coin…"

"We're going to get trouble no matter what," I said to Ritt while making a stabbing motion with the knife. "And we'll deal with it appropriately. But not all adventurers are going to be complete dicks when they get here. Some will be more than happy to work with us. Integrate themselves into our village here."

"Say that they do," Ritt said with a disbelieving grunt. "What then? Pay them to behave?"

"Don't be silly." I began slicing another ragged piece of chitin off. "I'll pay them to work."

"Work?" Ritt asked quizzically, piling all his markers, string and tools into a wooden box with convenient handles for carrying. "What do you mean?"

"Whatever we've needed so far, one of us has managed to find it, or hunt for it." I used my hands to indicate myself and the absent party members by pointing at the armor. "That's working out now when we only have a small number of people in the village to support. But if we start adding in a few dozen adventurers or more. What are we going to do for food? For supplies? Hell, what about the village development?"

Understanding dawned on Ritt's face. "You're going to buy their stuff! Make them go out and supply the village. The promise of work will keep them in line."

"Damn right!" I continued to explain, making the universal *money* hand gesture, as I rubbed my fingers together. "A copper or two for every decent quality leather square they bring us, maybe a silver piece if they can cut and deliver a thick enough tree for our palisade. You get the picture."

"I do!" Ritt said excitedly. "I see where you need my help with that too. You want me to be your broker in a sense."

"You got it!" I nodded at Ritt. "We can sort out all the details when the time comes, but I'd be counting on you to do the buying and selling. We should probably get a village tax in right at the start..."

"Hang on, selling?" Ritt asked.

"Well, yeah!" I exclaimed with a nod. "We can't just keep buying, right? We'll run out of money. But if I start selling crafted goods right back to them…"

"Then we'll end up with more money and Aldford will grow!" Ritt finished for me, fully on board with the idea. "You're sure they'll go for it? It'll be a pretty mindless and repetitive process, just hunting, prospecting, or logging nonstop."

"There's one thing I've learned in all my years, Ritt," I said with a smile. "Adventurers will do *anything* if given the proper motivation, even if the job is a mindless, repetitive grind."

A COUPLE HOURS LATER, I badly needed to stretch my legs and was walking through Aldford with a box of broken and shredded spider chitin destined for the fire pit. I'd managed to repair the four sets of armor without too much of an issue, directly replacing the shredded chitin with new pieces, along with fixing torn stitching and covering any tears in the leather itself.

Unfortunately, with all the damage that had slowly been accumulating on Drace's and my armor, I figured it'd just be a matter of time before I was forced to craft a brand-new set of armor from scratch.

Oh well. Maybe I'll be able to make something new by that point.

As I strode through the village, the ever-growing azure oak tree caught my eye, having doubled in size and height since I saw it yesterday.

Is that thing going to ever stop growing? I wondered idly to myself as the full tree came into view. *Before long, it'll be a notable sight on the horizon.*

As I walked by the tree, I spotted Donovan leaning against it, pressing his ear firmly against the bark. Angling my path towards him to see what he was up to, I cautiously called out.

"Hey, Donovan," I started, not to startle the mage. "I…uh, don't think that works the same way a seashell does."

"What?" Despite my best efforts, Donovan flinched at my arrival. "Lyrian! Good! You may have answers! What in the world is this?"

Pausing to glance at the tree, I looked back at Donovan. "By my guess, it's an ætherwarped oak tree."

"I can *see* that!" Donovan hissed with exasperation. "But how did it get here? This…shouldn't be possible!"

Offering Donovan a shrug, I set the box I was carrying down, then began to explain yesterday morning's events in more detail. "… and now it seems to grow a hand span every hour or so. Sometimes a little more, sometimes a little less."

"That's…" Donovan shook his head at a loss for words. "I have never seen anything like this before, I don't think *anyone* has."

"Really?" I asked in disbelief. "No one has tried pouring a vial of æther on something to see what happens?"

"Hardly anyone *has* a vial of æther!" Donovan exclaimed. "Let alone uses it so frivolously! The effort that it takes to create æther… staggers the mind."

"Hold on, *create* æther?" I jumped on Donovan's statement. "You can do that?"

Donovan nodded intently. "Certainly! Almost any mage could, if they had enough power."

"What do you mean, power?"

"Well, as I'm sure you are aware…æther is intently concentrated mana," Donovan began to explain. "If a mage is able to capture and harness enough mana, it can then be distilled into a liquid form."

"How much mana would it take to create æther?" I pressed out of curiosity. "If it's that rare…"

"There is no easy comparison…" Donovan shook his head as he tried to find a way to explain. "It would take at least as many motes of mana to create a *liter* of æther as it would copper coins to equal a single platinum coin."

At least ten thousand points of mana. Making the mental conversion in my head. "If æther is so rare in Eberia, then I take that it has no ley line then?"

"No, it does not," Donovan said after a moment. "And that is most unnatural. There is a prevailing theory that something has damaged or redirected the natural ley line system that spans across the continent."

Like an explosion at Crater Lake? The thought crossed my mind.

"Leaving Eberia dry in a magical sense," I finished, receiving a nod from Donovan.

Now I understand why they were looking for that ley line.

We both fell silent, looking up towards the tree.

"Lyrian..." Donovan spoke after a moment. "I would ask your permission to study this oak in more detail. Last night, Natasha told me she managed to rescue a pack when she fled our camp. When I looked inside this morning, I found that it contained a handful of arcane tools including an *æther*scope and a magosphere. I would appreciate the opportunity to get a better understanding of how the æther is integrating with the tree. This is an unparalleled opportunity."

"Uh?" I crooked an eyebrow at the mage in surprise. "Sure, just don't hurt the tree. If we could also have a copy of your results..."

"Of course!" Donovan said enthusiastically, starting to inch his way back to the town hall. "Thank you, Lyrian! I'm eager to get started on it right away!"

"Let me know what you find!" I called out at the departing mage's back. *At least he'll be out of trouble for the day.*

Grabbing the box once again, I set off towards the fire pit, which was also conveniently near the yard where the militia was drilling.

Seems like Caius is getting more than he bargained for. I saw the spindly half-dark elf surrounded by four members of the militia, each taking turns to attack him with their spears. In his hands he twirled a practice staff, methodically batting the attacks out of the way. *But he's learning quickly and will probably need to apply a few levels worth of points into Strength and Agility.*

Continuing to watch Caius fight, I tossed the chitin into the fire pit without any ceremony, happy to be rid of the mess. Someone would light a fire at some point during the day to burn any other garbage that was collected.

"Ho, Lyrian!" I heard the bann's voice shout out. Turning, I saw Aldwin waving me over to the militia yard where the whole group, along with Caius, had just taken a break from their training.

"I had heard that Caius volunteered to put himself under your tender clutches," I said with a smile as I stepped out onto the yard. "So I figured to stop by to make sure I was going to be getting my warlock back in one piece."

"Ha! He's doing fine!" Aldwin exclaimed with a laugh. "He's a natural with the staff, and with a little bit more conditioning and practice, he'll be able to knock you down without breaking a sweat."

"That's great news!" I replied nodding happily at Aldwin and the sweat drenched Caius that had gingerly walked over. "How are you making out, Caius?"

"Everything hurts, and I want to die," Caius gasped as sweat continued to pour down his face. "But it's something I need to do."

"Oh?" I asked, with curiosity. "What's on your mind?"

"I had a hard time yesterday," Caius said slowly as he sucked in air. "Especially with landing a touch on a creature, and I don't really have a fancy shield like Halcyon to hide behind if things get rough."

I nodded in understanding. "You want to be able to keep up."

"Yeah…I just feel like I've been scrambling up to this point," Caius replied with a sigh. "Making great progress so far, but I'm hoping to pick up on some more unarmed skills as well. Aldwin is just teaching me everything as it comes."

"Best way to do it," I said in full agreement.

"Are you off to dig, Lyrian?" Aldwin asked, indicating the neatly measured section Ritt had staked out before Jenkins's wrath caught up to him.

"Not yet." I shook my head, indicating the direction of the workshop. "Just felt a little cooped up in the workshop, so I decided to stretch my legs and throw some scraps in the fire pit. I'm headed back to make more tribuli for the other ditch still."

"Ah," Aldwin said with a nod. "We'll be drilling a bit longer, then it'll be off to digging for us. Speaking of which, we best get back. Muscles don't earn themselves, after all."

"They sure don't," I agreed, waving goodbye to the group. "Have fun, Caius!"

THE REST OF THE MORNING for me was a blur of wood and sawdust as I sat in the workshop with Jenkins crafting tribuli after tribuli. I lost count of how many I made over the course of the day, losing myself in the simple, yet rewarding task. There was a steady stream of villagers that popped into the workshop, dropping off handfuls of wood, or grabbing as many of the giant caltrops as they could safely carry, and emplacing them in the ditches for us. It allowed us to continue crafting without our work piling up around us.

By the time the late afternoon had arrived, Jenkins and I got word that the second ditch had been appropriately filled with enough tribuli to thwart even the most determined attacker from safely making it across. Grabbing a pair of shovels, we wasted no time in joining the rest of the village in digging out the final, and longest stretch of our defenses.

Despite needing to put the finishing touches on the second ditch, the rest of the village had made excellent progress today, largely in part to Drace's incredible strength and stamina. Working a line all by himself, he was able to carve through the earth like butter, tearing huge shovelfuls of dirt from the ground with every thrust. While not able to match Drace's speed, Halcyon was right beside Drace, waist deep into the ditch and working tirelessly without complaint.

<*I return.*> Amaranth's voice echoed in my mind.

<*Amaranth!*> I flinched at the unexpected voice that had been missing all day. <*How was your day? Did you find anything interesting?*>

<*The Many-Legs, spiders, have begun to retreat to their old territory,*> the cat replied. <*Their numbers have been greatly diminished and should not pose a threat if they are culled frequently.*>

<*That's good news! It'll give us some breathing room,*> I sent back <*Where did you patrol today? Any sign of the goblins or adventurers?*>

<*I returned to the lower ridge, then circled towards the rising sun,*> Amaranth said <*I caught faint scents of goblins throughout the wood. However, it was stale and many nights old.*>

North and then east. I mentally made a note to try and teach Amaranth about compass directions when I had a chance. <*That's unfortunate, I wonder where the goblins have hidden themselves. Are any of the others with you?*>

<*The Dirty Ones will be found. The hunter must be patient.*> Amaranth spoke with a confident mental voice. <*No, we divided our tasks today. The others proceeded riverward, as I could cover more ground through the woods without them.*>

<*Did they say when they would return?*> I asked, after mentally converting "riverward" to mean south.

<*Before the sun set,*> Amaranth replied quickly. <*Hunger takes me, and I have spotted prey. I will return to the den shortly after feasting.*>

Happy to know that my familiar was capable and willing to fend for himself, I returned to digging. With the added hands today, it looked like there was a good chance of being able to finish the final ditch before the day was over. That left us with plenty of time tomorrow to craft the needed tribuli to fill it.

Fortunately, it wasn't much longer after I spoke to Amaranth that Sierra, Constantine, and Natasha returned from their day in the field. The sight of our scouts returning back safely was met with waves and cheers, quickly followed by a trio of outstretched shovels to help with the dig. With the extra help arriving and the ditch nearly completed, everyone quickly found a second wind, eager to finally be done the hard work of digging and have the majority of the defenses completed.

Sliding up beside us, Sierra and the others quickly filled us in on their day.

"Not too much to report for the day today," Sierra began. "We ranged about half a day's travel to the south and a bit to the east, mostly retracing the steps that we originally traveled to get to Aldford.

"There's hardly any cover out that way," Constantine added as he dug. "But it's also pretty easy ground to travel over. No sign of any adventurers out that way so far."

"Stronger predators are moving into that region, though," Sierra continued. "I don't know what changed in that area, but most creatures are in and around level eight now, and we saw a handful of those level ten wolverines Drace fought the other day too."

"Yeah," Constantine said in full agreement. "We had a reasonably easy time of it since we're well-leveled and decently geared. But unless the coming batch of adventurers are a hell of a lot more leveled than we're expecting, any that wander into that area are going to regret it."

"Happy to hear about that." I breathed a sigh of relief, knowing that we still had a bit of breathing room around the village.

"Natasha also managed to reach her base class today," Constantine added bringing the scout into the conversation.

"Ah!" She squeaked, hearing her name. "I did! I am now a fully-fledged scout like Sierra! These two have been so wonderful in sharpening my skills! I had never thought I'd be able to progress so quickly!"

"That's great news, Natasha!" I beamed with a smile. "I'm happy you're fitting in so nicely here."

"Me too!" she added with a shy smile as she continued to dig.

"Have either of you seen Donovan today yet?" I made a motion indicating the glowing tree at the heart of the village.

"We did…" Sierra started to say with a shake of her head.

"He's camped out under the tree," Constantine finished with a shrug. "Found a table and chair from somewhere and dragged it out there, writing furiously."

"He barely noticed us when we walked by," Natasha added with a shake of her head.

"Is that unusual for him?" I asked, remembering the bann's words about House Denarius, along with my own assessment of the man.

"No, not really," Natasha admitted. "He's always seemed driven by his work, and a little too focused at times."

"Hm. He doesn't really seem like the type that should have been chosen to lead your expedition," I said bluntly.

"I…had thought the same thing," the young scout said with some embarrassment. "But I didn't think it was my place to say anything, I was the least experienced novice in the expedition. I just focused on doing what I was told, and tried to learn from some of the more experienced scouts."

"Hm." I paused to think for a moment. "Did anyone else step up to fill Donovan's…gaps, in leadership?"

"Well, the scoutmaster did his best. His name was—*is*—Bax Rafferty," Natasha said with a sigh as she thought about her missing comrades. "But ultimately, the mages directed where the expedition went."

"There were other mages?" Constantine asked.

"Yes, three," Natasha replied. "They kept to themselves really, constantly focused on all of their equipment and barely spoke to any of us. To be honest, they seemed rather agitated most of the time. I don't think their experiments were going that well."

"Donovan mentioned the same thing," I confirmed, wondering if whatever agent House Denarius deployed was one of the mages. Given her relative youth and inexperience, it was hard to suspect Natasha as filling that role. *Would they have chosen a non-spellcaster to be an agent?*

"Amaranth mentioned that he smelled traces of goblin throughout the wood," I told Natasha. "With any luck, we'll be able to track them down, and see if we can find out what happened to the rest of the expedition."

"Hopefully," Natasha said softly.

We dug until the sun went down, everyone working tirelessly to have the final link of our defenses completed. As the distance shrank and space to work became tighter and tighter, a sense of eager anticipation arose, as a handful of us worked to bring down the final patch of dirt. If someone tired, another was ready to step in and take their place.

Unable to stand up to our determined effort, the final wall of dirt succumbed to our shovels, connecting the entirety of Aldford's defenses into one near seamless piece, save for strategic patches of dirt that could be quickly used to enter and exit the village without having to wade through a sharpened wall of tribuli.

"We've done it!" I called out to the crowd, being greeted by the enthusiastic cheers and applause of the gathered villagers. "We have taken the first steps to ensuring the safety and prosperity of Aldford! No longer will we be threatened by goblins or harassed by spiders!" I continued. "We will finally be able to sleep in peace, knowing that we can be safe in our own homes! You should all be proud at what we have accomplished here over the last few days!"

Pausing for a moment, I looked around the cheering crowd, trying to make eye contact with as many people as I could.

"Our work is not yet done, however! For we will have to prove that we have the strength to stand on our own, that we are a beacon of surety in these lands for all those who wish to live in peace!" I raised a fist up high. "In the coming days, other adventurers will begin arriving to Aldford and our surrounding territory! Among those, there will be wicked and greedy hearts that will look upon our work and seek to steal it for themselves! By my word, their craven hands will find Aldford a thorny prize to grasp!

"But fear not!" I assured the crowd. "For every heart that holds malice, there will be two filled with virtue! Hearts that will understand and appreciate the hard work that we have put into the village! These are the souls that we will invite into our village, to better strengthen us, and to better strengthen Aldford against those who would wish it harm!

"Should any doubt of my words cross your mind, look upon the spider queen's skull, now mounted on the town hall wall!" I saw tired determination on the faces of the villagers as they nodded at my words.

Having withstood both a goblin *and* spider attack in the same week, they were no longer unbloodied settlers staking a claim far from home. They were now *pioneers* living on the very edge of a dangerous and uncharted frontier. On a primal level, they accepted it now and were prepared to rise to any challenge put before them.

"As for tonight! Let us rest in the glory of a day's hard work!" I called out, finishing my speech. "I don't know about you all, but I am certainly ready to sit down!"

The crowd continued to cheer all the way to the town hall.

THIRTY-FOUR

Sunday, February 10th, 2047 - 6:21 am
Aldford

Good morning, players!
CTI would like to remind all Long-Term Play Players about the 10-day (240 hour) limit for continuous play. If you do not log out before you reach the play time limit, you will be automatically logged out by the system!
Minor play time extensions may be granted by the system while in Combat or engaged by a Story Event on an ad hoc basis. However, CTI encourages players to plan accordingly and to log out ahead of their play time limit expiring to prevent any issues from occurring!
Thank you, and enjoy your time in Ascend Online!
-CTI Development Team

THE NEXT MORNING FOUND ME in a grumpy mood as an impatient Sierra and Constantine dragged me out of bed early to have their armor repaired before they departed for the day again. Our earliest estimates had the adventurers arriving late today or by the end of the day tomorrow, which understandably had everyone more than a little nervous and short tempered.

"We need to get moving, Lyr," Constantine said impatiently as he progressively dressed himself in the gear that I had managed to repair so far.

"Calm your shit!" I snapped at the rogue, stripping a large piece of chitin from the armor I was working on. "If you want me to move faster, then you should avoid getting yourself stabbed in the chest."

"But—"

"I don't care!" I interrupted whatever Constantine was about to say. "Go be useful and create me another mana-infused carapace."

"Gah!" A sound of frustration escaped Constantine as he left to do as I had ordered.

"You're headed off to the southeast today." My clipped words came out as a statement, rather than a question as I looked at Sierra.

"Yeah." Sierra nodded quickly, sensing that I wasn't overly amused at the moment. "There's quite a bit of ground we haven't covered yet. If the adventurers have taken a direct path here, we'll hopefully be able to spot them."

"And *when* we spot them," Constantine added optimistically, placing the requested carapace on the workbench. "We'll have Amaranth and Sierra shadow the adventurers, with Natasha and myself coming back to warn the village."

"Good," I stated, tying off the stitch I was working on and grabbing the carapace. "We'll know where the both of you are via party sense, and once the adventurers get closer, Amaranth can give me real time updates via our mental link."

"What are we going to do then?" Sierra asked quietly, for all the planning that we had done so far, the adventurers arrival to Aldford was one that we had no idea how to predict.

There are just too many contingencies.

"We'll play it by ear," I said with a shake of my head. "My gut could be wrong, and they may be happy to have a place to rest and relax, or—"

"We'll run into an organized guild," Constantine said with a sigh, echoing the worst-case scenario we could come up with.

Our greatest fear was that one of the massive gaming syndicates would be knocking on our door. Huge guilds with thousands of members, all choosing to start in the same location and follow their leaders to wherever they decided to set up shop. If something like that happened to Aldford, there was little we'd be able to do about it, even with the defenses we'd managed to create so far.

Quantity has a quality all its own. I reminded myself of the old quote, hoping after everything we'd gone through, we wouldn't just be overrun by sheer numbers.

"We'll manage as best as we can," I told the both of them, tossing Constantine's fully repaired chest piece at him. "Here, you're all patched up."

"Thanks, Lyr," Constantine said nervously.

"No problem." I exhaled deeply as I tried to banish the stress that had steadily built up overnight. "You'll both be great, and it'll all work out in the end. I know we're all a bit on edge today."

"Yeah," Sierra agreed with a sigh. "I haven't felt this stressed since I nearly slept through that exam back in university."

"I think I remember that. Wasn't there a huge RPG released around that time? Ugh, what was it called?" Constantine said while scratching his head. "That's going to bug me all day now."

"I don't even remember." Sierra smiled, thinking back to the day. "I barely even remember what the exam was about now."

I chuckled, my nervousness bleeding away slightly. "All right, both your armors look in good shape, try not to be too hard on it today, if possible. These things are getting towards the end of their lifespan."

"Heh." Constantine barked a dry laugh, as he slipped on his chest piece. "Something tells me that won't be up to us."

"We shall see," I said softly as I motioned the group outside.

Natasha and Amaranth were waiting outside in the cool air as we stepped outside the workshop. Natasha chewed on a piece of dried meat as she quickly ate her breakfast, giving us a wave when she saw us. Amaranth, in typical cat fashion, had curled himself into a ball, using a crate outside the workshop as a convenient perch as he dozed.

<Is it time to begin the hunt?> Amaranth's eyes opened as we walked by.

<Looks like it,> I told my familiar. *<Everyone's armor is fixed, and they are eager to be on their way.>*

<Good.> The azure cat leaped off the crate and coiled its body into an arch as it stretched. *<We depart.>*

Flicking an ear at Constantine in greeting, Amaranth set off, nudging Sierra's hip with his head as he passed, moving directly towards the nearest village exit.

"Oof," Sierra exclaimed as the giant feline knocked her elfin figure off stride. "Good morning to you too, you brute."

"I guess it's time to go," Natasha said, wiping her face with the back of her hand, moving to follow the cat. "Have a good day, Lyrian!"

"I guess Amaranth is ready to go," Constantine muttered under his breath as he waved goodbye to me.

"Don't worry." Sierra waved as she turned to follow the rest of the group. "If there are any adventurers in the area, we'll find them! *Before* they find us!"

I watched the group leave the village, biting my lip slightly as they vanished from sight. I finally began to understand the expression "hurry up and wait" that I heard people use before. Short of adding the last bit of tribuli to our defenses, everything else depended on what came down on us.

Speaking of which, I probably should get started on those. I wasn't looking forward to another day filled with sharpening the spiked lengths of wood. With the items having long since become trivial for me to create, there weren't going to be any more skill increases for me to look forward to today.

Maybe Jenkins will get a few people helping us craft them. I made a mental note to mention it to the man when I saw him this morning.

So far, everything was quiet in Aldford, the majority of the villagers enjoying a morning to sleep in, as a reward for the amount of work we'd accomplished yesterday. I looked back at the workshop, debating with myself just how long I could afford to procrastinate before starting on the endless task of manufacturing tribuli.

I sat down on a crate for a moment, appreciating the silent stillness of the village. Even if everything went perfectly over the next few days, this morning would probably be the last truly quiet day Aldford would see for a while.

With any luck, the future would have friendly adventurers waking up early and getting ready for their day in the wild. The same would go for the merchants that I hoped would one-day open shops here, along with all the other pieces that would come together once Aldford became a fully functioning town.

Looking upwards, I spotted the azure-tinted oak tree once again, its massive form stretching over twenty feet tall, easily the tallest feature in Aldford now, with no end to its growth in sight.

Shit…when was the last time I saw Donovan? I struggled to remember if I had seen the mage yesterday evening. *Probably not since yesterday morning.*

I sighed, pushing myself off the crate and walking back towards the center of the town in search of Donovan. True to Constantine's words yesterday, I spotted a table pulled up beside the now massive base of the tree, covered in a heap of papers. Donovan and the rumored chair were nowhere to be seen.

Scattered on top of the mess of papers and conveniently doubling as a paperweight was a thick, intricately engraved iron rod. A quick glance at the rod prompted a tag to appear, informing me that it was an *[Ætherscope]*.

Picking the item up in one hand while holding the papers down with the other, I felt the faintest tingle of energy while grabbing the ætherscope. As I examined the engravings on the cool rod, I started to feel a faint, *tugging* motion in my hand as the rod began to nudge itself towards the oak tree.

Huh, maybe some sort of magical dowsing rod? I thought to myself. *I guess that could be somewhat useful.*

The ætherscope was pointing directly at the tree when I felt it begin to tug harder in my hand, moving downwards towards the base of the tree, until it was pointing nearly straight down into the ground.

That's where all the ichor was spilled when the Webwood Horror exploded. I frowned as the ætherscope began to vibrate in my hand. *What the hell is this thing doing?*

Curious as to what could be causing the ætherscope to react so strangely I activated True Sight, gazing towards the ground.

My vision brightened, my newly augmented ability cutting through the dark shadows cast by the rising sun. But it did not stop there. Thick, vibrant white lines appeared in the ground around me, causing me to flinch in surprise. The longer I held the ætherscope, the more lines I saw, the range I could perceive the lines increasing gradually, second by second.

Are those...roots? My eyes opened even wider as I stared at the ground, tracing the lines through the earth. There were hundreds, maybe even thousands of the roots, burrowing far into the ground, far deeper than the tree was tall. The further away the roots descended, the more of an azure tinge the roots acquired. *Shit! What is that?*

At the edge of my vision, a faint deep blue vein of energy appeared, running from the east and then curving to the northwest, flowing so slowly that I could barely perceive it. I knelt down to the ground as if the short distance would be enough to change what I saw.

It was then I noticed the acrid smell of burning flesh, quickly followed by blinding pain in my hand.

"Shit!" I yelled, dropping the now red hot ætherscope from my hand, instinctively deactivating my True Sight. The second it struck the ground, it began to smolder sending up smoke as it burnt through the grass surrounding the tree.

"Aaah, what the fuck?" My stomach roiled as I looked down at the charred mess of my palm. Had I still relied on food for nourishment, I was pretty sure I'd have thrown up from the sight. Sucking in a deep breath, I closed my eyes as the pain peaked, then thankfully it began to fade. A quick glance had shown me losing a full ten percent of my health from clutching the searing rod.

What the hell just happened?

"Wha-what? Whoa!" A sleepy voice greeted my ears, followed by a crash. I heard some scrambling on the ground before footsteps came rushing around the tree. "Lyrian! What happened?"

I opened my eyes to see a disheveled Donovan standing over me. "Your...*æther*scope fucking burnt my hand to the bone, is what happened!"

"What?" The mage sounded concerned; whether it was for me or the ætherscope, I couldn't tell. "It's not supposed to do that!"

Donovan spotted the thing lying on the ground nearby in a patch of smoldering grass. He waved a hand over it, testing the temperature, before gingerly picking it up. "It's cold now. Tell me what happened."

"I-I—" My voice caught as I tried to flex my hand, sending shooting pains through it as the regenerating pink skin cracked under movement. "I came to check up on you but didn't see you nearby."

"I fell asleep in the chair." Donovan indicated a nearby chair that was on its side. "I was just on the other side of the tree."

"Fuck." I shook my head, with how quickly this tree had grown, the simple thought to check on the other side of it hadn't even crossed my mind. I took another deep breath and continued talking. "I saw the ætherscope lying on the table and was curious to what it was. Once I had picked it up, it pointed itself at the tree first, then the ground. At that point, I activated my Arcane Sight…"

"So you saw the root system." Donovan nodded expectantly, not knowing that I had mentioned the old version of my skill. "That shouldn't have caused the rod to overheat."

"I saw more than that," I told Donovan, explaining the change in color of the roots and the massive blue tinted river of energy beneath us.

"*You saw what?*" Donovan practically leaped out of his skin as he absorbed my statement. "How? Even with the ætherscope, you should not have been able to see so far!"

"What do you mean 'even with the *æther*scope'?" I shot back at Donovan. "I don't even know what the ætherscope does!"

"What? Why did you even touch it, then?" Donovan hissed back in surprise. "Normally they aren't dangerous except possibly as a club, but gods you've proven that wrong!"

"I get it, Donovan," I replied acidly. "I was an idiot and touched something magical I didn't fully understand. It's not the first time that's happened and likely not the last. Now tell me, what does an *æther*scope do?"

Donovan took a deep breath, his face coloring like he was about to tear a strip off my hide. But he caught himself and exhaled muttering under his breath. "Like a babe in a naphtha factory playing with matches."

He looked at me for a moment before beginning to explain.

"An ætherscope is a device that is able to detect major sources of magic nearby, as well as enhance the detection range of our Arcane Sight's ability to perceive magic. Depending on the distance, the ætherscope will also shade any magic it perceives in shades ranging from white for the closest auras, to a dark blue for the furthest. It was primarily used for reconnaissance during the war, to maintain a watch for magic-oriented attacks. However, we have repurposed it for our expedition. Not that it did us much good, all things considered."

"How far does it extend your vision?" I asked after taking a moment to absorb Donovan's information about the ætherscope.

"Five hundred meters, in all cases, since we've begun designing them," Donovan stated. "How you saw further is a mystery to me."

"I think it has to do with my fall into the ley line," I told Donovan vaguely. "I have felt more in tune with magic since I emerged."

"Perhaps that has granted you a better sensitivity," Donovan conceded thoughtfully. "Though I am loathe to try and replicate such a gift. Anyway," the mage continued. "You were saying that you saw a massive river of energy beneath us?"

"I did," I said with a nod. "I think it is a portion of the ley line. It was extremely faint."

Donovan nodded excitedly as if he suspected that all along. "Likely that is what burnt the rod from your hand, it was never designed to withstand detecting such power, a good thing to know for the future."

"I'm glad nearly charring my hand to ash was of *some help*." I flexed my hand a second time, feeling less pain as it had nearly healed itself. *If that happened in Real Life, I'd have lost my hand.*

"Perhaps it will teach you not to touch things you don't understand," Donovan replied sagely.

"Doubt it," I grunted as I stood up and indicated the tree. "The roots that I saw were growing straight down, towards the ley line. They had a fair distance to go, but not much longer I'd say."

"Are you certain?" Donovan asked looking towards the glowing tree, still cradling the ætherscope that I had dropped.

"Certain enough that I don't want to check again." I indicated the rod. "Should we be concerned if the tree reaches the ley line?"

"Eh? I have no idea, this is new ground to me," Donovan admitted with a shrug. "I have no frame of reference for such magic."

"Great," I replied with a sigh, looking up at the tree.

"All I can say with confidence," Donovan said softly. "Is that when this tree touches the ley line, it's likely to get *much* larger."

"Fantastic."

AFTER MY RATHER POINTED LESSON in the value of keeping my hands to myself, I returned to the workshop, content to stick to the task of crafting the needed tribuli to complete our defenses. At the very least, the pointy lengths of wood wouldn't spontaneously catch fire on me if I gripped them too tightly.

I really need to figure out the rules of magic in this world, along with ten thousand other things. My mind spiraled as I tried to assess everything I had learned about Ascend Online over the last week. *Even a week into the game and I have yet to scratch the surface of what this world has to offer. If only I had a few more days to catch my breath and find my footing...*

I felt like a drowning man trying to keep his head above water as the responsibility for the defense and development of Aldford began to weigh on me. I had never expected to be in a position of such responsibility when I had first logged onto this world. Now here I was, quite literally preparing for a war I might have no chance in winning about to land on my doorstep.

Even if everything worked out flawlessly, the weight and pressure on me would only increase, the impending adventurers merely being the leading tip of the challenges facing us. Aldford would become the focal point of everyone turning their gaze to the frontier, if only for its strategic location as a safe haven.

Adding onto all of that, if I wished to truly secure the area, I would have to follow through on the bann's advice, potentially pitting myself against an ex-queen and putting myself into a world of politics I knew nothing about.

I think I know why most political leaders have gray hair now. I found myself constantly taking deep breaths, trying to calm my hammering heart before it leaped straight out of my chest. *I wonder if I can somehow put this on my resume. "Led virtual village and all inhabitants to destruction," "experienced in biting off more than one can chew," "ability to repeatedly touch strange and unknown magical artifacts without proper safety precautions."*

"Lyrian, are you okay?" Jenkin's voice cut my spiraling thoughts off.

"Hm?" I looked up at Jenkin's unexpected question. "Yeah, I'm okay."

"Are you sure?" His eyes dropped down to the tribuli I was working on.

"Huh?" I turned the wooden caltrop around, to see that I had tied a hammer in place of one of the wooden spikes. "Oh…"

"I think you need a break," Jenkins said gently, taking the tribuli from my hands.

"But—"

"Lyrian, you've made close to *fifty* of these in the last couple of hours alone! The rest of us have barely made twenty-five, each, in that time," Jenkins soothed me as he waved to a handful of helpers nearby. "Take a break. We'll be able to finish the rest by lunch time."

"Sorry." I let a deep breath out. "Bit nervous today."

"I know what you mean," Jenkins said sympathetically. "Take some time to wind down and let the day work itself out. Don't stress yourself out."

"Thanks, Jenkins. I think I'll do that." I felt my heart flutter a bit as I stood up. "Maybe a bit of a walk will soothe my nerves."

I left the workshop in a bit of a daze, losing myself in thought once again. Walking through the village, I sensed an underlying current of anxiety. I spotted a handful of nervous villagers focused on relentlessly cleaning and sharpening tools, past the point of reason. Gleaming pitchforks, knives, and spades all rested in a line as if they would have to be picked up at a moment's notice to repel invaders. Others dealt with their stress in a more traditional way, simply by burying themselves in whatever work they could find.

Clenching my hand at the memory of the burning ætherscope, I saw Halcyon talking animatedly with Donovan while cutting through the center of the village, both of them so deep into a conversation about magical theory they didn't notice me pass by.

I gradually circled the village, double checking the ditch that we had dug out around the village. Seeing the defenses soothed my heart, realizing how imposing they would look from the other side. Anyone bearing ill intent would have to ford their way across the river, scramble across nearly four feet of tribuli, and then claw their way up a five-foot berm of dirt to get into the village proper. A task that would only get more difficult once the ground became soaked with water and blood.

My feet slowly led me towards the militia yard, where I saw Aldwin, Caius, and Drace sparring with one another.

"Hey, Lyr," Drace greeted me with a wave as Caius and the bann faced off hand-to-hand. "You guys finished already?"

"Not quite yet," I replied with a shake of my head. "Nerves have been getting the better of me. Jenkins decided it'd be best for me to take a bit of a break."

"I know what you mean," Drace said with a sigh. "I've been *nervously excited* all morning long so far."

"Ha! I think that's an apt description." It felt good to laugh and have some of the stress bleed away. I cocked my head towards Aldwin and Caius still sparring with one another. "So you guys just tendering Caius up today?"

"Heh. If anything, I'd say Caius is tendering us up now!" Drace chuckled, a grin spreading across his face. "He's learning fast and I doubt he'll have any problems with his touch attacks now."

"Perfect!" I was happy to hear that Caius was progressing well. I could only imagine how frustrating Friday had been for him, trying to keep up with the rather nimble spiders.

"Aldwin is just showing him a few pointers for his hand to hand work and teaching him a few abilities."

"Abilities?" I asked curiously. "Which ones?"

"Nothing too crazy, just Shoulder Tackle and Kick," Drace explained. "Good for getting some quick distance between you and an enemy or disrupting an attack. I use them all the time."

"Shit! I saw those available to me when I hit level ten!" I exclaimed, stepping closer to Drace. "When did you learn them? Can you teach me?"

Drace's eyes opened wide at my sudden flurry of energy. "Y-yeah, calm down! Aldwin taught me the shoulder tackle maneuver yesterday, and I just picked up Kick back on Friday while we were dealing with the spiders. Surprised you haven't learned it already, actually."

"I tend to lean more towards punching things, rather than kicking them." I began stripping my tunic off as I motioned towards an unused part of the practice field. "Mind if I work on Alteration too? My mana takes a bit more time to regenerate now."

"Hm? Yeah, that's no problem, man," Drace answered waving the question away as he followed me onto the field. "Wish we had a few days to do nothing but catch up on skills. My skills are...everywhere."

"Fuck, don't you know it." I was in full agreement with Drace. "So how do you want to start?"

"Hm..." The warrior paused as he looked thoughtfully at me. "Let's start with Kick first."

I gave Drace a thumbs-up, motioning for him to proceed.

"So the first thing you have to do is make sure that your non-kicking leg is planted firmly into the ground." Drace began to explain as he indicated his left leg. "When you kick, you're going to want to kick *through* your target, like you're trying to break a door down..."

"LYRIAN!" NATASHA'S BREATHLESS VOICE ECHOED through the air as she jogged towards us.

"We found them!" Constantine added, quickly following on Natasha's heels. "Three or four hours out from Aldford."

Finally.

Aldwin, Caius, Drace, and I had spent the entire afternoon sparring under the hot sun, each of us trying to work past the crushing stress that gripped our hearts. The handful of skill increases in Unarmed Combat, and Alteration helped take the edge off of the stress away, but a single careless thought would bring it crashing back down.

"What are we dealing with?" I asked, my mouth suddenly dry. "Is it...*bad?*"

"I...don't know." Constantine shook his head with a grimace. "Not our worst-case scenario, but not good either. It looks complicated— better yet, *fucking complicated.*"

"Great." I let out a deep breath, feeling the stress in my stomach curdle into nausea. Beside me I could see Aldwin, Caius and Drace visibly tense too. "How many are there?"

"In total we have a little over a hundred adventurers coming our way, my guess is around a hundred and thirty or so. They definitely know without a doubt Aldford is out here," Constantine started to explain. "Thing is, I think that the adventurers have split into different factions within the group and that it's not all happy within their camp."

"What do you mean?" I asked Constantine. A divided camp between the adventurers would certainly make our problems easier to bear.

"Well, we've noticed that there are three different groups within the adventurers' ranks," Constantine explained. "First, there is a rather well-equipped group of about fifty that are obviously running the show. They're all wearing leather armor with decent looking weapons. Their primary job seems to be to keep any roaming creatures off the group."

"The second group," Natasha chimed in, taking over for Constantine. "Seems to be a go-between, between the first and third group, roughly twenty of them. They show quite a bit of deference to the better-equipped group while treating the third group like, well, *prisoners*."

"Which is what I think the third group are," Constantine said softly. "At first glance both the second group and the third group are roughly geared the same way, in the same sort of threadbare clothing we all started in. But damned if the third group looks *rough*. Just in the time we were watching, we saw a handful of stragglers beaten for falling behind the group. I don't know *why* they're doing it, but it's definitely been brutal."

"I don't understand," I hissed slowly shaking my head. "Why bother with prisoners? Especially if they're adventurers? I'm not saying it's the best option, but why not just kill them and have them respawn back in Eberia? I'd be loads easier than dragging them along and torturing them."

"I don't know, Lyr, but on top of all that almost all in the third group are walking wounded, which means that they haven't eaten in at least a day," Constantine continued. "There are quite a few that are actually being *carried* by others, simply because their wounds won't allow them to walk."

"Fuck," Caius spat. "They're intentionally keeping them weak."

"Did you notice any leaders in the mess?" Drace asked, nodding at Caius.

"Not too sure," Constantine answered with a shake of his head. "Soon as we had a decent count and direction of travel, we decided to head back and report."

"Sierra said that she and Amaranth would keep pace with the adventurers," Natasha said, cocking her head towards the south. "We have plenty of time to get ready for them."

"Okay." I exhaled another deep breath, feeling the stress bleeding away now that the moment of truth had arrived. I looked around at everyone, finding them all looking back at me. "If they're dragging that many prisoners, I think it's safe to assume that they're not coming here in peace. Inform the villagers and make sure everyone has something sharp or heavy on hand."

I began to call out orders.

"Split anyone able and willing to swing a weapon along the defenses inside the village. Those who can't, have them hunker down in the town hall. Make sure that there are a pair of militiamen to anchor each side of the village, Jenkins and Shelia can decide for themselves where they need to be." I motioned for everyone to start following me back to the heart of the village. "Aldwin, Caius, Drace, Halcyon, and I will meet them outside the village, on the other side of the river. Until we can figure them out, I don't want them any closer to Aldford than they need to be."

"Where do you want us?" Constantine asked, indicating Natasha and himself.

"Back out in the field," I replied. "See if you can meet up with Sierra and Amaranth again. I want the both of you covering our flanks. If they send out any scouts to flank us, I want to know."

"And if they attack us?" Constantine spoke softly. "Or look like they'll attack Aldford?"

I turned my head to look at Constantine, steel in my eyes. "Then kill them."

THIRTY-FIVE

I T ONLY TOOK AN HOUR for Aldford to ready itself for war. Weapons and sharpened tools were passed out to grim-faced villagers, each taking positions along the village perimeter. We checked and rechecked the tribuli filling our defenses, reaffirming our confidence that none could pass without paying a heavy price in blood. Instructions were given, with various contingencies depending on the situation. Everyone knew what was expected of them.

All that was left to do was wait.

Standing under a pair of tall, widely branched trees just outside of Aldford, the five of us watched the sun trace across the sky as it began its inevitable descent on the western horizon. Closing my eyes, I could sense Constantine flanking outward to the east, with Sierra and Amaranth doing the same in the west.

"I see them." Aldwin was the first to break the silence as he pointed. "There, coming around that distant batch of trees."

Eagerly, we all followed his gaze. From this far out, the adventurers appeared to just be a single blob moving in the distance. The blob slowly grew larger as the distance shrank, becoming somewhat more distinct.

< Three of the interlopers have broken off towards us. > Amaranth's cool mental voice could not fully conceal his impending excitement. *< They glide ineptly through the wood, playing at being hunters. >*

< Where are they going? > I sent back to Amaranth, signaling the others to walk out from the trees. My plan was to meet them in full view of Aldford. Close enough for us to be able to escape behind our defenses if we needed to, but far enough away that they wouldn't be able to actively threaten the village. At least not until they've fully declared their intentions.

< They speed through the wood, seeking the Den's flank. > I could feel Amaranth quickly moving in the distance as he and Sierra paced the scouting adventurers. I felt Constantine's presence begin to move in the distance as well and assumed that he too was tracking another set of scouts. *< Shall we end them? >*

< Not yet, > I sent back. *< Let them get closer and make the first move. >*

My familiar closed the link with a mental acknowledgment, leaving us watching the mass of adventurers slowly begin to sharpen into distinct humanoid shapes.

"Amaranth tells me they've sent out scouts to flank us," I told the group. "They're keeping track of them right now but won't hit them unless they're a threat."

"Good," Aldwin replied somewhat uneasily as he watched the advancing horde. "Gods, there are so many of them. We would have been caught completely unaware."

"I expected more," Caius whispered softly. "A hundred or so isn't that bad."

"Probably easier places to go much closer than here," Halcyon suggested.

"Too bad the majority of them are likely assholes," Drace said pessimistically.

"This is far enough," I spoke confidently to the group, motioning for us to stop. There was no way that the arriving adventurers would miss us where we stood. Our presence here was a challenge. They would have no choice but to approach us if they wanted to get any closer to Aldford. "Game faces on, everyone."

We watched the approaching horde grind to a halt a bowshot away from us, milling about as their ranks came to a halt. Looking closely at the first few rows of adventurers that I could make out from this distance, my eyes easily picked out a number of different races from within the crowd.

All the common races were thoroughly represented, humans, elves, dwarves, along with countless half-breeds of every kind imaginable. I caught the sight of a handful of feline, lupine, and saurian races intermixed throughout the crowd, bringing an exotic touch to the travel-worn mass. A few other feathered or furred races stood out, but at the moment, I had no frame of reference to what they may be.

The longer I watched the group, the more details my eyes drew out. Echoing Constantine's earlier observations, I quickly noted the differences between the two groups of poorly geared adventurers. Some merely looked dirty and ragged, while others wore scraps of cloth that could barely even be considered clothes anymore, dried blood evident on the few scraps that remained.

I could feel the weight of their hungry eyes as they watched us, afraid to make a move, but unwilling to back down after such a long journey. It was a crowd driven by momentum more than anything else, and now that they had come to a stop, they looked around aimlessly, unsure of what to do.

As the adventurers settled, my attention focused on the armored adventurers that gradually appeared at the head of the crowd. All of them wearing matching sets of tan-colored leather armor, covering everything except their heads.

A row of adventurers parted ahead of me, a brightly armored human striding confidently out towards us, immediately standing out from all the other adventurers. Even from this far away I could see his armor glitter in the fading sunlight. His long black hair billowed in the wind as he walked towards us, the leather-clad adventurers falling in line behind him.

As he approached and his features sharpened in my vision, I revised my earlier guess, marking him as a half-human of some sort. His skin was far too unnaturally pale to be either a human or an elf, and I noted that he lacked the typical pointed ears elven kind normally had.

What are you? I kept my face impassive as the armor-clad man approached, watching him intently. On closer inspection, I could now see that the armor was a finely crafted suit of antique looking chainmail, made in a style that my mind couldn't quite recognize. A rather ornate-looking sword, complete with jewels stuck in the hilt, hung at his waist. The man rested his hand on the pommel of the blade as he and his entourage stopped a short distance away from us. *And why are you dragging so many prisoners with you?*

The man's gaze silently measured us, his eerily gray eyes roaming over our weapons and armor before focusing on Aldford nearby. Seven leather clad adventurers stopped an arm's length behind the man, my gaze shifting momentarily to identify the motley group as being a pair of half-orcs, a trio of humans, an elf and a dwarf.

"Well...fuck." The man frowned as he looked at us, his eyes carefully looking at our faces. "This is an annoying surprise."

"Uh. Nice to meet you too." I frowned looking at the adventurer standing in front us, caught a bit off guard. Out of everything that the man could have greeted us with, I didn't expect him to simply curse at us as if he spilled a glass of milk.

"In other circumstances, it might have been." The man exhaled with a huff, shaking his head. The rest of his entourage carried hard looks on their faces as they carefully assessed us, unsure of what kind of threat we posed. "I'm guessing you guys either have Isaac, Killian, and the others tied up somewhere in that village, or you killed them, and they're back in Eberia."

I felt Drace stiffen beside me, and let out a short laugh that echoed through the air. "Those were your guys?"

Halcyon and Caius couldn't help but echo Drace's chuckle.

"Isaac, Killian, and the others are all dead, likely in an Eberian prison, too," Drace said bluntly, not bothering to keep the acid out of his voice. "They got a little uppity with us, killed a pair of guards, there was some fire involved. In the end, it turns out Isaac can definitely *not* fly."

Those must have been the adventurers they encountered on their way here. I noted, remembering the shortcut they took to climb up the ridge, and the subsequent fight at the lift system that had been still under construction.

"Knowing them, I can't say I really blame you. They can be rather excessive at times," the dark-haired man ground out slowly with a sigh. "What's done is done. Unfortunately, though, that might make this next part a bit of a pain."

"How about we take a step back," I said, watching the man carefully. "And you tell us who you are and what it is exactly that you want?"

"You're right." The man nodded in agreement. "There is no reason to lose our *civility*. You can call me Graves."

Graves made no move to introduce the guards beside him, an awkward pause filling the air before we caught on and introduced ourselves. Even as I focused my attention on the adventurers behind

Graves, the game world didn't supply any identifying tags to who they may be.

"A pleasure to meet you all." Graves slightly inclined his head in greeting, then focused his gaze on Aldford in the distance. "As for what I want, I think that's pretty obvious."

Well, at least he's straight to the point.

"And I think that with us standing here, you should realize that we're not going to give it up that easily," I replied slowly, looking directly into Graves's gray eyes.

"Of course." Graves nodded understandably. "I wouldn't do anything different were I in your shoes either. At least not without significant recompense."

"You've just met us, and now you want to *bribe* us?" Halcyon exclaimed incredulously. "To just step aside and *let* you take Aldford?"

"Calling it a bribe would be a rather rude way of describing the generous offer I am willing to extend." Graves began to pace in front of his men, inspecting us intently. "Judging by your equipment, along with the fact that you took care of Isaac and his group, tells me that you're all rather decent players. Ones I'd rather have on my side than against me.

"So instead of us wasting energy fighting against one another, I would instead prefer to recruit you." Graves stated. "There are other… *events* closer to Eberia, which are currently attracting the majority of the other Eberian adventurers' attention. If we work together, we can solidify our power in this region before more start heading out this way."

I suddenly get the feeling that we're not the first ones to hear this pitch. My jaw clenched as my eyes flicked towards the larger group of adventurers, only to see that more of the armor-clad followers had moved to the front of the group.

"As great as you may think that offer is," I replied looking at Graves. "What's exactly in it for us? From where I'm standing, it looks like we're going to be selling all our hard work pretty damn cheap."

"You mean aside from us simply storming the village and taking it from you?" Graves said coolly, resting his hand on the hilt of his sword.

"Yeah, aside from *that*." I stared Graves in the eye, unwilling to be intimidated in such a manner.

Eyes boring into me, Graves stared at me silently as he tried to gauge the depth of my resolve, his guards standing behind him, doing their best to look intimidating.

"You've got spine," Graves admitted after a moment, a grudging tone of respect in his voice.

He glanced briefly at his guards behind him, some unspoken communication passing between them.

"Very well, I suppose I *could* tell you what my vision for this land is. A few days ago," Graves began. "I happened to come across an *opportunity*, the details of which are largely unimportant. However, it allowed me to discover a rather interesting quest chain that coincidentally led to this area. You can imagine my joy when I realized it was the same place I had sent Isaac to."

"Of course," I replied, feeling somewhat uneasy. *I'm sure the game did that on purpose!*

"So a long story short, without delving into needless minutia, this quest affords me an opportunity to found my own kingdom. Completely separate from Eberia, and under my own personal rule." Graves paused to indicate the guards. "And of course, the ability to reward those who choose to follow me."

"A kingdom, huh?" I repeated slowly. "That is quite a lot of responsibility to take onto oneself."

"I assure you, I am *more* than capable of such a burden," Graves declared confidently. "The only question is whether or not you are all willing to surrender peacefully, join my ranks, and enjoy the spoils. Or...if my coronation is going to be one marred by bloodshed." Graves held up a finger in warning. "I assure you, we've become *quite* adept at bloodshed on our journey here."

"No doubt," I replied, my eyes narrowing. "I'm sure it takes quite a bit of cajoling to keep so many prisoners in line."

Graves's eyebrows rose at that statement. "Ah, you've been watching us. I am impressed. I have had yet to see such initiative in this game thus far."

Graves glanced back at his guards once again.

"Nor did my scouts *notice* we were being watched. As *distasteful* as it may be, the quest I spoke of requires a certain amount of...*followers,* shall we say, to successfully found my kingdom." Graves's voice took a regretful tone. "Specifically those followers must also be broken, and completely obedient to my rule."

"You mean broken as *slaves,*" Aldwin stated, biting the word as it came out of his mouth.

"And you thought that that was a good idea? Just because you had a quest?" I couldn't help but keep the venom out of my voice. *Just a handful of days into Ascend Online and just because he has a quest, he considers enslaving dozens of people not only acceptable but actually follows through with it?*

"It is quite a temporary measure." Graves shrugged as if the matter was unimportant. "Once the kingdom is founded successfully I plan to free them to whatever ends they wish. Until then however, they will have to remain with me. I can't have them getting away and spreading word of my kingdom until it's truly ready to defend itself."

"I'm not so sure I believe you will free them at all," I hissed at Graves.

"Whether you believe me or not is irrelevant." Graves smiled as he spread his arms out wide. "What I am more interested in at this moment is your answer to my offer."

< The scouts have moved against the Den. > Amaranth's voice floated

through my mind. *<One has forded the river and fallen into the pit of teeth. Shall we strike at the others?>*

He was just stalling. I felt my heart skip a beat as I looked out towards the increasing unsettled mass of adventurers in the distance. *Waiting for his scouts to get into position.*

<Stop them,> I sent back to Amaranth, doubting that Graves had any intention of honoring any deal he had struck with us. *<Take prisoners if possible, but if not...>*

<Then their blood will water the earth.> My familiar's voice finished with a mental smile.

"I am prepared to discuss surrender," I answered the man, clenching my fists. Everyone beside me would take that as a sign to be on their guard. "There is no need for anyone to get hurt."

"Splendid! I was hoping you were all men of reason as well as ability!" Graves clapped his hands with a smile that didn't quite reach his eyes. "My followers will need to secure the village, as well as get a proper count of ho—"

Graves stopped speaking mid-sentence, his eyes immediately glancing to the west then back towards the east.

"My apologies," I said as I took a step forward, silently praising Amaranth's and Constantine's timing. "Perhaps I wasn't clear. I am prepared to discuss *your* surrender."

"So...that's how you want to play it," Graves hissed after a moment of shock, his eyes blooming with a crimson light. He visibly trembled with fury as he drew his ornate blade from his hilt, pointing it directly at me, all of his guards quickly doing the same. "That was a mistake."

Did...his eyes just change color? I focused intently on the man at a sudden loss for words, alarm bells ringing silently in my head.

"I think the mistake was coming here with a horde of slaves in tow," Drace replied hotly, less affected by the sudden change of color in Graves's eyes. "What the hell is wrong with you to think that is okay? Those are all other players!"

"God, you are all such sensitive pricks!" Graves's voice boomed as he scowled at us. Following his shout, I heard murmurs of concern and rustling from the distant crowd of adventurers. "This is just a game! We can do whatever we want in this world! Real Life moralities don't exist here!"

"Like shit, they don't!" Caius shouted back.

"Idiots! After all this time, you still have no idea what the *true* purpose of this game is?" Graves hissed at us with anger in his voice. "We are all entertainers! Actors to play out a grand drama for the real world to watch!"

"What?" Graves's words stunned me. I had completely forgotten about one of Ascend Online's key features. From the instant that I had spawned in Aldwin's study, right up until this very second, everything that I, *we*, had done in Ascend Online had been recorded.

"You're doing this all because you want to sell your feed?" I asked with disbelief. The party and I shared a similar goal, but our intentions were to simply cover the costs of subscribing to Ascend Online and keep playing. Graves, on the other hand, seemed to have much grander plans.

"Ah! Finally, comprehension!" Graves mocked as he slashed his sword through the air. "I have bigger plans than merely selling my game feed. I plan to make myself a feature attraction for Ascend Online! The first player to become a *king!* People will want to watch me just for that novelty alone, but more importantly, they will *pay* to watch me!"

"That's it?" Halcyon exclaimed in disbelief. "You're doing all of this, just for a few bucks?"

"I am doing this, for a few *million* bucks!" A greedy grin crossed Graves's face as his red eyes bored into ours. "We *all* are."

"What the fuck are you talking about, Graves?" I shook my head at the deluded man.

It was Graves's turn to look at us in disbelief. "You all really have no idea just *how* popular this game has become over the last week, have you? As of right now, Ascend Online has over fifty million sub-scribers, and yet, there aren't enough pods across the *entire* world to accommodate them all, let alone the hundreds of millions on waiting lists until construction can catch up!"

"Are you fucking serious?" I heard Caius gasp.

"The world is desperate for *any* news, footage, or information about the game." Graves's eyes gleamed with undisguised greed. "By the time we're allowed to release our feeds, the world will be in an absolute *frenzy*, one that I damned well plan on capitalizing on."

"You think people will watch you after they see you treating other players as slaves?" Drace gaped at Graves.

"How many people do you even think will be able to tell the dif-ference between players and non-players?" Graves asked with a shrug. "Even if they do, how many people do you think will even *care* about what happens in virtual reality? To them, this will be nothing but a brand-new show to watch as they trudge through their dreary lives."

As crazy as Graves sounded, I couldn't help but agree with what he was saying. By majority, people *wouldn't* care what happened within the game world, writing it off as either a scripted story or super realistic animations within a video game. Only the people who actually *played* the game and suffered through the experience would fully understand.

"I have heard enough!" Aldwin interrupted with a shout, his face bright red with anger. "You have come into my domain, openly declar-ing yourself to be a *slaver*, with the intent on bringing harm to my people, and usurping my village! I would be a fool to stand here any longer and not take action!"

I saw Graves's crimson eyes narrow as Aldwin continued to speak. "By my right as the bann of Aldford, and a knight of Eberia, I hereby proclaim you and all under your banner to be outlaws in any and all domains that hold loyal to the kingdom of Eberia!

"You are hereby forbidden to seek food, fire, shelter or passage, from any law-abiding citizen or trespass in any Eberian domain, under penalty of death!" The bann's words echoed through the air. "Furthermore, any Eberian Citizen can turn in proof of your death in exchange for a single golden coin. May the Gods have mercy on your soul!"

Standing this close to Graves and his guards, I noted a small tag appear above their heads.

Outlaw – Current Bounty: 1 Gold Coin.

Surprised that such a feature existed, I looked over at Aldwin, his eyes meeting mine. He nodded almost imperceptibly, then turned back to look at Graves.

"What an interesting feature. I shall have to remember it for my reign," Graves spoke, unperturbed by his newfound status, his eyes unfocused as he read a system alert we could not see. "I'm certain there will be quite a number of powers available to me once I become king."

Graves held up his free hand, conjuring a ball of crimson energy in it.

He's a caster too? I eyed the ball of energy, instantly coming to a decision. *Here we go!*

"Be sure to watch me when this is all over." Graves smirked, as his guards began to move forward. "I promise to make this entertai—"

I flicked my hand in Halcyon's direction.

Following the prearranged cue, Halcyon detonated a Pyroclap directly in front of Graves. The blast sent him and his two closest guards, a pair of half-orcs, sprawling backwards onto the ground. The sudden attack caused whatever spell Graves had been conjuring to dissipate harmlessly in a spray of scarlet light.

"Take them all out!" I shouted to the party as I saw the increasingly agitated horde of armored adventurers starting to press forward after seeing their leader fall. "I'm going after Graves!"

Despite all their bravado, Graves's guards were slow to react to Halcyon's sudden escalation, giving us precious seconds to close the short distance between us. Focusing on one of the human adventurers ahead of me, my feet dug into the ground as I leaped forward, giving me much needed momentum as I triggered Blink Step.

Suddenly appearing an arm's length away from the surprised adventurer, I drew Razor from my sheath, my momentum carrying me inside his guard. The blade sang through the air as it carved a furrow of blood across the adventurer's body, stretching from waist to shoulder, splitting the leather armor with ease.

Stepping in even closer, I caught the adventurer's ax on my blade, driving my knee viciously into his groin as I collided with the man. Overwhelmed and outmatched, the man's eyes rolled up into the back of his head as he crashed to the ground, stunned, my foot trampling over his face as I sped towards the fallen form of Graves.

As I sprinted towards Graves, a surprised-looking elf stepped in front of me, conjuring a spell in his hand. I thrust Razor forward, at the same moment a tiny ball of fire burst from his hands and splashed across my chest.

[Unknown Elf] hits you with [Flare] for 13 points of fire damage!

"That's it?" I exclaimed more in surprise, rather than mockery as Razor's point punched through the elf's armor, burying itself straight up to the hilt in his chest.

"No—"The elf's scream was choked off, a spray of blood fountaining from his mouth as he died on my blade.

You critically [Power Attack I] [Unknown Elf] in a vulnerable location for 594 points of damage!
You have killed the Outlaw - [Unknown Elf]!

They're still novices! The revelation struck me as I pulled Razor free from the now dead elf's chest, noting that even the combat log had hidden his level and name from me. Having lived through countless battles up until now, we had learned to fight with every level of brutality and viciousness that we could muster. Something I was surprised to find both of the adventurers I had just trampled over sorely lacking.

I guess your skills don't improve that quickly when you practice them on prisoners that can't fight back!

Shoving the dead elf to the side, I finally had a clear path to Graves as he struggled to get back onto his feet. Pumping my legs hard, I sprinted at the fallen leader, intent to remove his presence from the battle as quickly as possible.

In all of our contingency planning, if things became violent, it fell to me to take advantage of any opportunity to decapitate the enemy leadership. My increased mobility made me the best candidate to burst past defenders and get into melee range before anyone could react. Our hopes were that by identifying and killing any leadership we found on the field, the adventurers would quickly collapse without anyone to drive them.

Springing forward, I leaped onto Graves, burying my knee deep into his gut as I barreled him back onto the ground. I used the weight of my attack to drive Razor in a brutal overhand blow, intent on cleaving straight through Graves's unarmored face.

Despite gasping for air, Graves had enough presence of mind to interpose his blade in front of his face, catching Razor with a wicked strength I hadn't accounted for, blunting nearly the entirety of my vicious attack. Fortunately, however, Graves's unforeseen strength wasn't enough to stop my blade from driving his own sword deep into his chin, just below his mouth, the doubled edged blade sinking deep into flesh and bone.

"Aaaaaaaah!" Graves let loose an unholy scream of pain as I gripped

Razor with both hands, sawing the blade forward and slicing it deep into his face. A line of blood bloomed between his left eye and nose, instantly blinding half of his vision. Desperately he heaved his unbelievable strength against me, his one visible eye wild with panic, forcing both our blades to pull free of his flesh with a wet sucking sound, the flesh across his lower lip tearing in the process.

Overwhelmed by his strength, I rocked backwards as I tried to use my positioning and weight to drive Razor downwards. *Shit! He's fucking stronger than Drace somehow! I can't hold him back!*

"Watch this!" I snarled at Graves, eager to put an end to the man. I let go of Razor with one hand, it shooting out to grab Graves by the throat. Clenching viciously, I felt my hands begin to crush his windpipe as I discharged a *Shocking Touch* deep into his body, forcing it to spasm as the electricity surged through it. No longer pressured by Graves's unearthly strength, I was able to slide my blade down and off of Graves's blade. I moved quickly with the intention to slice Razor straight across his throat.

But before I could get my blade into position, I was bodily tackled off of Graves by one of the half-orc guards that had finally recovered from Halcyon's earlier attack.

I slammed into the ground shoulder first as the half-orc pinned me to the ground, pushing my free arm down as he straddled me. *Damn it! Razor is trapped under me!*

Falling in a convenient pose to see the thundering horde of Graves's followers closing the gap as they charged towards us, I desperately tried to spin my body to face the half-orc pinning me down. I was able to buy a few precious inches of leverage as I angled my body towards him.

Craning my head upwards I could see wild anger on his face, his snarl exposing row after row of jagged teeth. He seemed intent on holding me in place long enough for the charging horde to come to his aid.

Shit! I have to get moving!

Bucking wildly, I quickly twisted back away from him, planting the balls of my feet on the ground as I faced downwards. Moving as fast and hard as I could, before he adjusted his grip, I pushed off with my legs, pulling myself straight out of the half orc's grip and onto my back. Grabbing Razor as I rolled, I swung it in an arc, chopping it directly into the side of the surprised guard's head.

Who says unarmed training is useless? Yanking the blade free, I quickly stabbed it into the half-orc's throat, kicking him off me before I was drenched in blood. I whirled to find Graves, intent on finishing him off if possible before time ran out.

"Lyr!" Halcyon's called my name urgently, interrupting my frantic search. "Leave it! We have to go!"

Stray arrows and flashes of magic began to pepper the ground around me as the charging adventurers started to find their range. *Damn! I'm out of time! I'm as good as dead if I catch half a dozen arrows and magic bolts!*

"Coming!" I shouted, scrambling to my feet. Chancing one quick glance behind me, I spotted Graves being dragged away by his one remaining half-orc guard, pulling him bodily by his armor's collar to safety.

Graves's face was a complete ruin, covered completely in blood. He seemed to be trying to shout something as his guard dragged him away to safety, but his ruined throat prevented him from making any sound.

An arrow thudded into the ground beside me. *Okay, time to go for real!*

Triggering Blink Step once again, I instantly sped to Halcyon's side. "I'm here!"

"Finally!" the mage shouted as his force shield shimmered into existence, catching a pair of arrows and a poorly aimed fireball.

"Well, this is shaping up to be a giant clusterfuck!" Caius shouted, indicating the charging horde of adventurers in front of us.

"At least they're not *all* against us!" Drace said optimistically.

"Small comfort right now!" Halcyon exclaimed as the outlaw adventurers thundered down on top of us.

"What's our plan?" Drace asked, looking at me. "We'll get swarmed if we stay."

"Yeah! Back to the bridge!" I shouted. "We'll hold them off there!"

"Dropping the shield!" Halcyon called. "Get ready to run!"

The moment that Halcyon's shield came down, we all spun, sprinting directly back to Aldford. For the first few yards of our flight, magic bolts and arrows sailed all around us before we managed to outpace the attacks.

Not pausing for anything, we all charged straight into Aldford, quickly running across the pair of stones that bridged the river. Originally intended as a temporary measure when the villagers had first arrived to settle Alford, the bridge was two roughly cut lengths of slate, each approximately three feet wide, a foot thick, and nine feet long.

More than enough for people to easily walk over, or a wagon to *very* carefully drive across. But as a chokepoint to fight over, all the while defenders tried to make your life difficult? It was going to be a nightmare.

There was no cover anywhere near the bridge on the opposite side of the river, forcing attackers to cross while under fire from the defenders. Even once they made it past the narrow bridge, both ditches filled with tribuli further extended the chokepoint, funneling the attackers between two earthen berms if they wanted to enter Aldford proper.

This design allowed us to make the most of our relatively few numbers and to reduce the amount of attackers that we had to deal with at the same time.

"Incoming!" I shouted out, rather needlessly, as we formed up right between the two earthen berms.

Once again Drace centered the line with both Aldwin and I flanking him on either side. Standing in front of us was Halcyon, hands outstretched as he channeled his Force Shield. I heard shouts behind me calling for Jenkins and Shelia to move to this front.

"I can't fucking believe I'm doing this again!" I heard Halcyon yell. "Mages aren't supposed to be charge breakers!"

"I *told* you, we'd make you into a tank!" Drace barked a short laugh as he tightened the straps on his shield. "Bwahaha!"

"This isn't funny!" Halcyon shouted back.

"They aren't stopping! What the fuck did you do to them, Lyrian?" I heard Sierra's voice call out, followed by a twang of her bow.

"You know me, Sierra. Just being my charming self!" I turned my head to see a flash of red hair near the top of the berm. *Sure glad she made it back in time!*

"We can break them!" Aldwin shouted. "Look at them! They are hardly more than a mob right now! They will shatter at the first sign of things turning against them!"

True to Aldwin's words, I saw that the charging adventurers had descended into complete chaos as they chased us, a booming voice egging them onwards. I had no way of knowing just how much Graves had shared about his quest or plan to monetize his feed with his followers. Judging from their rage and complete lack of strategy as they stormed towards Aldford, I felt that they knew *something*.

Either way, *time was up.*

"Here we go!" Halcyon shouted as he leaned his body forward, preparing to receive their charge and pushing his Force Shield just a little bit further forward.

Having never seen the magic that Halcyon was channeling before, the attacking adventurers simply didn't know what to make of the slight distortion that was Halcyon's Force Shield. Nor did they stop to question *why* we'd conceded the bridge to them without a fight. Instead they dug in their heels, and sprinted directly at us, intent on crashing right through our ranks and into Aldford.

Halfway through their stride, the front ranks of the outlaw adventurers suddenly slammed into the shield with a massive crunch of bone and flesh. The first few rows were flatted against the barrier as the weight of those behind them drove them forward.

With nowhere else to go, those unfortunate enough to follow in the fourth and fifth ranks of the charge found themselves tripping over their companions and falling directly into the nearby ditches of tribuli.

Screams of pain and terror quickly broke out as a handful of adventurers found wicked stakes of wood protruding through body parts, their cries quickly silenced as the weight of other falling adventurers fell atop them, driving them deeper into the ditch, and onto even more of the sharpened stakes. A handful of slower, luckier, adventurers were fortunate enough to avert their fall, choosing to tumble straight into the river instead.

The impact had Halcyon's feet skidding across the ground as he tried to keep himself standing until the charge abated. With a snap of his hands, he canceled the Force Shield, sending the pinned adventurers crashing to the ground in a heap, the faintly shimmering distortion vanishing instantly with a faint popping sound.

"Go! Go! Go!" Halcyon shouted as he ducked between Drace and me, detonating a Pyroclap right on top of the adventurers' front line as he passed.

"Forward!" I ordered, stepping forward into the chaos while activating my True Sight. The narrow battlefield suddenly lighting up, banishing the long shadows the setting sun cast across the berm.

Smashing into the line of fallen adventurers with little mercy, the first few seconds of the melee was completely in our favor. Nearly a dozen of outlaws had fallen over one another after abruptly colliding with Halcyon's Force Shield, leaving them tangled in a massive heap of limbs and weaponry, struggling to stand.

Wasting no time, Drace launched himself forward, his wicked bladefang sweeping through the tangle of adventurers mercilessly, leaving vicious wounds everywhere it passed. Following closely, Aldwin and I anchored Drace's flank, our weapons slashing at any within our reach.

We held nothing back as we began to scythe through the tangled pile of adventurers.

I ruthlessly thrust Razor into an adventurer's exposed throat, instantly wiping seven days of travel away, as they respawned in the distant Kingdom of Eberia.

Nearby I saw Aldwin brutally chop his ax directly into the side of an adventurer's skull, quickly kicking him free and doing the exact same to another adventurer following too closely behind.

Arrows flew through the air like deadly wasps, Sierra and Natasha focusing their efforts on any adventurers that dared to cast a spell.

A kaleidoscope of colors and echoing thunder fell upon the densely packed adventurers as Caius, Donovan, and Halcyon burned through their mana with reckless abandon.

Watching the death pile up around me, my stomach roiled as I tried to figure out what Graves promised to these adventurers for them to go along with his plan.

Maybe he promised to share the money he earns from his game feed? I slapped aside an inept sword thrust, rewarding the adventurer with a bleeding cut across the forehead before I kicked him into the tribuli-filled ditch. *Perhaps they'll see the error of their ways after they realize they've wasted a week for nothing.*

Seeing nearly a dozen of their friends fall, the outlaws redoubled their efforts, scrambling to press forward and fill the gaps of the fallen or wounded.

Arrows and magic bolts quickly lost their threat as the crowd pressed in around us, the distant outlaws across the river unable to find a clear shot at us in the melee. The fight dissolved into sheer butchery, blood spraying everywhere as Drace, Aldwin, and I battled with our attackers. Before long, Constantine, Jenkins, and a handful of the militia had joined our ranks giving us much-needed support as the outlaws pressed us harder.

With little room to maneuver and sheer numbers pressing down on us, we all accumulated countless wounds, Shelia's healing efforts being all that kept us from crossing over death's door.

Looking across the river, I saw hesitation appearing on the adventurers faces as they waited to press forward. So far they had lost nearly half of their number and now were having second thoughts of crossing the river.

"NO! WHAT HAVE YOU DONE?" I heard Graves's hoarse voice bellow from the other side of the river. "YOU IDIOT! You sent them all into prepared defenses! Fall back! FALL BACK!"

Hearing their leader's cry, the ragged mass of outlaws ground to a halt and started to pull away from the edge of the river, those finding themselves stuck on the Aldford side leaping straight into the river, as opposed to waiting for the tiny bridge to clear.

"They're retreating!" I screamed, charging forward. "Hit them hard, now!"

Yelling at the top of my lungs, I shot forward, the rest of the melee fighters not far behind. We thrust forward, abandoning our desperate defense, chasing after the fleeing enemy ranks. I bullied my way forward, intent on causing as much pain as possible.

We had barely made it to the edge of the bridge before Sierra started to shout loudly towards us. "Heads up! The other adventurers are moving! Hold on! They seem to be fighting one another!"

The other adventurers! My eyes shot open wide as we ground to a halt. I had completely forgotten about the two other groups of adventurers that Constantine and Natasha had identified. Looking through the crowd of fleeing outlaws, I could see bursts of magic flaring into the night.

A sizable group of adventurers broke off, fleeing towards the east, while even more adventurers leaped into the water, as they dragged themselves through the river and began to run westwards.

Shit! The slaves are scattering! What the hell is happening over there?

"GRAVES!" A loud feminine voice roared through the air ahead of me. "WHERE THE FUCK ARE YOU, GRAVES?"

A portion of the enslaved adventurers split apart from the chaos, all moving directly towards Aldford. My enchanted vision easily pierced through the gloom of the setting sun, giving me clear sight of a tall blonde-haired woman leading the group towards us.

This is just getting more complicated by the moment!

"GOD DAMN IT!" I heard Graves roar, my eyes quickly turning towards the sound of his voice. I saw him screaming at a nearby subordinate. "THIS IS WHY I TOLD YOU TO STAY BACK! NO MATTER WHAT!"

I lost whatever else Graves was shouting as a bright crimson aura bloomed around the man. Gone was the bright gleam of the armor he wore, now replaced with glowing red chains that coiled around him.

What the fuck is that? I gasped as the rest of the aura coalesced, forming into a ragged crimson spirit that hung over Graves. As it took shape, it assumed a vaguely human form, dressed in similar looking armor to what Graves wore with an ornate crown on its head. *Is that a ghost?*

Somehow detecting my gaze, it turned to look at me with bright scarlet eyes. My heart skipped a beat as a wave of incredible malevolence suddenly washed over me. Staggering back, I saw Graves flinch and turn to look directly at me, rage burning in his gaze.

Gone was the smooth, pale face that I had first seen when Graves approached Aldford. Now, it was completely covered in blood, with a piece of his lip hanging freely from his mouth, exposing a row of teeth. The two twin wounds on his face continued to bleed freely, turning him into a horrific parody of his uninjured self as blood dripped down onto his armor, marring its once pristine appearance.

Graves looked at me and spat out a mouthful of blood, saying something I couldn't hear. I saw the spirit raise one of its ethereal hands to point towards me, quickly followed by Graves mimicking the motion. *Is that thing controlling him?*

Before the spirit could finish whatever it had planned, the one remaining half-orc guard grabbed Graves by the shoulder, intent on pulling him away from the battle. At first, Graves resisted, turning to yell at the man, but the guard was insistent and said something to cause Graves to relent, the spirit suddenly fading away as the crimson aura dimmed. They both spun and ran towards the east, all of the outlaw adventurers moving to follow, before the rebelling slaves could come into range.

Running towards the trees, the outlaws quickly vanished from sight, the rebelling slaves continuing to chase them to the edges of the distant woods.

It's over. I looked around the once peaceful field that bordered the southern river of Aldford, finding it now trampled, the ground muddied with blood. I could hear cries of pain, coming from wounded adventurers that had fallen into the tribuli-filled ditches, begging for someone to come and pull them free.

"Lyr, are we going to go after them?" Drace asked, blood still dripping from his bladefang as he indicated the direction that Graves's group had fled.

"No." I shook my head, looking at the scattered groups of adventurers now loitering around Aldford, all taking furtive glances in our direction. "They likely won't stop running for a while, and I don't trust having these people on our doorstep while we fuck around in the woods."

"Not to mention only Amaranth, Caius, and Lyrian can see in the dark," Constantine added, panting heavily as he slid up to us. "If we're running straight through the woods with Light spells shouting where we are, we're begging to get ambushed. There's more than enough of them left over to ruin our day still."

"That's probably a good idea," Drace conceded, shaking the blood off his weapon. "Fuck, what a mess."

I nodded silently in agreement, distantly searching the crowd of adventurers for the woman that had spoken out earlier. *Maybe she'll have some answers.*

I let out a heavy sigh. *Shit just got a lot more complicated.*

THIRTY-SIX

LESS THAN AN HOUR HAD passed since the battle outside of Aldford, with the last rays of the evening sun vanishing below the horizon. Once it was evident that there would be no more fighting, we had begun the process of pulling out a trio of lucky adventurers that had somehow managed to survive their fall into the tribuli pits. They were quickly stripped of their gear and placed under the militia's close supervision.

In addition to the other adventurers taken prisoner, I found out that between both Sierra and Constantine, they had each managed to take a scout prisoner before the battle had begun. Deciding to keep these scouts separate from the other prisoners for the time being, we locked them in separate rooms in the town hall, planning on interrogating them separately from the prisoners rescued from the ditches.

After a quick assessment of Aldford's defenses after the battle, we found that they had held up rather admirably. Granted, Graves's adventurers practically ran headlong into the strongest part of our defenses with little thought for strategy, but they still came closer to succeeding than I was comfortable with. Had Graves's forces been a level or two higher, and if he had joined the fight himself they may have been able to break through into the heart of Aldford.

He lived in fear that the slaves would rebel if he split his forces, and they did. I had a feeling that Graves had focused too much on getting *everything* done at once, never realizing that he had hamstrung himself in case something went wrong. *I wonder what happened. Someone clearly disobeyed orders while Graves was incapacitated after my attack and decided to press against Aldford.*

It's not over yet, though. As far as I knew, Graves was still alive, along with a fairly large group of the other outlaw adventurers, which meant whatever quest he had was likely still active. *He'll try to rebuild and come back stronger.*

I sighed as I thought of the other group of adventurers now encamped outside of Aldford. They had taken little action after rebelling against the few guards that stayed behind during the battle, content to settle themselves along the river peacefully as they came to terms with their newfound freedom.

"Are you ready to go, Lyr?" Constantine's words snapped me back to the present as he motioned towards the adventurers, Aldwin following close behind him.

"Yeah." I nodded. So far we'd had no contact with the "rebel adventurers" as I called them in my head. The few that we had seen walking about had stayed close to their main group, respectfully keeping their distance from Aldford. It was time to change that and hopefully get a better idea of who exactly was squatting on our front door. "Let's go and hope this works out better than meeting Graves."

"*Anything* would be an improvement over that," Constantine muttered.

With those words, Aldwin, Constantine and I strode out of the village, walking towards the bulk of the rebel adventurers. We stopped a short distance away, hoping to communicate our peaceful intentions as we waited for someone to come out and greet us. Casting Light on myself as we walked, I made sure our presence was brightly evident in the growing darkness, even if I didn't need the light right now, thanks to my True Sight illuminating my vision.

After a few minutes of waiting, I saw a group of three adventurers start making their way towards us. I recognized one as the blond woman I had seen earlier. *She must be the leader.*

She was dressed in tattered rags, clenching a rusty sword in her hand. As the distance closed between us, I could make out wild streaks of blood still coating her face and hair suggesting she had just recently made use of her blade. Her pale skin was coated in days' worth of dirt and grime, obviously not being afforded the same opportunity Graves and his men had to wash themselves. Coming to a halt, she brushed her hair away from her face, tucking it behind human ears. She stared at us with a mix of appreciation and hesitation from behind deep green eyes.

On her left followed a dark-skinned dwarf, with an ebony beard covering his face. The faint gleam of my Light spell reflecting off his completely bald head, making him appear like a solid brick of obsidian. His completely black eyes made me feel unsettled as he looked at us, if only because I couldn't tell where exactly he was staring. Dressed in similar dirty rags as the woman, I noted that he carried a single rusty mace, hanging from a rope tied around his waist, which also doubled as a belt.

Lastly, on the woman's right was a massive saurian, a lizardman, which towered over all of us. Completely bare chested with only a rag to hide their shame, I noted thick muscles shifting and twitching under emerald scales as the green beast approached. The saurian was easily tall enough to rival Drace in height and nearly just as broad. Cool blue eyes met mine, raptor-like head bobbing in greeting as they came to a halt.

"Thank you," the woman said plainly, breaking the awkward silence that had formed as we appraised one another. "I don't know what happened between you and Graves, but we wouldn't be free without your standing up to him. I'm Freya, and these are my friends." Freya introduced herself, then indicated the dwarf, followed by the lizardman. "Thorne and Helix. I wouldn't have made it this far without them."

"Pleasssure," the massive saurian hissed in greeting first, his sibilant voice surprisingly easy to understand.

"Hello," Thorne spoke softly, giving us a nod.

"My name is Lyrian," I replied, everyone else taking the cue to introduce themselves. "So, Freya, can you explain to me, what the *hell* that was all about?" I asked the woman softly, stress still evident on my voice. "We have a hell of a lot of adventurers, *bandits*, loose in the area now, all of whom have a *clear* reason to hate us. Not to mention, I'm sure Graves is going to be holding a hell of a grudge because we've fucked up his plans to become king and get rich in the process."

"Yeah…" Freya crossed her arms defensively as she shifted her weight to lean in closer to Helix. "It's been a rough few days and a rather long story on how we got here." She let out a loud sigh before continuing. "But I—*we*—have nothing to hide from you."

"Rough sounds like an understatement." I paused, looking at Freya silently for a moment before nodding. "What happened?"

"Well…" Freya sighed again as she began to speak. "Where should I start? I…" Freya paused and took a deep breath. "I spawned in Eberia, way back on launch day. First suffering through that stupid Call to

Arms ceremony King Swain pulled out of his ass and like the thousands of other adventurers, left in search of riches and glory.

"I started Ascend Online by myself and didn't meet Thorne or Helix until a few days later." Freya's eyes had glazed over as she started to recite her story. "I joined up with a handful of adventurers looking to explore the east and see if we could find anything interesting. You know, typical adventurer stuff.

"Unfortunately though, there were close to ten thousand adventurers doing the same thing." Freya shook her head. "Have you ever seen those old photos of the wagon trains settling the American West? With people stretching from horizon to horizon? It practically looked like that, a massive horde of adventurers, all heading east from the capital.

"In hindsight…those days weren't too bad," Freya mused. "Enough creatures for us to kill for food and the players hadn't turned violent, yet. After travelling for a couple days, we made it to Coldscar, a new Eberian city being founded at the top of the ridge, near a series of natural chokepoints. I think the king plans to make it his new line of defense, should the orcs decide to return." Freya made a face as she spoke. "Or if the dark elves decide to press their claims too far."

"Hang on, dark elves?" Constantine interrupted. "Their empire you mean?"

Freya's eyes flicked over to Constantine before nodding. "Yes. There had already been a few incidents near Coldscar by the time we had arrived."

"What do you mean?" I asked with a frown. "What sort of incidents?"

"The kind that prelude war," Thorne replied with a bitter voice. "Settlers have gone missing, a handful of villages burnt to the ground, and a few dozen skirmishes against other dark elf players."

Damn. This sounds like what Graves was referring to when he said other events were keeping the adventurers' attention focused elsewhere.

"They're testing Eberia's response," I stated, to which Thorne simply nodded. "Would Eberia pick a new war so soon after ending the one with the orcs?"

"If it meant keeping Eberia unified, most definitely." Aldwin's voice was bitter as he spoke. "We've been at peace for a year, and the kingdom has practically torn itself apart. Eberia does not know how to be at peace."

We all paused at that uncomfortable thought. *I guess a war would be great entertainment for players, and those watching us play.*

"All right..." I said, steering the conversation back on track. "You arrived at Coldscar?"

"I did, or should I say, my group and I did," Freya said, picking up her story from where she had left off. "Coldscar was a very different city than Eberia, if only for the reason that they are trying to build a settlement straight from scratch, right into a major city.

"There were a ton of opportunities there...*if* you were lucky enough to get there first," Freya said with a bitter tone to her voice. "The city needed everything, from resources to crafters, guards, and everything in between. Problem was, by the time we got there, all the major resource areas had been claimed by emerging guilds, and the amount of players around meant any non-guild labor was dirt cheap.

"So our choices boiled down to joining up with a guild and sitting on top of a mine or quarry, competing with the hundreds of adventurers milling about the city for odd jobs, or pushing onwards towards the northwest, north, or eastern frontiers." Freya paused for a moment to lick her lips. "The overwhelming majority of players that decided to leave Coldscar chose to go east. That's how I lost my group.

"They were more interested in fighting dark elves and 'avenging' the lost settlers and raided villages than anything else," the blond woman stated with a shrug. "I, on the other hand, just wanted to level, work towards a base class and maybe find a decent set of gear. I doubted that I'd find any of that heading eastwards.

"So I found a new group, Graves's group, as they were getting ready to head out to the northwest." Freya said with a sigh. "At first it seemed like he knew what he was doing. He had apparently just come through with a huge score, finding an abandoned tomb of some sort, and had earned enough money to outfit all of his friends in leather armor, not to mention looting the gear you all saw him in. He was considered a lucky leader.

"There were over a hundred people looking to get out of Coldscar, in addition to the thirty or so already following Graves. That was when I first met Thorne." Freya paused to look at the ebony slab of muscle at her side. "Though we didn't become friends until *later*.

"Once we were a day away from Coldscar, Graves put whatever plan he had in motion. We noticed anyone who was over level six had an 'interview' with one of his followers. What they were promised, I have no idea." Freya shook her head at a memory that we couldn't see. "Then on the morning of our second day away from Coldscar, he told us all about the quest that he had and what *our* role would be in it.

"More than half the group was in on it, even the ones that weren't originally part of Graves's group. They just *turned* on us, almost instantly." Freya winced as she spoke. "They beat us and terrified us. We barely had enough time to understand what was happening before it was too late."

"Graves told us it was a temporary thing." Thorne spat on the ground in disgust. "Just something that we would have to suffer through until he completed his quest, and then we would be free to go. First time those damned red eyes of his appeared, too."

Freya looked a bit ashamed as she spoke. "There were so many of them, all stronger than the rest of us. What else could we do but stay in line and just wait until it was over? We couldn't even provoke them to kill us, and after a few beatings everyone just…stopped trying."

"Then they found us." Helix spoke, waving his clawed hand towards a handful of distant lizardman adventurers. "Our race, the Arakssi, doesn't spawn in Eberia or in any 'city' really, but within the fens of Swyn.

"Unfortunately for us, Swyn was not popular for new players, as well as being too poor in resources to be worth staying," Helix explained with a hint of frustration. "Ssso a handful of us left the fens, in search of civilization and other players. We had been traveling for many days before we crossed paths with the others…"

"The guards nearly killed them. Stopping once Graves realized that they were players." Freya took over for the giant saurian, who nodded as she started to speak. "Graves and his men just…dragged them into the main body of players and kept walking."

"You guys didn't fight back?" Constantine asked Helix.

"We did!" Helix hissed angrily as he motioned to his lack of equipment. "Arakssi ssstart off poor! No weapons or armor, only our natural claws and scales. We did the best we could, but there were too many."

"I sought out Helix as soon as he *joined* the group," Freya said, looking over to the giant lizardman. "I wanted to let him know what he had gotten himself into. Thorne found him first."

"Freya and I had the same idea." The dwarf spoke, nodding his head at Freya. "We wanted to make sure that Helix and the other Arakssi hoarded whatever food they still had. So that if an opportunity provided itself to be rid of Graves we could take advantage of it in the future."

"Food?" I asked with a confused look. "What do you mean?"

"Graves didn't bother to feed us and without food, our regeneration stopped." Freya winced as she traced a line down her arm, eyes briefly lost in memory. "We wanted to be sure that Helix and his friends hoarded their food and didn't just waste it until we could put it to use."

"Unfortunately, with the lack of food," Thorne explained, "It was starting to become impossible to keep up the twelve to fourteen-hour marches Graves insisted on. We just couldn't regenerate stamina fast enough to keep up with his pace."

"Graves wasn't happy about that. He thought we were purposefully slowing him down. So he ordered his men to beat any stragglers that fell behind the rearguard. When that caused us to slow down even more, he was livid." Freya's expression took on a dark look. "By that point, I was so exhausted I didn't care if I lived or died; *truthfully*, I was hoping to die. A respawn in Eberia would have been a gift. I marched right up to Graves and told him we needed more time to rest or that he needed to start giving us food."

"I thought he was going to kill me with how angry he looked, those goddamn red eyes of his nearly burning a hole in my head while he stared at me." Freya exhaled deeply, shaking the memory off. "He just looked off into the distance for a while, then told me that he was going to 'take care of it' and that I shouldn't concern myself with problems 'beyond my station'. Then he had his guards run me off."

"That night, his *scouts…*" I saw muscles clenching in Freya's jaw as she spoke. "Dragged a large pack of level seven wolves right into the heart of the camp. The majority of us at the time were still level five."

"Shit," Constantine swore.

Freya nodded. "I woke up to one of them gnawing on my arm. Thankfully Helix was nearby to help. But others…weren't so lucky. Hardly anyone had the energy to fight back. Dozens were maimed, and a handful were even killed by the time we rallied a large enough group to kill all the wolves. Graves *really* wasn't happy about that."

"Hang on," I interrupted. "Why didn't you just log off and log back in once the group passed you? Or even reroll your character."

The three of them looked at me like I was an idiot.

"I take it that you haven't logged off if you're asking that question…" Freya answered shaking her head. "First of all, logging off just removes your consciousness from your avatar. You don't just *vanish* like in other games. Your character is forever a part of this world, even when you stop playing."

"Shit, really?" Constantine exclaimed, taking the words right out of my mouth. "What happens to our...*avatars* when we're gone then?"

"The game takes over." Thorne pointed up towards the sky. "Apparently, it *learns* our personality as we play and creates a temporary NPC while we're gone."

"That's..." I was at a complete loss for words. *All the NPCs in this world are so alive, they could be people in their own right!*

"A little terrifying?" Constantine supplied, sounding a little spooked.

"Yeah..." My voice trailed off.

"Persistent characters controlled by the system is not a new idea for online games, just not a popular one. This game just happens to be better than any before it." Thorne shrugged, as if it was an inevitable progression for games. "Either way, it's fairly limited and won't involve you in any major decisions, and will do the best it can to keep you safe. You can even queue certain kinds of tasks behind that it will focus its time on while you're away, such as crafting or building, not that we could do anything of the sort. It's not like you really miss anything, either," Thorne continued to explain. "The game just *updates* your memories with everything that had happened since your last time logged in."

"What?" I said with shock. "The game can do that?"

"Why not? I'm sure you've all had skill ups before," Thorne explained with a shrug. "It feels no different, to be honest."

"I'm not sure how I feel about that," I said, more to myself, reminding myself of our forced log out time Wednesday morning.

"Yeah, well, it is what it is," Freya replied with a rather fatalistic shrug. "Anyway, rerolling a new character wasn't much of an option either," Freya continued after a moment. "First of all, you'll need to shell out the subscription cost *again,* which I'm sure you remember, wasn't exactly cheap."

I nodded at that statement; with us playing as a group, on a long-term play subscription, we received decent discounts as opposed to playing and paying individually. But the total monthly cost was pretty close to a thousand dollars a month. *Each.*

"Then, if you still want to reroll, you have to go to the end of the *waiting list* until your name comes up." Freya's voice was tinged with frustration when she spoke. "Do you have any idea how *long* the waiting list is?"

I shook my head slowly. Graves had mentioned something about that earlier.

"As of this morning, when I checked it, it is approximately one hundred and ninety-eight million people long." Freya stared at us numbly. "At current production rates, it would take us nearly two years to get a chance to reroll. CTI is scrambling to increase production rates, but pods are complicated pieces of technology, not to mention even finding a place to house them."

"Fuck." My head spun as I tried to do the mental math of just how many people wanted to play Ascend Online, quickly followed by the sheer amount of money that CTI would find themselves swimming in. *They'll be richer than most countries. That doesn't even include anything they'd get from media events!*

There was another long, somewhat uncomfortable pause before Constantine spoke up this time. "So...logging out got you nowhere, and rerolling is rather *pointless* considering how long it would take to get back into the game."

"After finding out a few people were killed, Graves banned the practice of dragging monsters into our group, realizing that we were on the verge of just *letting* them kill us, just to get away from him," Freya explained morbidly. "Many were on the verge of losing hope. We had even started to talk about a plan to just start killing one another, to deprive whatever Graves needed from us to finish his quest."

"Thankfully, things worked out for the better," Thorne said smoothly, revealing coal black teeth as he smiled at us.

"It did." Freya nodded, a small smile breaking out on her face as she looked at the dwarf.

"We saw quite a bit of fighting happening within your group earlier." I probed, nodding towards the rest of the adventurers. "What was that about?"

Freya's smile vanished at my question. "There were some scores that needed to be settled. People did things that couldn't easily be forgotten, or forgiven."

"What do you mean?" Constantine asked hesitantly.

"When the food ran out, some players started to prey on weaker players, extorting whatever scraps of food or supplies we managed to horde. They were brutal, intent on causing pain and suffering just because they *could*. In some ways, they were worse than Graves." Freya looked at me with a hard expression. "While you were having your *tête-à-tête* with Graves, we were busy solving a few other problems of our own. *Permanently.*"

Judging the blood I had seen on Freya when we first met, I knew exactly how she had solved those problems.

"Ssolved all of them but one," Helix hissed, clenching his claws menacingly. "He may be among the dead, or escaped, but if he lives…"

Dealing with other hostile adventurers in addition to Graves would have been a living nightmare. I couldn't help but feel a tinge of respect to the three standing before me, given how brutal their journey had been.

"For the last few days, we've been saving and pooling whatever scraps of food we could find and keep, waiting until we found an opportunity." Freya looked at me, then out towards the large group of adventurers behind her. "It gave us the edge we needed to survive today."

"So we saw," I said, following her gaze. *Might as well ask the big question now.*

With a sigh, I looked back at Freya and the others. "What are your plans now?"

Both Thorne and Helix looked towards Freya, who had clearly been expecting the question, but didn't have an answer for me.

"We...don't know yet. Everyone is still a bit in shock after everything that happened today, and after the week we had, only a handful have been staying logged in consistently. Many have been popping in and out every few hours to see what's changed." Freya put up both her hands in a placating gesture. "But we don't mean any harm to you or your village. I know we don't have much to offer, but I think the majority of us would actually be interested in joining your village, well, *if* they ever log back in again. That is, if you'll have us..." Freya added hopefully. "I know our arrival wasn't the best first impression."

"It definitely wasn't what we were expecting," I replied carefully. "But I—*we*—won't hold anything you did to survive Graves's reign of terror against you."

I chanced a quick glance at Aldwin and Constantine before continuing. "Unfortunately, the decision to let you join the village isn't mine alone to make, and it's something that we'll have to discuss between ourselves before we can come to a decision."

"That's more than fair," Freya replied gratefully. "Thank you."

"We'll meet out here in the morning tomorrow and let you know what we've decided," I said, signaling the end of the meeting. "Until then, if there are any issues that come up, send a runner over to the village."

THIRTY-SEVEN

"**T**HIS IS A COMPLETE FUCKING mess." Sierra sighed, slumping into a chair.

"That's what I said," Caius grunted as he sat down beside her.

"Yeah, well," I replied slowly, staring at the ceiling of the town hall as I leaned back in a chair. At the moment, only Sierra, Caius, Halcyon, and I were in the town hall, Constantine having gone to verify Freya's story against the scouts'. Drace and Aldwin gone to do the same with the other adventurers, now temporary prisoners, we'd picked up off the field. "It's probably the best we could have hoped for."

"*I guess*…at least they didn't make it into the village," Caius conceded as he rubbed the bridge of his nose. "Would have been better if they killed off all the ones that got away, though."

"No kidding!" Halcyon exclaimed. "What kind of fucking quest not only *allows* a player to take slaves but actively encourages it?"

"Is it really any different than other games we've played?" I asked, still staring at the ceiling.

"Sure as shit it is!" Sierra replied. "I don't recall any game that forced me to beat, maim, and enslave people!"

"Really?" I answered, my eyebrows raised as I turned to look at Sierra. "I can name at least half a dozen space-empire games that all have governments based around slaving."

"That's not the same!" Sierra scoffed at me.

"Why not?" I challenged. "Slaving is slaving."

"Because those games aren't *real!*" Sierra replied with a bit of frustration.

"*This* game isn't real either, Sierra," I said softly.

"It's *realer* than any other game I've ever played!" Sierra replied, with an angry expression on her face. "Lyrian, *Marcus*, are you seriously trying to rationalize what Graves did right now?"

"No, not at all." I held up my hand in a gesture of peace as I looked right at Sierra. "But answer me this, when you played all those space civilization games, did you ever *choose* a slaving empire?"

"N-no," Sierra answered after a moment. "I didn't. Never have actually."

"Why not?" I asked.

"It just didn't sit well with me." Sierra paused as she struggled to find a way to explain. "I just found it more fun to play as a 'good' empire or a 'merchant' based one. If anything, I was fighting against the slaving empires."

"But the option to play one was there if you wanted to," I finished, nodding sympathetically at Sierra. "Just as it is here."

"But it's immoral!" Caius exclaimed. "*Why* is it here?"

"Never thought I'd hear a *warlock* complaining about morality," Halcyon muttered. "Fucking hypocrite."

"Ha!" I couldn't help but laugh at Halcyon's comment. "I don't think it's the game's job to dictate morality. I think all the game does is present us with options, good, bad, neutral. It's not like it forced Graves or his followers into doing what they did."

"What's the point of all that?" Caius replied while flipping Halcyon off.

"What's the point of anything in a game like this?" I asked rhetorically. "To create conflict and entertain."

"Yeah…but, this time, it's just not entertaining *us*." Halcyon waved his hand upwards. "If we sell our feed, people will watch what we say and do every step of the way."

"It's like…fantasy reality television." Sierra tried the word out on her tongue. "People will tune in to watch good people or evil people, doing whatever it is they want, depending on how they want to play the game."

"Exactly." I nodded, waving my hand indicating everything around me. "All of this is just a stage, literally anything is possible."

"Fuck, this is making my head hurt," Caius complained rubbing his forehead.

"Do you want me to explain it to you using smaller words?" Halcyon asked mockingly.

"Do you want me to set you on fire?" Caius hissed back.

"Oh, please," Halcyon scoffed. "Your *morality* will probably get in the way. After all, you wouldn't set one of your dearest and closest friends deliberately on fire, thereby causing him intense physical pain, *right?*"

"Fuck you," Caius swore with a laugh, flipping Halcyon off a second time. "What's taking Constantine so long?"

"Still interrogating the scouts, I guess," I replied with a shrug. "I don't hear any violence, so I guess things haven't progressed to stage two of interrogations."

So much for morality.

"Fat chance getting them to say anything." Sierra rolled her eyes while shaking her head. "Constantine would have an easier time getting water from a stone than getting one of those two to talk."

"Well, I guess that makes me a fucking magician, because this stone is wet!" Constantine's voiced echoed from the back of the Town Hall as he walked down the stairs. "I got one of them talking, and his story matched up almost perfectly with Freya's."

"You got them to stay something?" Sierra exclaimed with surprise. "What did you do?! Did you..."

Sierra's words trailed off as she made a sawing motion with her hand.

"Nothing," Constantine said with a goofy grin on his face. "I didn't even touch him."

Sierra shook her head in disbelief. "What the hell did you say then?"

"Well, I first explained to him how the logout feature in Ascend Online works, just in case he wasn't aware of it," Constantine explained, giving me a nod. "Then I asked him if he wanted to be buried neck deep in the outhouse or never play Ascend Online again."

It took us a moment to process exactly what Constantine just said.

"You did not!" Sierra squeaked, as she fought back a roar of laughter.

"Oh no!" Halcyon's face quickly turned beet red.

"Oh, god." Caius had a hand over his face as he struggled to keep himself together. "You're evil!"

"Does this look like the face of mercy?" Constantine pointed to himself, sporting a wicked smile on his face.

It was at that moment Aldwin, Amaranth, and Drace walked

into the room.

"Hey-" Drace started to call out in greeting, before sensing something was amiss. "Hold on? What's with Constantine's shit-eating grin?"

"I told him that's how he could get out!" Constantine quipped, making eye contact with me as he smiled even wider.

That's it, I can't hold it anymore! A loud cackle escaped through my lips, quickly followed by the others as we all collectively, pardon the pun, lost our shit.

The stress of the day instantly burned away as we nearly fell out of our chairs laughing. With tears filling my eyes, I could barely make out Aldwin, Amaranth, or Drace staring at us all, completely dumbfounded.

"What did I say?" Drace looked around with a slightly confused look.

<Lyrian, are you all right?> Amaranth's voice was tinged with concern.

It took us a minute to settle ourselves down before we could explain Constantine's success and the joke to Aldwin and Drace, as well as reassuring Amaranth that we were all all right.

"The stories of the prisoners that we picked up match Freya's version of events as a whole as well," Aldwin said, sporting a smile across his face, the infectious laughter of Constantine's joke not yet completely gone. "Graves had apparently promised many of them positions of power within his...*kingdom.*"

"Yeah, the scout said the same. Apparently, Graves was in the process of building his own feudal kingdom on his way here, promising titles left, right, and center," Constantine added. "But that wasn't all, though. He promised them cash payments once he started making money from his game feed in real life, probably to help them stomach the slaving he had them doing."

"Really?" Drace exclaimed with surprise. "He didn't seem the type to share. How much was he offering?"

"Fifty grand," Constantine stated. "Each."

"Are you fucking kidding me?" Halcyon shouted as he leaped out of his chair. "There was at least fifty of them right? That's like, uh, two million and eighty—"

"It's two and a half million even, Halcyon." Sierra quipped. "Also, remind me to never trust you with counting money."

"I'm an illustrator, not a mathemagician, woman!" Halcyon shouted. "I don't deal with numbers!"

"How the hell did Graves expect to earn that much money?" Caius's face was skeptical. "He must have been lying."

"I don't know about that," I answered, shaking my head. "Freya told us that there was nearly *two hundred million* people on the waiting list just to play. Even if a fraction of them gave a few dollars…"

Everyone went silent at that mental calculation.

"Lyrian, I want a raise." Drace looked at me suddenly. "I think I am a valuable member of the team and that my services deserve adequate compensation outside the framework of this game."

"I couldn't agree more!" I said empathetically. "I'll double, no, *triple* your salary!"

"But you aren't paying me anything!"

"How is that my problem? You should have gotten a better agent when you signed with the team." I couldn't help but laugh at the absurdity of it all. "We'll figure it out when the time comes, man. Not to worry!"

"Did the scout know anything about the group Graves supposedly sent to take over Aldford?" Drace asked Constantine while chuckling. "Isaac and the others?"

"Didn't volunteer anything about them, and I didn't ask, in case it shut him up," Constantine replied shaking his head as he sat down beside me. "Though I don't feel that bad about killing them anymore and burning the lift down."

"We'll consider that a lucky bullet dodged then." I motioned towards Aldwin. "What's your opinion of the prisoners? Will they cooperate with us and behave until we can figure out what to do with them?"

"I feel they have been honest for the most part, if a bit shocked by recent events," Aldwin said after a moment of thought. "We've stripped them of their gear and stowed them away in the house that you crashed through the other night. Jenkins said it was unstable and will need to come down at some point, so it wasn't in use."

"That wasn't my fault!" I muttered, mostly out of reflex at this point.

"No tears from me if it collapses on them in their sleep." I heard Halcyon whisper to Sierra behind me.

"Their accommodations are better than what they would find sleeping in the wild all night." The bann paused for a moment before continuing. "We'll have to figure out what to do with them eventually."

"A problem for the future," Sierra said copying my favorite phrase. She turned to look at Constantine, indicating the upper floor where the scouts had been locked into separate rooms. "Did the scout say anything about Graves specifically?"

"Eh, the only other thing he mentioned was that Graves wasn't always the way we saw him today," Constantine replied. "He said he first started playing with Graves on launch day and he was a bit more...calm. If I recall right, his words were 'Graves was always kind of a dick, but not *I'm-a-fucking-king* kind of a dick.'"

"Well, *that's* helpful," Halcyon muttered sarcastically. "Did the scout know what race Graves chose? The way his eyes changed color, I bet he's part demon or something."

"Yeah, that was fucking creepy," Drace said quickly, glancing over at me. "Not the same as your glowing eyes, Lyr. His just made me feel on edge."

"I know what you mean," I agreed, nodding at the warrior. "But his eyes weren't the only thing I noticed, there was some sort of *aura* and spirit hovering around him."

"There was?" Halcyon asked, surprise evident on his voice. "I didn't notice anything."

"I think it was something I could only see with my True Sight ability; it lets me see a hell of a lot more than just magic now." I focused on a corner of the room as I recalled the thick red chains all wrapped around Graves. "I didn't have True Sight activated before the fighting started, so I didn't see it earlier, but towards the end of the battle, before Graves retreated, I saw him.

"He had all these *crimson chains* coiled tightly around him, pulsing with a strange sort of energy." I tried to explain, using my hands to mimic what I had seen. "After a bit of time, the aura formed into a ragged-looking ghost that wore similar armor to what Graves was wearing."

"Maybe it's a racial or class ability, or something like my patron demon?" Caius suggested. "He conjured that ball of crimson energy before Halcyon dropped the hammer on him."

<It sounds like a controlling spirit,> Amaranth hissed in my head, his eyes narrowing at the memory of when he was under control of the nemesis spirit.

<Maybe,> I replied, sending back a mental shrug. *<But what does it mean if the threads are red?>*

<I know not.>

"Did it seem like he had a base class?" Sierra asked glancing between the five of us that were there.

"Not particularly," Drace replied, his brow furrowed as he searched his memories. "I really didn't see him do anything, to be honest."

"Me either," Caius chimed in with a shake of his head.

"I think the armor he's wearing is giving him some pretty sweet stat boosts," I added, remembering Graves's unexpected strength. "But nothing really specific other than that."

"Hang on," Constantine said, getting a faraway look in his eye. "Freya said he *found* the armor and sword he was wearing, right? Also, he somehow got enough money to buy all of his friends' armor?"

"Yeah…" I nodded slowly, recalling Freya's story. "Something about a tomb they found."

"Okay, so Lyr saw a strange spirit hovering around Graves wearing similar armor, plus his personality isn't *quite* the same as people remember it being." Constantine quickly listed on his fingers. "To top it off, he seems to have a pretty rare quest aiming to make him king."

"Where are you going with this, Constantine?" Halcyon asked, exasperation evident in his voice.

"What if the armor or sword he found was *cursed*?" the rogue said with excitement. "What if it's changing his personality or forcing him to behave a certain way?"

That idea stopped everyone cold.

"*Shit.*" I thought back towards our encounter with Graves. "I think the spirit hovering around him had a crown on now that I think about it."

"Maybe he dug up the spirit of a dead king?" Constantine suggested.

"It fits," I agreed. "I think it may have been controlling his actions or at the very least powerfully *suggesting* things."

"That might explain how the slaving idea took root in Graves's head," Sierra said thoughtfully, before breaking into a wide yawn and changing the subject. "Moving on, *before* the sun comes up. What are we going to do about all of these adventurers on our doorstep?"

"It's a pretty large group of people to just absorb into Aldford…" Caius motioned around the group. "Did anyone have a rough count of just how many there are?"

"About sixty, maybe a little more," Constantine replied, waving his hand back and forth in an unsure gesture. "Plus…how many prisoners?"

"Three," Drace replied. "Not including the scouts."

"Who I doubt would want to stick around if it was up to them," Halcyon commented.

"That's nearly three times the amount of villagers we have already," I said quietly.

"That is, quite a considerable increase," Aldwin said hesitantly, concern written on his face. "If nothing else, it would put quite a strain on our resources."

"Not to mention having a place to physically put them," Caius added. "If they want to camp outside, that's fine. We have plenty of space for that, but short of having everyone asses to elbows here in the town hall every night, we'd need to start building."

"Would definitely have the labor for that," Drace said optimistically. "And incentive if they want their own space."

"But can we trust them to behave?" Halcyon asked, raising possibly the most important question. "I don't know about you all, but I don't want to be playing 'town guard' day after day."

"I definitely don't want to be a prisoner in our own village." I nodded at Halcyon. "Right now we're likely the strongest adventurers within a few days radius around Aldford, but as more players make their way out towards us and other players start to level, that gap will decrease, if not vanish entirely. But I don't want to pass up this opportunity as well."

"Opportunity?" Constantine looked at me with a confused expression.

"Yeah." I motioned my hand in a circle, indicating the village around us. "Let's face it, Freya's group *needs* us a lot more than we need them. We can make that work for us."

"How exactly?" Halcyon asked skeptically. "They're going to need to be fed *and* geared before they even come close to being useful. Even then the majority of them range from level four to six. If they're anything like the ones we fought, they'll barely know which end of their weapon they should be holding."

"That's exactly it! Practically all of them are hungry and weak," I replied, waving my hand towards the south. "You saw them, all huddled by the river. A third to a half of them still don't have food and aren't regenerating their wounds. Most are all still in shock. If we walk out there tomorrow with food and helping hands when they are at their weakest, they'll remember it and appreciate it. They know how much it sucks to be stuck in the wild."

"All that is only temporary, though," Sierra said. "Now that Graves isn't holding them down, they'll be able to hunt for their own food and support themselves."

"They probably could," I replied, completely agreeing with Sierra. "But the longer they see us here, all cozied up in the village, while they struggle just outside, it'll breed resentment. I know it would for me. Plus, we can offer them protection *from* Graves. Let's not forget that he's still out there, after all."

"As concerned as I am about the safety of Aldford, there is wisdom in Lyrian's words," Aldwin spoke up, having been lost in thought the last few moments. "When we were fleeing Assara, most of us only had the clothes on our back and very little of anything else. I know for certain that if it weren't for those more fortunate helping us, while we were packed into those tight ships, we would have never made it."

"Helping I can agree is a good thing." Halcyon nodded sympathetically at Aldwin. "That still doesn't answer the question of *how* to get them to behave."

"We'll need laws," Sierra said, looking at Aldwin. "System-enforced laws. If we do this, Aldford isn't going to be a village anymore. It'll be a town, well on its way to becoming a city, even. If there are penalties that are above and beyond ones that require *us* to enforce, they'll hesitate more in breaking them."

"We should also get them to buy-in, before formally joining the village. A special one-time offer to get a stake in the early development of the village," Drace added. "If they feel a sense of ownership and belonging here, they'll be less likely to cause problems. They also need to know that this will be a *frontier town*. They'll need to earn their keep, one way or another."

"Have them buy-in with what?" Caius shot back at Drace. "They just trudged halfway through the wild under Graves's thumb. They have nothing!"

"Likely they don't," Drace agreed, holding a hand up as a placating gesture. "But I think Lyrian is onto something. If we go out there tomorrow with a few crates of food, enough to see them through the day and regenerate their wounds, they'll be ready to go out and hunt again. It's not like they're going to sit on the edge of the river forever."

"I can also do a quick sharpen of any weapons they have to get them started," I added. "That won't take me long at all, and I'm sure it'll improve the weapons' stats."

"After that, we can present them with our offer," Drace continued, nodding at my idea. "If *they* want to join our village, then they'll need to invest some supplies to help us keep Aldford running. I'm not thinking anything crazy, maybe a few chunks of meat, or an equivalent amount of leather, wood, or ore. More than easy enough to get that much in a day's worth of hunting."

"That…would actually help make sure that everyone is fed," I said thoughtfully. "Plus give us a good reserve for materials. We're going to need to start building houses sooner than later, if nothing else."

"In exchange for that, we'll allow them to set Aldford as their resurrection point and live within the village, with the understanding that they'll be under Aldwin's leadership, as well as observing the basic rules of law." Drace started talking more confidently as the others started to nod in agreement. "They'll need to agree to actively defend Aldford in time of need too."

"I like it," Constantine stated, nodding his head emphatically. "We can offer them skill training too, if they want it."

Everyone else quickly agreed with the bones of Drace's proposal. There would be countless details that would still need to be worked out, but by majority, we felt that we had a good base to work from and present to the other adventurers.

"There is a way we can formalize their rights and responsibilities and have it bound by the weight of law," Aldwin stated, motioning towards the stairs. "Let us go to the study; I can explain more there."

Intrigued, we all followed the bann upstairs, stuffing ourselves into the smallish office once again. Moving behind the desk, Aldwin unlocked and opened a drawer, pulling out a rather ornate scroll case.

Placing it on the desk, Aldwin carefully opened the case, removing a large scroll of vellum. He slowly unraveled it, pinning each corner down with a paperweight, shiny gold calligraphy glinting in the light of the room.

"This," Aldwin said reverently, "is the Charter of Aldford. The document that recognizes Aldford as a legal settlement affiliated with Eberia, outlining both my rights and responsibilities as bann, and the rights and responsibilities of those having signed it.

"Any who have proven their worth and wish to join our village can affix their name on this document and be counted as a citizen of Aldford with all the rights and responsibilities that come with it." Aldwin gently turned the document to face me. "With this, we can enforce the rule of law for all those who live within Aldford and legally punish those who choose to break it."

I looked down at the intricately detailed document, recognizing the names of all the villagers in Aldford, including the handful that were killed in the goblin attack earlier last week. There was plenty of space left on the document to accommodate more names as Aldford grew before a new sheaf of vellum would be needed.

This would work. I nodded to myself as I read over the charter. Despite the ornate design and scrollwork, the verbiage in charter was plain and concise, covering all the common points one would expect for a town. Any who broke the laws outlined in the charter could quickly find themselves declared as outlaws at worst or merely shunned in all Eberian settlements as an oathbreaker. Nodding in agreement, I spoke with excitement. "This is perfect for what we need and very clear to understand."

I looked up to see Aldwin offering me a golden pen, a smile across his face.

"This is something that has been a long time coming, and I wish I had gotten to this sooner," he said, looking at me and the rest of the party. "You have all done so much for Aldford and truly are heroes in every sense of the word. Would you do me *and* Aldford the honor of being the first adventurers to formally join our growing settlement?"

Taking the pen from Aldwin, I couldn't help but smile. "I thought you'd never ask."

THIRTY-EIGHT

Monday, February 11th, 2047 - 12:04 am
Far East of Aldford
Graves

"**D**ANIEL, WAIT! I SAID I'M so—" Micken's pathetic cries for mercy ended with brutal finality as his head toppled from his shoulders, blood spurting in the air as it thumped to the ground face down.

Sidestepping the spray, I flicked the blood off my sword, barely having felt it pass through his neck. I turned to face the others gathered around me, cold anger written on my freshly healed face. Today had been a complete disaster.

Not only did Isaac and his group fail to take Aldford like they had been told to, they didn't even manage to stop other adventurers from getting there in the first place, giving that *fucking* adventurer Lyrian and the rest of his friends enough time to fortify the village.

Then to top it all off, despite telling him to stay back and watch the slaves "no matter what" and "so they don't fucking escape", Micken decided it would be a good idea to kill off half my troops by sending them into a suicidal charge against fixed defenses *and* let the slaves escape! *God damn that idiot!*

Rage surged through me as I remembered my helpless terror watching all of them charge straight at Aldford, unable to call them back as my crushed throat healed itself. By the time I could make a sound louder than a whisper, it was too late.

I had badly underestimated those adventurers. Part of me expected that just showing up with a massive group of people would cause them to cave in and surrender. *Did they somehow know I had no intention of keeping them alive? If I didn't kill them, someone else in the group would have after hearing about Isaac.*

Now here we were, barely two dozen of us left, sheltering in the woods like some sort of wounded animal desperately seeking a place to lick its wounds.

"Not only did Micken disobey orders..." The words fell out of my mouth slowly, the combined light from a pair of Light spells and a large bonfire casting wicked shadows around me. "But he compounded that error by another one and needlessly wasted the lives of our *friends*, in a battle that he should have known not to fight. It is because of him that we are where we are right now and it's going to be up to us to find a way to make this work."

My eyes scanned the crowd, searching and taking measure of my remaining followers. Micken was a popular presence within the group, and I was worried that signs of rebellion or defiance would appear. Seeing nothing but hard and angry eyes, some nodding in agreement with my statement, made me relax. No matter how popular someone was, few would be able to forgive a screw up of this magnitude.

Especially when it cost them tens of thousands of dollars.

After a moment of silence, I was pleased to find that none disagreed with what I had just done, their minds already preparing for the next challenges to come.

Wait. I saw a face staring at me in the crowd.

A grey-skinned half-orc caught my eye, staring at me intently with a crooked frown on his face. He shook his head at me slowly, his eyes flicking to the body on the ground and then back to mine.

<What is this?> A familiar voice slithered through my mind, causing me to frown.

Damn, the fucking ghost woke up again.

An alien curiosity bloomed in my mind, compelling me to focus the entire weight of my gaze on the man. Not for a second did the half-orc look away.

<How...interesting.> I felt my armor tighten in anticipation. *<Bring him to us.>*

"Get some rest, everyone. We'll be moving once the sun rises." I dismissed the crowd, curious as well to hear what the half-orc had on his mind. I sheathed my blade, not taking my eyes off the half-orc.

The adventurers slowly began to disperse, the majority simply collapsing where they stood around the fire, a handful of others walking to take shelter under nearby trees. I motioned for the half-orc to join me as I stepped a short distance away from the fire.

The half-orc glided smoothly through the gloom, his eyes easily piercing the darkness around us as he approached without fear. Looking at his garb, I noted that he was one of the other adventurers that I had enlisted once we left Coldscar, dressed in threadbare clothes without any armor at all.

"You disagree with what I have done?" My words came out harder than I intended as the half-orc approached, likely interference from the spirit that now shared my mind.

"Not at all." The half orc's yellow eyes bore intently into mine.

<Arrogant half-breed.> The dead king's voice whispered through my head again. *<Just like his forbearers.>*

"Personally, I found it too *abrupt*. There was not enough time for him to suffer."

"And you think he deserved to *suffer?*" I cocked my head, watching him closely.

"He cost us *millions* of dollars. Tens, maybe even hundreds of millions." The man scowled at me. "He should be fed into a fucking meat grinder, *feet first*. I don't mean in-game, either."

< On second thought, I like this one's passion.> I felt the king's spirit stir in excitement, his metaphysical claws wriggling through my mind.

"What's your name?" I struggled to push the king's influence away from my mind, feeling slightly sick as I stared into the half orc's eyes. There was something inside them that made me feel incredibly uncomfortable. *Even for me.*

"Carver," he said with a fang-filled smile.

"Well, *Carver.*" My tongue tasted ash as I spoke the half orc's name. "I feel Micken's punishment has been more than sufficient, given that he no longer has a stake in our kingdom."

"Because of him, there is no kingdom." Carver's voice was flat as he spoke, completely emotionless.

<Let him have his head.> The voice hissed through my head. *<A bloody example would go far to solidifying your rule.>*

I felt the spirit's compulsion dig into my mind as it urged me to give into Carver's bloodlust.

<SHUT UP!> I roared in my head, focusing the entirety of my energy solely on Carver. *<You may watch and advise, BUT STOP TRYING TO INTERFERE!>*

"And you think roughing him up or even *killing* him outside of the game is going to change that?" The half-orc was oblivious to the battle raging inside me, my eyes narrowing at him as I measured my words carefully. "All it'll do is land you in prison and keep you far, far away from being able to play this game. Is losing the chance to play this game worth that much to you?"

A flash of concern and anger passed through Carver's eyes. "No. There's nothing in life that's worth losing the chance to play this game."

"Then I *suggest* you watch what you say and think." I pointed up to the sky. "Lest the game catch on and send the police to drag you out of your pod because it thinks you're actually going to murder someone in reality."

Carver's jaw clenched as he stiffly nodded his head. "You have a point."

"There are going to be growing pains," I soothed, feeling the king's presence recede from my mind as I spoke, hopefully falling asleep for the night. "We will have much to learn in what it means to wage war in this game. There are going to be mistakes."

"I understa—" Carver's words were suddenly cut off as the bonfire behind him suddenly *exploded*, sending him sprawling forward against me.

As I instinctively reached to catch the falling man, screams and shouting echoed into the night as figures in the dark ran through our camp, attacking the half-asleep adventurers.

Shit! They found us! I couldn't believe the other adventurers had followed us so quickly! We had purposefully pushed deep into the forest to discourage any chance of pursuit. *But after losing all our scouts, it's not like we'd know if anyone was following us.*

Pushing Carver off of me, I drew my sword as I raced towards an adventurer that managed to cast a Light spell, giving us at least a small zone of illumination we could fight from. "They've followed us! Group up on me!"

"No, it's not them!" Running quickly behind me Carver called towards me. "They're all goblins!"

"What?" I didn't have enough time to fully process Carver's information before spotting a pair of goblins charging towards an isolated adventurer standing by herself on the edge of the Light spell. As they ran, I noted that they were dragging a rather large net behind them.

Before I could shout, the goblins leaped at the adventurer, easily catching the woman in the net, their momentum completely knocking her off her feet.

"No!" I shouted, raising my hand at the pair of goblins as I ran, channeling one of the abilities the king's spirit had granted me. A ball of crimson energy formed in the palm of my hand before shooting forward and splashing against one of the goblin's back.

Immediately the goblin's flesh withered and rotted as the corrupted energy devoured the goblin's life-force, sending it into mad convulsions as it fell to the ground. Wide, loping steps brought me into melee range with the second goblin, my blade effortlessly slicing through the rusty weapon it held, continuing straight through its body.

A massive fireball shot from the darkness, smashing directly into the adventurer at my feet, almost instantly reducing the woman to ash. What few adventurers I could see who were not caught in similar nets, all froze at the display of power.

"Surrender!" A gravely, high-pitched voice shouted in the darkness. "Surrender and be spared! Resist and you will die!"

A burst of light bloomed from nearby, illuminating a large, blue-skinned goblin dressed in a patchwork of leather armor and fur. In its hands, it wielded a massive bone staff, nearly as long as it was tall, complete with the skull of some unknown creature on its tip. The skull's eyes glowed with fire and tendrils of smoke wafted from its outstretched mouth.

<*A Tal'oshka!*> The ghost's voice roared through my mind as it awoke from its slumber. <*A Gifted Servant!*>

<*What?*> My head reeled from the spirit's sudden shout, worse

than anything I had experienced so far. *<A gifted what?>*

"We have waited far too long for you to leave your village! To have vengeance for those killed!" The azure goblin looked at me intently as it bared its fangs. "Submit now and we will be merciful!"

"We aren't from Aldford!" I heard one of the adventurers shout. "They drove us out!"

"We care not about the wars between your kind!" the goblin hissed, a ball of fire beginning to grow in the mouth of its staff. "This is your last warning! Submit and live! Resist and die!"

<Tell them your purpose!> The king's spirit pressed against my mind with an urgency that I had never felt before. *<QUICKLY!>*

"We aren't from the village! We were attacked by them! We are here to restore the slave-king's throne!" I screamed into the night, causing all the goblins nearby to pause, and turn their attention back onto me. "I seek to rebuild his fallen kingdom and resume his rule!"

"*You?* A *human*, seek the master's throne?" the blue goblin asked in disbelief. "You tread dangerous ground, uttering words of blasphemy your tongue was never meant to bear!"

"I am telling the truth! I have found his tomb and have awakened his spirit!" The words flew out of my mouth as the ghost urged me to divulge all that had happened. "I bear his sword and armor, and now he guides me in search of his lost crown!"

Shit, I didn't tell anyone about that part…

"You openly admit to defiling a tomb of the Old Masters?" The wizened goblin seemed to tremble with rage. "You are foolish beyond measure if you believe such lies will buy your freedom! If anything you say is true, I *demand* proof of your claim! Lest you and *all* of your followers be roasted on an open flame as we draw out your entrails!"

Proof? I panicked. *How can I prove anything?*

<Let me in.> The king's voice whispered seductively, pressing hard against invisible barriers in my mind. *<This servant has long forgotten*

his place.>

<I don't trust you!> I felt the armor I wore constrict as I refused the king's access into my mind. *Damn it!*

<LET ME IN!> The armor locked completely as the spirit raged in my mind.

"As I thought." The goblin seethed as the skull on his staff burst into flames. "A pretender, full of lies. I rescind my mercy! You shall all di—"

Damn it! Everything I had worked towards over the last week was crumbling all around me! *I have no choice!*

"Wait!" I shouted, completely surrendering to the spirit's will. I felt the mental barriers I had worked so hard to erect shatter as the king entered my mind. *<Do what you must.>*

<At last!> The spirit exclaimed with ecstasy as it settled deeper into my being, overlying itself on top of my consciousness. Disjointed memories flashed before my eyes as control was slowly taken away from me, my hands moving of their own accord in front of me, a bright crimson ball of light forming between them.

"**BEHOLD!**" A voice that wasn't my own erupted from my throat.

The orb exploded with brilliant energy.

Then everything went black.

THIRTY-NINE

"AND THAT'S THE ENTIRETY OF our offer," I finished, looking out towards the assembled crowd of adventurers that had camped out on Aldford's doorstep for the night. I wasn't quite sure how Freya had spread the word through real life and managed to get everyone logged in at the same time, but I was happy she did.

Having everyone "metaphysically" present to absorb the information and ask questions in the moment was a much better arrangement than having a crowd of adventurers logging on later to find themselves confused and alone while trying to absorb their new memories.

I had just spent the last half hour of the gray, cloud-covered morning, fully outlining the scope of our offer if any adventurers wished to join Aldford, what we would expect of them as citizens and what services we had to available if they decided to join.

Truthfully, it was an awful recruitment pitch.

I took great pains to emphasize that joining Aldford in no way guaranteed safety, explaining both the goblin raid earlier in the week, in addition to the attack by the Webwood horror. I made sure that everyone knew up front that they would be expected to work hard to help make Aldford a success, to truly take it past being just a tiny little village, to an actual living and breathing town.

"For those of you itching to get yourself out into the wild, a few quick notes about the area." I held up my hands hoping to keep everyone's attention a bit longer. "You'll find creatures ranging from levels two to five around Aldford here, with stronger creatures closer to level five if you head north and into Crater Lake. Next to Crater Lake there is the Webwood, a forest full of level seven and eight spiders which can and will poison you.

"To the west of Aldford creatures range from levels three to six, but truthfully, we haven't really explored that area too well, so be careful if you go that way," I cautioned the crowd. "About an hour away, south of Aldford is a huge patch of creatures ranging from level eight to level eleven. I highly advise *not* going there until you've chosen your base class or have a decent group with you.

"Finally, we have reason to believe that there are goblins of un-known levels somewhere east of Aldford, not to mention Graves and his followers. We don't recommend traveling in that direction at all until you've bound yourselves to Aldford." I motioned my hand to-wards the distant tree line as I spoke. "For anyone who is interested in getting their weapons sharpened before they leave to go hunting, please see our smith Jenkins over by the grindstones. I will be over shortly as well to help out.

"If you have any other questions or concerns, please come find one of my friends or myself. I urge you all to think about it carefully before making your decision. There is no rush to make it right at this second. Good hunting everyone and be safe!" I stepped off the crate I had been using as an impromptu stand while addressing the adventurers, finding Freya, Helix, and Thorne standing nearby.

"That was well put, Lyrian." Thorne greeted me with a nod. "I don't think anyone here is expecting a free ride, but it's good to know upfront that they're buying into more than just a place to rest their head."

"It is more than a fair offer," Helix agreed. "Better than we had when first spawning in Sywn. All the Arakssi plan to join your settlement, myself included."

"We'll certainly be happy to have you." I smiled at Helix, craning my head upwards to look at the towering Lizardman.

"I'm in too, if there was ever any doubt to that," Freya said excitedly before a worried look crossed her face. "We'll still need to deal with Graves, you know. Until we're sure that quest of his is no longer active, he's going to be a threat."

"Yeah…" I replied with a sigh. When we had started preparing for the adventurers' arrival, I had assumed their arrival would be something easily resolved all at once and then we could all move on with other problems. Unfortunately, with Graves's forces fleeing into the woods, they had turned that into a long-term problem.

Part of me wanted to take off right into the woods now that the sun was up and hunt the man and his followers down before they fully regrouped and turned their attention back onto us. But unfortunately, pragmatism and a healthy dose of caution had us staying back.

Our first concern was making sure that the adventurers successfully integrated themselves into Aldford and stayed true to their word. The last thing that we needed was a handful of them suddenly reneging their commitment to be law abiding citizens of the village and start causing problems.

Judging by the relieved yet determined looks on the handful of adventurers who had already bought in and received their Aldford citizenship, anyone who dared to step out of line would soon find themselves answering to a dozen angry men and women who were more than ready to defend their new home.

Our second concern revolved entirely around the issue of bodies and how many people we could afford to send out looking for Graves. If I counted everyone I completely trusted, the entire party, plus Amaranth, Natasha, and myself, we had a fighting force of eight that could reliably move and fight outside Aldford. That left only Aldwin, Donovan, Jenkins, and Shelia as a strong force to defend the village while we were gone.

The problem was, despite stripping Aldford nearly bare, we'd be outnumbered at least three to one, based on what we saw Graves escape with. On top of that, I didn't want Graves somehow slipping in behind us while we were gone looking for him, and him easily taking Aldford while we were gone.

If it were only two against one odds, I would have considered going after Graves right away, confident that even without the element of surprise we'd be able to overwhelm his lower level followers. But three to one odds? That made me uncomfortable. There'd be little room for error, and we wouldn't be able to count on using the terrain to the same advantage like we did yesterday.

We had to look at other ways at evening the odds, and with sixty adventurers to choose from. I was hoping to find a handful of people I could trust to take hunting for Graves. Adventurers like Freya, Thorne, and Helix.

In the meantime, however, I had sent Amaranth out to see if he could find and shadow Graves's forces from afar. The idea being that Amaranth could move the fastest through the underbrush and even if he was spotted, no one would think twice of seeing a prowling creature in the wild and trace it back to us.

"We'll find him eventually," I finally said, my mind coming back to the present. "We just need to get everyone settled first."

"Speaking of settled," Thorne spoke up, quickly motioning towards the spot where Aldwin and Ritt had set up a table and a few crates. "How about we get ourselves signed up for this village and see about getting our souls bound here. Then we can see about helping the others."

"Ah…" Freya replied hesitantly. "I still need to hunt a bit before I have enough."

"Ssame," Helix chimed in. "I only have a handful of sscrap leather and I am not certain how much the others I came with have either."

"Eh?" Thorne frowned. "Nah, don't worry about that. I have more than enough copper ore to buy in for the three of us."

"Y-you do?" I couldn't help but interrupt with surprise. We weren't asking for an overwhelming amount for those looking to join the village, just twenty pieces of food, herbs, leather, or ore.

With metal being probably the most valuable item on that list, I was surprised, yet happy, to see that Thorne was willing to part with so much of it just to help Freya and Helix out.

"Sure," Thorne shrugged as if it wasn't a big deal. "I managed to mine quite a bit before we left Coldscar, but with how low prices were there, I never sold any of it."

"Thorne, are you sure?" Freya asked with disbelief. "You don't have to."

"I've yet to even see any raw metals, so I can truly appreciate its value," Helix added quietly. "I really don't mind hunting to earn my own keep."

"I am *very* sure," the dwarf stated clearly. "Freya, without your leadership we'd have all likely committed virtual suicide a few days ago. And without your help, Helix, Freya would have likely been killed by that wolf. Not to mention all the food you and your other friends brought with you. It is really the least I can do."

With their protests completely quashed, I led the three adventurers directly to Aldwin and Ritt. After depositing sixty pieces of copper ore with Ritt, Aldwin was more than happy to have them write their names down on Aldford's charter.

"That makes fifteen that have joined us so far, Lyrian!" Aldwin whispered to me with a confident gleam in his eye, while we watched Freya, Helix, and Thorne sign the Charter. "I hadn't expected things to move so smoothly after yesterday…"

"Me too," I whispered back with a nod. "I imagine nearly a week under a tyrant's thumb puts quite a few things into perspective."

"That it does."

"So, Lyrian," Helix asked me, having been the first to sign the charter. "You said something about offering training to those who wished to improve their skills?"

"Yeah, between all of us, we have a pretty wide range of skills that we've all learned." I nodded at the giant lizardman. "Was there something specific you wanted to learn?"

"My friends and I wisssh to learn weapon skills, any weapon skills really." Helix hissed with excitement as he waved over a handful of different colored Arakssi that had been waiting on the edge of the milling crowd. "All we have done is fight creatures with our talons, which as useful as they are, are not ideal for all kinds of fighting."

"Yo-oh!" I couldn't help but gasp as five massive Arakssi suddenly surrounded me as they joined Helix and I in a circle. Craning my head upwards, I found myself staring upwards at the nearly seven-foot tall creatures, all of whom wore simple cloths tied around their waists and nothing more.

"Sspeak for yourself, Helix." A heavily muscled, black scaled lizardman spoke, his bright green eyes sending a primal chill down my back. "I rather enjoy rending creatures with my claws."

"Hussh, Cadmus. Not all of us have taken to the bloodlust as readily as you have." A smooth, feminine voice admonished the eager lizardman. Turning my head, I was surprised to see that the soft voice had come from a blue scaled *lizardwoman,* her pale gray eyes twinkling as she spoke. "Don't let our most gracious host regret letting us join his settlement."

"He will regret nothing after sseeing me fight, Theia," Cadmus replied confidently as he displayed his claws. "I am *oof—*"

"Lyrian, allow me to introduce you to my friends." Helix interrupted, his large tail swatting Cadmus in the back. "We have Theia and Cadmuss, whom you have already met."

"Next we have Zethus," Helix continued indicating a lizardman with similar emerald scales as himself, though Zethus proved to be a much smaller and lithe specimen than Helix.

"Nice to meet you," Zethus greeted coolly waving a claw in my direction, his eyes the same blue as Helix. "Thanks for letting us join. It's been a rough week out in the wild."

"Then thiss beast here is Abaddon." My eyes had to crane even higher as Helix introduced the largest lizardman in the circle. Well over seven feet tall, I was confident that the crimson scaled lizardman possibly had an inch or two in height over Drace.

"Hi." Abaddon's voice was calm and kind, his head bobbing as he looked down at me with bright yellow eyes. "Don't lissten to Cadmus. Our claws may be useful, but I am looking forward to sswinging a sword or ax around instead! If nothing else, it will be cleaner."

"It's not like we have anything to get dirty, Abby," the last and smallest member of the group quipped, as she elbowed the massive saurian in the ribs, then looked at me with crimson eyes. "I'm Myr."

"Happy to meet you." I smiled at the brown-scaled lizardwoman, noting the contrast between her lithe and sleek form when compared against the other, more muscled Arakssi of the group. "Happy to meet *all* of you."

Myr is the shortest one out of the group, and she's still three or four fingers taller than I am! I couldn't help but feel uncomfortably small while being surrounded by the group of massive saurians.

"Hey, everyone." Freya joined our group, having finished signing the charter. "How are you guys doing on materials? Do you need to go hunting still?"

"We are nearly there," Theia answered quickly. "We have quite a bit of leather between usss, but we still need a little bit more before we all have enough to join the town."

"Thank you for the food by the way." Zethus motioned towards an impromptu cooking area where Ragna had started a fire and was busy handing out meals to the hungry adventurers. "I had never thought spider meat to be so *tasssty*."

"And I had never thought ssspiders had *meat*," Cadmus said with a faint tone of revulsion in his voice.

"It was better than the Flitt—" Myr's reply was cut off as someone began calling my name in the crowd.

"Lyrian! Where are you?" I heard Constantine's voice getting louder as he approached. He poked his head under Abaddon's massive arm "Lyrian! There you are! Are you trying to hide in this pack of Thunder Lizards?"

"Thunder Lizards?" Abaddon exclaimed, repeating the name. "That…"

"Is a wonderful name!" Myr laughed giddily. "That sshould be our group name!"

"Ha!" Cadmus's voice boomed in laughter. "I like it!"

"Oh dear…" Theia's voice sounded exasperated as she shook her head. "I keep forgetting that I am surrounded by children."

"Here come the Thunder Lizardsss!" Zethus hissed with a toothy grin.

"What's going on?" Thorne called from behind Freya. "God damn it, you snakes are too fucking tall! I can't see anything."

Constantine looked alarmed for a second as all of Helix's group broke out laughing, but quickly motioned to me.

"I guess I'm needed elsewhere." I joined in laughing as I pointed to Constantine.

"We'll be back in a bit," Freya said, stepping to the side to let Thorne into the group. "We're going to help these... *Thunder Lizards* get their buy-in materials!"

"Sounds good!" I waved to the group as I ducked under Abaddon's arm, spotting Constantine quickly backpedaling with a vaguely lion-like feline adventurer following him nearby.

"Fuck, finally found you!" Constantine exclaimed. "Jenkins asked me to find you, he's literally being swarmed by all the adventurers who want to get their weapons sharpened."

"Oh, shit!" I rapped my knuckles on my forehead, having forgotten that I was due to help him out.

"Yeah, no kidding, right?" Constantine shook his head at all the excited adventurers around us. "I had no idea people would be this excited."

"You have no idea how bad Coldscar was," the feline adventurer behind Constantine muttered, waving a claw-tipped hand in dismissal. "Nor how much Graves's fucking stunt screwed us."

"What was bad with Coldscar?" I asked the adventurer.

"Oh Lyr, this is Léandre. He's a Tul'Shar—cat people, catfolk, cat... man?" Constantine frowned as he stumbled over the introduction trying to find the right word. "Anyway, I was taking him over to Ritt and Aldwin to sign the charter."

"Léandre?" I smiled looking at the lithe and slender Tul'Shar. A stark contrast to the Arakssi that I had just been hanging out around, I was happy to see that Léandre was of average height, not forcing me to crane my neck up high. "Lion-man?"

"Well, it fits." The adventurer smiled, revealing large canines as he indicated his tan-colored fur and bright yellow cat eyes. "Happy someone got that reference!"

"What reference?" Constantine looked at us confused, before thinking better of it. "You know what, on second thought, never mind. There's no time. Go find Jenkins before he starts hitting people. Last I saw he was pretty overwhelmed! You two can talk later."

"Okay! Okay!" I held up my hands waving to the pair. "I'm going! I'll catch you later, Léandre! In the meantime, welcome to Aldford!"

"LYRIAN!" JENKINS SOUNDED OUT OF breath as he found me walking out of the workshop, having just spent the last few hours crafting a few sets of armor and weapons after getting all of the adventurers' weapons sharpened out of town. "Lyrian!"

"Jenkins!" I saw the wild look in his eyes, immediately suspecting the worst. "What happened? What's going on?"

"Lyrian…" The burly black man was wheezing as he spoke. "I can't keep up with them. Gods…those adventurers are *possessed!*"

"Possessed?" I gasped, my hand going to Razor's hilt. "Hang on, you don't mean possessed by ghosts, do you?"

"What? No!" Jenkins shook his head, sweat dripping everywhere. "They just won't fucking *stop!* A handful of them asked me if they could start building a large log house within the city. After listening to that cat's plan, I allowed it."

"Okay…" I said slowly. *That cat?*

"Then there were three other adventurers talking about the workshop!" Jenkins looked distressed as he indicated the building behind us. "I heard them talking about building an addition to the workshop, so they had more room to work. Then that fucking cat somehow hears them talking about it, and the next thing I know, they want to knock the back wall of the workshop out to build an even larger addition in the back!"

"Jenkins, slow down!" I waved my hands in a calming motion at the distressed man. There had been a handful of adventurers making their way in and out of the workshop over the last few hours as they started to hone their craft, but I hadn't noticed anyone talking about the workshop. "You have to tell me, what *cat?* I don't understand."

"What do you mean, *what cat?*!" Jenkins looked at me crossly. "I mean that fucking Léandre you just recruited! He's been in this village for barely three hours and he already has a huge log house measured out, with nearly two dozen *trees* stacked to dry. Now he's eying my workshop! I need you to rein him in!"

"Léandre?" I repeated the name with a bit of surprise. "Is there something wrong with the plans he's giving you for the workshop?"

"No, not at all." Jenkins shook his head. "The plans he gave me make sense, but…"

"What's up, Jenkins?" I asked with a bit of impatience in my voice. As much as I wanted things to run smoothly in the village, I had an endless list of things to do, and this conversation wasn't going anywhere fast.

"What he's proposing for the workshop is *insane!*" Jenkins handed me a sheaf of papers with half a dozen sketches on it. "He's talking about making it into a two-story *factory* that will stretch nearly—"

"Jenkins." I interrupted the man while taking a cursory look at the designs. There were more ideas on these papers than just expanding the workshop. I saw sketches and notes that indicated quite a few more buildings within Aldford. "This is the opposite of a problem. These are some pretty good ideas here, but they aren't going to sprout from the ground today. Especially since it looks like, it's going to rain any minute now."

"Uh, it…" Jenkins looked up to the sky, seeing the dark overcast clouds. "*Okay*, rain should slow them down. But what are we going to do about Léandre? He's practically taken it upon himself to redesign the village!"

"Then give him the job and make it official," I stated, looking at Jenkins as if it was the simplest answer in the world. "Oh, and pay him too."

"Give him the job?" Jenkins looked incredulously at me, before something in his head clicked. "*Oh*! If we do that, then he'll have to submit everything for Aldwin to review, then I won't have to deal with it! That's brilliant, Lyrian!"

Without another word Jenkins spun on his heel towards the town hall in search of Aldwin, not even bothering to take the papers from my hand.

"Hey, wait, you forgot your—and he's gone," I called after Jenkins, before realizing that he had already moved on. "I guess these are mine now."

After folding the papers together and gently sticking them into my pack, I managed to make it all the way to the glowing oak tree in the heart of Aldford before Ritt practically ran me down.

"Lyrian! Fuck! I'm so happy I found you!" Ritt exclaimed with a panicked expression on his face. "I need some of your money."

"Oh, hi, Ritt, how's your day going?" I answered back sarcastically while looking over the nervous merchant. "Nice day today, isn't it?"

"Cut the shit, Lyrian! I don't have *time!*" Ritt looked around carefully, before whispering confidentially to me. "Remember that brokerage thing we set up? Well, I just ran out of the money you gave me."

"What the fuck Ritt? I gave you twenty gold!" I hissed back at the merchant with surprise. "That can't be gone already!"

"Sure as shit it's gone, Lyrian! Else I wouldn't be here!" Ritt waved his hands in the direction he just came from. "I have three adventurers waiting for me because I didn't have enough coins to make change for the stuff they were trying to sell."

"Are you fucking serious?"

"Like a heart attack." Ritt made a snatching motion with his hand. "If you want me to keep buying, I need more money."

"Fuck, just take the whole thing," I told Ritt handing him my coin purse. "Only buy leather, ore, and wood from here on out. If anyone's selling meat or herbs, that's up to the village to buy it."

"Thanks, Lyrian!" Ritt's expression was filled with relief as he took my money. "Okay, I can do that. Aldwin told me replenishing our stock is a priority over anything else at the moment." Ritt turned to leave but stopped as he remembered something. "Oh, also. Practically all of the adventurers have asked about buying armor or weapons…"

"I've already managed to craft a few sets of weapons and armor," I told Ritt. "But they're already spoken for, unfortunately. I'm looking to recruit and train a few people to hunt down Graves before he does something to fuck our day up."

"Probably a good idea," Ritt grunted, followed by a quick shrug. "I just wanted to let you know. You're the best crafter here right now…"

"But others will catch up," I finished with a sigh. "I'll see what I can do, Ritt. No promises, though."

"Sounds good. Catch you later, Lyrian." Ritt waved goodbye to me as he ran off.

Watching Ritt run away, I couldn't help but feel slightly over-whelmed at how quickly just a handful of adventurers had begun affecting Aldford. New buildings were going up, and long term plans were being made that would definitely impact the development of Aldford.

How will things look when we have sixty adventurers running around through the village?

"Huh…" I heard Freya's voice sound out from nearby. "Neat!"

"Are you kidding me?" I heard Halcyon mutter in disbelief.

Turning around to face the glowing azure oak tree I caught sight of Freya, Thorne, and the rest of the Thunder Lizards gazing upwards as their eyes followed the tree into the sky.

"Hey! You all made it!" I called out to the group, ignoring Halcyon's exasperation at everyone's rather reserved response to the ætherwarped oak tree.

"Nice, uh, *tree*." Helix flicked his tail at the glowing oak. "Isss it safe to be standing sso close to it?"

"Halcyon told us about your run in with the Webwood horror." Freya waved at me while touching the side of the tree. "You guys have *definitely* had an interesting week…"

"Yeah, that's *one* way of putting it," I said with a sigh, as I shook my head at Helix. "Should be fine, standing close by. I don't think you have anything to worry about."

"It feels rather pleasant on the skin, *err*, scales." Zethus commented as he stepped closer to the tree.

"It does," Helix admitted after a slight delay, causing the other Arakssi to move a step closer to the tree. "Hm."

"Have all of you seen Shelia yet?" I asked, looking at Freya and Thorne while indicating the rest of the Arakssi in their group. "Has she bound you to Aldford?"

Thorne nodded jerking a thumb backwards from where they had just come. "Just a moment ago, by the town hall."

"So what's the plan now, Lyrian?" Freya asked, nodding her head at Halcyon. "Halcyon said that you sent someone named Amaranth to go scouting for Graves?"

"Ah, yeah." I nodded. "Amaranth is my familiar actually, a puma that I accidentally bonded to the other day."

"Wait, familiar? Puma?" Freya frowned, looking at me with confusion. "Are we talking about the same thing? The way Halcyon explained it made him sound like a person."

"How do you *accidentally* bind with a familiar anyway?" Thorne added.

"He kind of is a person…" I sighed, not really knowing where to start, "…and that's a bit of a long story."

"Before that, *what* are you?" Freya waved her hand dismissing her earlier question. "All of you already have to have your base classes by now, right?"

"We all are," I replied with a nod. "And I'm a spellsword, a magic-based melee fighter with high mobility."

"And I'm a mage," Halcyon said before helpfully explaining the rest of the party's class choices.

"*Damn*, we are so far behind." Freya shook her head. "Even with a bit of hunting today, Thorne and I are only level six."

"We are all fairly close to level seven," Helix chimed in, indicating the rest of the Thunder Lizards. "But our sskills are greatly lacking. Our greatest skills are all unarmed combat, with some stealth and perception."

"Zethus and I have some magic sskills too, but we are sorely un-dertrained as a whole." Theia motioned towards the smaller lizardman.

"You two are magic users?" Halcyon said with surprise.

"Hoping to be," Zethus answered with a shrug. "I wish to become a necromancer, while Thelia aimss to become a shaman."

"Awesome!" Halcyon looked exceptionally happy to have other spellcasters around. "How about the rest of you? Any thoughts to what you want to do class-wise?"

"Rogue or scout for me," Thorne replied with a bit of hesitation. "Haven't quite made up my mind at this point."

"Warrior mosst likely on my part." Abaddon shrugged his massive shoulders as if it was an obvious choice.

"I rather enjoy using my fissts and claws," Cadmus said as he cracked the knuckles in his hands. "I plan to take the brawler classss."

"Scout," Myr replied simply, then looked towards Helix.

"How about you, Helix?" I replied looking at the giant lizardman, who had yet to answer.

"I am consssidering becoming a disciple," Helix said slowly as if embarrassed of his choice. "I would very much like to end up as a paladin or warpriest."

"A lizardman paladin or warpriest?" I was a bit surprised at the combination, but then I smiled and nodded emphatically to Helix's obvious relief. "That would be cool!"

"Have you thought about a class choice, Freya?" I turned to look at the woman, who simply shrugged at me.

"I don't know, to be honest." Freya looked conflicted as she spoke. "I'm not really sure what I like so far. Part of me wants to be a warrior, to be able to stand up and fight anything. While another part of me wants to be a rogue or a scout, so I can sneak and finesse my way through things."

"You can always do an agility-based warrior build," Halcyon suggested, then pointed to himself. "Certain classes may have higher preferences for certain skills and a particular way of playing, but I can still train my stealth skills as a mage. Hell, our warlock, Caius, just spent the last day training his unarmed and staff combat skills to help keep up when fighting things. There's more than one way to play."

"Really?" Halcyon's words went a long way to alleviating whatever concerns Freya's may have had about her choice. She nodded to herself as if making up her mind. "I think I may go warrior then and see where it takes me."

We all looked at one another in silence as we mulled over one another's class choices.

"If we are to go after Gravesss, we must start training and work towards our base classes," Helix declared, his eyes focusing on me. "You offered us training before. We wish to take advantage of it before we go out hunting once more."

"Yeah." Freya nodded. "We have a hell of a long way to catch up, but any pointers or skills you can get us started on would be super helpful, hopefully we can catch up in a day or two without Graves trying anything on the village."

I shook my head. *I can't wait that long. The party and I have to log off come Wednesday morning. I can't afford leaving Graves in the wind while we're logged out.*

"What if I told you I had an idea of how we could catch you guys up faster?" I asked the group, as I reached into my pack to pull out a piece of armor that I had crafted earlier in the day. "I warn you though, it's going to hurt a lot, and you may die, on top of likely spending the rest of the day covered in blood and shit."

"Well, when you put it that way..." Freya replied, her eyes lighting up as she saw the armor. "Tell us more."

LIGHTNING FLASHED THROUGH THE NIGHT, illuminating the wolverine's bloody maw as it reeled backwards from Freya's desperate thrust.

Thunder crashed down from the sky, drowning out the creature's wounded cry as Cadmus leaped on the creature's back, claws sinking deep into flesh.

Rain splashed into red pools of blood, streaming down from the creature's fur, as Helix's gleaming ax buried itself deep into the side of the creature's skull.

The wolverine fell.

"Next!" My voice pierced the air, quickly followed by a flare of magic nearby. A white-haired dark elf shot past me, a snarling roar not far behind. Gracefully, he leaped over a large puddle, vanishing in between two massive Arakssi.

"Wait! Lyrian!" I heard a voice call out. "Just a quick breather."

"After this one!" I called back as I leaned back into my hiding spot, hearing cursing as my answer reached their ears.

A second wolverine thundered past me, wildly chasing after Caius. It didn't even pause in its stride as it saw the dark elf vanish, wildly charging forward. It splashed through the rain, intent on barreling straight through the two lizardmen.

Its foot came down on the puddle Caius had cleared and promptly fell forward with a splash as the ground disappeared under it. Lightning flashed through the sky once again as a trio of weapons descended on the creature carving wicked wounds in its tough hide. As it struggled to stand, twin flares of magic slammed into its face sending it reeling wildly as it instinctively tried to defend its eyes.

The massive form of Cadmus leaped on the creature's back once again, this time grabbing hold of the beast's raging claws. Leaning his weight backwards, Cadmus yanked the wolverine upwards, exposing its vulnerable throat.

Without hesitation, a blade shot out, stabbing deep into the creature's gullet, a spray of blood shooting out before disappearing into the rain.

Slumping forward lifelessly, Cadmus let the creature fall, its body splashing into the deceptively deep puddle.

"Good work, everyone," I said, stepping out of my hiding spot and into the torrential downpour, looking at a small circle of illumination that Freya and the others stood in. "We can take a break."

"Is this what you all did?" Freya asked while panting, water running off of her armor and weapon as the thunderstorm raged above. "Just fight and kill non-stop for hours on end?"

"Sort of." Caius had to speak up over the sound of the falling rain. "Except it was a shit ton of spiders."

"*Lovely*," Freya replied with a sigh.

"At least the rain is warm," Thorne offered cheerfully, despite looking like a drowned cat.

"At least you all can *see*." Freya shook her head, stifling a yelp as fresh water ran down her back. Out of our group, she was the only one that didn't have any sort of night vision and was completely dependent on the feeble Light spell that Zethus cast on himself.

With the allure of a new set of equipment and a chance to quickly catch up on levels while training their skills, Freya and the rest of her party were more than willing to try out a power leveling plan that I hoped would bring them up to speed quickly and allow us to go after Graves before our forced log out time Wednesday morning.

After giving Freya and the group their new gear, I conscripted Aldwin, Constantine, Drace, and Halcyon to help me whip them into shape. I was intent on giving them enough confidence and skill levels so they would survive once we set off into the wild.

Over the course of the next few hours, we barely let any of them rest for any longer than it took for Shelia or Theia to cast a healing spell, brutally passing down the lessons that we had painstaking learned for ourselves as we sparred with barely any restraint.

Eager to make up for lost time, Freya, Thorne, and the rest of the Thunder Lizards rose up to our challenge. Never deigning to quit as their skill slowly improved against ours. Tempers flared, and harsh words were exchanged more than once as we trained, but we pushed through it, intent on preparing them for the realities of combat as we had experienced ourselves. We didn't want them ending up like Graves's followers, flinching at the first moment of pain.

Once I felt that their skills had improved enough, we left Aldford, taking only Caius with us as we traveled to the southern hunting grounds that had only recently become overrun with higher leveled creatures that I had warned the other adventurers about.

Now here we were, late into the evening, the rain that had been threatening all day having finally broken into a colossal summer thunderstorm. Water was everywhere, falling faster than it could drain into the ground, turning the soft dirt to mud. It was impossible to tell what was safe footing and what concealed a hole or patch of ground ready to swallow your ankle, if not your entire body.

As the wolverine had just painfully found out.

Hopefully, no one gets struck by lightning, I mused to myself, looking up into the sky and frowning. *I also hope that Amaranth found some trace of Graves before this rain washed all of it away.*

"How's everyone doing?" I asked, watching Freya and Thorne both huddle close to the Arakssi in an attempt to keep themselves out of the rain, while Helix and the others seemed completely content being wet. "How's your progress now?"

"Little more than halfway through level eight," Abaddon answered cheerfully as if he were on a sunny beach.

"Almost exactly half way through eight here," Freya answered with markedly less enthusiasm.

"Good!" I clapped my hands in a spray of water as I stepped backwards into my hiding spot, checking my own experience bar that had been steadily building, despite doing little to help. "Just a few more, then we can start heading back."

This little hide hole is doing wonders for my stealth skill. I smiled to myself, seeing that it had risen three levels tonight, just having reached level five. *As well as my regular experience too. Not bad for just standing out of sight in case something goes wrong for most of the time.*

"All right, here we go again," I called out to Caius, who had been more than happy to help pull creatures for us. Not to mention that it was a good opportunity for him to work on his situational awareness and learn to move under pressure.

"Incoming!" Caius shouted as something roared in the distance.

Just a little bit longer, then we can go home to rest.

FORTY

I T WAS LATE BY THE time we returned to Aldford. The raging
storm more than doubled the time it took us to return from our
hunting grounds as we made our way back. We slogged our way
through the rain and mud stoically, guided by Caius and my party
sense so that we didn't lose our way in the storm.

As we made our way closer to Aldford, I sensed that Amaranth
was still far towards the east, out of range of our mental link. It worried me slightly that he hadn't returned, but at the same time, I knew
that the cat would be loath to travel through a raging storm and get
himself wet unless he absolutely had to. Hopefully, once the rain broke,
he would begin making his way home with some news to share.

Crossing into Aldford, we were greeted by a pair of militiamen, along with a pair of dwarven adventurers who had agreed to take a night watch. Both adventurers seemed enraptured by the summer storm, content to watch the lightning play across the sky as they maintained their vigil, ensuring no one snuck into Aldford using the cover of the storm.

Eager to reach the town hall and finally take off our waterlogged armor, we sped through the sleepy village, quickly pushing open the heavy doors and taking shelter inside. Heated voices and murmuring greeted our ears as we stepped inside, the slam of the door catching everyone's attention.

"What's going on?" I called out, seeing dozens of eyes upon me, a wide range of emotion between each of them. The majority that looked at me were torn between concern and anger.

What the hell happened while I was out? It seemed like nearly all of the adventurers had taken our offer to join Aldford and now found themselves huddling inside the town hall to keep away from the storm.

"Lyrian!" I heard Constantine's voice call out from the other side of the crowd. "Come on everyone, let him through!"

The crowd of adventurers pushed away from one another, giving me some space to walk towards the other side of the room where the rest of the party waited. I noted a pale elf dressed in a ragged thread sack sitting on a chair, looking out at everyone with concern. Another half-elf adventurer I hadn't met before stood idly by to one side with his arms crossed over his chest, an angry expression on his face.

That's one of Graves's scouts in the chair. I frowned, as I moved my dripping self across the room, trailing a small puddle behind me.

Walking up to Constantine, I nodded to him in greeting. "So… uh. Catch me up?"

Constantine sighed before starting, shaking his head with frustration. "Two separate problems, kind of."

"Of course there are, why would I assume things start being simple now?" I muttered sarcastically before thumbing my wet hand towards the half-elf. "How about we start with that angry-looking adventurer with the crossed arms."

"His name is Cerril," Constantine spoke as he waved the adventurer over. "He and a few of his friends were among the first to join Aldford this morning and immediately went out hunting. He just spawned back here a couple of hours ago and started telling us that his friends had been captured by goblins *and* Graves's adventurers working together."

"Fuck," I hissed to myself, turning to acknowledge Cerril as he approached. "Okay, Cerril, Constantine just gave me an outline of what happened. Walk me through it."

"S-sure," Cerril stuttered, speaking hesitantly as he looked me over. Whatever attitude the half-elf seemed to have earlier had quickly burnt away now that he was talking to me. "W-where should I start?"

"Where ever is best," I replied softly, trying not to consciously intimidate the adventurer but also wanting him to hurry up. "Constantine said you left Aldford this morning after being soulbound here, did you go straight east?"

"N-no, well, not at first. The four of us actually went north, towards Crater Lake." Cerril paused for a moment to take a deep breath, before continuing. "We were pretty excited to be *free* this morning and we wanted to make up for lost leveling time."

I nodded, completely understanding that motivation. "Okay."

"We hunted for a bit through Crater Lake, and after reaching level six, we decided to try out the Webwood." Cerril continued, glancing up at the Webwood queen's skull on the wall. "We got a fair amount of experience hunting the spiders, but after hitting level seven, we were tired of their poison and decided to go exploring for a better hunting place.

"We had gone pretty far northwest by that point and knew we'd have to take the roundabout route to get to a higher elevation," Cerril explained with a shrug. "So we decided to make our way east, out of the crater, then angle back towards Aldford."

"Is that when you ran into the goblins?" I asked with a frown. Based on what Cerril had told me so far, they hadn't really gone that far from Aldford, nor that far east if they hugged the edges of Crater Lake.

"N-No," Cerril said hesitantly. "That was still fairly early in the day, and the storm hadn't started yet. After reaching the northeastern edge of the Crater, the forests cleared away into a huge plain filled with creatures." Cerril shook his head. "I don't know if you've explored that far?"

I shook my head. "No, not yet. We've only taken the most direct route to the Webwood. We haven't gone in that direction at all."

"I see. Well, it's kind of a higher leveled version of this area, ranging from level six to ten." Cerril waved his hand in a circle to indicate the outer edges of Aldford. "Practically every step we took we found snakes, beetles or other critters. We even saw a bear in the distance!"

"Hm, good to know." I nodded at the half-elf, hoping he would get to the point a bit faster. "How about we jump ahead to the goblins? When did that happen and where were you?"

"The goblins happened a few hours later, once it started to storm," Cerril quickly answered. "We were caught out in the middle of the plains hunting when it started to rain and quickly ran towards the tree line towards the south to take shelter. We made it into the trees without getting too wet, but we barely had enough time to catch our breath before the goblins attacked," Cerril said. "Over a dozen of them came charging out of nowhere, with a handful of them dragging nets between them. I didn't even have a chance to move before I was tangled up in one."

"I think they may have been watching them," Constantine told me.

"Yeah, while the plains do have a few small hills here and there, it's largely flat, with waist-high grass everywhere." Cerril explained, indicating the height of the grass against his body. "In hindsight... it would be easy for anyone to hide in the tree line and have a clear sight of anything for a mile or two away. Probably even further if they climbed one of the trees."

"If they were so intent on capturing you, how did you end up dying?" I asked with suspicion.

"With how many goblins that attacked us, we knew pretty quickly that we were fucked. I saw one of my other friends get caught in a net seconds after I fell to the ground," Cerril explained with a slightly haunted look on his face. "Jordan, one of my friends, must have remembered what you said about the goblins. Because one of the last things I remember him doing was stabbing me in the neck."

"Hold on! Your friend attacked you?" I exclaimed with surprise, seeing Constantine nod with a grim face. "Why?"

"Because he wanted me to get back here and tell you what happened!" Cerril visibly flinched at the memory of what happened. "He didn't kill me on the first stab though, which gave me enough time to see a half-orc and a handful of other adventurers come running out of the woods, shouting for someone to stop Jordan, but they were all too slow."

Fuck, I don't know if I would be willing... or even able to kill one of my friends. It's one thing to spar, another to brutally murder them, even if they don't die for real! My mouth was open and I was at a complete loss for words for a moment before I finally managed to reply. "You recognize any of them?"

"You better believe I did!" Cerril scowled as he spoke. "The half-orc was *Carver*."

All the adventurers in the hall, who had been calmly listening up to this point now jeered with anger. I even noticed the scout in the chair wincing as the name was mentioned.

"You saw Carver?" Freya's voice echoed through the room, as she and the rest of her party bullied their way through the crowd.

"I-it was him!" Cerril stuttered, taken aback at having so many people shouting. "I'm sure of it!"

"Who's Carver?" I asked Constantine, just to see him shrug with confusion. "Freya, who is Carver?"

"*Carver*...is a broken man." Freya's voice was laced with anger. "Graves may have been a colossal asshole and completely selfish, but there was a *reason* why he did things. Carver, on the other hand..."

"Iss a sociopath," Helix hissed, quickly followed by words of agreement from the adventurers in the hall. "He tormented people for his own amusement."

"He extorted food and supplies from anyone and everyone he could," Thorne added. "If you so much as looked at him the wrong way he'd shank you, just once, and walk away."

"Or hobble you, so you couldn't walk," Cerril said softly. "Which would then get you beaten once you started to fall behind."

"He paid attention to who could and couldn't regenerate." Freya's fists were clenched as she spoke. "If he noticed you ran out of food, he would find you and *hurt you*, giving you a wound that would always be there, day after day."

"I see," I whispered after a moment of silence, feeling the anger in the room beginning to boil. I had only seen a small piece of everyone's experience in getting here to Aldford. I couldn't imagine surviving in an environment like that, day after day. "Is there anything else you can tell us about the goblins?"

"It all happened so fast, I really didn't notice anything else." Cerril shook his head. "All that I have in my combat log is that I was immobilized by a level seven goblin stalker."

"Well, at least they aren't a higher level than us," Constantine commented hopefully. "Are you still grouped up with your friends? Can you tell where they are?"

Cerril nodded as he pointed to the east. "Yeah, we're still grouped, and I can feel that they're over *that way*, somewhere. But I'm not quite sure how far."

"We'll go looking for them, right, Lyrian?" Freya asked me. "And try to rescue them?"

"And maybe kill Carver?" Helix added hopefully.

The two questions caused the full attention of all the adventurers in the town hall to fall on me, everyone falling silent as they held their breaths for my answer.

"Yeah, of course," I answered with nod, feeling a sense of relief wash over the room. "We all signed up to help one another in time of need."

"Thank you, Lyrian," Cerril said earnestly. "Though, I'm not sure why the goblins would be willing to work with Carver, or how Graves managed to strike a deal..."

"Do you think there are other players?" Sierra entered the conversation. "Goblin players?"

"I hadn't considered that," I whispered softly, looking towards Cerril.

"I don't know," the adventurer replied with a shrug. "Like I said, I only have the logs for the one goblin that netted me."

"Damn," I cursed, the last thing we needed was to have Graves pairing up with an unknown amount of goblins. Especially since they've already proven to be hostile towards Aldford and practically everyone else that wandered through this area.

Hang on. My thoughts ground to a halt as that realization crossed my mind.

"How the fuck did Graves manage to get the cooperation of the goblins in the first place?" I grunted. "The goblins haven't exactly been all that welcoming to anyone that's crossed their paths."

"Like our expedition," Natasha commented softly, standing beside a morose looking Donovan.

"Or Aldford," Aldwin added heavily, his eyes flitting to scrapes and scratches around the town hall that still lingered from the goblins attack last week.

"Uh…" The scout hesitantly spoke up with a small voice. "It could be his quest."

"His quest?" I asked, watching the scout shrink under the combined gaze of all the adventurers in the room.

We should be doing this somewhere private. I tried to keep my face impassive as I made eye contact with the scout, trying to ignore all the other adventurers in the room. *But we literally have no comfortable place to stick everyone, short of sending them out into the storm. If we did that though, they'd all think we didn't trust them.*

"What do you mean?" Sierra took a step towards the scout. "I thought he needed to take Aldford, along with all that slave bullshit he subjected everyone to. How do goblins have anything to do with his quest?"

"Um, well you see…" The scout started off nervously. "The tomb that we, I mean, Graves found his armor and the quest in was Naffarian."

"So?" I looked at the scout, motioning for him to continue.

"Lyr, Eberia is a Naffarian ruin, remember?" Sierra whispered to me. "Both the orcs and the goblins revere the Nafarr. That's how the war started."

"Shit, *right*, I forgot about that." I rubbed my head, realizing that exhaustion was starting to set in.

"She's right." The scout nodded. "The tomb wasn't anything excitingly grand; it looked like the king was pretty hastily buried, but he definitely was Nafarrian."

"And what do we even know about the Nafarr?" I asked aloud. "That they just vanished at some point in this world's history."

"Not vanished." The scout shook his head. "They were largely killed by the Irovian Dynasty."

"Killed?" I echoed with confusion. "Irovian Dynasty? Who were they?"

"They were the previous dark elf empire," the scout replied. "But they're not around anymore. The empire eventually reformed itself as the Holy Ascendancy of Eligos, which is the name of the current dark elf empire."

"How do you even know that?" Sierra asked with a scathing tone. "And what the hell is your name anyway?"

"My name is Hux, well, actually Huxley," the elf quickly replied flinching under Sierra's tone. "And I know that because I'm a huge lore guy. While Graves was busy prying open the king's sarcophagus, I was busy translating the inscriptions that were carved into the walls."

"You can do that?" Halcyon couldn't help but exclaim.

"Sure! There's a skill called Linguistics that helps you do it," Huxley confirmed with a nod, visibly looking more confident after seeing Halcyon's interest in what he was saying. "But to answer your other question. The Nafarr used to be a major power in this area. Their kingdom ranged all the way from Eberia straight up to another coastal city somewhere in the north. From what I could decipher, there should actually be one of their cities in and around this area, assuming it still stands after all this time."

Likely it stood where Crater Lake is now. Comprehension flowed through me as I realized that whatever conflict there was between the Nafarr and the last dark elf empire must have resulted in the large crater to the north.

"I'm more interested in hearing about this king that was buried in the tomb and how long ago this all happened." I traded a guarded look with Sierra and Constantine, hoping that they wouldn't say anything about Crater Lake.

"Well, the second part of that may be hard to answer. One of the inscriptions in the tomb dated the king's death as happening in the year 983, but how that translates in game time, I don't know. We would probably have to ask someone in the dark elf empire about that," Huxley answered. "As for the king, he was apparently killed at the very beginning of whatever war there was between his kingdom and the dark elf empire."

"Does this king at least have a name?" Drace chimed in, no longer content to just listen to the conversation.

"Uh, y-yeah." Huxley nodded. "His full name and title was Slave-King Abdiel, and based on what I understand he was a very powerful mage or warlock, the translation uses both of those words interchangeably."

"Well, that explains more about Grave's motivation," Freya said bitterly, as murmurs of agreement echoed from the assembled crowd of adventurers.

"Yeah." Drace nodded at Freya in agreement. "And because the orcs and goblins have a soft spot for everything Nafarrian, you think Graves might have used his quest to sway them to helping him."

"I do," Huxley affirmed. "But I don't think Graves is *entirely* in control of his actions. He hasn't been quite the same since we came back from the tomb."

"We know," I told the scout, my eyes watching him as I spoke. "During your tomb robbing session, Graves managed to somehow wake that king's ghost in the process, which promptly latched onto him."

"It-it did?" Huxley seemed taken aback. "I *knew* he was acting differently, but I couldn't completely tell how…"

The room fell quiet for a moment as I continued to stare at the elf. Everyone seemed to have difficulty in accepting that Graves may have not completely been in control of his actions.

"Why are you telling us all this?" I asked after a while. "You barely said two words yesterday until Constantine threatened to drown you in shit. Why the sudden change of heart?"

"I was afraid Graves was going to come back," Huxley admitted shamefully. "I figured it was only a matter of time until he regrouped and tried for Aldford again, I didn't want him learning that I had spoken, in case he took it out on me after. Truthfully, I hated being with him."

"Why did you stay, then?" Freya practically shouted. "You're a scout, and you were fed! You could have easily snuck away!"

"You think so?" Huxley stared back at Freya while shaking his head. "I was *watched* every moment I was with the other scouts. They were, *are,* all firmly in Graves's corner. If I tried to escape, the five of them would have easily tracked me down and killed me."

"It would have been better than doing nothing!" Freya hissed.

"Maybe it would have, and I'm sorry I didn't at least *try.*" Huxley looked towards all the adventurers with a sad expression. "I was afraid, all I wanted to do was survive. I'm hoping to start helping now."

"What do you want?" I asked looking at the elf, sensing the subtle undertone to his voice.

"Amnesty," Huxley quickly answered. "Protection from Graves until he's dead and his quest foiled. After that, I can leave and find my own path if you really don't want me here. I'd understand if you didn't."

At Huxley's words, many of the other adventurers called out in disbelief. "After what he did! No fucking way we should be trusting him!"

"Lyrian…" Thorne looked a bit concerned as he looked over his shoulder to a handful of angry adventurers.

"Quiet!" My voice boomed over the noise, halting the protests cold. "Settle the fuck down, or go outside! This isn't a group negotiation! If he has useful information to offer, we would all be idiots not to listen!"

The grumbling continued for a few minutes, but no one seemed to be willing to challenge my statement.

"What about the other prisoners?" I asked Huxley after everyone had quieted down.

"Don't care." The elf shrugged. "If you want my recommendation? Hang them."

"We may very well end up doing that," I replied to the cheers of a few in the crowd. "Okay. Say we give you amnesty, what do you have to offer in return?"

The room quickly quieted as everyone focused on the elven scout.

Looking right at me, a small smile crossed Huxley's face. "Graves is still in my group."

My eyes widened.

"I can lead you right to him."

FORTY-ONE

THE FAINT RAYS OF THE morning sun poked through the thick foliage of the forest as our group made its way east under the cover of trees. After hearing Cerril's story yesterday, we didn't want to take the risk of walking out in the open as we searched for the lost adventurers and Graves.

"How are you guys doing?" I asked for the first time since leaving Aldford an hour ago, turning to look at both Huxley and Cerril following me nearby. "Party sense is still okay?"

"Yeah." Cerril nodded, pointing straight ahead. "Still a long way to go, though."

"Same here," Huxley replied, pointing in the same direction as Cerril.

"Good," I said cheerfully, happy that we had some redundancy between Cerril and Huxley. Right now their party sense pointed in roughly the same direction, however, if the kidnapped adventurers were moved over the course of the day, or if Graves decided to go hunting himself, we would quickly be able to adjust and, if necessary, split the group to go after both.

Plus, I liked having Cerril with us to help verify where Huxley led us. I didn't completely trust the elf scout, and likely wouldn't until I physically saw Graves with my own eyes.

The old expression "trust, but verify" came to mind with regards to Huxley. I was willing to believe the bare bones of his story, and the insight that he shared with us regarding the lore of the world seemed to be sincere. But it would take time, along with a hell of a lot of work on his part to fully cleanse himself of his association with Graves.

Unfortunately though, with the impending forced logout time coming up tomorrow morning for me and the rest of my friends, we didn't have the luxury to casually scout out where Graves and the kidnapped adventurers had hidden themselves, which was why we were out scouting in force, and the reason I had dedicated nearly the entire day to training Freya and her party yesterday.

We needed their help to hit Graves and, if need be, the goblins, hard enough to keep them from threatening Aldford while we had our downtime. With any luck, we would be able to permanently take care of both Graves *and* the goblins, giving us some much-needed time to regroup before the next crisis reared its head and more adventurers started to spread out into our region.

It'd be nice to have a week or so just to relax and build. I rapped the side of a tree with my knuckles as I walked past it, hoping I hadn't jinxed myself. *I could spend three or four days doing nothing but crafting.*

My thoughts were interrupted as Constantine appeared out of the woods ahead of us.

"Nothing to report, Lyr," Constantine said quickly. "I just checked in with Sierra, Myr, and Thorne. We have quite a few creatures in and about the wood ahead, but nothing over level five. We're making good time overall."

"Good," I replied with a nod as Freya stepped closer to join our conversation.

"Everyone holding up well?" she asked looking at Constantine.

"Yeah, they're doing great." Constantine waved a hand in reassurance. "Thorne's and Myr's stealth skills are great and they naturally have sharp eyes. I actually wouldn't be surprised if they unlocked their base classes today."

"That's great! But that also makes me feel a little bit jealous!" Freya replied happily, sounding relieved. "I still need to work on weapon skills."

"Don't we all," Abaddon croaked from behind us. "Hopefully we'll get plenty of practice today."

"*Hopefully.*" I could hear the smile in Drace's voice behind me.

"You think everything will be okay in Aldford today?" Constantine asked with a slightly concerned tone. "With us gone, along with Freya's group and Natasha, we only have Aldwin, Donovan, Shelia, and Jenkins to mind the village in case things go bad."

"I do," I replied confidently. "Honestly, I didn't expect all the other adventurers to integrate so...*easily* into Aldford. But with how driven everyone was yesterday to join us, and how protective they are to have a place they can rest, I think they'll keep it safe while we're gone."

"They will," Freya said matter-of-factly. "Everyone saw the benefits of being among the *first* to help settle a new city when we reached Coldscar, now that they have a chance to do the same thing for themselves in Aldford, they don't want to lose it."

"Not to mention the safety Aldford provides," Helix added. "Many are truly happy to finally be out from Graves's rule and appreciate the help you gave everyone to get them back on their feet."

"That too!" Freya agreed cheerfully.

"I heard a few adventurers talking about starting a farm to the west of Aldford," Drace chimed in. "Quite a few of the villagers seemed on board to help out."

"Really? I guess that does make me feel better," Constantine admitted, looking back to nod at Drace before turning to me. "Say, Lyr. Have you heard from Amaranth today?"

"Not yet." I shook my head, checking to see if my familiar was still out of range of our mental link. "He's getting closer, though."

"Okay. Let me know when he really gets close. I can go warn Thorne and Myr, so they aren't surprised when they see him," Constantine replied with a nod, poking this thumb backwards. "Going to go check on Natasha at the rear, I'll be back."

"Sounds good." I nodded at the rogue as he started to make his way to the back of our group.

"Why would they be surprised when they see him?" Freya asked me with confusion. "You said he's a puma?"

"Well," I started to explain before trailing off with a smile. "You'll see…"

<*I HAVE BROUGHT YOU A gift!*> Amaranth's mental voice was tinged with pride as he quickly closed in on us.

<*A gift?*> I sent back with surprise, not expecting to hear that my familiar was bringing me something. <*What is it?*>

Amaranth didn't reply back as he approached, and before long I began catching glimpses of his azure fur in between the trees ahead of us. *There's something in his mouth?*

Trotting with barely a care in the world, Amaranth emerged from the bushes and into clear sight, carrying a dead goblin in his mouth.

<I have caught one of the Dirty Ones!> The cat declared happily as it dropped the goblin a short distance in front of me.

The bigger the cat, the bigger the…uh, gift? I was momentarily taken aback by the prize that Amaranth had dropped by my feet.

"Oh!" Freya and the rest of the Thunder Lizards let out a gasp as they saw Amaranth emerge from the woods. "Wow."

"Hey!" I patted Amaranth as he nuzzled his head into me in greeting. "You caught a goblin!"

<I did!> Amaranth leaned into my hand as I scratched him behind the ear. *<He was far too focused on watching the plains and did not pay enough attention to his surroundings.>*

"Was there just one?" I asked the cat, while moving to look at the goblin.

<Yes.> Amaranth quickly replied. *<I found signs of others in the forest yesterday. However, the storm has washed away their scent and tracks since.>*

"Where did you find this one?" The goblin was dressed in simple, if crude, leathers and furs, much better equipped than the goblin raiders I had fought in Aldford last week. Turning the goblin over, I noted that it had been killed by a single powerful bite to the head, and judging by the rather *fresh* smell of offal, recently.

I definitely remember how those teeth felt.

After a moment of inspecting the goblin, I didn't find anything else of interest, the creature beginning to dissolve as I stood up.

<A fair distance sunward—east.> Amaranth quickly corrected himself, slowly getting the hang of using compass directions. *<I spotted this one hiding in wait upon my return.>*

"Lyrian, *that's* Amaranth?!" Freya asked, her voice breathless. "He's…*huge!*"

"And blue!" I heard Theia's voice exclaim with excitement, quickly followed by a faint whisper. "He looks so soft…"

"Oh, right!" I blushed, realizing how bizarre it must have looked to welcome a blue-furred, seven-hundred-pound puma with a hug, then proceed to inspect its kill while talking to it out loud. "Yes! Everyone, this is Amaranth."

Once again I underwent the surreal experience of introducing the newest members of our group to my familiar, explaining the nature of our mental link to one another. Everyone greeted the big cat with a bit of reservation, intimidated by Amaranth's rather large size. Everyone, except for Theia, who hugged Amaranth hard enough to make him squeak.

<*Oof!*> Amaranth winced over our mental link as Theia let go of him.

"T-this is y-your familiar?" Huxley managed to stutter out as he shrank away from the big puma. "I didn't know…"

<*You've brought one of the inept hunters that tried to raid our den?*> Amaranth flicked an ear at me as he focused his gaze on Huxley. <*Why?*>

<*He believes he can lead us to the man who led the raid,*> I told Amaranth, as I began to fill him in on everything that had passed since he was gone. A short glance at Huxley told me that his entire attention was focused on Amaranth. <*With any luck, we will be able to put an end to him today.*>

<*I do not trust him,*> Amaranth stated as he broke into a wide yawn, showing Huxley his wicked teeth. <*I will watch him closely.*>

<*I don't either,*> I told the cat truthfully while motioning for all of us to start walking again. <*Anyway, tell me about yesterday. Did you get caught in the storm?*>

<*I did.*> Amaranth sent back as he started to walk beside me. <*When I left yesterday, I took a wide path through the forest, following the scent of the fleeing raiders. At first, their flight was wild and without direction, each running along their own path, however, after a while, they regrouped and proceeded to travel eastwards. They traveled quite a distance*

through the woods, further than where we are now, before settling for rest,> Amaranth explained to me slowly. *<As I followed their path, I began to smell the Dirty Ones that had traveled through the forest long before them. This is the furthest I have traveled from the Ridge, so I am not certain, but I believe the raiders had unknowingly crossed into goblin territory.>*

< The raiders may be working with the goblins now.> I told my familiar, going on to explain everything that had happened to Cerril and the kidnapped adventurers.

<Are they?> A wave of confusion flowed from Amaranth as he spoke. *<Before the sky broke yesterday and I was forced to take shelter, I scented spilled blood belonging to both the raiders and the goblins, along with signs of battle where the raiders stopped to rest.>*

<Really?> I sent back with surprise. *<Can you take us there?>*

<It is not far.> Amaranth replied, trotting forward ahead of me. *<We already move towards it.>*

"Amaranth says that he found signs of the goblins fighting with Graves and the rest of his followers," I told the others, who were still getting used to Amaranth. "I don't know how much of it survived the storm yesterday, but it's on the way anyway."

"Really?" Freya said, casting a doubting look at Cerril. "I wonder what happened…"

"What did he say about the goblins, Lyr?" Halcyon asked from behind me. "You know we can't hear you two when you do that mental link thing between one another."

"Oh, right!" I rapped my head with my knuckles once again, silently looking forward to having some downtime tomorrow to recuperate. *I really need a break. I'm starting to make silly mistakes.*

"Amaranth said that he found the goblin on the way back to us today and that it was busy watching the plains when he snuck up on it."

"You think they are expecting more of us to walk that way?" Cerril asked.

"I don't know," I replied with an honest shrug. "Maybe you guys surprised them, and they're keeping an eye out now. Or maybe they've always had an eye out, and we've finally wandered far enough to trip over them."

"They must have a place somewhere out here if they're posting pickets in the wood," Drace said thoughtfully. "We can get away without them since the area around Aldford is reasonably clear of trees, and we have decent visibility all around us, except for the forest on the east side. If they've settled somewhere in the forest, we might not find any scouts unless we trip over them."

"True, though don't forget, they must have planned to take the villagers they tried to kidnap from Aldford somewhere," Caius added. "Plus, the Mages Guild expedition."

"A Mages Guild expedition? Is that what Natasha mentioned yesterday?" Freya asked with surprise. "How much has happened to you guys this week?"

"Oh, it's been a marathon of crises," Halcyon exclaimed dramatically. "All week long…"

"I think it is time that we were fully caught up," Helix plaintively hissed behind me, quickly followed by rumbling agreements from the rest of the Thunder Lizards. "We have only caught bits and pieces since we arrived. Words of a goblin invasion along with giant spiders in the foressst. What *has* happened since you all arrived here?"

I turned to glance at Drace over my shoulder, who merely shrugged. "It's your story here, Lyr."

"Ugh, all right." I started by taking a deep breath. There was a lot I hadn't yet explained to Freya, Thorne, Helix, and the rest of the lizards, only briefly highlighting the major events that happened around Aldford. There had always seemed something better to do with our time than just rehash everything that had already happened in detail. "It all started with me spawning completely naked, in the middle of a goblin raid…"

WE WALKED FOR NEARLY THREE more hours until Amaranth told us that we had arrived at the camp where he had detected the spilled blood between Graves's followers and the goblins. As we approached, we saw Sierra waiting for us in the middle of the clearing, her relaxed posture telling us that our other scouts were in the woods around us.

Not far, my ass, I sighed to myself as I made my way into the clearing, seeing two large patches of scorched ground. *I guess my next task should be trying to teach Amaranth the concept of distance and time.*

Despite my grumbling, I had to admit that catching Freya and the others up on the details of our week made the journey pass by reasonably quickly. I had freely outlined every detail of our adventures up until this point, save for mentioning my theories about the ruin we had found being a translocation hub. While I felt I could trust Freya and her friends with that information, I wasn't ready to share that information in front of Huxley or Cerril.

I'll have to tell them later, I told myself while making a mental note. *Then I'll probably have to do something about that ruin too, and make sure no other adventurers break Donovan's lock and wander into it.*

"Yet another abandoned camp," I said feeling a tinge of déjà vu as I inspected the area.

"We're in the middle of the wild, Lyr," Halcyon grunted as he followed me. "It's not like they can just check into a hotel in the middle of the night out here."

"I guess," I replied while looking at the two scorched patches of ground, one had a ring of stones surrounding it, while the other didn't. "Once people figure out proper fieldcraft and start *hiding* their camps after they leave, maybe we won't be tripping over them all the time."

"To be fair, goblins did attack the other camps," Caius pointed out. "Hiding a camp while under attack doesn't rate high on my list of things to do in the heat of the moment."

"Are you guys done? We're on a timeline here," Sierra grumbled with a bit of frustration before indicating both of the scorch marks. "If you look, there's a decent-sized crater in each burn spot, but this one here, with the stones, has the most ashes in and around it, even after the storm."

"Maybe they started the fires with magic?" I offered, remembering how handy it was to be able to kindle some wood with my Flare spell.

"With a fucking fireball?" Halcyon was looking at the second scorch mark. "Crazy overkill if you ask me, look how deep these are. A tiny flare is more than enough to light some wood."

"Amaranth, where did you smell the goblin blood?" Freya asked, looking at the cat with curiosity.

Flicking an ear at her, Amaranth walked over to the second scorch mark without the ring of stones. < *The smell of goblin blood was strongest here, but so was the smell of burnt flesh.* >

"Amaranth says he smelled both goblin blood and burnt flesh in that spot," I told Freya, passing on Amaranth's message.

"Hm." Freya nodded, then continued to look around the camp.

"I'm not sure what else there is to find here," Cadmus spoke up as he walked the perimeter of the camp. "All I'm finding is mud, damp grass, and fallen leaves."

"Any theories?" I asked Sierra as everyone quickly searched through the area.

"If this was done by goblins and they used a similar strategy as when they attacked the expedition camp, they would have destroyed the fire first, to disorient everyone, probably from that direction." Sierra pointed slightly towards the northeast. "Then, once people started panicking, they would have started raiding the camp."

"Is that what Natasha said happened to her camp?" I asked softly, knowing that Sierra had been spending quite a bit of time with the younger scout. "She didn't tell me much of what happened beyond the basic details."

"It was similar," Sierra replied with a nod, before looking at me with concern. "It still bothers her that she ran off you know."

"Running off is probably the only reason she's alive," I said with a sympathetic tone. "Hopefully she understands that."

"I think she does, just not all the time." Sierra shrugged, knowing it was beyond her control. "So what do we do now? I don't think there's much to go on here."

"Keep following Cerril and Huxley's party sense, I guess," I said after thinking for a moment. "We have to be in goblin territory now, and they've both said we're getting closer. Unfortunately, party sense doesn't convey distance very well."

"We have to be getting close," Sierra replied with a sigh, nodding her head to the sun high in the sky. "The day is already halfway done, if we don't find something soon, we'll have to start heading back."

"Yeah," I agreed, following her gaze upwards. "If we really needed to, we could make better time over the plains on our way home."

"It'd still take us a bit of time to get back to the plains." Sierra thumbed her hand sharply to the northwest. "We left the plains back there about a half hour ago when the forest started spreading northward. We're deep into these woods now."

"Shit, really?" I felt a brief wave of claustrophobia wash over me before I managed to shrug it off. If everything went to hell and we were forced to run, it'd be easier to use the terrain to our advantage in the forest, than if we were out and exposed in the plains. "I'd feel better if we knew how big this forest was."

"Guess you could climb a tree and take a look around," Sierra suggested half-jokingly. "They look sturdy enough."

"You know what," I trailed off, looking at the nearby trees. "That might not be a bad idea."

"Eh?" Sierra frowned at me as she held up her hands to slow me down. "I was just kidding, Lyr! We don't need you killing yourself by taking a dive off a tree!"

"Maybe you were, but it's still a good idea." I pointed to a tree that appeared to be taller than all the others nearby and started moving towards it. "That one over there looks like a good one."

"Lyr, the lowest branch that could hold you on that tree is twenty-five feet up!" Sierra called after me, catching the attention of the rest of our group. "How the hell are you going to even climb it?"

"I don't have to *climb* it." I shook my head while smiling.

"Then what are you even—" I heard Sierra start to say, right before I triggered Blink Step.

The world blurred as I teleported myself a short distance into the air, just below the branch. Feeling myself beginning to fall, I quickly threw my hands up to catch myself on the thick branch, hanging nearly thirty feet above everyone.

"—going to, *hey!*" Sierra shouted below me. "That's not fair!"

"Ugh," I grunted as I quickly heaved myself up onto the branch, grabbing hold of the trunk to steady myself. Chancing a look down, I put on a brave smile and waved to the party while silently fighting a wave of vertigo. "Why bother climbing, when you can just use magic?"

"Sure, sure! Rub it in!" Sierra called from below. "Now how are you going to get down, smarty-pants?"

Shit. I felt my balance sway for a moment as I considered that. *For some reason, this doesn't feel quite the same as when I leaped off that cliff, probably because the ground looks a hell of a lot harder than water.*

"That's a problem for future Lyrian!" I replied, trying to project a sense of confidence in my voice as I tore my gaze upwards, and focused on a higher branch. "First I still need to go a little bit higher and hopefully get above the tree line."

Repeating my Blink Step trick a second time, I managed to bypass another seven feet of sparse footholds and weak-looking branches, teleporting into the highest reaches of the tree, this time wrapping my arm around the trunk.

Fuck, it's been close to fifteen years since I last climbed a tree. My foot scraped along the tree's bark as I pushed myself higher, using my free hand to guide my way upwards. As I climbed towards the top, I started to feel the tree beginning to sway under my weight, instinct warning me to stop climbing. Holding onto the tree tightly, I quickly glanced around, seeing that I had climbed past the other neighboring trees. *Okay, I guess this is as high as I'm going to get.*

Wrapping one arm tightly around the trunk of the tree and bracing one foot on a branch, I carefully leaned away from the tree, using my free hand to push away the smaller branches around me.

Looking to the northwest first, I saw what Sierra had mentioned earlier, barely making out the distant edges of the plains before the forest began. Green trees filled my vision as I slowly turned my gaze to the north, the forest continuing as far as I could see, gently rippling into small hills and valleys in the distance. *We must have traveled along a finger of the forest as it stretches out to the east.*

Shifting around the tree I looked towards the south, seeing the forest continue further, gently sloping downwards into a large valley. *This forest is huge! Easily ten times the size of Crater Lake and the Webwood. It looks like it's much older growth too.*

Completing my awkward shimmy around the tree, I carefully gazed out to the east, catching the distant sparkle of a lake towards the southeast that was part of the valley I had just seen to the south. *Just more trees out that way, except for over there.*

Looking straight east from my position, I noted that the ground sloped downwards ever so slightly before rising again in the distance. A small patch of the distant forest seemed to be a noticeably different shade of green than the surrounding trees. Watching it intently for a moment, I noticed that whatever was there, didn't sway in the wind like the other trees did.

A grass or moss-covered hill? I thought to myself as I tried to make out details, noting bits of brown stone as my eyes focused. *Can't tell from here, though aside from the distant lake, it's the only other notable feature from this vantage point. Guess we'll find out as we head there.*

"You see anything, Lyr?" I heard Drace's voice shout up from far below.

"Eh," I called back down as I readied myself to begin my descent. "Nothing overly exciting. An overgrown rock cropping or landside out east, and a rather pretty looking lake in a valley towards the southeast."

Tuning out any follow-up questions, I carefully climbed my way down the tree, taking care that I didn't slip and fall headfirst into the ground. After a few minutes of gradual descent, I found myself once again on the branch I had first grabbed onto.

"All right, *future Lyrian.* How are you getting yourself back onto the ground now?" I heard Sierra call up to me, a devilish grin on her face.

"Well…" I replied hesitantly as I mentally worked out a plan of action, hoping that it wouldn't end up with me splattering all over the ground. "First I'm going to do this!"

I gently stepped off the branch.

"Oh, shit!" Drace shouted as he saw me begin to fall, moving forward to catch me.

Before I could build up any sort of momentum, I triggered Blink Step and found myself effortlessly landing on the ground as if I had just stepped off a street curb, leaving everyone staring at me dumbfounded.

"Ta-da!" I made a mock flourish, flashing a grin at Sierra. "Safe and sound!"

"Fucking spellsword and your magic," Sierra muttered as she shook her head and then looked around at everyone gathered nearby.

"I hereby vote that in light of Lyrian's superior climbing ability, that he be the designated group climber."

"Seconded." Drace deadpanned as he cocked his head at me.

"Hang on a second, guys." I waved my hands into the air, sensing the popular opinion going against me.

"All in favor?" Sierra raised her hand, quickly followed by the rest of the group, including Freya and the rest of the Thunder Lizards currently present. "All opposed?"

"Uh, definitely opposed!" My hand shot up into the air as I looked around for my familiar. *Where the hell did Amaranth go? I could use some help here!*

"The vote is twelve to one." Sierra looked at me with a blank expression. "Congratulations, Lyrian! You are now the designated group climber. We all stand humbled by your climbing prowess!"

"Fuck," I cursed softly, trying not to reveal just how uncomfortable I was with heights as I tried to save face. "Well, whatever is best for the party, I guess."

"Whatever is best for the party, indeed." Sierra wiggled her eyebrows at me as she motioned for everyone to get moving again. "Let's—"

"Seriously! What the fuck are you all thinking?" Constantine's venomous tone stopped all of us in our tracks as he stalked out of the nearby woods. "What the fuck happened that has you shouting so fucking loud?"

Looking at Constantine, I noticed a line of blood dripping down from his hand. "Shit, Constantine! Are you okay?"

"I'll be fine," the rogue replied flatly as he shook the blood free of his hand. "I was six feet away from sneaking up on a goblin stalker when you fuckers started shouting and sent him into a panic. He got a lucky stab in on me."

"Fuck! I didn't even think of that." Drace winced while waving his hands apologetically. "Sorry, man, did you manage to get him?"

"Of course I did," Constantine replied testily. "But where there's one…"

"There maybe more." Sierra sighed as she rubbed her eyes. "Ugh! Damn it!"

"Uh, sorry to interrupt," Huxley interjected hesitantly. "But where is Amaranth?"

"Good question." I trailed off as I tried to pinpoint Amaranth through our link, while everyone else glanced around the clearing. *<Amaranth, where did you go?>*

<I am chasing a Dirty One trying to escape to its den!> Amaranth's mental voice came back sounding annoyed. *<Your roaring can be heard across the entire forest!>*

"Shit, Amaranth is chasing down another goblin that heard us too!" I hissed pointing east and started to move. "He's heading east!"

"Let's move!" Sierra motioning us to follow her. "Quickly, but quietly!"

<Can you catch it?> I quickly sent back to my familiar, my heart jumping into my mouth. *Shit! I hope we didn't just blow the element of surprise!*

Amaranth didn't reply right away to my question, forcing me to stew as we followed in his wake. *Such a stupid thing to get tripped up over! All because of a lack of mental discipline!*

Constantine and Sierra led the way, the threat of discovery adding a spring in our step as we sped through the woods. My eyes flitted from tree to tree as we moved, hoping that my somewhat neglected perception skill would be able to spot any other hiding goblins. With every step I took, I felt my internal panic rising, fearing that something had happened to my familiar.

Finally, after what seemed like an eternity, Amaranth's voice echoed through my head. *<I have caught and killed the Dirty One. He was far too*

focused on flight and did not sense my pursuit.>

I couldn't help but let out a sigh of relief, as I gave everyone the thumbs up sign. "We're okay. He caught it."

< Thanks, Amaranth!> I sent back, a broad smile on my face. *<We're making our way to you slowly.>*

<Arrive with great caution and stealth,> Amaranth advised, his mental voice tinged with nervousness. *< There is something here you must see.>*

<Is everything okay?> My smile disappeared after hearing the concern in Amaranth's voice.

<I believe I have found the goblin den.>

FORTY-TWO

"**W**HAT THE HELL IS THAT?" Freya's voice whispered, barely loud enough for me to hear, even while crouching beside her. "It looks like a toppled watchtower, maybe?"

"Eh." I barely breathed while looking between the foliage, worried my breath would catch the attention of the distant goblins. "I think you're right."

<Quiet!> Amaranth's mental voice hissed as he leaned into me to get my attention. *<Do not make any more noise! They have not yet sensed us, but they might if you do not stop!>*

<Sorry.> I sent back to the cat while looking at Freya then putting my finger across my lips.

Following Amaranth's report that he may have found the goblin base, we immediately slowed our pace to a near crawl while we approached his position. Taking a moment to collect our other scouts, we carefully made our way eastwards, watching the surrounding forest nervously.

After a slow and patient advance, the azure-furred puma finally came into view, firmly nestled against a shallow ridge of eroding dirt that allowed him to peer overtop through a nest of leaves while concealing his rather distinctive coloring from afar.

Arrayed in a line, half of us pressed ourselves against the ridge as we took in the bewildering sight ahead, while the larger members of our group were hidden a short distance away, waiting in suspense as we didn't want to risk the goblins spotting their larger forms from behind our cover.

Barely two hundred meters in front of us lay the decaying ruins of what must have once been a truly tall watchtower set further on top of a hill ahead of us. Tragically, however, it had long since fallen over, breaking itself into three separate pieces as it fell westward down the hill.

Now the pieces of the tower were slowly being reclaimed by nature, having sunk deep into the soft ground. Thick green moss and various plants now grew on top what once used to be the side of the once great tower. Gaps of weather-beaten brown colored stone could be seen along the sides of the fallen tower where the overgrowth was thin or couldn't find purchase. Tall trees dotted the approach to the tower, albeit at a thinner density than the surrounding forest.

Finding such a well-preserved structure in the middle of a verdant forest would have been enough to take our breath away, yet our wonder of the tower was overshadowed by the discovery of the goblin village built in front of it.

And *into* it.

Under the shadow of what once used to be the peak of the tower was the beginnings of a settlement, complete with the tips of half a dozen red-roofed hovels poking over the top of a crude, crescent-shaped palisade that blocked entry and sight into the goblin village. Bits of red tiles and discolored lengths of wood gave the goblin palisade a ramshackle appearance, almost as if it was constructed in haste with whatever materials were easily available.

A handful of distant figures could be seen walking around on ramparts behind the improvised fortification, occasionally looking out at the only approach towards the settlement.

Barely containing our excitement we looked past the patchwork fortifications, towards the broken tower that hung over the village. We noticed that the goblins had found a way inside the structure, carving a massive hole through the red tiled roof of the tower as they scavenged pieces from it to use as building materials. From this distance, we could make out a crudely built stairway leading deeper into the gap and inside the broken tower.

Watching the sentries on the ramparts for any sign of threat or alarm I quietly signaled everyone close to me to retreat backwards a short distance, so we could fill the rest of the party in on what we saw, leaving both Amaranth and Sierra to keep an eye on the goblins in our absence.

"What'd we find, Lyr?" Drace was the first to ask, speaking barely above a whisper as we all huddled close together to prevent our voices from carrying.

"A goblin village from the looks of it, built under and into a decaying watchtower of some sort." I didn't waste any time, going on to describe what I had seen, intent on quickly bringing the rest of the group up to speed. "I'm pretty sure this is what I saw earlier from a distance when I climbed the tree, I thought it was a hill from far away."

"A watchtower?" Abaddon echoed with confusion. "Here? What would it even sssee? You could lose an army in the cover of this forest."

"I think it was here before the forest was, it would have been in a great spot overlooking the area," I suggested softly, glancing at everyone as I explained. "We've found two different ruins closer to Aldford on our own already; we're definitely not the first people to settle this region."

"Thisss is true." Abaddon bobbed his head. "Though I am ssurprised that it has lasted that long."

"It does look rather well preserved," Constantine said thoughtfully. "Even with nature taking its toll."

"What about the goblin village?" Drace asked, moving the conversation back on track. "Does it look like they've been there a while?"

"Not really," Freya replied shaking her head at Drace's question. "There are a few buildings built in the shadow of the tower, and they have a very basic looking palisade directly in front of the village, but the surrounding area looks rather wild and untouched."

"I think you're right, Freya. It looks like they took a lot of material sstraight from the tower when they built the palisade, especially the red tiles." Myr nodded at Freya while motioning back toward the goblins. "Did you notice the treess in front of the village?"

"Yeah, it wasn't as dense as the rest of the forest," Constantine replied thoughtfully. "But there were quite a few of them."

"But there weren't any stumps or signss that they had cut any trees down," Myr quickly stated. "With all the trees around, it'd have been easy to get better building materialss than pieces of a moldy old tower."

"These trees are pretty big, and goblins aren't that strong," I reasoned, looking up at the nearly forty foot trees surrounding us. "Maybe they didn't have enough manpower, uh, *goblinpower* to cut them down?"

"I don't know." Freya replied, glancing over at Myr who shrugged. "Looking at the palisade, I got the feeling that they were in a bit of hurry to build it."

"Why build anything at all?" Helix asked. "They could just live in the tower."

"Maybe they are," Drace said with a distasteful expression on his face. "And they ran out of space."

Now that's a terrifying thought. I looked over at Drace and then to the rest of the party who all gaped at the half-giant, each of us imagining a horde of goblins nesting within the watchtower.

"*Hopefully* that's not the case," Constantine said fervently, before looking over to Huxley and Cerril. "To be sure though, are we in the right place?"

"Yeah," Huxley replied with a nod, pointing towards the goblin settlement. "Graves is straight that way and reasonably close."

"Same for me," Cerril agreed, pointing slightly higher than the elf scout, but also in the same direction.

"If we're going to do something, we should do it quickly," Huxley suggested. "The party sense works both ways. Graves may notice that I've suddenly gotten closer over the course of a day."

"That's a good point." I nodded at the elf. "Though, we haven't seen any sign of Graves's adventurers yet."

"You wouldn't happen to have any of the other adventurers in your party?" Freya asked Huxley, suspicion coloring her tone.

"No, just Graves and the other scouts," he replied quickly, while pointing to the south towards Eberia, then back to the Aldford in the west. "The rest of them are way off that way, likely in Eberia, with the other scout being back in Aldford."

"Hrm," Thorne grunted. "Makes me a bit worried that there aren't any signs of the other adventurers."

"We can't let that hold us back," Drace said heavily. "The goblins have already attacked Aldford, not to mention the Mages Guild expedition. If we have the opportunity to take them out, we should."

"I agree." I looked out at the group surrounding me. "Even if we don't know where Graves's adventurers are, I think it's safe enough to assume that they have someone in there with him."

"Hang on, if we think they're all in there, is it even a good idea to attack?" Freya asked with concern. "We're outnumbered by Graves's forces alone, and could easily find ourselves swarmed and killed if the goblins come to help."

"I know what you mean, Freya, and I'm thinking the same thing," I replied, making eye contact with her. "But I really don't think we can pass up this chance to take a chunk out of both the goblins and the outlaw adventurers, even if it makes this a suicide mission."

"All of us are bound half a day away at Aldford and can get back here easily enough, whereas Graves and his group are bound back in Eberia or Coldscar," I continued. "Every single one of his followers we kill, will put them out of the picture for days, if not longer, now that they're marked as outlaws and will likely end up being arrested as soon as they respawn."

"Plus any goblins we kill won't be coming back at all," Drace added. "Really, the only person who isn't expendable here is Natasha."

"Thanks for that!" Natasha whispered dryly, though she couldn't conceal a slight smile. "I rather enjoy being alive, and I'd really like to keep it that way!"

"They're right, Freya," Thorne stated after a moment of silence. "Right now we have the respawn advantage, and the risk for failing is minimal. We'd be stupid not to use it."

"I know, I'm just not used to thinking that way," Freya said with a sigh. "I'll do whatever needs to be done, but if there's a way we could all live through this, that'd be *great*."

"That's the goal," I promised.

"Speaking of goalssss," Helix spoke while indicating Natasha with a clawed hand. "What about her expedition and the other missing adventurers?"

"We could probably use a complete rundown on our objectives,

Lyr," Constantine told me before I could reply to Helix. "We have quite a few irons in the fire here, and once the shit starts flying, we aren't going to have time to stop and figure things out."

"Yeah, that's a good point," I agreed before taking a moment to think everything over. "Okay. The way I see it, is that we have two primary goals. The first being to rescue the missing adventurers and anyone from the Mages Guild expedition that we can find. The second, to kill Graves or somehow disable his quest.

"Depending on how things work out, I want Freya, Thorne, Natasha, and the Thunder Lizards to take the lead on rescuing the prisoners if we have to split up, which means you'll also have Cerril to lead the way." I quickly scanned their faces, looking for any signs of concern or doubt. "Any prisoners we find will hopefully recognize you all quickly, which will hopefully translate into them *moving* quickly."

"With more of us in the group, we can also cover more ground sssearching once we're inside that tower too," Cadmus reasoned with a bob of his raptor head.

"Right." I nodded at the black-scaled lizardman in agreement. "The other group is going to go straight for Graves, focusing more on speed and chaos than anything else. Once we kick this show-off, it won't take long before everyone knows that they're under attack, I'm hoping if we move fast enough, we'll be able to take them by surprise."

"That leads to our secondary goal." My voice hardened as I spoke. "We need to kill as many of Graves's adventurers and goblins as possible. We're not here to take prisoners or make friends. We're here for vengeance, to return the favor for both of the attacks on Aldford, and to remind them of the only rule this world has."

"And what's that?" Thorne asked curiously.

"Only the strong survive."

THE SUN WAS HOT ON my back as I launched myself from behind the tree and into the light. I inhaled a quick breath as my foot bore down into the soft ground, quickly kicking up a spray of dirt as I quickly pushed off and gained speed.

Eyes fixed forward, the ramshackle palisade quickly grew with every powerful stride I took, the patrolling sentries oblivious to my approach. Thundering towards the barrier, I had almost made it halfway there before I saw one of the goblin sentries halt and gaze in my direction, its eyes unable to completely focus through the glare of the afternoon sun directly overhead of my approach.

It took precious seconds for the goblin to squint past the bright sunlight and precious more before it realized what was happening.

By then it was too late.

I appeared at the top of the goblin palisade in a burst of magic, Razor slicing through the surprised *[Goblin Sentry]*'s chest as my momentum sent me sailing over the edge of the ramparts and into the goblin village. After a short fall, I slammed into the ground with a bone-jarring crunch, instinctively rolling forward to reduce the impact. Coming to a stop, I spotted half a dozen goblins across the village staring at me incredulously as they tried to understand what had just happened.

Shit! I can't believe that worked! Forcing myself to stand up, I had a wild grin on my face as I dug my feet back into the ground, turning to run back towards the goblin palisade and away from the goblin shrieks that began to echo through the air. *Come on, come on, where is that gate?*

I looked around at the crude goblin architecture that was the palisade, finding it to be a near incomprehensible network of improvised material, ranging from scavenged timbers and red roof tiles taken directly from the fallen tower, intermixed with lengths of deadwood, lashed together with animal sinews and bone.

How the fuck did they even put this together? I raged, a momentary flash of panic shooting through my heart as I searched for an entrance into and out of the goblin settlement, the goblin shouts getting louder as the alarm was raised. If I couldn't find a way to open a gap in the palisade, things were going to get very *messy*.

My search became frantic as I looked over the improvised design, cursing at every single wasted second. A heartbeat before I was about to start tearing pieces from the palisade, my gaze fell upon a massive white bone that appeared to be fixed in place. *Hold on, is that…a giant femur? Wait, behind it! That's a gate!*

Grabbing the rough bone with both hands, I practically tore it from the wall causing a small part of the palisade to swing inwards.

"Yes!" I exclaimed, throwing the bone down onto the ground and tugging the cunningly concealed gate open. I shoved my head out into the bright glare of the sun ready to signal the rest of the group. "Hey! Over he—"

"*Move, Lyr!*" Drace's sudden bellow barely gave me a second's warning to get myself out of the way as his massive body crashed into the still opening gate. Despite tucking his head and shoulders in close as he ran, the half-giant was far too tall and wide to simply pass through the portal, his arrival shattering the surrounding frame as he bulled his way inside.

Flinching from the spray of splinters, I quickly moved away from the gate as Abaddon followed closely on Drace's heels and the rest of the group mere steps behind his. Both groups split into their respective parties as they advanced deeper into the village, overrunning the handful of goblins I had seen earlier with barely a thought.

It had only taken us half a minute to overcome the goblin's fixed defenses, counting from the moment that I had begun my sprint until the last party member stormed through the shattered gate. I couldn't help but feel disappointed at how easy it had been to bypass the palisade using Blink Step, making a mental note to explore ways to prevent the same being done in Aldford.

The river plus a ditch full of tribuli wouldn't have stopped me from doing this exact same thing to Aldford. The thought suddenly floated into my head, while I moved forward to catch up to Drace, Amaranth quickly falling in beside me. *Though, anyone looking to do the same to Aldford would quickly find a few dozen people ready to fight back.*

"Heads up!" Drace shouted as he bodily crashed into a horde of disoriented-looking goblins that suddenly poured from a nearby hut, giving Halcyon and Caius enough time to send a wild spray of magic at the goblins. "We have incoming!"

Shit! I forgot that goblins are nocturnal! I watched as Halcyon's and Caius's magic quickly set a nearby hut on fire. *We caught them while they were napping!*

"Burn the huts!" I ordered, motioning towards the flimsy looking structures within the village that began to stream panicked looking goblins as sounds of our assault reached their ears. "Half of them are still asleep!"

Sprinting deeper into the goblin village as Freya and her party turned to clear the ramparts, I quickly tossed a handful of Flares at a nearby hut, causing the deadwood to smolder. A flash of light caught my eye as a pair of large magic bolts belonging to Theia and Zethus flew overhead from their new perch on the ramparts, causing the crude hovel I had targeted to burst aflame, the acrid smell of burning leather and refuse instantly filling my nose.

Half a dozen goblins spilled forward from the slowly burning hut in a panic, all coughing furiously as the smoke filled the tiny enclosure. Not wasting a second, Amaranth and I quickly charged into melee range, intent on putting the goblins out of their misery.

Razor shot out like a bolt of lightning, carving through a pair of goblins before they could even acknowledge my presence. A third quickly joined the other two on the ground as I landed a vicious punch, charged with a Shocking Touch to the side of its head. Circling around me, Amaranth pounced upon a fourth goblin, his wicked teeth quickly ending its struggles.

Something feels wrong here, these goblins can barely even take a punch! I frowned at our easy dispatch of the goblins, quickly focusing on the two remaining terror filled goblins that cowered in front of me.

[Young Goblin Raider – Level 1]

"Level one?" I exclaimed in surprise, despite mercilessly swiping my blade through another goblin just as a swipe of Amaranth's paw ended the last goblin before it could flee deeper into the village. Looking over the fallen goblins closely, I remembered seeing these exact type of goblins when they first raided Aldford. "What the hell?"

"Nothing but scrub level ones here, Lyr!" Halcyon shouted to me as he and Caius caught up to me. "We've must have burned through at least two dozen of them!"

Quickly turning my head, I saw Drace nearby, looking oddly confused at the relative lack of resistance from the goblins he had just dispatched. So far the highest level goblins we had encountered today had been the few scouts in the forest and the handful on the ramparts.

"This can't be right!" Caius quickly followed behind Halcyon, a hand holding a glowing bolt of magic. "Why are they all so low leveled?"

Before I could reply, a booming clap of thunder echoed through the air, causing all of us to flinch and hide behind a nearby burning hut opposite to the noise. Halcyon quickly turned to look at me, his face pale. "That was a Pyroclap, and it wasn't mine!"

"Oh, fuck." Caius winced momentarily before pointing with his staff. "I hear a ton of heartbeats just over that way, coming from the tower. No idea how many!"

"We need to move and regroup with everyone else!" I quickly

replied, before sounds of shouting broke out a short distance away from us, followed by another thunderous bang. "Shit! What's goi—"

"Lyr!" Drace hissed my name as he ran towards us, using the now blazing huts as cover. "A dozen of Graves's adventurers just charged from the tower! They have half of Freya's group pinned on the stairs to the ramparts, with the rest on top!"

"Was this all a trap?" Caius exclaimed as he tried to peer around our cover. "Fuck! Sierra and Constantine got caught too! They're all stuck with no cover!"

"If it was, they shot their wad early!" Drace replied as he motioned for us to move around the hut. "We need to hit them from the flank and give the others some breathing room!"

"Okay!" I slapped Drace on the back as he moved ahead of us. "Take the lead! I'm one step behind you!"

Quickly circling the burning hut in front of us, we found ourselves just south of the tower's gaping entrance, almost perfectly behind the attacking adventurers. The adventurers' sudden attack had caught Freya's group in the middle of the stairs leading up to the ramshackle ramparts the goblin sentries had just been perched on. The four of us began to rush forward, struggling to close the distance before the party was overrun.

I saw Abaddon work furiously to hold back the assault, his bulk filling the entirety of the stairs, forced to contend with not only a pair of attackers in front of him, but two others that threatened his lower half from the side of the exposed stairway. Slick blood coating the lizardman's feet and legs spoke to the success of the adventurers' strategy, a panicked-looking Theia barely able to keep up with the wounds accumulating on her defender's flesh.

An azure spray of magic illuminated a faint distortion over the heads of attacking adventurers, bespeaking to the presence of a mage channeling a Force Shield within the mass of attacking adventurers.

Seeing the futility of attacking the shield, Sierra, Zethus, and Natasha ran along the ramparts attempting to find a better angle of attack, and hopefully find a gap under the near horizontal shield for their ranged attacks.

While the two scouts and mage moved to flank the adventurers at range, a trio of adventurers armed with bows took advantage of their absence, darting forward as a group out from under their magical cover, firing a barrage of arrows at Theia.

With a desperate shout as the group's only healer was targeted, a brown-scaled blur leaped into the path of the arrows, each thudding sickeningly as they pierced deep into already burnt flesh.

A momentary gasp of shock fell upon the battle as Myr fell lifelessly off the ramparts, Theia instinctively rushing to catch her falling companion but failing. Sensing Theia's exposure, Abaddon desperately gave up ground, bodily shoving the stunned lizardwoman to safety before a second flight of arrows rendered Myr's sacrifice moot. Seeing Abaddon's urgent retreat, half of the adventurers pressed forward up the rampart stairs, intent on bowling the lizardman straight off the palisade.

"Damn it!" Caius's curse crystallized the realization that our party had just shrunk by one member, Myr's party sense presence now reappearing far to the west, towards Aldford.

"Faster!" Drace's voice roared with anger, finding an extra burst of speed as he continued to sprint forward, pulling ahead of me, his massive strides quickly eating the distance between us and the adventurers.

Having lost nearly all of their situational awareness, Drace, Amaranth, and I were barely ten feet away before a pair of the adventurers saw our charge. The gleeful expressions on their face quickly turned to terror as Drace slammed into their ranks, bowling them completely over as he plowed through the tight cluster of adventurers hiding under their mage's Force Shield.

I had enough time to see Drace's momentum carry him up the rampart stairs, his bladefang chopping deep into the shoulder of an adventurer in his way, before a vicious jerk of the blade sent the unfortunate soul tumbling down the stairs behind him.

Then it was my turn.

My feet carried me through the hole that Drace had left when he smashed through the crowd of adventurers, my arm swinging Razor wildly as I tried to find the enemy mage. I felt Razor take a shallow slice out of an adventurer's arm, discharging a Shocking Touch into their body in the process before glancing off a piece of armor, uselessly slapping a second adventurer's back with the flat of the blade. There was a brief yell and a glimpse of azure fur as I pushed past the adventurer, trying to follow Drace's path of destruction.

"Rah!" I snarled in pain as I felt something stab into me, quickly seeing that a human adventurer had managed to thrust a dagger into my ribs. Flinching away from the pain, I shoved the adventurer away from me, the same instant I leaped sideways, deeper into the crowd and tearing the dagger free from the attacker's hand, leaving it sticking out of my side.

[Unknown Human] [Sneak Attack II]'s you for 73 points of damage!

Fuck! Another one with a base class! I swore to myself as I caught the combat log's message out of the corner of my eye. I couldn't help but cough a spray of blood as I tried to suck in a breath of air, feeling a disturbing watery sensation in my left lung as blood began to pool.

Reeling from the pain, I quickly grabbed the dagger with my free hand, roaring as I tore it from my flesh. Shifting my grip on the dagger, I promptly stabbed it deep into the kidneys of a dwarven adventurer in front of me that had his hands in the air above him. Screaming in pain, the dwarf fell to his knees, a soft popping sound filling the air as the gleaming distortion above us vanished.

That was the mage! I looked down at the dwarf with a bit of surprise, subconsciously not expecting such an unusual race and class combination for a caster. *Have to finish him off quickly!*

Out of the corner of my eye I saw the rogue that had attacked me begin to desperately scramble in my direction before a thunderclap of magefire knocked him off his feet and scorched a handful of the tightly packed adventurers that still struggled to find their feet after Drace's assault had knocked them down.

"Thanks, Hal!" I shouted the same instant I slashed Razor into the neck of the fallen dwarf, sawing until I felt the blade bite bone, I was in no mood to take chances and wanted to ensure that the mage was truly dead. His presence alone had been more than enough to render our ranged attackers ineffective, making it difficult for those trapped on the ramparts to fight back.

"*Incoming!*" A sibilant cry screeched through the air as two giant shadows leaped from the ramparts, slamming into the stunned group of adventurers.

Fueled by the loss of their comrade, Cadmus and Helix fell upon the adventurers with a level of ferocity never seen before, no longer prevented from joining in on the melee by the Force Shield's presence. Cadmus's deadly claws rent flesh as he pinned his victim to the ground, quickly biting deep into the adventurer's throat and tearing it free in a spurt of blood. Helix roared as he swung his ax with rage, cleaving deep into the shoulder of one of the archers responsible for Myr's death.

With a final slice of my blade, I ensured the death of the dwarven mage, throwing his body to the ground in front of me. An angry yowl had me turning quickly, in search of my familiar. Spinning, I first saw a brutally savaged adventurer, the one that I had cut earlier, bleeding out slowly on the ground.

Continuing my glance around, I found that Amaranth had turned his attention to the rogue that had stabbed me earlier, having traded a pair of blows with the man. Blood flowed freely from a cut across Amaranth's face, while the rogue held a mangled arm closely to his chest.

Before I could begin to move forward, the rogue flinched from twin impacts to his back as Sierra's and Natasha's arrows thudded home, quickly followed by a trio of azure missiles following the scout's lead. Overwhelmed by the sudden magical and ranged assault, the rogue didn't have a chance to avoid Amaranth's brutal tackle, which had the adventurer's head disappearing in the creature's maw, followed by a life ending crunch.

"How do you like it when we can actually fight back?" Freya's rage-filled shout caused my heart to skip a beat in fear, before I remembered that she was on my side.

"No! Wa—" The adventurer's cry ended with a stomach-wrenching wail, quickly followed by a wet-sounding thrust.

With all the nearby adventurers subdued or dead, I turned towards Freya's shouting. I saw her standing like a blood-covered Valkyrie amid a pool of blood and carnage at the foot of the rampart stairs. Her body shook with rage as she practically hovered on top of two wounded adventurers, one forcibly held down by Drace, the other by Thorne.

Looking past her, I saw Abaddon lying on his back, his chest rising in a desperate quest for air as dozens of wicked wounds bled from his body. Theia's hands were covering a massive wound on Abaddon's chest, and she looked towards us in panic.

"I'm out of mana, and Abaddon is bleeding out!" she screamed. "He needs healing!"

"Caius!" I shouted at the warlock, who had already begun to run towards the fallen party member.

"Where are they?" Freya continued to rage at the two broken adventurers by her feet, having placed the point of her bloody longsword over the heart of the struggling adventurer that Drace held. "Graves. Carver. Where. Are. They?"

"F-fuck you, bitch!" the half-elf adventurer spat at Freya as he struggled to pull himself free from Drace's grip.

"Wrong answer!" Freya shouted as she swung her sword up high, hefting over her head.

"Freya, wait!" I called out, knowing what was about to happen. I scrambled to close the distance between us, but I was far too slow to stop her in time.

Truthfully, a part of me wasn't sure I really wanted to stop her.

With a yell of fury, Freya unleashed a brutal coup de grâce, her sword biting deep into the head of the belligerent adventurer, barely missing Drace in her swing.

Not missing a beat, she stepped towards the other adventurer, her boot stepping on the man's blood-soaked knee. "I'll ask one more time. *Where are they?*"

"Aaaah! What the fuck?" the adventurer screamed as Freya ground her foot into the wound, the reduced pain threshold that the last patch had modified not enough to completely mitigate the sudden spike of pain. "They're inside! In the hill! Please stop!"

"We know they're in the tower, you idiot!" Freya hissed, leaning harder onto the wound. "Stop wasting our time!"

"N-no!" the man stuttered. "Not in the tower! In the hill! There's an entrance in the tower they dug out that leads into the hill! Graves, Carver, and the others disappeared into it early this morning!"

"What's in there?" I asked while watching Caius quickly run past me and up the stairs to tend to Abaddon.

"I don't know! We weren't allowed to go in there!" The adventurer's eyes clung to me as if he had found a life raft while being lost at sea. "We were told to watch the perimeter!"

"What about the goblins?" Freya barked, causing the adventurer to flinch in fear.

"Some went in too, but others are in the tower!" The adventurer tried to pull his leg out from under Freya's boot. "They know you're here! Please, just let me go! I-I'll disappear and leave you all alone!"

"Lyr!" Caius called out to me, first tapping his ear, then his heart, and pointed towards the tower. "Abaddon doesn't have much time. *I* won't have much time afterward either."

"I understand, Caius." I looked at the warlock, giving him a slow nod. "Do what you have to."

"What's going on?" The adventurer struggled to look backwards at Caius, who stumbled weakly down the bloody stairs. "Are you letting me go?"

"In a manner of speaking..." Caius whispered weakly as he placed his hand on the adventurer's shoulder. "Yes."

"Oh," the adventurer said as Caius's hand flared red. "Good."

"I'M *FINE*, LYRIAN," FREYA REPLIED to my question testily as we stormed up the crude stairs the goblins had built into the roof of the tower leading inside. After a moment, Freya sighed and continued speaking at a whisper. "No...I'm not fine, but I will be. When Myr died, all I could remember was our trip here with Graves and how angry I felt at being helpless."

"That's understandable," I replied softly. "But what Myr did, it saved Theia's life and possibly Abaddon's too."

"I know, and I would have done the same in her place," Freya said with another sigh. "It's just getting harder and harder to remember all of this is just a game."

"I hear you there."

Not wasting any time after Caius's warning that his Bloodsense had picked signs of life from the tower, we quickly ensured that none of the enemy adventurers remained alive, their bodies quickly dissolving into dust a few moments after they died. We then continued our assault, leaving the now burning goblin settlement behind as we entered the fallen tower.

Climbing up the stairs and into the massive hole the goblins had carved into the tower, we found ourselves running through what once was the rafters of the tower. Activating my True Sight to pierce through the gloom, I noticed dozens of wooden beams missing that would otherwise be helping to support the weight of the roof, scavenged by the goblins to be used as building materials.

I couldn't help but notice that there was a lot more material missing from the rafters than the tiny huts and palisade would account for.

As we ascended upwards, the stairway joined a thick supporting pillar at the very center of the room, just long enough for us to sprint along, serving as a makeshift bridge as it spanned the length of the rafters. It led towards a large door, set in the middle of a wooden wall, which by my guess, was once an access hatch to reach the rafters and affect any needed repairs on the roof.

Moving with urgency, Drace led the way through the access hatch, with Abaddon, Cadmus and myself close behind. We stepped out of the rafters onto a crude four-foot wide scaffold hammered into the wall that spanned the entire length of the room to our left, before circling around the distant wall and joining another scaffold set upon the opposite stone wall that inclined upwards, leading to a higher level of scaffolding above.

Well, that explains where all the material went. My brain was instantly caught off guard as we entered into a massive room that completely defied expectation. What was once a flat, wide open room at the peak of the tower was now a narrow, multi-leveled network of scaffolding and platforms. Quickly glancing around the room, I guessed that the chamber was around sixty feet, both in height and width, yet was only fifteen feet deep. *This room is like you stood a coin on its edge. Tall and wide, but also very thin!*

Before we could even begin to make sense of all the scaffolding and platforms that the goblins had built into the room, a hail of arrows suddenly rained down on Drace and Abaddon from above and to our right, piercing deep into their shoulders.

"Fuck!" Drace shouted in surprise, raising his shield up high to cover himself and Abaddon from a quartet of goblins on a scaffold, positioned perfectly to cover anyone entering the room.

"Don't stop! Circle around!" I shouted, making a snap decision as I came to a stop and looked up to the goblins readying another volley. "Go! I'll cover you!"

Triggering Blink Step, I instantly reappeared on the scaffolding in the middle of the four goblins, surprising them all with my sudden arrival and nearly cracking my head off the underside of a ramp that led even higher into the room.

Desperately waving about, I was able to disrupt the aim of three of the goblins closest to me, their arrows harmlessly flying off into the distance. The fourth and furthest goblin, however, merely shifted his aim, firing an arrow at me from near point blank range. I didn't have a chance even to tense for the blow before the arrow buried itself into me, a few fingers above my hip.

A [Goblin Stalker] hits you with [Focused Shot I] for 97 points of damage!

I felt my guts curdle from the impact of the arrow, causing me to howl in pain as I wildly swung Razor in an arc. My wild swing missed all of the goblins in front of me but managed to buy me some much-needed time and space until the pain from the goblin's attack subsided.

Instead of cowering before me like the goblins outside of the tower did, the four goblins all dropped their bows and drew wicked-looking daggers from sheaths hanging around their necks. Without even a glance between one another, they leaped towards me, intent on carving me to pieces. Caught off guard by their sudden ferocity, two of the goblins landed long, slicing cuts across my arm and leg respectively.

Oh damn! These goblins are definitely a cut above the rabble we fought outside! The small tags in my vision noted all four of the goblins to be level nine stalkers. I quickly found myself without any room to maneuver on the small platform, the goblins moving to surround me in an arc with my back exposed to the edge of the scaffold. I fervently worked Razor through a complicated parry to keep all four of the goblins daggers at bay. *They're going to carve me up before everyone gets here!*

Hoping to buy myself time, I channeled a Shocking Touch into Razor, causing it to crackle with electricity as I slapped the blade against the dagger held by the right most goblin threatening me. With a squawking cry, the goblin instantly let go of the dagger as the electricity shot through its body, affording me the chance to pirouette and shift myself away from the scaffold's edge placing my back to the wall.

Following the lessons that Drace had taught me the other day, I planted a vicious kick on the goblin that had instinctively bent down to retrieve its fallen weapon. I felt the jagged edges of the arrow still embedded in my hip tear at my insides as my foot made contact with the goblin's shoulder, but judged it a fair price to pay when I saw the goblin sail clear off the edge of the platform.

One down and three to go! I recounted to myself, feeling a sudden weariness overcome me. Concerned, I quickly scanned my health bar, only to find it at sixty percent and falling, *fast. What the hell is going on? Why am I losing so much health?*

With a mental thought, I brought up my combat log the same instant I cut a slice along a goblin's forearm, hoping to keep the trio at bay a few seconds longer.

You take 6 internal damage from a [Goblin Stalker]'s [Serrated Arrow]!
You take 4 internal damage from a [Goblin Stalker]'s [Serrated Arrow]!
You take 9 internal damage from a [Goblin Stalker]'s [Serrated Arrow]!

The fucking arrow deals damage every time when I move! My hand bent down to grasp the half still sticking out of my hip, feeling a jolting pain shoot through my body as I touched it. Wrapping my hand around the wood, I steeled myself before sharply yanking it out of my body. Even then, the pain nearly brought me to my knees as I swore I felt the tip of the arrow grate along my hip bone.

Despite having knocked one of them off the platform, the other three goblins showed no hesitation in taking advantage of my sudden spike of pain, each of them attacking all at once. While no longer being hampered by a twisting pain in my guts, there was little I could do to evade all three attacks with so little space available to me.

I only managed to parry one dagger, knocking the blade out of the way, the other two moving far too fast for me to react to. The second dagger sliced a thin line across my stomach, its sharp edge cutting through my armor, serving as a distraction for the third as it nearly buried itself in the same spot I had just pulled the arrow from.

"Ugh!" I felt the goblin's dagger quickly punch in and out of me, the goblins quickly retreating back as I cut upwards with Razor, in hopes of catching an outstretched goblin arm in front of me.

Okay! I'm getting my ass kicked here! The latest two blows from the goblins had sent my health spiraling below fifty percent, and I had barely even managed to scratch the trio. I just didn't have enough room to effectively maneuver around their attacks, especially while my head was cramped under the ramp above me. *This place wasn't built with regular sized people in mind!*

Casting a look over the edge of the platform, I tried to come up with a plan of action to escape from the goblins in front of me. Looking down through a mess of scaffolding far below me, I confirmed Drace's earlier fears that the goblins had made a home within the tower. There was easily a dozen goblins below that were rushing up similar ramps set into the walls as they moved to join the fight.

Can't go that way! I'll end up in even more trouble! My eyes fixated on the scaffold below me and towards the center of the room, the one that I had just teleported from a moment earlier. A quick scan told me that the rest of the party had made great use of my distraction, having already managed to circle around to the far side of the room. *Alright! That's enough! I need to fucking go!*

Sweeping Razor in a wide cleave, I bought myself some precious space as I turned to leap off the platform. Thankfully, the distance between the two platforms wasn't far, roughly ten feet lower and twelve feet further from my current perch, well within what I considered my normal jumping range.

What I didn't account for, however, was the strength of the kludged-together platform, or the relative lack of it.

After leaping away from the goblins and sailing through the air, I slammed into the edge of the platform and grabbed hold, with the intention to pull myself up. The impact of my landing, however, tore an entire length of the crudely designed platform from the wall, causing my grip to falter as wood cracked and snapped as it pulled away from the wall.

"Oh, no, no, no!" I tried to swing my weight towards the wall as a five-foot section of the platform twisted sickeningly before completely collapsing.

The world turned into a blur as I fell, wildly waving my arms in hopes of catching something to save myself. After falling a short distance, I felt my feet slam into something hard, turning my fall into a mad tumble as I spun head over heels. Razor flew from my grip as I crashed through another platform, finally coming to a stop at the very bottom of the room in a tangle of shattered wood.

"Oh...fuck, *that hurt*," I wheezed as pain shot through my body, forcing me to lay still as I collected myself.

<Lyrian! Are you okay?> Amaranth's concerned mental voice rang through my mind, causing me to wince at the sudden intrusion.

<I think so...> I replied slowly, waiting for my head to stop spinning. *<Hold on a moment.>*

Looking around, I realized I had fallen to the very bottom of what was once the lookout point for the tower when it still stood, the tower's fall having shattered the wall that now rested on the ground. Dirt was intermixed with broken stone fragments, giving a ragged, if firm terrain to move around. For the first time since entering the room, I noticed a handful of arrow slits and larger dirt covered windows that adorned the walls, casting beams of light that weakly illuminated the room.

Ugh, that fall took another twenty percent off my health. I looked at my greatly depleted health bar, seeing only 115 hit points remaining out of my 594 maximum. *I really need to be more care—hang on, what's that burning smell?*

Pushing myself up into a seated position, I immediately planted my hand onto something hot, causing myself to yelp in pain and surprise. "Ah! Fuck!"

As I flinched to move my hand away from the heat, the motion sent a spray of embers tumbling onto the ground beside me. Quickly looking about, I instantly realized I had just fallen onto a small cooking pit that the goblins had set against the far stone wall, where it wouldn't set the opposite wooden wall on fire, and by extension their carefully built platforms and scaffolds that led up and out of the room.

"Of course with my luck, I had to fucking land right on top of a fire!" I cursed as I quickly tried to free myself from all the debris that had fallen on top of me, only to have pieces spark and catch fire as I moved them. "Oh, shit!"

The dry and aged wood almost instantly caught aflame, spreading quickly as it began to consume the wood. Out of reflex, I began to slap the fires out before catching myself and stopping.

Hang on a second. I looked towards the western wooden wall that spanned from floor to ceiling. *What do I care if this place burns down? In fact, since we're here to cause a little bit of destruction, maybe I can help this along.*

With a demonic smile on my face, I happily indulged my inner pyromaniac. I began to pile burning debris against the far wooden wall, in hopes of setting the structure aflame. If nothing else, it would damage the front section of the tower and eventually burn itself out once it consumed all the wood in the old roof of the tower.

While looking for more kindling, I found the broken form of the goblin that I had kicked off the platform, having landed badly from its fall. *Well, at least I don't need to worry about him down here!*

Taking my eyes off the dead goblin, I resumed my search, seeing that the goblins had taken advantage of the internal space of the tower, setting up a number of homes at the bottom of this room, indicated by crude fences of sticks driven into the dirt or, an array of stones laid out in a square. Inside the spaces, I saw lengths of crudely cut fur on piles of dried grasses serving as beds for the goblins.

Grabbing armfuls of the rather foul-smelling thatch, I threw it onto the smoldering debris, quickly being rewarded by a flare of heat as it caught fire.

"It's working!" I had to cover my face to shield myself from the heat as the fire caught onto the wooden wall and began to spread rather quickly. "Oh, this is catching *fast*."

Hungrily consuming the ancient, dry wood, the fire had no problems finding purchase on the wooden wall as it began to spread outwards from the burning debris, growing in size and intensity every second that passed.

"Uh, okay. I *may* have overdone it," I said worriedly to myself as I saw the pillar of fire begin to tickle the only platform leading back up and out of the room. "I need to find Razor and get the fuck out of here!"

Retreating quickly from the increasingly intense heat, I returned to the spot where I had crash landed, urgently tearing through the debris looking for my sword. It took a moment of frantically clawing through the pile before I found my trusty blade in the mess. Quickly sheathing Razor, I broke into a sprint, moving to run up the ramp before the fire spread too far.

<I'm coming back up!> I sent to Amaranth as I stormed up the ramps, feeling an intense wash of heat as I passed over the flames that were quickly climbing up the wall. *<How is everything there?>*

< The Dirty Ones fight hard, and more have joined the fight from below!> Amaranth replied back to me, a nervous note in his mental voice. *<Drace and Abaddon struggle to hold the goblins at bay, while the others attack from afar. They are desperate in the defense of their den!>*

<As soon as I get there, we will need to move quickly!> I felt my lungs beginning to struggle as I climbed higher, the smoke of the burning wood wafting upwards as I ran. I could hear the sounds of battle above me as I ascended from an adjoining ramp and got closer to the fight. *<I'm almost there!>*

< What is happening?!> Amaranth asked me urgently. *<I smell smoke and fire!>*

<Yeah, that was me!> I sprinted across another platform before climbing up another ramp, appearing just behind a crowd of goblins attempting to swarm Drace and Abaddon who were both holding off separate goblin assaults, their large statures forcing them to adopt an awkwardly cramped stance in the tight space.

Drace had positioned himself to hold back the goblins attacking from the lower level I had just come from, while Abaddon fought against goblins descending from a ramp above. As the two warriors kept the bulk of the goblin horde in place, Halcyon defended the rest of the party, channeling his Force Shield to provide some degree of cover on the otherwise exposed platforms. This gave our two scouts and mages a chance to focus fire on the rest of the goblins, who were almost all equipped with similar bows to the stalkers I had just fought earlier.

It's like I've stumbled into a bizarre shootout! A goblin collapsed to the ground ahead of me, as a combined spray of magic and arrows finally overwhelmed it, but not before I heard Cerril's voice cry out as an arrow snuck past Halcyon's shield into the lower leveled novice. *Shit! I need to move faster!*

Chancing a quick glance over the side, I found the fire practically leaping up the wall as it burned faster and faster. *Oh, please be an exit somewhere up top!*

Gritting my teeth, I quickly checked my health, seeing that it thankfully regenerated just over forty percent in the time it had taken me to climb up the goblin made structure, giving me a little bit more confidence in jumping back into the fray.

Putting power into my sprint, I charged the crowd of goblins that had their backs turned to me, hopping over a trio of dead goblins as I ran, their bodies riddled with arrows and magical burns. Lowering my shoulder, I plowed into a goblin aiming its bow at Drace, sending it flying off the platform and into the fires below.

"Lyr!" Drace shouted out in surprise as my timely assistance caused the goblin's arrow to fire high over the warrior's head. Seeing the look of urgency on my face, he quickly shouted back. "What's going on?"

"We need to go up! Quickly!" I shouted at the warrior, ruthlessly shoving a goblin from behind, sending it falling off the edge of the platform. "Don't worry about killing them! Just knock them off! The fire will take care of them!"

"Fire? What fire?" Drace couldn't help but follow the descent of the goblin I had just thrown off the platform, instantly spotting the growing blaze climbing up the wall. "Holy hell, Lyrian! What the fuck did you do?"

"Fuck! I knew it was getting hot in here!" I heard Caius shout over the noise of combat. "Not again with the fire!"

"*Aw, yeah*! This is getting to be my kind of party!" Constantine's laugh boomed through the room. "Lighten up, Caius!"

The four remaining goblins having finally caught on to my presence and clearly able to understand our shouting, recoiled from Drace, looking down at the now raging fire below. I saw a flash of panic cross their stunned faces as the significance of what was happening caught up to them, followed by a howl of rage. Almost as one, they all ran from Drace, charging directly at me, intent on avenging their now burning home.

Note to self: setting someone's home on fire understandably puts you at the top of the aggro list! I drew Razor as I sprinted towards the goblins, ready to meet their charge head on, carefully calculating the timing of what I was about to attempt.

As the distance between the goblins and me closed, I quickly triggered Blink Step, teleporting me barely five feet forward, directly in front of the leading pair of goblins. Once again I crashed into the smaller goblins, my sudden teleport catching them all off stride. Barreling directly between the four goblins, I felt a dagger pierce into my thigh as I shoved my way through the goblins, pasting the left most goblins hard against the wall while sending the two goblins on my right sailing over the edge of the platform and into the fires below.

Running past the other goblins, I felt another dagger tag me in the back as I ran towards Drace, shouting at the warrior to move.

"Go! Go! Go! We need to start going up!" I urgently motioned towards the ramp that Abaddon had been fighting at, seeing that the goblins had retreated upwards.

"What about—" Drace started to ask me something before a thunderous echo of a Pyroclap filled the room as Halcyon dropped his shield, centering the spell on the two goblins I had just ran past.

Wasting no time to zero in on the two exposed goblins, the rest of the ranged group members quickly overwhelmed the pair, sending them both crashing to the ground.

"Lyrian, what did you do?" Freya shouted out at me as the rest of the party started to press forward along the platform.

"I'll tell you later! Abaddon, *go!*" I shouted at the concerned looking lizardman, who stood at the base of the ramp leading upwards, watching the fire below. "MOVE!"

"Moving ssounds good!" the aspiring warrior hissed, my shout finally pierced through his shock. "Follow me! Don't ssstop for anything!"

I nervously watched the group charge up the ramp, waiting for everyone to go ahead of me. Bringing up the rear, I spotted both Huxley and Cerril for what seemed to me like the first time in hours. Both looking terrified while following Drace as he awkwardly crab walked up the ramp. I noticed Cerril favoring his blood-soaked side as he walked, having already pulled the goblin arrow free.

<*We must go!*> Amaranth glared at me as a wave of heat wafted up from below. The temperature was on the verge of becoming unbearable.

"Go! I'm right behind you!" I waved the puma ahead as we both charged up the ramp, finding that the goblin design followed the same pattern as below, forcing us to run the length of the room before ascending to the next level. As we climbed higher, smoke began to fill the entirety of the room forcing me to hold my breath as I climbed.

"Heads up!" Halcyon shouted, a clap of thunder echoing through the air above me, quickly followed a by spray of debris and a pair of screaming goblins falling past me. "Keep going! Jump!"

"Ah!" I covered my face as shards of wood from the blast glanced off my helmet, forcing me to focus on the path ahead of me, keeping my eyes turned downward. As I ran, I caught sight of the now blazing inferno below.

By the time I reached the top level, my eyes were watering, and my lungs were beginning to burn. Blinking through tears, I saw Freya leap across a shattered section of the platform that lead directly into the stone wall. Stumbling forward, I tried to keep my head as low as possible while running towards the remaining group members.

Yes! A stairway! I felt an intense wave of relief wash over me as I saw Halcyon leap across the shattered gap just behind Freya, revealing a passage heading further into the tower. With True Sight cutting through the smoke, I risked a glance upwards, seeing that nearly everyone had made it, leaving only Cerril, Huxley, and Amaranth on the ledge ahead.

Wasting no time, Huxley followed Halcyon over the gap, quickly followed by a coughing Cerril. My heart leaped into my mouth as I saw Cerril stagger on the edge of the platform, windmilling his arms to catch his balance. Just before I thought Cerril would fall, Huxley's hand shot out, grabbing the man by the collar and pulling him down the stairs out of sight.

"Phew." I couldn't help but exhale as I motioned to Amaranth. *<Go!>*

Flicking an ear at me, Amaranth shot forward leaping across the gap easily. As soon as he landed, Amaranth glanced back, a look of panic crossing his face as both of his ears pointed forward towards me. *<Hurry!>*

I felt the platform around me suddenly shudder, the sound of cracking wood filling the air. A huge gap opened along the wooden edge of the ceiling as the wooden wall began to pull itself apart, sending me reeling backwards into the wall.

This place is coming down! I pushed myself forward as the platform shuddered a second time. Forcing myself to run against the pull of gravity, I stormed across the shaking platform, leaping into the air towards the stairway.

Flying through the smoke, I landed hard beside Amaranth, rolling to a stop. Looking back behind me, I saw the entire wooden roof of the tower tear itself free as it collapsed from the burning blaze right on top of the goblin village below.

"Fuck! That was close!" I gasped heavily trying to suck in fresh air. I felt a wave of energy surge into me, the same instant a message flashed across my vision.

Congratulations! You have reached Level 11!

FORTY-THREE

"**W**OO! LEVEL ELEVEN!" I HEARD Constantine exclaim as I slid down the smooth ramp with a set of stairs hanging overhead. Sliding to a stop as I gently bumped into Amaranth, I saw the rest of the party ahead of me, crammed into one another as the stairway twisted to our right with another flight of stairs above us leading even deeper into the tower.

"Okay, maybe that wasn't so bad *this time*," Caius whispered cautiously.

"Don't say that!" Halcyon slapped Caius on the shoulder while waving an arm at me. "You'll give him ideas!"

"*Lyr!*" Sierra turned to hiss at me as I came into sight, her eyes boring into mine. "What the fuck?"

"I, uh…" I looked around nervously, to see everyone except Constantine and Amaranth glaring at me. Constantine had a broad smile on his face as he gave me a wink, followed by a thumbs-up.

"Don't stop, Lyr." Sierra cupped a hand to her ear. "I'm curious to know just how the tower just *happened* to fucking catch fire and why you were running like a fucking guilty bat flying out of hell!"

"So, uh, after I fell." I looked at all of the unsympathetic faces, seeing everyone covered in ash and smoke. "I landed right on top of a dragon, you see…and it wasn't happy that I woke it up…"

"*A dragon?*" Zethus exclaimed excitedly as he squirmed to get out from under his friends. "There was a dragon in there?"

"Ha!" Constantine barked a short laugh at Zethus's naiveté, while Sierra just rolled her eyes.

"No, Zeth, Lyrian's just full of shit." Freya shook her head, a small grin crossing her face.

"Oh," Zethus replied, sounding disappointed.

"Seriously, Lyr?" Drace looked at me pointedly. "What happened?"

Looking at the big warrior, I let out a sigh. "I fell on a cooking pit, panicked when some debris near me caught fire. Then instead of putting it out, I decided to pile it against the wooden wall to set the place on fire."

Everyone looked at me with an incredulous expression on their face, their mouths hanging open in disbelief.

"Okay," Drace finally replied, shaking his head slowly, breaking the spell that had everyone fixated on me. "At least we hit level eleven."

"Is fire a regular thing with these guys?" I heard Freya whisper to Sierra, as she jerked her thumb in my direction.

"It's starting to be." Sierra rubbed her eyes as she spoke. "Constantine suggested setting fire to the forest once…"

"It would have saved time!" Constantine grumbled. "Fucking spiders…"

"Oh, dear." Freya cast a sympathetic look at Sierra while patting her on the shoulder, before the two began to untangle themselves and follow the rest of the party, who had begun to climb up the adjacent stairway, which angled upwards and deeper into the tower.

Waiting for my turn, I brought up my character sheet looking over the much-anticipated bonuses a new level always brought. *I haven't had a chance to check, but it looks like we do get experience for killing other players, a little bit more than a regular monster at the same level.*

Putting my newly earned attribute points into strength, I double checked my stats, wistfully looking at the experience bar that had now reset itself with an even higher mountain to climb before reaching the next level.

LYRIAN RASTLER – LEVEL 11 SPELLSWORD

Human Male (Eberian)
Statistics:
　HP: 638/638
　Stamina: 580/580
　Mana: 640/640
　Experience to next level: 54/23,200
Attributes:
　Strength: 41 (48)
　Agility: 36 (43)
　Constitution: 36
　Intelligence: 42
　Willpower: 16

Looking good! I thought to myself with a nod as I confirmed my choices and dismissed the sheet. *I should probably focus on Agility for the next few levels, but at least Intelligence is steadily improving with only my racial and class attribute increases every level.*

"Come on, Lyr," Constantine called to me as Cerril and Huxley climbed up the ramp. "We're up."

Following Constantine up the ramp, I took care not to crack my head off the stairs above me, sliding down the next adjacent ramp as we descended across the fallen length of the tower.

After repeating the process twice, we found ourselves climbing out onto a ledge overlooking a wide open space within the now hollow shell of the tower, the damaged middle section having bent slightly upwards as it slid down the hill ages past.

"Whoa," I said nervously, looking out over the edge, seeing everyone else caught by the same sight.

An arc of sunlight shone through a crack where the two pieces of the tower had broken, illuminating long vines and other plants that had grown downwards into the gap between the broken fragments. Following the plants downwards, I saw that the far ground was almost entirely covered with dirt and shattered stone, remnants from the rooms that once were the innards of the tower.

"Lyr!" I felt Halcyon grab my wrist as he pulled my attention over to the northern side of the ledge pointing at something that hung suspended in the air. "Look!"

A two-foot thick metallic pole connected to the far western wall of the tower, directly underneath the room we had just escaped from and spanned the entire length of the stairway we had just traveled through, before burying itself into the dirt below us. Turning my head, I saw a second length of the pole, having snapped during the tower's fall, protruding from the slowly rising dirt at an odd angle, running away from us and into the second section of the ancient tower.

"The center of the tower was hollow?" I asked Halcyon with confusion, indicating the two huge shattered lengths of metal. "What the hell is that thing for?"

"I don't know. Doesn't look like it'd be used to support the weight of the tower," Halcyon replied with a shrug. "Seems like a huge waste of space, but it must have been for something, especially with metal being so fucking expensive."

Everyone quickly crowded the edge of the platform overhearing our conversation, looking out at the strange contraption.

"Better quessstion for the moment," Cadmus began, waving at the edge. "How are we going to get down? I'd rather not jump."

We all looked around, seeing that Cadmus had just hit the nail on the head with his question. Whatever room once connected the stairway that we had just passed through had long since collapsed, leaving us with a rather long, forty foot drop until we reached the dirt packed bottom that had filled the lower third of the tower.

"I see a ledge down there," Caius said, peering over the edge. "It's about twenty feet down, though."

"Well, that solves the problem for Amaranth," Constantine replied looking at the big cat. "That sort of fall might hurt for the rest of us."

"Hey," Cerril suddenly spoke up, pointing downwards. "There are hand grips carved into the wall here, looks like they've just recently been widened to human size, too. Looks like they lead straight down along the outer wall."

"That'll do for us," Sierra replied bending to look down at the hand grips. "Might be a bit tight for the bigger guys, though."

"We'll manage," Drace said with a shrug. "After cramming myself up those ramps and platforms, and having them creak and crunch with every step I took, I can deal with small handholds."

Taking turns, we each stepped out over the edge and slowly made our way downwards, thankfully without any mishaps along the way. Once reaching the bottom, our feet sank into the wet, muddy ground, the water that had found its way in from the storm not yet having drained away in the closed environment.

"My friends are really close," Cerril grabbed my arm as he whispered softly, pointing east and upwards, towards the second section of the tower. "I wasn't paying attention earlier, but I think they've moved."

"They did?" I asked, while everyone quickly stopped to huddle around Cerril. "Where? What happened?"

"I think they moved higher," Cerril struggled to explain as he pointed in the same direction as before. "I think they used to be further away and not quite as high. But with us running through the other section of the tower and climbing down now, I'm not entirely sure."

"What about Graves?" Sierra asked, looking towards Huxley.

"That way," Huxley quickly replied, pointing almost straight ahead, despite the upward incline in front of us. "I think that other adventurer was telling the truth; Graves might have found a route into the hill. He seems too low to be anywhere in the tower."

"We'll figure that out after we find Cerril's friends," I said, nodding at Huxley. "Good to know we're on the right path."

Continuing forward, we slowly ascended the gentle incline that separated the two offset sections of the tower, momentarily stepping into the sunlight as we crossed the gap. We took care not to disrupt the long hanging vines that hung from the gap above any more than we had to, pushing them gently aside as we passed. Once on the other side of the sunbeam, we looked upwards, seeing the other half of the massive metallic pole jutting from the ground beside us.

Ours eyes followed the mysterious pole, seeing that it had sagged from bearing its own weight for untold ages, a gentle bend appearing along its length. Hanging limply in the air ahead of us, it led deeper into the second fragment of the tower, vanishing into a large hole cut in the center of a damaged stone wall. As we continued walking, we found the lower third of the wall completely missing, having shattered from the fall that knocked the tower over.

Finding it easier to move, I noticed that the ground on this side of the space was completely dry, the water from the storm having run downwards to the opposite end of the room. Looking at my feet, I saw that the ground had been disturbed, torn up even. *What happened here? This looks fresh.*

"They should be here," Cerril whispered, looking upwards, his gaze going towards the gap in the wall where the pole had vanished. "They should be right there."

We all looked upwards where the pole was resting on the stone, all surprised to see a man suddenly step out onto the ledge.

"It took you all long enough to get here," the man's unfamiliar voice called out as he looked down at us. "Once I felt everyone else dying outside, I never doubted that you all would."

"Carver!" Freya shouted, at the same instant the Thunder Lizards all hissed in rage.

"Ah? Freya!" The half-orc smiled, rubbing his hands together with delight. "I had *hoped* you would come, and you brought your friends too! How delightful! I was worried you had forgotten about me."

"How I wish I could, you sick son of a bitch!" Freya yelled up at the man. "I don't know how the fuck this game is still letting you play with half the shit you've pulled!"

"*Oh, my,* it's a pity to hear such coarse language from a lady." Carver clucked his tongue in disapproval, wagging a finger at Freya. "If only there was time to teach you some proper manners. Perhaps another day, you see, I am rather in a hurry."

"Running away again, Carver?" Thorne shouted back. "Are you afraid to fight us on even terms, without needing Graves to hold your hand?"

"Needing Graves? Ha!" Carver's laugh boomed through the hollow tower as he sneered down at us. "He was useful for a time but, unfortunately, has since lost his way. It is *I* who no longer have any need for him, and your arrival gives me the perfect opportunity to cut and run."

"What are you talking about?" I finally decided to enter the conversation. "What happened to Graves?"

"Oh, I guess you could say he's not exactly Graves anymore." Carver flicked his eyes over to me as he smirked, lifting his hand up. "Maybe you'll find out if you survive what's coming next. Either way, thanks for giving us the chance to escape!"

Seconds after Carver's signal, a handful of other adventurers appeared behind the half-orc, roughly pushing three other people ahead of them.

"Jordan!" Cerril shouted, rushing forward towards his friends high on the ledge ahead.

"Cerril, RUN!" Jordan shouted while struggling to get away from the adventurer that held him from behind. "They—"

"Do it!" Carver snapped, slicing his hand through the air. The other adventurers immediately kicked Jordan and Cerril's other friends off of the ledge.

As they plummeted towards the ground, I noticed something dark trailing their fall before they suddenly jerked to a stop with the loud snap of breaking bone. The three of them hung limply, their heads lolling at an unnatural angle as I saw a set of ropes looped around each of their necks.

"Carver!" Freya shouted with rage. "What the fuck did you do?"

"I believe that's fairly obvious, my dear," Carver replied with a laugh. "I killed them."

"WHY?" Cerril screamed rushing forward to the bodies of his hanging friends, eyes brimming with tears. "They were no threat to you!"

"Of course they weren't." Carver waved his hand dismissively, looking down at Cerril. "But the *other* things down there *are.*"

As if on cue, I saw nearly two dozen azure auras bloom to life ahead of me, a short distance past where the broken wall ended. Standing awkwardly, they began to shamble towards us, their auras becoming more and more distinct as they approached.

"Hal…" A worried tone escaped my voice as I looked to the other mage to confirm what I saw. "Cerril, get back here!"

"I see it too, Lyr." Halcyon's eyes had gone wide as he too saw the shuffling forms in the distance with his Arcane Sight.

"Really, I did your friends a huge favor!" Carver laughed once again, joined by the other adventurers standing beside him. "A long drop with a short rope will be much easier to get over, compared to what these creatures will do to you all! They seem to rather enjoy *rending* the flesh from their victims, be they dead or alive, before they eat it!"

"Haha! Goodbye, for now, kids!" Carver waved mockingly at us, the other adventurers turning to walk away from the ledge. "Uncle Carver will drop in sometime soon, once he and his friends find a place to bind themselves! Until then, enjoy playing with your new toys!"

"Get back here!" Freya shouted at Carver's retreating form, darting forward before Helix grabbed her by the arm. "Helix, let me go!"

"Freya, stop!" Helix pointed towards the darker shadows where I saw the auras approaching from. "*Look!*"

"Oh, God!" I heard someone gasp, as the creatures stepped out into the light.

A horde of emaciated humanoids shambled out of the gloom from under the stone wall, stumbling across the rough rubble. Some appeared to be grotesquely deformed goblins, while others were once clearly humans, dwarves, or elves. Whatever vestiges of sapience they once possessed, had long since been consumed by their transformation.

Their skin was now a charred black color, with scraps of clothes still hanging from their flesh. Milky white eyes gazed blindly into the distance, seemingly no longer used for sight. Crowding around the hanging adventurers they reached upwards with wicked groping claws, tearing strips of flesh from the bodies effortlessly.

"What the fuck!" Constantine couldn't help but gag as the creatures began to feed, shoving chunks of meat into their mouths.

"*Cerril!*" I hissed at the adventurer, having slowly backed away from the feasting horde. "Hurry up and get back here!"

"I-I—" Consumed by fear Cerril stuttered, his eyes fixated on the abominations in front of him.

"No!" Natasha let out a sobbing cry, her hand reaching out towards the creatures before us. "Noooo! How did this happen?"

"Natasha, I'm sorry…" Realization dawned upon me as I saw the familiar symbol of the Mages Guild appear on a scrap of clothes one of the creatures wore. "I don't—"

A gleaming azure light flared from the stomach of the feasting creatures, all of them turning their now glowing eyes towards us. Nearly two dozen tags appeared in my vision highlighting the creatures.

[Ætherwarped Ghoul – Level 10]

"Oh, fuck me," I gasped, the entire horde of ghouls shifting to face us. "Form up! Cerril! *Move!*"

"Ah!" Cerill began to turn, my voice finally breaking through his fear.

A bloodcurdling scream sliced through the air the second that Cerril turned his back on the ghoul horde. Almost as one they leaped forward, charging at the elven adventurer with their claws outstretched. Suddenly fueled with energy, they instantly closed the distance between them and the fleeing elf, driving their claws brutally into his body as they bore him to the ground.

"Aaaaah!" Cerril screamed as the ghouls fell upon him, a pair of arrows and a quartet of magical missiles doing nothing to stop the ghouls from rending apart Cerril's flesh. "Heeelp—"

Cerril's voice ended with a brutal finality as the creatures began pushing and crowding one another with snarls as they fought for position to devour Cerril's flesh. Pushed far from the circle of feasting ghouls some of the outliers turned to face us.

"Charge them!" I shouted, taking a step forward. "Before they all focus on us!"

Howling, our entire melee line charged forward, managing two entire strides before the ghouls leaped to meet us. Focusing on the ghoul ahead of me I managed an extra step forward, leading with my shoulder as I slammed into the ghoul's chest, knocking it to the ground.

Amaranth, quickly appearing to my right, swiped his claws across the fallen ghoul's legs, drawing forth foul and putrid smelling blood.

Fuck! That smells just as bad as the queen did! Unbidden memories couldn't help but surface at the familiar rotting stench.

I stabbed down with a Shocking Touch-charged Razor, the tip of the crackling blade thrusting into the creature's pelvis, twisting the blade and widening the wound as I pulled Razor free. Hissing with rage, the ghoul showed no sign that either of our attacks had even hurt it. It swiped a claw at me as it scrambled to its feet.

As it shot to its feet, I couldn't help but notice that the ghoul had once been a woman, remnants of long hair clinging to one side of the ghoul's scalp. Shrieking, the ghoul ignored two more long cuts that I managed to land on it, attacking wildly with its claws.

Damn it! I swore to myself as it carved a long gash into my arm. *How do you fight something that doesn't even feel pain?*

With its wickedly sharp claws slicing across my arm, the ghoul finally displayed some emotion. An unearthly squeal of pleasure erupted from the creature as it brought its blood covered claw to its open maw, a black barbed tongue shooting out to quickly lick it clean. The ghoul trembled like a drug addict finding their favorite fix, its stomach and eyes pulsing with an azure light.

What the fuck? Did it just fucking eat my blood?! It was one thing to see someone else being eaten or even bitten, but quite another to have it happen to you! Especially right in the middle of a fight! *What the fuck is going on with its stomach?*

Fueled by my blood, the ghoul fought with a heightened level of ferocity, clawing and biting as it tried to repeat its earlier success. Deciding to accept the risk of being clawed or bitten, I baited the aggressive creature close and grabbed hold of the creature's claw, stabbing Razor into its glowing gut. I felt something fight against the blade as I drove it into the creature. Gritting my teeth I bore down into the thrust, pushing past the resistance until I felt something give way.

With a wailing scream as Razor drove itself home, the ghoul panicked against my grip, its other claw grasping the blade and trying desperately to pull it free. With a smile I decided to indulge the ghoul, letting go of its arm at the same instant I pulled Razor free, planting a heavy kick in the center of the ghoul's chest.

The wailing ghoul fell backwards, sending glowing, azure-colored liquid spewing into the air as it crashed into the ground. Attempting to close the gaping wound in its stomach, it desperately pressed its claws to its abdomen while trying to scramble away from the rest of the ghoul horde.

Somehow sensing the weakness of the ghoul I had injured, the other ghouls spun towards the fallen one, a hungry expression crossing their decaying faces. A handful leaped upon the wounded ghoul, their claws and teeth sinking into the flesh of their companion as they hungrily drank the glowing fluid.

"What the fuck?" Drace shouted in surprise, the ghoul he was fighting being among those that had suddenly abandoned their fights in favor of an easier target.

"Stab them in the stomach!" I shouted down the melee line. "That's the only place they feel pain!"

A roaring cry broke out over the din of battle, the line beside Constantine suddenly faltering.

"Lyr! Cadmus just went down!" Drace called to me as he glanced down our battle line. "I got this! Go!"

"Okay!" I slapped Drace on the arm as I ducked out of the line, Amaranth moving to fill in my gap.

Running behind the line of battle, I saw Cadmus on the ground with a pair of ghouls straddling his body as their claws easily tore through his armor and scales. They rent apart flesh with reckless abandon as they devoured the fallen lizardman, his spirit having fled his ruined body.

Hard pressed to keep up with the higher-leveled creatures, Abaddon, Freya, Thorne, and Helix were forced to retreat a step backwards as all of the nearby ghouls abandoned their fights and leaped to devour Cadmus's corpse.

"Cadmuss!" Abaddon roared while chopping through a ghoul's wrist as it fled from him. "No!"

I'm seeing a pattern here. They all fixate on any source of food they can find! I ran towards Freya and her group, shouting as I arrived. "They are driven by hunger! Take advantage of it and stab their stomachs!"

"Their stomach?" Freya's face looked haunted as she looked towards the feral pack of ghouls.

"*How*, Lyrian?" Thorne hissed at my advice. "I have a fucking mace! I can't stab shit!"

"Do your best and don't die then!" I snapped back at the dwarf, stopping next to Freya and replacing Cadmus's spot in their line. "Let's go! While they're distracted!"

Leaping forward with Freya and the others at my side, I thrust Razor into the back of a goblin-sized ghoul feasting on Cadmus's body. The blade easily driving through the dry and emaciated skin before I felt it hit the familiar resistance of the stomach. Twisting my blade, Razor sliced through the glowing mass, the goblinoid ghoul instantly writhing in panic.

"Yes!" Freya shouted in joy as she found similar success, carving a large gash through a second ghoul's stomach and sending the glowing liquid spilling across the ground.

From there the battle descended into chaos, the ghouls attacking and savaging us along with any of their wounded that bled the azure fluid. Before long, our armor was rent by dozens of vicious claws and blood streamed from countless wicked wounds. Caius and Theia strode the line of battle like angels of mercy, their timely ministrations keeping us from joining the fallen.

But despite all their efforts, they couldn't be everywhere, nor could they save us all.

Overwhelmed by a thousand ever bleeding cuts, Thorne fell, his body vanishing under the horde of ravaging claws and teeth. Amid the rampaging ghouls we found ourselves pressed by their relentless fury as they swarmed around us, our lines of battle becoming desperate pockets of blood and metal as we fought back to back, leaving a wide-open path towards our scouts and mages in the rear.

Stepping up to defend the others from the ghouls that rushed through our broken line, Halcyon met the charging monsters, his Force Shield shimmering in gloom. To his surprise, however, the creatures passed through the barrier as if parting a curtain. Their claws sank deep into his flesh, overrunning the brave mage. Mere steps behind, Drace and Constantine, arrived far too late to save Halcyon. Instead, they took out their rage on the ghouls that slew him.

Fighting desperately, our tactics slowly began to turn the tide, the ghoul's hunger unable to resist the flesh of the fallen, be it ours or theirs. Their numbers dwindled, allowing us to reform our lines and focus our teamwork to wear the ravenous ghouls down.

In what seemed like ages later, I thrust Razor into the belly of the final ghoul as I pinned it to the ground. Panting from the exertion of the battle, I stepped onto the creature's flailing claw, having long since severed the other. Its struggles grew weaker as its azure lifeblood bled from around Razor's edge, shuddering under me.

Raising my other boot high, I looked down at the creature under me, seeing the tattered insignia of the Eberian Mages Guild on its breast. Its gleaming eyes stared up at me, its teeth snapping as it tried to bring its body close enough to bite me.

Sorry, we were too late. I looked down at the ghoul with sorrow.

Then I stomped on its head.

NO ONE SPOKE AS WE walked further into the tower, Carver's show and the fight with the ghouls having taken a toll on our spirits. Halcyon, Cadmus, and Thorne had fallen during the battle, joining Cerril and his friends in death. Granted, we could feel through the party sense that our friends had respawned distantly in Aldford, where we knew Myr was as well, but the loss of their presence here was felt in every step we took.

Thankfully, the system worked its subtle magic on our psyche, dulling the memories and pain from the battle, lest our minds snap from what we had experienced. As a whole I still wasn't sure how I felt, knowing that the game was effectively editing my personality every second I played Ascend Online. But at the moment, I was happy to have the carnage of the battle fade from my mind.

There was no sign of Carver or the other adventurers deeper into the tower, save gaps in the stone ceiling where we could spot the massive pole running overhead of us. Carver had clearly known about the presence of the ghouls and how they would react to the presence of interlopers, baiting them into attacking us so he could escape.

Was he trapped up there? I wondered, looking up at the ceiling, realizing there must have not been a route to escape from up there. *He had others with him too. What did Graves do to drive them away? Maybe the spirit possessing him caused it?*

How the hell did those expedition members end up becoming æther-

warped? We locked the Translocation hub down! Unless there's another ley line here? I scowled at the thought. *These fucking ley lines seem to be dangerous to anything that touches it! If they're this fucking common, we'll be wasting all of our time running around the region and plugging them up!*

Lost in my thoughts, time passed quickly while we walked through the second fragment of the tower. Light spells providing the much-needed illumination for those who could not see in the darkness. Much of this portion of the tower had shattered from the fall, giving us a reasonably clear path as we delved deeper into the ruin. Twice we were forced to zig-zag our way through long horizontal stairways, reminding us once again of how tall this tower must have been.

After climbing out of the second stairway, we found ourselves inside a completely hollow portion of the tower, only the outer shell of the structure remained. Looking around, my True Sight easily pierced through the darkness surrounding us, revealing large piles of dirt in the distance and of course, another broken length of the long mysterious pole that had traveled the length of the tower resting on the ground nearby.

"Where are we?" Sierra asked nervously, the first to speak since the battle with the ghouls ended. "I can't see anything."

"We're in the third section of the tower," I whispered, pointing off into the darkness to show where the two pieces of the tower had broken apart and then crashed into one another as they slid down the hill. Realizing too late that no one else could make out where I was pointing, the ceiling above us far enough away that even those with night vision couldn't see. "The pole we saw along the tower is also here."

"I really wish we knew what it was for," Zethus said softly.

"Maybe once we put Graves to bed we can look around here in more detail," Constantine replied. "Halcyon will have to come back here anyway to claim his Soul Fragment."

"Oh, that's right." I mentally winced, having forgotten about the death penalty that Halcyon now carried. With a sigh, I mentally pushed that problem to the future and motioned for everyone to follow me. "Let's keep moving, we have to be getting close to whatever the goblins dug into. I see a ton of dirt ahead."

"We're almost there," Huxley affirmed, pointing almost straight ahead. "Graves is close."

Leading the way, I stalked forward carefully, my eyes watching for any sign of goblins or other adventurers as we wove our way around piles of dirt that had obviously been carted and dumped here. Looking at the ground, I saw marks where a wheelbarrow or something similar had cut a rut in the hard dirt from repeated passages.

Dirt from digging through the hill? I continued to creep forward, following the rut in the ground as it slowly angled towards the center of the room. It was there we found the pole again, the rut running parallel to it. As with the other lengths of the pole we found throughout the tower, it being completely featureless and smooth, giving us no clue to what its function may have once been, save that it extended from the very base of the tower to nearly its tip.

"Well, what could cause it to do that?" Constantine whispered in surprise as the pole finally came to a rather abrupt end, mushrooming and splintering outwards as if something had exploded inside it.

"Whoa," Caius echoed, as he inspected the broken end metallic pole. "It's solid metal on the inside, through and through, but it looks—"

"—like you stuck a gigantic firecracker inside it and set it off," Freya finished.

"Yeah." Caius nodded, scanning the ground around us. "Must have happened during the tower's fall. I don't see any fragments of metal around us."

"That's because all the fragments are up there," I said in disbelief, staring nearly straight up at the ceiling towards the eastern half of the room. "Something exploded close to the base of the tower when it still stood. I just noticed it now, but the entire ceiling and walls past this point are charred black. I can see pockmarks in the walls from debris, along with cracks from the heat."

Everyone looked out into the darkness, before looking back at me.

"This wasn't just a watchtower, Lyr," Constantine said to me.

"Yeah, I'm starting to get the same feeling," I replied worriedly.

"What could it have been then?" Helix asked.

"I don't know." I turned to keep walking. "But we're about to find out."

IT DIDN'T TAKE US MUCH longer to find the tunnel that the goblins had dug into the side of the hill, having just continued to follow the seemingly endless piles of dirt that littered the way. At the mouth of the tunnel I saw a pair of crudely built wheelbarrows turned over onto their sides, dirt spilling from them. All around us, discarded tools carelessly littered the ground, having been rudely cast aside as if a great hurry had overcome the laborers.

"At least it's human-sized," Drace said wearily, looking at the width of the tunnel ahead of us. "I don't think I'd be able to make it through if it was any smaller."

"I think—" Natasha swallowed hard as she spoke, her voice on the edge of tears. "I think they had the expedition members dig this tunnel. I-I recognize some of these tools."

"I'm sorry, Natasha," Sierra whispered touching the scout's shoulder. "If any goblins remain, we'll be sure to avenge them."

"Thank you, Sierra." Natasha sniffled, her cracking voice reminding us that she was likely the youngest in the party, NPC or not. "I'll be okay."

"We'll take the tools with us," I said, grabbing a *[Steel Pickaxe]* from the ground and putting it into my inventory. Everyone else quickly following suit, until no other tools remained on the ground. "We'll find a better use for them, rather than leaving them behind for the goblins, or to rot down here forgotten."

"Uh, Lyrian?" I heard Huxley call my name, as he picked up a square piece of metal from the ground. "I think I found something, a *plaque* of some sort."

"A plaque?" I echoed with curiosity as I moved to the elf. "What does it say?"

"Uh." Huxley brushed the sheet of metal off, carefully reading the inscription. "It's in another language, kind of elvish, but not. My Linguistics skill can only make out the words 'annulment spire' and the number '985'."

"I think it's in the dark elf language, which I don't know," Huxley continued after a moment. "And that 985 is a year, maybe the one that this place was built?"

"Makes sense," I replied slowly. "But annulment spire? What does that even mean?"

"I don't know." Huxley shrugged, waving the plaque around. "Could be the wrong word, or might be the wrong meaning."

"Hang on, didn't you say the war between the dark elves and the Nafarr started in 983?" Constantine asked. "If this place is dark elf made..."

"Then it took at least two years for them to make it this far once the war started," Huxley answered with a nod. "Minus the time to build this tower, which I guess might have taken them a year. Or maybe the plaque could indicate the day they *started* building the tower."

"It's an interesting bit of history," I agreed. "But it doesn't do anything for us right now, and we really should get moving."

"Yeah, probably a good idea." Huxley quickly put the plaque away into his pack.

After a quick check to ensure we were ready, we set off into the tunnel with me in the lead. All of us were eager to finally put an end to both Graves and any other adventurers or goblins that followed him.

Creeping through the tunnel at a cautious pace, I found myself having to duck my head slightly to avoid cracking it off of the bracing set into the roof and wall. The now-familiar color and shape of the wooden braces told me that they had been one of the many pieces scavenged from the rafters of the tower.

It's a miracle the roof tower didn't collapse on its own with how much wood the goblins tore from it. I thought to myself, shaking my head at their recklessness. *Though that does make sense why it fell apart so quickly once it started burning.*

I had no idea how far we descended down the tunnel before I noticed a faint azure light in the distance ahead of us, causing us to slow our pace as we approached.

The light's pulsing, almost like a heartbeat! I suddenly realized, rubbing sweat off my brow, noticing that the temperature had been rising steadily. *I really hope we don't need to worry about bad air in here.*

A hand touched my shoulder, causing me to flinch in surprise as I quickly spun to see Caius staring at me with a finger across his lips. He pointed ahead, then to his heart and ears before looking at me expectantly.

He can hear blood ahead of us. I nodded at the warlock to show I understood his message, motioning to my sword then miming running feet with my fingers. Caius nodded, holding up a hand as he passed the message down the line, eventually giving me the thumbs up. *Here we go!*

With my heart thundering in my chest, I gripped Razor tightly and padded down the final stretch of the tunnel. Shattered white bricks crunched under my feet as I approached the passage's mouth.

Holy shit! I was forced to momentarily shield my eyes as an intense wave of magic washed over me, revealing a blazing pillar of azure energy centering the room ahead, spanning from floor to ceiling. After my eyes readjusted, I saw that the tunnel had breached a huge vertical chamber, set deep within the hillside, directly under where the tower had once stood. Impossibly white bricks covered every facet of the chamber, somehow reflecting the pulsing aura of the pillar and casting the center of the room in a deep azure tint.

What the hell is that? Nestled in the heart of the azure fire was a fist-sized object of near infinite darkness, hungrily drinking in every iota of energy directed to it. So strong was the draw that the edges of the pillar seemed to constrict and deform around the dark shape, as if it were a miniature black hole, consuming everything around it.

A short distance below me, a crimson aura bloomed in my vision as Graves stepped into sight, walking along a raised dais that surrounded the base of the burning column. He gazed upwards into the storm of energy before him, a familiar looking, blue-skinned goblin carrying a skull-tipped staff following him close by. A tag helpfully appeared in my vision, pointing to the goblin below.

[Goblin Shaman – Mtadr – Boss – Level 12]

That looks like the same kind of goblin that we fought at the transloca-tion hub! But this one is named and a boss creature! My eyes widened as the aura around Graves formed into a familiar-looking shape. *There's the king's ghost!*

The spirit I remembered shadowing Graves when we last fought no longer hung high above him, but instead was now superimposed over his very body. Both Graves and the spirit now moved in sync, as if the ghost had somehow settled deeper into Graves's flesh.

Movement in the corner of my eye had me turning my head to see a dozen *[Goblin Stalkers – Level 10]* standing on the very edges of the chamber, pressed hard against the outer wall. Writhing on the ground before them, lay three ragged prisoners, their faces contorted in pain.

Some of the expedition members are still alive! I could see the familiar white insignia flash in the azure light as one of the distant figures tried to push themselves closer to the outer wall the goblins had huddled against. *What are they trying to do here?*

Looking back I saw the blue-skinned goblin raise its staff up high, a ball of fire forming in the maw of the skull. The ball shot forth and slammed into the dark sphere hanging high above them. The impact causing it to rock back and forth, bending the energy of the pillar as it moved. A second fireball quickly followed, crashing into the sphere at the apex of its arc, forcing it outside the bounds of the pillar.

Instantly the darkness of the sphere faded, falling to the ground with a weak thump as it rolled across the floor. No longer inhibited, the blazing column of energy intensified, coating the entire chamber with even brighter azure light.

"**AT LAST,**" a discordant voice echoed through the room as Graves spread his arms wide, stepping onto the dais. "**I CAN RID MYSELF OF THIS PRISON OF FLESH.**"

Oh, shit, he's going to walk into the pillar! I swallowed hard as I leaped down from the mouth of the tunnel and into the chamber. I heard Caius and the others hit the ground behind me, close on my tail. *I need to get closer! It's too far away to Blink Step!*

"GRAVES!" I shouted, my voice booming through the chamber as I ran. I hoped that the surprise of our arrival would buy me enough time to get close. "DID YOU THINK I WOULDN'T FIND YOU HERE?"

Spinning at the sound of my voice both Graves and Mtadr looked at me with surprise, their gaze shifting to see the rest of the group emerging from the tunnel behind me. I heard shrieks as the other goblins rushed to intercept me.

Hope this gets me close enough! Lunging forward I triggered Blink Step, my vision blurring as I teleported across the room, arriving just ten feet away from Graves. The familiar warmth of æther coming from the pillar greeted me, my body instantly feeling energized in its light.

"GO!" the goblin shaman shouted as it stepped into my path, blocking my route to Graves. Fire blazing from the skull on its staff as it spewed forth a torrent of flame.

I instinctively covered my face with my arm as the flames washed over me, feeling my eyebrows and beard burn away. I felt the armor covering my arm and shoulder melt into my flesh under the searing fire the shaman channeled, all the while flashing red alerts appeared in my combat log.

[Goblin Shaman – Mtadr] burns you with [Spewing Flames] for 38 points of fire damage!
[Goblin Shaman – Mtadr] burns you with [Spewing Flames] for 43 points of fire damage!
[Goblin Shaman – Mtadr] burns you with [Spewing Flames] for 47 points of fire damage!

Relentlessly pushing forward, I broke through the flames, slashing Razor downwards in the spot where I last saw the goblin shaman. The flames cut off, the goblin quickly interposing its bone staff to keep Razor from chopping into its head.

"**YOU ARE TOO LATE, MORTAL!**" Graves's discordant voice boomed in front of me. A sneer crossed his face as I momentarily took my eyes off Mtadr to look at him. Taking his gaze off me he stepped into the blazing furnace of power, the crimson aura of the king's spirit immediately tainting the well of magic causing the chamber to vibrate. "**WITNESS MY REBIRTH!**"

"NO—" The skull of the goblin's staff slammed into the side of my face, sending me staggering to the side. I dizzily swiped Razor in an arc, cursing myself for taking my eyes off the shaman for so long.

Forcing my attention back onto the large blue-skinned goblin,

I charged towards it before it could point the flaming head of the staff at me. I kicked out at the staff the same instant a fireball spewed forth from its maw, harmlessly splashing against the chamber floor. Continuing my stride I slammed my shoulder into the goblin's body, sending it reeling backwards a step.

I followed up with a crackling Razor, discharging a fistful of electricity into the shaman and cutting a shallow wound through its fur armored shoulder. My hand shot out, intent on grabbing the goblin by the throat and strangling the life from it. However, the goblin shaman quickly recovered from my Shocking Touch, throwing a hand forward, which flashed with an intense flash of light, temporarily blinding me.

"Fuck!" I ducked my face, arm reflexively shielding my eyes once again as I fervently tried to blink the gigantic white afterimage out of my vision.

<I'm coming!> Amaranth's concerned voice echoed in my mind. *<Hold on!>*

<Hurry!> I mentally shouted back at my familiar, feeling another torrent of fire splash over me.

Running forward, the edges of my vision began to clear, only to be replaced by a pulsating crimson light bathing the room. Casting about wildly I saw Graves's silhouette floating high above me in the heart of the æther column. Molten metal began to drip from the ceiling, as the increasing vibrations began to shake the entire chamber.

A large drop of metal splashed to the ground, nearly hitting me as it sizzled atop the stone. Looking upwards, I saw the rapidly melting tip of the pole we had followed through the tower earlier, centered in the middle of the ceiling. *The pole was buried this deep?*

The shaking quickly grew in intensity, knocking everyone in the room off their feet. Bricks began to shake themselves loose, crashing to the ground all around us as the chamber shook itself apart. Lying sprawled out on the ground I couldn't help but twist myself to look back at the tunnel, expecting to see it collapse and trap us here.

With a final gut-wrenching quake, a thundering flash of crimson energy exploded from Graves's floating form, shattering the well set in the ground. The burning column of magic instantly vanished, momentarily plunging the room into darkness. I felt stone shrapnel slam into me, some piercing through my armor and into my flesh as the blast sent me sliding across the floor.

What the fuck just happened? I moaned in pain as I collected myself.

Slowly pushing myself up off the floor, my augmented vision easily cut through the darkness, revealing everyone slowly picking themselves up off the ground. I looked towards the center of the room, suddenly seeing a crimson apparition burst into being on top of Graves's floating form, filling the room with a bright malevolent light.

"I LIVE AGAIN!" the apparition roared, as Graves's body fell to the ground with a crash. "THE SECOND REIGN OF SLAVE-KING ABDIEL BEGINS!"

My mouth hung open in shock as the slave-king's transparent form burst into flames and began to grow.

For every second that passed, his appearance seemed to gain more solidity and detail as his form came into being, touching down on the ground slowly. Wearing the same armor that Graves wore, Slave-King Abdiel's new body stood nearly seven feet tall, complete with an ornate crown on his head. Holding a hand up high, a flaming sword conjured itself into being, centering itself in his grip. Hefting the blade high, his featureless gaze roamed the chamber as if in search of something.

Oh, what the fuck did you do, Graves? The spirit before me blazed with immense energy, my True Sight displaying the creature as one blinding mass of magic. With a blink, I deactivated the ability, instantly feeling relief as the aura vanished from my sight, leaving me only seeing its corporeal form. Heart clenching at what I might see, I focused on the reborn ghost, bringing up its tag, which was quickly followed by the chime of a new quest.

[Slave-King Abdiel – Ætheric Manifestation – Elite Boss – Level 14]
▷**NEW QUEST! THE SLAVE-KING REBORN!** *(Multi-Group)*
(Evolving Quest)
  Slave-King Abdiel, a Nafarrian king of an ancient age, has
  found a way to return to life! He has set his sights on rebuilding
  his old dynasty and bringing the region under the reign of his
  iron fist! Stop him before he regains his full power!
  Slave-King Abdiel Slain: 0/1
  Difficulty: Very Hard
  Reward: Experience & Renown

Don't we have enough shit to worry about? I quickly felt my heart sink as I scanned the king's level, followed by the system's new quest before dismissing it from my vision. *An ætheric manifestation? Does that mean he's made of magic now?*

"**AH! THERE YOU ARE, GRAVES!**" The newly formed king called at Graves's crawling form, temporarily ignoring the rest of us. "**DID YOU THINK YOU COULD ESCAPE ME?**"

Scanning my surroundings while the king's focus was elsewhere, I saw a savagely burnt Amaranth straddling the goblin shaman, having bit down into the creature's arm. Running to aid my familiar, I saw that the rest of the party had already resumed hostilities with the other goblins in the room and appeared to have formed a pocket of defense around the captured Expedition members I had seen earlier.

<*Lyrian, help!*> Amaranth's mental voice sounded desperate as a feline yelp of pain reached my ears.

In the split second that my attention had been focused elsewhere the goblin shaman had somehow knocked Amaranth off of him, sending the puma flying a short distance through the air. Seeing the skull on shaman's staff blazing with flame, I desperately cast Blink Step, appearing half a stride behind the kneeling shaman, tackling it from behind.

The fireball shot uselessly into the air, splashing against the far wall as I rode the goblin to a stop. Twisting under me, the goblin shaman's elbow shot out, catching me on the edge of my helmet as it spun onto its back. Recoiling from the blow, I blinked repeatedly, trying to get rid of the spinning stars in my vision.

Reaching out blindly before the goblin could attack me again, I felt my hand grab the arm holding the burning staff, pinning it against the ground. I felt bones snap under my brutal grip as I began to squeeze with every ounce of strength I had. The goblin shaman screamed in pain as the staff fell uselessly from its grip, the eyes of the smoldering skull winking out as it clattered to the ground.

Angling Razor downwards, I stabbed the blade deep into the goblin's shoulder the same moment its still functional hand touched my chest. I didn't even have a chance to see what spell the goblin cast before I was suddenly blown off the goblin by an intense wave of force. I sailed through the air, spinning wildly before slamming back into the ground with a crunch.

Wheezing, I slowly collected myself as the stunning effect of the shaman's spell began to wear off. I forced myself into an upright position, seeing that the goblin shaman had recovered his staff. The skull on the tip of the staff blazed with fire once more as the shaman chanted the final words of the spell that would send a massive fireball streaming towards me.

I'm fucked. The realization crystalized in my mind as I tried to stand, the effects of the shaman's spell on my mind preventing me from casting Blink Step in time.

<No!> Amaranth's voice pierced into my head as he suddenly leaped onto the shaman's back, sending him crashing into the ground once more as his deadly teeth sank into flesh, disrupting the spell in the last possible instant.

I heard bones crack and snap as Amaranth shook the goblin shaman by his neck, thrashing the creature against the ground. Blood splattered everywhere as Amaranth dug his claws into the goblin's flesh, working to rip and tear the shaman's head free from his body. In one violent motion, the puma tore the filthly creature's head free of its body, the sound of tearing flesh and crunching bone filling the air as the goblin shaman died.

Amaranth spat the goblin's head onto the ground, roaring with victory as he celebrated his kill, causing the slave-king to turn his attention towards us, sensing the goblin shaman's death.

"YOU HAVE DARED TO KILL MY SERVANT!" His voice boomed from the far side of the dais, his body slowly turning towards us, an orange glowing orb forming at the tip of his blade. **"SUCH AN AFFRONT WILL NOT STAND!"**

Before I could even fully comprehend what the king had said, the orb shot forth, crossing the room with blinding speed. It crashed into Amaranth's form, unerringly changing direction as it compensated for the cat's attempt to dodge midflight. An explosion of fire consumed my familiar, leaving nothing but dust behind.

"No!" I felt something tear deep inside me as Amaranth died, taking a piece of my soul with it. A heavy weariness instantly settled over me as a pair of messages appeared in my vision.

Your familiar – Amaranth has been killed by [Slave-King Abdiel]!
Your Soul is weakened! All abilities scores and skills have been reduced by 10% for the next 24 hours until your familiar respawns!

"AND NOW YOU!" The incandescent slave-king began walking towards me, his long strides allowing him to quickly cross the room.

"I was thinking the same thing!" I forced myself to meet the king's advance.

"We're with you, Lyr!" Caius's voice called out from behind me, a trio of magic bolts and an arrow sailing over my head, splashing against the corporeal spirit.

Glancing behind me, I saw that the rest of the party had taken care of the goblin stalkers, though not without injuries or casualties themselves. Along with the missing presence of Amaranth, I now noticed that Sierra was no longer with us, party sense now telling me that she was far away in the direction of Aldford.

One more time! I thought to myself tiredly as I started running towards the slave-king. *Just one more boss, then we can log off and rest.*

I charged up the dais noticing that the king had stopped advancing, shielding himself with one arm against the magical attacks of our mages.

"**PITIFUL!**" His voice took on a mocking tone as he shouted at us. "**I ONCE WIELDED MAGIC THAT COULD RUIN ENTIRE CITIES! YOU INSULT ME WITH YOUR PITIFUL SPELLS!**"

"And yet you died!" I shouted, unable to keep myself from taunting the king as I closed the distance.

Choosing not to reply to me, the slave-king instead hefted his flaming blade, extending a hand towards me.

Here goes nothing! I gripped Razor tightly as I watched the slave-king's blade. The moment I saw the sword begin to move, I ground to a halt, needing to shed every bit of speed I could for what I was about to try. Abdiel lunged forward swinging his blade in a wide arc, not intending to give me any space to escape. But I didn't plan to escape.

The world blurred as Blink Step took me directly behind the slave-king's outstretched form. Spinning, I sliced out with Razor, the blade passing through the corporeal spirit's leg with a flash of magic before resealing itself. Seeing a delightful message appear at the bottom of my vision.

You [Power Attack I] Slave-King Abdiel for 52 points of damage!

Yes! We can hurt it! I managed a second cut across Abdiel's back before the slave-king spun on me, planting a brutal kick on me that sent me flying across the room.

[Slave-King Abdiel] hits you with [Mighty Kick] for 123 points of damage!

I flew through the air a short distance before slamming into the ground and skidding to a stop. Coughing, I clutched my chest reflexively as I gasped for air. Lifting my head up, I looked back at the slave-king who had turned to meet the rest of the group's assault. Magic flew through the air, slamming into the slave-king's body, temporarily streaming æther from every blow.

As I stood up to rejoin the fight, I caught sight of Graves barely twenty feet away from me, digging desperately through the rubble on the ground. With a cry of triumph, Graves picked something up off the ground, immediately cursing and throwing it. It landed with a heavy thump and began quickly rolling across the ground. I spotted the object as it rolled past me, a heart-stopping tag appearing in my vision highlighting the item.

[Annulment Sphere]

That's the thing that was floating in the pillar! I instantly realized why the goblin shaman had forced the sphere out of the pillar before the then possessed Graves stepped into it. *He was worried it would consume him! We can kill the slave-king with this!*

I lunged towards the sphere the same instant Graves recovered from his fumble, his eyes landing on me.

"You!" he spat, pure hate crossing his features. "This is all your fault!"

"What the fuck did you do, Graves?" I shouted back at the man as we both moved to chase the rolling sphere. "You fucking unleashed this monster!"

"You gave me *no choice!*" Graves drew his sword, abandoning his pursuit of the sphere, instead choosing to advance on me. "You *ruined* everything I had planned! I was going to be *rich*! I was going to be *famous!*"

"Cry me a fucking river, Graves!" I sliced Razor through the air as I assumed a defensive posture, baiting Graves to attack me. "You made a play for Aldford and lost! Grow up and move on!"

"NO!" Graves shouted, his glance momentarily turning towards the annulment sphere, before looking up at me and rushing forward. "If I can't have Aldford, no one will! The world will see my vengeance first hand! They'll watch your precious village burn to ash! I'll take that sphere and hide it somewhere where no one will ever find it! *Everything will burn!*"

Our blades slammed together as I met Graves's charge head on, his overwhelming strength having vanished with the spirit's departure. He seemed surprised to find me not only having blunted his assault, but to be forcing his blade aside.

"Give it up, Graves!" I taunted the man, suddenly pulling back on our exchange and landing a heavy kick in his stomach and sending him reeling backwards. Disengaging, I quickly ran in the direction I had seen the sphere roll. "I beat you senseless when you still had your armor's fancy stat boosts! Without those you're nothing but a scrub novice now!"

"I'll show you how well I fight if you ever stop running from me!" Graves roared as he gave chase, swinging his sword in a vicious overhand chop at my head as I ground to a stop, spinning to face him.

Easily sidestepping the wild swing, Graves's charge carried him rushing past me, allowing me the opportunity to land a bleeding slash across his arm.

"Last chance Graves, surrender!" I called to the man, as he reflexively clutched his wounded arm.

"I would rather fucking die!" Graves spat at my feet as he launched into another set of attacks attempting to beat my defenses into submission.

"If that's what it takes!" I was forced to pick up the pace as I worked to parry Graves's increasingly desperate attacks. After nearly nonstop combat since we arrived at this tower, mental fatigue had begun to set in, exacerbated by the attribute and skill penalties I was suffering due to Amaranth's death.

I have to end this! I felt myself breathing heavily as I forced myself to keep up with Graves. A huge flash of light burst from behind me, instantly making me worry on how the others were faring against the slave-king.

Catching Graves's blade on Razor, I channeled a Shocking Touch into the metal. The shock instantly traveled through both our blades and into Graves's hand holding his sword. With a yelp, Graves's grip faltered long enough for me to knock the blade from his hand.

With no blade to block with, Graves was helpless as I ruthlessly thrust Razor into his gut, his mouth opening wide to scream. I followed up with a vicious kick to the side of his knee, shattering the joint as he instantly fell to the ground writhing in pain.

"Sit tight here for a second!" I told a screaming Graves, kicking his sword far away from him. "I want you to watch what happens next."

Having tracked the direction of the Annulment Sphere's journey, I found it nestled amid a pile of debris. Reaching for it, I paused for a heartbeat, steeling myself for what was about to come. *This seemed to hurt Graves when he picked it up.*

Grabbing the sphere, I instantly felt a freezing cold sensation run up the length of my arm. Fighting the instinctive urge to drop the sphere, I tucked it under my arm as I turned to sprint towards the middle, where the slave-king loomed over my friends. Time appeared to slow as I ran, giving me a chance to read the alert messages streaming into my combat log.

You have picked up an [Annulment Sphere!]
Warning! Holding an [Annulment Sphere] will drain your mana
at a rate of 10% per second! If you run out of mana while carrying
an Annulment Sphere, it will begin draining life 10% per second
instead!
[Annulment Sphere] drains 64 mana from you!
[Annulment Sphere] drains 64 mana from you!

This is going to be close! I saw my already diminished mana pool bleeding away at an incredible rate, giving me seconds before it started draining my life. I charged forward, hoping to make every single step count.

Glowing like a blazing furnace, I saw the slave-king standing ahead of me, my friends scattered around him. In one hand, he held a struggling Caius by the throat, a wicked laugh echoing through the air. With a flash of magic, I saw Caius's body fade to dust, his presence vanishing from party sense.

I hope this works! I triggered Blink Step one last time, a heartbeat before the last dregs of my mana was consumed. My world blurred in a kaleidoscope of colors as I reappeared barely ten feet away from the slave-king. Continuing my desperate sprint forward, I banished the sudden pangs of thirst and hunger my lack of mana brought upon me, not wavering in the slightest.

At the last instant, before I collided, the slave-king turned, somehow sensing my approach, but it was too late. I leaped from the ground the same instant a deafening shout filled the air, the annulment sphere outstretched before me. I passed into the slave-king's corporeal form, the sphere suddenly anchoring in the heart of his being, jerking me to a halt as my hands stuck to it, leaving me suspended inside the spirit.

As with the ley line I had fallen into days before, the æther contained within the slave-king's manifestation burned me right down to my very core. This time, however, there was no relief, my mana starved body desperately craving the fuel that it had grown accustomed to. My body began to draw on the æther within the slave-king, the annulment sphere then hungrily drinking from me and forcing my body to draw even more.

I lost track of time, as the cycle repeated itself. Hunger and thirst at one moment satiated, then the next starving. I felt something change within me as my body struggled to find a way to survive.

The next thing I knew, I was falling, blacking out as I fell to the ground.

I awoke almost instantly, only to find the remaining members of the party standing over me, concerned looks over the faces.

"Lyrian!" Freya called to me, rushing to bend down beside me. "Are you okay?"

"I-I don't know." I felt strange, in a way I couldn't quite pin down. Flashing system alerts danced in my vision, causing a spike of pain to shoot through my head as they cried for attention. Dismissing them for the time being, I tried to stand.

"Careful there, Lyr." Drace's hand appeared before me, as he helped me stand up. "You don't look so great."

"I'll be fine—" As I reached for Drace's hand, I caught sight of mine, the glove having been completely burnt off and seeing that it had suddenly become emaciated. It reminded me of the ghouls that we had fought just a short time ago, minus the razor-sharp claws. *Nothing left but tendons, muscle, and bone.*

"I don't know what you did, Lyr...but you killed the slave-king," Drace told me as I wavered on my feet unsteadily. "After you jumped into him, that orb you were holding went completely black. It just... sucked him up."

"I'm glad it worked out." I slowly scanned the room, seeing Natasha in the distance, kneeling amongst the expedition members held prisoner by the goblins what seemed like a lifetime ago.

"Where is he?" I asked Drace, feeling my balance steady under me. "Where is Graves?"

"Over here, Lyrian," Constantine called to me from a short distance away. Both he, Helix and Abaddon stood around the kneeling form of Graves, his head staring down at the ground. "We haven't decided what to do with him. We were waiting until you woke up."

"We can't take him back," Freya said softly. "Best case scenario, it'll start a riot."

"We can't leave him here either," Drace replied. "He'll escape."

I slowly began walking towards Graves, my feet echoing through the near silent chamber. There was only one way that this could end, only one way to be sure that Graves would leave us alone for a time.

Graves's head slowly rose as he heard my approach, his expression widening in fear as he saw my face.

"If only you came with an open hand, Graves." I stopped directly in front of the man, forcing him to look nearly straight up at me. "We could have worked something out, something better than this."

Graves swallowed hard as I put both of my hands on either side of his head.

"Either way, you gambled and *lost*." I bent down slightly, angling Graves's head so he could see my face clearly. "I don't *ever* want to see you in this region again, Graves. Go play your game somewhere else, far, far away."

"This wasn't how it was supposed to work out," Graves whispered, his eyes fixated on me. "I was supposed to be king! You can't do this to me! I-I…"

I gripped Graves's head tight, looking him straight in the eye. "Goodbye, Graves."

And then I snapped his neck.

FORTY-FOUR

I LET OUT A WEARY SIGH as I dismissed a menu from my vision, my eyes having gone far too blurry to see straight as I attempted to categorize and note the dozens of items laid out on the table before me. Walking over to a nearby stool, I gently sat down, my eyes staring out blankly at the now overflowing workshop.

It had been close to nine hours since the battle with the goblins, Graves, and Slave-King Abdiel. Night had fully fallen by the time we arrived back at Aldford.

After watching Graves's body dissipate into nothingness and hearing Huxley confirm his revival far away to the south, a sense of relief came over us as we began to decompress from the final battle. The region was safe, the dead were avenged, and those that still lived were rescued. Only Carver's escape marred our otherwise successful day. But given the alternatives, we felt it was a small price to pay.

He'll either turn up at some point, or we'll never seen him again, I thought to myself with a mental shrug, rubbing my face as I tried to clear my blurry eyes. Blinking slowly, the workshop came back into focus, my gaze falling on a long bone staff that once belonged to the goblin shaman, resting on the far side of the table before me. *I should probably double check everything again, because for the life of me I can't even remember what I was just looking at.*

With a grunt I forced myself back onto my feet and shuffled over to the staff, bringing up the item's information.

Flamespit

Slot: Primary Weapon

Item Class: Rare

Item Quality: Mastercraft (+20%)

Damage 22-42 (Bludgeoning)

Intelligence: +4 Willpower: +4

Durability 180/180

Weight: 2 kg

Favored Class: Any Arcane or Divine.

Base Material: Bone

Special Ability: Wielder gains the ability to cast Fireball and Spewing Flames. Effect scales based on Class Level and Evocation Skill.

Level 12

"I think Caius is going to get dibs on this one," I whispered to myself, slightly envying the warlock and his future prize. *Whatever gets in his way after he gets used to wielding this, won't have enough time to regret it!*

Setting the staff down, I moved over to a rather foul-smelling pile of furs that had also been taken off the goblin shaman, something that I had claimed for myself. *Maybe I'll wear it after I wash it in the river, two, three, or nine times! Gods, this stinks!*

> **Fur Mantle of Swiftness**
> *Slot: Back*
> *Item Class: Magical*
> *Item Quality: Good (+15%)*
> *Armor: 19*
> *Agility: +4*
> *Durability: 80/80*
> *Base Material: Fur*
> *Weight: 1 kg*
> *Favored Class: Any Martial*
> *Level: 12*

I'll need to make some modifications to it. I made a face as the pungent smell of goblin funk wafted up from the furs, forcing me to let go of it. *And sew a longer second length of furs in, to have it cover my lower back.*

Stifling a gag, I took a step away from the foul-smelling mantle as I searched for cleaner air, coughing slightly to clear my throat. I looked back down at the table, my eyes falling on a pile of chainmail. *Maybe I can turn this mess into something useful too.*

I picked up the remains of a damaged chain shirt, my eyes following a long slice of broken links. I reverently ran a hand over the break, wondering what long lost battles it had seen, that had since been forgotten by this world's history.

Thinking back to the chamber under the tower, I realized now that it had taken an embarrassingly long time after Graves's execution before we all realized that we hadn't quite explored the underground chamber we had urgently rushed into. I vaguely remembered walking around the perimeter of the room, finding only two points of interest.

One was a collapsed stairway leading upwards to where the tower once stood, having filled with debris when it fell.

The second was a small storage room that had somehow remained intact over the countless years since the tower's fall, filled nearly to the brim with a variety of supplies, sundries, and cast-off pieces of equipment in desperate need of repair and re-forging.

Among the dozens of prizes we found within the room, one was a barrel filled to the brim with broken and incomplete lengths of chainmail. Judging by ragged cuts and missing links in some of the samples we looked at, it was our belief that they had been deemed too damaged or too time-consuming to warrant repairing at that moment in time and had been stowed there out of the way.

A few of these pieces still bear the remnants of ancient enchantments, just like Razor did when I first found it. My eyes narrowed as I inspected the chain shirt even closer, feeling the coolness of the dark colored metal in my hands.

> **Blackened Chain Shirt**
> *Slot: Chest*
> *Item Class: Relic*
> *Item Quality: Fine (+10 %)*
> *Armor: 0*
> *Strength: +3 Agility: +3*
> *Durability 0/0*
> *Weight: 2.5 kg*
> *Note: A skilled smith might be able to re-forge this item.*

I should be able to repair a few of these semi-intact shirts, and build a new set of armor from the rest of the scrap. I'm need a new set of armor for myself anyway. I turned my head over towards the charred mess that was once my Webwood Striker Armor Set, having been forced to cut the melted remnants of the armor from my flesh.

Looking at the tattered scraps of the armor I felt a momentary sense of loss wash over me, knowing that the first set of armor I had ever made was destined for the fire pit. *If nothing else, studying these chainmail scraps should teach me how to properly make chainmail.*

Setting the chain shirt down I moved to the next item on the table, spotting several glowing jars of *[Mana-Infused Ectoplasm]* that one of the group members had looted from the remains of the slave-king's corporeal manifestation. The jars cast an eerie orange light on everything around them, and I wasn't quite sure what I was going to use the goopy substance for. Given where it had come from, I had half a mind to destroy the slime. But pragmatism had stilled my hand since I didn't get the impression that it was actually dangerous.

Maybe I'll find a stick later and stir it for a bit, see what happens. I moved on with a shrug, my tired brain unable to come up with any other ideas for the time being.

Unfortunately, the ectoplasm was the only item that the slave-king had dropped. Since for reasons we didn't quite understand, the annulment sphere had shattered itself after absorbing the slave-king's essence, leaving two broken halves of what appeared to be plain, mundane iron on the ground.

Probably for the best, I thought to myself, remembering the deadly touch of the sphere, a*t least for the time being. Now that we know such an item is possible, we'll find a way to make a new one if we really need one.*

The next item on the table was a finely lacquered rectangular box. I carefully spun the box to face me and unclipped the clasps that were keeping it securely closed and gently opened it. Staring back at me were a dozen intricately crafted *[Ætherscopes]*, all laid out perfectly with little metallic clips to hold them in place. Running a finger along one of the wands I found it to be somewhat rough and grainy to the touch, a huge contrast to the one Donovan had.

But that was because these ætherscopes appeared to have been made of bone and not metal, something that Donovan said had never been attempted back in Eberia. Every ætherscope ever made since the start of *the war* had always been metallic. He and Halcyon were both eager to see how these ancient bone ætherscopes would measure up against the metallic version.

So long as they don't burn my hand to a crisp when I use them, I'd consider that an improvement. I snorted to myself while closing the box carefully and sliding it back into place beside a pile of carefully stacked scroll tubes. *Ah! This was probably the best part of our haul!*

Tucked deep away in the room we'd uncovered, we had found six scroll tubes filled to the brim with a variety of common spells. Each tube containing nearly a dozen spell scrolls each, with multiple copies of the same spell. We now had access to spells such as Jump, Force Shield, Lesser Shielding, Flame Dagger, Fireball, Fire Whip, Pyroclap, Shocking Touch and a handful more that we had yet to successfully interpret due to their complexity.

The new spells would give our immediate circle of spellcasters a chance to greatly increase their versatility and not have to spend precious class skill points on learning lower level spells. Whatever our casters couldn't use, I planned to sell to the other adventurers in town or offer them up as rewards for the endless list of tasks and projects that Aldford needed to have done. *I can probably sell these spells for two to four gold each, and start earning back some of that gold I spent buying crafting materials.*

That's of course after I take a few of those spells for myself! A spark of excitement couldn't help but flare through my exhaustion as I looked forward to experimenting with a few new abilities. I smiled to myself, already imagining the future possibilities as I turned my attention towards a large crate on the floor. *Almost done, just this last box, and that hunk of scrap.*

Bending down, I cracked the lid of the crate open, revealing eighteen gleaming prisms. Gently removing one from the crate, I lifted the near translucent crystal into the light, turning it over in my hand. Completely smooth to the touch, each of the crystals were as long as my forearm and half the length across. We managed to identify them as all being *[Translucent Selenite Crystals]*. However, we weren't quite sure what their purpose was for.

After some debate between Donovan, Halcyon, Caius, and myself, we believed that the crystals may be mana batteries of a kind. Unfortunately, none of us had any real idea how to fill them. We did decide that pouring raw æther onto a crystal was probably not the best idea, and sounded like a good way to lose two rare items at the same time.

Placing the crystal gently back in its place and sealing the crate, I was eager to be done inventorying our loot before logging off for the next day. I walked towards a familiar colored length of scrap metal that leaned against the side of the forge and picked it up, turning it over in my hands excitedly. *Finally, the last item, and what will eventually become a massive long term project in itself!*

On our return from the underground chamber, we had crossed paths with the massive metallic pole again, a sudden revelation stopping us in our tracks. The entire pole was made completely out of metal and had long lain abandoned since the tower's fall. It no longer served any purpose that we could discern and would continue to molder until the tower one day collapsed around it. Saddened by the waste of such a precious material, a burning question entered our mind.

What if we could somehow scavenge the pole and smelt the metal down for our own use?

With Aldford on the verge of an incredible growth spurt, its burgeoning industry would soon begin to thirst for vast quantities of all metals imaginable. Recycling the already refined metal of the pole itself would serve to jump start local development and give us much needed time to find and begin exploiting other ore filled veins in the surrounding land.

Given the size and density of the pole, however, I knew it would be a long-term challenge to figure out a way to somehow cut and transport large chunks of metal back to Aldford. A challenge I was more than willing to pay the other adventurers in the village to solve for me. *Nothing motivates people better than a fistful of coins, or a few sets of magical armor crafted by yours truly.*

"Not a bad haul!" I declared, talking to myself as I looked over all the items for the last time, putting the piece of scrap metal down.

That quest paid off in experience just as well as the tower did in loot! I remembered my jaw nearly hitting the ground when I saw the experience and renown reward for completing the *The Slave-King Reborn'* quest.

▷**QUEST COMPLETE!**

THE SLAVE-KING REBORN! *(Evolving Quest) (Multi-Group)*
  After a fierce battle and many losses you and your companions
  have managed to kill Slave-King Abdiel! The region is now safe
  from his reign of tyranny! Congratulations!
  Slave-King Abdiel Slain: 1/1
  Difficulty: Very Hard
  Reward: (Granted to all members of participating groups)
  Experience Points: 14,000
  Renown: 1000

In one fell swoop, all of us had earned little more than half a level's worth of experience and a sizable chunk of renown. We were also happy to find out that Ascend Online's quest system took into account that Freya and her group were still stuck on their final novice level, and was delaying the quest's experience reward until they reached level ten, but our biggest surprise was that even those in the party who were unfortunate enough to die in the tower had also managed to receive the quest and still get credit for completing it.

I had a feeling that the quest system had been designed to account for attrition and death within dungeons and special events, given how punishing it could be to respawn hours, if not *days*, away from where your group members were.

Without such a system, I could see groups fighting far too conservatively, each member focusing on their own personal survival, rather than actually working together to successfully finish a quest, likely leading to everyone failing the quest altogether.

We still have no idea what renown is for. I brought up my character sheet, seeing that I had already managed to accumulate a grand total of 1105 points of renown. *Best guess is that it has something to do with how involved you are in the world's story. Maybe it'll become more important down the road at some point.*

As I scrolled through my character sheet, my attention wavered to the dull outline of an alert I had read several times but refused to dismiss completely. With a sigh, I compulsively brought it up once more and read through the description of my new condition.

> **Warning!**
> *The Trait – Ætherwarped, has been modified!*
> *You have gained a new Ability linked to the Ætherwarped Trait!*
> *Due to prolonged exposure to raw Æther while under the effects of an [Annulment Sphere] your Sub-Trait Mana Starved has been enhanced to Mana Void!*
>
> **Mana Void** – *Your body's hunger for Arcane Energy has become ravenous, turning your appearance gaunt as it desperately craves more and more mana in order to fuel your metabolism. For as long as you have mana, you do not require to eat or drink. However, if your mana reaches 0, your body will immediately begin to consume itself at a rate of one hit point for each second in mana deprivation state, per second, until mana is restored. All mana regeneration is permanently reduced by 100%.*

You have received the new ability: Mana Leech

Mana Leech *– As a result from prolonged contact with an [Annulment Sphere] your body's hunger for mana is so powerful you are now able to leech mana from any object or creature that you come in physical contact with, regardless of intervening armor or clothing that is not specifically designed to block the flow of mana. When this ability is activated, mana will be leeched at a rate of 30 mana per second, any mana leeched will be added to your current mana pool and any excess mana will be lost. This ability scales with Class Level and Intelligence.*

"Ugh!" I let out a grunt of frustration as this time I finally dismissed the alert, instead of simply minimizing it. I looked down at my bony hands for a moment, clenching and unclenching them as I watched the tendons play through my skin. I took a deep breath and let it out slowly, willing myself to move past this new development. "Okay, appearances aside, it's not all bad. I can still fight, run and move around. I'm a bit lighter than before, but still just as strong. While not ideal, I can still cast spells if I manage my mana *carefully* and focus on targets I can drain mana from." I slowly talked myself through my new abilities, trying to come to terms with them. "I guess I'm kind of a mana vampire now, and if I ever run out of mana I'll die in about…"

I paused for a moment, doing the math in my head.

"Thirty-six seconds, assuming I'm at full health."

Fuck. I sighed, realizing that in the heat of combat, thirty-six seconds could easily range from a lifetime to a single instant. *What are the odds that if I've run out of mana, I haven't also been injured? Hell, if someone mana drains me I could be dead before I even knew what was happening!*

"Hopefully that won't happen," I whispered to myself, the same instant Constantine walked into the room.

"Hopefully what won't happen?" Constantine asked me, before looking around the room and seeing that no one else was there. "Talking to yourself, Lyr?"

"Yeah, a little bit," I confessed as I waved the question away. "Nothing serious though."

"You sure you're doing okay?" Constantine replied raising his eyebrow in concern. "It's been a rough day, hell of a rough *week*."

"I agree with you there," I said wholeheartedly. "I'm all right, just tired. You know what they say, 'What doesn't kill you—'"

"Gives you a lot of unhealthy coping mechanisms?" Constantine interrupted me with a slight grin on his face.

I couldn't help but laugh. "Yeah, that sounds about right."

"Just a little bit more, then we can unplug for a day or two," Constantine said warmly before beckoning me to the door. "You said you wanted to talk to everyone in Aldford before we logged off, right? We managed to get everyone waiting in the town hall."

"Ah, I'd forgotten about that." I rapped a bony knuckle on my forehead as I moved to follow Constantine. "All right, let's go. This shouldn't take too long."

There's just one more thing I need to take care of.

THE TOWN HALL FELL SILENT the moment I walked in, dozens of heads turning to see my arrival. I heard gasps of surprise as I stalked towards the far end of the room, whispers of my new appearance quickly spreading throughout the crowd as everyone watched me with bated breath. Crossing the room, I saw the entire group waiting for me. They all stood in a line as they faced the gathered adventurers, purposefully showing off their battle-damaged armor. A crate had been dragged to the center of their line, serving as a makeshift stage for my coming speech.

Hopping up onto the crate, I looked over the crowd as all the whispering voices began to quiet. I waited until I felt I had everyone's full attention and then spoke the three words I knew everyone was waiting to hear.

"Graves is dead."

There was a pregnant pause as everyone absorbed my statement. Then a single cheer broke the silence, followed by another, and another as applause began to thunder through the room. I saw looks of relief spread across nearly every face as days of built up stress vanished in a heartbeat, everyone wildly celebrating the would-be tyrant's demise. With a smile I basked in the celebration, waiting for everyone to bring their attention back to me.

Sensing that I had more to say, the adventurers slowly fell silent, watching me with renewed anticipation.

"Today, we have faced a major trial that not only threatened Aldford, but the entire region itself." I paused, giving a chance for my statement to sink in. "All because of one man's greed.

"In his blind quest for power, Graves unleashed a terrible evil on this land, an evil that would have consumed everything we have worked so hard to build." I waved my hand to indicate all my friends standing in front of me. "But thanks to these heroes before you, we not only managed to stop Graves, we also managed to permanently put an end to the evil he let loose.

"We would have not been able to do this without the selfless sacrifice of Myr, who bravely stepped in the path of arrows destined for her friend, Theia." I saw the lizardwoman flinch at the sudden attention the crowd directed at her. "Or Huxley, who caught Cerril just in time and prevented his fall into a burning inferno.

"When we were pressed by a horde of vicious creatures, spawned from nightmare itself, Cadmus, Halcyon, and Thorne did not hesitate to give their lives so that the rest of us could have a chance at living." I continued speaking, watching the adventurers' attention shift with each name I mentioned. "To protect our rescuees in the heat of battle,

Sierra willingly stood a forlorn defense, sacrificing herself to ensure their survival."

I quickly glanced at the three Mages Guild expedition members that we had rescued from the tower, having barely talked to any of them. I recalled Natasha quickly telling me their names as she excitedly introduced her former scoutmaster, Bax, and the two mages, Samuel and Quincy.

"We were victorious because we fought together and trusted one another completely, knowing that if one of us fell, the others would continue onwards and honor our sacrifice." I paused once more, scanning over the faces of the adventurers. "Graves, on the other hand, died alone, a broken man, his greed having pushed everyone away from him."

The crowd began to murmur its approval, a second round of applause echoing through the room. Holding up a finger, I motioned for silence, indicating I still had more to say.

"I stand here before you all to tell you that Graves is only the first to raise his hand against us. There will be countless more behind him that will also be driven by greed and lust for power as they try to carve out a piece of this world for themselves, uncaring of who they take it from." I held my hands up high to indicate the surrounding village. "It will be up to us to defend what is ours, and define what sort of world we want to make for ourselves. We must all stand together as comrades, resolute in the protection of our community and future.

"To that end, I am announcing the formation of a guild, one that will defend against those who wish Aldford and this region harm." I saw looks of surprise and excitement cross the faces of the adventurers in the crowd. "This guild will be governed by the very idea of virtue as we transform this region into a shining example of what cooperation and hard work can accomplish.

"In honor of that ideal, we have chosen to call the Guild 'Virtus', a word that dates back to the days of the Roman Empire and a name that I hope will constantly inspire us to be better than we were the day before.

"All members within Virtus will strive to embody the ideals of valor, excellence, courage, character, and worth, in every aspect of their lives. Our goals as a guild will be to ensure the safety of Aldford and the surrounding region, providing a safe haven for any who choose to make their homes within this land.

"We will protect those who ask for protection, we will stand against gross injustices, and if necessary, we will be the hand of vengeance for those who cannot stand up for themselves!

"Standing before you all, are the founding members of Virtus! All of whom have bled in the defense of our new home today!" I spread my hands out wide, indicating the group for a second time as the crowd began to cheer. "It is because of them that we are all safe tonight! It is because of them that we can all lay our heads down in rest and know that there is no evil lurking in the night!

"It is because of them, that we are all *free!*"

With my final words, all of the adventurers leaped to their feet in applause and began to press forward, eager to congratulate every group member in person.

Hopping off the crate, I saw a panic-stricken Constantine backing away from the advancing crowd, quickly looking over at me.

"What the hell, Lyr? You were supposed to wind them down gently, not rile them all up!" He shouted to me over the roaring cheers. "This is going to take ages to get out of!"

"Sorry!" I yelled back with a smile. "I just wanted a head start!"

"A head start?" Constantine looked at me with confusion. "To what?"

"The bathroom!" I couldn't help but bark an evil laugh as I waved goodbye.

And then I logged off.

EPILOGUE

Eberia
Tower of Atonement
Graves

I SAT HUDDLED IN THE DEEPEST and darkest corner of the room that I could find, gripping the crude bone shiv I had fashioned so tightly I was worried that it would snap in my trembling hand.

And leave me defenseless, again. I relaxed my grip ever so slightly, daring to exhale a short breath in hopes of calming myself.

"Where are you, Graves?" A familiar voice called out for me, causing my heart to start thundering in my chest as I gripped the shiv tightly once more. I saw a shadow pass by the doorway before me, the soft patter of feet announcing the stalker's presence. "You can't hide from us forever, Graves! We'll find you eventually! *We always do.*"

I held my breath until the shadow passed, moving onwards into the dark.

Just ninety-seven more days, I told myself, swallowing hard as I suppressed a momentary spike of anger. *Ninety-seven days, trapped in a prison full of inmates that want you dead, in a prison where death is but a minor inconvenience.*

I'd lost track of how many times I'd been killed since I first arrived here three days ago, having stopped counting past my tenth death. Everything since my first death at that *bastard's* hands was a blur. I barely had enough time to realize that I had respawned back in Eberia before I was unceremoniously tackled by a Justicar, stripped of my gear and put before a magistrate.

All I remembered was that damned gavel banging and the sentence being read aloud.

One hundred days of imprisonment in the Tower of Atonement, the highest security prison Eberia had. A thirty-story prison where they just threw the prisoners in and locked the doors behind them until their sentence was over. A prison full of angry killers with nothing to lose.

It wouldn't have been so bad, had none of the other inmates known who I was. I stared out of the doorway, trying to judge if it was safe enough to take a quick nap. *When was the last time I slept? Yesterday morning?*

I blinked through sleepy, exhausted eyes, the darkness doing little to counter the weariness hanging over me. Unfortunately, nearly everyone from my group had been thrown into the prison before me, giving plenty of time for resentment and hate to fester. *I was barely in the prison for ten minutes before Micken found me and beat me to death with a brick.*

Ever since then word of my arrival had spread and nearly everyone in this prison spent their time hunting me, day or night. It was all I could do to hide in whatever nook or cranny I could find, doing my best to stay ahead of those searching for me. I knew all too well what they would do to me if they found me.

I did my best to stifle a yawn. *I need to catch some sleep, or I'll start making mistakes.*

"Oh, how the mighty have fallen." A feminine voice caused my eyes to widen in panic as I tried to find the source of the voice.

Who said that? Where did that come from? I didn't dare move while I fervently scanned the room before me, gripping my shiv painfully tight. My heart hammered in my chest as I saw nothing but shadows before me. *It has to be a trick to flush me out!*

"You were on the verge of becoming a king!" the voice continued. "But now you hide in the shadows like a *rat*, struggling to survive, all while your killer prospers. How does that make you feel?"

Angry. I thought to myself, feeling the embers of rage kindle within my breast, still searching for the source of the voice. *But there's nothing I can do about that now.*

"What if there was?" Pale white eyes suddenly appeared in front of me, just inches away from mine.

"Ah!" I barely stifled a yelp as I instinctively stabbed out with my shiv. But before my crude blade could even reach the eyes before me, they vanished, leaving me alone in the darkness once again.

Fuck, I'm starting to hallucinate! I ground the palm of my hand into my eyes, trying to banish the exhaustion that had crept over me. Holding my breath, I strained my ears, trying to hear if anyone was coming to investigate my gasp.

"You aren't hallucinating, Graves." With a burst of light a pale-skinned woman appeared a short distance away from me, watching me with the same unsettling pale eyes I had seen before. "I am really here."

"Turn that light off!" Fear of being discovered by the roaming death squads searching for me overrode any concerns I had about speaking. I learned the hard way that light would draw them to me almost instantly. "They'll find us!"

"Oh, don't worry about anyone interrupting us," the mysterious woman said dismissively. "I've taken steps to ensure that we will be left alone for a time."

I pointed my feeble dagger at the woman before me, wincing at the sudden bright light. Looking over her, I saw that the mystery woman was dressed in a pure white dress, save for a dark black mantle that covered her shoulders. Waiting for my cold appraisal of her to finish, she cocked her head at me, sending her raven black hair cascading to the side.

"Precautions?" I echoed, while continuing to watch her intently, expecting that at any moment a dozen prisoners would come charging into the room. *There's no dirt on her clothes yet; she must be new here. Maybe she wants to use my head to gain entry to one of the gangs?*

"I am *not* a prisoner." An amused expression crossed the woman's face. "As if *this place* could contain me. To answer your second question, *yes*, I can read your mind, after a fashion."

"W*hat* are you?" I asked hesitantly, realizing she had sensed the budding question in my mind before I had even had the chance to fully form it. "And *why* are you here?"

"The 'what' is much less than important than the 'why'." The woman smiled at me. "I am here to give you an opportunity for revenge, should you be willing to take it."

My eyes shot open in surprise, before narrowing suspiciously.

"I've had my fill of *opportunities*," I replied bitterly. "Look at where they have landed me! Take your cursed offer elsewhere and leave me be."

The woman made a show of examining the surroundings, her expression forming one of distaste. "I can understand your apprehension. Yet, are you so enamored of your surroundings that you would not even care to listen to my offer? Or would you wish to continue being hunted for the remainder of your sentence?"

I stared at the woman before me, my gut wrenching at the thought of another ninety-seven days in this hellhole. "*Fine*, I will listen."

"*A wise choice.*" The woman took a short step towards me, clasping her hands together. "I have grand designs for the city surrounding us. However, I am limited in the actions I can take on my own. I find myself in need of an agent that can act on my behalf in areas I cannot reach."

"And how will that help me get *my* revenge?" I asked scornfully. "I have been a puppet once before, and I would be a fool to not have learned my lesson from the events that led me here."

"And *I* would be a fool if I haven't learned that compelling obedience leads to unruly subjects." The woman cocked an eyebrow at me as she spoke. I suddenly found myself questioning just *how much* she knew about me. "Worry not, you will have full independence without my overt interference.

"As for your *revenge*, that entirely depends on you." The pale-skinned woman stopped before me, extending a hand. "Once you are firmly established where I need you to be, you should find yourself with near unlimited resources to pursue *any* goal you may have."

"That is *hardly* enough for me to even begin to trust you," I looked down towards her outstretched hand, then back at her pale eyes. "Everything you've just said is vague and insubstantial at best, coupled with promises that can be broken at any time."

"Perhaps it is," the woman agreed. "But unless you take my offer, I will not tell you anymore."

"Then you can take your off—" A shout from nearby interrupted me.

"Hey! There's a light! It has to be Graves! Go! Go! Go!" The sound of rushing feet and laughter began echoing through the hallway.

I looked up in horror at the woman standing before me, a devilish smile crossing her face.

"*Tick, tock, Graves.* The offer is about to expire." She waved her extended hand in front of my face. "You know what they are going to do when they get here."

I swallowed hard, as I looked up at the hand hovering before me, the sounds of rushing bodies closing fast.

"Damn you," I croaked as I grabbed the woman's hand, feeling the world shift out from under me, leaving me falling through an infinite abyss.

Discordant laughter filled my ears.

Lyrian's Character Sheet at the End of Book 1

LYRIAN RASTLER – LEVEL 11 SPELLSWORD

Human Male (Eberian)

Statistics:

HP: 638/638

Stamina: 580/580

Mana: 640/640

Experience to next level: 14,000/23,200

Critical Hit Chance: 11.5%

Attributes:

Strength: 46 (48)

Agility: 36 (43)

Constitution: 36

Intelligence: 42

Willpower: 16

Abilities:

Sneak Attack I *(Passive)* – *Attacks made before the target is aware of you automatically deal weapon damage +14.*

Power Attack I *(Active: 50 Stamina)* – *You slash viciously at the target putting extra strength behind the blow. Deal weapon damage +7.*

Kick *(Active: 20)* – *You kick your enemy for 10-20 points of damage, and knock them back 1-2 yards. Depending on your Strength/Agility score, you may also knock down the target.*

Shoulder Tackle *(Active: 40 Stamina)* – *Stun enemy for 1-2 seconds with chance to knock enemy down based on Strength and/or Agility attribute.*

Skills:

Evocation – *Level 10 – 66% (Increases knowledge of Evocation*

Magic and improves related Abilities.)

Alteration *– Level 9 – 88% (Increases knowledge of Alteration Magic and improves related Abilities.)*

Unarmed Combat *– Level 8 – 21% (Increases knowledge of hand-to-hand fighting and improves related Abilities.)*

Stealth *– Level 6 – 14% (Decreases chance of being detected while attempting to stay hidden. Improves related Abilities.)*

Swords *– Level 10 – 75% (Increases knowledge of sword fighting and improves related Abilities.)*

Wordplay *– Level 3 – 11% (Increases chance to persuade others, resolve differences and/or get information.)*

Perception *– Level 9 – 55% (You are skilled in spotting hidden creatures and places. Depending on your skill level, hidden creatures and places will be highlighted in red.)*

Tradeskills:

Blacksmithing – Level 10 – 1%

Carpentry – Level 6 – 51%

Cartography – Level 2 – 3%

Cooking – Level 5 – 54%

Herbalism – Level 7 – 14%

Leatherworking – Level 10 – 1%

Mining – Level 5 – 13%

Spells:

Flare

Light

Blink Step

Shocking Touch

Racial Ability:

Military Conditioning *(Passive) – All defenses are increased by 5% and total hit points are increased by 10%.*

Traits:

Open Minded *– Accepting of racial differences and radical ideas,* *you have learned to accept wisdom and the opportunity to learn no matter what form it takes, allowing you to make intuitive insights where others would give up in frustration. Grants a substantial increase in learning new skills, and the ability to learn all race locked traits, skills, crafting recipes, and abilities that are not otherwise restricted.*

Re-Forge *– You have learned the basics of how to recreate a broken relic and are able to bring back some of its former glory. This skill will function across any and all Tradeskills you acquire.*

Improvisation *– Your study of goblin craftsmanship has given you the insight to make adjustments to standard and learned recipes by replacing required materials with something else. E.g., Replacing metal with wood in an armor recipe will create a set of wooden armor instead of metal. The higher your level in Improvisation, the more changes can be made and the fewer materials they will require.*

Ætherwarped *– Due to high exposure of Raw Æther, your body has undergone unpredictable changes! You have gained the following Sub-Trait(s) and Abilities as part of your condition.*

True Sight *– Your eyes have been enhanced by exposure to Æther to the point where they are able to pierce through natural darkness and all facets of magic to see things as they truly are. This ability replaces Arcane Sight and can be suppressed at will. When this ability is active, the player's eyes will visibly glow a bright blue.*

Mana Void *– Your body's hunger for Arcane Energy has become ravenous, turning your appearance gaunt as it desperately craves more and more mana in order to fuel your metabolism. For as long as you have mana, you do not require to eat or drink. However, if your mana reaches 0, your body will immediately begin to consume itself at a rate of one hit point for each second in mana deprivation state, per second, until mana is restored. All mana regeneration is permanently reduced by 100%.*

Mana Leech – *As a result from prolonged contact with an [Annulment Sphere] your body's hunger for mana is so powerful you are now able to leech mana from any object or creature that you come in physical contact with, regardless of intervening armor or clothing that is not specifically designed to block the flow of mana. When this ability is activated mana will be leeched at a rate of 30 mana per second, any mana leeched will be added to your current mana pool and any excess mana will be lost. This ability scales with Class Level and Intelligence.*

Familiar:

Name: Amaranth

Type: Ætherwarped Puma

Level: 11

Relationship: Fanatically Loyal

Status: Dead (13 hours until respawn)

Familiar Abilities:

Mental Link – *The magical bond linking you and your familiar has created an intimate mental link between the two of you, allowing each of you to communicate mentally between one another for a distance of up to one mile, regardless of intervening objects. Magical wards, however, will block this form of mental communication.*

Soul Bound – *During the familiar bonding process, you have anchored the being's soul directly to your own. Should the familiar be slain in your service, you will immediately suffer a 10% penalty to all attributes and skills for the next 24 hours until the familiar is reborn. Should the familiar survive your death, it does not suffer any penalties, but will be compelled to travel to your place of rebirth as quickly as possible.*

AFTERWORD

Thank you for reading my story! Hopefully if you've made it this far, you've also enjoyed reading the story! As a first-time author, the entire book writing process has been one huge learning experience and I hope to consistently improve with every following book!

One thing I would like to ask of you, is to consider leaving a review of this book in any way that is possible, be it on Amazon or Goodreads! Reviews are critical to both help me improve as a writer and to help gain exposure! If there are things that you like or didn't like in this story, please let me know!

You can get in touch with me directly at LyrianRastler@gmail.com I welcome questions, comments, and suggestions!

CPSIA information can be obtained
at www.ICGtesting.com
Printed in the USA
LVHW112241290722
724754LV00002B/156